BEING MET TOGETHER

BY

VAUGHAN WILKINS

'. . . And I do swear that I will to the utmost of my power, support, maintain and defend the said United States, against the said King George the Third, his heirs and successors and his or their abettors, assistants and adherents . . .'
GEORGE WASHINGTON'S OATH OF ALLEGIANCE, 1778

'The President of the United States and the Prime Minister, Mr. Churchill, representing His Majesty's Government in the United Kingdom, being met together, deem it right to make known certain common principles in the national policies of their respective countries on which they base their hopes for a better future for the world.'
THE ATLANTIC CHARTER, 1941

NEW YORK   ❦   ❦   ❦   ❦   1944

THE MACMILLAN COMPANY

Copyright, 1944, by

WILLIAM VAUGHAN WILKINS

First printing.

A WARTIME BOOK

PRINTED IN THE UNITED STATES OF AMERICA

TO
GEORGE LAW
of Pass Christian, Mississippi, this book is inscribed with much affection

AUTHOR'S NOTE

THERE is nothing in the story of the St. Helena venture of the submarine *Mute* that transcends contemporary report and surmise. According to Lord Rosebery's *Napoleon: the Last Phase,* the possible employment of a submarine to rescue Bonaparte from captivity was 'the constant bugbear of British Governments'.

Sir Walter Scott gives some detail of such a scheme in his *Life* of Napoleon. The plot came to light in 1819, two years before the fallen dictator died and was carried to his grave in a coffin made out of a table-top. The organizer of the affair was a desperado named Johnstone, 'a smuggler of uncommonly resolute character, and whose life had been a tissue of desperate risks', including a 'memorable' escape from Newgate Prison.

'A submarine vessel, that is a ship capable of being sunk under water for a certain time, and of being raised again at pleasure by disengaging certain weights, was to be the means of effecting this enterprise', writes Sir Walter. 'It was thought that by sinking the vessel during the daytime, she might escape the notice of the British cruizers, and being raised at night, might approach the guarded rock without fear of discovery.

'The vessel was actually begun in one of the building-yards upon the Thames; but the peculiarity of her construction having occasioned suspicions, she was seized by the British Government.'

Another submarine 'on the Sommeriva system' was said to have been planned for the same purpose at the Brazilian port of Pernambuco.

Incidentally, at the time of his death in 1815, the inventor, Robert Fulton, had so far improved upon his early plans for a submarine that he was engaged — according to his friend and biographer, Cadwallader Colden — in the construction of a submersible capable of carrying a hundred men below its iron-plated deck, and armed with torpedoes and submarine guns.

VAUGHAN WILKINS

CONTENTS

BOOK FIVE

SILAS AND DEANE

BOOK SIX

CAPTIVITY

BOOK SEVEN

THE GUARDED ISLE

BOOK ONE

PRELUDE TO ANTHONY

Virginia 1781

★

CHAPTER I

DAYBREAK

DOCTOR and priest stood side by side in the long portico with which the house fronted ghostly dawn. The tumult of wind, that had raged throughout the hours of darkness, had at last abated; but the unfriendly stillness held no promise for the coming day. Against the pallid façade of lofty columns and blank windows, in the half-light, the two men resembled a pair of exploring crows.

Behind them the door closed softly, the bolts slid almost stealthily into place, and a chain rattled gently home.

The doctor shivered; drew his cloak more closely about his leanness; turned to his companion. His expression was not discernible, but there was something predatory in the manner in which immense bony nose, hunched shoulders, and — most particularly — black three-cornered hat, were stooped toward the other.

'Well, Mr. Chancellor?' he said in a tone of genial inquiry — and the faintest Scottish accent marked his speech. 'Well? So what do we now? . . . Pray for our immor-rtal souls?'

But Mr. Chancellor was unprepared with answer. He stared straight before him, across wide driveway and sloping lawn, to the line of trees — cedars and poplars — that fringed the road, and the grey unshining river which showed between the dark trunks and blur of foliage. His body was small and shrivelled, and his face was small and shrivelled and puckered in very anxious speculation. In one hand behind his back he clutched the horn frame of a pair of spectacles with shattered lenses.

'Pf-f-f!' he exhaled; threw out his narrow chest; drew in wheezily a great breath of the raw morning air. 'It is good to be out of doors again!'

'You ought to take something for that chest of yours,' commented the doctor. 'I'll make you up a linctus — as well as a sleeping-draught.'

He chuckled rather unpleasantly; paused a moment whilst he sought

in his memory; found what he wanted, and then quoted with infinite
gusto —

> ' "O merciful Lord by whose gracious gift mankind is increased:
> we beseech thee, assist with thy blessing these two persons, that
> they may be fruitful in the procreation of children."

Procreation of children! . . . Gracious gift!'

All night long his thin lips had been compressed as though in battle
with a smile: now he suddenly burst into so furious a bout of harsh
laughter that he had to prop himself for support against a column.
Laughter that awakened echoes along the colonnade, and horrified
Mr. Chancellor.

'For God's sake, Dr. Earle, restrain yourself!' he said in a low voice,
and looked nervously over either shoulder down the shadowy length of
the portico . . . Beneath one of the tall windows to his right lay a pool of
broken glass . . . 'Why isn't the chariot here? Rasselas said that it was
on its way round. It is monstrous to keep us waiting in this fashion!'

Dr. Earle's laughter slowly subsided.

He lounged easily against his pillar. He meditated on the small
gnome-like figure standing at the top of the steps, swathed in a rusty
black coat so large that only a few inches of rusty worsted stocking
showed between the skirts and the still rustier shoes. He started afresh —

'When you dragged yourself from bed last night — You were a little
muzzy as usual, I suppose! — you little guessed what you would be
called upon to do! Or what you *would* do! It must have been a great
shock, instead of merely ministering to the sick, to — '

The lines about the small man's eyes and mouth had deepened when
he swung about. Even in the sullen light that was neither night nor day,
Earle saw his whole face darken. His mouth opened and shut for a
moment without emitting any sound. Then he held up the ruined spectacles in the fashion of one producing a piece of irrefutable evidence.

'How could I tell?' he asked in a high-pitched voice. 'I can see nothing
without my glasses. I am as blind as a bat — as you well know . . . I
dropped them, and walked on them.'

Said Dr. Earle quietly —

'My fee as medical attendant on this auspeecious occasion — or is it
not auspeecious? — was precisely one thousand dollars. And *not* Continental currency, I would have you know! One thousand dollars in
minted money. And paid on the nail! . . . Now I wonder how Mrs.
Purvis compensated you for those broken glasses? Was it just by honorarium? Or did she do something else more delicate and considerate?

Really delicate and considerate? A promise to remain silent about some little peccadillo, perhaps? About Susie Green, for example?'

'Hush!' said Chancellor angrily. 'Can't you let things alone? You have a most poisonous tongue sometimes, Dr. Earle! You said that you would never — ' Light suddenly broke on him. He gave alarmed challenge to the black figure that stooped over him. 'It was you who told her! . . . You! There was no other way in which she could have learned.'

'I may have been a trifle unguarded,' admitted Dr. Earle. 'I apologize. But she is a clever woman, a very clever woman — as we both have reason to know! She knows how to turn anything — a scrap of information no matter how small — into a weapon to her hand. In circumstances like these she comes into her own! She would make a fine Lady Macbeth, or Medea!'

He regarded thoughtfully the disorder of the drive before the house. The grey shell surface was scored with the track of wheels and pitted with hoof marks. In the middle of the roadway lay the tall bearskin of a British grenadier — almost conical and absurdly like a dunce's cap of fur. A squat bottle had rolled to the verge of the colourless grass, and something — rag, or bandage, or handkerchief — lay at the foot of the steps with a great dark stain upon it.

'New Orleans after *Mardi Gras,*' he commented: descended the wide flight with a peculiar bent-kneed, prancing motion. Mr. Chancellor thought that he walked something like a spider.

Earle brought back the cap, regarding with a quizzical smile the tarnished brass plate on its front bearing King George III's coat of arms. Then he set the thing bolt upright on the marble threshold of the fan-lighted entrance to the house.

The fur was very wet and muddy, so that it resembled some small and bedraggled woodland creature beseeching shelter.

'They'll like,' said Dr. Earle, 'some wee souvenir of the occasion!'

Mr. Chancellor stared for a little at it in a fascination of horror: to him it symbolized the something obscene which, he felt, lurked in the precincts of the unhappy house. He averted his wizened face and blood-shot eyes.

'You should no' concern yourself too deeply,' said Dr. Earle yawning, 'with what has transpired. Even though you're a puir Episcopalian. Other sects will do as much — aye, and more — for their followers. Far, far more! . . . Pre-natal baptism, for instance!'

Mr. Chancellor showed no sign of drawing comfort from this statement. His professional interest, however, was aroused.

'What's that?'

Dr. Earle made certain that the cap-beast would not topple over when the door was opened. He flicked his muddied hands together as though on an imaginary towel.

'Aye, according to the records there have been quite a number of cases of pre-natal baptism — a christening of the embryo, you will understand. Quite offeecially per-rformed! It is a prettily ingenious and interesting method. It is like this — '

Mr. Chancellor was, temporarily at any rate, spared instruction. His ears had caught the rattle of quick wheels.

'At last!'

He heaved a sigh of relief.

But it was not the sober chariot that had fetched him from the parsonage during the windy night. It was a smart two-seated sulky with high yellow wheels, driven by a negro servant in a livery of light red and gold that was startling even in the grey twilight of daybreak. Its passenger was a large lady completely enveloped in large cloak, head invisible within large hood.

'Aha!' said the doctor with glee. 'And again, Aha!'

The large lady was on the ground. Came ballooning up the steps. Ignored their salutes. Flung from the secret cavern of her hood a brusque question —

'Is my daughter — is Lavinia — here?'

She looked from one to the other with arrogant bearing, as though defying them to dare lie to her.

The doctor drawled an answer for both, bowing as he spoke with a deference that was almost a parody of politeness.

'She has not yet left, so far as I am aweer, madam!'

She passed on without a word, and, finding the door barred, tugged most furiously at the iron bell-pull.

The carriage that was to restore them to their homes was even then drawing up. As he made to follow his hurrying companion down the steps, the doctor cast a last sardonic glance at the dark figure blotted against the phantasmal whiteness of the imposing door. Even at a distance he could see its sidelong regard of the cap-creature which, with it, sought admittance.

He turned and descended to the equipage with a dry smile.

'"Sero venientibus ossa,"' he remarked, hand on silver door handle. 'And that, Mr. Chancellor, as you doubtless know — or perhaps don't — means: "The late comer only gets the bones".'

He plunged within the nest of green morocco leather.

'Bones, mark you, Mr. Chancellor! Bones! Ve-e-ery suitable!'

The noise of wheels, and hoofs, and harness, as they drove past the long frontage of the house, drowned his sudden shout of laughter.

CHAPTER II

STRANGE NEWS FOR THE MAKER OF A CITY

At dusk on the night before there had been no broken glass lying on the floor of the wide porch — spacious as a temple aisle — that shadowed the three tall windows of the library.

The curtains were undrawn, and the long panes full of the desolation of nightfall — dark trees shivering against darkening sky; tattered clouds streaming across the heavens before the wind like the broken crests of billows across the sea; sullen river in whose waters there was no light.

This desolation was, however, as remote from the silent room as though not reality, but a decoration in three panels of grey and black, placed there to emphasize utter detachment from the outer world. It was a room painted apple-green, candle-lit, and walled with books, which crowded, shelf upon shelf, to the very ceiling — not merely a tapestry to mask the panelling, but an arras of dreams to shut out the present. Only over the malachite fireplace had space been left for Colonel Beriah Purvis — enormously peruked and jack-booted, and clad in a dark green coat with silver sash — to stare with contemptuous negligence at the countless volumes out of his Florentine frame.

Directly beneath his great-grandfather's portrait, back to the melancholy of the windows, Anthony Purvis — in a flowered gown of silk — sat at a chess table, its top checkered with ebony and ivory. He was established in a wing arm-chair mounted on small wooden wheels, and read intently in a book propped against a decanter, chin supported on hand and black locks very ruffled.

He read on. He turned a page. He extended long fingers absent-mindedly towards an empty wineglass. Within the isolation of his library he was in his turn isolated; was as aloof from his surroundings as they themselves were withdrawn from the fading landscape. While he read night crept about the mansion; war flickered up and died down about the countryside; retreating soldiery trailed through the dusk past his gates like shabby ghosts, as they had trailed at intervals all day long.

Now and then there had been scattered musket shots; and once there had come from very far away, beyond the wet woods, a muffled thumping as a distant battery of artillery went into action. But Purvis had not raised his eyes. He was not even distracted now, when the shuffle of weary feet along the road was drowned by the tattoo of hoofs that clattered to a sudden halt before the house; nor when someone walked crisply up the steps. Neither did he so much as look up a minute later, when a gentle knock sounded upon the library door, and there entered an elderly negro servant with solemn wrinkled face and closely cropped grey hair. A big man in dark blue livery coat and white cotton trousers. He halted at deferential attention just upon the threshold —

'Sah!'

Mr. Purvis traversed twenty centuries of time.

'Sah!'

Mr. Purvis travelled across seven thousand miles of space — he was reading in an antique translation of Herodotus, of Babylon the great city, whose walls were two hundred cubits high and pierced by an hundred gates of brass.

Even then, had not the small buhl clock on the mantelpiece, under Colonel Beriah's portrait, chimed the hour, it is doubtful whether Mr. Purvis would have returned to the American continent and to the year of grace one thousand seven hundred and eighty-one. He raised reluctant regard from printed page.

'What is it, Rasselas?' he asked indifferently.

'Sah, dere's a red-coat — an' English milerterry n'orfficer — '

'What, again?' commented Purvis. He slowly closed his book, yet leaving imprisoned between the worn covers a forefinger which he appeared unwilling to withdraw — as though such action would have been the symbol of too complete a divorce.

'Yes-sah. He ax — '

'Make the usual arrangements. Warn Mrs. Purvis. Apologize for me. If he should ask you, say — as usual — that it is true my mother's personal maids sleep in the house, but that they are locked in their quarters at night, and that she keeps the key.' He relinquished Herodotus at last; drew forward his wineglass; remarked its emptiness with mild surprise. 'Get me out Camelot! I will amuse myself with it for half an hour or so before starting work.'

Rasselas swung about on his heel; went cat-footed to a red lacquer cabinet close to the wall of books, and returned as noiselessly, carrying a tray covered with a cloth. This he placed on the long table which stood in the middle of the room, under a lighted chandelier whose pendant lustres sparkled and glistered as though the many candles had dripped into long icicles instead of wax. He snuffed the wicks in the wall sconces;

placed a cherry-wood log on the fire; as he straightened himself, said —
'Jedge Campbell's barn wuz burned las' night, Marse Tony!'

'How did that happen?' asked Mr. Purvis without much interest.

'De red-coats — dey say Jedge Campbell sot fier to hit hisse'f 'n try to roas' 'em alive. Jedge Campbell sez, sezee, dat dey wuz a-smokin' in de straw. Howsummuver, dey wuz all er-sleep w'en hit happened, 'n some uv 'em come nigh ter jumpin' de eberlastin' gates!'

Rasselas's tone was one of regret at the escape from death of the troops of His Majesty King George the Third.

'They'll be out of the country soon enough,' said Purvis indifferently. 'They are making for Yorktown as fast as they can go . . . Move me now!'

A moment later he was being wheeled in his chair toward the windows. The wide skirts of the heavy silken gown that hid his useless limbs rustled over the carpet in his progress. For a brief instant he faced the desolation that pressed against the panes — the blackness of the trees barely distinguishable from the blurred grey of nightfall. Then the vision was blotted out as the chair was swung gently round to anchorage at the head of the dark and shining table.

With the studied solemnity that the rite demanded, Rasselas lifted the veil from the tray before his master . . . To reveal an enchanting toy city some two foot square. A city of red roofs and grey spires and gilded pinnacles — of winding alleys, and houses with overhanging storeys and pointed gables, and churches, and cloisters, and colonnaded market-place — clustered about a tall castle that might have come from a fairy-tale.

On either side of this city's lord, close against his wheel-chair, Rasselas placed a small wine-table. On one was a litter of thin pasteboard, cartridge papers, scraps of all sorts, slivers of wood, gluepot, box of water-colours — the raw material of city-building, as well as an array of knives and scissors and compasses and ivory rulers. On the other was an enormous stack of manuscript, more than a foot thick at a moderate computation.

As he thus made ready for Mr. Purvis's evening entertainment and labours, the negro looked with never-failing interest upon the magical thing spread beneath his view as though it were a city of reality seen from a mountain top. Almost automatically his gaze sought out the landmarks; was held for a moment at one point. A discreet smile irradiated his melancholy face: he felt urgently that comment was called for.

'Dat new house at de en' er Lady Lane sutt'nly looks good, Marse Tony,' he said in respectful approval. 'En' I see dat las' night you done bin ter wuk 'n fixed up cullud winders fer de church. Dey look mighty nice ter me.'

The unsought tribute eventually reached those secret places wherein pererrated the thoughts of Mr. Purvis.

'So you noticed that, did you, Rasselas?' he said, his dark eyes still lowered to the model. A slight smile twisted the corners of his mouth. 'And what else?'

'I reckon dat I need my specs, Marse Tony,' answered the other slowly, peering down afresh. 'But ef desyere ole eyes don' fail me dere's a sot er contrapshun stickin' outer what I call Miz' Simmonses' house.'

There was. To one of the whimsical little houses in a crooked little lane had been added an oriel with mullioned window, a trifle less than half an inch high.

But Mr. Purvis's gratification was clouded. It was not Miss Simmons's house. No such person as a Miss Simmons could ever dwell in Camelot.

'It's —' he began; and fell silent, for he did not choose to make his servant a partaker of his imaginings.

Rasselas awaited revelation for a moment or so in silence; and, when it was obvious that none was forthcoming, shook his frosted head to clear his mind of the cobweb of dreams; gave his master a peculiar and somewhat unhappy look; hesitated, and then moved silently away.

Before he reached it, the door opened.

A lady entered, and — as she entered — imperiously beckoned to him, with black-mittened hand, to remain. She had a high and bitter nose, and thin and bitter lips; and scanty black hair that was drawn fiercely back from the forehead as though to strain the sallow skin of her face without a wrinkle over the bones of the skull, and anchor it securely. She wore a gown of black brocade, and the white neckerchief that was folded over her thin shoulders was fastened in front by a large mourning brooch ornamented with a sarcophagus bearing the words, 'Affection regrets; Heaven rejoices.' About her there was an almost conventual bleakness; and her presence in the book-walled sanctuary was as unfriendly and frigid as the dusk pressing against the windows — but could not be ignored.

Rasselas shut the door after her, and she went up the room with a susurration of wide skirts like the stirrings and the whisperings of dead leaves.

'Good evening, Anthony,' she said, coming to a halt at the far end of the table. 'Permit me to disturb your meditations for a few moments.'

Her voice — precise, chill, flat — recalled him from Camelot.

He bowed, and, with hands pressed upon the table, sketched the gesture of rising — a politeness that it was impossible for him to perform unaided.

'Good evening, Mother,' he replied; guessed at the reason for so unusual a visit — for they lived wholly separate lives in his great house; continued — 'I suppose you have come about this Englishman. But what can I do? We can't turn him out. We must just congratulate ourselves that it's one Englishman, and not a crowd of Hessians.'

'That *this* house —' began Mrs. Purvis; checked herself, and went on: 'I did *not* come "about this Englishman", but about a far more serious matter. I came to ascertain how far your knowledge went in its regard. I came to consult you as head of the family.'

Anthony realized that her tone implied how unsatisfactory a head of the family she found him. Once such implication would have irritated him, but now long usage had rendered him completely indifferent. As she turned her head slightly he noted the usual large drip at the end of her nose, and that it was ready to fall; he found himself speculating — as he had a thousand times before — on its destination, and upon the insensitiveness of certain noses to the presence of drips. He said —

'You may go, Rasselas! . . . Will you not be seated, Mother?'

She ignored the invitation, and remained standing. Indeed she was never seen to sit except at mealtimes, and appeared to pass her waking life on her feet, as though perpetually on the point of departure on some urgent errand. Stilly and unhurried as she was, yet she thus inevitably bore with her an atmosphere of restless expectancy.

'Forgive me, Anthony,' she said, darting command in a glance at the negro who stayed waiting by the door. 'But Rasselas must *not* go. Unless he has told you of the part he and his daughter are playing in our affairs. *Our* affairs! . . . Come here, Rasselas!'

The unhappy servant came drooping to her side.

'Has he informed you of his movements this afternoon? Of where he went? Of what he obtained? And why?'

Anthony Purvis, looking up quickly and then looking as quickly down, saw them for an instant posed against the faint background of the tapestry of books, like puppets in the traditional attitudes of denunciation and despair. He smiled secretly.

His mother suddenly lowered her eyes; sought for an instant in the black bag of woven horsehair that was pinned to a fold of her dress; extracted a small square of coarse linen.

When she spoke again her face was down-bent, and her speech punctuated by pauses in which she deliberately drew threads from an edge of the stuff and let them flutter to the floor. She always carried with her a supply of such pieces of tormented material, which on all sorts of occasions she frayed with deep fringes, or knotted with innumerable tassels, or caused to disintegrate into something like a cobweb. No one ever knew what it was she manufactured, or had viewed the finished article.

It was a strange hobby, and the stranger because it cut across all those other habits of precision and orderliness which she rigidly observed in public. On the other hand it was in keeping with the only weakness in which she permitted herself to indulge in private — the nibbling of all sorts of small dainties and sweetmeats at all sorts of times, and the leaving of tooth-marked relics in all sorts of unlikely places in her bed-chamber and sitting-room.

Said Mrs. Purvis, satisfactorily busied with the linen —

'Did he say that he went slinking through the dusk' — A thread went out — 'to the Swamp' — Another thread — 'to old Hannah's hut!' — Thread — 'to bring back some potion for which his daughter was waiting' — Thread — 'in our kitchen?'

' "Potion!" ' repeated Purvis slowly. His mind revolved all the witch-brews of literature. ' "Potion?" ' he repeated again with rising inflection. ' "Potion?" '

He looked at Rasselas with one lifted eyebrow. The man, he noted with private amusement, was the very personification of guilt.

Said Mrs. Purvis —

'Poison!' — Thread — 'Murder in a bottle!'

What mare's nest had his mother discovered now? — he wondered. Poison! . . . Socrates and his draught of hemlock . . . The shirt of Nessus . . . Pope Alexander the Sixth . . . Toffana . . . Madame de Brinvilliers . . . Rasselas! He raised his eyes again from Camelot to steal another glance at this member of the confraternity of the Borgias.

'Poison for some of our English visitors, Rasselas?' he inquired.

Mrs. Purvis's chill black regard was lifted; fastened upon him.

'It was poison' — Thread — 'to murder the unborn!' — Another — 'That is what Deborah was waiting for!'

So to this, then, had come the solemn little beauty who was Rasselas's daughter, a demure small person who walked with the proud and enticing carriage of the Queen of Sheba! A bad business! A sad business! But not unusual. He did not understand, however, why his mother should be so concerned over the morals of a slave girl who was not even a member of their household, but of her sister-in-law's. Mrs. Purvis was ordinarily interested neither in negroes nor her female relations.

'I am sorry about this, Rasselas,' he said: and there was genuine sympathy in his voice. 'We must do what we can for Deborah — but not in that way. Perhaps — '

'Deborah!' interrupted Mrs. Purvis, and she dealt with the square of linen in her hand as though it were an enemy. 'Deborah! Should *I* care whether Deborah spawns or not? Whether she slaughters her bastards or not? . . . It was for her mistress — for Lavinia . . . To murder Richard's unborn child!'

' "For Lavinia to — " '

He began to repeat his mother's statement, not loudly or angrily, but in a slow quiet voice, as though trying to impress it upon his understanding: and then, even before reaching realization, sought proof:

'How do you know this?'

'I saw him leave the house — from my window. I saw where he went. I saw him return. He was so furtive that my suspicions were aroused. I went down to his pantry. He was about to give his daughter *this!*' She suddenly produced and let fall upon the table a small phial, like a scent phial, full of black liquid. 'I asked an explanation. I was put off with lies. I demanded the truth . . . I got it!'

'How do you know it is the truth?' asked Purvis. Again he looked up, and then addressed Rasselas directly — 'How do *you* know about Miss Lavinia and Mr. Richard?'

The man squared his shoulders, and met his master's gaze. His voice held the deep song and resonance of wood wind.

'Miss Lavvy done tole Deb'rah, Marse Tony.'

Purvis's physical regard shifted to the golden pinnacles of the castle shining above the jumbled roofs of the entranced city of Camelot; but it was the dark proud face of his cousin Lavinia Fell that the eyes of his mind saw as he spoke. His critical faculty found it but little more appalling that she should have discussed the avoidance of motherhood with her negro maid, than that he should now debate her shame with a negro servant.

'Why?'

'Miss Lavvy ax Deb'rah ter git her med'cine las' Saddy night. She do'n say whaffor she want hit, en' Deb'rah was dat skeered outen her skin ter go ter ole Aunt Hannah in de dark dat she up en 'clar dat she ain't a-goin' — not no-how. So den Miss Lavvy tole her jes' zackly why. En' she went . . . De med'cine wuz mighty pow'ful med'cine, I cackerlate, fer Miss Lavvy wuz took tu'ible sick. But hit wuzn't no good. So Miss Lavvy ax fer some mo' an' pow'fuller. But Deb'rah dassen't go agin, en' tole her mammy, en' her mammy tole me. En' I fotch't hit.'

Even yet the story was as one read in the printed page, and not con-

cerned with real life — with his own life — with Lavinia's life — with —
'Doesn't anyone else know about this? Hasn't Mrs. Fell guessed?
Deborah has spoken to no one except you and Vera Lou?'

'Nobuddy don' know nuffin',' insisted Rasselas. 'Deb'rah sez dat she
sho' dat nobuddy hab a s'pishun. Eben ole Miz' — yet!'

Purvis reflected —

· 'Deborah didn't misunderstand Miss Lavinia? She is quite, quite sure
about — everything?'

'Spang sho', Marse Tony.'

With that Rasselas halted awkwardly, looking everywhere save at his
master or the still woman at his side, and fumbled for euphemisms:
found none: ambled into a morass of disconnected words and phrases
amid which Purvis distinguished a constant repetition of the statement
'Three months'.

Three months!

Three months ago Richard was still alive, although that hazy morning
of battle was very close when he was to fall amid his men at Hobkirk's
Hill under a hail of lead.

Three months! . . . He recalled the formal good-byes said in the
parlour under the dispassionate regard of four pictured generations of
Purvises and the watchful eyes of his mother and Aunt Fell: good-byes
indeed so formal that some instinct had told that there had been — or
were to be — other and less restrained farewells between his brother
and his cousin. No flicker of emotion had quivered the girl's icy composure; but after she had gone with her mother back to Fell House,
he had watched Richard standing — blue-coated, booted, spurred — lost
in reverie before the fire. Guessed at a love story without envy, and
with a selfless pleasure which overmastered all regret that Lavinia might
no longer figure, pale and proud, even in the unending tapestry of his
dreams.

He sat very still, staring at Camelot. Mrs. Purvis remained motionless. There was no sound within the room but the snapping and fall of
a log on the hearth. There seemed, indeed, to be no sound within all
the house; but, in the ghostly dusk without, once more ghostly feet
dragged and shuffled and tramped.

He saw the face of that much-loved brother in the mirror of his mind:
saw the high-bridged nose and the bright grey eyes, the high cheekbones and the arching eyebrows, the leanness and the weathered ruddi-
ness, the long strong chin with the faint cleft, the golden glint at the
temples in his fair unpowdered hair. He saw, too, his cousin's loveliness
— the long white throat, the blue-black hair sweeping back from a

widow's peak on the broad forehead, the upward slant of the eyebrows which gave her such faint air of mockery as a fairy lady might wear.

Had their love, their beauty, and their passion ended then in this — that negroes should whisper of their sin?

'Suppose that you emerge from your day-dreams, Anthony,' said Mrs. Purvis, 'and consider what can be done.'

She looked at him directly as she spoke, and he was aware that on the yellowed mask of her countenance, the skin was only white where it strained over the bones. That mask, he knew, would never crease with the lines of laughter or of sorrow; in it, indeed, life showed but faintly and far-away through the eyes — and even their blackness seemed to quench light rather than reflect it. He still feared her almost as much as he had done in childhood: and for the same reason — a shrinking from something inhuman in the violent spirit that raged furiously behind features which it could yet hold as impassive as those painted on a mummy-case.

He nerved himself for the battle to come.

'You may go, Rasselas,' he said. 'Has Deborah gone home yet? . . . Then tell her to wait for a little. You, or one of the older men, can see her back to Fell House in a short time.' He hesitated; steeled himself: 'With all respect to Mrs. Purvis, you did quite right — in my view. I don't see what else you could have properly done, in the circumstances . . . You may go!'

'He did right, did he?' quoted his mother's colourless voice almost before the door had shut.

'Rasselas was only being loyal to his daughter. Who was loyal to her mistress.'

'He did right, did he, to connive at the murder of your brother's child?'

'I should imagine,' said Anthony, staring at Camelot, 'that your use of the word "murder" is definitely arguable.'

'Arguable! . . . Is it on such terms that you can discuss the slaughter of Richard's child — Richard's heir — Richard's *son*?'

He remarked —

'Son? . . . Still another matter that is arguable, Mother.'

'Son!' she asseverated.

And then again repeated the one word 'Son' with such conviction that he, too, found himself believing in her foreknowledge. With that selfsame chill mien (he thought) the Pythoness of Delphi and the Oracles of Dodona or Amphiaraus must have prophesied of old to the embassies of kings.

Mrs. Purvis said a monstrous thing without emotion —

'You envy Richard having a son, I suppose . . . You were always envious of him in life. Not unnaturally, perhaps. But your envy appears to reach beyond the grave. You — '

'That is not just and not true,' interrupted Anthony. 'Your love of Richard — both during his life and since his death — has always been so exclusive that it has deliberately sought to deny to others the privilege of loving him.'

'For Lavinia,' continued Mrs. Purvis, ignoring his protest, 'I care not one whit. But she *shall* bear Richard's child, even if I have to act midwife myself. Whether she lives or dies is immaterial so long as Richard's blood is carried on . . . I shall go to your Aunt Fell. She will be glad enough for the matter to be taken out of her hands and quietly arranged. I shall then take the girl away. At once. To my Long Island house . . . I shall bring up the child myself.'

Better — thought Anthony — that Richard's child should remain among the unborn than that it should be brought up by his mother — a Cupid nourished by Medusa. What relentless hate — what continuing envy — what unnecessary malice — would be implicit in its education! Scorn for its mother — contempt for him — blind hatred for the English stock whence they had sprung! It did not bear imagining that Richard's and Lavinia's child should be left to the mercies of his mother in that far-away paint-blistered house of hers facing the grey Atlantic.

'So after all there will be a Purvis to avenge poor Richard!'

Her words came pat upon his thoughts.

'In twenty years' time all this confusion and horror will be forgotten.'

'Forgotten! . . . Forgotten! . . . Do you think that these things will be so easily forgotten? It will take more than one generation to forget massacre — treachery — rapine — murder! It will take three generations — four generations — five generations.'

'I pray to God, No!' . . . He also prayed in his heart that she would soon go: promised himself solution of his problems in peace, whilst shaping and painting the turret that should overhang the two inch long garden of the Lords of Camelot.

'You have condoned the attempted murder of your brother's child. You would forgive his murder, too?'

'Murder?' said Anthony irritably. He stared at the rows of books behind her and the quiet sheen of their gilt and of their rich leather. 'You really make very free with the word "murder", my dear Mother. Richard was killed in fair fight — unless he was shot down by one of his own men, which is unlikely.'

He pushed Camelot away, and drew toward him a silver standish with ink-pot, and sand-castor, and taper-holder.

His mother did not speak for a moment.

She was looking beyond him, at the tall windows, now panels of shining darkness, in which the candle flames were reflected as in black still water.

From the invisible road faintly sounded the creak and rumble of slow-turning wheels. At that very minute, too, there came to them a gust of drunken laughter, shreds of a raucous song, and the delighted squealing of a woman.

'They crawl with their drabs from defeat to defeat,' said his mother, without any inflection of the voice. Out of Isaiah she drew the text which her soul required; went on in low and even tones —

' "Their slain also shall be cast out, and their stink shall come up out of their carcases, and the mountains shall be melted with their blood." '

Although no muscle of her face moved, yet well he was aware that behind its mask the spirit of Henriette Purvis viewed the mounds of the unburied with joyful ferocity, and snuffed up the reek of blood and corruption, revelling therein.

'You have left three important factors out of consideration.' While he spoke he examined the bright-hued flowers embroidered on the sleeve of his banian — the point of a quill — the edge of the mother-of-pearl penknife in the tray of the standish. 'One is Lavinia herself. The second is her mother — and you should know by now something of the idiosyncrasies of Aunt Fell. Lastly, you have ignored me. That — in parenthesis — is not unusual, if I may say so. Now I am not merely Richard's elder brother and executor *and* friend, but also a very rich man. Although I am a wretched crippled creature — as you frequently remind me — I can offer to Richard's child and the girl I choose to consider as Richard's widow more than you can. Far, far more! And I propose to . . . You know even better than I do that Aunt Fell will always take the highest bid . . . I shall bid high. Very high! Richard's child and Richard's wife will be *my* care!'

She had battled and argued with him for half an hour — still standing and staring above his head into the solid darkness — before she realized his immovability. Then she regarded him with impenetrable face for a moment; turned on her heel, and went silently from the room.

For ten minutes after she had gone, perhaps, he remained peering at his little city — tracing the course of its winding streets, peopling its steep-roofed houses, recalling the romantic histories of its spiked towers. Then, as one refreshed by sojourn in Broceliande or Emain or some other realm of fantasy, he returned to the present.

He rang the hand-bell at his side.

When Rasselas came, he said —

'No letter— no messenger — will go from here to Fell House to-night except by my orders . . . You understand? No one at all! In a little you and one of the other men may take Deborah back — there are too many troops about for it to be safe for her alone. She will give Miss Lavinia a letter I am going to write . . . Come back for it in a quarter of an hour.'

He drew to him a sheet of paper: dipped quill in ink-pot.

'Dearest Lavvy,' he wrote— and with those two words came to a full stop.

'Dearest, dearest Lavvy — '

'My adored Lavvy — '

'My dearest Lavinia — '

Any of these forms of address he would have liked to write, continuing in a swift rush:

'I know *everything*. Would not the easiest remedy be for you to marry me at once? I beg you to do so, for Richard's sake as well as your own. You know without being told that I shall never ask anything of you except the right to protect you. — Anthony.'

But there must be no humiliation, by bleak directness, of a proud lady already humbled to the point of seeking aid from the potions of a witch-doctor.

It must be such a letter as should show beyond question that she retained all his homage, all his reverence, all his love. An affectionate letter, therefore — but a rather formal letter. A letter that would evade truth rather than emphasize it, and still be explicit. A very humble letter that should offer everything, and demand nothing . . . A very difficult letter!

He sat, folded arms upon the table, contemplating the greyish square of paper in front of him for a long time before he tore it across, and began again.

Rasselas had already twice reappeared when Purvis finally laid down his quill pen, dusted the sheet with sand from the silver castor, and set himself to read the last of many versions —

'High Pale, Wednesday.

'Dearest Cousin and Sister,

'Altho' it is so short a time since Richard died a hero's death in the cause of American freedom, I think I may now venture to write of what has been in my mind ever since the dreadful news arrived.

'It is this.

'Richard's sentiments in your regard were no secret from me, and I know that he proposed seeking Aunt Fell's consent to a union immediately upon returning from the campaign in the Carolinas. In this so happy event, which jealous destiny has denied us, it would have been my right, and my privilege, and my pleasure to make adequate provision for the two persons whom I most loved in the world. As my lawyer will shortly inform you, I have refused to be deprived of the consolation of making the same settlement on you that I should have made if our beloved Richard had lived.

'Furthermore, because I well know that once having given your love to Richard you will never supplant him in your heart by another, I venture to make a proposal which may seem to you at the outset a little strange. First, however, let me beg you to believe that my sole purpose is your happiness, and I can see no other way to make certain of your escape from intolerable dependence and subjection — even humiliation — or to establish your complete and unquestioned freedom of thought and word and deed.

'My proposal is this.

'Let me give you the name which you would have taken had Richard lived — Richard's name. Let me have that right to protect you which Richard would have had. In short, let me be in the eyes of the world your husband, tho' still before God only your — and Richard's — loyal, and humble, and very loving brother,

'Anthony.

'By this same messenger I send you a token that you well know. — A.P.'

It would do! . . . It would not do! . . . It was stilted and not sufficiently explicit. But how else to word it? . . . How?

With sudden desperate decision he folded the sheet, enclosed it in another, superscribed the cover, and sealed it with a great ring which he wore on the little finger of his left hand.

It must do. It was a poor ill-written letter from a poor mis-shapen creature, but, for all that —

He rang the small bell shrilly.

'Bring me the Muscovite casket,' he told Rasselas, and tossed a key on to the table.

In a corner near the door stood a large geographer's globe, blue-shining, and imprisoned (like a captive planet) in a heavy stand of mahogany and brass. Rasselas bent over it; busied himself with it for a few seconds. When he turned and approached the table he was carrying a little casket covered in faded blue velvet, and strapped with bands of tarnished silver. He brought it to his master flat upon one enormous pinkish palm as though he had it on a dish.

Purvis raised his head, and looked at the servant. It seemed to Rasselas that his dark eyes had become quite black.

'Before you go to Fell House with the letter and a package I shall give you,' said he, 'you will bring Vera Lou and Deborah to this room with you. The three of you will swear on the Holy Bible' — he paused, ransacking his recollection for imagery that would impress the negro mind; continued — 'on your fear of Hell — on your hope of Heaven — by all you hold dear — by the memory of your mother — by the Nine and Ninety Names of the Living God — by Israfel, the Angel of the Resurrection, that you will never again speak one word of this matter on this side of the grave! Never! . . . Never!'

He pushed the inkstand to one side, and opened the casket.

He poured on to the shining dark surface of the table a necklace of great diamonds so that it lay before him in a mound which held all the qualities of starlight, and ice, and the fire that burns in the sunlit spray of a cataract.

He quenched its brilliance with his cupped hand: he unveiled its glitter.

. . . Invisible in the darkness that pressed against the windows, the never-ending stream of baggage wagons and guns went creaking by. Women's voices were raised in shrill and drunken chorus. A command was bellowed out, and hoarsely repeated down the line till beyond hearing. . . .

'Draw the curtains,' said Anthony Purvis — as one who might say: 'Shut out the world!'

The wooden rings slid drily behind the carved and gilded pelmets as the negro drew the great tapestry folds before the sightless windows.

Night was shut out; war shut out; time shut out. The room became once more the ante-chamber of that other world in which alone he found reality . . . The diamonds, the waiting letter to Lavinia were merged into the fabric of his dreams.

CHAPTER III

THE VOYAGE OF AN HISTORIAN

RASSELAS was long in returning, but Purvis did not remark the fact. He sat in deep thought, staring at his toy city without seeing its jumble of roofs and towers. In such deep thought that he did not hear a peremptory knocking, and only looked up as the door was abruptly opened and a young man appeared on the threshold — a young man in a scarlet coat faced with green, and green breeches, and high riding-boots. A very trim young man with a deeply tanned face, and a high forehead that was very white a little above the brows; his powdered hair sculptured rather than curled into a rigid wave on either side of his head.

'Mr. Purvis?' inquired the young man in a staccato manner.

Purvis acknowledged his identity by a nod. He wondered how immaculate cravat and ruffles at wrist — how so much of elegance — had sustained without visible blemish the rigours of warfare.

His visitor quietly closed the door; walked with quick step to the table; bowed in very formal fashion across the length of mahogany.

'Hurrell. Brevet-Captain. Fourth Dragoons,' he announced himself.

'I am honoured,' said Purvis returning the courtesy. 'I was unaware that any of the Fourth Dragoons were in America. And what can I do for you, Captain Hurrell?'

As he spoke he took stock of the Englishman.

In the keen tanned face that confronted him he traced a surprising resemblance to his dead brother — not so much in individual feature as in type. There was about him the same air of eager youth and intelligence, of hardiness: the grey eyes were clouded with hostility in just such a manner as at times Richard's had been: the formal tones were an echo of the chill voice that Richard himself would assume towards a misliked stranger.

'I am attached to the Foreign Legion under Major Tarleton, sir,' said Captain Hurrell grudgingly, and continued — 'I have taken the liberty of intruding upon you, sir, with reference to your message to me!'

'My message to you?' echoed Purvis, knitting his brows. 'What message, may I ask?'

'There was some message which I failed to comprehend — it was delivered by your negro servant — with reference to the key of the maids' quarters!'

The soldier spoke with a stiff, offended face.

'You require it?' asked Purvis maliciously: relented as he saw the angry flush mount to the young man's forehead. 'No! I apologize, sir. I did not mean that. The message was only to have been given if my guest showed signs of desiring ancillary adventure. It was a mistake on the part of my servant.'

The word 'ancillary' was presumably new to Captain Hurrell, for his eyebrows mounted doubtfully as though he suspected it of connoting something indecent or unnatural.

Purvis, with inward appreciation, went on —

'I am an invalid — I have been one all my life — and I am rarely able to meet my guests personally and assess — if I may put it so bluntly — their probable code of behaviour. You must forgive Rasselas: he lacks judgment in some things. On the other hand my mother declines to be waited on by negresses: she has two very personable French maids. *And* we have had some very strange visitors here lately. Very, very strange. visitors!'

'I was afraid,' said Captain Hurrell, his austerity relaxing, 'that you must have had some unpleasant experience. I won't inquire into the details. I can guess them, sir! I apologize very humbly.'

Purvis, considering in not unfriendly fashion that pattern-book of a young officer before him, felt that pride and social correctness entered into the apology rather than any degree of humility.

'There are scallawags in every army,' he conceded.

Captain Hurrell acknowledged the truth of the statement by a grave bow.

'I very much regret that you should have had cause of complaint in the conduct of any English officer,' he said. 'More particularly since, I imagine, you are of English descent yourself.'

Purvis indicated the portrait of Colonel Beriah over the fireplace by a nod —

'The old gentleman — my great-grandfather — removed himself rather hurriedly from England in 1685. After the collapse of Monmouth's rebellion. He would certainly have been hanged if he hadn't!'

Hurrell regarded with interest the arrogant face and heavy-lidded eyes of that magnificent gentleman who might have dangled with entire lack of dignity at the end of an executioner's rope.

'A fine picture, sir,' he remarked.

'One of Huysmans' best . . . If you are interested in pictures you might care to examine those in the drawing-room. One or two are quite good. There's a portrait by Smybert of my grandfather as a young man, which almost makes you forget that the artist started life as a coach-painter. A painting of my mother in a red dress by Robert Feke that the connoisseurs praise very highly. And a Copley — too flattering, I'm afraid — of my younger brother and myself.'

'One has few opportunities to learn the appreciation of art while campaigning,' said Captain Hurrell. He had moved to the fireplace, and stood there for an instant examining more closely the lineaments of Colonel Beriah, the toe of a beautifully made riding-boot resting on the malachite curb. His survey passed to the book-lined walls. He added — 'Or of literature . . . You have a very fine library here, sir!'

'Fair — quite fair!' replied Purvis with a modesty that was obviously not genuine. His kindling eye ranged the shelves that mounted, from polished floor spread with Chinese rugs of apple green, to ceiling decorated with fat rosy cherubs on fat rosy clouds. 'Without looking at the titles, I am sure, you would never guess to what subject a very large section of my library is devoted!'

Hurrell shook his head.

'It includes,' said Purvis, offering a clue, 'the works of Apollonius Rhodius, Lucian, Homer. Of De Bergerac, Swift, Paltock. And Dante and Bunyan at the other end of the scale!'

As this obviously conveyed little or nothing to the Englishman, in whose countenance an expression of polite interest struggled with the blankness of non-comprehension, he further expounded —

'It is a section devoted to imaginary voyages — to fantastic journeyings through fairy seas; to the exploration of the unexplorable.'

He sat back in his chair, and regarded the roofs of Camelot a-shine under the brilliance of the great chandelier overhead, with a whimsical smile, as though he were some happy traveller viewing a haven in whose existence he had but half believed — 'I mean mythological and legendary voyages; such as that of Jason and the Argonauts in search of the Golden Fleece, of Bran the son of Febal, or St. Brendan. Pure efforts of fancy, like the journeyings of Lucian. Or of Cyrano de Bergerac to the sun and moon. Or of Peter Wilkins to the land of the Gawries. Travels — such as those recounted in the *Pilgrim's Progress* — that are allegories, or narrated as the vehicle for satire, like *Gulliver.*'

The young man nodded. His bright grey gaze moved from contemplation of Purvis's face to the unveiled pile of diamonds lying before him unheeded; to Camelot . · . . He was astonishingly like Richard! Richard, too, had used to stand in just such a manner under their great-grandfather's portrait, shoulder against mantelpiece, foot on curb, listening with polite attention to the narration of his elder brother's literary activities. Purvis found his heart warming to the Englishman —

'I am compiling a history of imaginary travel,' he confessed. 'On the lines of Hakluyt's *Voyages.*'

'An immense task!'

'I have already written three-quarter of a million words,' said Purvis, patting the mountain of manuscript on the small table at his left hand. 'But even so I am barely half-way through.'

This astronomical figure impressed Hurrell. He stepped two paces forward, the better to regard the mighty work, and Purvis shifted the pile so that he should view the title-page — a piece of the most artistic penmanship — which ran —

A History of
The Principal Voyages
Explorations and Discoveries
of
Fabulous Travellers

By Anthony Purvis Esq.

Underneath had been pencilled the words 'New York. Printed for H. Gaine?' — the mark of interrogation presumably indicating that the author had not finally decided who should have the honour of publication.

The Englishman was so close that Purvis could see the thread-bareness of his scarlet coat, and that there were rents in it which had been most exquisitely mended; and that his beautiful riding-boots had been patched and re-soled.

After Hurrell had returned to his fireside post he rained statistical questions upon his host about such matters as the total of words to a page of manuscript, daily output, average hours of work, and number of books used for reference, analysis, or quotation.

They were much at their ease by now — these two; soldier lounging against the mantelpiece, a rather consciously splendid figure that vied — by candle-light — even with the magnificence of Colonel Beriah at his back; cripple toying absent-mindedly with the necklace of immense gems while he told of strange wayfarers and yet stranger journeyings. So much at their ease, in fact, that Rasselas, looking into the room, was unobserved and withdrew.

'And the little town?' asked Hurrell at length. 'What part does it play? Is it a scale model of the capital of Lilliput or Blefuscu?'

'It is to me what her knitting is to a woman . . . I occupy myself with it for half an hour every evening. While I am shaping or colouring house or tower, my mind is at work upon problems of the *opus!*'

He spoke a trifle defensively, but the other appeared to comprehend.

'When I want to think anything out, *I* clean my pistols,' he said. 'A soothing occupation!'

Hurrell surveyed the library afresh, as though it would take on a new aspect in light of what he now knew of its master. He scanned the quiet tapestry of books that hid the walls, soft-coloured in the light of the sconces upon the green pilasters dividing the shelves into bays; viewed globe and red lacquer cabinet and the long mahogany table whose surface shone like a lake of dark wine beneath the glacial chandelier; brought back his regard to Camelot and Camelot's constructor with his long pale face and faintly twisted nose and dark eyes. The survey was done swiftly and without offence.

'The war seems very far away from here,' he said at length. 'One might be in another planet.'

'I sometimes wish we were,' replied Purvis. 'I try to convince myself that the war has nothing to do with me . . . Of course I can take no part in it . . .' He paused; went on, 'But my brother was killed in action barely three months ago.'

'I am sorry,' said Hurrell. 'He was — er — on the other side?'

Purvis nodded assent.

'He was what we call a Patriot, and you call a rebel . . . He had served throughout the campaign in Carolina. He fought at Camden, Cowpens, and Guildford. He was killed at Hobkirk's Hill.'

'I am sorry,' said Hurrell again: added with an air of relief — 'I was not there . . . The casualties, of course, were heavy on both sides. But it was an interesting engagement. Very interesting! Young Rawdon had picked up some useful tips from your people. It was a remarkable victory for a young man against superior numbers and an experienced general!'

Purvis meditated upon a second view-point of the battle which had cost him his brother's life.

'You take your profession seriously?' he commented.

'When you're a poor man, you've got to,' said Hurrell in a matter of fact sort of way. 'I am not only interested in soldiering, but like a lot of other fellows I have to make a living at it.'

'I thought — ' said Purvis, and left the sentence unfinished, implying by uplifted eyebrows his established belief that the English army was solely officered by the sons of the squirearchy and the plutocracy.

Captain Hurrell read his thoughts: he smiled a little wryly.

'Don't forget, sir, that the English army system is the most extraordinary in the world. An officer must buy his commission and pay for each step of promotion in solid cash. A poor man's son has to be exceptionally industrious — and exceptionally lucky — if he does not want to remain where he started.'

'Good God!' said Purvis. 'I had forgotten that — if I ever knew it. Something like buying an annuity!'

'Precisely. And a very expensive one.' Hurrell's grey eyes were again caught by the string of diamonds. He speculated about them as he spoke. 'My commission as cornet in the Dragoons cost my poor father seven hundred guineas, and my pay was exactly sufficient to keep my horse and my servant. By scraping and saving he just managed to buy me the next step. And that is as far as he will ever be able to go without robbing my sisters of their dowries.'

'But you are a captain now!'

'Brevet rank. There was a fellow I knew in the 55th. Got a brevet lieutenant-colonelcy. Commanded his regiment in action several times. A first-class soldier. What happened? He couldn't put up the cash for his promotion, and a young captain who had never been on active service put down six thousand pounds and got the command. Poor Tom had to go back to his company. I heard that he'd got killed the other day. I am not surprised.'

'Six thousand pounds!' commented Purvis slowly.

'A man who bought his way up in one of the best regiments would have spent anything in the neighbourhood of twelve thousand pounds by the time he was colonel!'

'A disheartening reflection for those without that sum!'

'Very,' said Hurrell with feeling. 'There was a man in ours. Before my time. Lieutenant and adjutant. In thirteen years he missed promotion twelve times. Junior officers purchased over him every time . . . He blew his brains out in the end.'

'That sort of business would not have suited Colonel Beriah,' remarked Purvis, raising his eyes to that dark and orgulous warrior. 'During the Commonwealth he went soldiering on the Continent. He fought for the Turks. He fought for the Austrians. He fought for the king of Spain. He fought for anyone who paid well. He finished by reorganizing the Russian artillery, and making a fortune. Here's the token!' He let the great necklace trickle through his fingers and rattle drily upon the table. 'The price of two colonelcies! . . . A mere casual gift from a Czar!'

Hurrell looked enviously for a moment again at the exponent of the art of soldiering for profit — and for a longer period at the necklace. He sighed.

'And they'd never even heard of de Gribeauval in those days!'

'Who was de Gribeauval?' asked Purvis with genuine interest.

'Is,' corrected Hurrell. 'He is the greatest artilleryist who has ever lived. A Frenchman. What he has done for guns will alter the entire science of war. But not one in a hundred of our people have ever heard of him. Nor ever will until we have been whacked on the Continent a few times. Mobility — and mobility at all costs is his watchword. And by God he has made it possible with what he has done for field artillery.

Do you know that one should be able now to fight a successful rear-guard action?'

The younger man approached the table. With the aid of silver standish, and Camelot, and — 'Permit me!' — the letter to Lavinia, he demonstrated. From that diverged to appreciation of Rawdon's pincer movement at Hobkirk's Hill — to general discussion on tactics.

Purvis listened with interest. He almost thought to hear Richard expounding the art of warfare. Richard and this young man would have been friends at once. He could vividly imagine an intense discussion between the two lasting until the small hours.

Captain Hurrell ran on. The bayonet was obsolete. The old solid formation even more so! Future battles would all be fought with as great a frontage of fire as possible. There must be much greater freedom of action for small units and the individual. Cut out some of the drill and concentrate on firing practice. Cut out the third rank in the infantry line.

He regarded thoughtfully the rosy Venus languishing among her cupids on the painted ceiling.

'Cut out the damned women, too!'

'A misogynist!' commented Purvis sympathetically.

So would Mr. Purvis be, if he had to deal not only with his men but with the cloud of women that surrounded them like blow-flies. Burgoyne's army of eight thousand men, for instance, had had two thousand women with them! Although the regulations only permitted sixty to a regiment — and that was sixty too many! . . . What women! Drabs from every city on the continent! Philadelphia — Boston — New York. Particularly New York. Half the trulls seemed to come from 'Canvas Town'.

' "Canvas Town" is a sore subject in this house,' said Purvis. 'Most of my mother's property in New York is in that area — between Whitehall Street and Broad Street. What wasn't burned down in the great fire of '76 was destroyed in the fire of '78, and what is left has been mostly wrecked by your people. My mother is by way of being an exceptionally vigorous — Patriot, so you may guess at her feelings!'

'When I was last in New York,' admitted Hurrell, 'it certainly seemed to me that a quarter of the town was in ruins . . . I think I must have seen Mrs. Purvis in the hall as I entered. A middle-aged lady. Dark. In black. I fancied at the time that she did not regard me with any particular favour . . . Thank you very much, I should enjoy a glass of sherry.'

He poured out a glass of the golden brown wine from one of the pair of ship's decanters which stood upon the checkered top of the chess-table, and held it up admiringly to the light.

'It looks a fine wine,' he said: drank — 'It *is* a fine wine, sir! Your good health! . . . As sound an East India as I have ever drunk . . . I also incline to the walnut flavour.'

Purvis gravely acknowledged the compliment — which privately amused him. The young Richard, too, would have set up as connoisseur in just such a manner, although he knew nothing whatever about wine. It was not a bad sherry; but it certainly was not good. The better wines were difficult to come at after years of war and blockade. When he expected no guest he invariably contented himself with the lesser renowned soleras.

Hurrell went on talking of strategy and tactics: analyzed the generalship of Washington and Greene, giving his verdict in favour of the subordinate leader. His comments were intelligent and Purvis was glad to listen, reminding himself that the letter to Lavinia must go before long. The diamonds! Perhaps it would be unwise to send them by night. Too many lawless characters abroad.

'You seem to have made a close study of operations in the North as well as the South, Captain Hurrell,' he commented when the young man stopped.

'I was hoping one day to write a history of the war,' said Hurrell, after a moment's pause as though to nerve himself to the confession. He flushed slightly. 'It is kind of you to let me talk to you, sir. It is particularly pleasant to be able to converse on such friendly terms with — one on the other side.'

'Perhaps it would not be so friendly if we talked politics?' remarked Purvis, smiling slightly.

'I never talk politics — know nothing about them,' replied Hurrell, contemplating the rowels of his swan-necked spurs. 'But if I can agree with you when you talk about books, and you can agree with me when I talk of military matters, we ought to find ground for agreement somehow on other things.'

'A pity, perhaps, that you and I were not left to discover a solution for the present mess.'

'Mess?' said Hurrell, considering the word. 'Yes — "mess" is exactly right . . . I like to know who the enemy is. I like him to be a different colour from myself, or to talk a different language. One knows where one is. But this is bedlam! First Benedict Arnold — the swine! — fights for you; then he fights for us. The Hessians, for whom we are paying God knows how many thousand pounds a year, desert at every opportunity; and the Americans change from one side to the other almost in the middle of a battle. Every one of your fellows whom we captured at Camden — a thousand of 'em — have 'listed to fight in the West Indies for King George. Did you know that? What do you think of it?'

Through the heavy curtains of green and blue brocade which shrouded the windows came suddenly vague sounds of shouting. A single shot cracked out from near at hand, to be followed by the loud shrieks of a woman.

'Damn those devils!' said Hurrell immediately alert. 'I wager it's the infernal Hessians. I must see what mischief they are up to . . . You will excuse me?'

His hand went to his side, but he had taken off sword and belt, and left them with the saddle-bags in his room. He made hurriedly for the door: paused —

'May we continue our talk when I come back?'

'I shall enjoy it,' declared Purvis, ringing his bell, and smiling at him again. 'In the meantime I will have some slippers found for you — and another bottle of wine.'

It should be good wine this time! The best! . . . As the door closed he laughed out loud at the thought of his mother's reactions to this hobnobbing with the enemy. It would have amused Richard! Perhaps it *was* amusing Richard!

With the departure of Captain Hurrell the noise outside appeared to have redoubled — to be coming nearer. He thought to hear a blur of scuffling and oaths from the driveway itself . . . Rasselas certainly should not take the diamonds with him to-night. They must go to-morrow.

Heavy feet suddenly pounded along the porch. A moment later some-one came fumbling at one of the windows behind him — a corner win-dow.

Purvis twisted in his chair, and, peering round its high wing, regarded expectantly the unstirring folds of brocade that hid the night and what-ever drama was in progress without. He felt no alarm — curiosity only, and annoyance.

Someone cried something in a high-pitched voice; was answered by a muffled shout; fumbled at the window again; crashed into the room amid a sound of splintering glass; and fell upon the floor so that the curtains bulged forward with the burden of the body though they did not part.

Purvis did not cry out. He sat very still in his chair at the top of the great table, head turned over right shoulder, quietly watching.

More feet thudded on the porch, and, as they approached, the someone on the floor rose with a convulsive effort, and burst through from the outer world of violence and night into the quiet room that housed Camelot and the three-quarter-of-a-million words history of fabulous travellers.

A woman stood in the gap in the curtains for a split second.

She was young, and might once have been pretty, but her trade was told in her face. Her hair was tangled, and her dirty pink cotton dress torn at the throat and dabbled with blood. Around her neck a small spirit keg was suspended by a string.

She flung herself forward those few paces to Anthony Purvis's wheelchair, so that she was on her knees beside him, clutching at his embroidered gown. Looking down on the suppliant he saw how bitten were the nails of the fingers that scrabbled at his knees — how matted the yellow hair. He was not revolted. He put out his hand and covered with his own those dirty urgent fingers, as though offering what protection he could.

Even as the woman broke into some hoarse plea, there was another crash of glass, the curtains were torn wide apart, and — as Purvis turned in his chair — a man appeared swaying in the opening. He was obviously very drunken, capless, and wearing a filthy blue uniform. His big face was of a startling red against the greyish whiteness of his powdered hair, and from his blackened lips poured a stream of incomprehensible words. A long pistol wavered in his right hand.

His voice rose to a scream —

'. . . so krepieren — .'

At the topmost note he fired.

The room was full of noise — of the smell of burnt powder; and a little cloud of grey smoke floated upward.

Anthony Purvis was aware of all this, even as his body was spun round by the sledge-hammer blow of the bullet — even as he sagged forward until head and shoulders rested upon the table. A little blood came from his mouth.

For an instant the man with the pistol stood regarding his handiwork with an entire lack of comprehension. Then he realized. He flung the useless weapon from him, so that it skidded along the polished oaken floor to the green malachite rim of the fireplace; hurled himself across the room, and was gone, upsetting two small tables in his flight and leaving the door gaping on to an unlighted corridor.

The woman rose to her feet. She leaned over the chronicler of fantastic journeyings — the creator of Camelot; and lifted his head against her breast. . . .

The room was full of men; was empty. The house echoed with hurrying feet, and shouts, and a nameless confusion; was silent.

Overhead — above rosy Venus and rosy clouds and rosy cupids —
there was a sudden piercing cry answered by a fusillade of shots, and
then a heavy fall . . . Hurrell reappeared in the doorway, a naked sword
in his hand; behind him a square-faced sergeant of grenadiers. He
spoke over his shoulder, without turning his head.

'Report that he died resisting arrest!'

'Yes-sir!'

'Any surgeon with your party, sergeant?'

'No-sir!'

'Send the people of the house here — and quickly!' He crossed the
room with swift strides. 'And take this bitch away! . . .'

The night wind streamed into the room through the black oblong of
the shattered window. The lights in chandelier and wall-sconce flickered
and guttered.

Hurrell set Purvis back in his chair, and moved it slightly away from
the table. He undid the closely fitting upper part of that magnificent
gown — now so wet and red; but knew well how little could be done
before ever he saw the hideous wound.

He was wiping the stained mouth when Rasselas entered.

'Linen — hot water — a basin — quickly! And tell Mrs. Purvis what
has happened!'

With one horror-stricken glance at his master the man was gone.

Hurrell found that Purvis's eyes were open, were watching his face
as he stooped over him. A faint smile — a very faint smile — creased
the cripple's lips. It was a smile of recognition.

'Richard!' said Purvis in a low, slow voice. 'Why, no, it is the enemy!'
And he smiled again. 'See that that letter goes to-night!' He lifted a
hand an inch or two as though to indicate the folded square of grey
paper that lay near the pile of diamonds on the table. There was a
smear of blood in one corner.

'Yes!' said Hurrell.

The dying man spoke again, almost immediately.

'The chronicler — of — imaginary — voyages — sets out — on — his
travels!'

He gave a ghost of a chuckle.

The wind poured in through the broken panes. The curtains streamed
into the room like the banners of a legendary fleet. Some of the candles
were extinguished, and hot wax dripped from the chandelier. The pages
of the manuscript were strewn over the table and the floor. For sixty

seconds the library was full of uproar, and confusion, and movement.

As though he had but awaited so favourable a gale to raise anchor and set sail, Anthony Purvis died. . . .

It was the sense of departure rather than of death that made Charles Hurrell say — 'He has gone!' when that black ghost, Mrs. Purvis, entered the room, followed by Rasselas and another servant.

She said not a word. She did not even look at him — nor when he stumbled into apologies and regrets. More — she did not come into a room profaned by the presence of an enemy, further than the door; but stood there, and signed to the two men with her that they should wheel away the chair with their dead master.

Hurrell sought under the litter of paper strewn upon the table, found the letter addressed to Lavinia Fell. He walked down the room to Mrs. Purvis bearing it in his hand.

'Your son's last words were that this letter should be delivered to-night, madam,' he said.

She made no attempt to take it from him; did not shift her regard from the gentle progress of Anthony Purvis from his library — except for one flashing instant to take in the superscription.

The young man remained awkwardly with the letter held out toward her until the wheel-chair approached the door, when she turned and left without a word, a look, or a gesture.

The big negro, Rasselas, with tears pouring down his wrinkled cheeks, was steadying the body in the chair, while the other servant pushed.

'You heard your master's wishes?'

Rasselas nodded. He could not speak. He took the letter, and put it on Purvis's knees, and backed through the doorway facing the dead man.

The wheels creaked a little down the long corridor and across the hall: the air seemed full of whispering.

Hurrell shut the door. He went to the broken window; pushed out one or two slivers of glass that still clung precariously to the frame; closed the shutters, and drew the curtains. Then he surveyed the confusion of the room — snowdrifts of paper everywhere — overturned table lying amid the wreckage of materials for Camelot — a shattered decanter on the hearth. Almost automatically he began to gather up the blood-dappled sheets of manuscript scattered about the great writing-table — and so revealed the cold splendour of the Muscovy necklace.

For long he looked at the jewels . . . held them up so that they dripped from his hand, shining like moonlight imprisoned in ice . . . counted the stones. It needed no expert knowledge to realize their immense value.

His expression slowly changed.

He suddenly flushed; stooped quickly for his sword, which lay where he had dropped it so few minutes before, rammed it into its scabbard, and marched resolutely to the door . . . Paused. . . .

At the end of a shelf by the green-painted moulding of the doorway, and level with his gaze, was a Bible, in two large volumes bound in rose-red leather. A childhood recollection of his old nurse searching for divine guidance came to him. He reached up and brought down one of the books, and opened it at random with shut eyes.

When he looked at the spread pages he saw that his right thumb rested upon a paragraph in the first chapter of Numbers —

' . . . Nahshon the son of Amminadab.
'Of Issachar; Nethaneel the son of Zuar.'

But it had been no fair test! For a thread marker had lain between the pages so that the volume would be inclined to open at that place.

He would try once again. Once only. This time he lighted upon Exodus. He read —

'And the Lord gave the people favour in the sight of the Egyptians, so that they lent them such things as they required. And they spoiled the Egyptians.'

It was curious — very curious, to say the least of it! . . . A coincidence? . . . An instruction? . . . Guidance? . . .

'They *lent* them such things — '

Fortified by a new idea, he came back to the place at the table where had sat the master of Camelot.

A quill pen stood upright in the inkpot of the silver standish — the pen with which Purvis had written so many letters that night to Lavinia Fell. Hurrell turned over a sheet of the scattered manuscript. The back was blank. He reflected for a minute or so, outstaring the contemptuous gaze of Colonel Beriah; then took the pen, and, with an air of determination, wrote on the virgin surface very swiftly:

'I O U
The sum of five hundred pounds (£500)
Charles Hurrell.'

Having thus regularized proceedings he took up the rope of great stones in his hands, and, watching the door all the time, wrenched off the diamonds one by one — like a child stripping currants from a branch. Six of the biggest gems he placed in the deep pocket of his green waist-

coat; the rest he sent skittering across the littered floor. They rattled
like pebbles as they fell . . . People would think the dead assassin had
snatched at plunder in his flight!

He then started to fold the I O U into a small square, but as he did
so remarked the page number of the manuscript on which it was written.
It was '1313' — figures of ill omen! Almost against his will he tossed
the sheet into the dying fire, and wrote out a fresh acknowledgment of
the debt on a page with an innocuous numbering.

It was as he was engaged in folding the document that he noticed the
inch-high gate of the fairy castle, whose gilded turrets dominated Camelot.
It was open. On the spur of the moment he thrust the paper through
the aperture under the fangs of the raised portcullis. Within the hollow
interior of the stronghold. Out of sight. Only then did he realize that
his hands were a little besmeared with blood. . . .

He stood once more at the door, the battle within his heart between
his honour and his needs not even yet decided; although there was no
hint of the conflict in his carriage, or in his tanned face and high white
forehead, or in his level gaze across the room.

But somewhere in space his spirit was clamouring to the ghost of a
man with a faint and friendly smile — an historian of the fabulous, a
builder of toy cities. Was clamouring of his needs — of the promotion
in his profession which he would never get except through the iniquitous
army system of purchase. It was a loan! It would be a debt of honour! . . .

Nevertheless he had started to return when someone approached along
the passage. It was too late, now, to make restoration! . . . He opened
the door. He turned to the room, hand on handle: it was as if he spoke
to the ghost in final affirmation — 'A debt — a debt of honour! You understand!' He went out.

CHAPTER IV

'AFTER GOD'S ORDINANCE'

AN unseen clock was striking twelve as Lavinia Fell came through the
cedarwood-scented darkness of the wide hall, and mounted the great
staircase to the yet more intense darkness above. A negro servant carried
a candlestick before her. In the pale radiance of the little flame she went
through the silence of the house, escorted by shadows.

She had been aroused from uneasy sleep an hour earlier by a gentle tapping upon her door; had read Anthony's letter through a haze of tears — divining all his knowledge; had read the postscript written in her aunt's hand — 'Come at once to High Pale. Come quickly. Come secretly. Without question. The carriage will wait you by the pinetrees. H.P.'

She had obeyed the summons at once — quickly, secretly, unquestioningly. Wonder at its urgency and suddenness was swallowed up in the wonder at a miracle.

During all the solitary jolting journey in the dark she had refused to weep: had travelled with clenched hands, staring into the wind-torn night. Only she had said his name below her breath, again and again, 'Anthony! . . . Anthony!' in passionate gratitude . . . He should be told everything — even of that frantic and horrible attempt to escape destiny. Nothing of sin or folly but should be proffered for the pardon he would give.

Now she passed down the gallery that overhung the black void of the hall. In the light of the one candle, the balusters cast their shadows across the well of the staircase, so that upon the opposite wall was printed another and ghostly gallery.

She came to a door — a mahogany door with heavily moulded architrave. A tiny flame in its shining panels answered the escorting flame.

The manservant knocked. Twice. There was no response, and, looking to her for instruction, he turned the handle. . . .

The room was sombre and immense — one that she had never seen before. At the nearer end three people stood in hushed talk, their figures silhouetted against the brightness of a large wood fire and of the candles burning in tall candlesticks on the high mantelpiece.

At the further end — to her right — was a vast four-posted bed, only half-visible, and darker than the gloom that enfolded it. Some small sad light — from a table screened from view by the curtains at the head — was quenched in the obscurity of the hangings, of the lofty canopy with its deep and tasselled fringe; illumined the interior not at all.

The bed dominated the room, swollen with its shadows until it seemed huge enough to be a chapel.

Even in the confusion of her thoughts she recognized it. For it was the 'Black Bed', whose sable hangings and coverings for many generations had been at the service of dutiful widows and widowers of the family during the period of their mourning. Until, in fact, Mrs. Purvis had retired to it on the death of her husband and resolutely continued to use it during her long widowhood.

Where was Anthony? . . . Why? . . . What was — ?

Her aunt's ice-cold voice cut across the stream of questions flooding her mind. Mrs. Purvis said — and she emphasized not one word or one syllable more than another —

'You can show me nothing to prevent it. There is nothing to prevent it. Nothing shall prevent it!'

Mr. Chancellor — small and shrivelled — to whom she spoke, was replying in a flurried mumble, when the group by the fire became aware of Lavinia Fell's presence.

Mrs. Purvis did not move: she said something in a low tone to the taller of her companions, who turned and came swiftly across the room to the girl. It was Dr. Earle, of hunched shoulders and great beaked nose, dressed as ever in professional black. When he spoke his mouth opened in a straight line across his leathery face, and deep ridges were scored from lips to nostrils.

'Good morning, Miss Fell! . . . This is an unexpected summons, I fear . . . You must be brave — very brave! . . . Mr. Purvis is very ill. We sent for you. It was his wish.'

He looked toward the bed as he spoke, and then quickly away again. His voice was very low, and he took her unresisting hand in his — not as though to comfort her, but almost as if to assure himself that she would not suddenly approach the bed, or escape from the room. She had thrown back the hood of her long cloak, and he examined her face critically, professionally.

'He is dying?' said Lavinia in a whisper.

She felt that she had known all along — from the moment when a silent servant had assisted her into the carriage — that the miracle would never be more than a tantalizing dream. She turned her proud dark head and stared steadily into the dim grotto of the bed; but tears for the man who would have helped — and for herself — blinded her. She could see nothing.

'I am very much afraid so,' said Dr. Earle . . . 'All his thoughts have been of you. So long as he could speak he called your name, and asked why you had not come.'

'I came at once. As soon as I had his letter.' She stammered a catechism of urgent questions — 'Can he speak now? Is he conscious? Could he hear me if I spoke to him — and understand? . . . I want to thank him for — for something. May I speak to him now? I know he will hear me! I *know* it!'

That cold and gentle hold upon her hand tightened, so slightly as to be no more than a sympathetic pressure; yet it conveyed to her confused mind a suggestion of possible restraint.

The doctor shook his bowed head.

'It is quite impossible. Might well be fatal. The spar-r-rk of life is very dim! The spar-r-rk of consciousness very far away! All his strength must be saved for-r —' He broke off: continued in a yet lower voice — 'Miss Fell, can you guess what his wish is — his dying wish? Why you have been brought here?'

She did not answer him. She could not answer him. She stood facing the vast shadowy bed, sightless and speechless, battling with her quivering lips.

'He hoped — he hoped so much — he *hopes* . . . that . . . you will even now — do as he asked . . . in his letter.' Dr. Earle paused for a long while. In that pause his quick ears heard Mrs. Purvis say just six words to Mr. Chancellor by the distant fireplace, very slowly — 'I know all about Susan Green!' He barely restrained a grim smile of appreciation. He went on, all the while straining to catch any further snatch of what passed between man and woman: 'May I guess your answer? . . . Is your coming the answer?'

Dear, dear Anthony — her 'loyal, and humble, and very loving brother!' She tried fiercely to will that her spirit should tell all its clamour of gratitude and abasement and devotion and sorrow to the spirit of the man who lay unstirring, without sound and invisible, somewhere within the tomb-like bed. That it should say to him that he must live, if only for her to prove the deepness of her love. . . . The child should be Anthony's and hers. Anthony's spirit . . . Her flesh. All her flesh. Not Richard's! . . . Never Richard's! . . . Least of all Richard, whose heartlessness she had found out too late.

Dr. Earle said again —

'Is — ?'

She looked directly at him, and in her tear-dimmed eyes he saw his answer even before she nodded, not trusting herself to speech.

'It must be very quickly done. It may be a matter of minutes . . . You will be brave, Miss Fell! . . . It — it will be a great consolation to him . . . We have only just been able to find Mr. Chancellor. Your aunt is now making arrangements with him.'

At that moment he heard something fall lightly to the floor, by the hearth. Chancellor stepped back a pace, and the something crunched under his feet. Dr. Earle wanted to smile. Very badly. So Chancellor had given way; was preparing the very evidence for his defence — if it should ever be required — that he himself had suggested! . . . Almost he rubbed his hands.

There was a chair against the wall near the door; beside it a console table topped by an enormous mirror whose gloomy depths reflected their pale faces. He pressed the girl into the chair; filled a glass with wine from a decanter which stood on the table, added a few drops of colourless liquid from a small phial, and made her drink.

'Sit here for a moment or two,' he said in a tone in which command was mingled with request. 'I will tell Mr. Chancellor that you are ready . . . It will only take a few minutes . . . You will feel better very soon.'

He returned to the conference by the fireplace; and she sat very still and dazed, staring before her, beyond the heavy curtains that hid the windows, into some unimaginable future.

A little later her aunt came silently down the room, followed by the two men. In the dim light and amid the enormous and shifting shadows, they seemed a procession of mimes wearing symbolic masks — monkey-mask, vulture-mask, and mask of Fate.

Mrs. Purvis gave her niece no greeting. She halted in front of Lavinia, but did not look down as she spoke — remained, instead, regarding the reflection of her own impassive face in the chill fog of the mirror; her hands were loosely clasped before her against the blackness of her wide-skirted dress. She said —

'I have here a ring belonging to Anthony. I thought that you would prefer it, Lavinia. It will have to do. The rest are all signets . . . Will you take charge of it, Dr. Earle?'

Dr. Earle took the circlet from her. He remarked with inward amusement that it was a mourning ring with a design in black enamel, and that upon its inner surface it bore the legend in Gothic characters — 'Prepared Be to Follow Me. A.P. 1770.' He overlaid an ill-repressed chuckle with a rasping cough.

'Are you ready, Mr. Chancellor?' he asked.

'Mr. Chancellor is quite ready,' answered Mrs. Purvis for the little man, who had placed upon the marble top of the console the shattered frame of a pair of horn-rimmed spectacles, and was eyeing them miserably. Under his white wig with its sausage side-curls his small shrunken face was grey and blotched with dull red.

'I shan't be able to see,' he declared in a small, uncertain voice.

'You don't need to,' remarked Earle. 'There'll be light enough for what you have to do.'

'I don't carry all the services in my head.'

'There is a wall sconce by the bed which will serve,' said Mrs. Purvis. 'Please to light it, Dr. Earle.'

The doctor walked to the bed. He lifted a fold of the long hangings that screened its head, and bent into the darkness within. He appeared to be whispering to the unseen occupant, or — perhaps — debating with himself in an undertone, for the merest breath of sound came to the listeners.

He straightened his back, and stood for a little, hand to chin, looking down thoughtfully. Then with unhurried speed he lit a taper at the fire, and illumined one — and one only — of the candles in the silver sconce. The small light, high up on the panelled wall at the bed-head, revealed the straight voluminous folds of the black velvet curtains and the silver fringe and tassels ornamenting the deep black border of the canopy, which nearly reached the ceiling. It showed, too, in vague outline, the heavy *prie-dieu* standing directly beneath it. It cast no ray into the blackness of the bed itself.

Dr. Earle moved the desk some little way from the wall and so that it faced the curtains of the bed; placed a kneeling-stool with a cushioned top before it.

He came back to the three people by the door.

'*Now!*' he said. 'The time, I am afraid, is very short. You will please be as quick as possible, Mr. Chancellor. No prolixity. Leave out whatever you may. If you stand directly under the sconce you will have enough light to read even the rubrics. Speak in a very even, low, quiet voice. I will guarantee that Mr. Purvis's consciousness will hear — however far-r away it is. Even if the effort of speech may be too much for him, I can interpret a breath — a twitch . . . Miss Fell, you will kneel at the *prie-dieu*. I shall be beside you to prompt you . . . Mrs. Purvis, perhaps you will stand on Miss Fell's left?' . . .

' "Dearly beloved, we are gathered together here in the sight of God — " '

Mr. Chancellor began. He mouthed and gabbled sonorous words — mumbled the Almighty Name — tapped light accompaniment on the floor with the toe of a muddy buckled shoe. The big prayer-book was held so close to his short-sighted eyes, that nothing was visible between the top of his wig and the dirty Geneva bands at the throat of his rusty coat.

Lavinia, kneeling before the shrine of the vast draped bed, was conscious that Aunt Henriette stood beside her as rigidly as though her whole body was stiffened and taut upon its frame in such fashion as the

skin of her mask-like face was strained over the structure of the skull.
On the other side stood Dr. Earle, just brushing her shoulder: he exhaled
a mingled scent of fine soap and expensive snuff.

> ' "For the mutual society, help, and comfort, that the one ought to
> have of the other . . ." '

There was a faint sprinkling of tiny silver stars and lilies upon the
sombre tissue of the great precipice of curtain at whose foot she knelt.
Amid the tumult of her thoughts and speculations she was aware of the
throaty voice babbling on —

> ' "Require and charge you both . . . the dreadful Day of Judg-
> ment . . . now confess it — " '

She *must* see Anthony for one moment before the irrevocable thing
was done — to make sure that he knew, to explain, to excuse, to thank.
She raised her head toward the curtain.

Even as she did so — almost as though to forestall her action — Dr.
Earle looped back the hangings. It was a very high bed, and all that
Lavinia could see from her knees was the blur of a head resting in the
middle of a long blurred bank of pillows. It appeared to be turned toward
her; but she could not be sure.

Then Dr. Earle leaned forward, low over the bed; and his body blotted out the vision. She felt his left hand resting lightly upon her shoulder while he remained bent within — reassuringly, restrainingly.

Mr. Chancellor came to a pause. He cleared his throat with a series of
small husky coughs. He remained silent.

'Go on!'

' "Anthony," continued Mr. Chancellor in gasping speed from behind
the barricade of his prayer-book, "wilt thou have this woman to thy wedded wife, to live together after God's ordinance in the holy estate of Matrimony? Wilt thou love her, comfort her, honour, and keep her . . ." '

Of a sudden she felt drowsy, obedient, hopeful. It was her wedding
day! Anthony would not die! She would make him live! She *could*
make him live — Anthony who had restored the fabric of her world!
One day — a long long way off — she would tell him about Richard —
Richard to whom the betrayal of her honour had been but an agreeable
incident and its consequences a maddening calamity.

The pressure of the doctor's fingers upon her shoulder was accentuated.

From very, very far away she thought to hear a mere flutter of sound —
a tiny sigh, a breath.

'He has said "I will",' said the doctor turning his head a little to the room without changing his position. His body still hid Anthony from her sight.

In increasing daze she heard Chancellor drone on — responded when she should — found her right hand taken and stretched a long way and placed against something cold — found her left hand taken and dragged so far across the black silken coverlet that she must lean forward over the ledge of the faldstool — found a small ring of gold and black upon her finger when it was released . . . She became conscious that the murmuring voice had ceased.

The doctor straightened himself and stepped back. The curtain dropped. Mr. Chancellor lowered his book and made a sound that was between a sigh and a groan.

In the ensuing silence her aunt said slowly and reflectively —

'Lavinia Purvis!'

She spoke as one judging the euphony of the combination of names. Then —

'Richard Purvis — Richard Purvis!' And yet once again repeated the two words, without accentuation, but as though to assure herself of the remembered music. 'Richard Purvis!'

'Richard?'

In one swift moment of clarity, actuated by what fear she did not know, Lavinia rose to her feet. She threw right back the star-sprinkled curtain with a sweep of her arm, and held it up on high so that the light from the wall-sconce should fall within.

But it was not Richard whose pale face lay upturned upon the pillows, whose body barely hummocked the wide expanse of black quilt.

It was Anthony.

And Anthony was dead; had, she knew, died long before. The slight smile upon his face had frozen there a while since: his white lips had been closed to speech before ever she entered the room: the bandages about his head were such as are wrapped about the dead.

She looked down upon her bridegroom, saying no word: and presently she stooped over him and kissed him on the cold forehead and the lips.

She let fall the hangings. She turned away. She walked across the room. Her face, too, was as the face of the dead.

Dr. Earle followed her to the door. He plucked her gently by the elbow, and pointed with a long hand to a paper lying on the console.

'Sign this now. Then you must get some rest. We will witness it later.'

She dipped quill into inkpot and wrote her name, 'Lavinia Fell', firmly upon the sheet.

'Lavinia Fell — Lavinia Purvis!' said Aunt Henriette at her side. 'Lavinia Purvis! Richard Purvis! . . . Purvis!'

She felt that her consciousness and her strength were fading fast. As she bent up with difficulty from the table, she saw reflected in the grey dimness of the mirror before her the expressionless yellow mask of Aunt Henriette's face. She addressed it without turning her head —

'He is dead!'

'Murdered!' said the lips in the mirror. 'Murdered — by the English!' said the lips in the mirror. And the mask was suddenly distorted so that every line and every feature proclaimed 'Murder!'

Dr. Earle caught Lavinia in his arms before she could fall.

Still supporting her, he answered the unspoken question posed him by Mrs. Purvis in a glance before she moved, unhurried, to the bell-pull by the fireplace.

'Ve-e-ery small dose. Can't possibly hurt her. Do her good. Acted more slowly than I thought it would. She should be put to bed and kept warm. At once!'

'I have rung for the maids,' said Mrs. Purvis. 'One of them will assist you to take Mrs. Purvis to the Red Room, if you will be so good. I will go first to see that the lights are already there. . . .'

In a short space Dr. Earle returned to the room.

Mr. Chancellor, warming rusty coat and rusty breeches and rusty stockings and rusty body by the fire, was regarding uneasily the black precipice of the bed.

'Meditating on the connubial pleasures of the marriage bed?' Dr. Earle asked easily, and poured himself out a brimming glass of wine. 'Better sign this paper according to for-r-rm and precedent! Nothing like attention to detail! Let us see! What is the date? — The fifteenth. No, the sixteenth . . . I'll get our friend to append his signature later.' He sipped his wine thoughtfully. 'Or, rather, his mark! Perhaps, though, you had better witness the operation. Then, if any question is raised — which there won't be — you could say that you saw the pen in the signatory's fingers, but that he was too weak — being *in extremis* — to do more than make his cross.'

'No!' said Chancellor violently. 'No!'

'Come, come,' reproved Dr. Earle, 'the man has been dead for over four hours. He can't — '

'No!' said Chancellor, and his voice rose almost to a scream. He clapped his hands to his ears. 'I know nothing about it! I can't hear you! I can't!'

The dead are buried; and hatred flowers upon their graves.

The unborn are born to a distracted world, to old hates and new hates, to the threat of wars even bloodier than those that went before.

General Washington will soon begin his second term of office as President of the new Republic. The foolish King of France has just lost his head, and the mad King of England has temporarily recovered his reason.

The American nation is concerned about its neutrality in the European War — about the peculiar activities of a foreign ambassador.

In England they have debated the lessons of the Revolutionary War: have questioned why an infantryman's kit should weigh one hundred and twenty-five pounds, or the scabbard of a dragoon's sabre three pounds; why a soldier should march to battle with greased, powdered, and pig-tailed hair; whether it would not be better to forsake the traditional scarlet coat and dress him, like the Virginia rifleman, in shirt and breeches dyed the colour of dead leaves . . . Have done precisely nothing about it.

An expeditionary force under an incompetent and royal leader has landed on the continent — soon to find itself in such difficulties at Dunkirk that it will be forced to abandon there a vast quantity of equipment and war material.

In the name of their new order of society Frenchmen are busy exterminating Frenchmen: a young artillery lieutenant, the frequency of whose ablutions has caused comment among his fellows, is already on the path that shall lead to an imperial crown and to the prison island of St. Helena: there are bread queues in France, and a refugee problem in England.

The suave elegance of the mid-century has vanished. Women's bosoms have become high and bolster-like, their heads as fuzzy as thickets. Men's breeches have lengthened to pantaloons — will soon become trousers. In Paris the enterprising Monsieur Quènin and Madame Teillard have already opened the first ready-to-wear shops for citizens and citizenesses.

It is 1793.

BOOK TWO

THE INVISIBLE COMPANIONSHIP

Virginia — The Atlantic — France 1793

★

CHAPTER I

THE PERIAPT OF MADAM PURVIS

ANTHONY PURVIS said his prayers, for the last time in the big nursery which was so much at the top of the house that all you could see from its two windows were a white and windy sky and the shivering crests of the trees in the garden.

The room — with the blue-painted cupboards on either side of the fireplace, and the faded Chinese wall-paper covered with pagodas and bridges and willows in blue and black — had been the nursery at High Pale for three generations; and it seemed to belong to the ghosts of the children who had played there years ago rather than to the eleven-year-old boy with ruffled black hair and grey eyes, kneeling in his nightshirt at the casement.

Its scanty furnishings were theirs; its shabbiness had been created by them.

Their battered toys — wooden dolls and tops and rackets — filled one of the big cupboards. The low trundle bed, wherein he slept, opposite the windows, had belonged to Aunt Octavia — who had eloped with an Englishman during the war, and had gone to England, and was never mentioned. It was her bed — not his. The rocking-horse, whose nostrils were still scarlet although it had no stirrups, was Uncle Richard's — not his. The rush-seated chair, in which he sat and ate his supper of bread and milk, had the initials 'R.E.P.' carved in inch-long letters on its back. So, too, the silver porringer was Great Uncle William's, and the clumsy table a first serious effort by his grandfather at joinery. Even the queer chair over which he threw his clothes at night was Grandmother Fell's. A very queer chair it was, too; with a seat only four inches wide, and a straight solid back with the straps still on it by which Grandmother Fell had been fastened to it for hours at a time — in an unimaginable childhood — to ensure upright carriage and correct deportment.

Sometimes he had tried to go to bed without touching anything that was not his. That meant eating his bread and milk without touching the sides of his porringer; washing — and Heziah always looked to see if the water was dirty when she came back — without any contact with the diminutive wash-basin that had been Great Uncle Andrew's when he was at sea; and getting into bed with careful avoidance of Great Aunt Lucy's patchwork quilt.

Incidentally the business of touching and not-touching was very complicated. There were certain doors and trees that always had to be touched; and the skirting at the right-hand side of the door in the dining-room; and the underpart of the tread of the fifth stair, counting upward from the hall. On the other hand one must never walk anywhere except on the patterned part of the enormous Chinese carpet of green and rose in the drawing-room.

In some way by touching things one averted misfortune — though misfortune of what sort he could not say. Just as by not-touching objects one avoided arousing the jealousy (was it?) of the wraiths that owned them.

In a minute Heziah would be coming to see if he was in bed . . . He began his prayers.

'*God bless Mother and Father —*'

Grandmother Purvis had said that there was no use in praying for the dead. But that was only after he had refused to include Uncle Richard's name in his prayers.

Once, when Mother was alive, his grandmother had heard him saying his prayers at her knee, and asked why Uncle Richard was omitted. Mother had given no answer.

'Would you not have the child pray for his — ?' said Madam Purvis — as she was always called now. She bit short the sentence, as though to show that she held the remaining word for a weapon, of which she might make use one day.

Anthony had been tucked up in bed and kissed, the curtains drawn, before Lavinia made any reply. Then she merely said —

'We had better talk about this — and at once! Not here. Shall we go down to the drawing-room?'

The Copley portrait of Anthony and Richard was hung over the mantelpiece in the drawing-room, between two great Chinese jars decorated with peach blossom and dragons: Richard very upright and suavely gallant in a red-brown coat, and Anthony seated beside him, thoughtful, melancholy, in a lavender banian such as he always wore — close-fitting to the waist and wide-skirted to the toes, with immense buttons of silver filigree — his head wrapped in a sort of silver turban, so that he resembled an Eastern prince.

In this room of delicately tinted elegancies, the two women confronted one another.

'Let us come to a complete understanding, my dear aunt,' said Lavinia taking up her stand beneath the picture.

'Quite!' said her aunt with much composure; and, drawing forth a small piece of black material from her horse-hair bag, she concentrated her attention, with bent head, upon the task of extracting threads.

'I accepted the situation you prepared for several good reasons — mainly for the sake of the child. But as you arranged for his paternity, so you will accept that paternity wholeheartedly and without any reservation at all. Otherwise you can hardly remain in this house. You will prefer to remain, I imagine?'

'Quite!' said her aunt.

'The very peculiar bridal ceremony in which I took part was planned by you, not to save my honour, but so that the child should be called a Purvis with every show of legality.'

'Quite!'

Lavinia turned her back on the room, and regarded the portrait of Anthony. The elder Mrs. Purvis seated herself in an arm-chair by the hearth; continued to pull threads from the square of material on her black silk lap and drop them on the floor with a flick of finger and thumb; she did not raise her eyes.

'Therefore,' continued Lavinia to the picture, 'I have every right to arrange for my son to resume the surname of Fell — if certain circumstances should arise. You may perhaps be able to guess what those circumstances would be. If — for instance — you were to suggest to him that Anthony was not his father, or to depreciate Anthony as against Richard. I gave you some inkling of this when he was born — when I told you that under no circumstances would he be called Richard. I want you to realize that I look upon him as Anthony's son — *Anthony's son!* Even although I was never held in Anthony's arms, or kissed him on the lips until he was dead. The flesh of which the child is born is mine. Mine! And the soul within him is Anthony's! . . . I am not telling you what I wish, but what I know. One day you will discover for yourself the truth of what I am telling you!'

There was a considerable pause this time before the older lady again said —

'Quite!'

Lavinia adjusted the black lace scarf about her shoulders. In the fading daylight, with her pallor and powdered hair and lavender dress, she seemed almost to belong to the company of ghosts that thronged High Pale — to be wraith rather than woman.

'My father,' she told the picture, 'would be gratified by such a change — by his own name being borne by the son of his only child — by the heir to his estate, such as it is.'

'Quite!' said her aunt, but she drew out two threads at once.

'Therefore, when I die,' said Lavinia with such finality that for an instant her aunt's busy fingers were stilled and she looked up at the slim girl, who stood proudly contemplating death and a dead husband. ' . . . when I die — and Dr. Earle, as you know, says that it will be in the next two or three months — I am leaving Anthony to you and Mother's *joint* care!'

Madam Purvis did not say 'Quite!' She became very still.

'I could wish — ! However, you and Mother are so dissimilar that perhaps, between you, you will together make one ordinarily reasonable guardian! . . . With Dr. Earle's assistance!'

Madam Purvis said nothing.

'He will hold the balance between you. He will have the casting vote in any differences.'

'An invidious position!' remarked Madam Purvis to the tormented linen.

'It will be made worth his while. He may be a bad man — more, an evil man! — but I happen also to know that his word is his bond — '

'He left Scotland rather hurriedly twenty years ago to avoid a charge of murder,' Madam Purvis told a thread, as though in happier circumstances it might have been part of the noose that should have adorned Dr. Earle's throat.

Lavinia ignored the interposition.

'He knows my views. He will carry out the course I have told you should the need arise — to the letter. I hope the need won't arise. I should like Anthony to bear his father's name.'

Until that moment she had spoken slowly and quietly, as though everything which she said had been long planned, with due provision for Madam Purvis's 'Quite!' Now suddenly her eyes filled with tears, and she turned to her aunt in desperate appeal —

'My poor little boy! . . . Aunt Henriette! You will — '

But Aunt Henriette, composedly folding her material, and composedly putting it back in the bag, composedly went away. . . .

Then one evening a long while afterwards — when all the agony of

Mother's death had been dulled — Grandmother Purvis, standing at his bedside like a graven image while he kneeled and said his prayers, interrupted the orderly recital. She interjected —

'*And* Uncle Richard!'

He had stopped while she spoke: recalled to himself the incident of months ago. Mother had not told him to pray for Uncle Richard, then. She would have said so if she meant him to! . . . He had continued: had accordingly omitted Uncle Richard's name.

Grandmother had said —

'You will remain here — on your knees — until you obey me! You understand, Anthony?'

So he had remained kneeling on the cold boards, tears trickling down between his fingers — for convention demanded that worship of the Creator should be performed with hidden face. She had returned after a long while, but he had been obstinately silent, and she had gone away again. He had wakened stiff and cold, to find himself being lifted into bed by Heziah under the supervision and authority of Grandmother Fell.

He was not to know that that lady, having ascertained the reason for the protraction of his religious exercises, went very gladly into battle with her sister-in-law: battle which ended in the complete exhaustion of one combatant and the complete destruction of a square of brown linen by the other. He realized, however, that Grandmother Purvis attended his evening communings no more, so that he was no longer obliged to divide his prayers into two parts — official and unofficial; which latter had hitherto been said secretly and hurriedly in any respectful position possible, and included petitions on behalf of Rasselas, and Heziah, and Deborah (Grandmother did not approve of a Purvis wasting his own and the Almighty's time over slaves), and various other creatures about coach-house and stable.

The only reference that Madam Purvis ever made to the incident was indirect, upon an afternoon soon afterward when Dr. Earle and Mr. Chancellor were debating in desultory fashion at the dinner-table on various doctrinal questions, on Manichaeism, free-will, predestination, and the efficacy of prayer.

' . . . And prayers for the dead?' asked Grandmother Purvis.

She spoke so rarely during a meal that her chill flat voice woke Anthony from his day-dreams at the far end of the table, and he looked up and saw that, though she addressed Mr. Chancellor, her eyes were turned on him.

Chancellor, his grey small face already mottled red from wine, mumbled some reply.

'Of what use can be prayers for the dead?' said Madam Purvis, holding her grandchild's regard with her own. 'Their bodies mildew — and rot — and seep away — in the damp grave, can be led into no temptation and commit no evil. Their record of sin or saintliness has been completed and closed. Nothing can be expunged or added. How can the "has-been" of the dead be altered or blotted out by the bedside mumbling of any man, or woman . . . or child?'

The words 'mildew — and rot — and seep away', spoken so slowly, filled the child's mind with horror. Did — had — ?

'The dead,' commented Dr. Earle easily, 'are capable, even in their unfortunate condition, of some very peculiar feats — as Mr. Chancellor and I well know, ma'am!' . . .

'— and Grandmother Fell, and Grandfather Fell —' (prayed Anthony Purvis.)

Grandfather Fell was a dreary elderly gentleman with a long red nose and watery eyes and a snuffy brown coat, who always agreed with his wife — especially about Anthony's delinquencies — very heartily.

Thus, if she said —

'Anthony, you are a very badly-behaved little boy!'

Then Grandfather Fell invariably chimed in —

'Worst mannered little boy in America! Worst mannered little boy in the world!'

The house girls always giggled and squeaked when Grandfather Fell was about, and Heziah had once said in one of her angry fits, 'Ef yo' arst ole Mars' Fell, Ah reck'n dat yo'll fin' dat yo' got mo' uncles an' aunties dan yo' guess, Marse Tony!' But he had never ventured to probe this matter.

'and Grandmother Purvis —'

This had been one of her good days, and her name remained on the rota. For he invariably punished her offences by omitting her from his prayers . . . What happened to anyone if you didn't pray for them? — he had often wondered. Supposing no one prayed for someone, what happened to that someone? Did anyone pray for *him?* Supposing nobody in the whole world prayed for him except himself! Oh, the loneliness of not being prayed for! On the night upon which he had posed and confronted that problem he had wept himself to sleep. And the next morning he had begged Rasselas to remember him in his prayers, but Rasselas said that he always did — so that was all right anyway!

'and Miss Buckley —'

She was the latest of a long succession of governesses over whose bodies

Grandmother Purvis and Grandmother Fell wrangled and fought. A large red-faced young woman in large billowy dresses which looked as if they had been plumped out with down. A quenchless poetess who had once made her appearance in the august columns of the *South Carolina Gazette*. She also suffered from frequent and prolonged bouts of hic-coughing, most punctiliously asking pardon after each individual spasm.

'*and Rasselas, and Heziah, and Deborah, and Dr. Earle, and President Washington, and Nibbler, and make me a good boy, Amen.*'

He leaped into bed, and pulled the bed-clothes up to his chin without touching Great Aunt Lucy's quilt. After to-night it wouldn't matter: he would be going away — far from all these other people's possessions. Far across the seas, and for a long, long time!

Grandmother Purvis had told him this the very next morning after his other grandparents had set off in much state to visit relations in South Carolina. She had not told him as if it were a matter of interest or an occasion for excitement, but just as though she were advising him of an appointment for an engagement book.

No one could have guessed that the opportunity for which she had planned ever since Lavinia's death had at last arrived. No one excepting, perhaps, her Philadelphia agent, grim Mr. Jarman of Girard's Bank, who had sent her grim little notes in a grim handwriting once a week for four years, telling of the transfer of funds or the sailing of ships, in the curtest of language. From the day of his birth she had waited for the time when she should have sole charge and care of Richard's son. From the day when Dr. Earle had taken the feebly stirring little creature from its mother's arms in the depths of the Black Bed, and Mr. Chancellor — sent for very hurriedly — had baptized it over a great silver punch-bowl at the marble-topped console table by the door.

'Anthony, I baptize thee in the Name of the Father, and of the Son, and of the Holy Ghost. Amen . . .' said Mr. Chancellor: but Madam Purvis, standing at his side, had already silently shaped the name 'Richard' with her thin lips. . . .

So now Anthony Purvis the Second lay meditating in bed, while the pallor of the early evening sky turned to dusk — to darkness — to a dis-turbed and shadowed silver in the light of a moon that was invisible from where he lay.

He heard steps in the corridor. Not Heziah's heavy tread, or the slov-enly amble of Miss Buckley, but a very soft swift step. He shut his eyes, and so feigned sleep, cheek resting upon a hand.

It was his grandmother.

She came in, bearing a candle — for he could see the light through his closed lids — and stood for some time looking down upon him.

Presently she said 'Richard! Richard!' in a voice so strange that he did not recognize it; not as though she were speaking to him by a wrong name, but as though she were calling in triumph to someone very far off. Then she was gone.

He wondered, vaguely uneasy, about the matter for a minute or so: dismissed it from mind: went on to think about the morrow's journey — about Philadelphia — about the ship. Would there be other children of his own age on board? He hoped so, yet half feared so; for all his life had been lived among adults . . . Would they be wrecked? Were there wrecks nowadays? There was a frontispiece to the big edition of *Gulliver's Travels* in the library showing a great ship in the very act of sinking in a stormy sea.

Thinking of the library reminded him of something that was his own — his very own. Mother had given it to him: she had said, too, that she was certain that Father had made it for him to play with when he was old enough — the magic city which stood upon the great table in the middle of that wonderful pale green room all tapestried with books.

He lay meditating on the city — and its spires and gay roofs and the turreted gateway in its walls, and all the little twisted houses in its little twisted streets.

On wet days he was allowed in the library after lessons, to entertain himself with books or with Camelot. He never needed to touch the city; but he would remain in a sort of trance before it, peopling it with the figures of his dreams, riding up its lanes at the head of his men-at-arms, pacing the ramparts of the castle of the golden towers, living through heroic dramas and desperate encounters. He could no more go away without saying good-bye to Camelot than to Rasselas or Heziah. The Lord of the City must bid his city farewell.

Hot on the decision, he slipped from bed, and went out of the moonlit room — avoiding the loose board by the door — into the darkness of the house. . . .

The library was silver and black in moonshine. But neither shadow nor beam directly struck the bookcases, so that all the massed wisdom of their shelves was grey; Colonel Beriah's arrogance, too, was thus obscured, but not obliterated. The polished surface of the long table shone like water — an enchanted lake from which rose the chiaroscuro of the roofs and towers of Camelot.

He kneeled upon a chair, and, leaning his elbows on the table, stared intently at the city.

He entered through the main barbican, on horseback. On a grey charger. With William on his right and John on his left — those invisible friends, those only friends, who accompanied him through all the dream life which was so much more real than reality. The visors of their salades were raised, for they were returning in triumph, and every window of the town was illumined in token of welcome. He wore a scarlet surcoat over his armour — no, cloth-of-gold — and William one of silver, and John of deep blue.

Through the barbican — up the narrow street with the overhanging houses — past the church — the people dropping roses on them, and shouting from the doors — into the arcaded square. His ears attuned to the inaudible (even as his eyes were focused on the invisible) heard the clatter of hoofs upon the cobbles, the roar of crowds and the voices of his friends.

'Look, William!' he said aloud. 'Look, John!'

For from the balcony overhanging the great gate of the castle leaned the three princesses.

The three princesses! The three fairy princesses! Those lay — and somewhat vague — figures who, in accordance with all precedent, inevitably welcomed home the returning warriors with high courtesy!

The leaves of the gate were wide open, the portcullis raised. Into the cavernous entry they rode, and all their victorious soldiery after them.

It was the end of an interminable adventure upon which he had been engaged for many months. He had, perhaps, hastened the conclusion a trifle so that the break in his outer-world life might coincide with the opening of a new inner-world romance — a story that should include ships and unknown seas and voyages to far bright lands; a new pattern, of story altogether.

With this idea of finality he put out his hand to close the castle gate after the procession. *They* were within. *They* were feasting at long tables under canopies of state . . . To-morrow he and William and John would be other — adventurers in high boots of untanned hide, with long swords at their sides, making their way to the sea. He saw for a moment quick flashing visions of scenes-to-be.

He inserted the second finger of his right hand within the entry to shut the gate.

There was something loose inside. Almost automatically he extracted it. A square of paper folded very small.

In his interest he got down from the chair, and tiptoed to the window, unfolding the packet as he went, so that he might read whatever was written upon the sheet in the bright moonlight.

Through the square panes the alternating cedars and poplars that fringed the lawns showed ink-black against the dark blue sky.

On one side of the paper was a long brown smear: also the words —

'I O U
The sum of five hundred pounds (£500)
Charles Hurrell.'

What did it mean?—he wondered: turned the creased sheet over. The other side was closely covered with a quite different writing — a small neat hand. He began to read —

'. . . and the woman who bore the branch of silver apples into the royal house, when it was full of kings, bade Bran the son of Febal to fare out into the Western Sea; to these islands of the Happy Otherworld — to Emain, and to Aircthech, whereon drop dragon-stones and crystals; having with him for companions —'

He had read so far when the light was of a sudden blotted out. He looked up: his heart seemed to miss a beat when he saw that a black figure stood in the silver radiance without the window. It was unstirring, its face undistinguishable.

He felt sick: he wanted to cry out loud: in his thin nightshirt he shuddered with the chill of panic.

Then his grandmother's voice said — and he heard it clearly through the panes —

'Go to my sitting-room, Anthony, and take what you are reading with you!' . . .

Madam Purvis's room was as forbidding as Madam Purvis.

It was small, and square, and lofty. There was no ornament whatever on the bare grey walls, for you could not count as such the dim hard-favoured portrait of some dead-and-gone Purvis over the empty grate. There were two bleak chairs upon which she never sat, and a bleak secretaire that she was rarely seen to open — on its top usually half a nibbled comfit, or a corner of some dry biscuit. The ice-like sheen of the polished floor was blotted by a single small dark rug. A candle burned in discouraged fashion on either side of the picture.

Madam Purvis entered.

She took without a word the paper from the shivering child, and proceeded to read the manuscript by the light of one of the candles. When she came to the end she turned it over; read the few lines scrawled on the other side; regarded for a while the signature and the rust-coloured stain in the corner.

Still without a word she pulled the long bell-rope hanging on the wall between fireplace and secretaire.

To Rasselas, who answered the summons, she said —

'The English officer, who came here the night Mr. Anthony was murdered, left a book behind him when he went. Where is it?'

It was still in the room he had occupied. Placed with the other books on a small hanging shelf.

'Bring it here! . . . And a shawl for Master Anthony!'

The big man brought book and black fleecy wrap, casting a glance of commiseration at the child as he did so; and was dismissed.

A small book it was; of a size to go into a saddle-bag; and entitled *Sims' Military Guide*. On the fly-leaf was the signature 'Charles Hurrell. Fourth Dragoons.'

Madam Purvis compared the two signatures — book and paper lying on the mantelpiece; examined afresh the smear. In the candlelight her face, bent intently down, was more yellow than old ivory; and there was a thin lustre in the satin folds of her black dress. The pale high walls gave out no reflections of light; a little cold draught whistled under the door beneath its breath; there was a faint smell of wetness, a faint sense of chill, a faint all-pervading greyness, as though the room had been excavated from a cloud or a night fog on East River.

Said Madam Purvis at last —

'Where did you find this?'

Anthony explained, anxiously watching her face for some clue to her attitude. But she made no comment, and gave no more sign of anger than she did of surprise. Although she had punished him but once; and, if she rarely commended him, equally rarely rebuked him, yet he always feared her far more in her seeming indifference than he did his other grandmother with her continuous querulousness and frequent hurricanes of temper.

He stood on the thin dark rug, a small peculiar figure with the black shawl round his shoulders, hands clasped behind his back, nervously rubbing together the bare toes that showed beneath the hem of his long nightshirt.

'Do you know where Emain is, ma'am?' he asked politely at length, to break the oppressive silence.

Madam Purvis ignored the question: continued to examine his discovery. After a while he ventured another question —

'What *is* a dragon-stone, ma'am?'

If his grandmother knew what a dragon-stone was, she nevertheless did not say.

Presently she turned her head a little, and looked down on the small and apprehensive boy.

'Look at this — Richard!' she said, and held out the leaf of manuscript so that he should see it. Obediently he regarded it.

'It's upside down, ma'am,' he said at length, uncertain what it was that he was expected to see.

'Look at that dark smear!'

He looked.

'It is a finger-print! . . . In blood! . . . A murderer's finger-print! . . . In your — father's blood!'

The child averted his gaze. He sickened with horror. He could not bear to see the rusty stain that cried out violence and death. He had always thought of his father as he was in the great portrait — a little fantastical, a little whimsical, keen and kind, quick to laugh or to sigh; not as a dead thing, clotted and stained with blood, to frighten people. In a sort of miasma of abhorrence he recalled the lolling head and ashen face (seamed with trickles of blood) of Mr. Chancellor, when his body had been brought to the house on a gate from under the ruins of his wrecked sulky.

'Take it,' said his grandmother, 'and look at it! And say to yourself, "That is my father's blood, and that is the name of the man who murdered him! I shall not forget!" '

He forced himself to take the page in his trembling fingers, by the corner furthest from the stain, and to hold it as though regarding it — but with tightly closed eyes. Between cold and terror he was near fainting.

'This man — this Hurrell — owed your father money. How or when he borrowed it I do not know. But instead of paying him, he undoubtedly murdered him, and cast the blame upon some other wretched creature. While your father was dying Hurrell robbed him — robbed *you* — of the great diamonds of the Muscovy necklace. Of that there can be no doubt. He was disturbed before he could get rid of the acknowledgment of the debt, and so hid it, as he thought, securely. He was a British officer! . . . You have a long account to settle with the British, Rich — Anthony!'

'Yes, ma'am,' he answered in something less than a whisper.

'You will remember to see that that account *is* settled, will you not, Anthony?'

She did not look at him as she spoke, but into the candle flame illuminating the left-hand corner of the dim picture on the wall. Anthony stared, as one mesmerized, at the mask of her face. His lips moved in obedient reply, but no coherent sound came, only a little croak.

'They owe us — you and me — for two lives! For your — for Richard Purvis! For Anthony Purvis! . . . You will never forget?'

His soul and mind were as numbed as his body. Automatically once more his lips parted.

And so that the child should have an unforgettable memory she drew for him — with every horrifying detail — the manner of the other Anthony's passing; blood-stained head sunk on blood-stained breast, body quivering to the gasps of the bubbling blood-filled breath . . . She told then of the dead Richard, as she envisaged him — a shapeless thing, shattered beyond recognition by hot lead and then trampled into the mud of the battlefield. It was as though the ravening spirit behind the still face drew ferocious nourishment from each imagined horror in that recital — from every detail she could fancy of the desecration of the bodies of her sons.

She took then the paper from her grandson's resistless hand, and putting it on the mantelpiece, scanned it again as though every crease, every pen-stroke, every detail of the blood-stain should be etched upon her memory for ever. Then she folded it up once more, this time so that the stain came uppermost, and the little package was, so to speak, bound in rusted blood.

With dry-rustling skirts she went to the secretaire; opened it; brought something from one of the small drawers. A locket with a crystal face, on a short gold chain.

'In this,' she said, 'is a lock of — Richard Purvis's hair.' She opened the trinket; put in the folded paper, and snapped it shut — 'And a leaf of Anthony Purvis's book stained with his life blood, and signed by his murderer!'

She turned to Anthony who was watching her every movement without the faintest comprehension.

'You will always wear this, Anthony, will you not? . . . So that you shall never forget.'

She had bent over him and placed the chain round his neck before he could have said any word. The locket slid down against his flesh — as cold as death.

A horror past words, past bearing, filled him. It was as though the life within him must always caress and keep warm the dead — as though he must always bear on him, and with him, and against him, a spell to conjure up the long-buried — as though the chain about his neck fettered him to ghosts.

He raised his hands in the feeble gesture of tearing off the dreadful burden. His body shrank from contact with that reliquary of the blood and hair of those who had died by violence so long ago: and he crouched his shoulders forward so that it might not touch him.

CHAPTER II

A YOUNG GENTLEMAN BEGINS HIS TRAVELS

THEY set out from High Pale on the following morning in immense state — high yellow-and-black travelling carriage, postilions liveried in blue, baggage coach (in which Madam Purvis's French maid, Louise, rode in prim solitude) and two outriders.

There were five travellers with this magnificent equipage.

There was Madam Purvis in her corner, sitting as upright against the upholstering of yellow and blue tapestry as though she were in her pew at church. She was enveloped in a black silk cloak, and wore a black calash bonnet, constructed on a framework of whalebone hoops, which could be pulled forward or pushed back from the face like the hood of a chaise. For the most part she was entirely invisible within the lair of her bonnet; but when she spoke — which was seldom — she would thrust back the whole extraordinary confection so that her head was entirely uncovered and would suddenly appear like the head of a tortoise projecting from its carapace.

Then there was the bosomy Miss Buckley, sitting opposite, resplendent in ample yellow dress and pink scarf and green bonnet.

Anthony himself, wide-brimmed black hat on the back of his head, sat on the same side as his governess, his nankeen-trousered legs a-dangle. He was very pale, and his small fingers never ceased plucking at the buttons of his short blue jacket, at the deep frills of the ruff of his shirt — as though he sought despairingly to disprove to himself the existence of what lay beneath the folds of cloth and linen.

And, finally, there were also — Father and Uncle Richard . . . Somewhere . . . Anthony was not quite sure where . . . Wraiths in the clouds of reddish dust that swirled in the wake of the carriage. Overtaking them and lurking in wait in the shadows of the woods. Galloping on invisible horses through the fields of maize and tobacco that lined the road so that the greenery was disturbed and shuddered with their passage — or

was it with the wind? Sometimes too, he had the conviction that they
rode on the very footboard behind the carriage, their blood-stained rags
fluttering about their shrivelled bodies, shaking and bouncing with the
lurches of the vehicle over the ill-made roads.

Despite the heat the windows had to be kept shut owing to the dust,
and the jolting of the carriage was so incessant that at the end of an
hour Miss Buckley showed every symptom of carriage sickness. Five
minutes afterwards the coach had to be brought to a quick halt, and
the steps let down so that the good lady could be sick in the seclusion of
a small wood.

A similar crisis occurred again half an hour later.

'You should exercise self-control,' said Madam Purvis with an entire
lack of sympathy as they slowed down. 'There is no need to be sick.
I am not sick. Anthony is not sick.'

As a matter of fact Anthony was nearly sick. In the haze of dust
that drifted past the window he had thought to see —

Nevertheless Miss Buckley, large handkerchief held desperately to her
face, extracted herself in a panicking haste and surged into refuge amid
convenient bushes.

Anthony and his grandmother sat facing one another in complete
silence for some little while. Then she said —

'You are wearing your locket, Anthony?'

'Yes, ma'am.'

He felt that her cold eyes could pierce jacket and shirt, and ascertain
that he spoke the truth. The — the Thing lay against his breast-bone.
He had put it on again that morning; had not indeed dared to do otherwise. Last night, however, when he had gone back to bed in the nursery
haunted by so many children, he had taken it off, and put it in a box,
and put the box in one of the cupboards, under a Bible. Even so he had
known that he had not escaped those Presences whom the locket and
himself — in some unexplainable way — enabled to break loose from
the narrow prison of the grave: that he would never escape . . . He had
left his candle burning and lay till dawn watching the cupboard door,
his nightshirt drenched with the sweat of panic.

As if she had read his thoughts, his grandmother added —

'You will never take it off, Anthony, until — '

And then suddenly pulled forward the front of her bonnet, so that
her face was completely hidden from him, as though the curtain had
been lowered at the conclusion of a performance.

All day long, as they bumped over ill-made roads on their way to
Philadelphia, his obsession grew that Those Other Travellers were with

them — were but barely out of sight. And as dusk came, and darkness, so his fears mounted.

But he was not destined to face his ghosts alone that night — or, indeed, on any of the succeeding nights. For the accommodation at the inns was so poor that he had to sleep with Miss Buckley — a greedy bedfellow, who was beset by small twitches and little whickerings and miniature explosions. On one occasion, even, they had to lie three in a bed with his grandmother, in a low-ceilinged room that harboured five other travellers.

Thus companioned, he thought that *they* would not dare invade his bed, cuddling their chilly impalpability to him for warmth, but must remain in the shadows behind the door, lurking at the stairfoot, or waiting amid all the stirrings of the night without the house. When the last candle was extinguished, however, he would cautiously remove the locket from about his neck and thrust it deep under the pillows. He lay, too, with one hand a little thrust out so that it touched — just touched — the warm body of the young woman at his side.

Each morning, when he rose, he strove to bring himself to leave the dreadful thing behind; but he was built for endurance rather than rebellion; and he knew, too, that it could not be thus abandoned, but would follow him and find him no matter where he went, or however fast he travelled. . . .

The journey thus was a continuous nightmare moving against a kaleidoscopic background of small towns, distant mountains, shoddy inns, wide waters, interminable fields of tobacco and corn, and swirling dust. They travelled without any sort of conversation; Madam Purvis withdrawn within the depths of her calash, and nibbling some small eatable so that her lap was always covered with crumbs; the governess knitting a strange garment in grey wool; and Anthony fighting hard to forget Father and Uncle Richard in the beginnings of a new dream story.

The day's travel would be punctuated by halts made necessary for Miss Buckley by the frequent calls of abundant Nature. Most of the pauses would be in the way of mere commas, so to speak; but occasionally they would range from semi-colons to full-stops. Madam Purvis made no comment until the third day, when she said without preamble, after the second stoppage in the early afternoon —

'Opium and lead pills are what you require, Miss Buckley.'

'It is constitutional!' apologized Miss Buckley, settling herself back in her seat. 'And hereditary! . . . My dear mother used to say that *her* mother — my grandmother . . .'

'We will procure some half-grain pills when we reach Alexandria,' said Madam Purvis.

'I assure you—' declared Miss Buckley.

'I insist,' replied Madam Purvis flatly. 'This afternoon alone the peculiarities of your constitution have caused us to lose at least fifteen minutes of travelling time. In other words, we ought to have been a mile and more nearer Alexandria, where there is one of the few decent inns in the State.'

'Nature—' began Miss Buckley in feeble rebellion, becoming extremely red.

'Nature,' said Madam Purvis, 'can be controlled. Nature must be controlled.'

And she terminated proceedings by pulling the strings of her calash, and retiring into that black silk lair.

Accordingly, after supper at Gadsby's Tavern, Madam Purvis herself fared forth to the nearest apothecary — attended by a manservant — and returned with a lavish supply of opium and lead boluses in a large cylindrical wooden box.

Miss Buckley had two pills after their seven o'clock breakfast, two more after the midday meal, and two after supper — taken under the personal and inexorable supervision of Madam Purvis. The results were highly satisfactory so far as the elder lady was concerned, although the younger showed considerable signs of wear and tear by the time that Philadelphia was reached. By the late afternoon she was generally comatose, and Anthony did not find her by any means improved as a bedfellow.

Two incidents only marked their journey. . . .

A broken pole delayed them for an hour or so outside the smithy of a small township of little white houses set about a wide green.

While the repair was being made, Anthony got out of the carriage and wandered along the dusty road past sun-blistered meeting-house, neat fences, and front yards overrun with flowers. It was a golden, sleepy afternoon in which the whole village seemed to slumber, and even the distant noises from the smithy were drowsily regular and slow.

Upon this peace the shrill shouting of children suddenly broke; and, with their shouting, laughter and a most extraordinary clatter.

From a little knot of small boys clustered about a tall wood-encased pump a short way off, there burst a half-grown pointer puppy with an old kettle tied to its tail.

The creature pelted down the road toward Anthony with the kettle leaping and bumping and clanking after it, like a thing possessed. Halted. Bit frantically at its tail. Span around in circles in its effort to get at the torment. Was overtaken by its enraptured audience, and renewed its panicked flight screaming as it ran. There was foam on its muzzle.

With some idea of rescue, Anthony stepped into its path, but the puppy swerved past him and continued its headlong career until the racket faded in the distance.

He watched its disappearance with tears in his eyes.

'Yah!' said the biggest of the little boys, who had now come up behind him and clustered about him.

'Yah!' said the smallest of the little boys, who appeared to be dressed in a shirt several sizes too large for him and nothing else.

'Coward!' said Anthony briefly, and without further ado struck the largest little boy on a very snub nose.

Further hostilities did not take place because at that moment a large fat voice intervened.

'You are quite right, little boy,' it said. 'Jake, leave him alone!'

At the first sound of that large fat voice all the little boys had frozen into attitudes expressive of the utmost consternation. Anthony swung about.

The large fat voice belonged to a large fat lady who had suddenly materialized at the garden gate of a neat white house, with a long neat porch, and shaded at either end by an immense oak tree. An enormous green sun-bonnet sat on the back of her head, and her face was very red and ornamented by a remarkable grey moustache.

'Jake Shaw, Edward Martin, Oliver Riddlesdell, Solomon Armine — disgraceful child! — you will bring that little dog round to my back porch within a quarter of an hour. You will also bring the kettle — separately! Otherwise . . . ! Do you understand, Jake?'

The eldest little boy (who wore a much patched pair of bright blue breeches) signified on behalf of himself and his companions that the instruction was understood, and then scampered off in obedience to the fat lady's nod.

'You don't endorse the principle of attaching kettles to dogs' tails, young gentleman, I gather?' said the large fat lady, regarding Anthony with approval.

'No, ma'am,' said Anthony, grateful for the double rescue.

'Unusual frame of mind for a small boy,' remarked the lady. 'You may come in with me and have some gingerbread!'

Certain of the acceptance of her invitation she turned, and, without a glance to see whether he followed, led the way up a narrow path into a shadowy old house and a shadowy old parlour full of shadowy old portraits. There he was regaled with spiced gingerbread and mint julep, and cross-examined very closely, until an elderly negress, who was nearly a cube dressed in a pink cotton frock, announced the arrival of Mr. Jake Shaw and his companions.

'A carpet-needle and my green string, Mary,' commanded the large lady, whose name it transpired was Bold.

Those articles having been procured, she shepherded Anthony to the back porch where the small band of offenders awaited her with trepidation, a shivering puppy, and a battered kettle.

'Your only breeches, Jake?' Miss Bold inquired, eyeing the patched blue unmentionables.

'Yes, ma'am.'

'Turn round!'

With swift stitches she attached the kettle by its handle to the baggy seat of Mr. Shaw's nether-wear: tugged at it to make certain that it was secure: stepped back a pace or two to admire her handiwork.

'You will wear that kettle to remind you *not* to tie such things to the tails of little dogs. You will come here to-morrow afternoon to have it taken off. You will not dare remove it until then. A very suitable lesson!'

Jake, after a short silence of stunned horror, burst into loud howls, and was led forthwith away by his companions whose feelings were obviously compounded of relief at their own escape, horrified joy, and sycophantic sympathy.

'And now some more gingerbread, child! No well-brought-up boy refuses gingerbread!' said Miss Bold, re-entering her house — which smelled most deliciously of cedarwood, lavender, and dried rose petals — and despatching Mary to the garden gate to ascertain in the meantime what progress had been made with the coach at the smithy across the green. . . .

The incident remained imprinted on Anthony's memory throughout his life, because it was the only occasion on which he ever deliberately struck another in anger — even through the years of war in which he was to become enmeshed. Thinking about it long afterwards he came to the conclusion that subconsciously his childish mind must have found a parallel between the puppy with a kettle tied to its tail and himself with his grandmother's periapt fastened round his neck. The blow that had fallen upon Jake Shaw's small nose had been delivered by no Galahad, but symbolized a desperate gesture of defiance against the fate that persecuted child and dog. . . .

The other business kept them prisoners for the whole of a day in a grimy Pennsylvanian inn. They had been about to set off — Miss Buckley's floridity by now become a greenishness — on a fine Sunday morning, when four select-men of the local meeting-house suddenly appeared at the horses' heads and forcibly restrained them from desecrating the Sabbath by unnecessary travel.

They were kept under surveillance until past dark, and on the next morning Madame Purvis appeared before an unshaven magistrate and was fined twenty-five dollars for profaning the Lord's Day. She made no comment and no protest, but the community had small profit out of the transaction, since she succeeded in effecting departure without paying a single cent of the long bill that awaited her at the inn.

So, at length, they came to Philadelphia. There the grim Mr. Jarman, of Girard's Bank, shepherded them to lodgings on Chestnut Street — opposite a carpet warehouse, from whose upper windows streamed out strips of floor-covering like cabbage-patterned banners; held grim conference with Madam Purvis; and, two days later, grimly escorted them aboard the ship *Chesapeake* bound for Genoa, and bade them farewell with no more feeling than if he were putting a ledger away.

They were dropping down the wide Delaware River before ever Dr. Earle had succeeded in notifying Grandmother Fell in distant South Carolina that fellow guardian and ward had vanished from High Pale.

CHAPTER III

THE PERIAPT OF MR. HARRADENCE

DURING daylight — except at odd moments — Anthony forgot those other travellers who had embarked with him in the *Chesapeake,* and of whom the captain had no record.

His mind was vastly busied. With the perpetual magic of the sea. With the miracle of the great ship that idled, curvetted, or battled across the hundreds of restless miles to another continent. With all his new friends; the one-legged cook who wore a red cotton nightcap and a tarred kilt; Mr. Harradence with his weather-beaten face and big nose and grey hair; and Garland Vane, a dark-eyed small lady in a muslin frock, whose tangle of curls was hidden ordinarily beneath an enchanting yellow silk bonnet with a very high crown and a very narrow brim.

As well as all this there were enormous and interminable meals, starting with breakfast at eight o'clock, continuing with lunch at noon, subduing him with dinner at three, and utterly defeating him with a most substantial tea at seven.

But at night it was far different, when the ship was dark; for then the song of the wind in the cordage, the whisper of the waters against the sides, and the complaints of the timbers were no longer friendly assonance, but took on a strange and sinister character.

After dusk he frequently just missed seeing *them* by the merest fraction of a second; was conscious that but an instant earlier they had stepped into one of the empty cabins off the darkened dining saloon. Or had slipped into the shadows of the fo'c'sle as the ship rode over the long Atlantic swells with no glimmer of light on the poop except from the lantern at the binnacle. Or had slid round the long-boat — which was housed over the main hatch — away from the moon. Or had lost themselves in the jumble of gear and rigging and obscurity by the foot of the main mast. Or —

And so after tea, when Garland had gone regretfully to bed and the handful of passengers were gathered at cards, or with their books, in a sort of snug inn parlour in the stern, Anthony would be there too.

It was a parlour which had six red-curtained windows looking out on the ship's foaming path across the waste; its white walls ornamented with a highly imaginative French engraving of the surrender of Yorktown, a portrait of General Washington fondling a large cannon, and a particularly anti-British cartoon by Paul Revere; and a tabby cat proprietorially asleep by the iron stove. There he would be ensconced on the long red upholstered window-seat, with Lord John Berners' translation of Froissart's *Chronicle,* lent him by Mr. Harradence. But he would not be reading, or even thinking; just sitting, a small polite automaton, paralyzed by fear of the moment when he must go to bed — go to the coffin-like berth in the small cabin which he had to himself; a small cabin that reminded him of the family vault at High Pale with its stone shelves and its shadows and grated door.

He never ventured out of range of the friendly lamplight except in company with one of his elders. Madam Purvis invariably withdrew to her cabin after tea, and was no more seen; Miss Buckley was immersed in her evening flirtation with Mr. Klinger, a young-old man from Delaware with a singularly flat yellow face. Anthony was therefore left, within reason, to choose his own bedtime. So when Mr. Harradence — who retired extremely early — drank off his nightcap of sangaree, yawned, remarked, as always, 'Well, sleep is better than medicine!' Anthony would hurriedly close his book.

In that way not only might he make in company the journey through the dim saloon to the small burial vault at the far end, but also was he able to do something that otherwise must be performed in the dark if

Miss Buckley supervised his undressing — after she had extinguished
the solitary candle-lamp affixed to a bulkhead, and withdrawn.

Outside Mr. Harradence's stateroom, which was exactly opposite his
own, they would halt.

'Good night, boy,' would say Mr. Harradence, shaking hands as if they
were about to part for a week or two.

'Good night, sir,' would say Anthony, and wait wistfully while the
big man entered the comfortable confusion of his cell. He had a glimpse
of books and clothes and toilet articles strewn on bunk and floor, before
the door shut.

'Don't forget your prayers, boy!'

'No, sir!'

'Good night again!'

'Good night, sir!'

And then the door would close; the mantle of Mr. Harradence's protection would be withdrawn; and he would be left to venture with quickly
beating heart into the haunted dimness of his own cabin. There he
would undress very quickly, don his long white cotton nightshirt, remove
his grandmother's locket from about his neck, and, after peering out to
see that the coast was clear, hang it on the latch of the empty stateroom
next door. Then he huddled into his berth, till Miss Buckley should
come perfunctorily to tuck him up, kiss him 'good-night' and blow out
the light. After that he would lie waiting tremulous (until the sleep of
exhaustion overcame him) for some faint noise that should tell that the
upper berth was no longer unoccupied; for the door to creak slowly
open; for —

One night, however, when he could no longer bear it, he slipped out
from the sheets and into the saloon, and sat himself on the deck propped
against Mr. Harradence's cabin door; and was so found asleep in the
grey dawn by a yawning steward.

That Mr. Harradence was a great and heroic figure, Anthony was
further convinced on the stupefying occasion when his friend flatly contradicted and browbeat Grandmother Purvis.

It was at dinner that this happened — dinner in the narrow saloon with
the afternoon sun streaming down through the glass panels of the companion on to the coarse table-cloth that had been dampened to prevent
the crockery slipping about if the seas rose; with all the mahogany doors
of the staterooms that lined the place complaining with the gentle movement of the ship.

Mr. and Mrs. Vernon Roscoe had been boasting to the small company
of their social successes, in a steep crescendo — New York . . . *Boston*

. . . PHILADELPHIA. At least Mrs. Roscoe had been so boasting, and Mr. Roscoe had repeated what she said like a rather feeble echo, for his lady had all the chin, all the chest, and all the character of the pair. Indeed Mr. Roscoe's only claim to distinction was that he was unable to partake of any meal unless he accompanied it by medicinal draughts, mostly of a nauseous grey complexion, needing a great deal of stirring.

Captain Banks, wooden-faced and very tightly jacketed in blue, sitting at the head of the table, had listened with his customary polite attention whilst he loaded an enormous cargo of boiled mutton.

'The President, of course, does not dance, but he was most attentive', said Mrs. Roscoe, flashing her black eyes round the table, as if challenging anyone to declare that there was not very good reason for General Washington's attentions.

'*Most* attentive,' said dutiful Echo.

'Yes-sir!' said Captain Banks, expressing thorough acquiescence in the presidential attitude.

'We took a turn round the room together', said Mrs. Roscoe. 'It was most refreshing after the turmoil of the ball.'

'*Most* refreshing, my dear, I am sure!'

'Yes-sir?' said Captain Banks, not interrupting for one instant the mastication of the largest potato which it was humanly possible to take on board whole.

'So interesting a man! So *very* interesting!'

'Yes-sir!'

'But sad — very sad! And a little silent!'

'Yes-sir?' said Captain Banks, still dealing with the potato.

'It seemed to me that the cares of state weighed heavily on him.'

'Yes-sir,' said Captain Banks in as cordial agreement as the potato would permit.

Miss Buckley and Mr. Klinger were evincing the greatest interest in these revelations of high society. Madam Purvis ate her dinner without the faintest display of attention. The enchanting Mrs. Vane — as blue-eyed and fair-complexioned as any Dresden shepherdess; mother of Garland, and niece of Mr. Harradence — made polite murmurings. The big man himself now proceeded to take part in the conversation, such as it was —

'Much more likely that it was his teeth which weighed heavily on him, ma'am,' remarked he.

'Teeth!' ejaculated Mrs. Roscoe.

'Teeth!' said Echo.

'Yes-sir?' said Captain Banks.

'The fact is,' continued Mr. Harradence, entirely unimpressed by the general atmosphere of hostility, 'that General Washington's reputation for solemnity and silence is due to his dentist. The fact is that he daren't laugh or talk too much for fear of dropping his teeth!'

'Yes-sir?' said Captain Banks, picking *his* with a wooden toothpick, which he afterwards wiped on the table-cloth.

'Really — ' began Mrs. Roscoe.

'I can assure you, ma'am, that it is so. Mr. Revere may have been a hero of the Revolutionary War, but he makes infernally bad false teeth. Infernally bad! Fact! And now the General has gone to a fellow in New York — fellow named Greenwood — and is very little better off. Although he has a set of pearlies made from sea-horse ivory! . . . Facts! — Thirty-two of them!'

'Yes-sir?' said Captain Banks.

'I fail to see,' commented Madam Purvis, who sat on the captain's right, opposite Mrs. Vane, 'how the President's teeth can be anyone's concern but his own!'

'And that is where you are utterly wrong, ma'am, if I may say so,' replied Mr. Harradence. 'The teeth of the President of the United States are — or can be — a matter every whit as important to the world as the sanity or insanity of King George the Third. A president in the exacerbation of tooth-ache may commit some egregious folly with disastrous consequences for his people. A presidential stomach-ache may result in national as well as personal convulsions.'

'Yes-sir!' said Captain Banks sympathetically — for his digestive apparatus was notoriously unsound.

'I think, sir,' said Madam Purvis, 'that you are inclined to push your theory to absurd conclusions.'

'Nonsense, ma'am — '

'Now, Uncle!' interposed Mrs. Vane in the most threatening manner.

'I won't be "Now-uncled",' continued Mr. Harradence in high excitement, and proceeded to emphasize his remarks by shaking a long forefinger in an admonitory manner at Madam Purvis. 'I said "Nonsense!" and I meant "Nonsense". At what point is absurdity reached, ma'am? At what point do the ailments of the head of a state leave off being a matter of public interest? . . . Answer that!' said he, stabbing the air.

Madame Purvis attended to her dinner.

'You agree that his sanity is a matter of national concern. If a king — or a president — becomes blind — or deaf — or dumb — or paralysed — you will agree that it is an affair of public importance? . . . You can't do otherwise! . . . If he suffers from a wasting disease, or a haemorrhage, or a tumour, you will still agree? Or if he loses a hand, an arm, or a leg? If he has jaundice, erysipelas, eczema, the influenza? . . . You agree, ma'am? . . . Do — you — agree?'

Madam Purvis wiped her lips composedly upon one of the black-bordered napkins of which she had brought a store with her.

Said she —

'I consider the subject an unsuitable one for argument, more particularly so at dinner-time.'

'And I disagree with you, ma'am!' said Mr. Harradence with much vehemence, leaning across the table toward her as far as he could. 'I utterly and entirely disagree with you! A royal stomach-ache may cost dozens — hundreds — thousands — of lives. And you dare tell me that it is an impertinence to take an interest in the royal intestines? Ph't, ma'am! Ph't! If I had my way no great executive — no chief of state — no legislator — should be allowed to start his day's work until he had been passed as physically and mentally fit by a committee of responsible doctors. Our lives are in Captain Banks's keeping. If he is unwell our risks are increased.' — 'Yes-sir!' said Captain Banks a little uncertainly. — 'Therefore, willy-nilly, all of us on board this ship must be vitally interested in Captain Banks's health — in his ears and his eyes and his stomach and his lungs and all the rest of him.'

Mr. Harradence was by now so excited that he appeared about to climb across the table. His niece removed his glass out of harm's way.

'Yes-sir?' said Captain Banks in an embarrassed manner.

'In the same way, ma'am, your health is a matter that does not affect you alone. It is a matter of interest to your family and dependants, apart altogether from an affection they may possibly bear you. Your illness may mean increased duties for them, or it may sour your temper and so make life an abomination for them. In the irritation of your gumboil, or stomach-ache, or other dolour you berate Mr. Anthony.' — Here Mr. Harradence winked most embarrassingly at the awestruck child sitting between grandmother and governess. — 'In his exacerbation Mr. Anthony behaves most pestilentially to his fair tutoress.' — And here he winked again; this time at the horrified Miss Buckley — 'She gets in a pet, quarrels with her betrothed, who takes to drink. Or the episode gives her such a distaste for the tutorial profession that she seeks refuge in matrimony. Wisely — possibly: unwisely, more probably! So there you have your gumboil affecting not merely your own family, not merely a wider circle of the community, but unborn generations! . . . I maintain that your gumboil — if you have one, ma'am — is a matter of vital interest to the whole ship!'

With that Mr. Harradence restored himself to his seat, drank off with much calmness a whole tumblerful of sangaree, and beamed on everybody.

'Yes-si . . .' began Captain Banks; eyed the silent Madam Purvis; said no more. . . .

'T'cha! And again t'cha! I will not be bullied, Elizabeth! The woman deserved it,' said Harradence. Dinner had come to a subdued conclusion, and now he sprawled beside his niece on deck, on a sort of garden seat that was sheltered by the high companion which lighted the saloon.

Overhead the great sails breasted out from the mizzen-yards, filled by the West Wind and by late sunlight. The ship pressed on across a sparkling light green sea, whose stirrings — told in quick-running shadows and criss-cross lines of foam — appeared no more than those of a field of young wheat.

Harradence was engaged desultorily, in moments of lesser idleness, in carving a large heart, pierced by an arrow, on the solid oaken arm of the seat. Now he yawned, stretching himself so vastly that every seam of his incredibly tight claret-coloured coat was brought to cracking point.

'Hey, Don Antonio!' he called.

The small boy — his dark hair all ruffled by the wind — looked up from the grave game of dominoes that he was playing with Garland Vane, on the deck a short way off.

'What is your grandmother's Christian name — given name — forename, my noble squire?'

'Henriette, sir.'

Harradence forthwith proceeded to outline with his pearl-handled penknife the letters 'H' and 'P' within the heart.

His niece laid down her book open on her lap: folded her arms in a menacing fashion — shapely arms sheathed past the elbow in green gauze gloves — and turned her head toward him slowly the better to examine him and his works from under the brim of her little yellow silk bonnet.

'What scoundrelism do you propose now, Harrady?' she asked.

'A love token — for remembrance,' said her uncle, adding his own initials, 'H.H.', to the design. Paused. Continued. 'I *was* rude. And meant to be! . . . I *shall* be rude. And shall mean to be!'

'Don't forget that she is no longer young!' said Mrs. Vane shaking her pretty head.

'She's an old harridan,' he replied, and added depth to the downstroke of an 'H' before he went on: 'She's also an old devil. A female Demogorgon! . . . The Virginian "tidewater" magnifico is generally a picturesque and useless sort of animal, but this one is a poisonous creature. A dash of Latin blood somewhere, I should think. Perhaps French planter stock from Louisiana . . . I overheard her this morning giving instructions to young hopeful — I don't know what the occasion was — in certain aspects of American history. I have no reason to love my country, but even, to my mind, she presented a damnably one-sided catalogue of British iniquities!

'Drunken governors signing death warrants of innocent men whilst in their cups — incompetent generals leading brave Americans to their doom against Indians or French — brutal soldiers firing on high-souled assemblages of patriots — redskins scalping fallen heroes amid applauding redcoats — armies whose sole object was rape and rapine and destruction! There was a gusto and glibness in production that makes me think that she often runs over the items to herself to keep their memory fresh! . . . It is a loathsome thing to do to a child — to charge it with hates and memories that should be forgotten! . . . No wonder he looks haunted!'

'Haunted!' said Mrs. Vane, regarding the pair with a smile. Anthony was obviously protesting — with much courtesy — against his opponent's predilection for rules of her own devising. There was much laughter and shaking of a dark head by the lady. 'Haunted! My dear Harrady, you have the most vivid imagination! The boy certainly doesn't look well. What he needs, without doubt, is a good dosing. Neither his grandmother nor his governess seem to give him what I should call sensible attention. He eats nothing — half as much as Garland does! *I* should give him — '

'You women,' remarked Harradence, brushing a few chips off the seat, 'read everything in the terms of stomach. Because the child is pale and his eyes stick out, you say at once "Liver!" Now *I* say he's sick in his heart, or his mind, or his soul — but not his body. Do you know that that small boy has practically never seen any other small boys; has lived all his days among ghosts and grown-ups and books and slaves — hundreds of 'em — in a sort of feudal state, with that snake of a grandmother as regent? Do you know what he and I were discussing yesterday afternoon when we were walking up and down the deck together?'

'Something absurd, I should fancy,' said his niece taking up her book again.

She had noticed with amusement the promenade of the pair — big man and small boy — in deep discussion, bare-headed, hands similarly cupped behind back. Her daughter had, indeed, been much displeased at the preoccupation of her playmate: had greatly desired to interrupt the conference.

'We debated Ossian and Homer! He had read the Iliad in both Chapman and Pope. I fully expected to have my views asked on the genuineness of Macpherson.'

'I suppose I have heard of them,' said Elizabeth Vane doubtfully, laying down the volume once more on her pink-spotted muslin lap.

'Intelligence was never your strongest point, my pretty,' commented Harradence, regarding her with admiration. 'But the nub of the thing is this. I get bored with playing cribbage with you or whist with those appalling Roscoes night after night, or drinking with Banks — a human cistern — or watching the unhandy spooning of Mr. Klinger and his Blowsabella. So last night I invited our young friend to a renewal of the discussion and a walk on deck after dark. I could sense his unwillingness, though he came all the same. But there was no talk in him, and as we walked up and down I could see him peering into the shadows as if he expected something to be lurking in them. Where the deck was moderately clear I knew that he was looking sideways at the bulwarks lest something should come clambering up out of the sea. And when we returned to the stern cabin, through the dark saloon, he came so close behind me up the narrow alley, between the chairs and the stateroom doors, that he was practically treading on my heels all the way. When we got into the light I saw that the child was as white as a sheet.'

'I have already noticed that he always seems to shoot off to bed at the same time that you do. I suppose that's the reason — ghosts in the dark! . . . The child needs someone to tuck him up and kiss him goodnight really properly!'

'I should hate to be tucked up and kissed by either the Purvis or the Buckley,' remarked her uncle in the tone of one who was a connoisseur in such matters.

'You are not likely to,' returned Elizabeth. 'I'd do it myself — I mean Anthony! — if — '

'If Hag Purvis were a trifle less terrifying! But then the situation wouldn't arise! . . . Coates, the steward, tells me that he found our mutual acquaintance asleep in the saloon soon after daybreak one morning last week! Huddled up against my door!'

'Poor lamb!' exclaimed Elizabeth. 'Someone ought really to speak to those women about it — but not me! . . . Perhaps one could drop a word to that French maid of his grandmother's — she looks human as well as pretty. I daresay Buckley is all right, but her mind is full of Klinger and poetry — what mind the old lady allows her to call her own!'

'About the French maid, Coates has already made the same discovery,' commented Harradence. 'You'll admit I'm right about the boy then — I usually am! — and that there's something on his mind?'

Mrs. Vane removed the book from her lap. From beside her on the seat she produced a very small round basket full of preserved plums — purple-black and frosty with sugar.

'Anthony!' she called; and then, almost as an after-thought, 'Garland!'

' "Everything in the terms of stomach!" ' repeated Harradence, selecting the largest plum. . . .

The *Chesapeake* drove on toward the darkness of the East, through a black and gently heaving sea. There was no moon, and the vessel passed across the face of the Atlantic as though she were a grey ghost; inaudible but for the faint creakings of timbers and cordage and the murmur of waters against her side; unillumined but for the tiny light at her binnacle.

Anthony woke up.

The lamp was out, and the cabin utterly dark. Someone during the day had locked the empty stateroom next door, and for the first time on board he was alone with IT, at night.

The door jarred within its frame far more than the movement of the ship seemed to warrant, and the latch of the fastening tapped very gently against the catch as though it had become undone. There was the minutest of sounds from the top of the locker under the porthole, which served for dressing-table and washstand, and whereon the locket lay; a tiny dry scratching sound, as though the trinket were being moved upon the varnished surface. At the same moment he heard — he *knew* that he heard — someone stir in the berth over his own.

There were thin straw palliasses upon the wooden ledges that formed the bunks, and it was impossible to shift on them without making a faint rustling noise. He himself had not moved at all — had been too panic-stricken . . . He lay and listened, his body suddenly clammy with perspiration . . . Distinct and unmistakable, amid all the familiar whisperings of the ship, there came again the sound of someone moving on the pallet just above him.

For a little he remained paralysed by fear, staring through the airless blackness at the upper berth, which was invisible to him, although so close overhead that he could have touched it without unduly stretching. In a short time, he knew, Someone would rustle again, would lean over the low rim of the bunk; and, next, its wet grey face would appear within a few inches of his own. He began to pray rapidly, but without any reliance upon the Almighty.

Then, as the ship swung upward to a steeper swell than those that had gone before, the cabin door crashed back against the panelling; there was a renewal of the small noises above; and his self-control was shattered.

In a paroxysm of terror he flung from his bed; leaped to the door as it closed again; wrestled with the latch; and hurled himself into the long dark tunnel that was the saloon, cannoning against one of the chairs that were fixed immovably along the narrow table down the centre.

As he started back he saw something hanging in the air before him — something tall and grey, which, though not luminous, yet held the vestiges of light within it. He had meant — so far as he was aware of any meaning to his flight — to have taken refuge with Mr. Harradence, but this menacing phantom seemed to lie directly in his path to the big man's cabin. With a choking cry he fled down the saloon toward the companion-way leading on deck.

Harradence had been sitting on the edge of his bunk, clad in a green and pink striped bed-gown with purple-tasselled nightcap, smoking a meditative cheroot — a thing entirely forbidden by the ship's regulations. He was in the dark, and, since it was a warm night, porthole and door were both hasped back.

He had heard the clatter made by the small boy emerging from the cabin; heard, too, the shapeless sound that burst from Anthony's lips when he was intimidated by the mirror-encased shaft of the mizzen-mast.

Now he came out into the saloon, which would have been pitch dark except for the faintest greyness that struggled through the skylight and appeared to lie against the glass, too feeble to be illuminant. As he did so he saw the small white figure vanish through the door that opened on the foot of the companion-ladder.

Harradence took the intervening space in two great strides: called 'Anthony! Anthony!' up the ladder after the child, who did not turn his head but only climbed the faster: himself followed. . . .

The poop-deck was deserted except for an obscure shape at the wheel, its head and shoulders thinly yellowed — and no more — by the faint sparkle of the binnacle light.

The night seemed a solid thing through which the ship must press her way, even as she forced a path through the inky sea. The restlessness of the vast waters about her sang a low rushing song. The *Chesapeake* shook herself as she topped another swell, and a splash of foam wetted the rail; and then she dipped a little as she slid down the long slope.

The door opening onto the desolation of the deck from the companion-hatch was shut. As he fumbled with the latch, Anthony cast a panicked glance behind him, down the ladder, which was dimly illumined by a small lantern suspended from the roof over it. . . . Something had begun to climb after him!

He screamed shrilly: tumbled over the coaming of the hatchway onto the deck: picked himself up: ran uncertainly — as though he were no longer in full control of his limbs — up the slanting deck: clutched at the rough coat of the helmsman and at the smooth spokes of the wheel, babbling appeals for succour.

'Christ!' said the man, his nerves shattered by scream and sudden apparition. 'Jesus Christ, what's this?'

He tore his coat from the child's grasp, and pushed him from the wheel.

'Anthony!' said Harradence very quietly; and halted by the great sky-light over the main cabin. 'Anthony, it's all right. It's only me!'

'Jesus Christ!' ejaculated the sailor, seeing yet another dim figure materialize in the darkness. He raised an alarmed shout, 'Mr. Mate! M-i-s-t-e-r Mate!'

From far forward a cry came in reply. Heavy feet started to run along the deck.

The refusal of his plea for aid, the sudden violent breaking of the silence, and above all, the appearance of that tall figure with its whispered summons — 'Anthony! Anthony!' — were the climax of his horror.

The child's mind no longer served him. In Harradence's still form he saw — Father — Uncle Richard — the ghost of a tattered body clothed in tatters; a dead thing which he himself in some way had warmed to a renewed and obscene life — a dead thing which had now come to make its ultimate and irresistible demands upon him. There was no escape! None!

Before either Harradence or the helmsman could guess his intention he had run to the starboard rail, and was clambering over. He was, perhaps, unconscious of the full purport of what he did.

He hung by his hands over the dark water, which rose up toward him at that moment as though it were some elemental god about to seize upon a sacrifice. The ship, too, rolled a little into the swell, dipping as if she would bring the offering within reach of the hungry Atlantic.

He cried out very loudly — 'Mother! Mother!'

He let go.

But as he released his grip so his wrists were seized. Harradence, babbling prayers and the most appalling blasphemies, drew him back into the ship, unconscious. . . .

'So now,' concluded Harradence, 'I am going to borrow your daughter!'

'Are you?' said Mrs. Vane.

She had thrown on a flowered wrap, and sat on the only stool the cabin possessed. A bracket lamp glimmered over a small travelling washstand near the open port, through which streamed in the roar and sighing of the sea. Harradence, in his preposterous bed-gown of pink and green, was propped opposite her against the dark panels of the bulkhead. His long bare feet were negligently crossed. The purple tassel of his nightcap had fallen over his nose, and while she meditated her reply he occupied himself in endeavouring to blow it to one side. He filled the tiny dim compartment to overflowing: his niece had the feeling that if he stretched he would push the walls apart; that his great voice — lowered though it was — reverberated within the confines as if it, too, would force an outlet.

'Here is the source of all the ghosts and other devilments,' he remarked, and held out a crystal locket on a thin gold chain. 'Here is the fetish — the evil periapt that has made our Don Antonio a prey to vampires!'

'What is it?' she asked curiously, following it with her eyes as he swung it to and fro like a pendulum before her.

'It's a locket which the Demogorgon insists upon her grandson wearing. Always! *Always!* A locket filled with the relics of men who died violent deaths!'

'Ugh!' said Elizabeth Vane, 'Take the horrible thing away, Harrady!'

'On this side, you may note,' he continued, swinging the trinket a little nearer to her, 'that something reddish shows through the glass. That's a bit of paper. It soaked up Father's blood when he was murdered! On the other' — he turned the gold and crystal oval so that she should see — 'you'll perceive a lock of fair hair. That was a curl of Uncle Richard's hair! He was killed in battle — battered, I gather, out of all resemblance to human shape . . . There is also something I don't understand about dragon-stones — whatever they are — and a debt.'

'Let me look!'

She stretched out her hand for the locket, but he withdrew it beyond her reach.

'I don't think it lies within our province to explore the contents, my beautiful! I, too, badly wanted to examine them, but restrained myself.'

'But why should the child have to wear such a monstrous thing? . . . Throw it out of the porthole, Harrady! It's obscene!'

'He's made to wear it for the same reason that Mrs. Demogorgon gives him lessons in American history,' said Harradence ironically. 'To promote love and fellowship! To remind him always of pleasant things! . . . What should you say of a woman who makes a ju-ju of blood and hair, and so infects it with hate and vengeance that the child fancies that ghosts come out of it like the Djinn from the bottle in the *Thousand and One Nights.*'

'Throw it out of the porthole, Harrady!'

'No! Even if you left the thing in the depths of the Atlantic, yet the ghosts would remain. It has done its work. Father and Uncle Richard have escaped from their graves and won't return there! . . . If the child is to be saved it must be in another way . . . I'll beat the damned woman! I've got a ju-ju stronger than hers! By God, I have!'

His voice, which had been very low, had begun to rise.

'S'sh, Harrady! For heaven's sake! . . . You'll wake the Roscoes . . . They'll think — '

'That you're the sort of niece whom elderly bachelors sometimes produce! . . . Let 'em!'

But he lowered his tone, and she ignored the remark.

'What's *your* mascot, Harrady?'

'Garland!'

Her eyes shifted to the upper berth where the child lay asleep: returned to the sorcerer.

She was silent for a minute or so, regarding him with a tiny smile that was, so to speak, the merest whisper of a laugh. He was so large, and, in some way, so preposterous in the pink and green-striped gown; his iron-grey hair was so tousled — for he had flung the nightcap on the floor; and on his ruddy leathery face with the great jutting nose, and in his grey eyes, was something of the expression of an adventurous and boastful schoolboy. . . .

'I think our young friend might quite easily lose his reason. Unless something is done at once. And the right something! . . . We — I and my talisman — can defeat Demogorgon for ever and ever. I know it! I swear it! I'd stake a hundred pounds on the efficacy of my sorcery! . . . Five hundred pounds, dammit! . . . Any money you like! . . . Will you take me?'

'Surely it would be easier to tell Madam Purvis what has occurred? She is not a fool, whatever else she may be! . . .'

'It is beyond her to undo what she has done, and you know it!' he answered with complete conviction.

'Have it your own way! . . . As you always do,' said Elizabeth rising to her feet. 'Where is Anthony now?'

'Lying on my berth. Engaged — unless it has already sent him to sleep — in reading the twenty-third psalm seven times and yet seven times again. You know —

' "Yea, though I walk through the valley of the shadow of death, I will fear no evil: for thou art with me; thy rod and thy staff they comfort me."

I have heard all his story — at least, so much as he is capable of explaining to me. I have silenced the crew with promises of what shall be theirs — when I have a garment with a proper pocket! Now I am going to undertake the cure . . . I'll come back for Garland in a moment.'

By a common impulse they both looked into the shadowy bed, the dimity curtains of which were drawn a little at the head. The child slumbered, her short black curls spread upon the thin pillow, her lips just parted, the flush of sleep staining the pearliness of her charming face. To see her and to hear her quiet breathing was in itself an act of prayer.

'You will lend me your talisman . . . for one night, Elizabeth?' he asked.

'There is very little that I wouldn't do for you, Harrady!' said Elizabeth, and swept him once again with a glance that was both mocking and tender. 'I have thought before that you were possessed of powers of sorcery, all the more dangerous because you have a way of behaving like an overgrown schoolboy. It may, of course, merely be persuasiveness, but I don't think so . . . In fact now that I have seen your bare feet for the first time, I know it isn't!'

'Bare feet?' said Harradence: looked down: most absurdly reddened: endeavoured to hide them under the hem of the long bed-gown.

'None but the fairy people have feet like yours. Long feet, and narrow, and pointed. You would probably have burned as a wizard in the Middle Ages, or in Massachusetts in the last century, without any other evidence being required. . . .'

Anthony sat up in his berth, back in the family vault: but it was a tomb no longer, for no tomb could have contained so brilliant and unfunereal a garment as the remarkable gown in which Mr. Harradence was clothed.

Harradence sat on the edge of the bunk, a little crouched because of the narrow space between it and the berth above. His elbows were set on his knees, and his long strong chin was cupped in his hands: his head was turned toward the small pale boy.

'. . . And so you see it is not age, or experience, or bodily strength that counts in such matters as this. I tell you that the weakest and most innocent thing in the world is also the strongest. Almighty God in his mercy has set special guard that it may be protected from strange perils

. . . You believe me, though it may be hard — don't you, Anthony?'

Believe him Anthony did. He was prepared to believe anything that the big man said. His mind was blank to everything except those words of confidence and reassurance. His memory was emptied of all the former horrors.

'And now,' said Harradence, 'I am going to bring you this weak and innocent thing, and you will see how it shall drive away for ever anything that is evil or frightening! So strong it is — so *very* strong!'

He was gone; and almost immediately was back again.

He bore Garland in his arms, drowsy, smiling.

For a second as he stooped with her to Anthony's berth, her eyes half-opened and widened in unsurprised recognition.

'Anthony Rowley!' she said below her breath, and then again — 'What fun!'

Her eyes closed as her ruffled head touched the pillow, but the smile of greeting lingered about her lips even after she had sighed with the renewed satisfaction of sleep, and after she had curved her body contentedly on the white honeycomb coverlet toward Anthony. Her cheeks had the exquisite texture and contours and colouring of a rose petal.

Anthony looked at her for a considerable time with pleasure and in puzzlement.

'Garland!' he said at last, half doubtfully. Not that for one moment he questioned Mr. Harradence's powers as a magician, but that he found it difficult to believe that his affairs could be judged of sufficient importance to justify the carrying-off of her from bed.

'Garland!' Mr. Harradence assured him.

The boy was sitting up: he was as pale as death, but his teeth were no longer chattering, nor was he shivering. He just sat up and stared down at the child; and then he suddenly smiled. Harradence found something extraordinarily beautiful in that smile, which was as if Anthony were at the same time offering protection and receiving it. He touched Garland's hand which was lightly curved upon the pillow, gently — very gently. In that moment and in that touch something passed from her to him. The innocent confidence of childhood — the Blessing of God. Presently he looked up, and smiled at Harradence, too.

Harradence responded to Anthony's smile; and as he did so, holding the small boy's eyes with his own steady gaze, he withdrew the locket and chain from the breast-pocket of his fantastic bed-gown, and held it toward him, cupped in a big hand.

Anthony's regard did not leave the other's face; but Harradence knew that he was aware of the locket by reason of the sudden intensification of that regard, by a slight tightening of the muscles about the mouth as though lips that might tremble were being steadied.

The big man dropped the amulet on the coverlet, and, leaning over the berth, deliberately and delicately undid the buttons at the neck of Garland's nightgown and opened the garment. In the half-light Anthony thought that the child's body — so revealed — seemed to be of silver.

Very gently Harradence raised that dark and sleepy head with the palm of his left hand. Just a little. He put the chain of the locket round the slender neck; clasped it, set the oval of crystal in its thin gold frame upon the whiteness of the chest between the faint stains of the tiny nipples.

'So weak!' said Harradence in a low whisper. 'And so very strong! See, she will wear it to-night, and *they* will not trouble her — nor you, ever again!'

With quick dexterity he whisked Garland between the sheets without awakening her.

'And now lie down, Anthony, beside her, and go to sleep. Sleep's better than medicine! God bless you both!'

As the boy edged down the bed, Garland turned toward him, sighed, and, flinging out a small bare arm, lightly encircled his neck.

Harradence blew out the candle.

'I knew I should win,' he crowed to the waiting Elizabeth. 'I knew I *must* win!'

'Sleep with your door open, all the same,' said Elizabeth, eminently practical, 'just in case they frighten one another!'

'I will. But they won't. The archangels themselves stand about that cabin in the darkness of the ship. There are no ghosts at all who shall pass their flaming swords.'

'Ah, the poor ghosts!' said Elizabeth slowly.

CHAPTER IV

HARRADENCE *v*. ENGLAND

'You may have gathered that I have no love for the British,' remarked Madam Purvis.

'I had a faint suspicion that such was the case, ma'am,' replied Harradence drily, leaning back on the red velvet settee, stretching his long legs straight out before him, and tapping his finger-tips together in a judicial manner.

It was evening. The *Chesapeake* was five weeks out from Philadelphia, with a wind which had steadily blown from the west-south-west. The Invisible Travellers had disembarked more than a fortnight since — had clambered over the ship's side into invisible boats, been ferried to an invisible haven over the rim of the ocean, were no longer ghosts; were barely memories.

The red curtains had been drawn before the row of square-paned windows which looked on the Atlantic. Two lamps, gently swinging from the low ceiling beams, filled the parlour with a snug glow which was reflected in the panelling and the large engravings on the walls. The stove had been lighted — it was damp and chill without — and the cat slept on the black and red rug in front of it. It was impossible to think of the scene in marine terms — of bulkhead, deck, and cabin: for atmosphere and setting were of a pleasant inn, and not of a ship.

Mrs. Vane, in a little white gown with cherry-coloured sleeves and sash, was playing cribbage with Mrs. Roscoe who adorned a light blue hussar jacket braided with green. The Echo — in a tight blue coat — scored for them, a tumbler full of some greyish healing fluid at his side. Miss Buckley sat soulfully with Mr. Klinger in the corner remotest from the light. At the far end of the settee, which ran the whole width of the ship under the windows, was curled Anthony Purvis endeavouring to write an important poem — suggested by Harradence — bringing in the names of every one of the thirteen tribes who originally inhabited Long Island. . . .

'You know, perhaps, something of the reasons for my dislike?' said Madam Purvis flatly. She sat very upright, very black, on the settee at the big Englishman's side.

He nodded: proceeded to a statement of his own position.

'I strongly disapproved of the war in America,' said he. 'I did not hesitate to say so. I thought then that its cause was an act of extreme tyranny. I think so still! It did no one any good, except a few German princelings who hired out their subjects as soldiers. Like the Landgrave of Hesse-Hanau who had seventy-four bastards to support — poor fellow! — and needed the cash. The war, of course, might have lasted for ever so far as he was concerned!'

'Seventy-four!' mused Madam Purvis.

Harradence found that her eyes were on him, and he was prepared to swear that in their blackness somewhere there was the ghost of a smile.

She did not, however, pursue the subject of princely philoprogenitiveness —

'Your niece tells me that you have abjured your country?'

'Well,' said Harradence thoughtfully, 'shall we say that the parting was mutual? I exercised my undeniable right of free thought — and free speech — to criticize the Ministry. They, further to confirm me in my opinions, withdrew from me that protection to which every citizen is entitled. In view of this incompatibility of temperament it seemed wiser and also safer to remove myself from England.'

'I doubt,' commented Madam Purvis, 'whether considerations of personal safety ever weighed very much with you!'

'I had others to consider beside myself,' returned Harradence. He indicated by a look Elizabeth Vane who was meditating on her card hand. 'I will admit, however, that the prime factor in my decision was a determination to live where liberty and justice were something more than catch phrases.'

'I presume, then, you consider yourself to have been very ill-used.'

' "Ill-used", ma'am!' exclaimed Harradence with a snort. ' "Ill-used" is a mild adjective to employ. Unless in Virginia they think that it is a merely casual incident to have your life menaced, your house burnt to the ground, and your place of worship desecrated!'

Madam Purvis foraged in her large black reticule; eventually produced a small fringed square of green linen, in which a perfect spider's web of a pattern had been nibbled and knotted and picked; said —

'Having had the pleasure of your acquaintance for the past five weeks, I should imagine that you must have held some peculiarly unpopular opinions. You probably maintained them in public with your usual — zeal!'

'Madam,' said Harradence very oratorically, sitting up, leaning toward her, and gripping a large black-silk-sheathed knee in each hand. 'Madam, I approved — I approve now — the principles underlying the French Revolution. I see in it a great step forward to the emancipation of man. I deplore the excesses — but childbirth must always have its pangs. I applaud the spectacle of a people tearing off the shackles of autocratic government — Liberty! . . . Tumbling down the nobility and privileged classes — Equality! . . . Proclaiming the great ideal of the brotherhood of man — Fraternity! . . . I say so now. I said so then!'

'I am sure you did,' commented Madam Purvis. 'In what you say now I seem to catch the echo of a public address!'

'You do?' asked Harradence unashamed. 'Very likely!'

And with that plunged into the dramatic story of Harradence *v.* England.

It had been (he said) two years ago when he and a number of friends, like-minded with himself, had decided to celebrate the second anniversary of the Fall of the Bastille with a dinner at Darbley's tavern in Birmingham . . . His home had been some four or five miles outside the city . . . They had a pleasant meal. They toasted the birth of liberty in France. They uttered no word that could be construed as sedition or treason. To show their inoffensiveness, he might tell Madam Purvis that the chief decoration of their banqueting-room was a medallion of cod-faced Majesty, George the Third.

After that quiet gathering a mob collected outside the hotel — at the instigation of the magistracy of Birmingham. Yes, ma'am, of *the magistracy!* Of the clergy! And smashed every window in the place.

With broken glass for an appetiser, the crowd had proceeded to a full meal of destruction: wrecked meeting-houses, and set fire to the home of every well-known Radical in the district.

They had burned Dr. Priestley's house and wrecked his laboratory, destroying the labour of years. — 'You know of Dr. Priestley, of course, ma'am?' Madam Purvis obviously did not. 'Priestley the democrat, the divine, the philosopher, the chemist, the discoverer of oxygen, the inventor of soda water! . . . Oh, lamentable ignorance!' They burned Gilbert Wakefield's house and library. — 'You will naturally know of Wakefield?' — And William Russell's house at Showell Green. And Ryland's house. And many others.

Mr. Harradence's own place had gone up in flames with all its contents. With wealth of language he described a peculiarly horrible scene when the blazing building had collapsed on top of rioters conducting a wild orgy in the wine-cellars.

But Madam Purvis was apparently unstirred: all she said, in a tone that almost suggested criticism, was —

'You were not there to defend your property, then?'

'I was not,' said Harradence. 'I was in Birmingham trying to arouse the magistrates to a sense of their duty. But could I? No! They were only too glad to see the damned Radicals being put through the hoop! The drunken, roistering crowds were Holy Crusaders upholding King, Church, and State against the forces of evil . . . Noble mob! The fire-raisers were allowed to do their worst for nearly four days before the troops were called out! . . . Magnanimous magistrates! . . . '

'America has declared her independence,' remarked Madam Purvis, sweeping a thread off her dress. 'And you have declared yours?'

'Precisely, ma'am,' said Harradence, much pleased with the comparison. 'So much so that I am purposing to live in France, although England is now at war with her. A monstrous war! An unjustified war! What business is the internal government of France to England? Every French soldier killed by an invading force is murdered to my mind — *murdered!*'

He took up a glass of punch from the floor — where it had had several narrow escapes from his mounting excitement — and drank off at a draught half the savoury contents of rum and lime and sugar.

His voice had gradually risen until the word 'Murdered' had travelled across the cosiness of the scene almost as a shout.

Elizabeth Vane cast an apprehensive glance over her shoulder, and Anthony looked up from his poetical task.

'You will forgive my curiosity about your personal history, I trust,' said Madam Purvis, preparing to rise. 'In the retired life I lead I rarely come in touch with people taking part in current affairs, or holding any except herd opinions.'

Harradence was on his feet.

'Not at all, ma'am. My private affairs are a matter of history — British history — very shady history! . . . As to —'

'Good night, sir,' said Madam Purvis, and made an abrupt departure, as though she had had her fill of excursions into the nearer past.

Harradence with a quizzical smile watched her pass into her cabin, where the demure Louise — with a lapful of sewing — rose at her entrance.

He turned his attention to the small boy so busy with pencil and paper on the settee.

'Hey, Squire! How's the poem?'

'It's very difficult, sir,' said Anthony. 'I have had to use a Latin word; do you think that that's fair?'

'A proof of scholarship, young fellow. Let's look!'

He stretched himself along the settee like a large schoolboy, and, propped up on an elbow, read the paper that Anthony diffidently handed to him. It was headed —

LONG ISLAND IN THE TIME OF THE RED INDIANS

and ran —

They murdered one another,
Did the Red man and his brother.
Matinecock
Killed Shinnecock.
Secataug
Slew Corchaug.
Marsapeague
Scalped Nessaquague.

Montauk *et*
Setauket
Behaved like rogues
To poor Patchogues.
The Manhassetts would choke
Man and woman Merricoke.
Canarsies drove the flocks away
From every shepherd Rockaway.

'Fine!' said Harradence. 'Heroic! . . . That's how I like my poetry! Plenty of rhyme and plenty of facts. That's why the oldest poetry is the best — it doesn't forget that there is a story to tell. Did you ever read the poem of "Beowulf"?'

'That's the story of Grendel and his mother the Water-Hag. I've read bits of it.'

Suddenly recalling the gruesomeness of the tale, Harradence looked quickly at his small companion.

Anthony sat on the edge of the window-seat, knees up and clasped by hands, black hair ruffled in poetic frenzy, dark grey eyes clouded with a far-away expression — but obviously by no unpleasant and disturbing memories.

Harradence deserted the subject of poetry. He was certain that no action or word of Madam Purvis was ever entirely motiveless. He sought, accordingly, information that might throw light upon this sudden affability.

'Do you know where you are going after we land at Genoa, young-fellow-my-lad?' he inquired.

Anthony had not the faintest idea.

'Do you know how long you are going to be away from America?' Grandmother had never said.

'Have you any relations in Italy?'

Anthony had never heard of any.

'Or friends?'

Again there was no information obtainable.

'Are you going to school there?'

Grandmother had never said anything about it: and Harradence himself was doubtful whether the educational facilities available in any of the wretched Italian states were likely to come up to the requirements of a Purvis of High Pale, Virginia.

Boy and big man regarded one another in silence for a minute, as though in unspoken comment on the queerness of travelling for so many weeks across so many hundred miles of ocean to a destination which was still unknown.

Harradence drew from the fob pocket of his black satin breeches a large old-fashioned gold watch enclosed in an outer case of worn tortoiseshell. As he consistently refused to indulge in 'any jiggery-pokery', such as adjusting it to the ship's time as they travelled eastward, there was always some considerable calculation before he could announce the hour.

'Seven minutes past ten,' he declared. 'No, seven minutes past nine . . . I feel certain, my lad, that your grandmother would like — '

No order, of course. Just a reminder as between friends. The usual evening formula — as usual as the scratch on the door after he was in bed, and the appearance of a big head round the corner with a last 'good night'. And Anthony, responsive immediately to the hint, rose and shook hands, and bobbed his little bow to the ladies and gentlemen — particularly Garland's mother — and took his departure: went through the door leading to the darkened saloon with never a tremor.

Some ten minutes later, Elizabeth, having escaped from cribbage, sat down beside Harradence. He was lounging back easily, nursing his glass of punch, lost in meditation.

'Your third!' she commented.

'My fourth,' said Harradence, and drank off the contents with an expression of infinite pleasure. 'I like my punch in large quantities. I like things to be large. Long books. Enormous meals. Great hearts. Large men. Vast spaces. Big ideals.'

He threw back his wide shoulders and thrust out his broad chest, so that the high arched collar of his dark red coat rose almost to his ears.

'Loud voices and wide gestures,' added Elizabeth. 'You are not preening yourself on your newest victory, I presume!'

'It is the first time that the Demogorgon has addressed more than twenty consecutive words to anybody except her grandson since she came on board!'

'You flatter yourself, Harrady! She spent half an hour with me after dinner. While you remained in the dining-saloon guzzling with Captain Banks.'

'She talked about me all the time, I'll wager,' said Harradence without modesty. 'She wanted to know what my plans were; what sort of income I had got; what I had done with my life. Isn't that so? . . . It is surprising what a compelling effect I have on all females — even those nearing the dusk of life!'

'It *was* a catechism,' admitted Elizabeth, smiling and nodding 'Good night' to Mr. and Mrs. Roscoe. 'She even probed our very tenuous relationship. And repeated "Sister's brother-in-law's daughter" as if it were a conundrum in sex!'

'Jealousy, I presume.'

'I have noticed,' said Elizabeth examining her father's sister-in-law's brother dispassionately — high-coloured weather-beaten face, great jutting nose, light grey eyes with bushy eyebrows, long upper lip; an intolerant humorous kindly face. 'I have noticed that Madam P. has taken a great interest in you ever since you were so rude to her at dinner. She watches you at table, and listens most carefully to what you have to say, without remark. And Heaven knows that you always have enough to say — and always say it loud enough! . . . Because I am sure that she never does, or says, anything without a reason, I tried afterwards to find out from — ' she indicated Miss Buckley by the faintest of gestures ' — something of their plans, but the creature knew nothing about them at all. Any more than she knew anything of the reason why they left America . . . You were trying to pump Anthony, too, weren't you?'

'Yes,' admitted Harradence, 'and feeling very guilty in doing so. Although God knows that my questions were innocent enough! Still, the child knew nothing. I didn't imagine that he would. . . .'

Madam Purvis was, however, in no hurry to reveal the motive behind her inquiries, if she had one.

Her routine was unvaried. She appeared at all meals, whatever the weather, precisely as the steward sounded the first tinkle of his little brass hand-bell. She sat on deck if it was fine, and in the stern-cabin if it was wet, until lunch-time, engaged in drawn-thread work and supervising Miss Buckley's educational efforts. The rest of the day she spent in her own stateroom.

One steamy, foggy morning, after listening to a breakfast-table disquisition by Mr. Harradence to his young friend on the works of Herodotus and Procopius, she stopped him as he paced the dripping deck afterwards, hands behind back, long-stemmed clay pipe well alight. The wet sails hung listless from the yards: the fo'c'sle was barely visible from the break of the poop: there was no movement at all to the ship, which lay embedded in dense white fog as though she were sunken in a snowdrift.

'A scholar, Mr. Harradence, I perceive!' she said, coming to a halt beside the rail.

He thought to hear almost a tinge of derision in her tone.

'Yes, ma'am,' he answered, taking the pipe out of his mouth. 'Something of one, but none the less a man of affairs!'

'My husband, too, was something of a scholar: my elder son even more so,' she commented, and her tone implied that she had suffered from the fact. She looked at Harradence a little sideways as she spoke, as though to see if he appreciated what she had not said.

He had: he quoted the old proverb —

'"Hell is paved with the skulls of scholars".' Added, 'I keep my scholarship, such as it is, for my lighter moments. The scholarship may suffer, but my other interests don't!'

She nodded black-bonneted concurrence in this attitude, and stood gazing thoughtfully into the fog. He waited at her side, sensing that she had more to say.

She was a remarkable-looking woman, he thought. Her face — yellowed as it was, and with the skin strained so curiously over cheekbone and bridge of nose — held the remains of a striking and severe beauty. He wondered whether he had not been wrong in suggesting that she had some Latin blood in her, and whether she was not actually of Jewish extraction. Wondered suddenly if she were not a little mad . . . More than a little mad!

Madam Purvis began without any preamble —

'You are a gentleman, I believe, Mr. Harradence, and — '

'Let us be clear about this, ma'am,' said Harradence, leaning back against the rail, punctuating his interruption with emphatic waving of pipe, and preparing to debate the question very seriously.

'Let us be quite clear! Personally I think I am. Against this you have the fact that I might equally think that I was the Pope of Rome, the Vice-President of the United States, the Queen of Sheba, or a boiled egg! Furthermore — which is much more serious — I have lived in, or near, Birmingham, and no gentleman ever did that! . . . I rather incline to this view myself! . . . Then I am a manufacturer, and no gentleman can be one! I am a Radical, and therefore socially impossible! I am also a Dissenter, and so utterly beyond the pale! Otherwise — '

'You talk, of course, a great deal too much!' mused Madam Purvis. 'But, despite that, you are obviously honest and sincere, and — I should imagine — capable! You are well read, and you have the manner of a gentleman; even when you decide to have no manners!'

'I consider that a flattering assessment, ma'am,' said Harradence approvingly.

Madam Purvis continued talking into the fog, without turning her head: 'You have entirely captivated my grandson. Your influence has been immensely to the good in these weeks in which we have been at sea. He has become manlier. He has opened out. He has become more self-reliant. The sea air may have had something to do with it, but suitable companionship far more . . . Curiously enough' — and here she suddenly looked once more at him — 'I am — attached — to my grandson, although perhaps a *Demogorgon!*' — Now, how did she overhear that? he asked himself. — 'He is all that I have left of my son. He is of my son's flesh, even as my son was of mine. He — I have made my plans for him.'

'He is a very charming, imaginative small boy,' said Harradence. 'I have conceived, as you may have seen, a real affection for him!'

'Too imaginative, almost, at present, for the purpose I have in view!'

He would have liked to ask what the purpose was, but her attitude did not invite inquiry.

She went on now, black-mittened hands gripping the streaming wet rail of the ship, staring into the white opacity, her low voice intense. The two of them seemed to be utterly alone in a silent and abandoned ship. Harradence had a sudden fancy that the Almighty must view them as two specimens of insect life nested in white wool.

'This child,' said Madam Purvis, 'is my son's son! He is an orphan. He belongs to me! To me! . . . *To me!*' — And she repeated her statement of ownership with such vibrant force as though to traverse the Atlantic with the challenge to Grandmother Fell and Dr. Earle.

'Quite!' agreed Harradence thoughtfully. 'Quite!'

'I don't propose to inflict any personal history on you,' she continued with a change of manner. 'I will just say that for my own perfectly good reasons I decided to leave America. I took the first ship sailing from Philadelphia. That the *Chesapeake* is bound for Genoa means nothing. All Europe is before us!'

'With some very definite limitations!'

'I should certainly not go to England,' she assented.

'France?'

'In theory I do not see why not. They are not in the least likely to interfere with Americans — an elderly woman and a child. You are going there yourself, with your — family! And *you* are — were — English'!

'Mine is rather a special case, in the circumstances of which I told you the other day!'

'I have imposed no limitations upon myself, with the single exception of England. But I should naturally not choose anywhere likely to be an invasion area or a general battlefield. Where are you going, if I may ask? I know it is somewhere in Provence.'

'On the outskirts of a small town between Marseilles and Toulon. A place called La Cadière. It ought to be peaceful enough. It was, when

I knew it many years ago. I have bought an estate there and got the purchase recognized by the authorities.'

Madam Purvis recognized his air of triumph by the slightest 'Oh, really!' arching of her eyebrows.

'My only consideration will be,' she went on, 'the facilities for Anthony's education.'

'With a long purse a good education can be obtained anywhere, ma'am'!

'I am a rich woman, Mr. Harradence. The question of expense does not enter into consideration . . . It is precisely this question of education about which I wish to talk to you. I have been interested in you for some time, and I think that your advice would be well worth having!'

'Thank you,' said Harradence, humbly enough for him. 'I am flattered!'

And knew that he was telling the truth.

'Also because I am quite unlikely in the future to come into sufficiently close contact with any gentleman to be able to assess his qualities as an adviser upon this subject. I do not go out into society. I do not choose to . . . No woman is entirely competent to plan the education of a man-to-be by herself . . . There are, of course, certain aspects with which I propose to deal myself, but I should be most grateful for your advice on the general scheme. I should like to land with my plans cut and dried, and ready to be put into immediate operation!'

'I should not have thought that a well-to-do Virginia planter would have acquired — '

'I do not desire my grandson merely to be a well-to-do estate owner!'

'You are planning a career for him, then?'

He leaned back on his elbows on the high rail, and put his extinguished pipe absent-mindedly between his teeth to aid cogitation. In the name of Fortune, what careers were there open to a blue-blooded magnifico of Virginia?

Madam Purvis made no reply for an appreciable space of time. Then she said to the fog, incisively —

'Not a career. A purpose. A purpose in life that may lead — ' She broke off: continued, 'I want him to be a man of action — and judgment. I want him to have knowledge, and to know how to use it. I want him to know the things that will be useful to him in dealing with his fellows. I want him to be . . . a dangerous man!'

'A dangerous man!' echoed Harradence, between amusement and surprise. 'Good God!'

'No man,' said Madam Purvis, 'gets the respect of his fellows unless he is potentially dangerous.'

'It seems to me, ma'am, that whatever scheme of education you may draw up, the most important factor must always be that of environment.'

'I grant that. But first I should like to obtain your advice upon the structure of education that must be erected. The subjects of instruction — their balance in relation to one another. The method of instruction — school or tutors. The — '

'A *schema!*' said Harradence in delight. 'Now I have always had very strong views . . .' He was away! The co-ordination of physical and mental education. The overriding importance of foreign languages. A sound knowledge of three, if not four, was essential — he himself, in parenthesis, knew five like a native! Universities — damnable waste of time! Schools — perfectly useless for serious purposes; except in adolescence as an introduction to the world.

Madam Purvis listened to the flood she had loosed, without comment; though she nodded her head at intervals as she watched faint stirrings in the fog about the ship.

Presently she said, as though suggesting that the lecture might be brought to a close for the time being —

'On some other occasion we must discuss the question of environment which you raised. It is of great importance. An old — or elderly — woman is always a great deal more remote from the workings of a child's mind — girl as well as boy — than a man of comparable age. Why, I do not know. Perhaps it originates in the passing of the appreciation of adventure with the vanishing of the capacity for it . . . Now I had no idea whatever that the locket which I gave him would have been the cause of so much — disturbance!'

'How — ?' began Harradence.

'How I know doesn't matter. I do. I thank you now for what you did at the time, and have done since, to repair my mistake. There were certain facts in our family history which I desired to impress upon his memory. I had no intention, or wish, to create an overbearing obsession of horror!'

A drift of wind travelled across the surface of the grey and oily waters: it raised by a little on its invisible wings the burthen of the fog, so that the whole length of the ship's deck came into view with startling distinctness, and the sea lay exposed as a leaden floor under a vault of dense mist in which the upper yard-arms were hidden. A few hundred yards ahead this vaporous crypt opened out on to sunlight and a sparkling Atlantic.

'I will occupy part of my spare time in drawing up a *schema* for you,' said Harradence.

CHAPTER V

INTRODUCTION TO LIBERTY

'THESE God-dam bloody Britishers!' said the first mate.

He stood at the ship's side with a small and very shabby brown telescope directed at the great vessel which lay pitching and rolling on their starboard beam across half a mile of grey sea.

An immense vessel she was; high out of water, her sides painted in bands of alternate black and white. Her courses were clewed up, and a puff of whitish smoke ambled away from an open gunport aft, whence had come the shot at whose warning the *Chesapeake* even now was heaving-to.

'These God-dam bloody Britishers!' said the first mate, who was a small bitter-looking man without a hat. He also said—though not aloud—'This God-dam bloody cap'n!'

For Captain Banks, swaying a great deal and supporting himself by the mizzen shrouds, was endeavouring to locate his right eye with the wrong end of a telescope. In this effort he was peculiarly unsuccessful.

'Yesh-shir!' said Captain Banks, dropping the telescope and executing a wild and involuntary sort of hornpipe. 'Yesh-shir!' He forthwith let go of the shrouds and collapsed on deck, mumbling indistinctly something about his birthday.

'He's fallen down!' cried Garland in enormous glee, clinging to Anthony's sleeve and dancing in her excitement.

'He's fallen down! *Isn't* he drunk!'

Captain Banks's bi-weekly performances were always a source of undiluted joy to Garland and horrified disgust to Anthony. Now, however, the small boy had no time to spare for watching the shipmaster's gyrations as he was removed by the steward Coates with the bo'sun's assistance. All his attention was riveted upon the warship with her three tiers of guns, her masts as tall as the tallest forest trees, and her gigantic complication of rigging and bulging sails. It seemed to him a miracle that so lofty and so clumsy a thing could float and move secure through the savage welter of the sea.

A string of signal flags suddenly fluttered up, extended itself between fore-top and main-top.

The bitter little mate appeared to know what it meant without recourse to signal-book, for he momentarily lowered his telescope so that he might curse the more fluently.

At the same instant the British colours, which had been idling at the peak of the mizzen-yard, were hauled down, and replaced by another ensign which spread itself out wide as it rose. An ensign of broad stripes of blue and white and red.

'They're God-dam bloody Frogs!' said the first mate.

'God-dam bloody Frogs!' repeated Garland to Anthony, enchanted by the ripple of bad language.

Infinitely slowly, with the wallowing travel of logs, the ships drew closer together. . . .

'It's like climbing a precipice,' thought Anthony, as he started to scale the swaying accommodation-ladder that hung down the warship's side.

He went up the face of this floating hill nimbly as a squirrel. The paintwork was stained, and dulled with the salt of spray. The port-holes of the lowest gun tier were all closed, but many on the deck above were open, and massed full of interested faces. The inside of the port covers, he noticed, was painted red.

A loud English voice greeted him from somewhere above.

'What cheer, mate?' it called: but he could not tell which shaggy head and unshaven face peering down had thus bidden him welcome aboard the French Republican first-rate ship-of-the-line, *Aventurière*.

He looked down for a moment at the lurching pinnace. It seemed incredibly crowded with shabby chattering sailors, with people he knew, with baggage. In the stern was Harradence — very cheerful — talking at the top of his voice, and with the most extravagant gestures, to a little wizened officer, who was extinguished in an enormous cocked hat with a large red, white, and blue cockade, and ornamented about the shoulders with a pair of tarnished epaulettes as large as saucers. Grandmother was about to venture on the ascent with a seaman escort fore and aft.

The precipice heaved a little, and the top of it slanted outward so that the ladder and he swung away from the side and right over boat and water. He was looking straight down into Mrs. Vane's upturned face, and Garland's. He loosed one hand and waved to them, and Garland waved back. She was as thrilled as he at the exciting adventure.

It had all happened with astonishing swiftness. The mate had been summoned — in place of the captain — aboard the man-o'-war. He had returned almost at once with a very glum expression, escorted by the pinnace, which was manned by a heterogeneous assortment of sailors armed with muskets and cutlasses, under the command of Cocked Hat. Once on board, the small officer — Citizen-Lieutenant Vernet — had demanded the ship's papers. He had studied the manifest, the clearance from Philadelphia, the passenger list. He had demanded passports. Only the Roscoes and Klinger had such documents. Regretfully, politely, firmly he announced that Madam Purvis and her party, and Harradence and his, being entered as British subjects, must accompany him back to the *Aventurière*.

Harradence burst into voluble and fluent French. He expostulated: he argued: he pleaded, pacing up and down the while that cosy red-curtained marine parlour from which he was to be reft.

'It is against the laws of war, Citizen-Lieutenant! It is against the common courtesy of nations! It is an insult to a sister republic!'

Citizen Vernet regretted, apologized, explained, by a shrugging of shoulders that brought the decayed glory of his epaulettes almost up to his ears.

'This is a neutral ship sailing from a neutral port to another neutral port. A man of your principles and understanding will appreciate the enormity of abducting innocent non-combatants from beneath the shelter of the American flag!'

Citizen Vernet again regretted. He even explained that the action was in retaliation for similar action by the English. '*They* had begun it!'

Pressed to refresh himself, he accepted a suggestion as to the merits of port wine and brandy topped up with English ale — preferably a bottle of Kenton's "Crown and Magpie".

'I am not an Englishman,' said Harradence, continuing his march up and down the reeling cabin. 'I have disowned my nationality! I have suffered for my republican principles. My house has been burned down because I maintained the justice of the glorious Revolution. I have been ostracized for that reason! I have been persecuted for that reason! I have been driven into exile for that reason! I do not say these things without proof, Citizen! I have here a document recognizing my position from Citizen Charles Genêt, your Minister in Philadelphia! Coates, bring the Citizen-Lieutenant a larger glass!' He produced, waved and handed (with the air of one submitting overwhelming evidence) his credentials from the remarkable intriguer who represented France in the United States.

Citizen Vernet was impressed. He pocketed the documents for submission to his captain. He quaffed his brimming beaker. He was inflexible.

'Perhaps you will explain *my* position, Mr. Harradence?' asked Madam Purvis, who, with the bitter little mate, had been sole audience of the big man's oratorical effort. 'I am American, as you well know, not English. We were entered upon the manifest as of English nationality, and under names not our own, to throw any unauthorized inquirer off the scent, at Philadelphia and at our port of destination. For reasons I have given you. Captain Banks knows all about this and could explain very satisfactorily, I am sure —'

'Cap'n Banks, marm, cain't 'splain nuthin',' said the mate. 'He cain't 'splain hisself neither! He ain't a-goin' ter do no 'splainin' fer a coupl-a days. A reg'lar spazzum is what he's a-sufferin' from. Gits 'em very perticler between longitood fifteen and longitood ten outward bound to Yurrup!'

Harradence proceeded to evolve an elaborate and wholly untrue explanation for the incorrect entry of Madam Purvis and her entourage upon the manifest.

Citizen Vernet was impressed by the explanation as a work of art, but stood definitely — in a squeaking high-pitched voice — by the orders he had received. Urged the need for speedy packing.

He then refreshed himself from the rummer once more. Mellowed he bent over the letter from Citizen Genêt again. Emerged from that second reading still more impressed though remaining adamant.

He permitted himself, however, to express the opinion that Citizen Harradence, '*çi-devant manufacturier de Birmingham*', was a child of fortune. Here was he proposing — according to the letter — to take up his residence in the South of France: and there, but so short a distance away, was a warship of the Republic waiting to take him in safety, luxury, and comfort to a French port. (Which port? . . . At the moment, the citizen would understand — !) But could there be any comparison between such a voyage and a journey to Genoa in the *Chesapeake* — he glanced disparagingly round the inn parlour — with all the subsequent trials of long and arduous travel in barbaric Italy? . . . And now, Citizen, and Citizeness — !

So it came about that Anthony Purvis climbed that tenuous, swinging cobweb of a ladder — and Grandmother Purvis (grimly) and Garland (gaily) and Elizabeth Vane (with resignation) and Miss Buckley and Louise (squeaking, and supported very closely from behind by grinning sailors) and then Harradence, still conducting an immense conversation on the principles of democracy over his shoulder with Citizen Vernet, as he mounted.

All his life long Anthony had vivid and confusing memories of the chaotic fourteen days spent in that chaotic ship. Kaleidoscopic pictures of hordes of men, dirty, shirtless, thin, gesticulatory, with grinning unshaven faces and red night-caps. Immense noise: shouting, singing, quarrelling — all to an accompaniment of the singing of the wind, the rustle of the sea, the creaking of the ship's timbers, and the complaining of the guns against the confinement of their lashings. Indefinable smells, among which predominated the acrid reek of humanity and the odour of garlic.

Particularly he remembered standing on the quarter-deck of the *Aventurière,* awaiting the arrival of the other passengers from the *Chesapeake.* Below him yawned the main-deck on which milled a crowd of the crew, all staring upward. There was a sea of faces.

Then Harradence appeared at the top of the accommodation-ladder, still talking.

The big man set foot on deck: fell silent as he perceived the mob: meditatively continued the upward journey to the quarter-deck.

At the top of the balustraded ladder he suddenly turned about, swept his wide-brimmed round hat from his head, and burst into an impassioned address to the crew in perfect French. Immediate silence followed his first words: he spoke, as though from a platform in a public hall, to as attentive an audience as orator could desire. Bursts of applause punctuated the speech, and cries of encouragement. A tall meagre officer — also with a large cockade in his cocked hat — who was advancing obviously to receive the new arrivals, paused in his tracks, and listened with restrained disapproval, thoughtfully scratching the calf of a much darned silk stocking with the scabbard of his sword.

It was not a long address. Anthony never knew what it was all about. Said Garland tolerantly, holding tight to his hand: 'Uncle Harrady has gone mad again!'

Harradence reached his peroration. It was magnificent! It was sublime! He held back his audience's applause for just one moment by a compelling gesture of his right hand. He turned violently on Citizen-Lieutenant Vernet who was at his side.

For a palpitating instant Anthony thought that he was about to embrace the citizen-lieutenant. He did not. With a word of apology he seized the cockade from the citizen-lieutenant's hat, and pinned it to his own, which he clapped on his head, pulling it well down over his nose.

Then with a dozen bellowed words, he folded his arms, and brooded over his auditory, as though he defied them — and the French Republic, and the National Convention, and anybody and everybody else, to improve on his sentiments.

The reception given speech and gesture was overwhelming. Citizen-Lieutenant Vernet clapped his old friend on the back: and the faintly disapproving officer now approached, and, introducing himself as the captain of the ship, commented in no measured terms of praise upon the purity of the doctrine, the oratorical skill, and the linguistic ability of the involuntary passenger.

Anthony was mesmerized by the performance. If anything could have set Harradence on a yet higher peak in his estimation, this would have done so. It added, too, a new scene to his repertory for those long involved stories which he told himself at all times of the day. He saw himself addressing his armies, swaying vast multitudes by his eloquence, opening debate from a crimson-canopied chair of state in a council of great nobles.

'Isn't Uncle Harrady funny?' said Garland, deciding after some thought to treat the matter as a joke rather than as a breach of conventions. 'I want my dinner.'

And in less than ten minutes they were being ceremoniously introduced into a large cabin, lighted, just like the inn parlour in the *Chesapeake,* now but a speck astern, by windows at the far end. It was walled with racks full of muskets and cutlasses in two tiers, and half-way down on either hand was stationed a dumpy carronade.

A table, covered with oilcloth that had seen better days, and crowded with steaming dishes, ran the complete length of the cabin which was darkish and more than a trifle smelly. In the middle — fumigated by a platter of fish boiled with onions — was set up a Tree of Liberty, a very brown and decrepit little bush some three feet high, blossoming at intervals into rosettes of red, white, and blue ribbon, and crowned with the red bonnet of the Revolution. This sacred emblem was symbolically guarded by a circle of intertwined bayonets and dirks mounted on a frame, and suspended over it like an extremely bellicose halo.

The cabin was full of officers — old and young; all very shabby, all very noisy, most none too close-shaven nor even particularly clean — as well as a mob of small boys, bare-footed and tattered-breeched, each burdened with a plate, knife, fork and spoon, and a bottle of wine.

The appearance of the captain was the signal for a general movement to the table and for a rush by the small boys to set their masters' dining utensils before them.

Places were politely found for the newcomers. Silence fell, and the whole company waited, still standing.

From the top of the table there came a sharp rap. It was answered in a great shout of song by everyone present with the first stanza of a hymn that Anthony was afterwards to know as the *Chant des Marseillais* —

> '*Allons enfants de la Patrie*
> *Le jour de gloire est arrivé . . .*'

After this grace they took their seats and flung themselves upon the viands without more ado. Anthony particularly noted a very fat man with a brown bald head who finished singing definitely two syllables ahead of his companions, and so had the first plunge into a savoury-looking mess that smoked in a white earthenware dish before him.

There was no pretence at elegance or etiquette. As each man finished, he rose with a little bow and departed, and his small attendant hooligan would remove the utensils.

Anthony always remembered that first meal in the *Aventurière*, but still more the tour of the ship which he and Garland made afterwards in the company of Lieutenant Vernet.

Vistas of long decks swarming with men — dim tunnels in which two ranks of clumsy cannon were stabled, their iron fodder beside them: great hatchways with precarious ladders, leading into darker and yet more noisome depths: vast black store-rooms — in which you sensed rather than saw an immense jumble of casks and cases — with clerks scribbling at ledgers by candlelight: a sick-bay below the water-line, lighted only from a distant hatch and reeking like a battlefield on a summer day: the galley with half-naked cooks sweating in the heat from brick ovens and coppers on a floor of iron plates.

It was from the cook-house that the pair of them bore off a lump of some remarkable confection — earth-coloured, hard as rock, and vaguely flavoured with raspberries — which was later to give Garland the stomach-ache and to cause Anthony considerable internal uneasiness.

The gift was, however, symptomatic of the general friendliness shown to two such young and tender prisoners of war. Everywhere they went the men pressed round them, offering small presents, essaying sentences in broken English, commenting — obviously favourably — upon their appearance and dress. The presence of an officer was no deterrent: in fact the citizen-lieutenant would be included, or would himself engage in the noisy discussions that took place.

Garland radiantly accepted the situation. She tossed her black curls; smiled back at the bizarre figures that greeted her; laughed at incomprehensible jokes; shook the grimy hands extended to her, and said '*Merci!*' and '*Comment vous portez-vous?*' and '*Oui!*' and '*Au revoir!*' with all the aplomb of a very small duchess.

Anthony greatly admired her complete self-possession, as he stood shyly beside the little figure in the high-waisted, sprigged-muslin dress, faltering polite replies to inquiries — after they had been repeated three or four times — in painstaking French. Citizen-Lieutenant Vernet watched proceedings with the benevolent air of a kind papa who has just produced some exciting treat for the delectation of a well-loved family of youngsters. . . .

By one of the guns on the lower deck, as they traversed it on their way back to the upper air, were half a dozen men squatted at cards. They were burlier, cleaner, better clad than the rest, and they spoke in English — mostly in oaths.

One of them looked up as Vernet approached, and said something to the others. Whereat they ceased their game: they watched him mince along the deck with the two children: they did not stir, and their eyes were very insolent.

The lieutenant was within three-four paces when the sailor who spoke had first seen him. A lean fellow it was, with a lean fierce face, shirtless, and holding his hand of cards fanwise against a hairy chest tattooed in blue and red and green. His eyes were a pale blue and turbulent.

' 'Oo 'ave we 'ere?' asked the tattooed man in a loud voice of mockery. ' 'Oo 'ave we 'ere, mates? Wy, a bleedin' cock-sparrer and two little Judas h'Iscariots! . . . 'Ow d'yer do, Miss Judas? 'Ow d'yer do, Master h'Iscariot? 'Ow d'yer do, yer little bleeders? And 'ow's yer bleedin' pa?'

So alien was the manner of the tattooed man's speech that Anthony did not comprehend a single word, but the insolence of intent was evident enough to him. He came to a halt before the group, looking uncertainly from one to the other.

'*Venez! Venez!*' said the citizen-lieutenant in an imperative squeak, hurrying Garland on, out of the zone of the recalcitrant Englishmen. '*Venez vite, mon gars!*'

'I don't understand! What do you want?' said Anthony to the tattooed man.

'Uncork yer y'ears then,' replied the sailor. He rose to his long lean height, and bent toward Anthony across the circle of card-players, shaking his fist. 'Uncork yer y'ears! And tell yer dad from me an' my mates that if 'e don't take that bleedin' cockade outer 'is bleedin' 'at, we'll do it fer 'im! 'N throw '*im* overboard h'arter the lousy thing as soon as look at 'im!'

'He isn't my father,' said Anthony, trembling not so much from fright as with anger at insult. 'Tell him yourself! But I suppose you're afraid to!'

'A-feared to? A-feared to, is it?' said the tattooed man furiously. 'See this!' — and he shook that enormous and bony fist, with the knuckles scarred and scratched, directly under Anthony's nose. The boy did not give ground before the menace of it: he merely leaned back his head a little, as though he found the harsh clump of skin and bone unsavoury to the nostrils and unaesthetic to the sight: he remarked the lean flat belly (of the pale tan of a mushroom top) girt about with a faded red scarf that sustained wide sail-cloth trousers. — 'A-feared to, is it? . . . You tell that lily-livered bastard ter come dahn 'ere wiv that perishin' bit o' ribbon 'n tike wot 'e'll bloody well get!'

Of course, in his fantasies he would have quelled so insolent a dog with one glance, one word; and he, with William and John at his heels, would then have passed proudly on. As it was, his eyes filled with angry tears, and he stammered out:

'*You*'re lily-livered! . . . *You* are afraid!'

And turned, and walked hurriedly away, expecting a long arm to seize him suddenly from behind, and humiliate him still further by revealing to himself how feeble his resistance must be. But nothing happened. Somebody said —

'Shut yer trap, Dick! Leave 'im alone! It ain't 'is bloody fault!'

The citizen-lieutenant had halted uncertainly a few paces away. There had already been trouble with the English prisoners on the previous day, and he noticed that the armed guard had discreetly made themselves scarce. It was with relief that he saw them resume their game of cards.

'Were they being rude, Rowley?' asked Garland, greatly interested. Anthony had become Rowley to her from early ship-board days: '"Heigh-ho! says Anthony Rowley": *You* know!' . . . 'What did they want?'

But Anthony was sick with anger at himself for being angry and for being afraid, and with anger at the long lean man with the pale stomach for being insolent and (which was much worse) for making him angry and afraid. He shook his head, and said nothing. . . .

At sunset — so red a sun, so grey a sky, and so swiftly-moving a molten sea, that Mr. Harradence said it was like looking at an egg frying in molten lead! — the song of the Marseillais was again performed. By the small disorderly hooligans who waited on the citizen-officers, on the ammunition hoists, on the citizen-scullions in the calaboose. Drawn up in two ranks facing each other on the main-deck, under the supervision of a battered master-at-arms, they sang the battle hymn with immense vigour, looking like a disreputable party of waits who had strayed into a marine setting. Incidentally the same performance was repeated at sunrise.

They slept that night (and while they remained in the *Aventurière*) amid their baggage, in a cabin hurriedly prepared on the lower-deck by the erection of sail-cloth partitions. It seemed a precarious privacy, and the ventilation from the one port-hole on a hot July night left a great deal to be desired.

Anthony and Garland lay side by side, their small whispering voices inaudible to their elders amid the noises of the ship, and talked themselves to sleep.

It was not until the next day that Harradence (who had slept soundly but stormily in a hammock hard by the entrance) heard of the man with the pale stomach. Only a very sketchy outline of the story he gathered, as he washed in a bucket of sea-water and brushed the tangle of grizzled hair which no amount of brushing could ever make orderly. It was, however, sufficient. He shrugged himself into close-fitting red coat, flicked an imaginary speck off close-fitting grey pantaloons, set widebrimmed black hat (with red-white-blue cockade) at a jaunty angle upon his head: nodded sagely to himself: departed.

He reappeared twenty minutes later in the ward-room, just as breakfast of coffee and pickled pork was about to be served. He was accompanied by a couple of young officers, and followed by a cloud of enthusiastic small mess attendants, who explained the reason for tardiness to their incensed masters with a wealth of gesture and volubility.

Harradence himself said nothing, but his expression was highly self-satisfied. There was a red mark on his left cheekbone, and the knuckles of his left hand were grazed.

The story of Homeric conflict, however, spread like wildfire, and from that time onward his domination of the ship seemed to his fellow-passengers to be complete. His lightest remark was listened to with interest and respect by officers and men: he developed and expounded to the sailing-master an entirely new method of cutting a mizzen topgallant stay-sail: he persuaded the cooks to make Cornish pasties for the midday dinner: he gained the support of the master-gunner for his theories in regard to the use of hollow shot in carronades; he even won over the English sailors, with the exception of the man Dick, who brooded sullenly over the loss of three front teeth and a flattened nose.

'I really believe,' said Elizabeth Vane to him, 'that if you were to suggest that the ship should take us to Genoa, they would do it!'

'Having watched the progress of the English lessons you are giving to at least half a dozen officers, I should think you may have even greater influence than I,' replied Harradence.

A singularly handsome lad in a sub-lieutenant's uniform was watching Elizabeth from the other side of the quarter-deck, secretly, eagerly, attentively.

'Our young friend over there would willingly set sail for you for Paphos or Cytherea!'

'Poor René,' said Elizabeth smiling, 'has already placed his sword at

my feet — and a heart slightly chipped in one or two earlier adventures.
He does not, however, believe in marriage! As a nicely brought-up
young woman I could contemplate nothing less . . . There the matter
stands for the present!'

'Blast his insolence!' said Harradence.

'His intentions are most honourable,' continued Elizabeth. 'In fact, too
honourable! He says that marriage is so material — it interferes with
worship! His theories are straight out of a fairy tale: passionate kisses
on hems of skirts; butterfly kisses on finger-tips; love paced to the tune
of an old pavane!'

'You've misunderstood him,' said Harradence. 'These are the preliminary antics to a good old-fashioned seduction! You ought to know that
by now!'

'I haven't misunderstood him,' she declared. 'His attitude coincides
with yours in all its essentials. *I* know!'

'H'rmph!' said Harradence, and gave her a sidelong look.

He pointed out to Garland and Anthony, who had that moment joined
them, a dark line upon the horizon. An iron grey line dividing the light
grey of the sky from the darker grey of the sea.

'France!'

Here was an even greater thrill than they had had on that afternoon
when they approached the perilous straits of Gibraltar and saw Europe
and Africa lying cloud-like on either hand.

France — the land of Charlemagne and Roland; of the Froissart
Chronicles, and Gaston Earl of Foix, and the Three Chamberlains of
King Charles the Sixth: the land of Monsieur Perrault and the White
Cat, and the Sleeping Beauty: of Joan of Arc: of — as Mr. Harradence
frequently reminded them — Liberty, Equality, Fraternity! The end of
the long road that had lain across Virginia and Maryland and Pennsylvania, and the vast width of the Atlantic.

The small boy, speechless with emotion, watched the enchanted coast
of an imaginary France of Chivalry and fairy-tale draw nearer with
wearisome slowness. The great ship idled through the sea, all her dingy
sails spread to catch the wind, the lithe frigates that now accompanied
her curbing their gait to suit her ponderous pace. He climbed into the
nets at the bowsprit, and so hung over the water, watching it part in a
lazy wave against the bows, splashing and slapping the huge hull as it
did, almost derisively.

Garland had to be restrained by force from accompanying him: and
her protests recalled him somewhat unwillingly to her side.

First sight of the shores of France coincided with the anniversary of the Fall of the Bastille — July 14. The occasion was celebrated by an epidemic of singing of the *Chant des Marseillais* by the disreputable choir of small boys. There was also much dancing by the crew — in wooden-soled shoes — to the music of flute and fiddle.

The Tree of Liberty in the ward-room had its hair done up, so to speak, in fresh curlers of blue, white, and red ribbons; a somewhat more sumptuous supper than usual was provided; and a small keg of Armagnac was brought in so that the toast of the Revolution should be drunk in all due form.

Whatever programme may have been devised, Harradence made the occasion peculiarly his own. For it was he who, remarking that most of the glasses were charged, suddenly rose to his feet, and, gathering the attention of the long table, proposed the toast of 'The Revolution — the Downfall of all Tyranny — the Reign of Liberty, Equality, Fraternity!'

It was a remarkable speech. Entirely without modesty.

He painted in graphic words his sufferings for his ideals, with side references to the suppression of liberty in England, the causes of the American Revolution, and to the scandalous mis-government of India.

In epic language he described his search for true democracy in the new republic across the Atlantic. His disappointment. The great principle enunciated in the Declaration of Independence that all men are created equal, had been foully betrayed, he said. Half the population of the South were slaves — the merest chattels of the other half. The rich and the propertied still withheld the suffrage from the poor in many states. Corruption and political intrigue were rife. Furthermore America, in his view, had not really earned her independence. Did they know that barely one man in twenty of military age had taken up arms against the tyranny of the parasitical oligarchy of Britain? American Independence had been won by the French — by Lafayette, and Rochambeau, and De Grasse, and De Kalb! . . . So now he sought his ideals of liberty and democracy in a free France. The coasts of that free France already loomed upon the horizon. The very winds were the purer because of it. . . .

Madam Purvis may not have understood much of this rapid rhetoric, but she nodded at intervals her restrained approval. For approve she did the violent vigour of the man, the self-assurance, the mastery which he had obtained over an alien audience.

'I, the Apostle of Liberty, salute the Tree of Liberty!' cried Harradence, looking down the long table toward the rather decrepit bush with its multitude of hair curlers.

As he looked he became aware of the small intent face of Anthony Purvis at his side — uncomprehending but intoxicated by rolling periods and sonorous language and enormous gesture. He stretched out a great hand and raised the child by scruff of coat so that he was set standing on his feet upon the seat of his chair. He said in his great voice —

'He, too — this child — this citizen-to-be of the youngest nation — salutes the Tree!'

How did one salute the Tree of Liberty? Privately Anthony thought it rather a poor sort of thing to pay any reverence to. For a moment there was complete silence, and then, moved by Heaven knew what inspiration, and encouraged by the nearness of that friend who seemed to him so little else than a god, Anthony exclaimed in his loudest tones —

'*Allons enfants de la Patrie* — '

Harradence, who had meanwhile swigged off half a tumbler of rum, took up the song in a gigantic bellow —

'*Le jour de gloire est arrivé!*'

And the whole table rose to its feet and joined in with noisy enthusiasm.

Very proud, and yet a little alarmed, at having loosed so great a volume of sound, Anthony remained standing on his chair, borne away into reverie in which he saw Vikings chanting their war-songs before they launched their long-ships into the grey seas — saw himself roaring hymn of battle to his comrades-in-arms in the vaulted banqueting hall of a dream castle.

He was suddenly conscious of a sharp pain in the ankle. He looked down. Garland was furtively prodding the leg nearest her, through the white nankeen trousers, with a sharp two-pronged fork. She was repeating with the fiercest intensity the while, only just a little over her breath, 'God save the King! . . . God save the King! . . . God save the King! . . . God save the King!'

In the explosion of shouting with which the toast was honoured, Anthony got down. He was very aggrieved.

'What did you do that for?' he asked.

'Why did you want to sing that beastly song?' said Garland. 'Rowley, I hate you!'

'But — ' began Anthony, his grievance swallowed up in surprise — 'but Mr. Harradence — '

'Uncle Harrady — !' said Garland in a whisper full of angry contempt. 'Him! . . . I'm not going to speak to you. I'm English and you're a beastly American! I hate you all!'

She turned her back on him: nor did she speak to him for the remainder of the day, and in her self-denying ordinance refused even to ask him for the continuation of the long and exciting romance with which he had hitherto beguiled bedtime.

He got up early, and finding Citizen-Lieutenant Vernet on watch — wrapped in a boat-cloak that had faded to a mottled green, and topped by a red night-cap — he mounted to the quarter-deck and thought out the problem, leaning over the port-rail.

The coast was very close now, across a gently heaving sea that was a clear pale green in the sunrise. It was a mountainous coast, smoke-grey and blue, seamed with the white threads of waterfalls, darkened with forest, with here and there a white house shining like silver on a hillside or at the water's edge. Its jagged outline was so definite against a primrose sky that it looked to be the edge of the world with nothingness behind it.

Garland was English. It was curious that he had never realized that. Then Mr. Harradence was English, too. And Mrs. Vane. Of the race who had oppressed America, killed his father and his uncle, and plundered his family! And yet he liked them better than anybody he had ever met! But then Mr. Harradence had disowned England — had issued (he said) his Declaration of Independence. Did that make him not English? Before the Revolution — before America became a nation, his own father must have been English! It was astonishingly puzzling.

The panorama of a wide bay was now spread before them, with lofty mountains in the background, and a great city strewn along the shore like a steep bank of white pebbles.

He suddenly realized that Garland was standing at his side, looking across the water. She was hatless, and the disorder of her black curls was lustrous in the light of early morning. He examined her cautiously as though he had never seen her before — golden skin and level brow, face wide at the cheekbones, short upper lip, and nose that was just tip-tilted and no more. It did not occur to him that here was a singularly lovely child: it was just Garland at whom he gazed, because she was Garland — and the first friend of his own generation he had ever possessed — and English — and very angry with him!

Presently this very grave Garland permitted herself to become aware of his regard. She looked at him directly. Very gravely. Reproachfully . . . Forgivingly. Then she smiled at him a little wistfully as if to imply that things would never be the same again, but — ! She raised herself on tiptoe and kissed him on the lips.

He was very glad.

'*Ah, voiçi une petite scène tout-à-fait charmante!*' said Citizen-Lieutenant Vernet in his high squeaky voice, regarding them with his head on one side, and clapping his hands — encased in tattered woollen gloves of bright yellow — as though applauding a pretty stage fantasy.

They stood side by side after that, perfectly content, exchanging no word. . . .

It was still very early when they came to anchor within shelter of the mole, a bare hundred yards away from the long quayside. Tall houses, with bedding thrust to air out of the upper windows, faced the harbour: already women with kilted skirts and mops and brooms scurried about the dark entries of dingy wine-shop and store at the base of those cliffs of discoloured plaster: drays drawn by large square horses clattered with infinite noise over the cobbles of the wide roadway to the accompaniment of furious shouting and furious lash-cracking by blue-bloused drivers. Along the stone edge of the quay was a dark fringe of spectators, mostly men. The grey water was lifeless, soiled with the ordure of ships, with moribund seaweed, and with the refuse of the shore.

A deep hum rose from the ship. Every shoreward port-hole was black with heads, and the bulwarks were lined thickly with men.

A clock in a neighbouring church tower struck the hour — six — in thin poor notes with little resonance. A chill wind swooped down on the city from far-off mountains, and streamed fiercely through the narrow gulleys of streets that opened on the Place du Port, scavenging as it blew, so that a fog of yellow dust momentarily enveloped the ships at anchor in the harbour, and then swirled in dense cloud far out into the bay.

As Harradence — a rather silent Harradence — joined them, a group of men entered a long white boat which had been waiting at the foot of the landing stairs directly opposite, and were rowed rapidly toward the *Aventurière*.

'I don't like France,' said Garland studying the landscape without approval. 'It looks as dirty as the ship! Why do they *all* beat their horses like that man?'

Glad as was Anthony that a reconciliation had been effected, yet he was not prepared publicly to forswear his principles by agreeing on political matters with a self-declared Englishwoman. His secret soul, however, refused to find in this sordid town the France of Roncesvalles, the Marquis of Carabas, Bayard, and the troubadours.

'I don't suppose it's as dirty as London,' said this American champion of France. And regretted the statement as soon as made.

'London — ' had begun Garland in hot defence, when three of the boat party made their appearance at the top of the companion-ladder leading to the quarter-deck, in charge of a worried young officer — Elizabeth Vane's René.

The principal of them was a small man in a very dusty green great-coat, which was unbuttoned, revealing the bright red sash that encircled the meridian between blue waistcoat and pink-and-white striped trousers. He had a face that seemed to Anthony to be an animal's rather than a man's, for the lower part of his nose and his mouth and his chin all projected forward together from the general line of his grey countenance. He wore a round brimless catskin cap with a large cockade in front. His companions, a pace or so behind, were a short and a tall soldier in equally filthy blue uniforms with once-white spatterdashes and battered cocked hats. They carried muskets with uncommonly long bayonets. None of the party had seen a razor for several days, and both the soldiers had flamboyant moustaches.

'Citizen Harradence?' said Animal-Face, coming to a halt four or five paces away, and pointing to Harradence with a roll of papers in his hand.

The Apostle of Liberty acknowledged the correctness of the accusation by a curt bow.

Animal-Face took a few paces forward, and extended his arms as if he would enfold the other in an embrace against dusty coat and wine-stained waistcoat.

'Fourichon!' he introduced himself. 'Agent for the Commission of the Marine. I salute thee fraternally! I bid thee welcome in the name of the Republic — One and Indivisible!'

At this greeting the anxious faces of Lieutenant Vernet and Elizabeth's admirer cleared.

Harradence bowed — rather formally — again. It seemed to Lieutenant Vernet that perhaps the big man would have better appreciated the honour done him by France if her representative had been less scrubby. Harradence realized this himself. He made a magnificent effort. He too stepped forward. With theatrical gesture took the dusty, ruffianly figure in his arms; pressed it for an instant against sprigged waistcoat; held it away as if to regard it the better; and, refusing to part with so precious an object, once again took it to his bosom.

'I greet the great and glorious Republic in thy person, Citizen Fourichon,' said he.

Great-and-Glorious-Republic, having recovered breath, then informed Apostle of Liberty how he had been advised of his presence in the *Aventurière* by a despatch boat which had arrived over a week ago from the squadron: how he had notified the Committee of Public Safety in Paris through the Commission for the Marine, forwarding the various documents that had been taken from him on shipboard: how the Committee of Public Safety apparently knew all about him; and how by semaphore telegraph he had been instructed to see that he and all his party were immediately set at liberty.

Nay, more! The Committee of Public Safety had addressed a personal message to the Citizen. It was this —

He unfolded a paper and read out loud to Harradence and a crowded quarter-deck:

'It is with satisfaction that the Committee of Public Safety of the National Convention have heard of thy arrival in France. The Nation will receive thee with sympathy for the persecutions thou hast undergone by reason of thy sentiments for liberty and the French Revolution. It will desire to employ in the cause of Freedom the knowledge and zeal of which its agents in London and Philadelphia have spoken most favourably.'

Great-and-Glorious-Republic, having read this citation at the top of his voice, rolled the paper up into one of his bulging pockets, and spat right and left on the deck in a hissing sort of way (which Garland was later to essay) through a gap in his front teeth.

'Citizen!' said Harradence, 'With what indescribable emotion shall I set foot in a few moments upon the sacred soil of a France that has purified itself from ancient tyranny and superstition!'

As he was speaking a cart clattered rapidly over the sacred cobbles of the Place du Port, the driver sitting on a shaft smoking a short clay pipe. It was piled high with large wicker baskets provided by the One-and-Indivisible-Republic for the reception of the crumpled bodies and severed heads of those from whom she was so busily engaged in purifying herself . . . Baskets waiting to be filled! No one paid any attention.

CHAPTER VI

THE MASTER OF THE GUNS

MADAM PURVIS sat in a lofty dim room, listening to the passing of the guns through the darkness.

She sat very erect in a high-backed elbow chair close to a shuttered window, feet on a little round footstool, hands folded on her black satin lap, ivory face expressionless within the frame of the narrow frill to her lace indoor cap.

Ever since they had halted at midday at the house in the mountains, the procession of great cannon and their attendant supply wagons had gone by, creaking, bumping, grumbling. Teams of horses — teams of mules — teams of oxen: ten, a dozen, twenty beasts, straining at the rope traces. Files of dusty troops, inconceivably ragged, with slung muskets, toiling alongside the lumbering gun-carriages up the steep road between the pines.

Now that night had fallen each section of the convoy was lighted by a multitude of lanterns which came twinkling and tossing up out of the darkness, as if on little ships in a choppy sea; drew into the calm water, so to speak, of the level space directly before the house; burned steadily and motionless there for precisely fifteen minutes, while man and beast were refreshed; and then twinkled out of sight on the way to further heights; were succeeded by more lights, more dim great shapes, more shouting, and a fresh trampling of feet on the bare flagstones of the bare rooms directly beneath.

Twelve years had gone by since Madam Purvis had last heard the heavy thunder of great guns going about their business. It had been the night on which her eldest son had died. Then it had been the cannon of the British growling in withdrawal from defeat toward the crowning disaster of the surrender at Yorktown. Now it was the cannon of the French Republic massing in their scores to bombard beleaguered Toulon and drive the intrusive British into the sea.

Madam Purvis listened intently to all the uproar — to every note of it; bourdon of gun-wheels, jingle of harness, cry of driver. As intently as though she hearkened to some fantastic symphony. She was content. And, since no one was looking, she permitted herself the luxury of a smile, and to sample a bon-bon which she produced from her reticule.

It was very hot, although mid-September. No breath of wind came in through the farthest of the three tall windows — which alone was unshuttered and wide open to the night — to flicker the naked yellow flame of the lamp placed on the little round table at her elbow. A copy of Young's *Night Thoughts,* bound in as black and shiny a binding as her gown, lay unopened on the table.

An immense tent-bed with a canopy of white net, resembling a small iceberg in the half-light, was set against either side wall, across a wide expanse of tiled floor that had faded to the red of dead roses.

Before the open window, at a larger table lighted by another lamp, sat Anthony, head in hands, stooped over a chessboard. His bowed back was toward his grandmother, but over it she could see, yellowed by the lamplight, the shapely face of his opponent — a dark face having in it something of the fullness outlined on the medallion of a Roman emperor, black hair rather lank, grey eyes that might be almost blue. They were strange eyes in so young a man, telling nothing; for at intervals, as though aware of but unconcerned by her continued regard, he would raise them and meet her gaze calmly and without embarrassment.

He had been standing, hatless, hands behind back, a slim young man sunning himself on the wide pine-needle-strewn patch of ground between the lonely house and the road, when they halted to breathe their horses. The grey building and its curtilage were projected from the forest-clad mountain-side on a sort of bracket that was edged with a thick fence of pines and overhung vast depths from which rose, above the susurration of the trees, the murmur of the invisible sea.

He surveyed coach and sweating horses dispassionately: turned his look to the escort of four men and a corporal, trusting in whom Harradence had ridden ahead.

Then he barked something at the men. His voice had a harsh, un-recognizable accent.

He approached the carriage door as they prepared to descend from the capacious mildewed interior: assisted the first two ladies down; assessed the other occupants as children and maids or near-maids; was not concerned with further politeness; addressed himself to Elizabeth Vane —

'May I see your papers, please?'

His accent certainly made his speech difficult to understand, but Anthony thought he had not seen so clean a soldier, or so well-shaven a soldier since he had landed in France.

Elizabeth produced the credential provided by the gallant General Dugommier. He read the document through at a glance, refolded it with white, well-kept hands: returned it.

'You will have to wait here until to-morrow. I am sorry!'

'Why, please?' asked Elizabeth. She was wearing a high-waisted frock with cherry-coloured hem, and cherry-coloured scarf, and little white bonnet with cherry-coloured ribbons. She felt, looked, and spoke at her most winning.

'Orders!' said he.

'Whose?'

'Mine!' he replied. And though he met her eyes unwinkingly, she sensed that there was admiration behind his gaze. She found herself re-specting him for his uncompromising firmness despite susceptibility.

'But General Dugommier has given us permission to travel. This lady is going to Italy, and I and my child are going to La Cadière. God knows that we have waited in Marseilles for nearly two months to get per-mission!'

'General Dugommier is not in command here, madame!'

'Then who is?'

'I am!'

'Are you then a general?' she asked, looking at his shabby (but very neat) blue uniform and tarnished gold epaulettes with the faintest depreciation.

'Not yet, madame!'

'The command is rather peremptory,' she said. 'I think, perhaps, that as a gentleman you might explain what you have ordered as an officer.'

He meditated upon this instruction in the art of politeness quite seriously for an instant. When he spoke again it seemed to Elizabeth that he had the air of one who had committed a *gaucherie*.

'I am waiting for my guns,' he explained. 'Many guns. Heavy guns. I dare run no risk of obstruction to them upon the mountain road . . . Also I want your horses. As a stand-by in case I need reliefs for some of my cattle.'

He turned his back on her with a curt bow; threw a word or two of command to the corporal in charge of the escort; began to walk slowly toward the house; recollected —

'All the accommodations of the house, such as it is, shall be at your disposal. It belonged to royalist *émigrés* and has been taken over by the military. One or two of the bedrooms are still furnished and there is a big front room upstairs which can serve you as a sitting-room, if you will permit me to use a table in it for a few hours. I may even be able to let you have army rations. . . .'

During the whole of the afternoon he had sat at the table, for most of the time as motionless as a lizard, his eyes fixed on the sheet of foolscap in front of him, or on the large silver watch which lay beside it. As a cannon crashed and rattled to a standstill before the house, he would flicker a look out of the window at it, mark off an entry on the paper, and then relapse into immobility again until ten minutes had elapsed, when he would bring a small silver whistle out of a pocket in his white waistcoat and blow a shrill blast. Five minutes later he would sound the whistle twice, and forthwith would begin once more the creaking, bumping journey of the great gun to its embrasure before Toulon.

When night fell the same procedure continued. Lanterns were slung on ropes stretched across the parking place from tree to tree, and, although a very square sergeant with a drooping moustache reported each fresh arrival, the officer seemed already, even in that uncertain light, to have ascertained all the essential particulars.

The others of the party went early to bed, but Madam Purvis kept vigil with the gloomy young artilleryman, as if she could not bear the thought of being beyond earshot of the orchestra of death; as though she drew nourishment for her soul out of the mere sound of the passage of those immense instruments of war — iron tubes nine and ten feet long, weighing over three tons.

Anthony stayed, too, sitting on a little stool by the open window whence he could watch everything that happened in the tangle of shadows and lantern-light without. Presently he ventured a question to the silent officer, for a fortnight in the *Aventurière,* and two months in a dark repressed hotel at the corner of the Rue Paradis in Marseilles, had given him a considerable fluency in French. It was an intelligent question, and the young man was at pains to answer it as clearly as possible. He encouraged more questions, and in half an hour the pair were very much engaged in a game of chess — made a trifle complicated by the fact that two black pawns and a white bishop were a-missing.

'Check!' said Anthony.

The survivors of his White army were putting up a last and desperate resistance in a corner of the board.

'Check!' said he, making a sudden surprise sortie with a knight.

The young officer glanced at the board, at the intent downbent head of his small opponent, at his watch. He leaned out of the window with the whistle to his lips, and shrilled it twice across all the confused noises of the night. As he brought up a piece to cover his king, so from outside came an intensification of the uproar and the heavy rumble of wheels.

'I have moved pieces on two chessboards,' he said with a slight smile. 'Check-mate!'

He sat back in his chair and regarded thoughtfully the bloodless battle-field. A lock of dark hair slipped down upon his forehead, romanticizing the classical outlines of his face.

'You learned French at school?' he inquired. 'It is useful to be able to speak foreign languages. I wish that I could speak English, but they taught me nothing of use or interest at school at all, either at Brienne or Paris. I can tell you about the Anglo-Saxon heptarchy, the Incas, and Cretan civilization — but because I taught myself.'

Anthony explained the system of education at High Pale — the succession of governesses, the lessons in French and German and Latin by visiting tutors, the instruction in fencing by a French veteran of the Revolutionary War.

'You had, then, no companions of your own age?'

'No.'

'A lonely life!' commented the officer; added with the matter-of-fact

bluntness of the Latin, 'But your family without doubt will be rich —
very rich?'

Anthony had never considered the matter. He supposed so.

'If you are rich you can never be so lonely as if you are poor. We were
— are — very poor, although noble, of course! I was very lonely.'

Anthony thought it very surprising that it was possible to be lonely
at a school.

The Poor-but-Noble, resting rather full chin on the folds of black
neckerchief, remarked that the presence of a herd of their own kind always
increased the sensation of loneliness that was the fate of the intelligent.

'I have always been lonely! I am lonely! I shall always be lonely!'

Anthony felt that perhaps he gathered his loneliness to his bosom, but
Poor-but-Noble, having once broken through the shell of his reserve,
revealed himself fully-fledged as an expositor of ideas and ideals. He spoke
in a rapid torrent of which a bare third was comprehensible to the boy.

In the middle of the address he was interrupted by the arrival of his
sergeant. Anthony thought that the man's long grey moustache looked
as though it were false and had been stuck carelessly on his upper lip
because it was so definitely lop-sided. It was really the only part of the
sergeant that was recognizable as he stood in the dark oblong of the
doorway.

Whatever words they were that he uttered in his peculiar harsh dialect,
they brought Poor-but-Noble to a full stop.

'I have a visitor. I trust it will not discommode your grandmother.
Please apologize to her. He will be here but a very short time.'

Madam Purvis, on interpretation, signified that she would not be discommoded.

'And perhaps you, Mister America, will act the interpreter for me, if
need be. I have a prisoner to interrogate.'

Whatever was the picture conjured up in Anthony's mind by the word
'prisoner', it was utterly shattered by the reality.

Here came no heavily guarded, dishevelled, and dejected captive.
There was a quick firm step on the stair followed by a heavier tread.
The door swung open, and a gentleman — obviously quite at his ease —
appeared; bowed to Poor-but-Noble; bowed to Anthony; walked with
nonchalant elegance across the wide waste of tiles between the two
ghostly beds, and came to a halt at the table under the window where
he stood looking from boy to soldier with one eyebrow slightly raised
as if he would ask which was his host.

The slanting moustache of the sergeant meanwhile had projected itself round the door; presumably satisfied itself that all was in order, and edged out again.

The prisoner now permitted himself the faintest of smiles, as though at the whimsicality of his position, whilst he surveyed the scene with bright grey eyes. Incongruous pair; chessboard; watch; pistol — hurriedly produced by Poor-but-Noble at the sergeant's first announcement, to Anthony's immense excitement, and tactfully shrouded by a rather dingy silk handkerchief. All illumined by the soft yellow glow of a Provençal lamp, a mere globe of glass full of lemon-coloured oil, with a naked wick, set on a brass candlestick.

He threw over his left arm the long cloak which had enveloped him, and stood before them revealed in a scarlet magnificence to which the grey monochrome of the room became but a setting. There was gold embroidery on the stiff high collar of his coat, and gold thread round the button-holes. Whatever had been his misadventures, they had not disturbed the set curls of his powdered and pomatumed hair, or the lofty equanimity of his tanned and handsome face. He was swordless, and the only fleck or speck upon his immaculateness was the grey mark left on the white gold-buttoned waistcoat by the rubbing of his sword-belt.

Now he bowed once more to Poor-but-Noble who, rather belatedly, rose from his seat. Anthony liked Poor-but-Noble, but he had to admit to himself that the Frenchman looked a little shabby, a little dusty, a little unimpressive beside his captive.

'You will forgive my interrupting you at your recreation,' said Captive Elegance in perfect French. 'I assure you that my visit is — well, involuntary!'

He flung his cloak over the back of a chair and sat down with a murmur of apology — 'I am rather weary. You will forgive me?' — crossing his legs in an easy manner . . . Anthony thought he had not seen such beautiful boots in all France — knee-high, as black and shining as the wing-case of a beetle, and fitting as though they had been moulded by an artist round the long slim limbs; very different indeed from the lacquered brown-paper efforts of the French boot-makers . . . 'I am completely at your disposal, Citizen-Captain!'

Poor-but-Noble also sat down. In the old days before the Revolution, as one whose nobility of birth was perhaps a little dubious, he had met with, and raged at, that assumption of lofty indifference and superiority. Equally did he resent the reminder that he was now the servant of mob-rule. His pale face, however, showed no sign of the irritation that possessed him. He only said —

'I am aware of that! . . . Your name and rank?'

'Name — Hurrell. Christian name (you didn't ask me, but I do not object to vouchsafing the information) — Charles. Rank — Lieutenant-Colonel.'

Madam Purvis, who had been sitting with her head a little inclined to the shuttered window the better to catch every note of the vast prelude to the symphony of death, had displayed no interest in the new arrival. She was too far away to hear anything of the low-toned conversation, and it was by the merest chance that she caught the single word — 'Hurrell'. She turned her head very slowly so that she might concentrate her gaze upon keen and hardy face with high-bridged nose and lofty forehead.

She knew it now. Twelve years had made very little difference to the Englishman. In the yellow glow about the far table she could recognize every line of the face that she had last seen against the tapestry of books in the library at High Pale, staring at her across the dead body of her eldest son propped in its wheel-chair.

She took the book from the table, opened it, and laid it on her knee. Satisfied as to the identity of the newcomer she bent her regard upon the spread pages, as though reading. Her eyes met a sentiment with which she found herself thoroughly in accord —

'*A God all mercy, is a God unjust.*'

'Your regiment?' said Poor-but-Noble.

'The Fourth Dragoons.'

Poor-but-Noble let his glance flicker over the uniform of Colonel Hurrell — scarlet and gold with white breeches.

'I should not have said that that was the uniform of the Fourth Dragoons,' he remarked with an expressionless face.

'No?' said Colonel Hurrell with the raised eyebrow of polite interest. 'What are you doing so far from Toulon?'

'There are three questions which you may ask a prisoner, and which he is compelled to answer truthfully. You have asked them, and you have been answered — truthfully.'

'It is peculiar, to say the least of it, that you should appear here at this precise moment.'

'It certainly has dawned on me since I landed that you are moving up a considerable quantity of artillery. I even thought to recognize one or two 36-pounders. Heavy stuff, that! But you can hardly suggest that I am a spy, in view of my uniform; or that I am an invasion, since my command was only three men — sailors whom your people succeeded in shooting, quite unnecessarily, I assure you.'

'Anthony!' said Madam Purvis, without raising her eyes from *Night Thoughts*.

The small boy obediently got down from his stool and approached his grandmother. Colonel Hurrell, his attention attracted momentarily, cast a quick glance at the lady, who was bent over her book; looked away again indifferently.

'What is that man doing here?' asked Madam Purvis in a very low voice, eyes still fixed on the book upon her knee.

'He is a prisoner, ma'am! An English prisoner!' whispered Anthony. 'He is a colonel.'

A fresh thought had occurred to Captive-Elegance —

'It is surprising, Citizen-Captain, to find a French officer conversant with the details of the uniform of the Fourth Dragoons!'

'There are many things that a French officer must know . . . With us promotion cannot be obtained by purchase!'

'Ah!' said Hurrell reflectively. And again, 'Ah! . . . I wonder, then, what qualities earned their appointments for your present commanders in this area. One, I believe, was a professional painter, and the other a physician!'

'Even so they are probably vastly superior to the officers commanding the forces of — let us say your Sardinian and Spanish allies.'

The conversation thus continued, Poor-but-Noble probing for information, Captive-Elegance straying into digressions on every conceivable subject. Forts Equilette and Balaquier on the La Grasse promontory had been strengthened by the British? Had they really? Suppose that, instead of trenching upon this subject, they debate the theories of the great artillerist Gribeauval, or of Gilbert, or Du Teil, or Bourcet!

'What are they talking about now?' said Grandmother Purvis in her low voice, eyes still glued to the epigrammatic pages of the Reverend Mr. Young.

But Anthony's keen ears and acquaintanceship with the French language were not sufficient to disentangle sense from the hum of distant conversation.

As a matter of fact, Colonel Hurrell had already enticed the younger man into an argument upon the manufacture of slow matches. A skirmish on this question of strong lye versus sugar of lead and rain water, eventually developed into a major action on the general subject of artillery and its use.

By this time it was obvious, even at a distance, that captor and captive had resolved themselves into a conference of professional gentlemen upon matters of common concern.

First Professional, with apology for the interruption, whistled the departure signal for his gun.

Second Professional, with polite interest — 'That will be the 36-pounder which I passed on the road. I was interested to think that you considered it worth while bringing up such heavy stuff.'

First Professional, realizing that this is merely an invitation to debate the comparative merits of English 32-pounder and French 36, hedges — 'When you strike, strike hard and with all you've got, and strike quickly.'

'When I was at Toulon I noted your policy. Almost every morning we woke to find a fresh battery in operation.'

'Duturbie estimates that a battery of four or five guns well posted is a match for a first-rate man-of-war.'

The Second Professional Gentleman obviously made some private calculations. Whatever the answer to the sum was, he made no remark, but smiled in a particularly knowing way.

'For a dragoon you are surprisingly conversant with artillery matters, Colonel Hurrell. You have read, I realize, Mr. Robins' *New Principles of Gunnery*. You have quoted to me from the *Essai général de Tactique*. I suppose you could even tell me without unduly cudgelling your brains what is the extreme effective range of one of our brass field-pieces — a twelve-pounder, for example?'

'If I said something less than five hundred toises — with round shot and a four-pound charge — I should not be far wrong . . . I perceive that you are startled to find that any senior officer in the British forces knows anything. I am not saying that the British system of promotion is good or equitable, but it compares very favourably with the French one, I assure you. Do you think that to refuse anyone a commission unless he was a noble with sixteen quarterings to his coat of arms — as you did in the pre-revolutionary days — was beneficial to your army? . . . Has there been much improvement since? In the last eighteen months you have nominated and superseded no fewer than five hundred and ninety-three generals! Five hundred and ninety-three! I kept particular note of the number. It is considerable!'

'I wonder which of us two will be a general first?' said French Professional at length, turning his pale face so that he could study every lineament of English Professional. 'I am two steps down in rank, but you are a prisoner.'

'It would be a more curious speculation to question which of us would remain longest in that rank, in view of your country's record,' said Colonel Hurrell. 'I have enjoyed our talk, Captain — ?'

'Buonaparte.'

'Italian?'

'Corsican.'

' — Captain Buonaparte, much as I regret the occasion.'

He cast a look round the dimly lighted room, with the pale large ghosts of beds ranged against opposing walls: regarded for a moment the little group in the glow of the lamp on the other table — small boy in short black jacket with frilled shirt collar standing beside elderly lady in black, whose eyes were never lifted for an instant from whatever book she read. He wondered what connection they had with the young artillery officer.

As if in answer to his unspoken question, Madam Purvis at that moment began to speak to Anthony. In English. Just loud enough for him to recognize the texture of the language, though not the meaning.

His mind worked rapidly.

As his captors had marched him up the steep path through the pines from the sea, he had identified the place at once, even by moonlight. Often from shipboard he had viewed through the telescope the steep wooded cove with trees descending to its fringe of silvery sand — the high promontory on its eastern wall capped with a few stalwart pines, the ledge high up on its seaward face, where lay the house behind a fence of pine and fir.

The boat in which he had strayed ashore in a dense sea mist, right into the hands of the coast-watchers, had been drawn up on the beach. It had not been immobilized when he last saw it. If once he could get to it and push out to sea, now that the fog had lifted, it was all Lombard-street to a China orange that he would be picked up by one of the vessels that kept continuous patrol from the fleet at Toulon.

These English-speaking people, if not actively helpful, must be at least neutral.

If —

He suddenly became a little indiscreet on the subject of the Sardinian garrisons of the forts at Cape Lebrun and Cape Lesset. It didn't matter. The Sardinians were of no account anyhow. Hood knew — Mulgrave knew, that when this young man had shepherded his hundred guns into position it would be all over.

The indiscretion worked the trick. Captain Buonaparte was interested, very interested. The interview would be indefinitely prolonged. Time was what he needed — time and the chance.

And then something happened.

There was an enormous crash without. A splintering collapse of something heavy, followed by a noise as of giants playing skittles. A horse screamed with pain, and a frenzy of shouting and curses rose over the never-ceasing din below. He gauged that an ammunition waggon had smashed a wheel and overturned, scattering its load of heavy cannon balls. Captain Buonaparte leaned out of the window in vain effort to investigate extent and nature of the disaster: leaned back: shouted instruction to Slanting-Moustache on duty outside the door.

Hurrell heard the man lumber quickly downstairs.

He leaned a little across the table as though to ascertain for himself what had happened. And as he did so struck, with the swiftness of a snake. With a sweeping savage blow of his clenched left fist he hit the other just below the right ear and sent him and his chair to the floor. With his right hand he seized the pistol that lay under the silk handkerchief by the chessboard, and the foolscap list of ordnance. He rose: he veiled scarlet elegance in long dark cloak, and so was no longer splendidly alien to the dim greys and shadowy whites of the lofty room, which he had dominated.

Captain Buonaparte was out! Out for far more than any count of ten!

With the elegant assurance of a gentleman of easy fortune taking leave of his hostess, he approached Madam Purvis. He bowed formally from the hips.

She did not look up for a moment: it seemed to him almost as if she were unaware of what had occurred and even of his presence. The small boy standing close to her side, regarded him, however, with undisguised hostility.

'I trust, madam — ' he began.

Madam Purvis looked up.

By what still trait or inflexible expression he recognized her after all those years, he did not know. But recognize her he did, although it had been for so few moments that he had seen her in the library at High Pale. Everything came back to him with horrible clarity — the confusion and disorder of violent death in an apple-green room tapestried with books — Colonel Beriah Purvis, vastly peruked, sneering contempt out of his Florentine frame over the mantelpiece — the lolling blood-dappled figure of Anthony Purvis, the historian of imaginary travels — even the round brown stains on the copper engravings in the illustrated Bible from which he had secured decision about the diamonds.

So horrified was he by the return of this undesired past, that — despite all his knowledge of the vital need for every second — he remained stone motionless. The air of assurance and competence dropped from him: he stood before Madam Purvis like peccant schoolboy before incensed parent.

Madam Purvis rose to her feet. Very slowly.

Premonition of some unimaginable calamity seized him.

'Pray do not apologize, Colonel Hurrell,' she said. 'On *this* occasion I have not been discommoded. I may as well tell you that I have no property worthy of your attention here. And, as you probably recollect, I have no sons left to be murdered.'

'Madam—' he began, and so quailed before her terrible regard that he half turned, proposing to escape without further word.

'You need not think about escape, Colonel Hurrell, I assure you! You will never escape *me*! Anthony, call the guard! Quickly!'

And then she suddenly took one step forward, and, before he could divine her intention, flung her arms about his neck and held him fiercely to her in the hideous parody of an embrace.

For a few instants Hurrell was paralysed by the attack: he was as a man in a nightmare; he could only struggle feebly to free himself from the bony clutch, thrusting back his face from the contorted face that was so close, its colourless lips compressed, its eyes glaring into his.

Anthony, appalled, watched the black figures sway together to and fro—just a little—almost rhythmically in a kind of vampire dance against a background of grey wall and grey shutter, to the accompaniment without of a mounting confusion of noise.

Then Hurrell panicked. Not at the prospect of frustrated escape, but from fear of the woman who held him fast—fear of her as though she were not human but demoniac. Women conversed with one in pleasant drawing-rooms, rode, dined, danced, slept with one—after various tactical manœuvres of an elegant and amusing nature: they did not strive with one in the hideous intimacy of physical combat, body to body.

He could not release himself without violence; could not tear himself loose from the arms clasped tightly round his neck without the exercise of ungentle strength. He set hands on her throat.

'Anthony!' she cried. 'Anthony! Quickly!'

As she choked, Hurrell set foot on the hem of her wide black skirts. Anthony saw the man slip, reel—still held, fall—still held. There was a thud: the dark struggling forms were on the floor—a writhing stain upon the faded red of the tiles.

He ran out of the door, and down the stairs shouting, screaming at the top of his voice.

The sergeant with the unreal moustache stood at the stair-foot in what had been the great entrance hall of the mansion—a hall lighted by a few candles, and now jumbled with cases and barrels, and full of men clustered about a couple of casks raised upon trestles. Slant-Moustache was quicker witted than his appearance suggested, for he realized instantly

that action and not inquiry was required. He called to some of the tat-
terdemalion crew, and leaped up the stairs two at a time. . . .

Anthony followed: waited trembling in the dark corridor, which was
barred by a broad beam of pale light from the big front room. He dared
not to enter, to see what was the outcome of that conflict which his
grandmother had begun — and in which she had cast off grandmother-
hood to become as a wolf. He knew nothing of Hurrell's part in his
own history; only he knew him as an English soldier, an enemy, the assailant of Poor-but-Noble, and the sinister figure which had evoked his
grandmother's metamorphosis. In that lofty dimly-lighted room something unnatural and beyond comprehension had happened. His lips
quivered, and he could feel the tears gathering along his eyelids.

A door beside him opened. Elizabeth Vane appeared, sleepy, wrapped
in a dark fur-edged pelisse, a pair of golden mules upon her feet; in her
hand a candle.

'What is it, Rowley?' she asked. 'Why did you cry out?'

'Grandmother — ' he stammered: felt for her hand. . . .

But nothing horrifying was to be seen.

Far from it. Madam Purvis and Captain Buonaparte were standing
facing one another across the table before the open window, with the
yellow-orange of the lamp and the chessboard and the muster-roll of artillery between them. Their faces were masks of calmness. Only those
who knew him would have remarked that the officer's grey eyes had
become almost black: he had curled the fingers of his right hand about
the cuff of his shabby blue coat and was twisting the sleeve to and fro,
corkscrew fashion, round his arm. It was that absent-minded trick which
came back to Anthony many years afterwards when he saw Captain
Buonaparte again.

Colonel Hurrell was held at the elbows by two hatless soldiers in dusty
uniforms some short distance away. He was no longer Captive-Elegance,
for cloak was gone, white sculptured head all disarrayed, and scarlet coat
considerably tumbled.

'I am glad to have been of service,' said Madam Purvis, obviously in
reply to some speech of thanks: and both Elizabeth and Anthony noted
with surprise that she spoke in excellent French, although hitherto she
had always allowed someone to interpret for her. 'Very, very glad! . . .
You will not, of course, shoot our prisoner?'

'I should like to, madame,' remarked Captain Buonaparte eyeing Hurrell with disfavour. 'Unfortunately it is not permissible to shoot enemy
prisoners.'

'No?' asked Madam Purvis. She, too, regarded Hurrell; but no one could have told from her expression what were her thoughts. 'I am glad. I should have been upset if anything had happened to Colonel Hurrell yet!'

'An old acquaintance?' asked Buonaparte, swinging his black gaze from Hurrell to the lady.

'I met him first twelve years ago,' said Madam Purvis, continuing to refresh her memory of the prisoner's lineaments and expression. 'I have always desired to meet him again, and then a few months ago I learned that I had even greater reason for this desire than I had known.'

'You would almost appear to dislike the man, if I may say so,' commented Buonaparte in his harsh accents. He glanced from her to Elizabeth in violet fur-trimmed pelisse and golden mules, and to small boy in yellow nankeen pantaloons; as though they might provide the clue to the elder woman's attitude.

'Dislike is a mild word for my sentiments . . . Eventually, I hope, my acquaintance with Colonel Hurrell will be terminated through the medium of rope or firing party. But only after I have —'

'As a prisoner of war —' began Hurrell uncertainly.

'Silence, Prisoner!' said the sergeant, who stood at rigid attention against the wall a pace behind his officer. His moustache now registered a clock position of ten minutes past eight.

'Now that I have met Colonel Hurrell again, I shall make a point of keeping in touch with him,' said Madam Purvis. 'I shall endeavor to bring the unexpected and the unwelcome frequently into his life . . . You owe me something, Captain Buonaparte, for preventing your prisoner's escape. You can very easily get out of my debt.'

'Well?'

'In my country we have a very practical and effective method of dealing with persons we do not like who are inclined to cause trouble.'

'Captain Buonaparte, as a prisoner of war —'

'Silence, Prisoner!'

'When our people wish to assure themselves of a prisoner's security with the minimum of trouble to themselves, they remove his breeches and undergarments and boots. I believe, sir, that a man feels — and is — singularly helpless without those articles!'

Hurrell started violently forward. He was as violently restrained by his escort.

Captain Buonaparte nodded thoughtfully. He had now started to corkscrew his left sleeve simultaneously with the right.

'It would even be a pretty fancy to return him thus to the English lines! A very pretty fancy!'

Captain Buonaparte again nodded. His sergeant permitted a wooden smile to alter once again the angle of his itinerant moustache.

Captain Buonaparte had been enraged by the bland superiority of his prisoner and the physical violence used to himself. The Corsican blood in him demanded reprisal.

'I think that might arrange itself,' he agreed curtly. 'We might even send him back wearing a placard, "Captured by a Woman"!'

Hurrell's immediate and violent protests convinced him that this New World treatment would prove the most humiliating retribution that could be exacted. And exact it he accordingly did, at the expense of another desperate battle on the floor between prisoner and escort.

When Colonel Hurrell stood upright again, he wore neither boots nor breeches, neither stockings nor drawers.

The splendour of his gold-braided coat of scarlet topped white dangling shirt-tails and long naked legs. For a moment he kept his head downcast, his gaze fixed on the floor; but, standing so, he was more than ever aware of the ugly nudity of his feet. He raised his head, and stared with set grey face at the grey wall.

'On a hot night like this,' said Madam Purvis, 'you will take no harm travelling in deshabille.'

Her eyes regarded him out of a smooth yellow face with obvious pleasure. Then suddenly she burst into laughter — prolonged harsh laughter that had not one single note of mirth in it. Anthony had never heard her laugh before; nor did he ever want to hear her again. From grandmother she had become successively wolf and hyena.

Wide-eyed, Elizabeth had watched the shame put upon her fellow countryman. It had been impossible to tear herself away from the scene while it was enacting. Protest to the two inflexible judges was useless, she knew quite well. Now she turned to go.

'Come, Anthony', she said to the boy who still clutched firmly at her hand.

'Anthony will remain,' remarked Madam Purvis coldly, in English. 'Anthony will like to see this elegant gentleman — this thief, this murderer — so that he may know him again! Look at him, Anthony! An English soldier, the enemy of freedom throughout the world! Who fought and massacred and murdered and robbed so that Americans should remain slaves of British tyranny. Who fights now so that France may be brought back into subjection to despotism! Who slaughtered and pillaged and ravished throughout the length and breadth of India to establish the domination of the London shopkeeper over its ancient dynasties.

. . . But there are other reasons for Anthony's special interest. Come here, Anthony!'

Elizabeth accompanied the boy across the dimly shining floor to the table by the open window. Her golden mules clattered on the tiles. 'The woman's mad!' she told herself. 'The woman's mad!' She dared not to look at the stony figure standing half-naked, wrists bound behind back, by the further bed between two soldiers — one of them with an unshaven face all bloodied from a bleeding nose.

'Now, Anthony,' said Madam Purvis, 'I will tell you why you should be so very interested in Colonel Hurrell.' . . .

A little later the devil of hate and anger, that had brooded within her frame for years, in furious outburst wrecked her body. She had poured out passionate denunciation of the silent man held between his guards before her . . . had flung with all her strength at him the locket (which Anthony had once worn) with its contents of ringlets and blood-stained paper, so that it struck him on the lips . . . and then suddenly and most horribly gave a loud cry like that of an animal, and dropped to the floor, felled by a paralytic stroke.

Two hours afterwards Elizabeth came out into the darkness of the landing. She carried over her arm a pair of Harradence's pantaloons and some stockings; in one hand a pair of soft leather top-boots, and in the other her gilt embroidery scissors.

The uproar in the courtyard had not lessened. Higher up the mountain road, in its narrowest part, the carriage of one of the heavy guns had collapsed; the whole programme had been disarranged, and Captain Buonaparte had departed to the scene of trouble.

In the big front room Miss Buckley, keeping watch over the smitten woman, meditated a poem to be called 'The Living Dead'.

There was no guard on duty at the locked door of the unlighted loft in which Colonel Hurrell was confined. None was needed, since she found him within, roped — legs, arms and body — to a chair set by the solitary dormer window. The chair was tilted forward on its front legs against the ledge of the window, so that the prisoner's head and shoulders were thrust forward through the open casement. He was staring so intently into the night that he did not hear her enter, or realize her presence, until she said in a whisper —

'Colonel Hurrell!'

By a great effort he restored the chair to an even keel: turned his head to regard her, although her face was but a blur.

'Colonel Hurrell — I've brought some scissors! And some clothes! . . .
You see, I'm English, too!'

He said, rather brokenly, in a very low voice —

'If you can help me get away, I shall thank you till my dying day —
and after! . . . God bless you!'

There could be no question of undoing knots, of unwinding the convolutions of rope in the dark. He was as enmeshed as any fly in a spider's
larder. With her absurd scissors she had to battle with tough new cord,
and it was not until nearly half an hour later that Hurrell was able to
stand up a free man.

'I can't thank you,' he said — blur talking to blur — 'I shan't try to!
But one day I will repay — no matter where, or how, or at what cost!
I promise it! . . . You had better go at once, in case — ! Bolt the door
after you! I shall collect the pieces of rope when you've gone and take
them with me. I shall climb out of this window, and go down the cliff
face. I stand a very fair chance of escape once I am out of the house.
They'll think that I was not tied well enough. There must be no possible
chance of suspicion attaching to you.'

He sought for her hand in the darkness: found it: raised it to his lips.

'Will you tell me your name?' he asked.

'I am Mrs. Vane. Elizabeth Vane.'

'You have heard my name . . . I beg you not to believe the worst of
me. I did a great wrong when I was young. A very great wrong! But
I swear to you before Almighty God that I am no murderer! I swear
it most solemnly!'

'I did not think so,' said Elizabeth.

He added — still standing so that the chair should shield his nudity,
despite the dark —

'I owe to Mrs. Purvis's dead son, Anthony, a very, very, great debt!
A debt which I had no right to incur! A debt which does me infinite
dishonour! A debt which ever since I have been endeavouring to pay!
One day I shall! . . . The ghost of Anthony Purvis is a kindly one. It
is not he that haunts me — but the ghost of myself! Good-bye!' . . .

It was soon after daybreak that the sergeant with the itinerant moustache
discovered Hurrell's flight. Broken tiles beneath the window told the path
that the Englishman had taken. He was not caught, and the boat in
which he had come ashore was missing. Nobody expressed much concern.

BOOK THREE

THE WITCH IN THE TOWER

France 1794–1800

★

CHAPTER I

EDUCATION OF A GENTLEMAN

ANTHONY began to forget High Pale.

Sometimes lying awake in bed at La Cadière, with the windows wide open to moon and rustling sea and the song of nightingales in the thickets of the wild garden, he would have a sudden vision of his old home. Perhaps of the long white colonnade with which it fronted its lawns. Perhaps of the endless repetition of pagoda and bridge and willow tree on the faded wall-paper in the nursery, or the blue doors with buff panels of the cupboards that had been so full of other children's toys. Or of the tangle of red roofs and golden spires of forsaken Camelot, in the cedar-scented library whose book-crowded walls were patterned by the thin lines of apple-green shelves.

But he did not like to remember these things. He tried, indeed, to forget; for inevitably with them came other memories. A whole train of memories, starting in grandmother's dim chill room near the stair-foot . . . The Copley portrait of his father and his uncle, exquisite in russet and in lavender until they dissolved into the tattered blood-spattered Things that had followed his journeyings . . . Dark cabin and creaking upper berth . . . And then a whole miasma of horrors . . . In some strange way those memories (in which the actual and the phantasmal were inextricably confused) were kept to the plane of reality and out of the realm of merely evil dreams by two other recollections. By recollection of the tall Englishman with the pale flat belly, who had cursed him on the gun deck of the *Aventurière* — of his grandmother flinging herself savagely upon Hurrell in that bare room filled with the noise of guns.

He had a hatred of the sailor out of all proportion to the offence. Before the menace of that lean body he had quailed — he, the unquenchable hero of so many imaginary adventures, who rode into battle at the head of his spearmen against a thousand odds; whose sorties and battles ended without fail in tossing church bells and garlands and the roaring welcome of vast crowds. Thus had the cold wind of reality torn the gossamer fabric of the tapestry of his daydreams. He knew himself little, and weak, and afraid.

So, too, with Hurrell. For long he represented to Anthony neither murderer and thief, nor scarecrow figure of fun; but the evil genius who had changed his grandmother from the still icy woman that he had always known into something ravening and violent, like the wolf in *Red-Riding-Hood*.

For months afterwards he had been unable to see her without imagining that she might spring, snarling, from the bed on which she lay for so long after their arrival.

It was Mr. Harradence who brought them to La Cadière.

'We can't desert them,' he told Elizabeth. 'The house is big enough, in all conscience! It's a barracks! They can have the West wing, and we'll have the East. But we can't possibly leave her with Rowley and that fool of a Buckley to get on as best they can. Personally I don't give a damn whether the woman lives or dies, but while she *is* alive we've got a duty to do. In any case I mean to keep my eye on the boy. I like him. *I* saved him. He's mine . . . Incidentally I'm sure that Madam P. had some such scheme in mind when we talked about environment and education on board the *Chesapeake*.'

Madam Purvis probably had; though she never said so.

Anyhow, after she got better they all continued to live together in the long weather-stained château. A house embowered in trees, and looking steeply down upon the sea from a dilapidated terrace set with two lines of acacias.

Garland said that it was like the palace of the Sleeping Beauty. That was because of the blunt round towers, roofed with dark red tiles, at either end; and the high blank wall that hid the house from the dusty road; and the weeds that grew in the flagged fore-court; and the small windows so deeply set in the thick walls that they showed nothing of the life which stirred within-doors; and the mysterious warren of small rooms it held, all opening out of one another like a Chinese puzzle.

The house itself was always very dark and still, as though something important and strange had happened in it long ago, so that it paid no further heed to the passage of time or the actions of its inmates, or events beyond its walls.

A magic thicket, indeed, seemed to interpose itself between the château and the bloody turmoil of the outer world. During those long months when the ideologists of the Revolution purged the nation by mass drownings, with grapeshot, and by the blade of the insatiable guillotine, the house and its inhabitants were undisturbed. Once only did a very minor emissary of the Terror foul its portals — to retire respectfully at sight of the august names of the Committee of Public Safety on Harradence's special permits and passports. Even the little town half a mile away drowsed virtually unmolested through the nightmare months, royalist to the core though it was, like many other less lucky little towns in the South. It awoke, however, just sufficiently, on a hot July night when the news of Robespierre's downfall arrived, to cut the throat of Very Minor Emissary — who had been too engaged in the pursuit of René from the *épicerie*, to attend to politics — and dump his body in the middle of the bay, attached to a large stone.

Garland said that Very Minor Emissary used to poke his head nightly through the surface of the sea: that the water bubbled round him; and that his eye sockets and wound glowed with yellow fire. For a month or so after he had heard her graphically describe this, Négrel, the fisherman who performed the unofficial funeral, declined to be about the bay unaccompanied of a night.

It was like Garland. She must always fit her imaginings to reality. That was the great difference between her and Anthony; for to him the world of his dream-fantasies touched not the material world at any single point, although it was as much part of his daily life as the air he breathed and the books he read. Garland had to impart her imaginings to someone else before she could realize to the full all their bright colours: Anthony's world was utterly private to himself.

Garland also had ideas about living people as well as about things and places, and the dead. . . .

They spent some time, one September afternoon in '95, in the great coach-house, watching Joséphine, the black retriever, produce a succession of shiny slug-like puppies to the world. An expedition planned by Harradence.

'The earlier they learn that the gooseberry bush and the doctor's black bag business is all nonsense, the better,' he told the protesting Elizabeth. 'Let 'em see for themselves. Instruction in the facts of life figures in my *schema* for both of them. Madam P. approves. You come, too!'

'You think Garland's mother might pick up a few hints against possible eventualities, from a retriever?' asked Elizabeth, a little dryly.

She declined the invitation, but Garland and Anthony attended the affair: listened to a short biological discourse by Harradence: watched the process of parturition. They were interested, but not greatly so; and after a little found greater amusement in exploring the enormous old coach (covered with brass-nailed leather) in which the Comte de la Cadière of more than a century ago had journeyed — long-curled peruke, red-heeled shoes and all — to the court of His Most Christian Majesty at Versailles. It had slatted shutters instead of windows, and was hung on great leather straps. Although its dark blue interior was cobwebby and smelled of mice and was grey with mildew, Garland said that it was the veritable vehicle in which Dick Whittington, the Marquis of Carabas, and the White Cat had ridden on various historical occasions.

They came back from these fairy-tale encounters, not through the arched gateway leading from the stable-court to the fore-court of the house, but through a little wicket that opened onto the far end of the moss-stained terrace overhanging the tangle of rocky garden, which rose precipitously from the sea. There, between the acacias, which ran its length, and the decaying stucco of the balustrade, Madame Purvis was walking across the weed-fringed flagstones with dragging steps, aided by an ebony stick.

As the sun sank into the sea, the steely waters appeared to absorb all its warmth; against a sky as colourful and chilly as a prism the trees grew black and their shadows very long. In the stillness of the early evening, although she was far off, they could hear the shuffle of her slow tread and the faint tap-tapping of her stick.

'She's a witch, Rowley!' said Garland, suddenly clutching him by the hand. 'I know it! I always say so!'

'There aren't such things,' said Anthony.

But he halted with her in the shadows and watched his grandmother's slow progress away from them. Perhaps it was because Madam Purvis's dress was of a shining slug black, like those newly born things in the coach-house, that Garland added —

'She can't ever have had babies, you know!'

Both of them meditated awhile upon the facts of life in their relation to Madam Purvis. Even Anthony found it difficult to believe that children had been produced by the normal means out of her body: but —

'But my father was her son,' he protested. 'And my uncle!'

'How do you know?' said Garland unconvinced. 'You weren't born then.'

It was true that all the evidence was purely hearsay. Still it seemed to have been generally accepted. He pointed this out, but Garland was not prepared to take it for granted.

'I shouldn't have liked to have been born out of her . . . I don't believe anybody ever was . . . I always say that she's a witch! She *is* a witch! I don't mind what you think!'

They did not quarrel about the matter — in fact they rarely quarrelled at all — because Anthony himself felt that there was much to be said for Garland's theory; even if he could not accept it.

It was from that day that Garland's obsession against Madam Purvis dated. She would not remain alone with her, and in her presence always drew closer to Elizabeth, or Harradence. Wild horses would not have forced the child over the threshold of the door at the end of the long gallery on the château seaward front — the door of the big room which Madam Purvis inhabited in the western round tower.

The room was lighted by four deep-sunk small windows, and hung with dusky tapestries depicting hunting scenes. Its circle was flattened on one side by pale green panelling in which there was a small door to a staircase to the floor above, and a wall-bed and enormous clothespress and *cabinet de toilette* behind sliding panels on which were painted fat cupids. Rather dingy cupids lumbering through foggy space with baskets full of faded roses.

There was a great deal of heavy furniture of antique design — oak and walnut — against the walls; and in the middle of the room, underneath the brass chandelier hanging from a beam, a most remarkable table. A heavy round table of mahogany so high that it seemed more like a dais, or a scaffold, or a platform, or an altar. Its fluted legs had been so lengthened by additions of some yellow wood (the colour of apricot jam) that Madam Purvis could stand upright at it, now she was recovered, resting her folded arms upon the wine-dark surface. The same things always stood in the same places on that table; mahogany brass-bound writing desk flanked to its left by a green russia-leather dispatch case, to its right by a pile of four or five books, and having in front of it a miniature of Richard lying on a clean folded white handkerchief.

Every morning at eleven o'clock Paul, the grey splay-footed major-domo, would paddle his way from Harradence territory across the neutral ground of the great hall of the castle — a dark barn-like place it was! — to the Purvis dominion, with the message —

'Monsieur Harradence's compliments to Madame Purvis. He trusted that she had slept well. Could he be of any service to her that day?'

The formula never changed; although until the Revolution of Thermidor 9 when the Incorruptible Robespierre was given to the corruption of the grave-pit with his brother monsters of the Terror, Paul with a wry face had adhered strictly to the official text of the message: '*Citizen* Harradence's compliments to *Citizeness* Purvis . . .'

Only on alternate Wednesdays was the reply other than a grateful acknowledgment of courtesy. On the alternate Wednesdays, however, as regular as clockwork came the response that Madam Purvis would be greatly obliged if Monsieur Harradence would make it convenient to call upon her in person at four o'clock in the afternoon.

That — with the exception of the weekly visits of Monsieur Corvisart, the apothecary — constituted almost her only physical contact with the outside world. She emerged from her room to take lunch at noon with Anthony and Miss Buckley in a small panelled parlour looking on to the fore-court, and to walk for half an hour in the late afternoon — when the weather was fine — upon the terrace before her windows. That was all.

'God knows what she can do with herself all day,' said Harradence, returning from one of the fortnightly appointments. 'And yet she stands bleakly there in the dusk scratching a little tune with her nails upon the table all the time I am with her, as though she were impatient for me to be gone . . . She doesn't read, I'll swear! The books upon her table have been there ever since we came. They are never opened. They have the forsaken look of unread books . . . She asks if I chance to have the household accounts. I do. She opens her dispatch box, and pays her share in gold. She inquires my view of Anthony's progress — and listens, I will admit, very attentively. Just remembers that you and Garland exist. Then becomes wearied of me. Obviously desires to return to her occupations. I back out of the presence. I ask myself — What *are* those occupations? How does she fill in her time?'

'You don't ask how *I* succeed in filling in my time,' said Elizabeth with a sigh. '*I* have the household, and Garland, and you to see to. But even then —'

She stopped abruptly. Harradence eyed her in silence for a moment.

'It's dull for a young woman living in exile,' he said at last, leaning back dangerously in the fragile chair in her little pink boudoir. 'I can't go back to England, you know, my dear. I should almost certainly get hanged. But there is nothing to prevent you going. In fact I have thought a good deal about it lately. There's no reason why a young and pretty woman should be sacrificed to the selfishness of an old bachelor. Paris is too unsettled at present for it to be safe for you to go there, but there is nothing to prevent you putting in six months in Rome, for instance. Nothing in the wide world! Do you good! Couldn't stay myself while negotiations are going on about the Marseilles shipyard, but at any rate could take you and see you established.'

He contemplated the shapely long leg that was cocked over the other — the lustre of varnished shoe. He shot a quick glance at the exquisite Elizabeth, all in rose-pink, intent on her embroidery, sitting in a tapestry-covered settee on the opposite side of the hearth in which logs of cherry wood and old apple burned.

When she was certain that he no longer regarded her, she raised her eyes from her work, and looked at him with exasperation, with speculation, with —

'My dear uncle,' she began rather coldly, and then hurried on very fast with what she had to say. 'You must think me curiously ungrateful if you can imagine me gallivanting off to Rome — or anywhere else — leaving you to your own devices. If you want to get rid of me it would be a different thing, but while you keep Garland and me — because nobody else will, or can — in comfort and luxury, it's my job, and my pleasure, to look after you. To see that your clothes are mended, that you get your dinner, that you don't drink too much, that you have some sort of home life . . . I oughtn't to have complained. I am sorry.'

'Poor little Lizzie!' said Harradence in a tone of very gentle mockery. 'Poor little Lizzie!'

Elizabeth swung her feet off the settee and faced him.

'I will not be called Lizzie!' she said. 'I will not!'

'Lizzie! Lizzie! Lizzie!' repeated Harradence softly.

'I will not — '

'When you are being Lizzyish, I call you Lizzie. And you are Lizzyish when you play the poor orphaned widow, or widowed orphan, and call me "Dear Uncle", and talk about your duties in a melancholy tone . . . Lizzie! Lizzie!'

'Widow!' said Elizabeth bitterly.

She was off the settee and standing over him. Three-quarters in earnest and a quarter in jest, she bent and seized him by the ears, and shook his great head to and fro.

He took her wrists in his big hands and stayed her. He did not shift his position, but remained lying back in the chair, holding her, and narrowly studying her face until she turned away.

He suddenly became conscious of the fact that Garland had come into the room, and was watching them curiously.

'Reverting to our original subject of discussion,' he said, 'I think that Madam P. stands motionless in her room all day before her monstrous table, brooding like a great spider in the middle of its web. And at night she climbs the winding stair to her upper room and makes potions and strange spells, and creeps about the house when we are all asleep, and then slips out of a window and flutters about the woods like a bat or a vampire in the dark.'

'She *is* a witch. I always say she is,' said Garland.

'Hush, Garland,' ordered Elizabeth. 'Harrady, I wish you wouldn't talk such nonsense before the child.'

Garland told Anthony of Harradence's speculation when they had their supper of bread and milk together by themselves, as usual, that evening in the great hall. They always sat at a little table spread for them in a wide bay under the musicians' gallery, divided from the dim emptiness of the hall itself by a carved oaken screen and lighted by a mullioned window full of stained glass. It was rather like having supper in the sanctuary of a cathedral.

Harradence's jest and Garland's embroideries thereon were in Anthony's mind therefore when he went, according to form, to bid good night to his grandmother a little later.

She stood at the table in the middle of the room. Her supper tray had been removed, and she was bent a little over some paper spread before her. In the dim light cast by the chandelier, directly over her head, he noted for the first time that the pattern of the circular carpet radiated from its centre — like the lines of a cobweb.

And when he approached the table he saw that on it, level with his eyes, was some little bitten piece of biscuit, or something of the kind, such as she was always nibbling (although nobody ever saw her so engaged) and putting down somewhere and forgetting. Again he thought of a spider and its hoarded food supply upon the web.

When at last she raised her head —

'Good evening, ma'am? I hope you have had a better day!'

'Good evening, Anthony!'

Pause while she looked at him, as though searching his face for something that was not there — as though vaguely disappointed.

'The news has been good to-day, Anthony.'

'Has it, ma'am?'

'The British have lost six thousand men in four days in their retreat across Holland. They abandoned most of their equipment when they evacuated Dunkirk, and their casualties were very heavy. Now they have lost a third of the force they had left . . . Six thousand men!'

She lingered over the phrase as though savouring to the full the thought of the icy wastes between the rivers Waal and Yssel strewn with the frozen British dead — of Guards and Hessians fighting over their bread rations — of barge-loads of untended wounded — of the Calvary of an army's march in broken boots and linen jackets through the worst winter of a century . . . She even smiled.

'Will the war soon be over then, ma'am?'

'I hope not,' said Madam Purvis.

Then by close cross-examination, as always, she drew from him the minutest detail of his day — how it had been spent, where and with whom. She made no comment. She never did.

At the end, however, as if she would present a *bonne bouche* to a good child, she remarked:

'I heard from London to-day. A letter written only a fortnight ago.' Which meant that it had been brought across the Narrow Seas by one of the great fleet of smugglers that kept up continuous, if precarious, communication between the belligerent countries. 'From Mr. Starkey!'

The name 'Starkey' conveyed a whole history to Anthony.

It recalled those days at La Cadière before Madam Purvis could do anything except lie, as if she had been broken, along a couch with only her head raised a fraction upon a small hard cushion of purple and dingy silver. In that reclining position she had dictated letters out of the side of her distorted mouth to the Buckley, to Elizabeth, even to Harradence. Letters for the grim Mr. Jarman of Girard's Bank in Philadelphia; letters for Captain — Colonel — General (his changes were meteoric) Buonaparte; letters for the Prisoners of War Bureau in Paris; letters for her London agents, Fielding's Bank in Red Lion Square; letters for all sorts of people in all sorts of places, taking months in many cases to get answered. From all that cloud of correspondence one name in particular had emerged . . . Starkey. And Starkey wrote immensely long letters, in very black ink, on faintly pencilled lines — as if to keep his calligraphy straight — on one subject, always discreetly termed The Subject. He told of the movements, and the debts, and the daily life of Lieutenant-Colonel Charles Hurrell; of everything except those thoughts that The Subject kept to himself.

Anthony visualized Starkey with bony wrists sticking out of his wristbands, and long sinewy throat sticking out of his neck-cloth, and low flat forehead sticking out over sunken luminous eyes, watching The Subject behind doors, round the corner of windows; listening to The Subject at keyholes; opening The Subject's letters; and reading every word that was printed about him in the twelve newspapers which, Mr. Harradence said, were printed daily in London.

Grandmother now edited Starkey's latest letter for Anthony's edification. It was from Buckingham Street, London, and dated January 14, 1795.

The Subject — read Madam Purvis — had been slightly wounded by a musket ball during a minor engagement in the neighbourhood of Ypres. 'Good!' commented Madam Purvis . . . The Subject had gone into hospital, and therefore had become considerably worse . . . 'Very good!' . . . The Subject had been disappointed in his suit for the hand of a young lady with a fortune of over £100,000 in Consols and East India Stock. This was due, it was said, to doubts as to his character raised in the mind of the lady's guardian by certain anonymous letters . . . 'Very good, indeed!' . . . The Subject would shortly be disappointed, too, although he did not know it yet, about an appointment he was expecting at the Horse Guards. It was wanted for a gentleman friend of a lady friend of His Royal Highness the Duke of York, until lately Commander-in-Chief of the British Expeditionary Force . . . The letter tailed off thereafter into a reminder of the high cost of delicate investigation and requests for a draft.

Although Madam Purvis had read that letter a dozen times since its arrival, the pleasure it gave her was unquenchable. She stood turning it over and over in her long yellow fingers, as though the touch of it were tangible evidence of vengeance. Eventually she folded it into a small square packet, and placed it on the table before her, so that it just touched the handkerchief upon which the miniature of the long-dead Richard lay. An offering upon an altar!

'God has been very good!' said Madam Purvis, raising her eyes to the small boy in short brown jacket and loose yellow pantaloons, whose eyes and brow just showed above the edge of her table.

'Yes, ma'am?' said Anthony.

His action being screened from her view by the rampart of books and dispatch box and writing desk, he pushed very cautiously out of his range of vision that indecent nibbled morsel of hard biscuit.

'He has delivered our enemy into my hands . . . He is exacting retribution from those who brought war and ruin and death to our country. They are threatened with invasion, Anthony! A dose of their own medicine! With foreign soldiery let loose on their own soil! That is no more than fair requital, Anthony! Is it?'

'No, ma'am.'

'There'll be Englishmen killed in battle on their own fields — as were Americans! There'll be Englishmen shot on their own doorsteps — as were Americans! There'll be looting of English houses — as there was of ours! There'll be burning and bombardment and destruction of English towns and villages — just as there was of ours! That is very just, is it not, Anthony?'

She never raised her voice at all, nor uttered any stress upon the sentences. She spoke with the neutral accents of a seer. But even to Anthony the words and phrases that she used were balanced for violent speech, a music score, as it were, that she could not herself perform.

'Yes, ma'am,' said Anthony.

He moved the little bit of nibbled food — upon which so much hate was nourished physically — a trifle further away, although he never shifted his regard from hers by a flicker. He tried, too, to forget the crystal jug of thin brown toast-water — looking like diluted small-beer or the tidewater at a jetty in some muddy estuary — by which the fires were presumably damped down; a jug that usually stood of an evening close to her right hand on a salver with a green tumbler and a plate of dry biscuits.

Then, as she apparently had no more to say, he said good night again with the quick little bow that he had been taught.

But she said —

'Why did we fight the English, Anthony?'

He was ready with the formula evolved from much specialized discussion —

'Because we wouldn't pay the unjust taxes which they wanted us to.'

'And — ?'

'Because we thought that all men are free and equal, and shouldn't be ruled by kings, and earls, and princes, and bishops, and — and — tyrants.'

He had his hands loosely clasped behind his back, and he faced his grandmother, across the wide round table under the chandelier, with the slightly glazed expression of a scholar who answers an interrogatory by rote.

He knew so well what the next question must be, that he had almost answered without waiting for it to be posed —

'They used Germans and Red Indians because they like other people to fight their battles for them.'

Madam Purvis nodded her approval of these sentiments. She poured out a glassful of toast-water as carefully as though dealing with a particularly choice vintage, and drank it with the idea presumably of restoring the chill to her blood.

'Good night, Anthony.'

'Good night, ma'am.'

As he opened the door he heard by the rustle of paper that she had unfolded the letter from Starkey once again. He half turned in closing the door after him, and saw her standing there in the middle of the grey web of the carpet, brooding over the document, a bleak black figure, utterly still.

Could she have ever been tormented as Joséphine, the retriever had been? . . .

At night did she — ?

He was rather glad that he slept in a room leading out of Miss Buckley's. . . .

And next morning, when he paid his duty call, it was almost as though she had stood there black and unstirring through the waxing and the waning of the night — cap with dead black ribbons, golden black neckerchief fastened with funereal brooch, lustrous black dress with a silver sheen.

The only alteration was that set in front of her on the table were a little feather brush, a folded yellow duster and a folded grey duster, and a pair of black knitted silk gloves. With the aid of these articles Madam Purvis would presently occupy herself dusting her room . . . As he approached he saw, too, that there were one or two sweetmeats lying on the table, nibbled and — presumably — rejected.

The morning conference was always a brief one. It began exactly as the clumsy grandfather clock between the two seaward windows struck nine: it never lasted more than five minutes.

Anthony proffered the day's educational *menu,* of which Garland partook whenever possible: for at long last the *schema* to which Harradence had devoted so much time and thought on board the *Chesapeake,* was in full working order. There were lessons in French — language, literature, and history — from Monsieur Jacquot, the old curé of La Cadière, who had never troubled to go into hiding, or to doff his *soutane* during the Terror. Lessons in military science, mathematics, and shooting from Lieutenant Courville, a threadbare veteran of many wars, who had reappeared at his lodgings that winter as if he had only been away for a day or so instead of for more than two years. Lessons in Spanish and Italian: lessons in riding and fencing: lessons in all sorts of subjects from all sorts of people who had emerged destitute from all sorts of hiding-places now that the worst of the storm was over-past. Invariably two hours of instruction in German from Dr. Baldamus, resident tutor-in-chief.

The doctor was a shabby old gentleman in list slippers, with two pairs of spectacles in steel rims balanced on his long nose, and an enormous pipe with a china bowl. He was supposed to be the greatest living oologist, and although his interest in, and knowledge of, life were confined to such forces as are oviparous, he had fallen under suspicion of the Berlin authorities as a Radical. After being fined one hundred thalers for passing a sentry in the *Tiergarten* with his pipe in his mouth, and one hundred and fifty for failing to salute a young officer with sufficient respect, Dr. Baldamus had become a political refugee; and Harradence had eventually encountered him in Avignon practically penniless, having for sole luggage a small hand-valise and a box containing a couple of eggs of the duck-billed platypus.

At the end of his recital Anthony gave a little bob, and nerved himself to ask a question to which the inquisitiveness of Garland had stimulated him.

'Does Grandmother Fell ever write to you from Virginia, ma'am?'

'She does not write to me, Anthony. I do not desire it.'

He paused: having ventured so much, dared still more: ' — Or Aunt Octavia?'

At the mention of that unforgiven daughter who had wed an Englishman twenty years and more ago — whose childhood's bed Anthony had occupied in the nursery that looked out on sky and tree-tops at High Pale — Madam Purvis cast a quick glance at him.

'She does not write to me, Anthony. I do not desire it. Why do you ask?'

'I was reading about a lady called Octavia in Shakespeare, ma'am. And I just — just remembered!'

Madam Purvis looked at the clock. She said, out of the blue —

'You do not forget, Anthony, that Garland is British?'

He had not thought about the matter ever since her quarrel with him on board the *Aventurière*.

He answered, trying to straighten things out in his mind —

'And Mr. Harradence?'

His grandmother took up the feather duster.

'He *was* British. He has disowned his country.'

He thought for a moment, and then put the question that always worried him —

'Were *we* British before the Revolution, ma'am? . . . Was General Washington British?'

But Madam Purvis offered no solution to the problem. All that she said was —

'You may go, Anthony.'

CHAPTER II

THREE LADIES

THE years of France's torment — of Europe's torment — went by, the faintest of shadows, the most distant of echoes in the peaceful life of childhood at La Cadière. So far as Anthony was concerned they provided but subjects for the after-dinner debate at the mid-week sessions of Mr. Harradence's parliament, which was informed by local rumour, by the gleanings of its president on his visits to Marseilles, and by the scanty columns of the *Moniteur*.

The new republic decided to permit itself to be ruled by a comic-opera government, whose five Directors held high state amid their wantons in the once-royal Luxembourg, attired in an insane splendour that was a sort of patchwork from the rag-bag of history: Mr. Harradence's parliament took cognizance of this.

General Poor-but-Noble Bonaparte wedded the cast mistress of one of these great men, and embarked on meteoric campaign in North Italy: much debate. Forty-five thousand francs in *assignats* were only worth twenty-four in hard cash: the British fleet mutinied at Spithead and the Nore: the elections were annulled in forty-eight Departments: thirty journalists were transported and thousands of political offenders herded in concentration camps: still more debate.

And now, in 1798, the invasion of England; the seizure of Egypt — what opportunities for theorizing and speculation!

When he grew up all Anthony's memories of La Cadière merged in the recollection of those discussions outdoors on summer nights by the circle that Harradence had drawn round him. So vividly could he remember the accustomed scene that he could conjure up the very texture of the shadows, the accents of voices, the pearly curve of Garland's face as she leaned forward listening intently, and the excited pressure of her knee against his when she drew his attention to some particularly outrageous rhetoric on Harradence's part.

Perhaps it became idealized, but nevertheless the picture in his mind had a solidity and a reality that made him feel that so very little an effort would be needed to walk back into the setting and resume the past. The debaters would look up indifferently as if he had been away for an instant or two, and would continue. . . .

All along the terrace over the moonlit sea on that May night the acacias sighed and rustled in the little warm wind. The stains and fractures in the balustrade, the worn hollows in the wide flags, were veiled and disguised by the unsteady shadows of the trees; the tablecloth ringed with the marks of coffee-cups and wine-glasses, and stippled with tobacco ash, was a sheet of grey silver before the parliament as it sat back and meditated with ponderous calm upon the world of the dying century and all its curious manifestations.

'No!' said Monsieur Corvisart, the apothecary. He regarded, as he spoke, the dark drop of old brandy at the bottom of his glass with an infinite regret — for he knew his capacity. 'Absolutely, no!'

But no English transliteration can give that value to the phrase which Monsieur Corvisart imparted to it. His whole professional standing was built upon emphatic negative or affirmative. When he said 'No!' or 'Yes!' he did not shilly-shally about it: he said '*Non! Absolument, non!*' or '*Oui! Absolument, oui!*' And all the rich consonants and vowels came rumbling and reverberating out of his vast interior as if they were echoes from some enormous cavern.

'*Non!* . . . *Absolument, non!*'

That was what Monsieur Corvisart said; and the deep thunder of his refutation enveloped and contained within itself the opinion of most of those about the table. Of lean sardonic Lieutenant Courville, who sat next the apothecary, twisting his grey moustache. Of Monsieur Jacquot, the old priest with a face like a bird, who measured every worldly occurrence by the yard-stick of his breviary and the Vulgate — a mystic for whom a miracle was a matter of course, but the progress of science a subject for alarmed wonderment. Of Dr. Baldamus who sat slumped in his chair, chin on chest, as if he had dropped there from a great height and had not yet recovered. Of one or two minor guests. But not of Harradence, lounging back at the head of the table, one hand curved about a goblet of the rose-coloured Rhone wine in which his heart delighted, drumming with the other a soundless tune upon the cloth.

'No! Absolutely, no!' said Corvisart, and he heaved himself in his chair as he spoke, and ran an exploratory forefinger round the inside of his white neck-cloth — for he had dined exceedingly well. 'Science says "No!" Salt water says "No!" — its resistance, its pressure! The atmosphere says "No!" — its rapid consumption; its replacement by the gross vapours and fumes of the human body! . . . A device for De Crac or Münchausen!'

'I don't think that I am a coward,' said the lieutenant, 'but I wouldn't shut myself up in an under-water coffin with a keg or so of gunpowder for the income of the whole Directory. And I wager that there are very few men who would do so. Your American will never get his crews — even if he ever succeeds in building his submarine ship.' Another thought struck him. 'Beside, how will they see?'

The priest, sitting opposite his compatriots, but turned on his seat so that he should yet face the great lounging figure of his host, could see over his right shoulder the black and silver of the almost soundless sea under the vault of a heaven that was both dark and luminous. Upon such waters the Christ had walked; and through such waters had a highway been riven by the All-Powerful for the fugitive Israelites so that they

went dry-shod. Christ had not submerged Himself and walked along
the sea floor; nor had the Jews marched in their ranks after Moses beneath
the waves of the Red Sea. Where the good God had not led the way it
was not for man to venture. No Christian thing, but only the pagan
deities — Neptune and his tritons and his mermaids — might frequent
the world under the water.

'It would be an impiety,' said Monsieur Jacquot. 'The good God — '
His voice trailed off. He rarely, if ever, finished any sentence except
when he comforted the faithful with simple truths from the pulpit.

'Quite!' said Harradence soothingly, as though he had followed the
little man's unspoken train of thought: but he always said 'Quite!' to
anyone with whom he could not be bothered to argue and when he proposed to take a discussion into his own hands.

He pushed the decanter toward the priest, and proceeded to discuss
historically, scientifically, psychologically, morally, the construction of
under-water war-craft. He talked learnedly of the pioneer work of Bourne
and van Drebbel; of the turtle-shaped submarine with which Bushnell
had attacked the British warship *Cerberus* during the War of Independence; of the use and construction of air reservoirs; of the force with which
a floating body tends to resist inclination in relation to the cube of the
ordinates of the plane of flotation; of sundry cognate matters; all tending
to prove his wide knowledge of the subject. Then he let his imagination
run riot. He saw the under-seas thronging with swarms of small and
deadly craft, that would attack and destroy great navies from out of the
depths, unseen and unheard. He saw ships crossing from shore to shore
unaffected by tempest, so deep beneath the roots of the waves would they
travel. He saw the valleys and the plains of the ocean bottoms being
explored, and treasure wrested from vessels that had lain in the green
submarine twilight since the time of Solomon.

He stopped.

He began again.

This time, however, he obliterated all the pictures he had painted —
expunged them as though from a blackboard. Wiped them out with a
single sentence —

' — But not in our time.'

'Why?' said Anthony, who, with his elbows upon the table, and his
chin resting on his clasped hands, had been listening most intently.

'How would such a craft be propelled?' replied Harradence. 'Not by
sails — not by oars. How then?'

The parliament meditated in silence the question of the propulsion of
a submarine vessel. Dr. Baldamus, losing interest, prepared to return to

his inward speculations on the subject of the generative habits of vipers.

Said Corvisart at length —

'Then how does this American, this Fulton, propose to make his *Nautilus* travel?'

'He plans that it should be driven by a two-bladed propeller from its tail. At the end of a shaft revolved by hand! Figure to yourselves the speed with which it will flash through the depths! Figure to yourselves how it will pounce on a great battleship, secure the torpedo to it, and dart away again before the explosion occurs! Figure to yourselves the celerity and navigability of such a vessel, whose greatest speed will be one or two miles in the hour!'

The old lieutenant arranged his wineglass, the nut-crackers, his fruit plate, in line formation before him; dressed them by the left; swept their parade ground clear of crumbs with his hand; said —

'I am glad of that. It would be a dirty kind of war to attack from under-sea. I like clean open fighting. There is something wrong about a great ship with perhaps a thousand men on board being at the mercy of a plunging-boat with a crew of three.'

'I don't see any difference,' said Anthony diffidently, 'between a submarine attack on a ship and a night raid on enemy lines, Monsieur Courville. What is the difference, too, between passing underneath a ship and attaching an explosive to her bottom, and tunnelling a mine under the wall of a fortress?'

He nudged Garland to draw her attention to this unanswerable argument, but she did not respond as usual.

'It is bringing war down to the level of the basest kind of murder,' insisted Courville. 'Like stabbing a sleeping man.'

'The age of chivalry is dead — if, indeed it ever existed,' remarked Harradence.

'Ah, no —' said the old priest.

Dr. Baldamus took snuff — noisily and carelessly: his long upper lip, his nose, his chin, and the folds of his neck-cloth were permanently browned by the fine dust of tobacco. He forsook reverie upon eggs for argument on morals.

'Be practical, my good Courville.' He spoke in intensely guttural French. 'Soldiers should be practical business men, not paladins. Killing's their business. What is the purpose of war? To kill your enemy as easily and quickly as possible before he can kill *you*. That is the only rule. War is not a game of cards. There should be no politeness about it — only ruthlessness. Kill, or be killed — such is the law of Nature; and it applies to mankind as much as to brute creation. Even although we have evolved a slaughter-house code of good manners and slaughter-house costumes of blue or scarlet with gold lace. The more people you kill quickly — and I don't see that it matters how; whether it's by poison, or submarine ship, or surprise throat-cutting by night — the sooner your war will be over, and the fewer will perish in the long run. One must be practical in such matters, my friend!'

'But — I mean to say . . . Christianity?' said Jacquot gently.

'What has Christianity got to do with war?'

The debate ambled gently onward into the mazes of the ethics of the battlefield; but Anthony was far away. He had no need of the single glass of *Château-neuf-du-Pape,* which was his ration, to stimulate his imagination. Already in his mind he was exploring the colossal ruins of lost Atlantis, swimming — a mile beneath the surface — past the porticoes of sunken palaces and fortresses and over the marble jetties of great harbours that had not been seen of man for ten thousand years.

'I wish I could go in a plunging-boat,' he said to Garland in a low voice.

The pair of them sat together at the far end of the long table. Elizabeth and Miss Buckley always withdrew at the finish of the meal, but Harradence had insisted from the very beginning that the two younger members of the household should attend the sessions: it was (he said) part of their education to listen to intelligent conversation.

'Why?'

Garland answered Anthony without turning her head.

He was not sure of the reason, and before he could analyse the workings of his mind, she went on in a fierce whisper —

'I suppose you would like to blow up a British warship without running any risk!'

It had been an unfortunate day. Harradence had arrived back very early that morning from Marseilles with a packet of English papers. He had read excerpts without comment while they sat over their breakfast *café-au-lait* and *brioches* on the sunny terrace. Madam Purvis, unusually enough, had joined them; had drunk half a cup of coffee, fiddling with her drawn-thread work, and listening with sombre joy to the story unfolded.

England was making ready in frantic haste to meet invasion. They were giving arms to every man who could bear them. Plans were being prepared to evacuate women and children from the threatened areas, to drive the cattle inland, to burn crops and destroy bridges, to provide peaceful citizens with hand-grenades. Ireland was in rebellion. Already there was talk of French landings on the sister isle. Any day, any moment, the semaphores might flicker out from South Coast to Whitehall the news that the invasion barges were in sight — that the enemy was violating British soil — that, unbelievably, the tide of war had swept across English fields and hamlets.

The tempo of Madam Purvis's work grew faster and faster as detail piled on detail, until her black gown was covered with white threads like the rime of frost.

Elizabeth said nothing. Garland's face grew redder and redder, until she finally burst into tears, and ran back into the house.

Anthony remembered this. Now he said diplomatically —

'I wasn't thinking of that at all . . . I should like to be one of the first to travel under the sea. I should like the adventure and romance of it.'

Garland said —

'That's not true! I watched you and your old grandmother sitting and gloating over all that Uncle Harrady read out this morning. I'll bet she's bitten bits off a dozen more bon-bons than usual to-day.'

'What do you mean?'

'Whenever anything beastly happens — what she calls "Good news" — she nibbles twice as much as usual. I know. Louise told me so.'

Anthony meditated for a while on this revealing habit of his grandmother. Garland went on —

'It *would* be an American who invented that filthy little boat! . . . She'ld like to go out in it and tie kegs of gunpowder to every ship in the British navy!'

Anthony returned to a major issue. He said diffidently —

'All the same, I don't see why England shouldn't be invaded. They invaded us first. They invaded France. Now it's their turn!'

'America belonged to us,' said Garland, as if that were a complete explanation of England's policy to her former colonies. 'And France declared war on us first.'

'You don't understand,' said Anthony, beginning to get annoyed. 'You're a girl. You're only fourteen!'

'A girl of fourteen knows a great deal more than a boy of sixteen. Mamma says that women grow up much faster than men. She says a girl of seventeen is as grown up as a man of twenty-three!'

'You aren't seventeen!'

'No, but I'm as old as a man of twenty. That makes me really four years older than you are!'

'You aren't,' said Anthony indignantly.

'I am!'

'You aren't!'

At this juncture Monsieur Jacquot rose to his feet: he always left long before the others. A buzz of leave-taking succeeded the ordered ripple of conversation. . . .

Anthony — parting unreconciled from Garland — accompanied the priest on the short walk to his home. Down the dusty hill between low stone walls with young pine plantations on one hand and, on the other, olive groves sloping to the sea. The small moon-washed town faced the moonlit bay, and at its far end small church and still smaller presbytery were cuddled together in the dark of a glade of tall eucalyptus trees, whose leaves rustled with a peculiar dryness — the old man always slept on pillows stuffed with them.

They parted at the low arched door. The priest paused. In the light of the small lantern hung over the doorway, Anthony remarked how threadbare and darned was the material of his cassock about the knees — his best cassock, which he wore when he was invited out to supper at the château. Although the garment was short, showing clumsy patched silver-buckled shoes and six inches or so of thick woollen stocking, yet the hem, too, was worn and frayed, and the material had cracked in front exactly as if it had been something brittle, because it was very old and had been knelt on for so many years.

The old man had said practically nothing all the way home; had begun something; had ceased: stood there with his broad-brimmed hat in his hand, his silver head and mild face very reverend in the dramatization of moonlight and lamplight. He said now in his abrupt, unhappy way —

'The good God . . . The same God . . . The same Heaven . . . Never forget! . . . Over us all . . . French and English — and Americans. *And* Americans, of course! Good night. God bless you, my son!'

He walked back through the town along the sea-front, past small white houses with unencumbered view of the shining dark mirror of the sea and the slow curtaining by clouds of the moon-bright heaven. Stood for a while against the low wall and watched the cradling of little boats tied to the long breakwater which was roughly built of boulders. Turned over in his mind a dozen things: dream things: realities — like the crossness of Garland; like his grandmother listening to the chronicles of war and stripping the while a broad band of white linen (so to speak) to the bare bones; like the plunging-boat of Mr. Fulton. Sighed a little at the incomprehensibility of life. Pursued his way.

As he passed the last houses of the town the faint song of a violin became audible above the rhythmic wash of the sea and the ripple of pebbles on the narrow beach. Fairy-lights glimmered against the shiny foliage of fig trees and in a vine-decked pergola from which the Café de la Plage looked out upon its garden. There were, too, light-hearted laughter and the shuffle of dancing feet.

Spurred by what motive he did not know, and feeling greatly daring — for he had never ventured within before — he went in through the gate, and sat down at a rustic table under one of the trees to watch the merrymakers footing it on a dance-floor of beaten earth.

It was still early enough for many of the other tables to be occupied by townsfolk, half-seen figures in the uncertainty of light and shadow. Some eight or nine couples were revolving gaily in the mazes of a country dance played by a little old fiddler squatting cross-legged on a table under a yellow lantern, his enormous round spectacles tied to his head with leathern thongs.

Anthony ordered a *vermouth-cassis* from a perspiring and deferential waiter in shirt-sleeves and white apron. As he did so a voice spoke in English from out of the shadows near him —

'Good evening, Monsieur Anthony!'

He looked over his shoulder. He could distinguish vaguely a girl's figure at a table a few paces away, a ghost in lilac under the faint light of a fairy-lamp somewhere in the foliage above. He rose and bowed, and responded politely though with obvious lack of recognition —

'Good evening!'

'You don't recognize me, then?' said the lady with a trickle of laughter. 'That is not gallant, Monsieur Anthony, even if the light is bad, and my costume is strange to you.'

He approached her table, apology on lips, and looked down — on the pretty, coquettish face of Elizabeth Vane's new maid, Hortense. A round, smiling face; a round plump body in a high-waisted dress that revealed a great deal of rounded white bosom.

He was utterly at sea. He had never thought of Hortense as anything other than a sort of furnishing of the château — something just a little more important than a tray or a coffee-cup; something rather like a shadow in room and corridor; something mechanical that responded only to direction and initiated no speech. But here she was alive — like people who were not servants. Very much alive. With a social life — for there were three empty wine-glasses on the table; a man's cane rested against one chair, and on another were two little bonnets and a reticule.

Hortense was, however, quite competent to deal with the situation that she herself had created. She patted the chair beside her, and said —

'Monsieur will, perhaps, offer me a glass of wine?'

Still astonished by the fact that Hortense lived and did not just merely

exist, he sat down, and beckoned to the interested and sympathetic
Antoine. . . .

'It was perhaps venturesome of me,' said Hortense, 'but — '

She was both voluble and imaginative in explanation of this venturesomeness.

A bemused Anthony heard, with increasing interest and sympathy, the
tale of an innocent young girl orphaned by the Revolution: how the
good, poor Papa had been spirited away and finally executed by the
Montagnards during the Terror, although his only crime had been that
he mildly favoured the party of the Gironde: how the dear little Mamma
had faded away from grief: how a delicately nurtured young girl had
had to face, and battle with, the realities and cruelties of life, and finally
accept a menial position in the Purvis-Harradence household! Needless
to say, the society of the steward's room was *peu sympathique* for a person
brought up as she had been.

Hortense sipped her *vin d'Oporto* in the genteelest manner, and regarded Anthony with large dark appealing eyes.

She was clever enough to make no further reference after that to
menial duties and the steward's room, or the château of La Cadière and
its inhabitants. Instead she commented gaily upon the dance, and the
wine, and the weather, and finally (with a faint malice, but great discretion) upon the personal history and peculiarities of many of the dancers.

To his surprise Anthony found that he was regarding her not as Mrs.
Vane's maid — as a servant; but as any other of the few young ladies
he had met, and as an exceptionally pretty one at that.

'That is my friend!' said Hortense as a tall slim couple revolved into
the field of vision.

Anthony had a momentary glimpse of a handsome man in a dark
green coat, and of a still handsomer girl in a light green dress. 'She is
dancing with her uncle. He does not permit her to dance — or be acquainted with any of the gentlemen of the town. He is her guardian,
and extremely particular.'

Anthony eyed the disappearing back of this exclusive guardian with
interest.

'It must be very hard on the young lady,' he adventured.

'Monsieur Pagan . . . Monsieur le Comte Pagan — ' said Hortense
underlining the title, and looking sideways at the lad to see how he was
affected by this revelation of her friendship with the aristocracy — 'is
excessively proud! He is an Irishman. He is descended from a line of
Irish kings. He is a Count of the Papal States. He is a soldier. He has
fought in a hundred wars. They are staying here for the benefit of my

friend's health. The count was a great friend of Papa's. He is — not well off; his estates in Ireland were all seized by the English, and his castle destroyed by — how do you call him? — Cromouaille.'

At this moment the dance finished and the Irish grandee and his companion came stepping proudly out of the shadows. They carried themselves with fairy grace, not as though they trod the earthy dance floor of an *estaminet*, but as if they walked over the celestial meads of Emain. Count Pagan was a little in advance of his niece: exceptionally tall, fantastically handsome, dowered apparently with eternal youth, with wavy dark hair and long straight eyebrows that slanted upwards at their outer edge.

As he approached the table with dancing steps, Hortense said — almost as if in warning —

'Monsieur le Comte!'

He halted at once, and as he noticed that she was companioned, his slanting eyebrows seemed to slope still further and to be suddenly linked by a thin line across the top of the bridge of his nose.

'Let me present to you,' said Hortense, indicating Anthony with a pretty, plump hand, 'Mr. Anthony — '

The Count seemed to freeze.

'Mademoiselle Gendrey is aware of my invariable — ' he began.

' — Mr. Anthony Purvis,' concluded Hortense, unintimidated. 'Monsieur le Comte Pagan . . . Mr. Purvis is not English. He is American.'

Monsieur le Comte's air of great gravity dispersed. His handsome face was lightened by a most charming smile. He bowed. He advanced with outstretched hand.

'Forgive me! Forgive me!' said he. 'I am enchanted to make your acquaintance, Mr. Purvis. Honoured, indeed, to meet any American. I should have known Mademoiselle Gendrey better than to think that she would have presented any Englishman to me . . . I do *not* meet Englishmen . . . Let me present you to my niece — and ward. Jasmine, my dear, this is an American gentleman — Mr. Anthony Purvis.'

He made a sweeping gesture with his hand, as though he drew aside a social curtain that had veiled his niece from the view of the unintroduced or the unpresentable.

Miss Jasmine Pagan sketched the faintest, swaying outline of a curtsey.

Anthony bowed very deeply again — to the loveliest creature that he had ever seen, or dreamed of. As slim, as tall, as faintly tinted as the wraith-like ladies that had welcomed him and the returning warriors home when they rode up the streets of Camelot in those self-told fairy-tales of his childhood.

The whole fabric of his social ideas was being shredded to the winds. He had found himself sitting at table with a servant—who turned out to be a remarkably pretty and self-possessed young woman. He now found himself being introduced by this member of the domestic staff to a member of the nobility and his ethereal relative.

'My niece will tell you,' said Count Pagan, handing Jasmine to the chair next Anthony, 'that the last American gentleman we met was in Vienna. A Mr. Bush, of Boston, if I remember aright, my dear, was it not?'

Uncle remembered aright, said Jasmine in the lowest and most musical tones.

Uncle had good reason to remember aright; and Mr. Bush had still better reason to recall the encounter—for his purse was rendered considerably lighter after two or three evening sessions at picquet.

'And then there was Mr. Wintle. Let me see—that was in Paris, last year. He came from Philadelphia. Quite the gentleman. Excessively charming! ... And General Dickens in Dublin in '94; and Mr. and Mrs. Platt, of Charleston. That would be in Madrid, would it not, my dear?' As the count mentioned a name, so did he scrutinize the ingenuous face of the lad before him, for sign of recognition. It was unnecessary, for Anthony had never heard of any of them. 'So you see that we have quite a large circle of American acquaintances. Friends, I may say. Very dear friends—some! But it is difficult for us to keep in touch, for we are such birds of passage, Miss Pagan and I. Here to-day, there yesterday, somewhere else to-morrow!—Copenhagen—Coblentz—Capua—Constantinople!'

He sat down between his niece and Hortense; took up his glass of wine, and toyed with it for a few moments, all his movements flowing into one another with an effortless grace. His tight dark green coat with the darker cuffs of velvet was admirable: on the little finger of a long white hand glowed a great green stone.

'This auspicious occasion—this new and welcome addition to our gallery of Americans, calls for something special in the way of refreshment,' said the count draining his glass. 'No, I insist, my dear Mr. Purvis! ... To expunge, too, the recollection of the frigidity of my first greeting ... Antoine, champagne!'

And though he clapped his hands as lightly as might a bashaw upon whose every gesture waited a hundred attentive slaves, yet Antoine saw and heard him through the crepuscule, and through the wailing of the violin, the shuffle of the dancers, and the buzz of conversation. It was obvious that Count Pagan knew how to get attention wherever he might be.

They drank a pink-tinged sparkling wine that reminded Anthony of the flavour of raisins. It was sweetish, and commented upon favourably by Hortense: but Count Pagan said —

'Pah! My dear Hortense, your poor papa would have thought it only fit for toilette water!'

Which was true; for the late Monsieur Gendrey (who had been a ship's chandler in a small way on the Vieux Port at Marseilles) cared only for rum — Martinique rum, for preference.

'Poor Papa!' sighed Hortense; and she and Count Pagan embarked on a sea of reminiscences of a high-coloured character.

So Anthony was left to talk to the glimmering shimmering phantom of a fairy-lady, compound of dawn and mist in the trees, and thin water reflecting the pallid colour of an early evening sky. Ventured at length to address her.

'You have been great travellers, Miss Pagan!'

She only said in reply that they had, indeed, been great travellers, but her speech was silvern — like her uncle's, without brogue — rippling with the music of water. As she spoke, too, she turned a little and looked directly at him: starry-eyed, she was, with long slim throat, and the piled curls of her head a ghostly gold. In fact, he fancied her a silver girl. Silver-skinned. Silver spoken. He could have stayed for ever listening, shyly watching her from under lowered lashes.

She may have known the spell she exercised: at any rate, she fell silent, so that it was not broken. She watched him surreptitiously, too. She had seen her uncle's question, expressed in a tilting of his fascinating eyebrows, and had seen Hortense's lips shaping the soundless answer, 'Très — très — tr-r-r-ès riche!' He was younger than she was, in years by but few, but in knowledge by a century. She liked his grave youthful face, and every quiet detail of his beautiful dress — prune-coloured coat, buff waistcoat, snowy neck-cloth, and the high-crowned broad-brimmed hat (which was the latest English style) slightly tilted to one side. He was utterly different from those haggard or hearty caricatures of manhood from whose foibles and follies her uncle drew his living — who eyed her as though they were fingering her.

'I think,' she added at length, 'that we have been travelling ever since I was born. I have lived in so many places that I cannot remember what any of them are like. They are all a blur — like the country you travel through when you are going fast in a four-horse post-chaise.'

How graphic and how true! — he thought, recalling that journey from Virginia. His memories of it were mostly of ghosts — not of geography.

'I think,' said Jasmine, 'that the only country in Europe we have never been to is England. Uncle says he will never go there until Ireland is free. He hates England and the English . . . We have lived in Rome, and Paris, and Vienna, and Madrid, and Venice, and Calais, and Boulogne, and St. Petersburg, and Copenhagen, and dozens of little German towns. I was even for a few months in Bangalore when Uncle was a general in the Sultan of Mysore's army . . . And you — have you travelled much?'

He confessed the slight extent of his journeyings.

'You have been here for five years!' she commented, regarding him amazed, as though he had spoken of whole cycles of time. 'I *should* like to be somewhere for five years . . . Don't you want to go back to America?' He shook his head. He preferred life here.

But Miss Pagan wanted to hear all about America: and he found himself describing High Pale, and its wide plantations, and its slaves, and what he recollected of the isolated princeliness of life.

Miss Pagan was interested — obviously. So, too, though not obviously, was Count Pagan, for he succeeded in doing two things at once — sustaining a conversation with Hortense, and listening attentively to Anthony's reminiscences of Virginia. Once he raised an eyebrow as if he would ask confirmation of the modestly worded tale of the magnificence of that home across the Atlantic: and Hortense had nodded quick warranty.

It all came to an end too soon: the lights began to go out; the violin uttered its final squeak; the dancers drifted to the shadowy tables; the fiddler shambled after them collecting *sous* in his round catskin cap, with his goblin spectacles hanging precariously and askew on the tip of his nose at the end of their leathern thongs; there was a general air of departure — of the paying of bills, of the gathering up of reticules, of a shaking into coats, and an assumption of bonnets.

Anthony suddenly found himself involved in a cloud of farewells: found himself walking up the dusty road to the château; pine-woods on his right, and twisted thorn tree or hedge of angular cactus on his left, sentinelling (against the dark blue sky) the steep slope to the sea: found Hortense dancing up the hill at his side, one hand resting lightly upon the crook of his arm, the other swinging her little lilac bonnet by its long streamers.

She chatted to him as to an equal, gaily, but not familiarly. The burden of her speech concerned the lineage of Count Pagan and his extraordinarily distinguished career as soldier in a dozen armies; and also the romantic and tragic marriage of his brother, the dead father of Jasmine.

Anthony had listened to her until then in a sort of daze. His mind was filled with pictures of Jasmine, the fairy-lady who was of the pale gold of spring sunshine in a swiftly-running brook . . . her every movement and gesture and intonation. On the reference to her he came to the alert from out of his day-dream —

'Romantic? . . . Tragic?'

'Ah, but how romantic! But how tragic! . . . Jasmine's mother was a Circassian lady. Of extraordinary beauty. A Christian and daughter of a noble. Her family were staying in Smyrna when the Turks massacred all the Christians. That would be — let's see, Jasmine is seventeen years old — eighteen years ago. In '80. Her parents were butchered, and the Count's brother, Colonel Pagan, saved the girl from the murderers as she ran through the streets. He was in the Genoese service at the time, and was returning to his ship. He fought his way to the harbour with her, but when he got to the quay-side there was no boat waiting. So he swam with her to the frigate . . . He married her . . . Two years after Jasmine was born she ran away with a Russian prince. One of the Demidoffs. Colonel Pagan went to Russia to look for her, and was sent to Siberia for his pains. He died there, and Count Pagan adopted the baby. What a history!'

Somehow Anthony had felt that no ordinary parentage could have been responsible for Jasmine.

Before them, alongside the road, the black hulk of the château was outlined against the sky, rising above the square mass of the stable-court with the little peaked belfry on the coach-house. Their pace slowed.

Hortense dropped her hand from his arm. The gesture — he knew quite well — was acknowledgment that they were no longer Mademoiselle Gendrey and Mr. Purvis, but Monsieur Anthony and Hortense.

She said —

'It would be kind, Monsieur Anthony, if you did not refer to me — to my . . . It might be misunderstood!'

It might, indeed. He murmured some reply, which was apparently adequate, for Hortense was profuse in her thanks.

'You will understand how it is, Monsieur Anthony. Everyone is kind. So kind! But it is not what one was brought up to. Sometimes one gets an unbearable — what shall I say? — *nostalgie* for the sort of social life one used to lead, for friends of the sort that one used to have — like Mademoiselle Pagan . . . One becomes despairing. One — '

She suddenly turned through a gap in the low roadside wall into a field-track that slanted gently downhill toward the dark blur of the terraced garden. Anthony automatically followed. She finished her sentence —

— 'One plays truant!'

Poor Hortense!

'It is very understandable,' sympathized Anthony.

'One has one's little secrets. I will show you one!'

Hortense and he had already such a full-sized secret, thought Anthony, that one extra was neither here nor there.

Hortense gave a gurgle of laughter. Now that they were out of sight of the château she became once again Mademoiselle Gendrey. Very definitely Mademoiselle Gendrey. For she took his hand in hers, as they approached the darkness of the thickets —

'If you let go, you will get lost.'

She plunged into the depths of the plantation, drawing him after her along a winding path. The moon was veiled by cloud, and such light as it shed was curtained by the dense foliage of young trees.

Once or twice she came to so sudden a halt that, involuntarily, he was brought rather disturbingly against her. Her small warm hand within his own was, too, rather distracting, even to a lad whose mind was filled with the image of a palely golden girl.

'Miss Pagan — ' he began, as though the magic of the name might prove a spell to raise the curious enchantment that was stealing over him.

'S-sh!' said Hortense: and came to an abrupt standstill.

He collided with her again.

She did not move away: he did not step back. He never knew afterwards how it began, but he found himself holding the girl in his arms and kissing her, or being kissed. They were exploratory, rather brusque kisses on his part. Brief kisses, amateurish kisses — the first he had ever performed for the sake of the pleasure to be extracted from them. And all the time, amid the crowding sensations attached to those kisses he was thinking how odd it was to be kissing Hortense when he was quite sure he was in love with Jasmine: and how odd it was to be kissing Hortense at all.

'Where are we?' he asked at length, removing his lips from hers under pressure of these reactions.

'It is not an abduction!' said Hortense with a ripple of low laughter. 'Look up, then, Monsieur Anthony!'

Before them, straight out of a thicket rose a high wall. It had a balustraded top.

'It is the end of the great terrace . . . And you do not know of this, then?'

As she spoke the moon came out, and he saw that they were standing against a low arched doorway.

A moment later they were climbing steep steps in total darkness that smelled of damp and earth. . . .

'It is the end — of the steps and our little adventure,' said Hortense. 'The door here is in the short passage by the butler's pantry. You will know where you are, then . . . Will you go first and see that the coast is clear . . . So, we say good-bye!'

Saying good-bye to Hortense was instructive. Anthony realized that he had a great deal to learn in the art of kissing. . . .

He went to bed in a state of great perturbation and confusion.

He had kissed a girl for the first time in his life for the pleasure of it. He had kissed Mrs. Vane's servant.

He had met the most wonderful, adorable, slim, tall, fairy-lady; the princess of his dreams, of whom to think in the terms of kissing was sacrilege.

He was tarnished for ever. For him to think of Jasmine, with Hortense's kisses yet warm on his lips was desecration. He was a leper, a pariah, an outcast, a worshipper of false idols. He tried to expunge from memory the last half-hour — but it would not be blotted out.

He said his prayers. He prayed to God — or was it Jasmine? — for forgiveness. . . .

'And where has my little rabbit been?' asked Paul, the splay-footed major-domo, as Hortense peered round the half-open door of the tight-fitting snuggery where he sat — like the kernel in a nut — surrounded by shelves of silver and crystal, a bottle of anisette sharing the small table at his elbow with a candle and a highly indelicate romance.

'About and about,' said Hortense.

'Come in and drink a *petite verre,* then, and cheer thy old gargoyle with tales of sin!'

'I suppose that I might as well,' said Hortense.

CHAPTER III

FURTHER EDUCATION OF A GENTLEMAN

'Was it nice, Rowley? Did you enjoy it?' asked Garland.

Dr. Baldamus had gone wheezing and panting out of one of the many doors of the school-room — almost every room at La Cadière had, as a minimum, as many doors as walls — leaving her and Anthony to the task of turning Molière's *Bourgeois Gentilhomme* into classical German.

They sat facing one another across a sunlit table with a large pewter inkpot between them. The inkpot had holes all round its edge, in which were stuck half a dozen quill pens, so that it looked something like the feather head-dress of a Peruvian Inca.

'Was what nice?' replied Anthony, with a sudden chill of alarm. He spoke as casually as possible, and pretended to be absorbed in what he was doing.

'Kissing Hortense!' said Garland with a trickle of laughter.

From above the fireplace the portrait of a grave Garland — painted soon after their arrival in La Cadière; in mob cap, cherry-coloured sash, and mittens — regarded the original with prim disapproval.

'Kissing — Hortense! Kiss-ing Hort-ense!' repeated Anthony very slowly and very stupidly, to gain all the time he could.

'You needn't pretend you don't know what I mean,' said Garland, still laughing. 'You've gone bright red, Rowley! Beside, I saw you. It ought to have been fun. I should think that she'ld kiss very nicely. I don't blame you. I always say I should kiss Hortense if I were a man. Tell me all about it!'

'You saw me?' said Anthony astounded. 'Where? How? When? It's nonsense you are talking.'

'It isn't nonsense. Tibby was missing, and I went out to find her after Mother had gone to bed. I was out on the terrace. I heard you say, "Where are we?" and Hortense say something about it not being an abduction . . . Do tell me about it! I shan't say a word. Where had you been?'

'Why should I tell you?' he asked.

'I think you might. I told you when Henri Courboin tried to kiss me, and I hit him on the nose. Did you — ' she hesitated for the fraction of a second ' — go to her bedroom?'

'Garland!' said Anthony horror-struck at this matter-of-fact suggestion of flagrant immorality.

'Well, I don't see why you shouldn't! . . . Are you in love with her?'

'Of course I'm not,' he answered indignantly.

He rose, as though to break off the conversation, and went to the window, and stood looking out at the cobbled fore-court, with the orange trees in green tubs alternating with flowering oleanders against the high grey wall that hid the road. A couple of small lizards skirmished along the coping. He turned at last.

'I wish you hadn't seen, Garland,' he said. 'But I give you my word of honour that it was nothing at all. Really — honestly and truly! I'm rather ashamed of myself!'

'Why?' she asked. 'I should have thought that it must have been fun.

Didn't you think it over first? I always say that kissing wants a lot of thought!'

'As a matter of fact — ' he began: came to a halt.

He felt that Garland would have seen the incident in its proper proportions if he had been able to explain about Jasmine. He felt the urgent need for a confidant with regard to the pale gold girl. He felt too, however, that the mention of Jasmine, in any relation whatever to the sordid happenings which Garland had overseen last night, might be misunderstood. The breath that spoke of Hortense must not utter the name of Miss Pagan.

'You've got your best blue coat on!' exclaimed Garland, suddenly awakening to this interesting fact.

He had. And the sprigged waistcoat of lightest green. And the close-fitting pantaloons of fawn kerseymere. He was proposing (although he barely admitted it to himself) to walk into La Cadière in the afternoon, on the chance that . . . With his dark romantic locks, and his fresh complexion, and his air of confusion, Garland thought that he looked very attractive. The awakening of adolescence within her soul and body was responsible for the smallest possible tinge of jealousy, or just perhaps a pang of faint regret.

All she said was, when he did not reply to her comment —

'Are you going to take her out? . . . You'll be making Paul jealous!'

'Of course I'm not,' said Anthony indignantly and flushing furiously. 'I don't care if I never see her again! . . . What do you mean about Paul?'

'Uncle Harrady says that Paul is sweet on her . . . I wonder if he kisses her, too?'

It could not be true. It was not possible that Paul and he should share Hortense's kisses — Paul with his queer duck-footed shamble, and his pale deferential face and plump deferential hands folded on his great round stomach, and his deferentially bowed head with the grey hair plastered across the bald patch. He felt almost sick at the thought.

At the sight of his expression Garland went off into peals of laughter. As he slammed out of the room in a fury — Molière could wait! — he saw her rocking to and fro in the straight-back chair, mopping her eyes with an efficiently large handkerchief. . . .

'Of course Garland didn't tell me!' said Harradence indignantly. 'She would never give young Rowley away. I overheard it all.'

'Overheard?' commented Elizabeth.

'I was just going into the room when Garland began,' explained Harradence without shame. 'It all sounded rather interesting and important, so I just waited outside the door and listened till my lord stamped out in a huff.'

'My God! At the key-hole?' remarked Elizabeth.

'I always try and hear things I'm not meant to,' said Harradence simply. 'It's the secret of my success!'

He crossed his legs, and leaned back most perilously in a very small damask-covered chair which faced the window in Elizabeth's boudoir — a little room fragrant of the France of eighty years before, in walnut furniture and old-fashioned hangings sprigged with rosebuds.

Elizabeth did not debate the moral issue. All she said was —

'Hortense will have to go!'

'Whatever for?' he asked. 'She's a pretty little creature who's quite capable of looking after herself. Very capable indeed, I should imagine. The boy's got to start sometime, and it's much better that these sort of things should go on where we can take a hand in the game if need be! My old mother knew all about my first goings-on, and didn't interfere for that very reason. A girl called Ellen Fowler, it was,' he added in reminiscent vein. 'A plumpsy creature with a pink-and-white face and straw-coloured hair. Lord, how well I remember her! I was fourteen. She was four or five years older than me . . . Oh, no, let Hortense be!'

'And you mean to tell me that Garland looked upon it all as a joke?'

'A roaring, terrific joke! . . . In fact she asked Anthony if he had been to Hortense's bedroom!'

'Good God!' said Elizabeth, stirred to the core.

'Garland and I are moderns,' said Harradence with dignity. 'But as a matter of fact I am not certain that she was not just a — the merest trifle — jealous!'

Elizabeth laid down her embroidery on her grey lap. She looked at him straitly out of honest dark blue eyes.

'That is a more serious business,' she said. 'Is that why you have told me this?'

'Garland is still only a child although she is tall,' answered Harradence. 'But I don't think that you will ever have to worry about her. I know she will be very good-looking. Anyone can see that with half an eye. I love her short nose, and her short upper lip, and the way that black hair of hers waves from her brow, and her determined small chin. In a year or two poetically inclined youths will be comparing her to a cypress, and the slim pale-handed princesses of Celtic legend — Deirdre, or Guinevere, or Gyneth . . . But she is armoured with intelligence, and determination, and character.'

'Let us get back to Hortense!'

'It's got beyond Hortense—'

'Oh!'

'I knew about Hortense a month ago. It didn't worry me. But two or three times since I have seen our young friend out and about in his go-to-meeting best with another charmer! He doesn't know that I saw him.'

'What a Mahometan!' said Elizabeth. 'Who is it this time?'

'One of the loveliest creatures I have ever set eyes on. You should have seen the expression with which our mutual acquaintance regarded her! Restrained even, as he was, by the presence of an uncle!'

'Uncle! I don't like the sound of this very much, Harrady!'

'Neither did I. More particularly so when I made inquiries and found that Uncle was a fire-eating Irish adventurer calling himself Count Pagan, staying here with his ward for the benefit of her health! One can deal with the Hortenses a great deal more easily than with the Uncle Pagans! He's as beautiful as the girl — and that's saying a good deal — and probably a thousand times more dangerous! There are one or two very odd stories about him. Very odd, indeed. The man's no seedy scoundrel, either — slim and strong as a rapier — eternally young — beautifully dressed. Wears an immense cocked hat so that he looks like a general. Which he is! A general with the Russkis, and an admiral with the Chinese, and a colonel to the Pope, and something else in Parma, and (I believe) an agent now for the United Irishmen. Wolfe Tone and Lord Edward Fitzgerald and that gang, you know! He's as dangerous and swift as a hungry tiger!'

'I don't like the sound of this at all!' said Elizabeth.

Neither did Madam Purvis when Harradence broached the subject on a special visit to the dark room with the cobweb-patterned carpet.

She had had a packet from Jarman of Philadelphia that afternoon which had not been too satisfactory. And a letter from Starkey of London, which had been very annoying. And the annual letter of reconciliation (to which no reply was ever sent) from her outcast daughter, Octavia Parrish, from some fenland manor in Lincolnshire. She pushed them all from her across the polished table, and out of her mind. She listened very attentively to what Harradence had to say.

'I have no objection to a man being a man,' she remarked. 'In fact I prefer them so. Girls like Hortense fulfil a very useful purpose . . . My son Richard — ' She broke off; continued — 'But this Pagan business is in a very different category. I suppose that the only thing to do is to leave. It is a pity. I had hoped that we might finish his education here!'

'I don't see why you should be driven away. Where would you go?

America? That might be dangerous in the circumstances which you have explained to me.'

'My sister-in-law is not dead yet,' replied Madam Purvis regretfully, 'although my agent tells me that she oughtn't to last more than a few months . . . It is five years since I left America. It took her two years to find me, and for three years I have successfully obstructed every effort she has made in every court in the States and in France to force me to take Anthony back. She has no power to appoint a successor to her guardianship. It would be quite foolish to run into all sorts of complications when everything may satisfactorily settle itself any moment. I do not know either that I particularly desire to return — yet. I can conduct my — certain business with greater ease in Europe.'

'My own view is that by far the best course would be to send Anthony away for a while,' said Harradence tentatively.

Madam Purvis looked doubtful. Her hand slid along the table toward a morsel of purplish lozenge lying nearby; halted; withdrew.

'In my opinion,' said Harradence walking up and down before the sea-ward windows with hands behind back under his coat-tails, 'the boy now needs a year's schooling. Not from the point of view of ordinary education — because he is far in advance of the average: his French is perfect: his German good, and his Italian quite fair. But so that he shall mix for a while with lads of his own age. There are none here. No one can call young Courboin anything except a young lady — and not a very nice young lady! If I had a son like that — '

'But Anthony has made good progress in other things beside his books,' protested Madam Purvis. 'He rides exceptionally well, and you yourself have told me that he is a first-rate shot, and more than fair with the small-sword!'

'Négrel tells me he can handle a boat with anyone in the bay, but even so he's got to emerge from the conventual seclusion of La Cadière sometime, and mingle with his fellows. Training in the knowledge of their foibles, habits, discipline, idiocies and idiosyncrasies is essential. Why not now? It would solve the other problem, too!'

'A year, only,' said Madam Purvis firmly.

'Twelve months will be quite enough! . . . You well know, ma'am, that I despise schools and abominate universities from the educational viewpoint. But there is a certain self-reliance, a certain team-spirit, to be learned at them. Sending a boy to school — a carefully selected school, be it understood — with this end in view, is like pushing him into the shallow water of a pool in order to teach him to swim in the open sea . . . Now Baldamus was telling me — '

They went into committee on the matter.

And so —

'Well, it's all settled at last, Rowley, my lad!' said Harradence a fortnight or so later.

He swept the space before him on the crowded breakfast table clear of empty muffineer, of drained coffee-pot, of ravaged dish of grilled kidneys; and sat back, hands resting upon the arms of his carving chair, as though conscious of great difficulties overcome. He cast his napkin on the floor.

'What's settled?' asked Anthony.

'We'll leave for Paris to-morrow morning — if the Buck can get you packed in time. Marseilles — Arles — Lyons — Chalon — Auxerre. And so to Paris!'

'Paris!' said Anthony, astonished. 'Paris!'

'Didn't you know it was at Paris?'

'What's at Paris, sir?'

Harradence evinced the greatest surprise.

'You don't mean to say that your grandmother has said nothing about her plans for you all the time I have been away?'

'What plans? . . . Not a word!'

'What plans?' asked Garland, watching her uncle narrowly, for she had a hereditary instinct for knowing when he was by-passing the truth.

'Gracious me, Rowley! I took it for granted that she had told you all about it!' said Harradence, thus justifying Garland's suspicions.

'She never tells me anything,' said Anthony, knowing without being told that the whole structure of life was about to be radically altered. An immortal despair clutched his soul . . . Jasmine! . . . Jasmine! 'I do think it's a shame, sir, that I should be pushed about as if I were a pawn! What have I got to go to Paris for?'

Garland said that it was a shame, too; although latterly she had not been inclined to agree with Anthony on any subject.

'To school! That's what for,' said Harradence. 'Bring me my pipe and tobacco jar from the mantelpiece, my pretty! . . . To school! To the super-celebrated Institut Putzger. Where they look after your health, as if it were the veritable Temple of Hygeia. Where they discipline you like the Prussian Guards. Where they teach all the languages of the Tower of Babel. You're going to have the corners knocked off, to be finished, and polished, and stained, and varnished. Oh, the references and testimonials that your grandmother showed me when I got back last night! . . . And, by the way, where were you, Rowley? Nobody could find you!'

'He —' began Garland, and stopped out of loyalty.

'I —' began Anthony, and stopped because he did not like to lie.

'Well,' said Harradence, rapidly sailing out of these dangerous waters, 'here you are, at any rate, come to see your reverend uncle eating the first decent breakfast that he has had for a fortnight. The French would be a wiser and better people if they learned the art of breakfasting. There's more charity and general loving-kindness due to ham rashers and fried eggs and grilled kidneys and toast at the right time of day than ever emerged from a million poor-boxes.'. . .

He was given no chance at all of escaping and bidding Jasmine farewell before he left — Jasmine whom he had seen almost every day for six weeks as the crosses on his calendar showed; Jasmine whom he was to have accompanied to the fair — chaperoned, of course, by her uncle — on the very day that he would be driving up the dusty road across the barren mountains, into exile. He could not bring himself to send a message by Hortense, that discreet young lady who would dip him a small curtsy of a morning with her '*Bon jour*, Monsieur Anthony!' and thereafter pass him without a flicker of expression. In the end he had to despatch a hurried incoherent note by a stable boy.

No one appeared to be devastated by his impending departure.

Garland was a little regretful, but envious. Harradence was only interested in the route and detail of the journey. Elizabeth Vane had many consultations with Miss Buckley on the matter of packing. Monsieur Jacquot prayed that he might journey so great a distance under the protection of the good God, and the lieutenant implored him to remember a grave failing with the foil.

His grandmother wished him good-bye the night before their early departure: desired him always to recollect that he was a Purvis: remarked that Mr. Harradence would make satisfactory arrangements for his financial needs: bestowed on him God's blessing at the same time as a leathery kiss which held no more savour, warmth or emotion than might have been extracted from the covers of Young's *Night Thoughts* or any of the other volumes lying unread upon her table.

Miss Buckley seemed to be the only person at all upset. She embraced him very fondly against her exuberant bosom, and pressed into his hand a folded paper which, on examination at later date, transpired to be an original poem on his departure. It was headed 'The Wanderer', and began —

> 'Go, youthful friend, across the wide French plains,
> Thy foaming nags can not out-race my heart,
> Which, bound indeed to thee with viewless chains —

CHAPTER IV ·

PAVANE OF THE CHAMBER-POTS

HARRADENCE abandoned Anthony at the front door of the *Institut Putzger des Langues Occidentales et d'Education Supérieure* on the morning after their arrival in Paris.

They walked there together through ill-kempt streets from their hotel, the fashionable Richelieu — 'Phew! The place reeks of profiteers and their concubines!' said Harradence. 'I'ld shift to the Battelière if it were for more than a night or two.'

Although the Terror was four years over-past, and it was three years since the big guns of Poor-but-Noble had taught the mob to respect their betters in a bloody lesson, yet still Paris wore the look of 'the morning after'. She was a *cocotte* facing daylight before making good the overnight ravages to her complexion.

Palaces had become warrens of gambling den, dance hall, and brothel: and looked so. Great mansions had become apartment houses: and looked so. Churches had become temples for peculiarly desecrating festivals: and looked so. But everywhere amid the ruins of ancient magnificence there was springing up the lush splendour of the new society, founded on currency inflation and pillage — pillage of the Church, of Belgium, of Holland, Germany, Switzerland, Italy — incredible in its dress, its manners, and its morals. The pageantry of the streets displayed the extravagance of a circus.

'Growing pains!' said Harradence, and brusquely swept from his path, with a swimming motion of large arms, a pair of obstructive caricatures of youth swamped in enormous coats, enormous hats, and choked by enormous neck-cloths up to the point of the chin.

'Growing pains!' said he again.

It had been his standard comment upon all the excesses of revolutionary France, even during the worst abominations beyond whose bloody fog he had still seen the shimmer of an earthly paradise. Nowadays even the unobservant Anthony remarked that he repeated his catch-phrase with considerable less certainty.

'I shall leave you at the door, Rowley,' he remarked, paying no heed to the indignant protests that followed them. 'You must learn to make your own way . . . You would have stepped into the gutter for those pups, I do suppose! . . . There's nothing like standing on your own feet. I had to . . . When I was eleven I was taken off to a boarding school forty miles away. My mother — God rest her soul! — put me into my best for the occasion. Plum-coloured velvet coat with cut steel buttons. Sprigged waistcoat. Lace at my wrists and round my scrawny little throat. Three-cornered hat bound with gold galloon. I think I was something of a shock to my poor father when he found me waiting for him by the carriage door. However he said nothing until we stopped to change horses — just sat and eyed me as though I were a troupe of performing monkeys. Then he said — 'Know where you are going? . . . Good! . . . You are too fine a little gentleman to need your old father's help in finding your way about! Good-bye to you, son, God bless you! Come back — when you do — with a black eye and your breeches torn!' With that he got out of the carriage and left me to do the best I could!'

'Do I look like a troupe of performing monkeys?' asked Anthony, a little shaken by the implications of the story, and examining the sober elegance of his attire critically.

'A little showy, perhaps!' said Harradence, disregarding the fact that he himself was, at the least, brilliant in a violet coat and primrose-hued waistcoat. 'No, in your case it is your mind rather than your body that has been dolled up a trifle too extravagantly. Not your fault, of course, Rowley. It comes of living among adults, women and cranks. For your grandmother most certainly is a crank, and, I suppose, some people *might* call me one!'

'I sometimes wonder if — Do you think it's possible that Grandmother's a little . . . mad?'

Harradence avoided direct reply with the Stoic tag —

'*Insaniunt omnes praeter sapientem!* . . . We are discussing you and not your grandmother. This business of being away from all — *all* — the influences of home will give you a chance to find yourself. Of getting out of the mental garments in which your grandmother has prinked you out — and I too, perhaps!'

They came to a halt before a door in a high white wall in a quiet street in the Faubourg St. Germain.

'Well, here you are! I don't suppose you'll like it at first. A queer place, but they've got ideas; and that's rare for a school anywhere! . . . Perhaps they are a little mad, too! . . . Old Putzger impressed me, when I saw him a month ago, as a man who knew his job. Stick it out! If you can't, let me know and I'll come to the rescue. It'll be a good training in guts! . . . Good-bye, Rowley, and God bless you!'

He shook hands vigorously: was gone. Anthony pulled the bell which hung in a sort of little belfry projecting from the wall by the door. . . .

The Institut Putzger was a low large chalk-white house, standing back from its neighbours and half submerged in a shiny green poo. or laurel bushes. The laurels were all-pervasive. Whenever you looked from a window you saw them before anything else: their smell tainted the air: and even the indoor paintwork glittered with their metallic sheen.

Dr. Putzger received Anthony in the smallest room possible, painted dark green, and illuminated from a lofty barred window with such light as was able to filter through the screen of laurels.

He had an enormous bald head — the lower rim of which was occupied by a most diminutive face — on a long and thin neck, whose length and thinness were emphasized by a very low and tight neck-cloth and a large shirt-frill.

He greeted Anthony in French — if such chilly phrasing could be termed greeting — and listened to his replies with the intentness of a physician in auscultation of a patient.

'Your French will do,' he said, 'although your accent is a trifle of the *Midi*.' Plunged into German. 'For how long have you studied German? What books have you read? Do you know anything of German history?'

And listened again: shook his head — a dangerous gesture, it struck Anthony, with so thin a stalk.

'That will not do. I will put you in the *Deutsche Ecke*.' He opened a ledger and examined some entries. 'You will have Bed 3 in Room B . . . Have you any French or English books?'

Anthony confessed to the possession of half a dozen.

Dr. Putzger shook his head again.

'You must surrender them to me. You must speak German, read German, think German, sleep German! Your instruction of every sort will be in German — for the present at any rate . . . You will understand that I do not fail . . . You have your keys? Good! You will open your luggage in my presence, and I will indicate what you will require. All your other things will be put back in your trunks and taken to the store-room.'

He rose slowly from a shiny horsehair-seated chair, a little thin man whose body appeared to consist only of bones without flesh or sinew or muscle. His hands were almost those of a skeleton. Anthony received the impression that the doctor's immense head (as though it were a balloon) upheld his little trailing body.

Dr. Putzger led the way upstairs through a silent house which was so clean and polished that it seemed to Anthony to smell damp — like a laurel shrubbery after the rain. Two square-faced men in black aprons followed with Anthony's baggage.

At the top landing long corridors branched off to the right and the left.

'*Deutsche Ecke*,' said Dr. Putzger explanatorily; and turned into the right-hand passage that was lighted by a window at the far end, with a number of doors facing a blank wall against which were arranged perhaps twenty chamber-pots, each one with a placard bearing a number, and a small slate hanging over it. There was a single yellow wood washstand under the window.

Toward the end of the passage Dr. Putzger opened a door, and they entered a chilly bare room. On the left were four truckle beds facing the windows, each having by it the smallest imaginable chest of drawers. There were no curtains and no carpet. At the right-hand side of the door, however, there was a large tent-bed with a bedside table bearing a glass-shaded candlestick. It appeared to divide the room in half, for through the aperture in the draperies could be seen more beds and more chests.

'Herr von Knötel is in charge of the *Ecke* and of this room,' said Dr. Putzger, casting a passing glance at the green-draped bed. 'And now — '

Under the hot reddish eyes of the head of the Institut and the indifferent gaze of his minions, Anthony unpacked the elaborate trousseau which Elizabeth Vane and Miss Buckley had thought essential for metropolitan requirements.

'I will take these books. You may retain as much clothing as will fill your chest of drawers, and no more. Your hat and great-coat, however, may be kept in the cloakroom downstairs . . . Your schedule of work will be planned by me in consultation with Herr von Knötel after further exploration. You will keep to that schedule. You will find that this establishment is run by observance of strict routine. That routine must be observed — in every respect. There is no idleness, or laziness, or indiscipline. We do not permit them. There are many means of enforcing the salutary rules and regulations that have been laid down. My fees are high because my methods are successful. I am honest. I have to justify my charges. I can only do that by succeeding with my pupils. Therefore I *must* succeed with them. I *do*. If there is a test of will it is I who win. I *must*. My livelihood depends on it. You understand me?'

'Yes, Herr Doktor,' said the worshipper of Jasmine.

They retraced their steps along the passage with its row of alphabetically numbered doors and its row of labelled chamber-pots. On the way downstairs the doctor pointed out various other darkly green burrows as being the abodes of other *Ecken* — an English Corner, a *Coin Français*, and so on. They reached the ground-floor; they explored a labyrinth of laurel-green passages, which smelled of laurels, and were darkened by laurels before the occasional barred windows. Every door was labelled or numbered in some way.

Dr. Putzger came to a halt before one of these. He turned the handle with his bony hand very silently and pushed open the door equally silently, not as though he desired to avoid disturbing those within, but as if he desired to spring a surprise on them.

A large man with a large face sat at the end of a long table purring instruction in German to a class of lads of about Anthony's age. No one looked up at their entry. The large man purred on — Was there an undertone of growling in that purr? — large head sunk in wide shoulders so deeply that he resembled an enormous cat. He was clean-shaven, but a little tuft of jet black hair projected from each nostril against the pallor of his face. He looked up presently from whatever he was reading, and directly at them, but there was no flicker of recognition of their presence in his grey chilly eyes that seemed as convex as a cat's. His class kept their disciplined attention upon their books.

'Herr von Knötel!' said Dr. Putzger.

The head of the Institut having thus decided to become officially visible, Herr von Knötel rose to his feet with the drowsy speed of a cat —

'*Achtung!*' he growled. 'Herr Direktor?'

The class rose to its collective and individual feet.

'This is your B 3, Herr von Knötel,' said Dr. Putzger. 'I will discuss his schedule with you to-morrow morning at — ' he consulted a little memorandum leaf of ivory contained in a silver case which he produced from his waistcoat pocket, ' — at two minutes after nine.'

Anthony was left to his fate.

'Be seated, B 3,' said Herr von Knötel. 'No. The B side of the table is on my left. The third seat, you will note, is empty . . . Pass this newspaper to B 3! Read out loud the paragraph marked in blue pencil in the third column and then expound your views to us.'

B 3 found himself sitting in a chair with a number painted on the back, and before a section of green baize table-cloth with a corresponding number painted on it in white; in his hands a copy of the *Schwabische Merkur* of about three weeks back, with the item marked for his attention having the heading 'Cryptic Policy of the British Government.'. . .

Anthony wrote to Harradence:

'Paris, 19 Fructidor, An VI

'. . . I still feel as if I were going to school in something that is a cross between a mad prison and a wild game of chess. Every Décadi night after supper I am given my moves for the following decade on a sheet of foolscap headed "DB 3" — that's me: D for *Deutsche Ecke;* B for the section; and 3 my number in it — divided into ten columns with times in the margin. In each column is a sort of cryptogram, like FC 1, or SA 2, which means that at such and such an hour I occupy such and such a seat in such and such a class-room.

'There are eight of us at present in A and B of the *Deutsche Ecke* — those are the two senior grades: C is elementary. A Dutchman, a Pole, two Swiss, three French, and myself. They are a dull lot except the Pole, who's got slanting eyes and high cheekbones. He's either extraordinarily gay or ripe for suicide. His name's Radomski. Every night he spits and washes out his mouth before he goes to bed, and will not speak another word until morning. He says it is to get the German taste out of his mouth, or he wouldn't sleep. When they chopped up Poland for good three years ago, his father's estates along the River Bug — a pretty name, isn't it? — were divided up between Prussia and Austria. His father says he's got to learn German to prevent the family being victimized by officials more than they need be. All he wants to do when he grows up is to fight the Germans.

'We never seem to be out of sight of the masters for an instant from when we get up at six until "lights out" at ten o'clock: except on the one "free" day in ten, and sometimes for a very little during day-time "recreation".

'After breakfast at a quarter to seven — getting up takes some time because there's only one washstand for our dormitory — we march upstairs in silence to the passage full of chamber-pots. There we sit, each on his own private pot, under supervision, until each of us has performed. Then Herr von Knötel inspects the result and chalks up something on the slate over it. By and by someone else comes and inspects, too, they say, before the pots are emptied, and marks up something more. Then the slates are taken off, and from them Miss Putzger — the only woman in the house, if she is one! — works out what each of us ought to have to eat and drink, and how much. It is a crime against the Holy Ghost to use anybody else's. The bedroom door is locked at night so that anyone who wants to go out must wake up old Knotty, who has to go with them! Even the plates are lettered and numbered to make sure you get your proper diet. . . .'

'There's sound sense in it, all the same,' said Harradence, laughing, when he had read thus far, to Elizabeth Vane 'although it does sound rather like a speculation of the philosophers of Lagado. I think Garland would enjoy that bit!'

'You have peculiar ideas of Garland's enjoyment!'

'Not so peculiar as yours, my dear Elizabeth!'

But Garland already knew about the chamber-pots long before. Knew more than anyone about the Institut Putzger. About the dreary 'breaks', which meant aimless walking in gloomy groups, speaking a foreign tongue, for half an hour on paths of crackling grey gravel among the hostile laurels. About his companions. About the daily six-mile march in the early morning. About the sullen system by which everyone was driven on to the limit of his capacity — watched, spied on, scheduled, fed, exercised, taught by the most approved method so that even the densest must progress or break.

After a while Anthony ventured to write to Count Pagan a polite letter, regretting that he had been unable to pay his respects to him and Miss Pagan before his departure. He trusted that they might meet again at the end of the twelvemonth which he had to spend in Paris.

And by and by there had come back an answer — in the prettiest Italian hand imaginable — from Miss Pagan herself. Poor Uncle had been called away on service — *dangerous* service! He might be away for many months, so he had taken a little house for her in La Cadière, and an old cousin had come to keep her company! . . . Perhaps — !

He folded that letter in a piece of tissue paper: carried it about with him in the secret pocket which was provided in the lining of his everyday waistcoat: kept it under his pillow of nights: shamefacedly — and apologetically — kissed it in the dark.

Later on, when it was getting very frayed and fingered and smudged, it was given the companionship of another such epistle. And another. And another . . . By and by there was almost a portfolio, making a thick, though holy, pad in his pocket.

He began to see himself even as a Jacob working and waiting for his Rachel for twice seven years: for, at the age of sixteen, a year is an almost astronomical measurement of futurity. . . .

Each *Ecke* was as self-contained and isolated as if it were a separate establishment. Anything more than acquaintanceship was practically impossible outside its boundaries. Of his companions there were only two with whom he had any community of ideas.

One of them was the lean, incalculable, indomitable Radomski: but he had little talk except of the beauty and the woes of Poland. His father, a once notorious *bon viveur*, had sworn to touch neither woman nor wine again until Poland was free. His elder brother was of the four hundred Polish *legionnaires* who formed the bodyguard of General Bonaparte, the flail of Austria. One day General Bonaparte would —. One day he himself —. One day Poland —. But the theme was invariable and in the end a little wearisome.

The other was the Dutchman, B 4, a lame red-headed Jew whose pale face held faint blue shadows, and whose hooked thin nose had a faint red glaze at the tip. A remote, lonely creature, humbly conscious of the Institut's ill-disguised dislike of the Jewish race; of the pitiable collapse of Holland before the invader; of the inferiority of his position as a pupil-teacher in embryo; of his unprepossessing appearance and uncouthness. He made sad little efforts at friendship, and was pathetically grateful that they were not utterly repelled. He talked intelligently — and apologetically — and practised the violin in an empty stable for hours together on every permitted occasion.

No friendship was possible with von Knötel — Knotty who hated all boys, the 'lower' orders, Poles, musicians, and the Jews.

Knotty who was always with them, like the gigantic nightmare of a huge black cat, creeping after them on his velvet silent feet, unsheathing his great claws at them, snarling at them, growling at them, spitting at them, until it came time for him to curl up — lazily purring to himself — behind the green curtains of the tent-bed! The purring seemed to go on all night through. No matter how late you might wake there still rumbled through the darkness the deep purr, as of a vigilant mouser on duty at a mouse hole.

Knotty who thought the day ill-spent if he had not reduced B 4 to tears at least once in the course of it; who visited upon B 4 the sins of omission and commission of the entire *Ecke* with the apparent concurrence of its members, with the exception of Anthony!

On one occasion, indeed, he had risen to his feet in protest while Herr von Knötel flayed alive the wretched lad who stood drooping in his place before the square of green serge that was numbered '4'.

'Sir! — '

' — but instead are incorrigibly idle and ill-conditioned! Your characteristics are those of the ghetto from which you spring! I have appealed to you! I have warned you! I have commanded you! I have threatened you! Now I strike — '

And all the time as he spoke, sitting with his heavy shoulders hunched, his great paws — resting on the table — rubbed and curved against one another, as might the paws of a cat sheathing and unsheathing its claws.

'Sir! I am equally to blame!'

Knotty did not show that he had heard by either movement or expression. He did not shift his gaze from the miserable, ugly face of his victim.

'The *Herr Direktor* has drawn attention, very justly, to the abominable condition of the *Ecke's* wash-place.' — Two very small basins on the single stand, for twelve students — 'I investigate . . . I find this miserable creature stark naked, washing his grotesque body while standing with his filthy feet in a basin on a floor that is swamped with foul water. The walls dripping with miniature cataracts. The window speckled with soapy splashes. The clean towel a damp rag. The whole place resembling a noisome cattle trough rather than a toilet for gentlemen! At two o'clock of an afternoon! Yesterday afternoon.'

As the Institut boasted no bath — a matter for no great astonishment since France and Germany generally found little need for such equipment — clean Jew and clean American had taken advantage of the one free day in the Republican ten-day week, to engage in more complete ablutions on that particular afternoon than was possible during the morning scramble.

At the time that Herr von Knötel had made his inspection, Anthony had already bathed to the best of his abilities, and had departed. He had probably scattered more water about the bare boards of the passage than B 4; he certainly had left the only towel so sopping that it was problematical whether the other would ever be able to dry himself on it.

'Sir! — ' he began again in resolute determination to take his share of the blame.

Knotty ignored him absolutely.

"Furthermore, the soap was on the floor. Where anyone might tread upon it and break a leg. The place for soap is not the floor. A joke, I suppose! A Jewish booby-trap! . . . Now, how shall we teach you the elements of order and discipline and decency?'

He appeared to meditate on the problem of fitting punishment to the crime. No one at the table stirred, but sat regarding books and papers, the green cloth, finger-nails, anything except the large pale face sunk into the broad chest at the head of the table. That is, except Anthony.

In the silence he said —

'Sir, I am equally responsible. I bathed there, too, yesterday afternoon.'

But no one looked at him, or appeared to have heard him, or be even aware of his existence. He found himself getting very red: he wanted to crash his fist on the table and shout . . . He sat down.

Knotty started to purr very gently, and his great hands opened and shut, and curved, and rubbed, against one another a little faster than before.

'We will kill two flies with one clapper,' said he. 'At the same time we will inculcate cleanliness and decency and relieve the domestic staff of one of their many duties . . . A moderate and wise punishment! Not so much a punishment as an *aide-mémoire!* B 4! Until further notice you will act as toilet orderly for the *Ecke!* You will be not only responsible personally for the cleanliness of the wash-place but for the emptying and cleansing of the chamber-pots! . . . B 3! This is not a debating society, nor a Roman Catholic confessional, nor a rehearsal of theatrical heroics! I earnestly draw your attention to this fact, for your own comfort and convenience and happiness!' . . .

Anthony had offered to share the blame. He did not offer to share the punishment. Although every time that he saw Klasing — B 4 — travelling through the laurels to the cess-pit with his loathsome burdens, his conscience pricked him.

He said as much once, while he listened to the other playing his violin in the disused stable where he was allowed to practise — a place of clouded and cobwebby windows, and rotting woodwork, and rusting hay-racks.

But Klasing shook his head —

'I am used to humiliation. You aren't. You say that we are a grovel-ling spiritless people. We are not! We are prouder than you! We hug our humiliations to our bosom, glorying in the knowledge that we bear a fate heavier than any other people — a fate that would have destroyed utterly any other race. A fate by which the Lord God is testing the worthiness of His Chosen.'

He swung into something on his violin that Anthony had not heard him play before — a rather noble tune in which ran a vein of mockery.

'What's that? That's new!'

'I've just invented it.'

'Composed it, do you mean?' said Anthony, eyeing with astonishment this amazing creature who not only could play the violin but compose the music out of his head.

The amazing creature — sitting on the edge of a dilapidated manger, shabby sleeves showing bony wrists and several inches of forearm; shabby pantaloons revealing a great quantity of once-white stocking; weak eyes staring through the discoloured whitewash of the ceiling into some other and splendid world where the humble and meek were ex-alted — just nodded as if it were the most natural thing on earth. He went on playing.

'Viotti taught me the fiddle when I was little,' he said. 'He said I'd got a natural ear for music — like Mozart. I have made up pieces ever since I was ten . . . I call this "Requiem Mass for a Dead Jew", or "Pavane of the Chamber-Pots".'

CHAPTER V

REWARD FOR AN ARTIST

WHEN he had been at the Institut Putzger for nearly a year, Anthony wrote to his grandmother in his monthly letter —

'I have heard from Uncle Harradence that I am not to come home until the spring of next year. 1800; next century! It seems a very long while off, written like that.' — He had been going to appeal to her, but realized as he put pen to paper how little anything he could say would influence her determination . . . He was rather pleased with the touch about the next century, and he repeated it to himself as he sat, pen in hand, at one of the few wooden tables with which the dark green cavern of a study was furnished. 'I have now been promoted to A section of the *Ecke* which means that I am expected to take turns in giving lessons in German to the more advanced of the day-boys. Herr von Knötel may be severe, but he is a good teacher. An Austrian here says I speak like a native — but with a Prussian accent! But then we talk practically nothing but German all day, except that Radomski (of whom I have written to you) is teaching me Polish.

'I am now taking a course of lessons in sketching and water-colour painting. We are allowed, as you know, to choose some subjects for ourselves. The teacher is an American from Pennsylvania, and, I believe, was a pupil of Mr. Benjamin West, the famous painter. He knows Virginia. He is a very pleasant man who also comes to the Institut as visiting teacher to help with the elementary English class.'

Anthony did not say that his whole purpose in learning the mystery of painting was portraiture — the portraiture of a lady as faintly tinted as the colours of a remembered dream, whose unpicturable grace lay in that suggestion of movement which there is in a garden at daybreak.

Mr. Fulton may have been a student of the celebrated West; may indeed have exhibited at the Royal Academy in London; may have been a professional miniature painter in Philadelphia; but he was a pedestrian artist and no teacher. Dr. Putzger, who looked upon all forms of art as unworthy of attention since they were incapable of being systematized, would not have discovered that fact in half a dozen years: Anthony discovered it in fewer than half a dozen lessons. . . .

Fulton arrived late that autumn morning — as he always did — with the air of someone looking in for just ten minutes between two more important appointments. He came bustling into the converted coach-house which served as the Institut's art centre, out of the rain and the labyrinth of dripping laurels, his threadbare coat glistering with wet, his dark luxurious hair flattened from the downpour.

He slammed the large portfolio he carried onto the table on the little dais where he sat; dried his head, his face, his coat, with a vast red handkerchief; studied an elementary lesson in perspective chalked on the blackboard affixed to the wall behind him; swept his eyes along the semi-circle of eight or nine widely spaced small tables in front; heaved an immense sigh.

'Hell!' said he in English: caught Anthony's eye, and grinned disarmingly.

There was no one else in the Institut Putzger who ever grinned like that — or grinned at all. Anthony grinned back. There was something very likeable in the man's roughly finished face with combatant nose and long cleft chin and big mouth. His combination of threadbareness and boisterousness made him seem something vital in that place of schedule and routine.

He sought in his pockets — in his coat pockets — in his waistcoat pockets — in his fob pockets.

'I've lost the *Schema*,' he said at length out loud with something of an air of relief: addressed himself more particularly to Anthony. 'Do I address the art class in English, French, or German?'

'French, sir,' said Anthony, bobbing up in his seat respectfully. 'There are none who speak much English here except myself!'

Mr. Fulton sighed again.

He proceeded to allocate tasks with great rapidity, and a great fluency of ungrammatical French, and obviously at extreme random.

'You at the end table — I don't know your number, and don't care! — Draw me a hand! Palm upwards, with fingers spread out as though awaiting money. Are you left-handed? No! . . . Then use your own right hand as a model. That will make it more difficult!'

A shelf ran round the bare whitewashed wall of the class-room. On it were a number of plaster casts of hands and arms and feet, of classical masks, of busts of Roman Emperor and Greek orator — a little yellowed by age, but none of them chipped or dusty, or disfigured by facetious pencillings: that would not have been the way at the Institut Putzger! Never!

He took an armful, and walked round dumping them on the various tables with quick instructions, until he came to Anthony.

'You — ' he began: changed his mind: added in English — 'I will find something for you to do later. Meanwhile, you can study these. You will find them instructive.'

He walked to his own table, and returned with the portfolio — a battered thing covered with green oilskin — from which he extracted two papers (Anthony thought that they looked like an engineer's drawings) before he placed it in front of him.

'Very — very instructive!' added Mr. Fulton with a pursed-up smile. Anthony did.

The portfolio contained a collection of Mr. Fulton's water-colours. Poor things in idea and in performance; chiefly concerned, it would appear, with the combination of prison and prayer. There was Lady Jane Grey on the night before her execution, reading in a most enormous Bible with a heart-rending expression and an hour-glass running out at her side: there was Queen Mary of the Scots also studying Holy Writ with an identical expression of countenance by a barred window: there was Katharine Howard doing the same thing in the same way: there was —

At the end, however, were a number of most intriguing little drawings and diagrams in pencil and wash. Of a boat which appeared to have sprouted wheels at the side. Of something which might have been a plough but was not, for it had got a sort of miniature windmill attached to it. Of mysterious canal-locks, and hoists, and wagons, and incomprehensible machines.

These Anthony studied with great interest until he heard Mr. Fulton say —

'Here, you! . . . I don't know either your name or your number — but you who speak English!'

Anthony approached the dais.

Mr. Fulton had been engaged with pencil and compass and ruler on some large diagram. Now he pushed them to one side.

'Well, brother,' said he, 'so you've seen through me! I suspected so the last time I came here. Now you've examined my efforts at high art your suspicions have become a certainty, haven't they?'

'They're all very nice, sir,' commented Anthony, standing in front of the table and endeavouring, without a display of undue curiosity, to make out the nature of the drawing upon which his preceptor was engaged.

'Very nice! Ve-e-ry nice!' repeated Mr. Fulton, tilting back his chair to a dangerous angle. 'Nice — the exact word! The sort of art — God save the mark! — that old ladies in Boston and Philadelphia produce! And, I suppose, old ladies in every other city in the world! Muck! Blather! Bosh! Balderdash! Tosh! Trash! Twiddle-twaddle! . . . I'm not an artist, and shan't be in twice ten thousand years! And don't want to be, Number-whatever-you-are!'

'DA 2, sir,' said the newly-promoted Anthony.

'And don't care either!' continued Mr. Fulton. 'You are the first lad that's looked at all human that has come my way. The rest are either automata or scared out of their lives. But then you're an American! . . . There's the Pole, of course — what's his name? — but he's a Slav and queer, very queer!'

'Radomski!'

'And don't care a damn!'

'No, sir!'

Mr. Fulton started to scratch his rather shaggy head with both hands at once, very vigorously, and in the most plebeian manner.

'Boy!' he said, 'I come here for varying times nine mornings out of the ten in the blasted Republican week. I don't mind telling you that these mornings poison my whole existence . . . Do you know why I come to this soul-destroying warren?'

Anthony could not guess.

'For cash, my innocent friend! For dollars and cents — or their equivalent in the local currency! And for why do I want dollars and cents? . . . Why, for my *real* work, for my life work! . . . And *what* is this life work, you ask with polite interest?'

He opened the portfolio; undid a pocket at the back, and extracted a large water-colour which he presented to Anthony.

It was a portrait of himself — a bit flattering perhaps; fresh colour toned down a trifle; eyes very large and brilliant; chin resting on the folds of a superb neck-cloth; high-collared modish waistcoat; one hand inserted between the buttons of a handsome blue coat, the other holding a large diagram of some sort over his knees like a table-napkin. By his left elbow a noble stream on which floated the demented craft Anthony had already seen — cross between boat and cart: on his right the plough windmill at work upon a field.

'That is a very good likeness, sir,' said Anthony critically — and truthfully, for it was.

'As a map of my face, yes!' replied Mr. Fulton, easing his chair back onto its four legs, so that he might regard the picture. 'As a map, yes. My nose, eyes, chin, etceteras are all in the right geographical positions: in proportion they are of absolutely correct dimensions. But there is no more expression, no more feeling, no more soul about it than there is in the seat of my pantaloons.'

Said Anthony —

'I've got it! You are an inventor!'

'X Y Z! That's the soundest thing you've said since you entered the portals of the Institut Putzger, *fondé en* 1770 "for the higher education of adolescents of the superior classes" — only they've dropped that bit since the Revolution — "with special reference to the knowledge of modern languages". I *am* an inventor. I have given up copying the awful faces of fatheads in favour of originating things. Ideas stream from me! Every day! Every hour! Practicable ideas! Ideas that will benefit man! Ideas that will make work easier — make transport easier — make navigation easier: that will save toilsome labour: that will arm democracy in its fight against tyranny!'

He cast his eyes round the industrious class.

'You — you — *Not* you! — You with the long nose who's drawing a cone!' — It was the Jew, Solomon Klasing — 'Ornament that cone at the base with a Greek key pattern; at one-third of its height with a dog-tooth pattern! On its top put a globe shaded so as to suggest that it's about to fall off! . . . He was beginning to get too curious. That'll keep him quiet for a bit — more than a bit! . . . Where did I get? Yes! I do everything to make money. I'm here to make it. Can you guess what else I'm doing? . . . I'm painting a panorama one hundred and thirty feet long for public exhibition. God in Heaven — forty-three yards and a bit to cover with paint! Mostly yellows and reds and blacks. Leaping flames — rolling clouds of smoke. The burning of Moscow! A safe subject because the damned town has been burned down half a dozen times in the last two hundred years — a lurid one, to wheedle the *sous* out of the Frog-eaters! The show'll be in the Montmartre. It ought to open next year — a new sensation for a new century! You shall come and see it!'

"Thank you, sir,' said Anthony with correct gratitude, wondering how it would be managed; for the boarders of the Institut never left their laurel-guarded seclusion except for an escorted march of six miles at half-past seven in the morning — rain or fine, summer and winter — up to the Palais Egalité, and back by the Champs de Mars.

'And why do I grub for money, and abase myself for money, and beg money, and borrow money, and owe money — mostly owe it! — and do all but steal money? Why? Not for myself! But for my ideas. To make my ideas concrete things! To turn my rope-making machines, my mechanical diggers, my plunging-boats, my torpedoes, my steamboats from designs on a drawing-board into reality!'

'Plunging-boat!' said Anthony.

His mind went back to the debate of the La Cadière parliament, more than a year ago, under the acacias, with the moon on the sea, and Harrady oratorizing on the subject.

He suddenly saw his preceptor, not as a shabby drawing-master, verbose and lazy, but as a genius, a hero — the man who would travel as and where men had never travelled before. He looked now directly at him, as he sat there in his tilted chair, head and shoulders resting against the blackboard with the roughly chalked lines of perspective ornamenting it. Something of this new respect and admiration showed in his demeanour. Mr. Fulton noticed it.

'Good boy, X Y Z,' he remarked, and his whole face lit with pleasure at the tribute of a schoolboy. 'So you've heard of the *Nautilus!* That is as it should be! That confirms my impression of you! That strengthens me in my decision . . . Bring me your sketch-book!'

He ruffled the leaves. Anthony had a certain mechanical efficiency as a copyist. He nodded to himself. Turned to a blank leaf.

'Put your class signature here, brother!'

Anthony, deferential though puzzled, inscribed at the bottom of the page his *Ecke* number with the number of the seat he occupied at the art classes —

'DA 2 Z3.'

Mr. Fulton tore out the page.

'Go back to your seat, Mr. Algebra, and amuse yourself as best you can for a quarter of an hour . . . Draw me a page of noses. There are plenty of odd ones round you! Outlines only. Use your softest pencil.'

For a while all was silence.

Mr. Fulton, bent over his desk, appeared to be very occupied. Presently he looked at the watch he had taken from his fob and set before him. He swept his work on one side, heaved a sigh, and rose to his feet.

'My good Numbers, *attention!*' said he, rapping with his knuckles upon the table. 'I am now about to address you on the mechanics of art. I will give you some advice that should help you to deal with the problems which I have set you.'

Still talking volubly, but standing so that he could watch the door, he proceeded to draw on the blackboard with great rapidity. A cone casting a shadow directly forward. A cube casting a shadow to its right front — to its right rear — illuminated from beneath — lighted from two directions at once.

His quick eyes noted, across the width of the studio, the slow turning of the door handle — very slow, and very silent.

He continued the demonstration faster and more fluently than ever.

The door now began to open. Through the gap came the damp breath of the laurels and the rattle of the rain upon their grim leaves.

Mr. Fulton continued at full tilt.

The huge bald head and little black-cased skeleton of Dr. Putzger appeared in the opening, followed by one of the two square-headed, square-built, black-aproned porters who were always in attendance upon him. The door shut after them.

Mr. Fulton continued to expatiate with the utmost glibness.

'Monsieur Fulton!'

'*Attention! . . . Monsieur le Directeur?*'

The little stalk of bones bore the balloon of head up to the dais. The little thin mouth at the very bottom edge of the diminutive face made some remark. Mr. Fulton made deferential reply. The small blue lips again just parted in speech. Mr. Fulton made even more deferential reply. Mr. Fulton initiated some topic deferentially. He pushed a paper across the table to the notice of the Director who glanced at it, turned his head on its thin neck — as if it were some mechanical device — until he had brought his hot pink-rimmed eyes under their lashless lids to bear on Anthony where he sat at the end table to the left of the dais.

'It is good,' said Mr. Fulton. 'It is extremely good!'

Dr. Putzger regarded for the fraction of a second the high-coloured face of the art master; regarded whatever it was that lay on the table; set the pivoting mechanism to work so that he could regard Anthony; committed himself to his highest meed of praise —

'It is not bad! . . . I accept your recommendation!'

He took a small gold pencil from a pocket in his black moiré silk waistcoat, and wrote something on the paper which had been presented to him: was gone. . . .

Mr. Fulton did not heave a great sigh upon the departure; but his whole attitude was that of one who did so. If ever a face, a figure, a bearing expressed the attitude of a man heaving a sigh, it was Fulton's. He wound up his lecture without ceremony —

'And now, my good Formulae, with this advice and my best wishes you will again settle down to your interesting pursuits! You with the red hair, put another globe on top of the first, falling in a different direction. The shadows will be cast by a light at the opposite side to that which you have planned . . . Y X Z, come here!'

Anthony approached with his page of noses.

Mr. Fulton waved it on one side.

'I don't want to see the damned things,' he said frankly. 'You will have noted my prescience? That comes from an observant mind. I have re-

marked that our revered chief arrives here on his surprise visits at precisely twenty-four minutes past the hour—I always have my watch in
front of me to make sure that I don't give a moment's more instruction
than I am paid for! — I plan accordingly.'

Anthony had remarked the prescience.

The Diviner-of-Futurity held out a sheet of cartridge paper toward his
scholar. The cuff of his coat — frayed and shiny — retreated a long way
up his forearm. The hand was calloused, and stained with acid· and ink,
and considerably chipped.

On the sheet was a sketch of the Diviner's head, a quick pencil copy of
it as it appeared in the water-colour portrait: a very recognizable likeness,
with the geographical exactitude and lack of expression of a map. The
curious and interesting thing about it was that in the bottom right-hand
corner was Anthony's own signature— 'DA 2 Z3'. And, furthermore, on
the top was written in Fulton's sloping hand the words 'Certificate Thesis:
Recommended for consideration. Robt. Fulton'. Underneath was pencilled the angular signature of the head of the Institut — 'R. P.'

Anthony regarded the production with astonishment.

'I consider it quite good,' said the Diviner. 'It is not unlike. It is not
unflattering — an important point when you are portraying your elders
and betters and instructors. On the whole I regard it as showing remarkable promise. I had no hesitation in showing it to Dr. Putzger, and recom-
mending that you should be given your recreation exeat on the score of it
. . . I congratulate you, Mr. Algebra!'

'But — ' began Anthony.

' "But",' echoed Mr. Fulton sending his black eyebrows up towards the
mane of dark hair that by now had recovered from its wetting. 'Give me
no "buts", brother. Did you, or did you not draw this little sketch of me?'

'Well — '

'Nor any "wells"! . . . I don't suppose that you imagine that this drawing evolved itself upon this sheet of paper without human interposition —
or that I did it for you?'

'No, sir!' said Anthony. Looked up. Met the bright humorous eyes of
Monsieur l'Instituteur. Grinned. 'Oh, no, indeed, sir! Thank you, sir!
My own unaided work, of course, sir. I am glad you like it!' Paused. Was
daring. 'I shall do better with more instruction, of course, sir.'

A recreation exeat! It was something beyond all his dreams. It meant
an end of that appalling 'free' day in every ten: a day marked by two
dreary marches instead of one: a monotonous percolation of the labyrinth
of laurels: a miserable effort at entertainment with book or chessboard in
the bare recreation room on the ground-floor, into which the light filtered

through barred windows and a denser wall of laurels than anywhere else. Holders of exeats — and there were very few of them — were permitted, during good behaviour, to pursue their hobbies during all the daylight hours out of doors on their 'free' day. Under supervision, of course. They botanized in the Bois; they listened to fine music at the *Exercices* of the Conservatoire or the Concerts Marbœuf or de Feydeau; they studied architecture among the stones of Paris; they made serious expeditions to the Muséum d'Histoire Naturelle; they —

'You with the red hair!' said Mr. Fulton easily, tilting his chair still further back, and assuring his equilibrium by propping his knees against the edge of his table. Very shiny knees, rubbed to a glass-like surface. Pantaloons generally powdered rather thickly with white chalk dust. 'You with the red hair, alter your shadow now, so that it falls as if your cone were standing upon a plane surface with a light directed on it from above and slightly in front . . . The fellow has got more eyes and ears than God ever intended he should have! . . . Brother Algebra, don't get any false ideas into your head! I am not doing this because I think you are an embryonic Old Master, or for the sake of your beautiful grey eyes! I'm doing it for the sake of the most important person in the world! And that's me!'

'No, sir! Yes, sir!'

'I'm doing it because I shall get a fee for escorting Youth and Innocence about the streets of Paris. All is cash that comes to my net. You'll like a day's freedom: I'll like a day's emoluments. You scratch my back, and I'll scratch yours. But you are mistaken if you think you'll see anything of me from the time we leave this shack hand in hand — or from the time we get out of sight of it — until we meet again at sundown somewhere round the corner and come back looking as if butter wouldn't melt in our collective mouths. Quite mistaken! I can occupy my time very profitably in other ways!'

Anthony did his best to look as if he would regret the deprivation of Mr. Fulton's company. Not very successfully.

Fulton surveyed the slim figure before him with whimsical appreciation.

'How old are you?'

'I shall be eighteen next year, sir.'

'You won't be sorry. At eighteen one does not like shabby companions. Even if they are geniuses or pedagogues from the Institut Putzger!'

Again Anthony was conscious of scrutiny.

'I shan't ask you to behave yourself, because I think you will. I shan't ask you not to let me down, because we are both lone Americans in a hostile and alien world . . . I shall call for you to-morrow morning after breakfast . . . You with the red hair — '

In this way it came about that Anthony was at last able to make some slight acquaintance with the Paris of the Directory. Bankrupt, tawdry Paris where women outdid the Classical Age in a nudity of muslin, and men masqueraded like apes in huge cocked hats and pink-striped pantaloons. Paris where the 'Sacrament of Adultery' had outmoded Holy Mass . . . Where, too, a slight dark man in modest costume quietly strolled the streets — as though he had never stormed across Italy and held princely state in the castle of Montebello; or delivered Egypt from the yoke of the Mamelukes; or had borne last year the title of General of the Army of England; or even now was plotting the overthrow of the Republic.

CHAPTER VI

INTRODUCTION TO A SHIP

MR. FULTON approached the fashionable elegance of the Café des Tuileries, with its blue and white striped awning over the pavement, where his student should be awaiting him. The black boughs of the tall trees in the gardens of the palace opposite were shaking off their foliage against the windy green sky of early evening. The air was full of fluttering leaves — red, and golden, and brown — on their way to dissolution in the thin shining mud of the broad street: they fretted the very smart grey mare of the very smart equipage that was reined in at the curb.

The turn-out was an American whisky — Gallicized by astonishingly high wheels, and by being painted almond green with the seat outlined in cherry red; its little golden lamps shaded like Grecian urns.

A young man with a vacuous pink face held the reins — a face so empty of meaning that there was more character in the enormous cocked hat shaped like a gargantuan slice of melon, which overshadowed it. Beside him sat a young lady in the most classical of costumes, with the most classical of hair-dressing, and the most Parisian of pretty faces. She was bidding an affectionate farewell in a very high-pitched voice to a slim youngster in a blue coat, who stood at the pavement edge.

'Au revoir, my poor, poor exile!' said the classical lady, kissing the bunched-up finger-tips of both little hands, and presenting the result to the gentleman's lips. Fulton noted with some amusement that the latter did not appear quite to know what to do with the gift.

'Till your next day off, then, when we shall not have Henri to discommode us!'

'Till then,' agreed Exile.

At the sound of his voice Fulton sat down on a rush-seated chair at the table nearest to him. To his general air of weariness was added a look of concern.

'You will be a horribly jealous husband, will you not, Henri?'

'*Inc'oyablement!*' said Henri without a flicker of expression.

'You will hurry back from Lyons very fast to assure yourself of my constancy?'

'*Inc'oyablement vite, ma pa'ole d'honneu'!*'

'I will be discreet even if not faithful, I assure you . . . *Au revoir* . . . Anthony darling!'

'*Au revoir* . . . Hortense!' . . .

'So that, young Algebra, is how you study art!' said Fulton, following the retreating equipage with his eyes. He shook his head. 'Examining female pulchritude through one fold of muslin and an equally transparent tissue chemise! To say nothing of the abbreviated tights which barely exist! And "barely" is the right word! What would they say now in Richmond, Williamsburg, Yorktown, or Alexandria — Virginia — and even more so in the celebrated Institut Putzger, 43 Rue du Magistrat, Paris, France, if they thought their little Alge were hand in glove with a *merveilleuse* and her *incroyable?*'

'It was sheer chance that she — ! They saw me as I came in here,' said Anthony facing his preceptor with a bright red face. 'I give you my word of honour!' — ' "Ma pa'ole d'honneu'!" ' echoed Fulton. — 'She is an old — that is to say, an — acquaintance of all my family . . . She — '

'Spare me!' said Fulton. 'Have you any money? Yes! Then you may buy me the least nauseous beverage this place supplies, and after that we must be getting back.'

He stretched out his long legs; dropped his somewhat decrepit hat on a chair, and moodily regarded a truncheon of rolled papers which he held upright in ink-stained fingers on the table.

'This damned Government!' he said rather wearily. 'It is next to impossible to get anything out of them — even a plain "yes" or "no". It's two years — very nearly — since I first put up the idea of the *Nautilus* to them. They're still havering about it. They're still buzz-buzzing. More than a year ago their own bloody commission reported favourably on it!'

Anthony made sufficiently sympathetic noises to induce him to undo the tape that secured the roll of papers. He fumbled with pursed lips among the litter let loose.

'This is the crux of the report of the commission appointed last year by Bruix, the Minister of Marine.'

He read out loud —

' "The arm conceived by Citizen Fulton is a terrible instrument of destruction, because it strikes in silence and in a fashion that is almost certain of effect. It is particularly suitable for use by the French Navy . . . The Commission recommends the Minister of Marine and Colonies to authorize Citizen Fulton to make the machine, and to grant him the necessary funds."

'*Am* I a scatter-brained lunatic, my gentle Alge, or am I not? Am I a fantastic dreamer, or am I not? Is that the report of a committee of technicians made more than a year ago, or is it not? Has anything been done about it, or has it not? Not! . . . You are right! In one word — *Not!* Not! . . . Let us go back to the saner atmosphere of the Institut Putzger!'

As they walked back, Anthony suddenly said a little awkwardly — 'May I say something, sir?'

Fulton, hands and truncheon behind back, lost in thought, absentmindedly gave permission.

'It's Klasing —'

'Klasing?'

'You know . . . "Red-head" — "Long-nose"!'

'I didn't know. I remember. Well?'

'He wasn't being inquisitive — really! It's a sort of enviousness. He has no friends at all. I don't know why! Except me . . . And me only a little! He just has to watch other people being — being friendly!'

'You are suggesting that I should amend my conduct toward him?'

'Well — ' . . .

Solomon Klasing limped into the dusk-haunted desolation of the study as Anthony was peeling off his gloves. His precious violin in its shabby case was cradled before him in both arms. He put it down on one of the bleak tables, and patted it as if telling it that it had been a good child.

He regarded the slim figure in the blue coat — the brown dogskin gloves — the broad-brimmed high-crowned hat — with gentle envy.

'Did you enjoy yourself?' he asked.

'It was wonderful,' said Anthony. 'He left me to myself at the corner!' — There was no one other than themselves in the twilit room — 'And I didn't see him again until half an hour ago!'

'Ah!'

'I went and had a hot bath at the Bains Vigier. It was marvellous! I felt quite new after it, and I walked and walked, and walked. Just anywhere. And I had dinner at a café next to the Théâtre des Variétés. I had lobster, and chicken, and an ice! Then I went to the Louvre. Then I went to the Galeries de Bois in the Palais Egalité. P-p-phe-e-ew! You should see the sort of things they've got in the little shops in the arcades there! Just filthy! You wouldn't believe it! Then I walked in the Tuileries gardens. Then I had two ices in the Café des Tuileries. And then I came back!'

He sighed regretfully and reminiscently.

Klasing sighed too.

'I've been here for four and a half years — no, nearly five! — and I've never been outside except on the official walks! And then nobody ever walks with me — because I can only just keep up, I suppose! Except you — sometimes!'

'So!' exclaimed Anthony in accent of self-reproach. 'I'm sorry! I'll — '

Klasing fumbled in the tails of the worn black coat which he had long outgrown: said rather awkwardly as he did so —

'Oh! It's all right! I am used to it. You have always been very good-natured to me! The only — '

He found what he had been seeking. A pencil, and a piece of paper folded small. He sat down at the table: unfolded the paper, drew rapid lines across it, and began to dot in notes of music. Anthony watched him in silence for a moment or so.

'What's that you're doing?'

'Jotting down a theme that's occurred to me. A good one, too. I shall use it for my thesis for a recreation exeat.'

'What do you call it?'

' "Minuet of the Hanged Jew"!'

'You won't get an exeat for a thing with a title like that!'

'Only to myself, of course! I shall just call it a Minuet. I shan't get an exeat anyhow. I'm a better musician than Schmelzer, and he knows it. I *am* good. Really and truly, without boasting. One day, I hope — ! But they won't give me an exeat! I have tried a dozen times, and I don't think that Schmelzer even looks for one moment at my compositions. Instead they let Uzanne go out, *and* Crété, though they don't know the difference between *pizzicato* and *placabile*! Still, I don't mind — not very much!'

He hummed a note or two: wrote a note or two: regarded the dirty sheet of paper with an enthusiasm which seemed as much too large for his shrunken frame as his coat was too small.

'It's going to be good! One of the best things I have ever done!'

Despite all the prohibitions he opened his violin-case, tenderly un-wrapped the instrument from an old red silk handkerchief and played — very, very softly — a stately and ironic tune set to the measure of a minuet.

It was very nearly dark. As he turned away Anthony cast a glance through the long barred windows, across the waste of laurels, to the high wall of the neighbouring convent. Against the dark ivy-clad back-ground, seen through the mists of evening, he almost thought to see a high gallows from which a grey figure, swinging by the neck at the end of a filament of rope, trod the thin air in a mockery of courtly dance. . . .

The appointment with Hortense proved slightly disturbing. He did not quite know why.

Madame Garnerey — for such was now her name — had a sumptuous apartment on the first floor of a famous and historic house that had once belonged to a famous and historic family. A family whose surviving members were now refugees in England earning their bread by copying music for the Drury Lane orchestra and teaching French and the use of the small-sword.

Hortense was not yet up when he was ushered into her presence by a formidable elderly maid with a dough-like face in which were set two very black currants of eyes.

Hortense was sitting up in bed. Large bed — of a severely classical outline, having a rose-pink coverlet: small Hortense — very classical too, in the transparency of whatever garment it was she wore. Every-thing very classical about the big room, from the Olympian grey of its walls to the curves and lines and ornamentation of chair, and table, and mirror, and couch, which were all scrupulously imitated from Greece or Rome.

He had to sit on the edge of her bed — rather self-consciously — and help her with the morning chocolate.

'My Anthony,' said Hortense, 'figure to yourself that you are an early visitor! It is only half-past eight! I have not been awake at this hour for a year. Figure to yourself the self-sacrifice, my poor exile!'

He figured it to himself: apologized, blushing. He also figured to him-self the reactions of La Cadière if it could see him sitting on Hortense's emperor of beds, eyes fixed on Sèvres cup and silver platter so that they should not offend by too frank an investigation of the alluring folds of gauze at Hortense's bosom.

Hortense beamed at him.

'As you have come thus early, you must make yourself useful. You shall help me to dress!'

This accordingly Anthony did, in the chaperoning presence of the bun-faced maid, who added to his embarrassment by ill-disguised laughter. He failed to see why Hortense needed any help, for she appeared to wear very little more when dressed for the street than when attired for bed . . . Afterwards they drove in a yellow and black chaise to Versailles where they walked in the park, and afterwards lunched in a tiny luxurious restaurant in a nest of a room that was grey and gilt and full of long mirrors.

An elderly gentleman in the height of fashion, having a pink face and a great quantity of white hair that stood on end, came in just after they had begun, escorting two very young, very lively, and extremely pretty ladies. Old — dear — friends of Hortense! A vast of kissing, and curt-sying, and chattering: a moving of glasses, and cutlery, and knives, and tables, and chairs by attentive waiters. Lunch accordingly prolonged itself till very late in the afternoon, the young ladies becoming even gayer than when they arrived — if that were possible — and the old gentleman more and more epigrammatic and delicately indecorous.

Anthony was appalled at the size of the bill which was eventually produced; working out agonizing sums in his head; but Hortense, who had examined it over his shoulder, quietly removed it, and handed it across the table to the old gentleman who tucked it under his plate with his own as if that was what he always expected to do.

'You will bring your friend, then, Hortense, to the party,' said the youngest lady, who at intervals had patted Anthony's hand and presented him with special smiles. 'It will be an orgy — a veritable Roman orgy, I assure you! Lark's tongues and peacock's brains, and all that!'

'Bring your friend, my dear Madame,' urged the elderly gentleman, rising and bowing to her as she prepared to go: paused; added rather slyly, 'You and I are of one mind, I see, Madame!'

Hortense raised her delicate eyebrows.

'We both like them young!'

Hortense had planned that they should go back to her apartment and talk, but it was already late, and she dropped him at the Café des Tuileries where he was to meet Mr. Fulton.

'You shall call for me the week after next,' she said. 'And we will see if we want to go to Monsieur Pontmartin's party. He was a bishop, you know! . . . But we will not go unless you pay no attention whatever to Rachel. She's a minx, and I shall get jealous, you know! Jealous! You wouldn't like me to be jealous, would you, now, my Anthony?"

The closed chaise had come to a halt. Suddenly, in the darkness of its interior he found himself kissing Hortense — or was it being kissed? Warm lips against his; fragrant breath warm upon his cheek; the soft exciting pressure of a warm body against his; the delicate scent of her hair! But it was not merely Hortense that he was kissing, but somebody else's wife!

Overwhelmed by this realization, he got out of the carriage quickly. He wanted to run away, so that in the very act of running he might forget the renewed disloyalty to Jasmine, and the treachery to the pink-faced Henri. . . .

'Woman! Woman!' said Mr. Fulton reprovingly. He was sitting at a table under the blue and white awning, his ink-stained fingers pressed together before him in the travesty of an attitude of propriety. 'No man should have more than three women in his life! If you begin your collection now, my young friend, I hesitate to imagine the figure you will reach!"

'Three,' echoed Anthony, sitting down, still shaken by the moral impact of one.

'Initial experiment! True love! Wife!'

'What about a mother?'

'A class apart!'

'Or grandmother — or mother-in-law — or — ?'

'They are *not* women! . . . I mean women like that alluring and naked young friend of — your family's! I mean women whom one could, would, or should invite between the sheets . . . Dangerous animals — but I am speaking to the initiated! Am I not?'

Said Anthony in a matter of fact manner —

'Oh, I've known — everything — since I was quite little. My uncle thought that I and my cousin ought to know. So we knew!'

'A sensible man!' commented Fulton. 'Still, there's a vast of difference between the theory and the practice — between doing a proportion sum in apples and eating them. In the one case you don't get stomach-ache, in the other you do! . . . Well, now you are here, I really believe that I could do with a large *fine*! . . . Waiter, bring a pen and ink and sheet of paper at the same time!'

He drank the *fine* — for which Anthony paid — at a gulp, and ordered another — for which Anthony also paid.

'They tell me,' he said with a sigh of satisfaction, 'that you speak and write French better than a Frenchman. I want you to translate this letter into French — here and now — so that I can take it home and copy it in my own handwriting. It's to Barras — he's got more power than anybody else in the Directory, I suppose . . . I've always written in English before. Which has added another hurdle for me to clear in dealing with this damned Government!'

He pushed two or three scrawled fragments of paper across the check table-cloth to Anthony.

This would do instead of running away: spiritually he rolled up his sleeves: he wrote, with scratchy quill and violet ink —

'Citizen Director, — From the report of the Commissioners named by the Minister of Marine it would appear that the machine and the means by which I have proposed to destroy the English Fleet are pronounced practicable . . . The enormous commerce of England, as well as its monstrous government, depends upon its navy. Should some warships be destroyed by so novel, so secret, so incalculable a method, the confidence of the seamen will vanish and the fleet rendered useless from the moment of the first alarm. In such a state of affairs the English republicans would rise . . . With England republicanized the seas will be free . . . If at first glance the method I propose seems inhuman, it is only because it is utterly new: in reality it is anything but inhuman. It is in reality the gentlest and least sanguinary . . . end of brigandage . . . Peace to earth.'

So on, and so on. Yards of it!

'Ough!' said Anthony. 'There you are, sir!'

'Thank you, young Alge! You are certain that you've got all the genders right? I never know myself . . . Talking of genders, on mature consideration I opine that it will be for the good of your soul if you spend next Sunday — or whatever they call the damned day — with me, instead of investigating feminine substantives in private chaises! It will be a tax on me, but I feel responsible for you — up to a point! No, I don't want any more brandy, thank you. I have as little to do with drink as with women. And small use for either!' . . .

Once back in the Institut, Anthony meditated with grave concern upon the events of the day. He gave but little information to the avid Klasing.

Even as those knights of Arthur's Round Table who might never see the Holy Grail by reason of their sins, so too was he in fair way to lose the vision of Jasmine. He had sat on Hortense's bed, furtively espying her daring loveliness — with Jasmine's letters in his pocket! He had kissed Hortense in the darkness of her carriage — with Jasmine's letters in his pocket!

Jasmine!

What fruition there should be of his love for her he could not imagine. But certainly no earthly one! The mere suggestion of physical desire would dissipate all the dream. At a gross touch she would vanish like the fairy-ladies of Outre-mer. A mystical union!

Henri — Monsieur Garnerey!

What treachery to an innocent and unsuspecting man to have kissed his wife! His conscience tormented him.

It was curious, though, how little evidence of Hortense's husband there had been amidst the charm and luxury of the apartment on the first floor of that great mansion which once had belonged to the ducal house of Reille. No trace of male inhabitant at all, so far as he had been able to remark, in the white and gold *salon*, with its Aubusson carpet, and *chinoiserie* in almond green and lacquer red: any more than in the bedroom or in the *salle-à-manger* which might have come from Pompeii — almost! . . . He was glad that so long intervened before he must see the place again . . . He could almost hear Garland saying, with laughter in her voice, 'Was it nice, Rowley? Did you enjoy it?' . . .

There was a brightness in Fulton's face which slowly faded through the week, until by the end of it he looked careworn, and only recollected the invariable routine of Dr. Putzger's surprise visit to the art class on Nonidi with a minute or so to spare.

'You've had no word from Monsieur Barras?' asked Anthony, already certain of the reply, as they walked down the Rue du Magistrat on the next day.

'Not a word!'

He snapped out the sentence as though it were an execration, and increased the length of his stride.

They seemed to walk for an eternity: crossed the Seine: plunged into a confusion of mean streets in the Faubourg Ste Antoine: came at last to a narrow steep lane, at the end of whose perspective of wet cobblestones and dingy overhanging houses was a grey segment of river.

At the entry was a little drink shop, its doorway — surmounted by the legend 'Café du Bon Jacobin' — two steps down from the street. Fulton stumbled down the steps, and dropped on to a wooden form close to a dirty lead-covered counter.

There was no one within except an itinerant vendor of hot sausages — a huge dishevelled woman — asleep on a stool against a wall on which was spread out and nailed the faded glory of a revolutionary flag of one of the battalions of the National Guard. A complicated affair showing a lion carrying the Cap of Liberty.

'I am going to break my oldest rule,' said Fulton, 'by drinking before midday. *You* can watch me! . . . I am very tired. Beside my ordinary work last night I made four copies of the letter I sent to Barras. One for each other member of the Directory. One for Sieyès, damn him! One for Ducos, damn him! One for Gohier, damn him! And one for Moulin, damn *him!* One for each of the five Kings of France, damn them! I wasn't in bed before three! . . . I wish there was something long and strong to drink, instead of these sickly French messes!'

'Champagne?' suggested Anthony.

'They haven't got it, and I can't afford it!'

But Anthony had just received his quarter's allowance, and so *could* afford it; and on inquiry the *patronne,* an old lady with fiery face and grey moustache, *had* got it — just one half bottle; without doubt the remains of loot from some great house five or six years ago.

In such case Mr. Fulton did not need much pressing, and furthermore was prepared to lace the beverage with a full tot of the best brandy to be had.

'This constant delay is fearfully disheartening! Even to me — and I am, on the whole, pretty much of an optimist,' he remarked, watching the bubbles rise from the straw-coloured wine, which had been poured into a blue and brown earthenware mug. 'Beside, I am very nearly at the end of my resources. I can't go on much longer!'

Anthony delicately inquired into the cash prospects from the *Nautilus.*

'I have been very moderate,' answered Fulton, swallowing half the draught. 'I have asked for the cost of construction, naturally, and reasonable pay for myself and my assistants. I then propose that they should give me so much for every English ship I succeed in destroying. At the rate of eight hundred dollars a gun. You see? If I get a first-rater, say a seventy-gun ship-of-the-line, then I make fifty-six thousand dollars. If it's a forty-gun frigate, then it's only thirty-two thousand. It seems to me a very fair way of doing it, don't you think so?'

Anthony thought that it was.

The other drained his mug and rose to go.

'It's all very well talking in thousands of dollars when you don't know where to — Come along! It's very close now!'

He watched with frank interest when Anthony produced his purse of blue netted silk and paid with a piece of gold. Checked the change for his charge with avuncular care.

The downward slope of the lane ended at a high wooden barricade and gate which had once been painted light green, and bore right across it the almost illegible inscription 'C. Perrier, *Chantier de Construction*'.

All the filth and rubbish of the alley appeared to be in the process of piling itself against the obstruction — rags, bones, broken crockery, straw, paper, and a litter of drowned kittens. From over the wall came a little crisp tapping and the subdued song of a saw.

'I rely upon your word of honour as a gentleman,' said Fulton, as they halted, 'to say nothing whatever of what you will see, until I give you permission.'

With that he set up a most enormous kicking and rapping at the gate. After the lapse of considerable time the noises beyond were stilled, while whoever was there listened.

'Heigh! Perrier, it's me — Fulton!'

After a further interval the gate was opened by a little man with the mild long face of a sheep. He was enveloped in a once-white smock and crowned with a filthy cotton night-cap, so that he looked like an ancient ram that had just got out of an extremely dirty bed in which a paint pot or two had been spilled. He carried a small smoothing-plane.

They came into a very minor shipbuilder's yard, littered with little boats in various stages of decay or repair, stacks of timber, windlasses, coils of rope, rusty anchors, stray spars — all resting on an oozy substratum compound of mud, green slime, wood-shavings, and old nails. Everything about the yard looked as if it had been left in a great hurry by someone who had been called away in a great hurry to leave something else somewhere else in an equally great hurry. Even the ancient ketch, which drooped wearily over on one side at the top of the stone slipway that slanted down to the grey water, looked as if it had been mislaid and forgotten after its battered hull had been patched with bright new timber. Beyond this forlorn ship was a long low workshop with steep tiled roof and leaded windows, from most of which the glass was missing.

The noise of hammering and sawing began again as they made their way to the building across an infinitude of obstructions.

The interior of the workshop was dark, and aromatic with the smell of tar and freshly sawn wood.

In the middle of its gloom shimmered a large, many-ribbed silver-grey skeleton of timber upon which two or three men were at work with plane and hammer — a skeleton such as a gargantuan sausage might have (if sausages were to have skeletons) thought Anthony, recalling the rather stubby wares of the *marchande de saucisses*.

'Well, what do you think of her?' asked Fulton, but did not await an answer; plunged forthwith into a most technical discussion with the sheep-faced man.

With a quick surge of excitement Anthony realized that before him was the submarine boat, *Nautilus,* materializing from an inventor's dream, sketch, scale drawing.

For an instant he was borne back to La Cadière and Harradence's parliament at table under the shivering acacias, with the black and silver Mediterranean whispering to itself far below; and Uncle Harrady laying down the law on under-water navigation; and all his imaginings; and Garland's outbreak . . . and Jasmine . . . and Hortense!

The hull of this fantastic craft that should float hidden from the eye of man beneath the tides, and bring destruction to towering ships of war, was both larger and yet smaller than he had thought.

In the dusky workshop, resting upon the chocks, the *Nautilus* seemed an incredibly bulky thing to swim or sink at will. A little man with a face grey with sawdust, was sitting straddlewise — as if riding her — on the top of one of the curved ribs, affixing some metal contrivance to the framework of a sort of cupola near her pointed bows: his feet hung far above Anthony's head.

She wasn't like a sausage, he decided; she was like a whale, as big as a cottage.

When he paced her, however, he found that she was only a trifle more than seven yards long, whilst from where her keel should have been to the top of the cupola, too, was barely ten feet.

Forward she had already been floored within, and he stepped up on the narrow planking, to realize that it would be barely possible to stand upright inside except under her queer little dome — *calotte,* or skullcap, was what Fulton called it afterwards. It was like being in a tunnel or large drain.

One of the shipwrights — another goblin with a dusty face — was nailing the skin on to the ribs, smooth slim planks with long copper nails. In the few seconds that he remained there unnoticed, Anthony visualized the bare bones of the ship clad with their timber covering, and himself still standing within the narrow vault, its white walls faintly illumined with greenish light, moving soundless through the silence of the under-sea. He could almost smell the brine, and see the sweat trickling down the curve of the vessel's ribs and wall . . . Or could you hear the roar of waves and the whine of the wind far beneath the surface, and the trickle of the sea along the sides?

'Now you're here, you may as well be useful,' said Fulton interrupting his day-dreams. 'Put that very fine hat of yours on the least dirty bench, and borrow a smock from someone! . . . Heigh, Perrier, can you find a night-shirt that'll fit my young friend? . . . Citoyen Perrier — Citoyen Purvis, an American — good Republican, like me!'

Citoyen Perrier grunted without enthusiasm: found a smock of re-

markable filth, without enthusiasm; and then left them to their own
devices.

For the rest of the day Anthony acted the part of fitter's mate to Fulton,
attending on him with carpenter's pencil and folding rule, with measur-
ing tape, cheap notebook — in which occasionally the inventor made
incomprehensible calculations — and set-square.

Fulton talked all the time.

Anthony gathered that in the cupola there would be a man-hole
through which the crew would enter the boat, and small circular lights
with very thick glass, as well as a device whereby the deadly burden of
explosives which the *Nautilus* towed would be attached to her victim.
The day's job had some connection with a metal shaft that was to drive
a four-bladed propeller.

'How?' he asked.

'There'll be a handle in the forward compartment which two of the
crew will turn. I calculate on a normal speed of two knots.'

Could one by just winding a handle drive that bulk through the re-
sistant sea? — he wondered.

They broke off at two o'clock — the ordinary workman's dinner time
— for refreshment. Taken at the Café du Bon Jacobin, which provided
them with beer and bread, while the itinerant sausage merchant sufficiently aroused herself at intervals from her doze to produce two brace
of sausages from a dirty canvas bag attached to her person, fry them in
the pan which was tied to her waist, over the small portable charcoal
stove on the tray which was slung around her neck.

After that interlude they continued work on the *Nautilus* until late
in the afternoon.

It was as they were preparing to leave that Citoyen Perrier sidled up
to Fulton, looking more than ever like a goblin ram that had just got
out of bed — on the wrong side. He said something that Anthony did
not hear. Fulton protested. He said something else, whereat Fulton protested still more vigorously. Then the citoyen's voice rose to a loud bleat,
like that of a demented sheep, while the various other goblins ceased work
to listen and watch and make approving noises and spit in the most fluid
manner.

The purport of Perrier's remarks appeared to Anthony to be that the
citoyen was an honest man, and that something-or-the-other would not do
— was not the French way — was not the Republican way! So what did
the Citoyen Fulton propose to do about it?

Presently Fulton came to Anthony standing at some little distance by
the door.

'Got any money, my young Algebra?' he said: and his naturally florid face was very red.

'Yes, sir,' said Anthony, seeking the blue netted purse. 'How much do you want?'

'The fact is that somehow these swine have scented out that I am in low water. They decline to go on unless I pay them their wages in advance for the week. A matter of two hundred livres — forty dollars. And I can't! By God, I have paid everything up to date, and they won't trust me even till to-morrow! The bloody lice!'

Anthony tilted the contents of his purse out into the palm of his hand. There was a little heap of shining gold — five-dollar pieces — representing the greater part of his quarter's allowance which was a not ungenerous one.

Fulton's face brightened.

'Lend me fifty dollars! That'll keep them quiet all right. They won't have seen so much gold in years! Not real good gold! . . .' He took the money, made note of the amount in a battered pocket-book, and walked across to Perrier — 'Here you are, you snot-nosed Shylock, you perverted pastry-cook! Here's the filthy money for your left-handed coal-heavers! And, by God, if there's so much as half an ounce of copper nails unaccounted for in the final reckoning, I'll have you up before the tribunal!'

Apparently he knew his man, because they were escorted to the gate by the citoyen and full staff, all protesting that they had been greatly misunderstood — that the poor must live — that in these uncertain times — that the price of bread — that the Government —

It was the first of many such days. Anthony played the truant from Hortense (to whom he wrote a regretful note) and from Monsieur Pontmartin's 'veritable orgy' of a party. He lived from one week to the next, and even grudged the occasion when he was introduced to a coldly bright Montmartre studio, one complete wall of which was occupied by an immense section of the panorama of the great fire of Moscow a century before. He was even unstirred by the presentation of a pot of yellow paint and a pot of red, and instruction in the art of depicting excessively lurid flames. Years afterward, however, Anthony recalled with grim amusement his small share in creating that ironic prophecy of the events of 1812.

Under his eyes the *Nautilus* took shape; her frame was clothed in timber; her metal cupola adjusted with its tiny port-holes and water-tight hatch; her rudder assembled with the fins that should direct her plunge or rise. He learned her every detail: he studied Steel's *Elements of Mast-making, Sail-making and Rigging,* an old French manual for ship-builders borrowed from Fulton, and a still older copy of *A Mariner's Hornbook,* which he lighted on at a book-stall on the *quais.*

There came at last the momentous day when the propeller shaft was finally bedded, and Fulton span it quickly for a minute or more so that the screw whirred round before the enchanted gaze of Anthony and Citoyen Perrier and his workmen.

The dream had become a reality; midwived by a goblin crew, and born in dilapidated shed in muddy yard lying between stinking river and stinking streets!

Fulton had always believed! So had Anthony! Now Citoyen Perrier professed that such, too, had always been his faith! He capered about the hull, rubbing a great ball of wood-shavings between his hands —

'Aha! The filthy English — she will sting them! Won't you, my beauty?' — Expectoration. — 'She'll give them a sore bottom! Won't you, my pretty sword-fish?' — Expectoration. — 'Old Perrier and his merry boys will help to teach the murdering pirates a bloody lesson!'

He clapped Anthony on the back, and all the merry boys growled agreement, and expectorated, too, in a juicy manner right and left, as if firing a salivary salute to the *Nautilus.*

Much remained to be completed. Collapsible mast for surface sailing — resembling a bat's wing or an insane umbrella: controls for towing, affixing, and firing the 'torpedo'; for anchoring; for altering the plane of natation: pumps for sucking in or expelling the water ballast that should make her sink or rise: caulking: painting.

But Citoyen Perrier made no further difficulties. Presumably Fulton had obtained funds, although he did not return to Anthony his fifty dollars. The source of supply was quite clearly not governmental, for at intervals the American would curse the Directory and all its works — or lack of them — with great fluency. . . .

Anthony came into the study out of the November fog and dusk. The shiny green walls had a yellow glaze on them from the light of the swinging oil lamps, which did not illumine so much as emphasize the darkness of a room as iced and hostile as though it were the recreation place of the tree-spirits that might frequent the laurels.

Klasing sat crouched at a table, his head buried in his arms. He was alone — but then he was always alone! He did not look up; although Anthony knew that he was aware of his presence. He had given up asking eager questions about the outer world, because Anthony, by very reason of his pledge to Fulton, was unable to tell him anything except a chronicle of weather and walk.

Anthony's heart misgave him.

'Cheer up, Solly!' he said. 'Heard the news?'

Solly lifted his head. His weak eyes were red-rimmed; his sallow face, green-shadowed, was ghastly in the hideous light of the hideous room.

'Good God! What's the matter?'

'Oh, nothing more than usual! Just the accumulation of the usual, in fact! . . . What were you going to tell me?'

'There's been another revolution! That's all!' said Anthony, a trifle hurt at lack of interest.

'Oh!' said Solly, obviously just registering the fact, and no more. Obviously uninterested in revolutions.

'You've heard about it?'

Solly made an uncertain gesture with his head —

'One of the day-boys said his father said that the Government had bolted to St. Cloud and Bonaparte was going to seize power. I heard him talking about it during my geography class. Then somebody fell on him, and they had a free fight! Somebody else hit the blackboard with an inkpot. They always have a conversazione and then a battle during the classes I take! . . . And then, of course, in the middle of it, Putzger came in!'

'Bad luck!' said Anthony, still full of his news. '. . . Fulton and I saw General Bonaparte this morning driving down to St. Cloud. In the Rue de Sèvres. There was an absolute procession of carriages and carts and vans, all going the same way through the fog. All of them packed. He was a bit pale, and people shouted at him! . . . But it was exciting to have seen the start of a new *régime!* . . . He'll pull it off, all right; He looks the sort! . . . Will he make himself King? . . . I remember him when I was a little boy . . . Fulton says — '

Fulton had said 'By God, and it's time, too! Now we may get something done! A man of action at last!' and had stamped on, swinging his arms like a windmill. Had spent a serious part of the day evolving fresh propaganda on behalf of the *Nautilus* to a fresh ruler, whilst his young companion absent-mindedly packed the plunging-boat's water-pumps with grease, recalling the encounter on the mountain road: recalling the noise of the great guns on their way to Toulon — his grandmother's leap upon Hurrell — the often-told tale of his father's death — the hideous stripping of a proud man into a scarecrow figure of ghastly fun.

Now Klasing said in his high weak voice —

'Well, it won't make any difference to me!'

'Don't be so despondent! I suppose it's those damned chamber-pots!'

'It's everything! . . . It's everybody — No, not you! — I'll always be an outcast! Even Radomski — and he's usually kind — said to-day that all Jews stink!'

'He's a liar! Why did he say it?'

'He saw that thing I wrote — the "Requiem Mass for a Hanged Jew." He said the title was blasphemous. I didn't mean it to be.'

'He's a fool. I'll make him read the *Pseudoxia Epidemica*, which says that Jews are the cleanest of all races! My uncle says it's one of the greatest books in the world!'

'Don't say anything about it. It wouldn't make any difference. I wish I had gone to an ordinary school. But this place had such a reputation that it seemed a wonderful opportunity. Still, I can't change now — all the money is gone, and I'm under indenture. Knotty has been after me all day. These Germans are frightful to my people! . . . Do you know that they made me an outcast the day I was born?'

'I thought you were Dutch!'

'I'm not anything! I was brought up by an aunt in Holland, but I was born in Berlin!'

'Then you're German!'

Klasing shook his head.

'I wasn't allowed to live there . . . You see, my father had already had two children!'

'But — '

'Father was reader at a synagogue. So he had what they call "hereditary right of residence", and he and Mother could have one child. That was my eldest brother. Then my sister was born. Father had to pay an enormous fine — seventy thousand thalers! The congregation raised the money. Then I came — I wish I hadn't! — and there was no more money, so they had to send me away as soon as I was born. To Holland — to an aunt. I've never seen my Mother or Father. They're too poor to come so far!'

He sighed.

'Oh, well! . . . I've thought of a new tune. Really good!' — He drew a piece of paper towards him — ' "Lullaby for a Latrine Attendant"! How do you fancy that?'

CHAPTER VII

THE UNKINDNESS OF THE LAUREL
BUSHES

THEY came back to the class-room from a morning walk in the drenching rain of February. The harsh brightness of the laurel-green walls was hazed with damp, and the small iron stove at the far end of the room did little but warm the back of Herr von Knötel, who was already seated in his place at the top of the baize-covered table like a croupier at some solemn game of chance. He sat with folded arms resting on the table, and watched his class file in, his pale convex eyes entirely expressionless, the little tufts of black hair jutting from his nostrils as if he were puffing out black smoke.

Uneasy under that unmoving stare the students settled in their numbered seats, before the numbered squares of the table-cloth, and made ready books and papers. It was a full gathering of both the senior sections of the *Deutsche Ecke* — now twelve, all told.

Von Knötel did not break silence for a full minute after the last student had ceased rustling. From long experience everyone knew that such silence was ominous: everyone, accordingly, sat looking straight before him at his opposite neighbour, or down at his work. Except Anthony, who — at the top of the class, on von Knötel's right — furtively examined the master's big square-ended fingers with square-cut nails as they slowly kneaded his upper arm. They were black with hair — no, fur! He wondered why von Knötel should have so much hair upon his hands when there was so little upon his head.

Knotty suddenly began to speak in the mumbling sort of purr in which Anthony imagined a priest of the cat gods of Bubastis adjuring worshippers. Another ominous sign! He continued, too, in measured periods instead of a staccato metre of snarls and purrs and growls. Still more ominous!

'This morning,' said Knotty, 'we are about to study history in its widest sense; and I am going to draw your attention to certain tendencies which have recurred again and again over vast periods of years. I will take, for example, that hatred of the Jewish race which has manifested itself in many ways in Europe during the course of many centuries. . . .'

Anthony stole a quick glance at Solomon Klasing on the other side of the table. He had gone even more deathly white than usual, and was shivering.

'. . . In antiquity the cause of that hatred was racialism — the dislike of the Western races for the Eastern. We are in the process of outgrowing that stupidity!

'In the Middle Ages the cause was religion. We are in the course of realizing that one God — if there is such a Being — is much the same as any other!

'In this New Age we have analysed the cause as nationalism — nationalism, which is the realization by the individual of his citizenship of a state, and of his responsibilities to that state. We have discovered that the Jew does not make a good citizen. He takes all from the nation: he gives nothing to it. In Germany he is the usurer. In Galicia he is the drink-shop keeper. In Russia the keeper of the house of ill-fame. In France — which foolishly enfranchised the Israelite at the time of the Revolution — he has been the *agioteur,* the principal participator in the traffic in funds and commodities which has ended in the bankruptcy of the country and the ruin of three hundred thousand families!'

Herr von Knötel paused for a moment. His great fingers never ceased to knead the great muscles under the tight-fitting black sleeve. Everybody was watching him. He switched his gaze from the blank wall at the end of the room to the trembling figure of Klasing, as abruptly and swiftly as though his eyes were controlled by machinery.

What's going to happen? — thought Anthony — The unjust, dirty swine! He could not bear to look at Klasing, and knew that Radomski was shifting uneasily in his chair.

Von Knötel's voice dropped to the gentle purr of a somnolent cat. He still regarded Klasing.

'The Jew is in fact anti-social . . . I will give you an instance.' The purring grew louder. 'From within our own walls — unfortunately! Stand up, B 2! Stand up, miserable youth! Stand up, I tell you!'

Purr had become growl. Growl had become snarl.

At the last yarr the wretched Klasing rose to his feet, and stood leaning and shuddering over the table, his mouth fallen open and his hands making little feeble gestures of self-exculpation for some unknown offence. His wristbands appeared to have travelled half-way up his forearms. The knot of his travesty of a neck-cloth had slipped, and the gills of his soiled shirt-collar fallen away from a neck as scraggy as an old man's.

'We are here all members of a community — the Institut Putzger, which is, so to speak, the microcosm of a state. We owe it loyalty, obedience, and certain duties. By due performance we earn certain privileges. Have *you* duly performed all your duties, B 2?'

Knotty's voice purred tender anxiety.

Klasing, hands twitching at side, croaked —
'Yes, sir!'
'In return for giving certain elementary instruction in Dutch and in one or two other subjects to the junior classes, B 2, you have been granted the privilege of a free education at this establishment. Is not that so?'
'Yes, sir!'
'You have justly earned this privilege?'
'Yes, sir!' said Klasing, and his air was one of apologizing for his very existence.
'Will you explain to me, then, why at four o'clock yesterday afternoon a class of small boys had been awaiting instruction by you in elementary geography for over an hour?'
Stunning realization of his offence was obvious in Klasing's unlovely face. His long stringy throat swallowed convulsively. He remained silent.
'That you are lazy and untidy reflects discredit on the Institut, but principally affects yourself and your future. That you lamentably fail in the small duty which you owe our community, shows how little you care for anybody except yourself. You are anti-social, B 2, a bad citizen. And bad citizens in good communities are punished.'
For God's sake don't prolong the fellow's agony! — thought Anthony, and shifted his regard from Klasing to the barred oblong of the window behind the lad, with its shabby vista of grey sky and harsh shrubbery.
'Dr. Putzger made this discovery. He brought his well-found complaint to me. I investigated. I found that, instead of performing your duties, you were engaged in scratching out tunes in the stable on a fiddle! You were lost to all sense of time and responsibility. I said nothing. This morning during your walk Dr. Putzger and I pursued our investigations. We found these —'
From under a sheet of foolscap he produced to sight a mass of manuscript on all sorts of odds and ends of ragged paper.
Klasing darted a horrified glance at them: looked back at the broken binding of the book lying on the table before him. His hands no longer twitched, but he swayed forward as if he were about to faint.
Knotty turned over the leaves, reciting in a gentle purr the titles of the various pieces —
' "Pavane of the Chamber-Pots" . . . "Prayer of Humble Access: from a Mass for a Dead Jew" . . . "Minuet of the Hanged Jew" . . . "Lullaby for a Latrine Attendant" . . . "Song of a Gelded Cat" . . . That is dedicated to Adalbert von Knötel! "Song of a Gelded Cat!" In G sharp minor, and dedicated to me! A questionable honour, I opine! . . . "Hymn to Jehovah" . . . And so on!'

Radomski—the indomitable—made no effort entirely to suppress a snigger: he even turned a sardonic face toward his preceptor as he did so, as if to draw Knotty's attention. Anthony wished that he had the moral courage to make such comment.

Von Knötel raised his eyes from the papers: he did not look at Radomski: he just stared for a second down the room into space, as though to advise the offender that he had taken note, but was too engaged to deal with him at that moment. He said—

'Our anti-social Jew has been too busy with the compilation of his obscenities to attend to his duties! He has been too occupied in offending against every canon of good taste—in blaspheming against the religion of his fellow-students—in mocking his instructor! . . . We must cleanse the place of this pollution!'

He rose to his feet: towered for an instant over his silent class—huge and threatening as Moloch. Then he turned to the small stove at his back, opened the lid at the top, and thrust into the orifice the mass of manuscript.

It was all done with astonishing swiftness, and he was sitting down again, leaning forward upon his folded arms, almost before anyone had realized what had happened; whilst Klasing with a broken cry yet jerked over the table and stretched out a restraining hand.

'Such are Dr. Putzger's instructions! . . . Furthermore,' said Herr von Knötel—and Anthony could almost have sworn that he licked his lips —'we must make certain that our friend attends to his duties. We must see that he devotes his time to imparting and receiving instruction and not to creating pollution. It has been decided—Dr. Putzger has decided —that his fiddle shall be impounded whilst he is under the roof of the Institut Putzger. It *is* impounded. It has *already* been impounded— during his absence! . . . I will now return from the specific to the general. I—'

Klasing uttered a feeble cry.

'Oh, no!' he said, and 'Oh, no!'

And the tears streamed down his ugly face.

'But—Ah, yes! Ah, yes!' mimicked Herr von Knötel.

'You can't do it! . . . You won't do it! . . . I've nothing else—nobody else! My only—Oh, please! *Please!*'

Klasing's voice rose to a scream. He stared at the big calm man incredulously, fearfully, hopelessly. He flung himself down on his knees and prayed to him with a babble of words and clasped outstretched hands as one imploring a god. A god without mercy.

Anthony was suddenly aware that Radomski had risen beside him and was speaking in the icy correct voice he always used to the Institut staff — the voice of one declining to weary himself with the trouble of emphasis or inflexion for a barbarian.

'In the matter of the geography class, Herr von Knötel, I — and I alone — am to blame. I promised B 2 to see to it for him, and forgot!'

By God, Radomski had guts! Why hadn't *he* said that?

Knotty was the only person in the room whose eyes were not turned on the Pole. He continued to search for some place in his book: he spoke without looking up — very gently, very contentedly, rather sleepily, like a cat that has had all the milk and all the mouse that it wants.

'Since when has a Polish nobleman — a descendant of the Jagellons, I believe? Correct me if I am wrong! — deputized for a Jew pupil-teacher? . . . We will revert to our studies. A 3, I want you to tell me in as few words as possible the effects of — '

But Klasing's crying had not ceased. Nor the stream of frenzied appeals, of frantic promises, broken by sobs and hiccoughs. It was rather horrible. Despair without dignity.

' — Put the wretched creature outside the door!' said Herr von Knötel.

Anthony found his blazing sympathy for Klasing quenched; was ashamed of himself therefor; found that Radomski had risen; found himself rising too; found himself helping to lift the sagged figure to its feet — to half-carry, half-drag it into the passage without, where it collapsed in a huddle on the floor. Pole and American exchanged glances and helpless shrugs.

'You are a stout chap!' said Anthony in a low voice, hand on door handle.

'Fellow feeling!' said Radomski with a bitter smile. 'He represents a race, and I represent a nation, that Europe wants to obliterate! . . . Besides, I am going at the end of the month — '

Half an hour later Dr. Putzger appeared in the doorway, stealthily as ever, hands behind back, huge head wilted a little on its thin stalk, black-aproned attendant behind him. As usual he said nothing for a few seconds. As usual Herr von Knötel ignored his presence. At last he materialized —

'Herr von Knötel!'

'*Achtung! . . . Herr Direktor?*'

Everybody rose to their feet.

'I wish to speak a few words with you in private, Herr von Knötel!'

With long soft tread the big man approached his chief. They stepped out into the passage. The door closed behind them. Through its panels the murmur of their voices reached the silent class. Presently the door half-opened again.

'Exactly!' said Knotty.

Continuing murmur.

'Just so!' said Knotty.

'My own view!' said Knotty.

'As you say, *Herr Direktor!*' said Knotty finally; and he came in to conclude the lesson.

Dr. Putzger presumably departed. Anthony pictured his great balloon of a head floating down the green darkness of the passage, with body and legs and arms trailing from it as if he were a cephalopod in the depths of a submarine cavern.

After the lecture was finished — and it was mechanically efficient like everything else he did — von Knötel drew his papers toward him; quelled the rustle of the class making ready for departure, with a prefatory growl; gathered their fixed attention with a cold stare along the ranks on either side of the long table.

'No reference of any sort whatever,' said he in his most rasping voice, 'will be made to the degrading spectacle you witnessed in this class-room a short time ago! In all circumstances it will be kept to yourselves! You will make no mention of it to any other person, or speak of it to one another within the hearing of others! . . . It is understood?'

Again the cold stare swept his class.

'Yes, sir!' said someone, and a ragged chorus of 'Yes-sirs' followed. Anthony noted that Radomski — like himself — said nothing. So, too, did Knotty. His chill eyes paused before the Pole.

'It is understood, A 2?'

There was an appreciable pause; but Radomski, with departure still a month away, was not yet prepared wholly to defy authority. He said curtly —

'Yes!'

— *I* won't say 'Yes!' stammered Anthony's soul to itself. — I won't! I swear I won't. Damn the cold-blooded pig! . . . In some occult way to do so would be a betrayal of the wretched Solly. But Knotty was apparently satisfied, and he was not asked to put his conscience to the test.

Anthony collected up pencils and sketch-book for the art class in silence. He was the only one of the *Ecke,* with the exception of Solly, to take the subject, and he went solitary down the corridor and out into the wilderness of laurels and gravel that was the recreation ground.

A watery sun was just visible through a veil of melancholy cloud. The wet slates of the roof of the convent opposite had a pale shimmer on them, and the dark repellent shrubs about the house returned a few sparkles and glints of the despondent radiance.

In the gap in the rampart of laurels by the door, one of the Institut attendants was busied, collecting slivers of glass from the ground into his wheelbarrow. He was Lacroix, a cheerful little fellow, French, nearly square, with a face as brown and wrinkled as a baked apple.

'What — ?' began Anthony: automatically looked back at the house.

All its rows of clean — too clean — windows had caught a little of the thin sunshine and gave back some glimmer of it. All except one on the top floor which gaped black, its empty oblong fringed with spikes and spears of jagged glass.

He knew instinctively what had happened. He went very white. He felt cold with sickness and with anger.

'Did — did he kill himself?' he asked.

'You know, then?' said Lacroix. 'They told me to say nothing. But if you know already — ! He got up on the window ledge, and jumped through the glass. Straight out! I was here. I heard the glass go and looked up. He was spread out in the air like a bat!'

'Did he kill himself?' repeated Anthony.

Oh, God! Poor Solly!

No: the laurels had declined to abet his escape. They had broken his fall, so that he should not die, although the breaking glass had sliced the tendons of his left wrist. There were, of course, some serious head wounds too.

Lacroix would have gone into details but for the sound of footsteps by the door.

Anthony, escaping, went into the shrubbery opposite the stable — that stable where Solly had composed the 'Minuet of the Hanged Jew' — burst into tears, and was violently sick. He eventually arrived, white and shaken, in the coach-house studio, with the stately and ironic tune of Solly's dance tinkling from afar off in his ears.

Fulton flicked aside his apologies for lateness, flicked him to his seat. He was engaged in dumping round the plaster casts at random before the students. When he had completed the operation and returned to the dais, he beckoned Anthony to him.

'I have had no word yet from the blasted Citizen-General,' he complained. 'I'll get you to help me compile a snappy reminder! Curse him!' Examined Anthony more closely. 'I don't know what has come to the class to-day. You are late and look as if you had seen a ghost. And somebody else hasn't turned up at all.' His eyes ranged semicircle of chairs and bent studious heads. 'Our friend with the carroty wig! What's the matter?'

'By God!' said Anthony. 'It's been a filthy, dirty, medieval business! Listen!'

In a very low voice, and leaning over the table, he recounted the story of Solly, so far as he knew it.

'If I could afford it,' said Fulton, when he had finished, 'I'ld rub Dr. Putzger's nose in every chamber-pot in the place — and I would make sure first that they were full! As for von Knötel, and his other bullies, I'ld — '

His eye caught his watch. He raised his voice.

'For a few moments now, before you become too immersed in your respective tasks — Go back to your seat, young Alge! — I wish to draw your attention to one of the simpler rules — ' . . .

But when the time for Dr. Putzger's surprise visit had been overpassed by a full ten minutes, he wearied, bade his class resume their tasks, and summoned Anthony to his side once more.

'Tell me it all over again,' he said. 'I want to make sure I've got it right.'

Listened intently to the narration, head supported on a hand.

'You are not exaggerating?'

'Not a word!' Anthony assured him. 'Every master trampled on him, and most of the fellows treated him as if he were mud. Except Radomski.'

' — And yourself!'

'I used to be ashamed of being so friendly with him — sometimes!' said Anthony in confessional, and red-faced.

'And he was really the genius you say?'

'I don't know, of course, though his music seemed to me awfully good — and clever! . . . But I saw a letter from Viotti — '

'Who's he?'

'The greatest violinist in the world — ' — 'Never heard of him!' — 'He was teaching Solly for some while. It was a long letter. He called Solly a born musician and prophesied a wonderful future for him. I think Solly had sent him the "Pavane of the Chamber-Pots"!'

'I doubt if Red-Head ever plays the violin again. You can't with cut wrist tendons, you know!'

They both fell silent. Anthony knew that his eyes had filled again with tears. He held his head down so that Fulton should not see.

Fulton had been leaning back in his favourite attitude, head against blackboard, chair tilted perilously, trodden over and muddy shoes resting on the table. He stared round the chill impersonal room — chill white

walls and chill plaster casts, and chill barred windows: cocked his head
back and found relief in the view of the cavernous blackness of the open
roof.

'They are dirty bastards!' said he in a fierce rumble that carried no
further than Anthony's ears. 'God in Heaven, I'd like to take it out of
them! There's nothing to choose between them and the slave-owners
of the South! . . . Sorry! . . . I hate this damned place! I loathe this
damned place! I abominate this damned place! There's no soul to it!
It's got an algebraic formula instead of a soul! It's got an alphabetical
schedule instead of a soul! It's got a twisted, distorted, mechanical mind
instead of a soul! . . . When I am rich — ! This half-English Putzger
and his German sergeants frighten me. I don't mind confessing it —
although theoretically I'm as free as air, and could walk out on them
this minute if I wanted to. And damned well would . . . if I could afford
to! What it must be like to be at their mercy, weak and poor and friendless, I hate to think!'

Here he paused for so long that Anthony made ready to return to his
own table and to a map of Solly's face which he was trying to sketch —
in rather inadequate gesture of revolt. Then a slow smile crept over Mr.
Fulton's ruddy countenance. He sat up with a bang. The decision of
character chiselled in big square chin, lips, and level brows was borne out
by the new expression that his face assumed.

'Take it out of them! My God, and I *can* take it out of them! And
nobody the penny the worse — except Putzger and Company! I'll — '
Stopped. ' — The less you know the better! . . . Christ, how they'll
squeal! And won't know who's stuck 'em under the fifth rib! . . . Go
back to your chair, young fellow-me-lad! You know nothing. Not even
that I have a literary bent by which I occasionally turn an honest penny!'

He took up a quill, and squared himself to write in his customary
rather clumsy manner. . . .

It was nearly dark when they came back the next day from Citoyen
Perrier's shipyard. The streets, wettened by a light rain, already glittered
with lamplight; and a young moon peeped through the curtain of clouds,
just above the house-tops. There were many people about, for it approached the fashionable dinner hour.

Both of them had been very silent all day. Anthony because he had
lain awake most of the night thinking of Solly — of the bitter melody
of the 'Minuet of the Hanged Jew' — of the black toothed void in the
landing window — of the bodiless Dr. Putzger, and of the grim Behemoth
that was von Knötel. He had thought also in a vague way of the night

on which he, too, had tried to escape from the imminent materialization of those tattered ghosts that had companioned him through America and on to the Atlantic. He shuddered now at the recollection. But for Uncle Harrady and but for Garland — ! His mind and heart went out to Garland, whose small white body had been a spell to drive away for ever those horrible things that would not let him be. He must write more often to Garland: he felt that, perhaps, he had taken her too much for granted.

Said Fulton suddenly —

'I reckon, young Anthony, that this is our last day at the yard — for a time, at least! There isn't a cent left in the "kitty", and I don't see any way of raising more. This bloody government! This blasted First Consul!'

They were half-way down a narrow street when he spoke. On their right was a drinking fountain against a high blank wall, the water gushing into a trough from a dolphin's mouth. Just beyond it a newspaper-seller had set up her booth: the rough pent-house roof had a gap in it through which rose the slim shaft of a young plane tree. On the green-painted stand before the woman were spread her merchandise, whitey-grey like dead flat-fish in the light of a small lantern fixed to the tree trunk. She was crying her wares in a gruff voice —

'Voici "Le Thè"! Prenez vôtre "Thè", messieurs! . . . Voici le grand "Miroir"! Qui veut se mirer, ce soir?'

Fulton stopped in full career. For the first time that day he laughed. 'I had forgotten! . . . Have you got any money? . . . Buy me a Miroir. It's a scandalous rag, but I know Souriguères, who edits it, pretty well!'

He took the paltry ill-printed paper out of Anthony's hands, and rustled the sheets to and fro, examining it by the light of the news-vendor's lantern: was about to throw it down with a curse, when his eyes caught sight of the headline of the principal article on the front page. His expression changed, and he remained standing under the light — a big shabby figure, hat on back of head — whilst he read, and chuckled. When he had finished he roared with laughter, straining his tight coat to bursting.

Then he seized Anthony by the arm, led him across the road into a café full of hazy mirrors and smoke and velvet; ordered two apéritifs and spread the paper on the round table in front of him. From somewhere further within, above the babble of voices, came the plaintive wail of a violin.

Anthony read —

ODIOUS PERSECUTION OF AN ISRAELITE. — Eight and a half years ago the Constituent Assembly implemented the Declaration of the Rights of Man by relieving the Jewish inhabitants of the Republic from all the imbecile disabilities under which they laboured during monarchical rule. Eight and a half years ago, thanks to the persistence of the Advocate Godard and the eloquence of the Citizen Talleyrand, the Israelite in this land was given the full freedom, equality, and fellowship which the tyrannies in Europe that surround us have withheld. . . .

There was much more to the same effect. Anthony read on, under the quizzical gaze of Fulton, and while the distant violin continued to scrape and complain —

The Institut Putzger, Rue du Magistrat, Faubourg St. Honoré, does not appear to have heard of the Statute of September 27, 1791, nor of the new principles governing human relationships which have succeeded feudalism, serfdom, autocracy, and barbarism. It is time that it did. Founded thirty years ago for the high education of adolescents 'of a superior class' by Dr. Rudolf Putzger — an Anglo-German inheriting through his mother the English aptitude for money-making, and from a Hessian father the callous Teutonic systematism — it is staffed mainly by teachers also of a mongrel breed. The Institut prospered under the monarchy, and, ever since the establishment of the Directory, has been exceedingly 'fashionable' among the new rich — speculators, monopolists, gangsters, who batten on the Republic — desirous that their offspring shall have an education that will fit them to retain their ill-gotten fortunes. This sinister academy for the wealthy has carried into the new century the odiousness of the soulless brutality of the Bourbons, of the Teutonic princelings, of the monster Pitt, of the Roman Pontiff, in dealing with those who have the misfortune to be poor and Jewish.

Among the wage-slaves, until yesterday, of this precious establishment there was an industrious youth, a pupil-teacher, named Solomon Klasing. . . .

Through the reek and chatter the violin went on wailing, 'They won't listen to me! They won't listen to me!'

As Anthony read on the Miroir's highly coloured and sensational account of the tragedy of Solly, he found himself hearing, as if from very far away, the thin ironic dance of the Hanged Jew. The article ended —

The authorities of the Institut refused all succour and shelter to the broken body of the victim of their ill-treatment. It was transported with haste and secrecy to the Hôtel-Dieu.

Thus has France, nay, the world, been deprived of a violinist whom the incomparable Viotti has declared to have shown every promise of supreme genius!

We call the attention of the authorities to the facts we have recited. They are beyond question.

'The fat'll be in the fire with a vengeance,' said Anthony with a fearful joy, laying the newspaper down, and regarding Fulton with awe. 'I should think Dr. Putzger will explode when he reads this! Can't you see that great head of his bursting with fury? Did you write it all?'

'Lord, no! . . . Well, *one* more before we go! . . . I just went along and saw Souriguères and told him about it. He knocked it into shape, sent down to the Hôtel-Dieu and put the flourishes in. He will always pay well for a story of that sort. Red-head has been avenged on his persecutors and I have got fifty francs — which is all I *have* got until the end of the month. So everything is for the best!'

'Supposing they find out!'

'They can't; how can they, unless one of us peaches? I don't know anything about it. And you don't, do you?'

'No,' said Anthony rather doubtfully. He did not fancy lying, or himself as a liar, but he certainly could never betray Fulton. And Solly most certainly had been revenged — and very thoroughly.

'Make quite sure that you don't!' remarked Fulton a little grimly. 'We have punished the brutality of some cold-blooded scoundrels. We don't want our altruism to result in penalties for ourselves. I do not wish to be turned out on the street — yet! And I should imagine that something singularly unpleasant, too, would happen to you, brother!'

Anthony, meditating on possibilities, thought it very likely. . . .

Thought it still more likely when he was summoned from a class in Russian to Dr. Putzger's study late on the following afternoon.

Found his heart beating the faster with apprehension as he followed one of the director's black-aproned janissaries along the corridor.

The man (his name was Franz; his comrade's Fritz) had all the look of an executioner's assistant, Anthony told himself. But what could they do, after all? If they expelled him, he had done nothing shameful to cloud his home-returning. He wasn't afraid of being expelled. Expulsion meant Jasmine — and Garland — and Harrady — and Elizabeth, all the sooner! No, he wasn't afraid of that! But he *was* afraid of **Dr.** Putzger, and of von Knötel, and of Fritz and Franz (those square-headed men with enormous hands) and even of Miss Putzger, and of the desolate bareness of the building, and of the repression that made it a place of low voices and whispers.

Franz opened the door and stood aside for him to enter the small room, laurel-darkened, that was the lair of the director of the Institut.

Dr. Putzger's vast mushroom-coloured head appeared to float about a foot above his table at the far end. Behind him towered von Knötel against a ceiling-high bookcase, of which the glass, dulled by the haze of reflections and of shadows, hid rather than revealed the volumes.

Fulton was propped negligently by one shoulder sideways against the wall of books that faced the doctor. He was in his usual seedy black. His legs were crossed at the ankles where his white woollen socks hung in wrinkles; and his attention appeared to be divided between the task of cleaning his nails with what might almost have been a quill pen, and the head of the Institut — whom he regarded insolently from time to time over his right shoulder with out-thrust chin. From his attitude Anthony knew instinctively what had happened, or was about to happen.

Anthony halted a pace or so from the door, the janissary, Franz, taking up his stand behind him. Prisoners under escort before a summary tribunal! — he thought.

'This young man is entirely innocent,' said Fulton examining a thumbnail. His eyes warned Anthony. 'My information came from an entirely different source.'

'That is a lie, Mr. Fulton!' said Dr. Putzger in his thin even voice. The face at the lower edge of the balloon-like head was astonishingly immobile even during speech. 'There is really no use in lying. By the process of deduction we have arrived infallibly at the conclusion that you contributed that tissue of lies to the *Miroir*. You have boasted too frequently of your acquaintanceship with the blackguard Souriguères. We know that you left this establishment immediately after your art class. We know that your only source of information could have been a member of the *Deutsche Ecke*. We know that this young man alone of that group had any contact with you . . . You are not here to discuss your guilt or innocence. That has been already adjudged. You are here to receive your sentence!'

'Save your breath, my dear sir!' implored Fulton.

Dr. Putzger folded his little skeleton claws upon the dark red leather surface of the table in front of him.

'First I should tell you that I have complained to the *Miroir,* and of the *Miroir.* Your story is a malicious and libellous falsehood. The unfortunate Klasing himself would tell you, that he mounted on the ledge of the window to open it, at my request. The hasp was beyond my reach and extremely stiff: it gave suddenly — so suddenly that he lost his balance and was precipitated out.'

'That,' said Anthony, 'is untrue, sir!'

'Hear! Hear!' said Fulton.

'I opened that window myself only the day before. The hasp works particularly easily. Klasing is as tall as myself. He could have easily reached it from the floor.'

Dr. Putzger ignored the interruption. His thin voice went on —

'I have spoken to Klasing this morning. He will confirm my account.' — A chill smile ruffled the frozen composure of the big man standing behind him. — 'He was only taken to the Hôtel-Dieu for immediate surgical treatment. He will be brought back here as soon as he can be moved.'

'He will try again!' said Anthony; and knew from the quick quiver of Dr. Putzger's lashless eyes that the blow had gone home.

'Meanwhile, Mr. Fulton, you are dismissed on the spot. Without notice. Without reference. Without pay. If you like to bring an action to recover arrears of salary you are welcome! I am reserving to myself the right to take legal proceedings against you.'

'I never liked Englishmen or Germans — from a child,' said Fulton easily, not changing his attitude. 'When I was a small boy in Lancaster, Pennsylvania, during the Revolution, we used to go and boo at the English and Hessian prisoners of war as they were brought in to the prison camp. I was ten or eleven at the time.'

'An exceptionally interesting reminiscence!' said Dr. Putzger. 'As for you, DA 1, you have proved yourself deliberately disobedient and disloyal! You will be given a month's segregation in which to consider those failings.'

He paused, and Knotty filled in the gap:

'Segregation Cell Number Two is vacant at present, Herr Direktor!'

Within that taciturn and unfriendly community the inhabitant of a segregation cell was a person set still farther apart from his fellows. He fed sparely; slept hard; worked slavishly; alone! He might neither be spoken to, nor speak, except in class. His was the life of a prisoner undergoing solitary confinement.

'Segregation Cell Number Two, then! . . . You may go — both of you!'

'Tut — tut, you and your Hessians!' commented Mr. Fulton in gentle reproval.

Said Anthony, hot with fury —

'I will go — but not to your damned cell!'

'No?' said Dr. Putzger, examining skeleton claws. 'No? . . . *Franz!*'

Anthony found his arms suddenly pinned to his sides in an unrelenting grip. Steel, he thought, was a foolish and inaccurate simile to use of such a clasp: it was a wooden grip by hands of teak or oak. The suggestion of violence outraged him; suddenly recalled the man with the pale stomach aboard the *Aventurière*. He flung himself forward; was restrained so forcibly that he was hurled back against the chest of the man behind him.

Until then the lazy figure of Fulton had not stirred. That singularly inadequate art master had watched the spasm of battle with an expression of slight amusement.

He now straightened up: held out for inspection the feathered object with which he had been cleaning his finger-nails. It was a dart.

'Do you know, Putzger-old-friend, that when I was in England I became singularly adept at a game that is played in practically every tavern in the land? . . . Darts! I have even introduced the pastime with marked success into one or two of the *bistros* to which I occasionally resort in Paris! I play every day — for the exercise!'

'You are, indeed, in reminiscent vein, Mr. Fulton,' said Dr. Putzger. 'Perhaps some other — '

'I have a certain inventive ability,' continued Fulton, idly swinging his hand. 'I like precision — accuracy. These were not to be obtained from the English wooden-bodied dart. So I designed one for myself with a brass shaft. It goes like a bullet — doesn't it, Knotty?'

As he spoke his hand flickered forward, and a feathered something shot out of it to shatter the thin glass of the bookcase just behind von Knötel's head. The missile must have passed within a hair's breadth of Knotty's right ear, because the big man raised his hand as though to assure himself that the organ was undamaged, before he turned automatically, with Dr. Putzger, to assess the destruction.

In the midst of that distraction the tail of Anthony's eye caught a glimpse of something that appeared to travel past his own head. There was a brittle crack and a thud behind. The grip on him was loosed, and his legs were nearly knocked from under him by the collapsing body of Franz.

'Very, very neat!' said Fulton in cordial self-approval, examining his knuckles, and then fumbling at a waistcoat pocket. 'Remove the body

from before the door, young Alge, and make a bolt for it. Unless you
want to stay!'

As Anthony stooped to shift the obstruction he saw that the great figure
of Knotty was already ponderously rounding the table on the way to attack, one big hand spread for leverage on the dark red surface.

'I shouldn't, Knotty! I shouldn't really! I've got plenty more! Stop
where —'

Von Knötel gave a loud cry of surprise and pain.

'They hurt, don't they?' said Fulton. 'Run for it, Alge! Run, you fat-
headed coon!'

Anthony straightened himself.

Von Knötel was standing frozen in an attitude of incredulous astonishment. One of Fulton's darts was stuck quivering in his upper arm.

'I'll put one through your hairy ear if you move,' said Fulton gaily.
'For God's sake run, you damned fool!' . . .

'Efficiency and Proficiency are my middle names,' said Fulton when
they emerged panting into the comparative safety of the Rue de Sèvres.
'But I should have liked to quote that bit of Milton to them — the only
bit I know!

> "Black it stood as night,
> Fierce as ten Furies, terrible as hell,
> And shook a dreadful dart."

Got any money, brother? Because I haven't.'

Anthony felt in his pockets. He had exactly twenty francs — five more
than the older man.

Which was why at six o'clock that evening he found himself sitting
in a Greek elbow chair ornamented with a key-pattern of inlaid brass,
watching the evening toilette of Hortense. She was seated before a pier-
glass supported by sphinxes, in her Pompeian bedroom that glowed softly
from the light of oil lamps disguised as Roman flambeaux of bronze.

'My poor angel,' said Hortense, 'the diligence does not go till the morning — if you *must* travel by it! To-morrow you shall have all the money
you want in the world for yourself and your ridiculous companion. To-
night we will make merry! Your first night in Paris! And afterwards
you shall have a bed on the sofa in the *salon!* Come, it all arranges itself! . . . Marthe, you will see that a really comfortable bed is made ready
for Monsieur on the big sofa!'

Marthe, grimly adjusting a gold filet about her mistress's dark shining

head, permitted herself a smile that was not quite secret as she gave the
required assurance.

'But, Hortense,' he protested. 'I'm not fit to be seen. I've got no hat,
and no money!'

'My angel,' said Hortense, 'my friends do not need fine clothes, or hats,
or — *sometimes* — any money!'

She rose; dabbled her finger-tips in the scented water of a tiny silver-
gilt washstand basin on a tripod stand intended to resemble the censer
in a temple of Aphrodite; flicked a sparkling drop or two at him, laughing; afterwards she examined herself with satisfaction in the mirror,
and took a dancing step or two, so that her long dress of grey-white
silk swirled about her. It was a very transparent dress, and the waist had
risen as far as it was physically possible for a waist to rise. The sleeves —
which barely existed — and the top of the bodice — which also struggled
for existence — were ornamented with flat marigold heads in gold.

Money — or the lack of it — seemed to mean nothing to Hortense.
Anthony did not see her pay for anything — did not pay himself — during the whole of that bewildering, crowded, incalculable night.

They went to Méon's for dinner; and there in a vast thronged room
decorated to resemble a garden in summer, among innumerable other
friends, she found Monsieur Pontmartin about to dine with two little thin
dark girls — almost children, and almost ugly.

'*Le bon Papa!*' exclaimed she with joy, kissing his pink face, 'May we
dine with you?'

Of course they might!

Thereafter life became a kaleidoscope of colour and excitement. Anthony found himself choosing at random amid the wilderness of a hundred unknown dishes on the menu handed him: drinking pink champagne; giggling with one of the little ugly girls who proved exceptionally
lively.

Found himself for a few minutes in the open air watching fireworks
burst into gold and silver blossom against the velvet blackness of the
night somewhere over Montmartre.

Found himself in a room that might have been the Presence Chamber
of a palace — its blue ceiling studded with silver stars — seated between
Hortense and one of the thin girls at a long and crowded table covered
with green baize like the table in the *Ecke* class-room; found Monsieur
Pontmartin leaning over and thrusting gold louis into his hands — into
Hortense's hands — into the thin girls' hands, and somebody else perpetually pushing little heaps of money with a small wooden rake across
the green baize toward him: 'It's all yours, pick it up!' said Hortense,

laughing as he stuffed his pockets. 'Bonaparte won three hundred thousand francs here at Perrin's before he went to Italy.'

Found himself drinking more champagne with all sorts of friendly men and pretty women — dancing with Hortense in the cyclopean vastness of the ballroom of the Hôtel de Longueville; supping in a pink and white nest — like a bridal cake turned inside out — where Monsieur Pontmartin became embarrassingly affectionate to both thin ugly girls at once; found himself finally regarding the rose and gold damask of the sofa in Hortense's *salon*. It had not been made up as a bed.

'The evil Marthe!' said Hortense, without rancour. 'It would serve her right to wake her up!'

She had thrown off her wrapping of gauzy silk, and her left breast had escaped from the unreluctant bodice of her dress. In such disarray, and amid the rococo graces of the radiant room with its cupids and damasks and almond-green *Chinoiserie* and cabinets of red lacquer, she resembled a roguish shepherdess in porcelain such as Elegance had loved before it went into eclipse in the shadow of the guillotine.

'It doesn't matter,' said Anthony lowering his eyes. 'I shall be very comfortable. I can sleep anywhere.'

'Can you?' said Hortense. . . .

The Chalon diligence clattered out of the cobbled courtyard of the *Messageries* into the Rue St. Honoré. They had the *rotonde* — perched like a covered-in rumble at the rear of the vehicle — to themselves.

Fulton, his shabby hat very much at the back of his head, a precious roll of papers on his knee, leaned a little forward to watch the streets through the window over the door. He talked to Anthony, silent in his corner, without turning his head.

'I hope it isn't a wild-goose chase,' he said. 'Ten days' journey there and back for nothing! You're sure your uncle will spring the needful!'

He had already made the same remark ten times in as many minutes.

'I'm sure!' said Anthony. 'Especially with the evidence of your drawings, and now that the *Nautilus* is so nearly ready!'

He spoke with stiff lips, automatically; because all the time his body and soul were talking about other things — about the fact that he was an adulterer; that he had betrayed Monsieur Garnerey (who did not matter so much) and — and Jasmine! How could he ever face Jasmine, or dream of Jasmine, or even think of Jasmine — polluted as he was? . . . Supposing there were a baby!

'It's lucky you were able to get some kit,' remarked Fulton, withdrawing his head from the window for a moment, and regarding Anthony.

'That's quite a good hat, too! Where did you buy it? You're a lucky devil to be able to buy new hats when you want to. I wish I could! . . . When I am rich —'

He looked out of the window again.

'Well, good-bye, Paris! Good-bye, Dr. Putzger! Good-bye, Herr von Knötel! As a free-born American, I say — Blast all Englishmen, and Blast all Germans! As a sometime resident in this city I say — *Je vous conspue!*'

CHAPTER VIII

INTRODUCTION TO TWO SHIPS

'So I hear that Mr. Harradence did not see his way to taking a financial interest in your schemes,' said Madam Purvis. 'Sit down, Mr. Fulton! Sit down there —'

And she pointed to a stiff relentless chair facing the light, set against the wall on her left, under a dim old tapestry representing Actaeon being torn to pieces by his hounds.

She was standing, as she always did, at her unnaturally tall table with its parti-coloured legs, her folded arms resting upon its wine-coloured surface.

The big man sat down where he was bidden, rather awkwardly, rather like a schoolboy — very upright; hands on shabby knees; feet set together and pushed a little forward, as though to draw attention to the new boots with rose-coloured tops that Anthony had bought for him (at his suggestion) in Marseilles.

The younger man remained standing in an attitude of deferential attention by the door. His grandmother's cold eyes dwelled on him thoughtfully before they were turned to Mr. Fulton.

The tall slim figure in the bright blue coat and fawn pantaloons and polished riding-boots might have been Richard's. Its chin was cocked up by many folds of white neck-cloth, so that the head was borne at just such a proud angle as Richard's. There was a wave to the dark hair, such as Richard's fair hair had had before it was powdered and tied. In bright grey eyes and arching brow, in high-bridged nose and high cheekbones she saw Richard, too. But — in an indefinable expression of the young face she found something that was not of Richard, nor yet of Lavinia. Then suddenly she recognized in her grandson's features the look of restless, melancholy inquiry that her eldest son had habitually worn: and with that recognition suddenly found the older Anthony in every lineament of the younger . . . Anthony to Anthony! . . . Was it possible that — ? It was not.

She returned her gaze to the shabby high-coloured Fulton.

'So Mr. Harradence will not help,' she repeated. 'Did he say why?'

'He will not, ma'am. He made me personally the most kind offers — for which I can't be sufficiently grateful — but with the *Nautilus* he will have nothing to do! I think he is making a mistake, but I guess he is entitled to his point of view.'

'What *is* his point of view?'

'It was not very clear, ma'am, to me! He talked about my invention not being of practical use until some new method of propulsion should be devised. But I am not proposing to make submarine voyages across the Atlantic in her! She is a surface craft until the opportunity arises of making sure and secret attack from beneath the waters . . . I think, if I may say so, that he had some other reason for his refusal than he gave! . . . Now I have here the report of a Government Commission to the Minister of the Marine on the *unimproved* model two years ago. Would it be troubling you too much to ask — ?'

He took up the roll of dog's-eared foolscap that lay on the floor beside him, rose, gave it to Madam Purvis, and resumed his seat. Anthony noticed that his hand trembled as he handed over the documents.

In his turn, Anthony regarded his grandmother as she read, holding the papers out almost at arm's length before her.

She stood, an immobile black figure, priestess at her queer circular altar in the centre of the grey cobweb of a carpet, as if she had not stirred since he went away. There in front of her was the brass-bound mahogany box that opened out into a writing-desk, with the miniature of Uncle Richard on the folded handkerchief lying before it; and the pile of four or five books on her left, and the green leather dispatch case on her right. The sunshine streaming in through the four narrow windows on the seaward side of the room even showed the black slanting script of Mr. Starkey of London on the letter which lay unfolded upon the nearer side of the table. She had given him a dry-biscuit kiss of welcome last night, and listened without comment to his account of the last moments at the Institut Putzger, while Harradence had bellowed with huge laughter . . . It was a pity that Garland should be with her mother in Marseilles choosing new bonnets, new dresses, new cloaks, when he came back! . . . Would he be able to get away and see Jasmine?

Said Madam Purvis, putting down the roll of foolscap —

'This seems quite satisfactory!'

'Yes, ma'am! But it would be more satisfactory if someone would do something about it! You know what governments are! The machinery of tape, sealing wax, spikes, dockets, files, hundred-and-one clerks, and waste-paper baskets, that has to be set going before any small matter can be undertaken. I don't doubt that when the First Consul gets thoroughly settled into the saddle, things will move fast. Meanwhile—'

'Is much money needed to complete your vessel?'

'A mere bagatelle, ma'am!' said Fulton earnestly. 'So small a sum, and so certain of great profit that a rich man should give no second thought to it! . . . Unfortunately I know no rich men!'

'How much?'

'A matter of a few thousand francs — really a few! — to complete her fitting. And a sum sufficient to pay the wages of a crew of three I shall need for demonstration purposes — say twelve hundred francs a month! With the cost of what I call the "torpedoes" and the voyage down the Seine to Havre for testing, you might reckon on three thousand dollars being ample!'

With her eyes, as though inattentive, on the miniature of Richard — Richard whose gay face and gallant body had been trampled into the mud of a battlefield so very long ago — she led Fulton on to tell of his *Nautilus* and the feats she would perform. Of her 'horn' by means of which the sinister burden of destruction that she towed behind would be affixed to the bottom of an enemy vessel. Of the appalling devastation — 'disintegration' he termed it — that could be wrought by the undersea explosion. Of experiments when the whole carcass of a ship had been hurled skyward, and lost its shape, and rained back upon the waters in fragments of shattered timber. Of strange tests and adventure and a weary waiting so that the narrator seemed to be a compound of Friar Bacon, Ulysses, and the Patient Griselda.

'Of course he isn't quite a gentleman!' thought Anthony. Recalled a large bloodstone ring that Fulton sometimes sported, engraved with armorial bearings and the motto '*Vi et Virtute*'; and tales told him of an ancestor who had raised a company of horse to fight for William of Orange. Chided himself for disloyalty to the genius who was his friend. Disloyalty — he told himself — was his great failing. He had been disloyal to Jasmine, and to Solly. In reaction against his worser self, he interrupted to re-tell some incident which Fulton had told him, magnified and embroidered into nigh upon an epic.

Madam Purvis nodded her head. She did not raise her eyes from the portrait of Richard.

'You were in England for some time, I believe. You have had no dealings with the British Government in this matter, of course?'

'Ma'am,' said Fulton a shade indignantly, slapping one of his shiny knees in emphasis with a large hand. 'I am a good republican! I am a good American! I have no truck with Hanoverian tyranny! I have offered my invention to France so that she may drive the English pirates from the seas, and give the freedom of the ocean to the world.'

Anthony told himself that he recognized the phrase as from one of the more recent letters to Forfait, the new Minister of Marine. Chided himself again.

Once more Madam Purvis nodded. In token of agreement.

With an effort she pushed away the high-backed chair behind her in which no one had ever seen her sit: crossed the room with short dragging steps to one of the windows looking across the acacia-sentinelled terrace to the far-stretching sea.

'Come here, Mr. Fulton! . . . You see those small islands at the far tip of the bay? . . . To your left!'

He went to the window beside her, and looked out across a bright green sea etched with swiftly-running lines of white foam. Anthony, too, approached the window-place. A small Louis XIV commode of elaborately carved acacia wood stood before it. Its sleek and silvery top was littered with the nibbled remains of comfits of green and purple and orange. — 'Grandmother must spend a great deal of time here,' he thought. — There was also a small pocket telescope with an ivory eye-piece, its red leather covering faded to an old rose.

'Now look at them through the spy-glass!' commanded Madam Purvis. Mr. Fulton levelled and focused the glass.

'The ships?' he ventured.

'The ships!'

He watched through the telescope in silence for a while. In the lee of the larger of two grey rocky islets, were two ships — a slim frigate and a raffish-looking brig, the broad white bands on their black hulls studded with gun-ports. They were hoisting sail. As he watched a cat's-paw of a breeze toyed with, fluttered, spread wide the ensign at the larger vessel's gaff: shook out before the enemy in the enemy's own waters the red cross and the white cross of Britain.

'British cruisers!' exclaimed Mr. Fulton. 'God! ma'am, what a target! Do they often visit here?'

He passed the spy-glass to Anthony.

'British cruisers!' assented Madam Purvis. 'They are most regular visitors! You might almost call them residents! They use the anchorage off the islands as if it belonged to Britain. They go thence on their marauding expeditions against the commerce of France. They lie in wait there to pounce on passing shipping. They flaunt the flag of piracy and oppression and murder as if British territorial waters were all the seas to the high-water mark of every shore.'

'Ah!' said Mr. Fulton thoughtfully. 'Their fast cruisers — their commerce destroyers — have got pet anchorages all along the coasts of France. I didn't know of this one, however. But I have had my eye for a long time on a very favourite anchorage off the Isles of St. Marcouf, near Isigny, between Cherbourg and Havre. That is where I mean to test the *Nautilus*. Bring her down the river from Paris — out into the Bay of the Seine — blow up a brig — and there you are!'

He put down the telescope, and pulled at his too-short sleeves in a reflective manner.

'There you are!' echoed Madam Purvis.

She stared for long and without a word at the distant islets and the white-sailed specks against their grey. When she turned and made her slow way back to her altar, Anthony saw that her eyes, black and bright as a girl's, were blazing.

'I watch them! And watch them!' she said. 'And pray that some great ship of war will suddenly round the point and blaze at them with a full broadside! . . . But it never happens! . . . If I were a man, I should row out to them at night and throw fire-bombs aboard them, or lead desperate assault up their sides! I would wipe out the insult with fire and steel! If I were a man — ! . . . I have good cause to dislike the English!' she added, not by way of apology, but in explanation.

'So young Al — your grandson has told me,' said Mr. Fulton.

'During the equinoctial gales last autumn they sheltered there for many days together. One moonless night two young officers were rowed ashore — midshipmen! They walked into the town and sat till past midnight drinking in one of the *estaminets!*'

'Did no one interfere with them, ma'am?'

'No, Mr. Fulton! . . . They became excessively drunk, and were escorted back to their boat by fisher-people! That is what I call damnable treason! I would have hanged the traitors along the shore!'

Mr. Fulton looked praeternaturally grave.

'Midshipmen!' he said. 'An adventure without the knowledge of their commanding officer! It probably ended in their being breeched and rope-ended by the master-at-arms!'

Anthony still stood before the narrow window. He had raised the spy-glass, and was watching the departure of the ships under the white towers of their sails — beautiful and deadly creatures, curtsying and prancing in the choppy sea as though they danced out light-heartedly and joyously to an errand of destruction . . . Solly would have written a tune for them — 'Solemn Pavane for the Ships of War' . . . He was conscious only of respect for their daring, mingled with a certain irritation at their insolence. He did not look upon them as representing people who formed the core of all resistance to the new order in France — the people who had endeavoured to trample American freedom underfoot — the people whose hirelings had slaughtered his father and his uncle — the people who had driven Uncle Harrady into exile. It meant little or nothing to him that they represented the England of King George the Third, and Colonel Hurrell. He viewed them as any small boy might view other small boys trespassing in his own back yard.

He closed the telescope with a click, and as he turned toward the table, his grandmother saw again in his bearing the bearing of Richard, and was glad. She put out a slim strong hand, of the colour of old ivory, and touched the miniature of her son, as if to convey physically to it her discovery.

She said —

'Mr. Fulton, I will personally advance the money necessary to complete and outfit the ship you have in building in Paris. Shall we say four thousand dollars? It will be a business arrangement between us, you understand?'

'Of course!' he eagerly assured her.

'Can I —' began Anthony.

But his grandmother continued —

'I see from the memorandum attached to the report you were good to show me, that you estimate the cost of a new larger and improved vessel at some fifty-seven thousand livres — approximately twelve thousand dollars?'

'A maximum, ma'am!'

'I am not haggling about cents! . . . Now I will advance you the four thousand dollars you require, immediately and free of interest on one condition!'

Mr. Fulton rose to his feet. He was transformed: his dark eyes, set cavernously, glowed; his rather ugly, highly-coloured face flushed still brighter.

'I accept, ma'am! I accept, no matter what the condition is! With the deepest gratitude! With the most devout homage! I —'

'And the condition is that you also borrow the twelve thousand dollars to build your better ship!'

He was speechless — stood yammering, with twisting hands, and his eyes full of tears.

'There is one condition to the second loan, too!' Madam Purvis still stood erect before her wine-dark altar: her arms rested upon it, and her long yellow fingers adjusted and re-adjusted the miniature of her son upon its bed of linen. 'That condition is . . . That you build the ship at Marseilles, or Toulon, or even La Ciotat, so that it may be tested in this bay . . . where I can see it . . . against the English! That will be the interest and the bonus that I shall require!'

She raised her eyes and looked through the open window and the gap between the acacias, out to sea where the raiders were hull-down on the horizon, white obelisks of sail. . . .

He left his grandmother and Mr. Fulton to settle financial arrangements, and went out on the terrace overlooking the steeply-sloping wilderness of the garden and the disturbed green of the sea.

Garland was there! Standing by the balustrade alone.

She wore a green-blue high-waisted dress with, short puffed sleeves and a wide falling collar of white frills. Her dark curls were piled up on her head, and she carried a cherry-coloured bonnet by its black ribbons.

She did not hear him come, and was looking out to sea.

'Garland!'

At the call she turned very quickly a bright and lovely face toward him — a face in which there was resolution, and humour, and intelligence, as well as beauty of outline and delicacy of colouring.

'Why, Rowley!'

For a tiny fraction of time the shining eyes under arched eyebrows explored his face.

'You — are *grown-up!*' she said with a little gasp, and kissed him on the lips, just as she was used.

He said nothing for an instant, for by that innocent and loving kiss was dissipated the miasma of shameful memories of the last night in Paris. It was, his subconsciousness told him, the kiss of healing and peace, although unwitting of the offence.

He looked at her with new eyes. There were long moonstone earring pendants from the lobes of her little ears; they gave him the clue to what was new and strange in her. She was grown-up, too!

'And so are you!' he said at last, finding his tongue.

'I am glad you are back, Rowley! . . . Don't you like my new dress? Isn't it Paris all over? . . . I *always* think that even a blind man could tell a Paris dress!'

There was now no fleck of white upon the dark etched line of the horizon, between sky and sea.

BOOK FOUR

MEN UNDER THE SEA

France — England — Prussia, 1801–1806

★

CHAPTER I

THE DAUGHTER OF THE SWAN

COUNT PAGAN opened the door, and walked into a room, with which — he found to his surprise — he was utterly unfamiliar.

A small and elegant clavichord in ebony inlaid with ivory and silver stood against the satin-white wall opposite, keyboard lid thrown back and a sheet of music open on it. Above was a portrait, in gilded frame, of an officer in green uniform with a crimson sash. There were a couple of Persian rugs, a few slim pieces of furniture of severe outline, a long mirror in a frame of ivory and gold, a clock of classical design surmounted by a gilded eagle, and a number of handsome engravings.

It was a room in which considerable taste as well as a long purse had been employed: a room that was expensively and fashionably bare. The count found it impossible to credit that it should be a room in the house he had rented from Monsieur Corvisart three years before — a house almost uninhabitable and unnavigable by reason of the jumble of ancient furniture in which the heart of the apothecary's widowed mother — recently defunct — had found much solace.

The glass doors that gave upon the garden were closed. Accordingly Count Pagan — looking like an inquisitive faun garbed in the attire of 1801; olive-green coat, grass-green breeches, and cypress-green boots — made a swift and efficient exploration of the room. The engravings gave no clue. One of them was the enchanting portrait of a girl by Godefroy, which won first prize at the Exposition of '99, the others classical subjects by Delvaux. The music on the clavichord lid — an Italian song — provided no information; nor did the morocco-bound book lying on a console — it was called, *Clélie, ou L'Enfant du Mystère,* and there was no name inside.

He was driven back to the portrait once more. The uniform seemed familiar, even if the face was strange. He stood before it, searching his memory, slanting eyebrows linked by thin line across bridge of nose. Suddenly he smiled. He knew, at last! It was himself, copied unrecognizably — except for the uniform — from a miniature taken when he was serving with the forces of the King of Sardinia.

Satisfied, he crossed the room to the glass-doors. A small buhl table stood on the threshold: it was littered with small and expensive trifles — a gold *bonbonnière* of silver-gilt and tortoiseshell, a painted chicken-skin fan, a watch, a miniature group in ivory. As he stepped out into the garden, the outer tilt of his eyebrows was accentuated once more. . . .

He stood aside to let Jasmine enter the house first — 'Cousin Kate's in the kitchen, and she's got ears as big as an elephant's!' — sat down elegantly on a small settee, and admired in a detached fashion the pale gold girl who was known as his niece. Her beauty and grace and purity of outline were those of a daffodil; her movements those of a goddess of the wind; her eyes the grey of freezing water. Like himself, there was about her the suggestion of immortal youth.

She remained standing by the clavichord, returning his stare.

'Now that the first transports of our mutual affection have subsided,' said Count Pagan in his mocking careless voice, 'we must exchange news, my pet!'

'Indeed we must, dearest uncle!'

'My own news can be told in a few sentences. There is little to add to what I have said in my letters — brief as they were, I fear! As a rebellion the Irish affair was amateurish. A fiasco! The French had all surrendered when I got there. I was arrested directly I landed and sent to Dublin. Someone had played the traitor!'

'A habit of the Irish, isn't it?'

'So I was tried and sentenced to death with remarkable celerity by the British. They'd had a lot of practice just then! They thought nothing of executing two hundred at a time!'

'But you should have turned King's evidence, of course!'

'Somebody else had already forestalled me, my precious!'

At this revelation of perfidy Jasmine shook her head in sympathy.

'The poor fellow had been treasurer for one of the republican committees: made a mess of his accounts: didn't see why the English should hang him when his playfellows were already after him with shot-guns: scooped the pool, got whisked to safety somewhere, and so made the best of both worlds!'

'How sensible of him!' said Jasmine warmly. 'But how annoying for you, dear uncle!'

'So I bribed my way out of prison!'

'So *that's* why you never sent me any money!'

'I got away to the Wicklow Mountains, where a ragged rascal called Dwyer was keeping a guerrilla gang together — still is, for all I know . . . Then the local priest said I was an atheist, so they tried to sell me to the British. However, I bolted just in time. By this means and that I transported myself to New York.' He paused for a few moments, while a reminiscent smile played over his beautiful face; continued — 'The dear Americans love an Irishman who has bled for Erin in the cause of freedom; they love a general — a colonel — or even a major; that's why every public-house keeper in the States is a colonel at least! Then most of all they love a title — even more than the English tradesman does! So, in the hunting phrase of my late dear master of Mysore, "there was a great killing!" A very great killing!' And he slapped a breeches pocket so that there answered the solemn clink of fat coin on coin. 'I went to Philadelphia. I went to Charleston. I went to Richmond. In fact I toured Virginia, which was both interesting and profitable!'

With so much meaning did he pronounce the last few words that Jasmine raised her eyes from contemplation of the ivory keys of the instrument at her side. She made no question, however.

'And how did my precious pet support her uncle's absence?'

'It is no thanks to dearest uncle that his precious pet supported it at all! Unless he thought that a thousand livres — two hundred dollars — forty pounds — two hundred and forty ducats, would maintain her in luxury for two and a half years! Unless he thought that she would be fed like Elijah by the ravens!'

The count permitted his eyes to range the room.

'Uncle's precious has presumably found a raven! And a good fat raven!'

Said Jasmine, uninformatively —

'Presumably!'

'A pleasant enough aviary!' said Pagan, examining her afresh. 'I trust that our raven was a gentlemanly bird! I trust that our raven realized that there was an eagle of an uncle in the offing! I trust that my little Jasmine's ornithological specimen, or specimens, have excited no ill-natured comment in the town!'

'Not so much comment, perhaps, as the peculiar coincidence that you and Hortense disappeared from our midst on the same day!'

'A most unfortunate coincidence, my precious!'

'I imagine you handed her over to someone better qualified to keep pace with her pecuniary requirements when you got to Paris!'

'She is a charming and agreeable girl,' said the count. 'She keeps a soft corner in her heart for her old lovers — always a good sign! I met her a week or so ago on my way through Paris. I had handed her over, as you express it, on my departure to a young industrialist of Lyons. I arrive back to find her at one and the same time mistress — if I may mention that word in your presence — of Eugène de Beauharnais, the First Consul's stepson, and of Monsieur de Talleyrand, who — my sweet will recall — was once Bishop of Autun! I heard news of our young American friend from her . . . I gathered news of him in America, as well! . . . I was interested to learn that he had returned here . . . I have wondered about our young friend. I have wondered quite a lot!'

'I feel certain that your interest would be appreciated!'

'Thank you, my pet! . . . Now I am certain that my Jasmine has been what is known technically as a "careful girl", as certain as I am that she may not always be what is also known technically as a "good girl". But perhaps you will satisfy your old uncle's mind with regard to this Mr. Raven before we talk about our young friend? . . . I presume Mr. Purvis still answers "Adsum"?'

'He does,' said Jasmine. 'Occasionally!'

She trailed her fingers along the keys of the clavichord at her side, so that the strings of the instrument responded, with her, in the sweet and hollow fashion of their kind.

'Well?'

'My Mr. Raven is fifty-five and has black side-whiskers and a white face. He has got a large stomach and hairy hands. He cries a great deal — because uncle's precious is not kind enough to him! The tears wet uncle's pet's lily-white hands because Mr. Raven mumbles over them while he cries!'

'Uncle's virginal treasure! . . . And has Mr. Raven never made any naughty suggestions?'

She raised her grey-green eyes to his face in which there was so much of mockery. In her very expressionlessness was there a mocking answer.

'Dear Monsieur Fraissinet — he is a great soap manufacturer of Marseilles — '

'Incredible that a soap-maker should amass a fortune in France!' murmured Pagan.

' — is animated by nothing but by feelings of the most platonic and Christian friendship! He has bought the Château de St. Pierre for the sake of his motherless little daughter who pines in town air! He has filled it with furniture — with so much furniture that it was a positive act of kindness (he said) for uncle's pet to choose enough to furnish two or three rooms! And she did! And of the best! . . . Then money! Surely an old — well, an elderly — man might help an unhappy child, destitute of her natural protector! What was a thousand livres here and there between friends? What was it to him? A bagatelle! His bank, like his château, was too crowded!'

'How much?' said the count curtly. His face had darkened: he no longer looked like a faun, but an angry arch-angel.

'Twenty-five thousand livres!'

'Christ Almighty! Does he — did he — ?'

She struck one bright, sparkling, mocking little note on her friend the clavichord.

'By God! You little bitch!' said the count, rising to his feet.

'Uncle's little bitch was so grateful to her big, kind, important friend! . . . And to make sure that the position was quite clear she spent forty francs on a lovely golden frame and got Mr. Anthony Purvis to make a large copy from the miniature that she treasured so much of her dearest uncle! Her dearest, ownest uncle!'

Count Pagan, thoughtfully regarding the girl's composed and down-cast face as she toyed with the responsive keys, sat down as abruptly as he had risen.

'Uncle's precious little bitch netted two birds at once! She hung the picture here to remind Monsieur Fraissinet — just in case! — that she was the niece of a noble, the descendant of the High Kings of Tara, and that uncle wore a sword — a long one! And Mr. Purvis admired the dutiful affection!'

'Now —'

'Let me finish! The upshot is that Monsieur Fraissinet — who always looks and smells as if he had been only shaved five minutes before — has fondled my hand respectfully, and mumbled my hand amorously, and wept over my hand despairingly, until I have allowed myself to throw out a faint hope that uncle might be brought — only might — to consider the possibility of a bourgeois nephew old enough to be *his* father!'

'Good girl! Good girl!' said the count, crossing his immaculate legs and caressing an immaculate knee. 'But I hope that this fragrant romance has not interfered with — business! I chanced — *chanced* — to visit High Pale! It is a palace! The estate is fabulous! The Purvises are in the same class as the Byrds of Westover and other legendary families of Virginia! Thousands of acres, and hundreds of slaves! I also gathered a mass of interesting information about our friend. Exceptionally interesting! He has another grandmother there — a roaring, rampageous old lady who should have died years ago! . . . There was a drunken old doctor, named Earle, who hinted in his cups at a great deal which might one day repay investigation. All very, very useful! . . . How does the affair go?'

'It has been a bit puzzling,' said Jasmine, thus frankly acknowledging her uncle's superior knowledge of the world.

She leaned a little over the instrument, and brushed her finger-tips upon the keys, so that the faintest and most ethereal chord was sounded.

'You remember how distantly reverent he was? Like someone worshipping a goddess! Well, since he came back from Paris he has become yet more distant and yet more reverent — as if I were even less attainable than a goddess; as though I were the ghost of Love, or the Blessed Virgin!'

'Hortense is on his conscience!' said the count with conviction.

'Hortense?'

'Hortense!' repeated Pagan. 'The fair, frail Hortense!'

'In God's name why should she be on *his* conscience?'

'You are dealing,' said Count Pagan with gentle disdain for one so lacking in elementary comprehension, 'with a youthful idealist who has had little experience of the world, although he is almost your own age. He finds himself no longer fit to touch the hem of your pure skirt, no longer fit even to be a doormat under your divinely chaste foot . . . In short, he is no longer a virgin!'

'Do you mean to say that Hortense — ?'

'I do!' said Count Pagan, with a display of charitable tolerance for the fallen.

'Damn Hortense!'

'Oh, no! A charming creature — but inquisitive! You may recall that she even seduced me when we were lodging over her father's shop! Before he unfortunately lost his head. She was fourteen then, and I was by no means the first subject she had studied very intimately. Oh, no! . . . I would lay ten maravedi to one that my reading of the situation is right!'

She nodded.

'I wish, Julian, that you hadn't told me that!'

He studied her pale beauty with quizzical interest, and a detached speculation.

'Uncle's precious appears to be experiencing a sensation that a woman of method and business has no business to experience?' he hazarded.

'*You* can hardly complain if I am!' said Jasmine. Paused to analyse: 'I don't know. He is so different from all the drunken fools — the fat rich men — the fatuous soldiers — the shoddy counts — all the mud from

the bottom of the pond which we seem to stir up wherever we go! . . .
He is respectful, and young, and—'

'I see that I shall have to ask his intentions! But you shall have him,
my beautiful! Trust uncle! . . . Any difficulty with his people? You
haven't met them, I suppose?'

'No. Grandmamma meets nobody, and Uncle Harrady detests the Irish!
They've got this town in their hands. They could buy it up, if they
wanted to. I think they suspect me! I believe they are plotting against
me! I'm sure they are! So far they've contented themselves with opening
negotiations with old Corvisart for this house! But you can see what
that means?'

Uncle could. He listened with a narrowing of eyes, and a thoughtful
cocking of eyebrows.

'Nothing else?'

'During the last few months,' she said, 'I fancied—I fancied—'

'Another woman?' inquired Pagan, permitting himself a faintly sympathetic attitude.

Jasmine did not answer immediately. She turned with slow grace to
the clavichord: with slow grace seated herself before it; with infinite
grace drew from it a little ripple of dancing, heartless melody.

'He has a cousin—a long-legged cousin,' she said at last, without turning. 'She is beginning to grow up! I think they are playing her against
me! She is certainly quite pretty. I fancy that he has begun to realize it.
He doesn't come here so often now. I have a feeling somehow that his
loyalties have divided. That he looks on me as the unattainable fairy lady
of a dream, and his cousin as a beautiful and companionable reality . . .
I don't want to be treated as a dream! I want to be treated as a reality!
I dare hardly say anything for fear it should be out of keeping with the
part he has assigned to me . . . If she knew about Hortense, I'll swear
she'ld say "How frightfully naughty of you! Tell me all about it,
Rowley!"—They call him Rowley, you know! But *I* daren't!—"Was it
exciting?" she'ld go on. "What did she say? . . . So what did you do?
. . . Did you really? . . . And what then?" There'ld be nothing dirty
about it—just interest! I'm interested, too. But I couldn't afford even
to hint that I know that there is such a thing as the bedding of man and
woman.'

'You couldn't manage to be seduced, I suppose, my pet? Our friend
is of the right age and exact temperament to handle very prettily with
charming results in such a case.'

'I have thought about it,' said Jasmine to the clavichord, 'but it's impossible, impossible, impossible!'

And the clavichord echoed her dismissal of the suggestion with a low sweet moan.

'Don't despair!' said the count.

He rose and surveyed himself in the long mirror in ivory-painted frame with gilt rosettes, beside the door. Jasmine did not turn. She remained seated at the clavichord, her lovely head — the colour of spun glass with the sunshine on it — lifted as though yearning toward the simulacrum of himself which faced her out of the golden frame.

'A seduction! A marriage! . . . Simple natural steps. Trust uncle . . . He's younger than you are, of course, and it will be a couple of years before he's his own master! Until then money! Money! But even that ought to be arranged quite comfortably! . . . Where is he now, by the way?'

'He should have got back last night from Marseilles. His grandmother sends him there once a month. Sometimes he's away for a week at a time. He sails there. She has bought him a schooner — the fastest thing on the coast. The cabin's most beautifully fitted up.'

'The very thing! You've been on board?'

'What do you mean? . . . Yes, several times! With Cousin Kate, of course!'

'My pet preserves the decencies of society! How nice! . . . But my mind is still running on seduction! . . . What's he go to Marseilles for?'

'His grandmother is financing some crack-brained inventor who's going to blow every English warship sky-high. I don't understand how or why. But she is; and Anthony goes in order to be able to report progress. Also he really seems to know something about the device, whatever it is. I'm not certain that he doesn't do some supervising. I wish he didn't. It's become a sort of mania with him. He sits here sometimes and talks technicalities to me by the hour! . . . Cousin Kate goes to sleep — or slips off to the kitchen. I wish she wouldn't always slip off to the kitchen. The *bonne* doesn't like it, and it's so degrading! . . . And I have to listen, and pretend to be interested in the number of pounds of gunpowder it will take to blow up an English sloop, or frigate or first-rater!'

'I wish he'd blow up the whole bloody race — exterminate every bastard — and send the women to compounds for the use of Cossacks!'

'He has been greatly stirred,' said Jasmine, 'by the wrongs done by England to the noble House of Pagan, lawful descendants of the High Kings of Tara and Ruaidhri O'Connor!' — Here the clavichord made a small tinkling ironic comment. — 'You and I have been the victims of odious oppression — particularly me! Like a knight errant he would fight any dragon to see me righted . . . He is really rather charming! . . .

His grandmother owes me a debt of gratitude. She is fanatically anti-British—'

'She has good reason to be.'

'—and I know that she has worked on him all her life by every means in her power to make him the same. She hasn't succeeded—she's too inhuman, I should think. Still I've done something to help by appealing to the romantic and chivalrous side of his character!'

'Not from any love of her, I imagine?'

'In order to romanticize myself.'

'Some day,' remarked Count Pagan, still approving his appearance, 'we must see what can be done about funds for the Irish republican movement. No, on second thoughts, no! I know of more deserving objects! ... But this, my pet, is a side-issue entirely! Although, perhaps, it would pay us to be a little more Irish—in our speech for instance! The merest *soupçon!* An occasional "Glory be to God and the Houly Saints!" Now and then a sound cursing of "The murthering bloudy-minded¹ English—may God blight them this day!" A—No! This is too serious a business, which will need our best attention, my girl! I don't mind saying that funds are tight—very tight! I had the worst possible luck in Paris. Practically everything I brought back from America went!'

'I want him,' said Jasmine, rising from the music-stool, and walking towards Pagan, and looking over his shoulder at his reflection in the mirror. 'I don't know whether it's because of the security he stands for; or because I want something clean and honest—for a change, or think I do!'

'Money is what you want! And what I want,' said Pagan swinging round on her. 'And when we've got it—'

He did not finish the sentence in words, but caught her to him; crushed her to him, and kissed her on the lips with a savage ferocity to which after a moment's passiveness she suddenly responded.

She went back to the instrument: sat down before it, her fingers on the keys.

'Damn! damn! damn!' said Jasmine.

And the very soul of the little clavichord vibrated to the burthen of the quivering strings—'Damn! damn! damn!' ...

On that same sunny afternoon in early March, Anthony Purvis sat writing poetry at the large untidy table in Harradence's small study.

There was not room for a single volume more in the crowded bookshelves, and the overflow, together with an assortment of papers, covered the surface of the table, except for the small clearing before him. There was only one chair in the room — 'When I'm in here I don't want visitors,' said Harradence — and the solitary other piece of furniture was a small buffet in the window on which was a great pile of newspapers in half a dozen languages, and a salver bearing a bottle of Madeira and other materials for making sangaree. Anthony was allowed to withdraw there for any profound meditation when Harradence was away from home. It was a privilege far greater than the appearance of the room would suggest.

Anthony had got as far as the title — written very fair on a sheet of blue-tinged foolscap —

'The Daughter of the Swan'

After that he was gravelled. There appeared to be no rhymes to the word Swan, except Con, Don, Gone, Shone, and Wan, and none of these particularly fitted into the pattern of the proposed poem or his notions on the subject of it.

He rejected his pen — with the feathered end of which he had been combing his thick dark hair — as being partly responsible for the breakdown. Chose another from the shallow wide box with seven compartments, in which Harradence kept his quills — three for each day of the week, one nib being broad-cut, one fine, and one oblique.

The simile (he considered) was perfect! 'Swanlike' was the only adjective to apply to Jasmine: it conveyed all the sense of the slimness, and effortless movement, and pallor, that were hers. And Helen of Troy, most beautiful of women, was known as Daughter of the Swan — so Miss Buckley said: thus it became extraordinarily fitting. He wished that he had borrowed Buck's rhyming dictionary — her constant companion, together with a number of russia-leather-bound albums in which she made fair copies of the endless poems — Odes, Elegies, Sonnets, Epics — that streamed from a too-facile pen.

In his mind there pulsed all the enchantment and music of deathless song: in his mind there was a vision of such pale beauty as is of ladies who dwell in the Other World beyond the Gates of Dreams . . . But the foolscap remained blank.

The new pen being of no assistance, he sought inspiration from the latest edition of Lemprière's *Classical Dictionary,* that had arrived recently, after Harradence had begun an immense enthusiasm for the lesser known classics — which he proposed to read in alphabetical order, starting with Alciphron.

'Leda — ' said the learned Dr. Lemprière, ' — was seen bathing in the river Eurotas by Jupiter, when she was some few days advanced in her pregnancy, and the god, struck with her beauty, resolved to deceive her. He persuaded Venus to change herself into an eagle, while he assumed the form of a swan; and, after this metamorphosis, Jupiter, as if fearful of the tyrannical cruelty of the bird of prey, fled through the air into the arms of Leda, who willingly sheltered the trembling bird from the assaults of his superior enemy. The caresses with which the naked Leda received the swan, enabled Jupiter to avail himself of his situation, and nine months after this adventure, the wife of Tyndarus brought forth two eggs — '

Eggs!

Dr. Baldamus might have been intrigued. Anthony was horrified.

Suppose he *had* written that poem, and suppose Jasmine *had* seen it, and suppose she *had* been sufficiently interested to inquire into the legend of Helen's birth, what a revolting tale of bestiality and unnatural sin would have been unfolded through his unwitting instrumentality, before her innocent eyes!

Eggs!

He dropped the foolscap, as though it were red-hot, into a waste-paper basket shaped like a Greek amphora and quite big enough to have served as a rain-water barrel.

'Damn!'

He went back to the task on which he was supposed to be engaged — a connotation of the immense correspondence that had been amassed in connection with the *Nautilus*.

There were letters of inquiry from Mr. Fulton into the progress of work at Marseilles; letters of advice, of triumph, of despair. There were letters about clockwork torpedoes, about the construction of copper air reservoirs, about the dimension of cranks. Notes made by himself on July 29, on that momentous day when he had assisted at the first plunge of the original *Nautilus,* in the Seine — a dive lasting eight minutes, and followed by another of more than a quarter of an hour. Memoranda from the shipyard in Marseilles distracted by repeated alteration in design. More letters from Fulton; recording fresh experiments in the open sea off the Breton coast and an attempted attack on the British brig *L'Oiseau;* telling of an enthusiastic official report to the First Consul, of a meeting with General Bonaparte himself, of the perfidy of the Minister of Marine; and then, latest of all, a hurried scrawl announcing that his project had been accepted — that ten thousand francs had been placed to his account — that the Government offered to pay him 400,000 francs for every enemy ship of more than thirty guns which he might destroy — that he hoped to start for Marseilles in a week or so, 'but meanwhile a small and very

temporary loan, say a couple of thousand livres . . . unexpected expenses
. . . journey . . .'

With a sigh Anthony prepared to reply, enclosing a draft by his grandmother upon her Paris banker. Mr. Fulton, he felt, would soon have
serious need to sink a British three-decker or two if he were ever to repay
the money he had borrowed.

Garland materialized in the doorway.

'Come for a ride, Rowley!'

'Can't! Wish I could!'

'Of course you can!'

He looked up at her from the littered table. She was already dressed
for riding, in a habit of biscuit-coloured cloth — short-jacketed, long-
sleeved — with green gloves and a primrose beaver hat like a man's.
There was a scarf of russet brown with stripe of primrose loosely tied
round the white ruffle at her throat.

'My goodness, Garland!' he said wide-eyed. 'That's new!'

'Don't you think it's nice? Isn't it superb? Uncle Harrady sent it from
Paris. He must have spent a fortune! It's made by Minette — Madame
Bonaparte's dressmaker. It only wanted ever such little alteration. Do
say you like it!'

Anthony said that he liked it. He continued to regard her with the
puzzled expression, which had become a not infrequent phenomenon
since Victor Radomski had paid them a two months' visit and had been
utterly subjugated: an expression which always sent Harradence stomp-
ing along to Elizabeth's boudoir, where he roared out boasts of fast-
coming victory, mingled with much self-commendation.

For Elizabeth had said to Harradence months before, when they had
finished their evening game of chess over the fire in her room —

'You can't dress up the child like this, Harrady! . . . They are beautiful
clothes you keep on getting for her, but most unsuitable for her age, and
for our quiet life. That last dress! — You would expect to see it in the
Parc de Bagatelle on one of the elegant young ladies who make life bright
for elderly grandees!'

'You're jealous, Lizzie!'

'Don't call me Lizzie,' snapped Elizabeth. 'And I don't understand
you!'

'Lizzie! Lizzie!' said the maddening Harradence. 'You are being
Lizzyish, that's what you are doing! You don't want the child to look
her real age — after all she *is* seventeen — because it reveals your own!'

'I'm not ashamed of being thirty-four,' said Elizabeth.

'You are! And you are missing, as well, the entire point of the proceedings. Garland is the strategy of the old and wily Harradence: her
dresses are his tactics in the campaign against sinister Irish invader and
sinister grandmother. In but a short while I shall say with friend
Marvell —

> "And now the Irish are ashamed
> To see themselves in one year tamed:
> So much one man can do,
> That does both act and know."

Garland is my periapt, my talisman! With her I drive away earthly
enemies as well as ghosts!'

'I don't see how you are going to effect that by dressing her up till she
looks as if she came from the Palais Egalité? I oughtn't to allow it!'

'My lovely and fading Lizzie — By the way, why don't you keep rum
in your room? — doesn't it occur to you that the Garland of post-Institut-
Putzger days has got to be evolved as something utterly different from
the Garland of pre-Institut-Putzger days? Young Rowley has to be
brought to the point where he'll say to himself "Who is this lovely, de-
sirable, exquisite lady? Who is this intelligent and magnificently dressed
creature? This is not my old tomboy child friend! Obviously this firm
has no connection with any other firm of the same name!" Once he
reaches that stage, the rest is easy! We'll not merely best the yellow-
haired siren, but the old witch in the tower! I have studied human nature!
It is one of the things to which I have really paid full attention! There is
little that escapes me! I say that we shall win all along the line! . . . The
old witch may be an efficient sorceress when it's just a question of han-
dling grandsons, but when it comes to dealing with me, or endeavoring
to remove sirens from her path by buying them off, or driving them out
of town by moral pressure, then she is the merest tyro! A pathetic and
futile anachronism!'

'But — ' began Elizabeth.

'Are you fond of Rowley, or are you not?'

'Of course I am, you idiot, but it's much too soon to start match-
making for him and Garland!'

'Idiot yourself!' said Harradence without offence, heels on fender,
elbows on mantelpiece, and coat-tails perilously close to crackling wood
fire. 'Until this damned plunging-boat is finished Madam Witch and her
grandson are anchored within range of the enemy. The very circumstances therefore compel us, my Lizzie, to reply to a match-making attack
by a counter-thrust of the same nature . . . For this purpose I am borrow-

ing your daughter. As I did once before! After all she is a year older than you when you were married!'

'Haven't I got a say in the matter, Henry? Supposing Garland got hurt!'

'You know as well as I do that Garland would be victorious! She inherits her mother's capacity for conquest!'

Elizabeth lifted her eyes from the candlelit chess-table at which she sat — from the board of ebony and white ivory strewn with her defeated host. She contemplated Harradence in silence for a little before she answered very slowly —

'And has her mother been so very victorious? Has she, Henry?'

He evaded this side-issue —

'We won't discuss the old folk!'

'Well, suppose, then, that Rowley got hurt!'

'Do you think it likely? It's as little likely as that Garland should — and you know it! Anyhow what hurt to him could be comparable to what he would get through being tied for life to a damned Irishwoman?'

'She may,' said Elizabeth weakly, 'be a very nice girl!'

'She *may!*' said Harradence. 'There *may* be nice snakes — nice tigers — nice scorpions — nice alligators! But it is unlikely. She comes from a race, my ignorant Lizzie, that in ancient times considered it etiquette to commit incest; in the Middle Ages invariably cut out the hearts of their enemies and ate them; and to-day fight for freedom by massacring their opponents in cold blood and then securing funds for further murder by betraying one another to the authorities.'

'But —'

'Do not interrupt! . . . Coming from the general to the specific, I would point out that apart from a tainted race, this young woman's only known relative — if he is one, which I greatly doubt — is a dyed-in-the-wool adventurer. A dangerous man. A very dangerous man. I have been at some pains to find out a little about his recent history. As for the girl, I can ascertain nothing about her antecedents. They've put out all sorts of romantic stories to account for her, but I don't believe a word of them. If town gossip is to be believed the relationship between the two is hardly that of uncle and niece!' . . . 'Uncle and niece!' echoed Elizabeth, thoughtfully examining her father's sister-in-law's brother, who reddened a trifle and hurriedly continued, 'There are queer stories, too, about her and old Fraissinet! It would be useless to say anything of this to Rowley, of course . . . In Garland I see safety for him from a man-eater, and from the abominations of his old grandmother!'

'But —'

'You say you are fond of Rowley. I know you love Garland. Well then — ! . . . We'll ask that fellow Rowley's always talking about, Victor Radomski, to stay. And see if we can't work up a little jealousy?'

With that he had left; returning a moment later to poke his head round the edge of the door to survey her as she sat thoughtfully staring into the fire — to survey the room . . . An old-fashioned room full of soft and friendly shadows in which old-fashioned furniture and old-fashioned china and old-fashioned hangings gleamed their response to golden fire-light and primrose candlelight. On a marqueterie commode against a wall was a dish piled with crystallized fruits. The sight of that glowing red and green and gold heap distracted Harradence from what he had intended to say.

He suddenly said, instead, without entering the room —

'Sugar-plums! . . . What wouldn't I give for that to be a dish of apples come straight from an English orchard! A great pyramid of apples — spice-apples, Keswicks, quarrenders, pippins! A dozen different kinds — wine-red, flame, dark green, light green, yellow, golden, streaky, shiny-coated, dull-coated! Big. Small. Round. Pear-shaped. Elliptical. Knobbly. Apples that one could take up in one's hand, narrating their history, knowing not merely their parent trees, but the very boughs from which they came. "Here's a little spice," one would say. "It comes from the tree at the far end of the orchard — you know, where the big hive was! Not the young tree — the old tree! I picked it up last evening, after the gale. I nearly missed it in the grass. It wasn't bruised at all." And you'ld hold it to the light, admiring its colour and shape and bouquet. And you'ld eat it with connoisseurship and enjoyment — not like an orchard-robber, but with a silver knife upon a porcelain plate — because it was a token of affection from an old and valued friend.'

'Your orchard is still there, even if your house is in ruins, Henry!' said Elizabeth, still looking into the fire.

'Ah!' said the large ruffled head non-committally.

'It is not apples that you want,' said Elizabeth without turning. 'It is the orchard. It isn't even the orchard that you want. It is England!'

'Ah!' repeated the head, and began to retire; paused before the operation was completed, and added in a rather embarrassed manner —

'I withdraw the word "fading". I withdraw the word "ignorant". I withdraw the word "Lizzie". In fact I withdraw everything that might lead anyone to imagine that I don't think . . . my Elizabeth . . .' The voice became an inaudible rumble accompanying heavy tread into the darkness of the passage.

Elizabeth turned: remained looking at the door, as though she hoped to see that ruffled high-nosed head again. . . .

Count Pagan dismissed the youth he had hired in Paris as body-servant, after he had unstrapped valise and trunk. The small bedroom that he had been given was whitewashed, and bare — still he liked bare bedrooms when he slept alone. But it was also rather dark, for the green persiennes were closed. He opened the window and flung the shutters wide.

Although the afternoon sun did not beat directly into it, the cobbled street was luminous. Opposite, by the door of Corvisart's shop, the buds of a plane tree were beginning to open their tender green against the grey house-front. Monsieur Jacquot, the old priest, ambled past in his shovel hat, listening attentively to the earnest conversation of a child who ran alongside, clinging to a fold of his shabby *soutane*. A moment later Monsieur Corvisart came out of the dark entry to his shop, and stood, pro-prietorially, puffing at a long china pipe, before the small window in which was paraded a rank of grey earthenware jars inscribed with mys-terious symbols, that had been old when Louis XIII was king.

Although it was the afternoon Monsieur Corvisart still wore his dressing-gown with a very high stand-up collar of green velvet, and list slippers.

What a town! reflected Pagan. Yet it was the battle-ground whereon he might win a mightier victory than even Paris could provide . . . He thought of the great house he had seen in America a few months ago, with its long white façade shimmering in the dusk; of the vast estate upon it — thousands upon thousands of acres, with hundreds upon hundreds of slaves. High Pale — the palace of the ruler of a domain as great as many a Serene Transparency's in the welter of Germany's sov-ereign states! . . . And then the lachrymose soap-manufacturer in reserve! . . . The lad Purvis would probably pay a call this afternoon, Jasmine said.

He was about to retire from the window to the task of setting out the manifold silver and crystal and ivory toilette requisites without which he never travelled, when he heard the sound of horses' hoofs on the cobbles. He looked out, screened from view by dark green curtains.

Monsieur Corvisart too glanced down the street, and then, obviously fearing to be caught in déshabillé, shot into his shop.

Pagan recognized at once the russet-coated lad riding the big bay and listening with a smile to his companion. He knew too, without need of telling, who was the girl on the chestnut mare: admired her looks, her habit and low-crowned beaver hat, her sleek and ruddy horse, the English saddlery, and the careless-seeming care with which the fiery gallant creature was restrained.

'I always say, Rowley — ' said the lady, 'I always — '

He watched them pass until they were out of sight, with a chill of foreboding. The 'long-legged cousin' was a dangerous foe — a far more dangerous foe than he had been led to believe.

Monsieur Corvisart caught sight of him: crossed the street, to give him greeting at the window. Then —

'What a romance unfolding!' said Monsieur Corvisart, jerking his head in the direction of vanished cavalcade. 'Both so young and so lovely! And so rich! So suitable! So much to be desired! It is a fairy-tale! A fairy-tale *absolument!* . . . Perhaps you could spare me half an hour for a little matter of business in a day or so?'

CHAPTER II

A PROBLEM IN LOYALTIES

'I AM acquainted with seventeen different ways of cooking a lobster,' said Harradence regarding the empty dish before him, 'but of them all there is none to equal the Spanish. I opine that these were cooked in my best East India sherry, and that Antoine with great judgment added what I might call a "breath" of red herring to the sauce. Is that so, Paul?'

Paul deferentially acknowledged the correctness of the assumption.

'Give Antoine my compliments, and tell him that with Mrs. Vane's permission I shall have a sweet-sour stew of carp for my breakfast on the day after to-morrow. He will *not* cook it in French beer. You may get him, instead, a bottle of Kenton's "Crown and Magpie" for the purpose from the cellar.'

'When I was in New Orleans at the end of the American war in '82 — no, '83 — I remember eating lobster cooked in brandy and red pepper,' remarked Lieutenant Courville.

'Creole cookery has its peculiarities,' commenced Harradence indulgently.

He surveyed the table.

The Parliament of La Cadière was in plenary and gustatory session about the round table in the Round Parlour. They were all there excepting Anthony — pontifical Corvisart with tremendous shirt-frill, bird-like priest, sardonic soldier of almost-forgotten wars and by-passed strategies, Dr. Baldamus with multitudinous chins slumped on chest and obese body slumped in chair. The business of debate not yet having been reached, Elizabeth and Garland and the bosomy and poetical Miss Buckley bore them company.

Although it was barely dusk the curtains were already drawn and the panelled room bathed in golden light from wall-sconces, and from the great candlesticks on the altar-like sideboards where the high-priest Paul and his attendant acolytes did reverent duty among decanters, bottles, sauceboats, chafing-dishes, *bains-marie,* and all sorts of tureens and platters. Each diner, too, had set before him, or her, a silver candlestick for personal use. For — had declared Harradence — the *gourmet* well knows that to appreciate good food sight is as important as the senses of taste and smell and touch. In fact — had argued Harradence — it was questionable whether all five senses must not be employed for full enjoyment: the music of a parting cork, the gush of wine into the glass, the clatter of knife and fork, the subdued and gentle rustle of movement at the buffet, the elfin sizzling of kidneys in a chafing-dish — these were all of vital moment to the processes of the cultured digestion.

'Where's Rowley?' he asked, inspecting the dish which Paul had wheeled round on a trolley and revealed for his examination from under an enormous silver cover — a whole lamb roast, bedded upon mushrooms, ornamented by a design in oysters, olives and tomatoes.

'Rowley's still in Marseilles,' said Garland rather flatly. 'We thought he would have come back with you to-day.'

'I stayed all the week at the Paradis, but saw nothing of him — not even a flashing glimpse of that marvellous new hat which I'll swear is a foot wide from brim to brim!'

'Mr. Fulton got there three days ago. I . . . I had a letter from Rowley in which he said so.'

'Ah!' said Harradence, noting the news with regret, and the hesitant admission of receipt of a letter with pleasure . . . 'Yes, Paul? What is it?'

He unfolded the billet which the major-domo presented to him — a tiny plait of paper, its complications secured by a small seal of black wax. Read with a puzzled expression. Rose reluctantly to his feet.

'If you will forgive me, Elizabeth! If you will excuse me, gentlemen! Here is Madam Purvis demanding my attendance in the very middle of dinner. A most extraordinary thing! God knows what the old lady wants! She has never done such a thing before . . . I suppose I had better see what it is all about!'

'Rowley!' said Garland quickly. 'Can anything have happened to Rowley?'

Harradence shook his great head.

'Most improbable!'

Said Corvisart with meaning —

'Perhaps, Mr. Harradence, you will be so kind as to tell Madame that I have done to-day as she asked. She will like to know as soon as possible. I had intended writing to her, but if it would not be troubling you . . .'

Harradence was away for so long a while that they had reached dessert when he returned, and decanters of dark wine and dishes of sunrise-golden oranges glowed like the treasure of Aladdin upon the bare and shining table.

He was pale — for him; and he stood by his chair in silence for a perceptible space of time before seating himself, as if he were weighing up his guests. He waved aside the dishes which Paul hastened to produce: had his glass filled with a wine that was almost scarlet: in a low voice dismissed the high-priest of the sideboard and his acolytes.

Garland looked up at the big figure dominating the table as though about to speak: tried to read whatever was written in the big leathery face and arrogant nose — what tale of trouble was told in the more-than-usual disorder of the iron-grey hair: divined disaster: paled: and, even as she lowered her lovely eyes to her plate, shot a quick glance of appeal to her mother.

Elizabeth knew the question that she would not ask again; spoke for her —

'There is nothing wrong with Rowley, is there?'

'Nothing has happened to Rowley, my dear!'

It was some while afterward that Harradence spoke again. He said, in what was for him a low tone, although everybody round the table could hear —

'I am afraid that this must be the last session of our Parliament — for me, at least!'

There was a murmur of surprised regret.

Looking up from under shaggy eyebrows, Harradence saw that Elizabeth's dark blue eyes were fixed on him; that something new, expectant, vital, had come into her bearing. Her slim hands were cupped one above the other at the table edge, and she was bent forward a little over them, head thrown up so that he could see the long curves of her white throat from chin to bosom.

'Does this mean that you are leaving us?' asked Courville.

'But this must not be! *Non, absolument non!*' declared Corvisart in his crypt-like tones.

Elizabeth said nothing. Garland said nothing. Dr. Baldamus said nothing — for he was presumably lost in some oological reverie. Miss

Buckley was not there to say anything: she had departed, as usual, to attend the bed-going of Madam Purvis — a ceremonial more akin to funeral obsequies than the initiatory rites of nightly slumber.

'My son,' said Monsieur Jacquot — and it was the first time that he had ever so addressed Harradence — 'this is sad news for us!'

In his old and gentle voice was implicit the recognition of crisis, and the offer of whatever spiritual help a Roman priest might bring to a Unitarian.

It was to this unspoken offer that Harradence replied, so low that none but the other could hear —

'I must go, and at once. To-morrow perhaps you will know how, and why. Do not think too harshly of me!'

Monsieur Jacquot said nothing out loud, but he whispered to himself between two sections of orange, the words of Thomas à Kempis —

'"My son, rest thy heart firmly upon the Lord, and be not afraid of the judgment of men!"'

Elizabeth still watched; still waited. She had rarely seen Harradence so deeply moved, but knew too that nothing, save death, would ever quench his volubility. Sometimes she wondered if even that would be sufficient. Once, indeed, she had said to him that she thought he would welcome public execution for the dramatic opportunity it offered of turning the scaffold into a rostrum.

What had happened? Would not these others ever go? Would he — could be — say nothing until all the partings had been said, and re-said?

Then suddenly Harradence drank off his wine at a draught, and leaned forward as though to impart confidences that must not even reach the panels of the wall.

They had all been watching him, either openly or unostentatiously: and at his movement a desultory conversation died away.

'May I inflict on you — my friends — a short personal explanation?' he asked. 'So that if at some future date the world should say "He was a traitor to his ideals and faith", you at any rate will know the truth?'

He paused for an instant to collect their consent, and then went on, sitting with arms folded on the table and big shoulders hunched, staring before him at the litter of crystal and porcelain and silver illumined by the circle of candles —

'It is almost exactly eight years since I first came among you — since I landed in France. You all know why I came — and with what hopes. You know, too, why I left my native land. Because I spoke too freely and too loudly of human rights and freedom: because I attacked what I thought was injustice and privilege. Because my home was destroyed by the deluded victims of oppression, and I was refused the common rights of a citizen.

'I became the Pilgrim of Liberty. I sought it across the Atlantic: I did not find it. In the very land where it was first proclaimed that "all men are created equal", I found instead hundreds of thousands of human beings the property of others — slaves subject to uncontrolled brutality, their lives patterned utterly to their owners' whims.

'Where would I find Liberty, then? In the states of Germany where a woman of the middle class may not seat herself nearer a great lady in a public place than six chairs away? In Russia where you must kneel in the snow when the Tsar's sledge drives by? In Spain where the Holy Inquisition has not yet been abolished? Amid the petty tyrannies of Italy, or the ghetto of Rome?

'I became a traitor. I sought refuge in the country with whom my own was waging — as I thought — unjustifiable war. The country of Liberty, Equality, and Fraternity!

'Through all the welter of blood of the Terror I said to myself, "These are the birth pangs of Freedom and the New Order of things!" I waited while in the name of Liberty thousands who were neither tyrants nor traitors died on the scaffold.

'When the days of Thermidor came, and Robespierre and his butchers went the way of their victims, I said, "It is the end of the beginning". It was not! There was no liberty, only licence! France was delivered to the speculator, and the profiteer, and the politician. I said, "This is a natural reaction from the horrors of the Terror". It was a reaction that lasted five long years!

'There came Brumaire and General Bonaparte's *coup d'état*. I said "Here is the strong man who will lift France out of the mire and set her again on the path of her ideals!" But Bonaparte has brought no liberty back to France — he has brought slavery. All the blood and tears and destruction of the Revolution have but resulted in a new and damnable despotism!'

'It is true!' said the republican Corvisart.

'I have seen wars of defence become wars of offence. I have seen Liberty gorged and gross with conquest — France bloated with the territory she has devoured in Germany and Italy and Flanders, ferocious foster-mother of new republics in Holland and Switzerland and Lombardy.'

'Alas!' said Monsieur Jacquot.

'This is not the France for which Mirabeau laboured or Moreau has fought — of which good republicans dreamed. Is it, Monsieur Corvisart?'

'It is not. *Absolument non!*' said Corvisart.

'Neither is it your France, Monsieur Courville!'

'My views are known,' said Courville. 'I fought at Toulon with the English against my own countrymen. I saw what I had never thought to see — the scuttling of a great French fleet so that it should not fall into the hands of Frenchmen. If I could have escaped to England then I should still be under arms with thousands of my brothers.'

'Nor is this France yours!' said Harradence, turning to the old man at his side. 'This France without God. Whose ruler two years ago contemplated turning Mahometan to forward his policies in the East! This France of desecrated churches!'

'France is always mine,' he replied. 'Nor is France without God, for "His compassions fail not; they are new every morning!" '

Before the simple statement Harradence's rhetoric came to a halt. When he spoke once more, after a brief silence, it was in short and abrupt sentences. Earnestly. Impressively.

'To-night something has happened. Something which has made me admit to myself that I was wrong. Made me admit to myself what in fact I had realized months ago. That the only liberty left in Europe is . . . in England! That the only hope for liberty in Europe is in England. In her refusal to admit defeat. In her readiness to stand alone. She faces a great enemy alone now. Where are her friends? Austria is broken. Russia is arming against her former friend. Prussia, Denmark, Sweden are organized to smash her commerce. Spain is about to invade Portugal, England's last ally. Practically all Italy is barred against her . . . I must return to my own land in this hour of her need, and to my old loyalties!'

His voice gradually raised itself; became a shout. He got to his feet: turned to the great buffet behind him, and took from it a black bottle and a large glass which he filled with golden-brown liquid, clear, sparkling, foam-capped.

'I can't ask you to drink this toast with me, gentlemen! It would not be right . . . I am drinking to Liberty, and to the only country where any vestige yet remains! I drink to England! In English ale! God save England!'

He raised the rummer; emptied it without drawing breath; smashed it with great violence upon the table, scarring the mahogany mirror of its surface with slivers of glass, flecking it with the creamy dregs.

As if the vehemence of the act had contented some deep spiritual need, he immediately turned to the old priest and began a conversation in his most normal tones on the subject of Gomarism.

His guests did not remain long afterwards, and he himself saw them to the wrought iron gates of the courtyard, where he bade Corvisart and

Jacquot an affectionate farewell, and stayed for some short time in very earnest talk with Courville. . . .

He went down the dark passage to his study. There was a light in the room, showing under the door, and he nearly turned tail, for it had been half in his mind to depart without further farewell and without explanation.

Garland was there, standing before the low sideboard on which two candles burned, with her back to the open window. A slim girl in a smoke-blue dress, against the blue-blackness of the night, slim arms bare, and slim fingers pressed against the top of the buffet behind her. She was facing him as he entered, and kept her bright eyes fixed upon his face.

Elizabeth was sitting in his great elbow chair — the only chair in the room — under the dark cliff of books, before the immense writing-table which occupied most of the floor-space. She shot one quick glance at him and then resumed her study of the fire.

It had to come!

Nobody said anything.

He walked to the fireplace, and stood for a moment apparently lost in contemplation of a couple of cartoons hanging on the chimney-breast. He had bought them in Paris last year because they had amused him. One showed a fleet of monster fire-balloons loaded with soldiers, cannon and horses, apparently traversing the English Channel. The other very graphically displayed invasion barges, the size of islands, propelled by windmills (it would seem) toward the cliffs of Dover. They did not amuse him now.

He turned round, and looked out, past Garland, into the night. Somewhere in the distance across the bay, the darkness that was sky and sea was pin-pricked by tiny points of light.

He regarded the dark youthful beauty of silent Garland. He regarded the fair beauty — that was youthful, too — of silent Elizabeth.

He said —

'Madam Purvis sent for me, because she wanted to show me a letter that arrived to-night. She lent it to me because she thought that you, too, would be interested! There's much of it that doesn't matter. I'll read what does . . . It's from Rowley!'

Garland did not cease to study him.

'Rowley!' she said. 'I knew it was.'

He fumbled in the long tails of his green dress coat, produced a stiff rustling sheet of paper; sought on the mantelshelf for the bright red leather case in which his spectacles were supposed to be always obvious to the searcher; found it in his pocket, and donned glasses that were horn-rimmed with oblong lenses — a fantasy of which he was particularly proud.

He read —

'Rue de la République 79,
'Marseilles

'My dear Grandmother,

'I write to tell you, as you asked, that *Nautilus II* has passed all her tests most satisfactorily. Mr. Fulton was very pleased with her behaviour last week when we put out into the harbour and submerged to a depth of twenty-five feet, where we remained for four hours and twenty minutes *without any discomfort*, by the aid of the copper reservoirs of compressed air. There was no need to burn any candles, as the thick windows in the upper part of the boat admit even at that depth enough light to read the barometer and compass. She sails well and looks like a small fishing-boat on the surface. Once you have lowered the mast the business of plunging takes just two minutes. Under-water progress, of course, is slow, even with two men at the crank of the propeller, but, of course, it is not proposed to attack a moving object.

'On the day before yesterday we went right out into the bay and manœuvred for something like twelve hours. Yesterday we sailed along the coast and attacked the hulk of a forty-foot sloop which the Maritime Prefect of Marseilles had had anchored to serve us as a target off Mourepiane. We struck it after we had passed underneath, with a forty-pound submarine bomb, and blew it to smithereens. Nothing was left except the buoy and the cable! Mr. Fulton managed the bomb, and I took the helm. It was stupendous!

'Thank you very much for letting me go on the *great expedition;* Mr. Fulton would not have allowed it without your written permission.

'We are hoping to make the attempt in the small hours of the day after to-morrow.' — 'That's to-morrow', commented Harradence looking at the small clock on the mantelshelf. — 'We shall enter the bay in the dark and attack the frigate the moment there is a glimmer of light enough for us to make certain of the target. It is a tremendous adventure!'

'A tremendous adventure!' quoted Harradence, folding the letter into a very small square in his big hands . . . 'There cannot be fewer than three hundred men aboard the frigate!'

'Dear God!' said Elizabeth, 'It is murder! It is plain murder!'

Garland said nothing articulate. She uttered something between a cry and a sob: turned suddenly and violently, and looked out of the window.

Across the black bay, against the blackness of sea or land or sky the two or three dim pin-points of light still showed the position of the English ships.

' "The moment there is a glimmer of light," he wrote,' said Harradence, and looked at the clock again. 'That'll be somewhere about five o'clock in the morning . . . It is barely half-past nine now.'

'He mustn't do it, Henry! He doesn't — he can't realize how horrible it is!'

'How can I stop him, Elizabeth? He has already sailed, and who could find a submarine on a moonless night in all the wide bay?'

'He has gone into this like a child seeking adventure — like a small boy playing soldiers — without realizing the implications of the game. He doesn't in the least realize that the "tremendous adventure" may cost three hundred lives. If the frigate were blown up without warning — '

'There would be very few who would live to tell the tale. Most of them would be killed on the spot. And those who were merely scorched and maimed would probably drown!'

'Don't! Oh, don't, Uncle Harrady! I can't bear it!'

Garland did not turn round as she spoke. She leaned forward on her hands further toward the open window, as if she were projecting her spirit through the starless night to do sentinel about those defenceless ships.

'What can you do, Henry?' asked Elizabeth rising to her feet, and coming to his side, and smoothing the great arm in the tight green sleeve of the tight green coat. 'You *must* do something!'

'What do you want me to do?'

'They are our own people. Yours and mine!'

'You needn't remind me of that! . . . What do you want me to do?'

'There are three hundred of them.'

'There are. At least.'

'From the only free country left in Europe!'

'Well? What have I got to do? . . .' He suddenly looked from the bronze-gowned figure at his side to the girl in the window whose face was turned away. 'Garland will tell you what I have to do! What is it I must do, Garland?'

'You've got to warn the ships! . . . You decided long ago! . . . Why must you make *me* say it?'

'Because I wanted you yourself to show and say that you knew what my duty was. I wanted you to admit that it was the only course to take, before I said that I had decided on it . . . I wanted you to realize that the warning which saves three hundred lives may also cost lives. Four or five lives! *One* life in particular!'

Elizabeth, still standing beside the big man with squared shoulders before the small fire, spoke to him again although she watched the slim straight back of her daughter —

'But Henry, surely the ships wouldn't just wait to be attacked, if they were warned. Wouldn't they hoist anchor and sail away?'

He shook his head. He, too, watched that still back.

'No, there are two things against it. One is that there is an on-shore wind, what there is of it. The other is that the best form of defence is attack. If I know anything about it, they'll arrange a cordon of patrol-boats — every boat they've got. Cram them with men with muskets and hand grenades and swivel-guns, and tell them to shoot first and inquire after. They might at the same time put out a sort of barrier of fishing nets. That's the French scheme of defence, I happen to know . . . I reckon that Fulton won't make his final plunge to attack until he has come in very close — as close as he dare without (as he thinks) being spotted by the ships' look-outs. A matter of a few hundred yards! Under-water progress is too slow. And then he'll run straight into the patrol-boats or get caught in the nets and be attacked before he can submerge.'

'It is hideously like betraying Anthony to his death!' said Elizabeth after a silence. She was very white.

'The alternative,' answered Harradence slowly, 'is to betray three hundred British sailors to *theirs!* So you see one has no real choice!'

He extracted his watch from a fob pocket, withdrew it from the chamois leather purse in which it lived, and compared it with the timepiece on the mantel.

Elizabeth without warning burst into tears. She laid her head against Harradence's arm so that her face was hidden; both hands clutched at his wrist, and she wept with quick catches of the breath.

Garland turned round. She was whiter even than her mother, and her face was set in rigid lines.

'Don't cry, mother!' she said. 'Not now! Afterwards — perhaps! . . . How will you warn them, Uncle Harrady?'

'Row out to them — although I haven't touched an oar for God knows how long! I can't ask anyone here to play the traitor to their own country!'

'And then?'

'Then? . . .' He paused for some time before continuing. 'I shall probably just have to remain on board. It's obvious I can't come back. My life will be forfeit. I shall have betrayed France. And even if no one were ever to know, my conscience wouldn't let me return as though nothing had happened.'

'So— ?'

'Well, I suppose that eventually they'll get me back to England. It'll be the best, in the end. Though what will happen I can't guess. I shall probably be arrested on the old warrants. Seditious utterances, and so on! Will lie in prison until the authorities have decided that my services have outweighed my offences. That they will certainly do — in time!'

Elizabeth raised her head. She had regained an outward composure. She spoke in a controlled and even voice, but still retained his large hand in hers.

'You are quite right, Henry! I know you are right: as well as Garland does. There is nothing else to do!'

Said Harradence with a sudden ferocity —

'Curse Fulton! And curse his filthy kind of war! He'd sink a French ship as readily as a British, so long as there was a four hundred thousand francs reward for it — so long as it enabled him to market his devilish invention!'

'It's Madam Purvis you must curse,' said Elizabeth. 'It's she — '

Harradence quoted Vergil —

' "*Vulnus alit venis, et caeco carpitur igni!*" — "She cherishes the wound in her veins, and is consumed by hidden fires!" '

'No,' said Garland; and she clenched her hands in the urgency of denial. 'No, mother, you are wrong! Wrong! She *didn't* succeed. Rowley has no hate in his heart at all! None! All her curses and witchcraft have come to nothing. He doesn't hate anything or anybody. If she had had nothing to do with the *Nautilus* at all, and he had been given this opportunity I am sure he would have taken it. Remember how interested he was before she knew anything about it! He's doing this for the adventure. Without imagination of the suffering and the heartbreak involved. He's doing it for the love of the danger, for the high exploit of a great journey under the sea, to be one of the first to employ a new and wonderful weapon. He's a small boy shooting wildly with a new gun!'

'Garland is right,' said Harradence. 'But the old woman thinks she has succeeded. She is triumphant! She wants the world to know that she is avenging her sons, and through her grandson! She was telling that maid of hers about it when I got there. She was most insistent that I should inform everyone I knew. She was physically quivering with the tearing glory of the immensity of her revenge. She sent for Buck to tell her and to write letters for her — not to be put to bed. When I left she was standing in the window with the spy-glass in her hand, menacing those distant ships with their fate with a malignity you cannot imagine . . . There was another thing, too — '

Garland interrupted —

'But supposing Rowley were to succeed, how could I ever — ?'

Harradence took off his absurd spectacles and examined the brave proud face.

She flushed bright scarlet under his inspection.

'We are taking too gloomy a view,' he said. 'Nothing at all may happen. Somebody else may have warned the ships. They may be hoisting anchor even now.' All three pairs of eyes sought the oblong of night that filled the window frame: but two tiny specks of light still pierced the distant darkness. 'Fulton more than probably will find night manœuvring quite beyond his capacity, and the upshot will be that I shall spend a month or so in an English gaol for nothing. And that we shall have to re-sort our lives a bit. Until the war is over . . .'

'Will it ever be over?' said Garland. 'How long has it been going on . . . Eight years! I never seem to remember it being peace.'

'The dictator will probably find that his Russian alliance will crack. Then there will be a makeshift peace that will last a couple of years or so . . . There is plenty of money here to see you through. I have already spoken to Courville asking him to get you on an American ship from Marseilles as soon as possible, and escort you home to England. He'll do it gladly. Very gladly! I have explained that he shall not lose by it. All I have to do now is to write a short letter to my agent in Marseilles, and another for him to forward to London. One of the men must set off with them immediately.'

He examined his watch again. Compared it with the clock.

'Clement should be here any moment with my valise. I must write those letters and go. There is no sense in running unnecessary risks.'

Said Garland crossing the room, and standing before him —

'Uncle Harrady, I am coming too!'

'What do you mean? You can't possibly! How will you get back?'

'I am coming, too. For the reason that you will never get there if I don't. There is no boat on our beach now except the *Mistraou,* and nobody in the world can handle her alone. You don't know the currents, or the bay, or the boat; and you haven't handled a boat for as long as I can remember. You never would get there. Never! . . . *I am coming, too!* Mother, I am going, too. I *will* go, too! I *must* go, too!'

Her head was back. Her eyes were bright. Her colour high. She even essayed a smile as she spoke.

'Everything is going to be right. Terribly right. And in a month or so we shall be laughing at all our melodrama. But I've got to go with Uncle Harrady, and *he* knows it. The reason is obvious.'

They held hands for a moment — woman in bronze dress who was so like a girl, and girl in smoke-blue who had so suddenly become a woman. 'There must be no slightest chance of Uncle Harrady failing, Mother! No chance of them succeeding! Rowley would be far far more dead like that than if he were just . . . killed . . . or drowned!' Her voice broke. She steadied it. 'I am right, Mother, aren't I?'

'She is right, Henry,' said Elizabeth. 'She must go with you. There can be no failure. For the sake of three hundred lives. For her own sake. For Rowley's sake . . . I've lent her to you twice before for Rowley's sake. Now I lend her again — and mostly for her own . . . God bless you, darling!'

She took Garland in her arms, and kissed the beautiful dejected face on lips and eyes and forehead. Became the brisk mother.

'Go up and get your thick cloak! You will need it. I will come in an instant and help you pack a few things very quickly.'

Garland gone, Elizabeth confronted Harradence. She put her hands upon his shoulders, but though he cupped his hands about her elbows in a gentle grasp he did not lift his hanging head and continued to regard the floor.

'Look at me, Henry!' she demanded.

He obediently raised his grey gaze to the level of her blue eyes, long-lashed, wistful, set in the pallor of her oval face. The gold of her hair, in the shimmer of the candles behind him, held every shade that fields of wheat, traversed by quickly-moving cloud-shadows, can hold in a swift wind.

They looked into one another's eyes for a little, and then Elizabeth said —

'You *do* know, Henry, don't you?'

He did not pretend to misunderstand. He answered just —

'I do, my dearest!'

And kissed her as he had never done before . . . .

He was by himself, hat and big coat thrown upon the table; valise attending his pleasure by the window. Garland should be ready soon.

He waited, still standing rock-like before the fire, his mind full of Elizabeth and himself, staring for a while unseeing at the ceiling-high tiers of books on the opposite wall. Then the golden glint of the binding of one of the volumes caught his attention.

What book was it? In midst of all his confused thoughts he found himself worrying over the identity of the volume. Almost automatically he approached the shelves.

It was a superbly bound edition of *Gil Blas* which Rowley had got for him in Paris as a present . . . Rowley!

How many, indeed, of the books on those crowded shelves had associations for him with the lad!

There was the glowing ruby red binding of the set of Smollett. What debate they had had over the question of the position that *Humphrey Clinker* should occupy in the Temple of Literature! Rowley had liked it better than any other, and had maintained that it was superior to Fielding's *Joseph Andrews*.

How had the *Pseudoxia Epidemica, or Vulgar Errors* of old Sir Thomas Browne got next door to it? A shabby volume, but he and Rowley had revelled in it. When Rowley had got back from Paris he had gone to its pages to re-read the chapter headed, 'That Jews Stink'.

His eyes ranged the shelves: caught sight of the slim tall Alciphron's *Letters*. Rowley said that he had learned more about classical Greece from it than from a dozen lectures. Next to it was Longus' *Daphnis and Chloe*. Odd that Rowley, who hadn't turned a hair over some bits in Alciphron, was definitely shocked by Daphnis' behaviour! Of course, he had been a little shattered — surprisingly enough — by the inserted tales in Montesquieu's *Lettres Persanes* . . . There, too, on an upper shelf was the self-same battered Berners' *Froissart* to which he had introduced the young Anthony eight years ago. He could see the small figure now, in its short black jacket and nankeen trousers, coiled up on the crimson cushions of the long seat under the stern windows of the good ship *Chesapeake*.

He was about to set out to betray that loving and lovable small boy to what might be his death.

There was nothing else to do now. There was much, however, that he might have done in the past . . . It was true that he could never have dissuaded Madam Purvis from financing the construction of the new *Nautilus,* but should it not have been his duty to point out all the horrible implications of the weapon to her grandson, to have discouraged his interest instead of ignoring it? Not on patriotic, but on humanitarian grounds. It was no consolation to tell himself that he could not possibly have known that Anthony would be allowed to take part personally in an expedition that had never been mentioned in his hearing.

He went down on his knees and prayed to Almighty God — for Anthony, for himself, and for a distracted world.

When Garland came a little later she found him writing as though for dear life, the floor about him strewn with the beginnings of a letter. . . .

All night long Madam Purvis sat in a straight-backed chair at the open window whence she could stare across the invisible bay to the invisible islands under the invisible sky, and watch the pin-points of light that shone their insult to France — and to her. For barely a single second did she take her eyes away.

There was no light in the room at all. Cupids and posies on the panels, elegant hunters and nymphs of the chase upon the tapestries, that central scaffold of a table — all were swallowed up in the darkness. She had, indeed, to fumble upon the top of the commode at her elbow at intervals to make sure that a very precious letter was still there — and her lozenges — and the quite useless spy-glass.

Even in that complete blackness, in which no one could have seen — had there been anybody to see — she did not relax for one instant a single muscle that controlled the mask behind which she lived. She sat, a woman of stone, staring out to sea — out to the lights — out to the English ships, with so quiet a respiration that she barely seemed to breathe.

It was some while before midnight that the sparks were suddenly extinguished. But it did not matter to her, since she knew without their guidance where to look.

Gradually the impenetrability of night began to fade; the darkness to lessen, to become a black-grey in which nothing could be distinguished — in which shadowy outlines became just visible in a sub-world of shadow — in which land and sea grew most vaguely recognizable.

Her hand was closing on the telescope when a flash of flame darted from one of the invisible ships: travelled upward as a lurid spark, with the hissing of a snake: burst into a great white light that arched across the sky, revealing the vessels surrounded by a flock of boats: was quenched.

Madam Purvis sought and found the spy-glass: began to raise it.

She had not completed the action before a short-lived even line of scarlet flame was suddenly stippled against the neutral tints of dying night. By the light of the broadside volley for a fraction of a second the hull of the frigate was rendered again visible. There was an echoing sound as though many great doors had been slammed violently in a vaulted passage. Persistent under the reverberations sounded the unceasing wash of the sea along the shingle.

CHAPTER III

FIRE AND WATER

IN the black void of night there began to emerge vague gradations of darkness. Soon the outlines of land would appear against the elemental formlessness of sea and sky. Anthony, awaiting that moment, imagined that so, in the lifting of shadow after shadow, had the world of Genesis been revealed — stark and frigid in the pallid birth of the first dawn.

On the surface of the inky sea was smudged the top of the hull of the *Nautilus II* and her squat metal conning-tower — just awash, like the back of some primal monster humping from out the depths, invisible at more than a few yards.

The mast and the sails, under which she had come from the open sea, had been lowered and were secured along her narrow low-sided deck. Upon this gear Anthony was squatted uncomfortably, peering into the blackness ahead as they moved slowly into the bay. His folded arms rested upon the *calotte* so that his body screened the faint light coming from the open man-hole which led into the hull of the ship. It was still so dark that he could distinguish nothing, not even Fulton's submarine bomb that bobbed somewhere in the oily water nearby as though it were a baby monster nuzzling at its mother's side. He could feel with his fingers, however, the deadly thing pulling at the end of the cord by which it was towed, and by which it would eventually be fired.

From down below rose maddening repetition of the song, which Fulton had hummed, almost without cessation, ever since night fell — a negro song learned during his one and only visit to Virginia, and (Anthony thought) peculiarly unsuitable to their circumstances:

'O Lord, O my Lord,
O my good Lord,
Keep me from sinkin' down!
O my Lord, O my good Lord,
Keep me from sinkin' down!
I tell yo' what I mean to do
— Keep me from sinkin' down —
I mean to go to Heaven too!
Keep me from sinkin' down!'

What did he want to hum that damned silly tune for? The last thing in the world that they wanted was to be kept from 'sinkin' down!' In fact if they could not keep to the scheduled plunging time of two minutes they might find themselves in a very uncomfortable position.

Fulton had only ceased humming it in snatches, or whistling it maddeningly through his teeth in snatches, to discuss what he would do with the four hundred thousand francs prize money. Experiments with a steam engine boat: the construction of a new panorama three hundred feet long to show the overwhelming of Atlantis in the Deluge: improvements on *Nautilus*, on submarine bomb, on rope-making invention, and a hundred and one other schemes. It did not concern Anthony, but he wondered at the possible reaction of Fleuret and Guillaume, who were paid fewer than six hundred francs a month between them.

He leaned back a little so that he could peer down into the dim white cellar that was below the sea. A very crowded cellar lighted by a single candle-lamp!

He could see the sail-cloth patches in the knees of Fleuret's trousers; the rest of the man was out of sight as he sat hunched against the side. All he could see, too, of Guillaume were a stooped bare shoulder aft, and a dirty foot splayed out for support on the floor grating with a scarlet snake tattooed as bracelet round the ankle. Fulton, naked to the waist, was squatted on his hunkers, back against the forward bulkhead (in which were set controls for anchoring and bomb-towing) staring straight upward. His large black eyes seemed to start right out of his sweating face, from which continued exertion had drained every vestigue of colour.

In the small compartment the three men's bodies touched each other. There did not appear to be room for another. Guillaume had quite obviously been sick again — recently.

My God! (thought Anthony, remembering the last frightful hour of trial submersion). How can we stand it down there again for another hour? For two hours — or three — or four? Every garment he had on was soaked and clammy with perspiration. Even now it did not seem real that he should be able to breathe chill pure air, to stretch himself unbounded by the white-grey walls, dripping with damp, of the underwater vault.

Fulton bit a huge semicircle out of a shaggy meat sandwich, and continued to hum his song whilst he chewed. His eyes encountered Anthony's.

In all his romantic dreams the lad had never associated high adventure with greasy faces and sweating bodies, and confined spaces. High adventure had not spelled stolid endurance of the barely endurable, the monotonous winding of a crank handle in a crazy hull that any whim of the sea or riposte of the enemy might turn in a second into an inescapable coffin. The pageantry of his childish imaginings fluttered against the ugliness of the present like a torn tapestry that could not hide reality. Only success could ever counterbalance the sordidness of their venture. It was of that sordidness, and not of the risk that he thought as he crouched in the night watching Fulton's eyes, waiting for him to clear his mouth sufficiently to speak. They *must* succeed. Their toil and danger *must* be repaid. He thought of the ship against which they moved on their deathly errand not as an enemy but as an obstruction to their return to the sanity of the upper air. Not once had it occurred to him that their attack would probably be accompanied by an appalling death-roll. He saw in the sinking of the ship the accomplishment of their purpose, a target struck — that was all.

Said Fulton's voice hoarsened by fatigue and foul air —

'See anything, young Alge?'

'Too dark! . . . There's a slight current here. We should be drawing in nicely with it. I'll lay anything we are dead on the frigate! I know the bay backward!'

'We'll go down at very first glimpse. Can't risk that packet of francs for anything! We'll come up to sight for attack as close to them as we dare. Up as far as the forward porthole and no more! We've got to come up so close that they won't have time to do anything about it, even if they see us!'

He mumbled on, repeating instructions that had already been reiterated until they were known by heart.

'No time to get away?' said the invisible Fleuret with sardonic glee, and his bony knees jerked as he spoke. 'No time to get away! P-f-f-f! That's how they'll get away! Up they'll go, and down they'll come! . . . They'll get away all right — and leave their tails and their heads, *and* legs, *and* arms behind them!' — His young son had perished when the great flag-ship *Orient* had roared skyward in dreadful culmination of the Battle of the Nile.

Guillaume's bare foot shifted a little, as he strained at the crank of the propeller: now he said something in his low grumbling voice.

Fulton began afresh —

'O my Lord, O my good Lord,
Keep me from sinkin' — '

'S'sh!' said Anthony in urgent whisper. 'S-s-s'sh!'

He strained his eyes forward over the top of the conning-tower.

'My francs in sight?' asked Fulton in a hoarse murmur, and began to rise to his feet.

Was that a darker darkness right forward? Was there something yet darker still against the darker darkness? Ships and islands?

'Get ready! . . . We're nearer than I — '

The enveloping silence was torn by the hissing as of a stupendous serpent: the enveloping darkness torn by an upward stream of white fire that burst against the black vault into a great blossom of light descending in rain of silver stars to the smooth uneasy sea. In the momentary brilliance he saw the ships ahead — perilously close — with a screen of boats about them, and that they had tow-ropes out.

'They've been warned!' he called. 'They've heard us! They — '

He had already one leg over the rim of the hatch when he saw a festoon of cord trailing across the grey-white orifice. The lanyard of the bomb, which was secured to the top of the conning-tower, had fouled the opening. It must be got away before the watertight cover could be shut.

He caught the thin rope in his left hand, and raised it well above his head to fling clear.

As he did so, a line of sullen flame licked out across the darkness ahead. It illumined luridly the yellowish-white stripe along the black hull of the frigate, studding it with many tongues of scarlet. Even as he realized this he was staggered by so enormous a blow that he felt the impact — though no hurt — in every fibre of his body and his mind . . . Or was it just the immensity of the concussion of the broadside?

For a moment afterwards, he saw — heard — felt nothing.

He dropped to his feet clumsily inside the hull, bumping Guillaume in his descent.

'That startled — ' he began, and wondered if he were speaking, or just imagining that he did.

He raised his hand to close the cover above him: saw Fulton's eyes follow the movement with a stunned expression: saw his lips purse in a soundless whistle of maddening ditty.

Then he saw, too, that the arm he had lifted above his head, ended abruptly . . . ended abruptly . . . ended without a hand . . . ended in streaming blood.

No! Of course he had a hand! He could feel the handle of the heavy lid! He could feel the pressure of his nails against the palm! . . . He could! . . .

CHAPTER IV

A HERO'S RETURN

ANTHONY PURVIS stood in one of the many doors of the small white-painted room that had been his and Garland's snuggery and schoolroom. He had stood there for some moments with a crumpled letter in his remaining hand, wordless, numbed, staring about the familiar place as though he saw it now for the first time.

Even Miss Buckley — silhouetted against a window full of sunset, as she peered over the bottle-green rampart of her bosom at a needle and

thread that would not unite — was alien, was somebody other than the
Buck who admired bad poetry and wrote worse, and lived in a chronic
state of sneezing, hiccupping, or wheezing, and apologizing therefor.
Still more alien was the little girl in mob cap and cherry-coloured sash,
with black-mittened hands folded primly on muslin lap, who looked
gravely down from the picture-frame above the mantelpiece — a little
girl whose name had once been Garland.

The twin presses on either side of the fire meant nothing to him; nor
the bookshelves atop, crowded with battered volumes that had been much
loved by two people he had known very long — very, very long — ago.
He did not recall the historic battle with which the pear-shaped ink stain
on the green tablecloth was associated: nor that someone he had almost
forgotten had, in the dim past, used the small square work-table at which
now Miss Buckley sat — a work-table with a pleated stomach of faded
pink silk.

He flung to the floor that shattering letter from Harradence which Miss
Buckley had given him within two minutes of his arrival at La Cadière,
with a babbled story of incredible incident, confused issue, and monstrous
import.

He said in a strange voice —

'I had better go and see Grandmother, Buck, hadn't I?'

Miss Buckley looked up from needle and thread that refused to come
into co-operative combination. She regarded him standing there in the
doorway, his maimed arm in its stained bandages strapped high up against
his chest in a once-white sling, his face haggard and drawn, his dark hair
disordered, and his blue coat grey with the dust of the forty-mile journey
from Marseilles. Globular tears welled up in her prominent eyes; rolled
down her florid cheeks.

She sniffled and apologized after every sentence.

'She won't know you, my dear! . . . S-she doesn't m-m-move at all
. . . Or speak . . . Or even open her poor eyes! She b-b-breathes just
like snoring! . . . It's dreadful! She just lies there like Lot's wife. She'ld
be quite dead — if she weren't alive! Or the King of the Black Mountain — was it? Monsieur Corvisart and Dr. Leroux say she may be like
it for years and years!'

'I'll go and see her, all the same, Buck!'

He *must* see his grandmother, for she was all he had left in a world
that lay in ruins. He was as yet filled with no anger against Harradence
and Garland: was still too stunned to experience anything but a sense
of utter desolation.

He had already, reasonlessly, been filled with forebodings of some unimagined disaster when old Pinaud, the porter, flung wide the wrought-iron gates in the high wall, and the chaise rolled into the courtyard on his return. They had grown as he wearily climbed the semicircular sweep of steps; they had become a certainty when he entered the dim and echoing emptiness of the Great Hall. The house seemed to him to be quite indifferent to whatever fortune attended these newcomers: the things which had happened in the past were of far more moment! There were so many, many little rooms that it could not be bothered by what befell the inhabitants of a mere dozen or so!

And then Paul had appeared, swimming in his splay-footed way through the gloom; and Miss Buckley, running, and panting, and crying, and giving him the letter and telling him not to read it and he ought to know and not to worry and that his poor dear grandmother . . . and that Mr. Mason had said everything would be all right — 'Money, you know, my dear!' — and that he must lie down, and shouldn't they have Monsieur Corvisart up at once to put on new dressings, and —

Now Buck put the needle into that part of her capacious bosom which she was accustomed to use as a pin-cushion, hung the loop of the recalcitrant thread round it, and went off to ascertain 'If it'll be convenient for you to see your poor dear Grandmother — because you know, my dear — '

It *was* convenient.

A moment or so later he stood in his grandmother's circular room with its circular cobweb of a carpet and circular altar of a table, and its deeply-sunk windows. There was no sound except of the harsh stertorous breathing from the wall-bed with its faded panels decked with faded cupids and faded bouquets and true-lovers'-knots. The ivory-yellow face was almost invisible among the pillows in the dusk of the recess.

Beside the bed sat a nun in black robes with immense starched white coif, her eyes downbent to folded hands on lap.

It was late in the afternoon; the room dim, the hunting scenes on the tapestry hangings barely discernible, and the heavy Provençale commodes and presses along the walls merged into grey shadows. In the half-light it seemed to be a fitting shrine for the half-life — less than half-life — which it enfolded.

Anthony noted the spy-glass still lying on the acacia-wood chest — books and writing-desk and despatch-box on the table in the middle of the cob-web — customary stack of newspapers on a chair. But there were no fragments of biscuit or comfit about, and their very absence gave him the impression that he was looking at a careless reproduction of the room he knew.

'She's been like that for a week now. Ever since *that* night, in fact,' said Miss Buckley in rather a proprietorial fashion, patting the bedclothes as though to emphasize her position of privilege to the silent nun.

> ' "She lies like bronze or carven stone,
> Without a twitch, without a moan!" '

Anthony stood still, regarding that yellow mask and the unhummocked bed.

That was all he had got left!

He turned away, and walked to the window whence he had regarded not so long ago the white-winged insolence of the English ships. The clack and buzz of Buck's explanations and regrets came vaguely to him. He returned to the table with its ritual spread in the accustomed way. His uncle's face stared back at him from the miniature lying — as it had done for so many years — on the folded handkerchief before the brass-bound writing-box.

'Mr. Mason opened the box,' said Miss Buckley. 'But there's nothing in it except a few trinkets. She can't have kept any letters at all. He says that her expenditure has been absolutely nothing compared to the income. He's going over the accounts now, in the Green Parlour.'

Mr. Mason was the Marseilles agent of grim Mr. Jarman of Philadelphia, a little man in drab clothes, whose face looked as if it had been carved out of a piece of yellowish timber and were filed or sandpapered every morning instead of being shaved. A little man with a touch of the lawyer and the doctor about him, sitting in a small draughty room off the Great Hall with all the doors open, and sheaves of accounts strewn upon the table, weighted down by piles of five-franc pieces.

He bobbed up when Anthony entered, took a pinch of snuff, shook hands — and his hand felt as though it were covered with sawdust — and spoke in a creaking voice, like two pieces of wood being rubbed together.

'Shocking business!' creaked Mr. Mason, 'Very shocking! Sorry for your misfortune! Only one eye, myself! Lost the sight of the right in the War of Independence. Nothing heroic! Hand-grenade practice at Valley Forge. Was a bit too slow. Still one soon gets used to going short! . . . Mrs. Vane — it was she sent for me — had already gone when your messenger arrived last night. Only just in time, too. Officials came from the Marine Prefecture at Marseilles to conduct inquiries a couple of hours after she left! However there was nobody here to tell them anything, so they went away as wise as they came! . . . It wasn't my business to repeat what Mrs. Vane had told me: she thought — quite rightly — that I ought to know the position . . . With regard to the *Nautilus*, I suppose that

Madam Purvis's investment is entirely lost. I had better write the amount of the loan off. There is no chance of getting it out of Mr. Fulton, I suppose!'

'None,' said Anthony.

'No salvage?'

'Not a screw! When we came to the surface we found that the mast-hoisting gear had been smashed . . . They had fired chain-shot and grape at us . . . We were carried helpless out to sea by a gale. Then we sprang a leak — two! We were taken off by a polacre bound for Narbonne just before she went down . . . There was an army surgeon on board going home on leave from Genoa, luckily for me! A good one!'

Mr. Mason absorbed this information. He rustled among the sheaves of paper that epitomized life at La Cadière.

'Fortunately your grandmother made adequate arrangements for such eventualities as the present. After her first attack eight years ago. Otherwise the position would have been complicated because of your minority and the disagreement between Madam Purvis and her co-guardian . . . As it is I am authorized to see that this establishment continues on its normal footing. With regard to yourself, there is a letter here of very considerable interest. Of more than considerable interest. It is the only letter or private paper of any sort I have been able to find. I imagine that once your grandmother had dealt with any matter she destroyed the papers relating to it. Legal documents of course excepted — I've got those."

From under one of the piles of five-franc pieces he produced a letter written on particularly thick paper; unfolded it, and thoughtfully flattened it before Anthony on the table. It was in the most appalling and illegible hand-writing he had ever seen.

'You'ld think the man wrote it with his foot,' said Mr. Mason, taking a pinch of snuff — or sawdust? — for refreshment. 'I succeeded in making it out after half an hour's labour. It'll be quicker, perhaps, if I read it to you. It is to your grandmother from the First Consul, General Bonaparte. Dated, *Paris, 23 Ventôse, An. IX.*'

Mr. Mason took up the letter again, and read it slowly, holding it out at some little distance from his eyes and so that what daylight was left should fall upon the dreadful scrawl.

'Madam,' the letter ran, 'I well remember the service you rendered to me eight years ago during the siege of Toulon. Nor have I forgotten the small and intelligent boy, your grandson, who played chess with me. I am interested in what you tell me of him. Too few Frenchmen are linguists. If his knowledge of modern languages is as you say then I can serve myself in repaying the debt I owe you. A sub-lieutenant's commission in the Chausseurs awaits him. He will report to Captain Bacler d'Albe at the Ministry of War as soon as possible, for service in the topographical and statistical offices of my cabinet.   Bonaparte'

'Signs his letters like a king,' commented Mr. Mason, refolding the letter and presenting it once more to Anthony.

'Of what possible use can I be as a soldier, now?' commented Anthony bitterly, stirring the bundle of stained bandages against his chest.

'T'cht!' said Mr. Mason, sitting down again and glancing at him not unkindly. 'You won't need two hands in a topographical office — whatever that may be! Any more than I need two eyes in my profession! You'll find in course of time that you think Nature absurdly lavish in providing man with limbs and organs in pairs. After a week or two I found that I was quite ready to joke about my monocular state. Whenever I go to the theatre I always offer to pay half-price — because I can only see half! That always causes great amusement to my friends! If I lost an arm I should enjoy a great deal of innocent amusement in deducting a percentage from my tailor's and shirt-maker's bills and over arguments with the glove-maker!'

Anthony was not yet prepared to take the loss of his left hand in any humorous light, and Mr. Mason, having exhausted his resources of sympathy, reverted to the First Consul's letter.

'Your grandmother wrote to me immediately on receipt of this letter. Her view was that, as there are two years before you attain your majority and can possibly return to America, this was an unrivalled opportunity of seeing the world and coming into contact with people who are making history. She may have had other motives as well — it is not for me to say! But I agree with her: you have here a wonderful opening, offered you by a most remarkable man — something to look back upon when you eventually settle down to the humdrum life of a Virginia plantation-owner. And that you should be able to enter this great world on an equality with *anyone* of your age — or even older — she told me that you were to be given an allowance of two thousand livres a month — four hundred dollars! Which is very — ve-e-ery handsome! . . . You will obviously have to make up your mind quickly.'

'You will be here to-morrow?'

'I've arranged for post-horses at midday.'

'I am feeling very weak,' said Anthony. 'And very tired. Let us finish this talk to-morrow at breakfast. . . .'

He went out into the darkening Great Hall, and wandered aimlessly through the long suites of small inter-communicating rooms to the Round Parlour in the eastern tower. The desolation of the orderliness of that chain of prim apartments was emphasized by the frigid dusk. They were rooms in which no one lived but merely passed through as ghosts on their way from a forgotten past to an unknown future.

There was a ship's decanter full of port among the impedimenta upon the big buffet, but no glasses. He drank perhaps a tumblerful of wine out of the vessel, although it was a heavy and awkward thing to hold to the lips with one hand. He had never drunk out of a decanter before: he felt a little ashamed of himself, and wiped its mouth with his sleeve.

Then he walked back again through all the warren of little deserted rooms. In at one door, out of the other, the echo of his tread upon the parquet being his only company amid that maze of desolation. Came once more to the small schoolroom where the picture of a little girl in a mob cap — now almost indistinguishable — looked down on the faded rosewood work-table of which she had been so proud. He stood before it for nearly ten minutes, regarding the blur without either seeing anything or even visualizing anything. He was conscious of no emotion except horror.

He re-entered his grandmother's room unannounced.

The candles had not been lit. The windows were four grey oblongs. In that twilight the nun remained unstirring beside the unstirring bed. He took the brass-bound writing-desk from the table; set it on the commode in the window looking across the bay: opened it almost mechanically.

The compartment under the green baize writing slope held only a supply of note-paper and unused quills. But a little drawer at the side contained a jumble of small articles — a man's engraved seals, a gold watch in a chamois leather pocket, one or two squares of folded paper with dark and fair ringlets within, but nothing to show to whom they had belonged: also a locket on a fine gold chain.

He put the trinket down on the top of the commode and regarded it. He had seen it before. A plaited coil of fair hair showed under the crystal face of one side. He turned it over and clumsily opened the back. A rust-smeared piece of paper was intricately folded within: and when he had eventually mastered its convolutions there was spread before him that well-remembered message out of the distant past, written on a leaf of his father's manuscript —

'IOU
The sum of five hundred pounds (£500)
Charles Hurrell.'

The ink had become brownish red in the passage of time — redder and less brown than the ominous smear to one side.

As if in very fact it were the spell his grandmother would have had it be, it evoked crowding memories and crowding ghosts. He saw High Pale again and Colonel Beriah, in green coat and jack-boots, staring contemptuously out of his frame at the tangled streets and roofs of the fairy city of Camelot — Colonel Beriah who had had to fly England for his life. Saw too the portrait of his father and his uncle — the one quizzically and wearily magnificent, the other consciously and carelessly gallant: the one wantonly slaughtered in cold blood, the other fallen in hot battle for the freedom of America.

How it all returned to him now — the invisible companionship of the dead upon that long journey to the sea!

As he stood staring into the gathering dusk, he saw, not the grey uneasy sea and the outline of the islands at the eastern peak of the bay, but himself — the small unhappy boy of eight years ago — jolting across Virginia in the high yellow and black carriage with the tattered phantoms in pursuit. Remembered the nights when he had lain awake listening for their ghostly tread outside the door, while Miss Buckley had fidgeted and whickered and rumbled in her sleep. Remembered the long dark saloon in the *Chesapeake*, and the creaking of the upper berth, and the black sea reaching up for him as he hung over the ship's side, and the silver of Garland's bare chest as she stirred in her sleep under his gaze. Remembered the pale belly and fierce face of the English sailor who had threatened him on the gun-deck of the *Aventurière:* the frozen anger of Colonel Hurrell wrestling against the grip of two dishevelled soldiers in the house in the mountains: his grandmother's furious attack — he even remembered so vividly the rush and rustle of her silken dress as she flung herself upon the Englishman that he thought to hear it again, and turned sharply as though he might find her leaping like a vampire or a were-wolf from her bed. Remembered the half-Englishman, Putzger, floating down the seaweed-green corridors of the Institut under his enormous pale head like an octopus . . . all his grandmother's stories of English misrule and treachery! Treachery! Garland — Harradence, than whom he had loved no one better! Who had betrayed him and the *Nautilus;* who had cost him a hand! Harradence, the republican, the democrat, who had renounced his country and adopted France — to sell her (and him) foully to the enemies of freedom! Without question Harradence had all the time been a spy — his speech, his thoughts, his way of life, his affections, had masked the real purpose of the man. He suddenly felt that same horror of Harradence that his grandmother had inspired in him long ago when she had revealed for just a few instants the violence and the hate of which she was capable.

A white pyramid of sail rounded the distant smokiness of the further island, swam slowly into its shelter.

He took up the spy-glass, though he had no need to do so. He did not require to count the sixteen gun-ports in the white streak along the vessel's side to know that it was the English frigate returned insolently to the scene of attack. She came placidly to anchor and proceeded to furl sail, for all the world like a bird preening itself deliberately before a sportsman, knowing that he has no gun.

He brought the telescope down with a crash upon the commode, brutally denting the lustrous silvery surface. He took up his grandmother's amulet in his solitary hand, and put the thin chain over his head, and permitted the locket to slide down behind folds of white neck-cloth. . . .

Once more he wandered through the dark, indifferent house, but now he had a purpose. He was in Harradence's study, sweeping the deep litter from the big table into irreparable ruin upon the floor: in Elizabeth's boudoir, hurling to destruction the pretty things she had loved, Dresden shepherdess and fiddler, ormolu clock, porcelain jars from China in apple-green and flame-red: in Garland's bedroom, where he smashed the shield-shaped mirror that had so often reflected her lovely treacherous face, and rent and trampled on the fragile lovely things of silks and satins and muslins that she had worn: in the schoolroom tearing down the grave-faced portrait, and stripping the shelves of much-loved books which he sent hurtling against the walls with flurrying pages.

Paul arrived with candles.

'Do you see that picture?'

Paul looked at the portrait lying amid the destruction of its frame on the floor. His face held no emotion, was utterly expressionless.

'Walk on it!' said Anthony. 'Trample on it!'

Paul walked deliberately up to the fallen picture, and stood on it, his large silver-buckled shoes splayed in duck-footed manner over charming face and white mob cab and cherry-coloured sash. Looked questioningly at Anthony as if to learn whether he could be of further service.

'Kick it!' said Anthony.

Paul accordingly kicked it; in just such deferential manner as a butler might be expected to kick a picture on instruction. In a rather ladylike way.

'Harder!'

Paul kicked harder: frame and canvas ripped into ruin under his toe. . . .

Again he walked up and down the tunnels of the dark rooms with all doors set wide, and lights twinkling at the end of long perspectives.

He was alone. Utterly alone.

He had no one.

Paul padded into view once more. He bore a great salver with a letter secured by a green wafer on it.

By the light of a many-branched silver candlestick on the marble top of a low bookcase, Anthony recognized Jasmine's handwriting . . . Jasmine, whom he had forsaken for the false Garland. Jasmine, the golden pale lady of a dream world —

> 'I have heard of your misfortunes — your tragedy. In the desolation that has befallen you — '

Jasmine!

CHAPTER V

THE REALITY OF A LADY—1

'OUR young friend arrives hot-foot in search of consolation!' said Count Pagan, as a low knock sounded on the street-door. 'I pride myself on composing a good letter!'

He scooped up the spread cards with which he had been keeping wrist and eye in trim; folded the satin-wood card-table and set it against the wall; swept the room with a quick glance to see that there was no trace of his occupation.

Jasmine rose slowly from her seat before the clavichord. In the candle-light her high-waisted gown was the faint yellow of the flower from which she drew her name. She was silver, and water, and moonlight, and the wind; the incarnation of a slim huntress nymph haunting the birchwood groves of Artemis.

'This,' said Count Pagan, 'is the last chance!' He slapped his pocket suggestively. 'It is either this — or the soap-boiler from Marseilles!'

Jasmine nodded. She continued her way toward the door.

'You are alone!' said Pagan, taking her by the wrist. 'Quite alone! The *bonne* has gone home! Your dear, dear uncle has had to take Cousin

Kate to Marseilles, and Heaven alone knows when he will get back!
Probably to-morrow morning! . . . Do you understand?'

She pulled her hand contemptuously away.

'You do not need to teach me my business!'

'You have not been too successful so far!'

'If you had been able to keep your hands off Hortense —'

The gentle knocking on the street-door was renewed, a trifle louder.

'I wonder if you can manage the affair by yourself,' reflected Pagan
out loud. 'Don't be a damned fool!' He barred her way to the door.
'Listen! If — *if* you can't get him up to scratch, put five drops of this in
his coffee, or his *fine*, or anything else you can persuade him to drink —'

He produced a tiny flat phial from a waistcoat pocket, and held it
up to view.

'What is it? . . . I must go — or he'll think we are all a-bed!'

'A compound prepared by our old acquaintance, Monsieur Corvisart,
not for this purpose, but admirably suitable! Five drops and our young
friend will know no more until he wakes hours later in your arms, to be
confronted by an infuriated guardian with the dust of journey on him!'

An indefinable expression, an inscrutable smile, flitted across Jasmine's
lovely face. She said —

'And you'll say: "Is this how you bring ruin upon my innocent niece,
you unspeakable young blackguard?" No, you'll pronounce it "Blay-
guard" in order to emphasize the dangerous swords-in-the-morning Irish-
ness of your nature! And I'm to say, "Oh, Uncle, forgive us! Forgive!
Anthony is going to marry me! I — He — You — !" and be red with
shame. You are out-of-date, *dearest* Uncle. That's the sort of thing one
reads about in old-fashioned romances! You stick to your card-sharping,
and high treason, and old women!'

But she took from him the small flat phial as she left the room; and
suddenly kissed him fiercely on the lips; and as suddenly wrested herself
away as though she had discovered in the close contact of the embrace
that she loathed him — or herself — or both. . . .

She let Anthony in; led him by the hand along the dark passage, and
then turned and regarded him as they entered the grey and silver *salon*,
that was so softly lighted that its imperfections were hidden and it took
on the quality of a room seen in a dream.

He stood before her, haggard, dishevelled, lost, his shattered arm so
obvious in its soiled wrappings, that her eyes filled with tears and her
lips parted in a low cry of compassion — something between a sigh and
a moan.

At that sound, and responsive to some unconscious movement of the slim hand that still held his, he murmured suddenly words she did not catch, stepped forward a pace, and bowed his head to her shoulder. It was the action of a hurt child seeking the comfort of its mother's dress; of one who in spiritual distress takes solace from merely touching the robes of an image of the Mother of God. His fingers twined in hers were unrestraining: his head did not rest upon the silveriness that rose from her faintly-tinted dress; it touched without pressure, and no more than touched. The contact was as of a ghost.

She stood quite still for a little, looking down on his ruffled head with a tenderness, with a half-smile, with thoughts that became her beauty. For so short a while his need, his worship made her what he deemed her. . . .

The clock behind her struck the hour. Only half-way through the course of its chime did she become conscious of the tinkling strokes upon the tiny gong. Then almost instinctively she began to turn her head: paused. But by the fractional movement she had brought herself closer to him. By so very, very little. By so very, very much.

Quite suddenly she became physically conscious of the contact of his body. There was a touch light as a leaf against her right breast. A bent knee was against her own.

An emotion, which she well knew, awoke. Seized upon her: demanded response.

She began to raise her free hand in order to smooth his head, to press it closer against herself — to precipitate the crisis that every fibre of her now demanded. She desired to be kissed hungrily, to be clutched brutally; that she should have to restrain ardour — if restrain she would — rather than herself be thus restrained.

But all the same she paused: dared not to stir or speak, lest by clumsy word or gesture she might break the spell she had cast upon this remote lover . . . There was a legend or a lay which she recollected from long ago, telling of a fairy lover who was held to his lady by so tenuous a bond of enchantment that he vanished when once she had touched him with her lips.

She did not stir. And if he had suddenly lifted his head and regarded her, he could not have told from her expression that she had passed in a few seconds from an almost divine pity to urgent physical desire, and then to nicely balanced calculations in which Count Pagan, and the Marseilles soap-boiler, and the phial with the five-drop-dose, and High Pale, were prime factors.

She met his stillness with her own: stood thus looking down upon his dark hair. Attractive hair, she thought; crisp, wavy, not quite black but a very dark brown with lights in it that were almost red. She would have liked to stroke it — but dared not.

How long would he remain in this worshipful attitude at her shrine? What was her next move?

His breathing that had almost been sobbing quietened.

Would he lift his head now? And what would he do then?

Would he *never* lift his head?

Odd unrelated thoughts passed through her mind. What was Julian doing? Lying on his bed cynically picturing the scene downstairs whilst he smoked a cheroot? The entire house would smell of it if he were . . . Anthony had really beautiful hair. What did he wash it with? Or did the barber do it? . . . How long had they stood like this? Two minutes? Ten? . . . Renée Tavernes had said this morning when she complained about the *épicerie* bill, that haricots had been up to fifteen hundred francs the bushel in Paris. Fifteen hundred francs! Paper francs, of course! . . . Renée knew too much — or guessed it! So did other people in La Cadière . . . They couldn't continue in this *tableau vivant* for ever! They couldn't! Flesh and blood . . .

She raised her eyes from the bowed head of the boy before her: looked at the reflection of the scene in the long mirror in its narrow gold and ivory frame near them, beside the door.

Tableau vivant!

The grey depths of the glass showed them, faintly hued in the subdued light, like a picture in a dream. Staring into her own eyes, she was suddenly seized with the fantastic notion that she might, indeed, be withdrawn by Anthony from the world of reality and become in truth but a passionless figure in the fabric of a vision.

Reflected in the mirror, too, was the silver candlestick standing on the top of her clavichord, its primrose flame casting a pale radiance upon the portrait of Pagan in uniform of green with crimson sash. It seemed to her that the portrait symbolized all her bygone lovers ironically watching from the past — from the very near past. Those urgent, desirous, satyr lovers!

She sighed. The merest whisper of a sigh. She caught her breath. The tiniest sound, as though she would have restrained even that smallest of suspirations.

At that he looked up; and as he did so, she bent and kissed him on the forehead, so lightly, so very lightly, that it was no more than a kiss out of a dream.

He straightened up; began to stammer apologies; would have loosed her hand, but she would not let him go.

'My poor Anthony!' she said. 'My poor, poor Anthony!' Her voice was like the sighing of the West Wind.

'What have they done to you?' she said.

'I don't know,' he answered brokenly. 'I don't know . . . I'm all alone. I've got nobody. Nobody at all!'

She led him to the small settee by a small round table set before the long curtains of grey and silver brocade that hid the glass doors to the garden: made him sit down: now disengaged her hand that she might fill for him the glass waiting beside a carafe of bright red wine.

Thus far (she felt) she had observed all the canons of romance: but what next? Did she seat herself beside him? Did she — ? . . . But what progress could she make if she held herself physically aloof?

When Anthony set down the goblet and looked up, she was standing by the clavichord, regarding him wistfully. He thought she had all the beauty of a field of daffodils in moonlight. Her spell was on him. Already he began to forget his wrongs.

'I'm sorry,' he said. 'But they've all been such —.! And then Grandmother! *And* this —'

He stirred the soiled bundle that represented all that remained of his left arm.

'I come back,' he went on, 'like this; and there's no one left! No one in the entire world of my own! . . . Uncle Harrady repudiated England and all her works! He proves his good faith by betraying me — and Fulton — and the men with us — and the *Nautilus!* . . . And Garland herself sailed him out to the ships!'

Jasmine felt too uncertain of her ground to do anything except sigh in sympathy.

Anthony rose to his feet. He paced up and down the room as he spoke. 'I still can't believe it! It seems too monstrous to believe! and yet I know it's true. I have Uncle Harrady's own letter saying what he was going to do. I didn't read it all; just enough to know! . . . But Garland — ! You would not have thought it possible that she would want to take a *personal* part. It's just as if she had loaded and aimed and fired the gun that smashed my arm!'

'Nothing in the whole world matters so much as loyalty,' said Jasmine.

Did the ghosts of bygone lovers snigger? Even to herself the aphorism rang false, and whilst she watched him go to and fro she repeated it below her breath with varied stress.

'I suppose I've got to hate them now! It's frightful when you discover that people have been living a lie all the time you have known them. Not Garland, of course! She never pretended that she didn't hate the

French — and the Americans. But Uncle Harrady — all the time spouting of Liberty, Fraternity, Equality! Of British interference — of the New Order that was to be — of the "Greatest experiment in history". Spouting catch-phrases! Declaiming against British tyranny! Taking British money all the time.' He stopped: apologized to the far-distant Harradence. 'No! That's not true, and I know it!'

Leaning against the clavichord she let him talk on, barely listening, asking herself all the while what must be her next move — not *her* next move, but the next move of the shadowy figure of his imaginings.

An idea suddenly occurred to him. He halted his pacing.

'How did they know about all this — the authorities, I mean?'

'The German at the château — I don't know his name — came down and warned people in the town as soon as Mr. Harradence had left the house.'

So Baldamus had been traitor to treason. He found himself, paradoxically, contemptuous of him.

'But why then didn't they — '

'Uncle told me that they all pretended to disbelieve him. I think they hate the Republicans worse than the British!'

He nodded.

'They've not forgotten the mass executions at Marseilles and Toulon. A lot of them lost friends and relatives.'

Baldamus must have afterwards gone to Marseilles. To the Marine Prefecture. Probably afraid of being implicated in the business himself . . . He had never returned, at any rate, wherever he might have gone.

She asked herself — What *could* she do? What *should* she do? Would he never sit down? . . . He would drink no more. He just walked to and fro, demanding sympathy. In a little while he would look at the clock and would see the time — or hear it strike — and be horrified at the lateness of the hour; and tear himself away in a cloud of apologies.

She brought him back to the present.

'But what are you going to do now, Anthony?'

He stopped where he was; against the silver and grey background of the curtains. A lock of his dark hair had fallen across his forehead: his deep blue coat and high boots were still dusty with his journeyings. His pale rather long face was not now that of a boy, but of an unhappy man.

'I can do nothing — up there. She may last for years! I am going to Paris to-morrow. I've been offered a post on the First Consul's staff. I don't know whether they will have me now. They may! . . . I should like to make someone pay for *this!* For the *Nautilus!* For everything!'

Paris! For one moment the word conveyed absolutely nothing to her beyond Renée Tavernes's assertion that there the price of haricots had been as high as fifteen hundred francs the bushel.

Then quite suddenly she realized what it meant . . . The Marseilles soap-boiler — a lifetime of him! . . . Julian Pagan — a lifetime of him and of the gulls and rooks and sordid half-world in which they moved! . . . In any case her own worse self — a lifetime of ever worsening, from which there could be no escape so long as Julian had any hold upon her. Unless . . .

But it was without premeditation or design that she burst into tears. He thought that it was for him she wept — for his world broken past repair. He was too humble to imagine that they were other than tears of sympathy she shed, or that they should be tears of frustrated love. He was too young to know that it is for themselves that women mainly weep.

She stood before him, beside the clavichord, with her head bowed and turned to one side, holding a trifle of a handkerchief to her eyes. She was Oenone: she was Psyche! No! — More! She was of the Other-World, mourning mortality's distress.

He was aghast at what he had done: took one step toward her: halted: gazed on her desolated loveliness, stricken by her anguish.

'Don't cry, Jasmine!' he implored her. 'I didn't mean to distress you. I shall get over things. They'll all come right in the end . . . Oh, Jasmine, please don't cry!'

And, because she still wept, he came a little nearer in the urgency of appeal.

He thought that only her beauty could equal her loving-kindness — that both were divine: when he dropped on his knees, it was no act of gallantry, but of reverence; and when he took her hand in his and carried it to his lips, it was in passionless adoration.

'Oh, Jasmine!' he said in little more than a whisper. 'You are too compassionate! . . . I did not believe that there were people like you! You make up — you more than make up for all that I have lost!'

He did not venture to kiss her slim cold fingers: He just held them against his lips so that they touched — and no more than touched.

And yet once again was the enchantment perfected, and she became such as he thought — the lady of a dream, half-saint, half-goddess, remote from desire, unsullied by the passions of Julian Pagan and surreptitious amours unknown even to that demon lover. She looked down upon the kneeling boy with a mind emptied of everything except tenderness toward him. He was young and unhappy. She was young and unhappy, too! She could be — she always had been — worthy of such worship! The past must be as if it had never been, and only the spell remain.

She said — and the confused words were meant as confession of the past, an appeal for pity for her weakness, not an enticement —

'I'm real, you know, Anthony!'

At that he looked up, half-comprehending only that some change in their relationship was impending, his grey eyes seeking the clue in hers.

'I love you very much, Anthony,' she answered the unspoken question. 'Too much to let you go without saying so! Too much to be ashamed of saying so. Too much —'

But already he had risen to his feet, was gathering her to him — a little to one side — with his one arm; and so held her in silence closely but without constraint, still looking into her eyes. Was satisfied at last that he had made no error, although it was still in incredulous whisper that he sighed —

'Jasmine!'

And after a long while, again —

'Jasmine!'

With gentle pressure he drew her head to his shoulder. He did not attempt to kiss her on the lips; only her hair, those scented tresses that held all the pale gold of moonshine. She was glad that he did not seek her mouth that had but a little while since been fiercely pressed to Julian's.

It was the love-making of a dream. So she would have had it. . . .

'S'sh! You will tread very softly in the hall when I open the door, Anthony? Very, very softly! In — in case he came back without my hearing.'

'Very softly, Jasmine!'

'And when we have got to Paris and are married, you promise that he shall never enter the house! Never! Never! Swear it again!'

'Your uncle shall never enter the house. I swear it, Jasmine!'

'Because if he did I believe that I should vanish — like the princess in the fairy-tale. But far farther than to the Castle East of the Sun and West of the Moon. I believe I should, Anthony! . . . Anthony, I don't want to vanish from you! You do promise, don't you?'

He would promise anything — everything.

A swift recapitulation of the plans for her escape and flight to-morrow after dark.

To-morrow!

In the darkness of the narrow hall of the house they clung together in silence for an instant or two; but he did nothing except murmur words of endearment and kiss the quenched glory of her hair.

'Well, shall I offer you my warmest congratulations?' said Julian Pagan. He was lounging on the little settee in a dressing-gown of peacock blues and greens and bronzes, his legs thrust out before him.

She had barely closed the house-door after Anthony, before he was downstairs and leading her back to the grey and silver *salon* by the wrist.

She seated herself on the stool before the clavichord, half-turned so that she should watch him. He was as beautiful as a faun — as well she was aware; and as soul-less and as dangerous.

'All simple! All settled!' said Pagan. 'You took far shorter time than I expected. Not eleven o'clock yet. Good girl! Very! . . . *Vogue la galère!*'

He produced from somewhere, like a conjuror, a pack of cards with which by one dexterous flick he sprayed the shining reddish tiles of the floor, the Persian rugs. They lay face uppermost. They flecked with their cheap dishonour a sanctuary of visionary love.

'When's it to be? . . . Where are you going? . . . Paris, I suppose! Come, Jasmine, I am making small-talk while you recover from an emotional crisis, but I can't go on indefinitely. Tell your — your business partner!'

She turned away from him then, and suddenly began to play upon the clavichord an old French nursery tune. To play it with an infinite mockery. To play it so that the soft blurred chords appeared to come from very far off, as though singing a triumph of elves over scarecrows and Jack-o'-Lanterns.

> *'Et moi de m'en cour', cour', cour',*
> *Et moi de m'en courir!'*

Pagan's eyebrows lifted at the outer tips, contracted in front. He did not, however, alter his easy posture. He said lightly enough, although there was a hint of steel in his voice —

'I hope, Jasmine, that your head has not been turned by the prospect of being made a respectable woman at last! I should be glad to hear, *now*, what has happened.'

> *'Et moi de m'en courir!'*

She made the instrument tinkle with elfin laughter at hobgoblin fears.

And then he said rather slowly, as if still turning over the thought in his mind —

'I do not suppose that by any chance you are meditating upon a *"m'en courir"*?'

With the question cold fear came to her. Whatever happened he must never guess that to-morrow she would be gone — would pass with her lover beyond his sight and hearing and touch. He must never, never guess.

She turned toward him a little and began to tell just the bare facts, her left hand still lightly moving over the keyboard. At least, such bare facts as she might. Marriage . . . In Paris . . . Soon . . . To be kept secret until he was of age.

'He is, of course, two years younger than you are!' said Pagan maliciously, and watched to see how she took the stab. Added, 'But you and I are old with an immortal youth!'

But Jasmine paid no heed. Her regard was toward the floor.

'Am I to be officially informed about this charming idyll?' he asked.

Anthony was to come, not to-morrow, because his grandmother's man of business was still at the château, but the next day to make formal application.

At this prospective regularizing of the affair, the guardian relaxed. He lay back on the settee, regarding his niece through half-closed eyes in a sort of travesty of benignity.

'Paris, I think you said! Well, well! And how do my turtle-doves propose to live in Paris — the dearest city in the world, as I know to my cost?'

'Haricot beans were fifteen hundred francs the bushel there last year,' said Jasmine irrelevantly, without looking up.

'An interesting enough fact to those whose fortune is in haricot beans,' agreed her uncle cordially. 'Alarming to the rest of us!'

He continued to watch her, but with increasing intentness as though he would read everything that was in her mind. Said in a mocking tone —

'As I said once before, I believe that you are half in love with the boy — with the child! Don't forget, my pretty, that your experience of life in the fullest sense ranges over seven years. His, over one — with, I should imagine, a solitary, but invaluable experiment with Hortense!'

Jasmine rose to her feet.

She looked at him for a minute without a word. He lay back, laughing, on the soap-boiler's settee, a faun peacocking it in his silken wrapper of green and bronze — paid for by the soap-boiler — against the grey and silver of the soap-boiler's curtains.

'Oh, God! You *would* remind me of that!'

He was suddenly upon his feet. So quickly that there seemed no intervening movement between his being seated and his being risen. Often, she felt, there was something inhuman about the speed of his actions, as though in verity he were the heathen half-god that he looked.

'It is Deirdre, Deirdre of the Sorrows, that you fancy yourself to be, my beautiful!' he said. 'It is a Deirdre that would be away with the Son of Usnach! But I am no Conchobar.'

He took her by the hand — that hand against which Anthony's lips had been pressed in reverence so very short a time before.

She tore it away. He recaptured it, and held it in such fashion that she could not wrest it from him without the indignity of physical combat.

'Remember, I *lend* you to this lad! I do *not* give you. And when I so desire I shall take my own. And I shall take it very often. And I shall take it how I choose!'

'Let me go!'

'And the pity it is, perhaps, that it's not the soap-boiler after all that is the lucky fellow! Maybe we must see into it! For then would you be sitting on my knee, and we'ld be laughing together, and planning great things, and kissing, and — '

'Let me go, Julian! Let me go! . . . Please let me go! I've been through a great deal to-night. I want to go to bed!'

'Alone? Not alone, Jasmine!'

In the same swift manner as before, his arms encircled her, gently, inexorably, in the embrace of Pan. His mocking beautiful face came close to hers.

She gave a cry.

'I *will* go!'

And fought against him with all the strength of her youth and anger, straining from him, beating his face with her hands, turning her head from side to side to escape the menace of his lips . . . So with but little noise they struggled for a while.

Then, as if wearied of the combat, Julian unclasped her; but before she could escape, or had even realized her freedom, he had grasped the bosom of her pale sleeveless dress with both hands and rent it — and whatever lay beneath — to shreds.

She clutched the falling garments about her, and so stood before him, frozen, in silvery half-nakedness.

She suddenly knew that the spell was breaking.

'I had forgotten,' said Julian, 'how beautiful you are!'

He took her within his clasp again. She made no resistance.

Of what use when all the tissue of dreams woven in that room had in some occult way been tattered with the primrose dress; when the very sanctuary of an idyllic love was desecrated by such a battle; when one man devoured her nakedness with kisses, where another had kissed her gown as though it were the robe of a saint.

'Remember! I *lend* you,' said Julian. 'I shall come when I list. I shall hold you — like this. I shall kiss you — like this. I shall call to you — and your body will bring your spirit, for you are *all* mine! All . . . Aren't you, Jasmine?'

The spell *was* breaking! How should it ever be restored?

And his kisses on the lips she had not dared offer to her other lover brought her the profound knowledge that no shadowy love, no passionless worship would ever fill her needs.

She suddenly laughed . . . At herself . . . Out loud . . . Laughed at the princess of dreams who had vanished beyond recall to the Land that is East of the Sun and West of the Moon. Farther yet!

CHAPTER VI

THE REALITY OF A LADY — 2

WAR became peace — a peace that was to endure for one year and sixteen days. A delirious mob had dragged the carriage of the French envoy through the streets of London, and the night of October 10, 1801, was bright with bonfires and transparencies and fairy-lamps as Lieutenant-Colonel Charles Hurrell concluded a letter, in his Bond Street lodgings, to Mr. Harradence, in Wales. He wrote —

' . . . I owe Mrs. Vane more than I can say: anything I may have been able to do for you with the authorities is the mere return of a tithe of that debt. I am glad that things have been so easily settled.

'And now I am *your* debtor as well. But for your information about the unspeakable Starkey I might have had to look forward to an indefinite continuation of the nightmare of persecution to which I have been subjected for the past eight years.

'When I was a very young man I did a grievous wrong — I will tell you the truth about it one day — but God knows that I have been punished indeed.

'Ever since 1793 I have been aware of a malign campaign to effect my ruin. All sorts of ugly rumours about me have been put into circulation — in town and in Carmarthenshire, in club and drawing-room, in the regiment and at the Horse Guards. When one lot died down, a fresh batch would spring up. They have dragged me into half a dozen duels, the only result of which has been to add to my reputation that of being a swashbuckler. They have lost me a bride, and twice cost me promotion — fortunately the Duke of York has always stood my friend. Wherever I have gone — whatever I have done, a whispering campaign of calumny has followed. Queer things have happened to my investments — few and small though they are. My creditors have invariably become pressing out of all reason at times when I could least well meet their demands.

'I was never able to find out who directed and carried out this deliberate design to destroy me professionally, socially, and financially. Now, thanks to you, I am at last freed. Yesterday morning I had the infinite pleasure of horse-whipping Mr. Starkey in his office, before his clerks: in the afternoon he was visited by my lawyer who put the fear of God into him: to-day he was summoned to the Horse Guards where he was warned of what happens to people who carry on such operations against a serving British officer, as agents for an alien domiciled in an enemy country. Mr. Starkey was very, very frightened, and is going to be very, very good. He has undertaken to advise me if he learns thro' his own peculiar channels of any attempt by Madam Purvis to renew the war thro' any other agency. But I do not think anyone will undertake the business for her: I fancy that the warning has already gone round the underground burrows where the like of Mr. Starkey lurk. . . .

'I shall give myself the pleasure, if I may, of calling upon you and your family very shortly, as I must go to Morfa to see my old uncle who has never recovered from the sudden death of his only son.'

Peace became war. Which was why Miss Buckley had no reply to the letter she wrote to England — and took to the post herself so that none of the household should be aware of it —

'Versailles, May 2nd, '03

'My dearest Mrs. Harradence — I had almost written Vane,

'How glad and happy I am at your *enchanting* news! How sincerely I congratulate you and Mr. Harradence! How much I regret that I should not have been present when Hymen's knot was tied! My every good wish and hope for you both. If you can find time amid the turmoil of setting up house, I implore you to furnish me with *every* detail of the ceremony. Please write soon, as they say here that war is inevitable and may be resumed any day — How I pray, not! — and then correspondence will become difficult, if not impossible, as Madam P. no longer has a London agent.

'I could wish that I were as happy and confident about our *other* marriage!

'Anthony has just returned to Paris — he looks *most* distinguished and romantic in uniform — after being away for nearly two years checking maps and topographical information in Germany. He says that the French War Ministry's maps are appallingly bad, none of them being less than forty years old!

'He says very little about *her* lately to me! How I wish it had been Another! During his absence Count Pagan resided with his niece. He seemed to be very much at home when I visited her once, as A. had asked me to. The house was full of smart, gay people who made me feel the middle-aged frump that I am, so I did not go again.

'Altho' he is only 21, A. has already been promoted captain. He is to be transferred to another branch of the Intelligence section of the First Consul's personal staff this month, although his chief has protested. He will be stationed at Boulogne. There will be no excuse for *her* refusing to go with him, as he has taken a small house in the town.

"We have still not ventured to tell Madam P. of the marriage for fear of another stroke, altho' since we moved to Versailles last year the improvement in her condition has been remarkable. She is *indomitable!*

'My own health too is greatly improved — in particular the digestion — ever since I started taking Dr. Burnier's Sea-weed and Silver Compound. It costs five francs the bottle, but my hiccups — . . . (*And so on, and so on!*)

'Yours most affly
'Susanna Buckley

'*Post-scriptum:* I take the liberty of enclosing a little Epithalamium which I composed to mark *The* Occasion. — S.B.

'*Post-post-scriptum:* Count Victor Radomski called on Madam P. recently. He asked me afterwards to remember him to you all. I once started to speak of you to A. but he desired me to desist. We must trust to Time, that Great Healer. — S.B.'

The Battle of Britain was begun. On the Invasion Coast the Dictator gathered a vast army, immense stores, a huge fleet of landing-craft: surveyed through a colossal telescope, from his camp above Boulogne, the white cliffs of England and the grey walls of Dover Castle. In the threatened island King George the Third prepared to evacuate his wife and daughters to the comparative safety of the Welsh border, whilst he with his subjects — armed with whatever weapon might come to hand — fought the invader on the beaches, in the fields, in the streets, in the hills, without thought of surrender.

Jasmine Purvis wrote from Boulogne to Julian Pagan in Paris, in July 1804 —

'You can have no idea how frightful it is here. The place is as unbelievably crowded as if a perpetual Grand Review were being held simultaneously with a continuous performance by a circus on a fairground on a market-day. There is no society except when the Emperor comes: the shops are impossible: the hotels are impossible: the theatre is impossible. The place smells of sweat, gunpowder, and the sort of scent with which women of the streets drench themselves.

'Firing practice and embarkation and debarkation exercises go on all day, and at night the British amuse themselves by bombarding the town! A week ago the house next but one to us was destroyed by a shell. It was appalling. Our windows were all broken by the concussion. A month ago they dropped two hundred bombs into the town, and occasionally they land a raiding party under our very noses!

'Anthony is liaison officer for the Imperial Headquarters Staff with the Corps of Guide-Interpreters who were, I imagine, mostly touts for the Paris brothels in civilian life.

'He spends most of his time interrogating British prisoners — spies, who seem to arrive here by the boatload. The other morning a batch of eight were shot on the sands; and yet the more they catch, the more there seem to be. They say that everything that happens here is known in London within thirty-six hours.

'Promise me that you won't go to Ireland again! These Irish risings always end in fiasco: they can't be worth the trouble and the risk. I dreamed of firing-parties all the time that you were away, and used to wake up with the echoes of the volley in my ears. It was a few days before I had your letter saying that you were safely back in Paris that they shot the eight men. Anthony had to see them the night before the execution, and I knew when he came back what he had been doing — I can always tell from the expression on his long melancholy face what he has been doing, although he never says anything . . . I got the idea that you, too, might be about to face a firing-party, and did not have a moment's peace until your letter came. I don't think I did or said anything foolish, but I feel that Anthony somewhere at the back of his mind has begun to suspect me rather vaguely. His manner has entirely changed since the spring of last year when I refused to have a child.

The practice of abortion was something new and horrible to him. He will never forgive me. I think he blames me for not being the woman he thought I was. He's found out that I'm real — perhaps too real! Don't be under any illusions! I don't love you in the least. I hate you — but I need you. I am only writing to you, just as I spend hours talking to "Cousin" Kate, because there is nothing else to do. I cannot bear to contemplate the possibility of your dying, but I know quite well that once you *are* dead I shall only heave a sigh of relief. Something like a toper surveying an empty brandy bottle and realizing that a period of sobriety has begun.

'I cannot stay here any longer. *Je m'ennuie à la mort.* I *will* not stay here. I hate the place. I am telling Anthony that I must go back to Paris . . . He does not even know that you have returned, and need not, if you can keep clear of Victor Radomski who is perpetually between Paris and Boulogne since he became an orderly officer to the Emperor. I rather fancy that he . . .'

The Battle of Britain was over — won at sea, hundreds of miles from the island shores. At Trafalgar the fleet that should have made safe the passage of the narrow waters for the invader was annihilated.

England was saved, but the Continent was laid prostrate. For the armies of invasion marched away from their camps on the Iron Coast — eastward to immense conquest, to staggering victory. Anthony went with them. From Berlin he wrote, in November '06, to Jasmine —

' . . . and after that we made our triumphal entry here, with the Emperor wearing his plainest clothes and a two-*sous* cockade in his hat.

'I have not heard from you for three months, altho' I write every fortnight regularly, and you never seem to tell me any news. If it hadn't been for Victor Radomski, who saw him in Paris the other day, I shouldn't even have known that your uncle had turned up again. Where is he living? I don't think it really necessary for us to house him again.

'Lafitte's have written to me that you are overdrawn by as much as seventy thousand francs. This is a very large sum, for even if we have a big income yet we are living up to every cent of it and the reports from the States are by no means satisfactory. I hate saying so, but I thought that we had agreed last time . . .'

BOOK FIVE

SILAS AND DEANE

Prussia — England 1806

★

CHAPTER I

INTERLUDE WITH AN EMPEROR

ALL the roads in Europe led to the castle of Lauchstein.

There was no purpose to any highway in any land but that it should at last come to that wide melancholy Prussian plain with the dark line of forest upon the horizon, and to the vast jumble of peaked towers and steep roofs fretting the sad sky and reflected sombrely in the coil of the reed-fringed river from which they rose.

Out of the tangle of alleys and lanes and streets in every capital city, the grey threads of highway unravelled themselves, wound over wide plains, bridged great waters, climbed mountain ranges, and pierced enormous forests, so that eventually they should meet before the lofty iron gates and the stone lodges with striped sentry-boxes and the avenue of giant pines.

Along those roads, from east and west, and south and north, the messengers of Empire travelled. They came on spur-marked horses and in mud-encrusted travelling-carriages from our metropolis of Paris; from Milan where our step-son ruled the Kingdom of Italy as our Viceroy; from our brothers the Kings of Holland and Naples; from Imperial Vienna which the Habsburgs had surrendered without a blow; from our governor in Berlin; from a dozen lickspittle sovereigns of feudatory Germany; from our Most Catholic cousin the idiot monarch of Spain — shortly to surrender his tarnished crown to our goodwill; from the dukes and princes — our marshals — who further eastward kept watch upon the remnants of broken Prussian armies and an uncertain Tsar. They came, too, with their budgets by circuitous and secret routes from London, the stronghold of the one enemy who could neither be placated nor intimidated, who could be beaten but not conquered.

They came by day and by night, jaded by the last long stage across the shelterless plain. Through the great gates; up the long avenue in which it was never lighter than dusk; over the bridge across a leaden stream; and so were swallowed up in the black portals of the gatehouse, like laden bees returning to the hive.

And their burden was always news. News, and yet more news; facts, and yet more facts. For one insatiable reader.

Of his own armies — daily movement returns; daily statistical returns.

Of the enemy — every scrap of information that could be garnered by the intelligence departments of each corps, by secret service agents of the Minister of Police, by unspeakable traitors bought by General Savary, by emissaries of the spy bureau organized by the sinister Schulmeister . . . Reports of conversations with peasants — reports of conversations with princes; notes scribbled while listening at key-holes; letters, deadly in import, and fatal to their writers if seen by other eyes than those for which they were intended. Notes of topographical reconnaissances sufficient to fill a dozen hand-books — word-pictures which coloured a dozen maps with the sheen of water and the slime of mud and the green of forests and the purple of mountains and the red or grey or yellow-thatch roofs of hamlet and city.

For one reader.

Reports on newspapers. Reports on books. Reports on publishers. Reports on new plays. Reports on harlots. Reports on generals. Reports on their wives. Reports on his own wife. Reports on agriculture, education, shipbuilding, road-making, local government, inventions, sermons. Reports on everything.

For one omnivorous reader.

To annotate and connotate for whom, to carry whose decisions into effect, there was herded behind those walls the complex and multifarious population of Grand Imperial Headquarters. The Emperor's personal staff, his business office, his household: generals, dukes, secretaries to the cabinet, secretaries of the portfolio, *aides-de-camp, aides-de-camp* to *aides-de-camp,* archivists, geographers, surgeons, valets, scullions. Eight hundred of them! *And* the Chief of the General Staff, and *his* personal staff, and *his* cabinet. *And* stray representatives of the General Staff that was housed meekly in a shabby wooden town somewhere on the horizon. *And* duty officers from the four regiments of the Guard which were bivouacked under the cyclopean trees of the avenue, along the banks of the river, and in the mud-coloured cottages and barns of the hamlet set about the muddy cross-roads a quarter of a mile away whence the yet muddier highways debouched from Paris, from Berlin, from Vienna, from Moscow, from — London.

At night the black bulk of the castle rose against the black sky, stippled with a hundred lighted windows, from a firefly nest of campfires and lights on horse-lines and wagon-parks.

Out there on the melancholy east-land plain was the capital of Empire. For a day — for a week — for a month — for so long as Imperial Majesty desired. That Imperial Majesty who twelve years ago had been flung into gaol because of his friendship with the fallen Terrorist Robespierre; at whose nod now frontiers were swept away and ancient nations obliterated. . . .

Count Victor Radomski climbed the narrow winding staircase of the circular tower in the pitch darkness, hands spread wide before him so that he might feel the rough stone of the invisible wall on either side. His sword, although hitched, threatened at any moment to capsize him as he stumbled upward, alternately cursing that he had no candle and praying that he had not mis-read the directions on the billeting list in the Imperial *salle-de-service*.

He reached the top: fell with a crash over the threshold of the narrow archway that opened into a completely obscure passage: lost his schapka: sought for the damned thing on hands and knees: found it, set it once more firmly on his head: as he rose, became tangled with his sword in some strange way, and sat down upon his spurred heels.

He went down the passage, restraining neither his language nor the loudness of it, the bare uneven boards protesting as he trod.

At the far end a light showed under an ill-fitting door. Somebody was awake — Thank God! — to tell him where Anthony Purvis's quarters were.

He entered without knocking.

Anthony lay asleep, covered by rugs, on a truckle bed in a white-washed attic little bigger than a cupboard. Before the curtainless dormer window was a small table covered with papers, and lighted by a couple of guttering candles. The plain dark green uniform coat of an orderly officer to the Emperor hung over the back of a rush-seated chair; a bucket of water — presumably for toilet purposes — and a battered valise were pushed into the angle where the steeply slanting roof met the floor.

Anthony slept.

Radomski dropped on to the foot of the bed with a thump.

'Lucky, lucky swine! A bed by all that's holy!' he said.

Anthony groaned, turned from side to back, brought up an arm to shield his face — an arm whose night-shirt cuff was frilled and pinned back over the stump in which it ended.

Radomski, his queer high-cheekboned countenance furrowed with a smile that was both affectionate and sardonic, regarded his victim for a moment — tangle of dark hair, high-bridged nose, cleft chin, black straight eyebrows with the faintest inquiring twist at their outer ends, face that was both imaginative and adventurous, that held the leanness of a soldier and yet — in sleep at least — something of the contours of childhood.

'Hey!' said Radomski. 'Wake up, my beautiful! Wake up, Apollo! Wake up from dreams of *her* to deal with *him!*'

'Blast you!' said Anthony waking. 'Bl——! . . . Victor! When did you get back?'

'To-night! Did sixty miles to-day on foundered horses! Got back here at eight o'clock. Am immediately detailed for orderly duty. To be relieved at seven! Have got one — *one* — ONE carriage cushion on the *salle-de-service* floor, and have already been routed out of it three times on messages which the half-witted son of a Prussian pederast could faithfully perform . . . The Little Man wants you!'

'Me?' said Anthony, stirring feebly beneath rugs and blankets. 'What the devil for?'

'Christ knows! He's in one of his moods, I suppose! At two o'clock in the morning he shoots out of his little green-curtained bed and into his plump little pantaloons. He calls for Méneval, and he calls for Fain — and he calls for his fiddlers three! And then he calls for Berthier, and he calls for d'Albe and he calls for Savary and he calls for d'Ideville! They can't find either Savvy or Iddy — out womanizing, I suppose! — so he calls for you! . . . By the time I get back to the *salle-de-service* he'll do what he did the night before they sent me off to Paris — want everybody waked up! Blast his soul to perdition!'

'Me?' said Anthony, throwing a long leg out of bed.

'Well, you're Imperial Topographical Office, or Statistical Office, or Intelligence, aren't you?'

'God knows! A bit of all of them! . . . Well, the Little Man will have to wait while I get dressed!'

'I'll stop here till you're ready! I'm not going to risk my neck on your damned stairs without a candle again!'

Anthony pulled on his shirt.

'How did you get on in Paris? Did you see Jasmine? Or anybody else?'

Radomski gave him a sidelong look before replying.

'Didn't see a soul! Not a soul *you* know! Had no time. Took Fouché his orders. Collected his reports about something or other. Stole *one* hair-raising night. And that was all! But what a night!' Paused. Added — 'Haven't you heard from her lately?'

'Not for over three months,' said Anthony, struggling into tight green breeches, and rescuing a long black riding-boot from under the bed. 'She's not a good letter-writer!'

'Odd!' commented Radomski, not thinking the matter in the least odd, and debating within his soul whether or no duty and friendship demanded that he should repeat some of the reports that were circulating in Paris.

Said Anthony, easing his foot down the boot —

'I calculated the other day that, though we have been married for nearly six years, we have lived together for less than six months!'

Radomski nodded: examined in absent-minded fashion the other's dark green coat, which was without ornament but for a golden shoulder-knot with heavy bullion tassel.

'We had two months together when we were first married, and I had joined the army and was doing my training under d'Albe. That was in '01. We had three weeks in '03 just before war broke out again. And three months in Boulogne in '04. I haven't seen her since. The Little Man has kept me on the run all the time.'

'It is hard luck!' agreed Radomski in a rather half-hearted manner: recollected a fresh topic, and broached it with an air of relief whilst Anthony sponged his face over the bucket.

'I was forgetting. I *did* see someone you know . . . I saw Solly Klasing in one of the passages of the Police Ministry. He says you got him a job there!'

'Well — '

'He says that you also — '

'Oh, well!'

'If you want to know what a grateful Jew looks like, you ought to see Solly! Except that you wouldn't recognize him. He's dyed his hair black. He says it's less conspicuous than red, and Fouché likes his people to be inconspicuous.'

'My God!'

'Quite! . . . You had better hurry up!'

'If the Little Man's got d'Albe there's no need to hurry . . . What's Solly doing?'

'So far as I could make out he spends his office hours cooking fake credentials for our agents abroad. He said quite proudly that he seemed to have a gift for forgery! The rest of the time he reads philosophy or listens to music. He's composed a dance, "Quadrille of the Secret Police".

But he says it's no good. He says that not having a workable left hand entirely throws him out . . . Hey! Don't forget your sword!'

What a foul world it was! . . . Solly, for whom Viotti had prophesied great things, with all the potentialities for music within him quenched, reduced to the job of forger of documents in a police bureau! . . . It seemed odd to think of a forger keeping office hours — hanging up his hat on a peg — climbing on to a high stool — entering up his forgeries in a business-like day-book, or whatever it was . . . He suddenly recalled Solly standing in the disused stable at the Institut, rapt in the queer, ironic, yet rather noble melody — 'Requiem Mass for a Dead Jew'.

While Anthony brushed his hair and set himself to rights, Radomski had risen to his feet, surveyed the mass of newspapers lying on the table in the window. He recited their names as he turned them over —

'Moscow News — Son of the Fatherland — Swabian Mercury — Hamburg News — Frankfort Times — Cobbett's Political Register — The Times — Morning Chronicle. What the devil do you want all those for?'

'To read, you ass! To pick out bits that'll interest the Little Man. Bits about himself. Bits about his enemies. Bits about their armies. Bits about all sorts of things you wouldn't understand! That's one of my jobs as d'Ideville's assistant. The Statistical Office is the place where we sort out the stuff that Fouché's people get, and Savary's people get, and the Foreign Ministry gets. We edit the Little Man's foreign news service. And we travel round with him when the Grand Imperial Circus is on the move — I'm ready now! — as his personal interpreters . . . Come on!'

'I thought that statistics had something to do with sums,' grumbled Radomski hitching up his sword, and preparing to follow out of the door.

'Well here they haven't,' said Anthony, and stalked into the passage. 'You'd better carry the candle, Victor! One wants a second hand to shield it with!'

In the darkness of the stairs Radomski remarked, and tried not to infuse any special meaning into his words —

'I should ask for leave, Anthony, if I were you!'

'No more hope of getting it than invading England! The Little Man would look upon it as tantamount to treason!' . . .

Two hard-bitten Polish lancers with schapkas of crimson and jackets of crimson, and braided breeches of dark blue, stood on guard before the elaborately carved double doors of mahogany which gave on the ante-chamber used as the duty-room.

It was a lofty room of beautiful proportions. At the great doors at the further end a tall page in green and silver yawned dolorously in his chair. A weary hussar subaltern of the guard made deferential conversation with the Prince of Neuchâtel's *aide-de-camp* — an orientally magnificent creature in plumed shako, black Hungarian pelisse, white furred dolman and scarlet trousers; who would have been less Oriental and more magnificent if his jowl had not been black with unshaved bristles. The floor was strewn with cushions and rugs from which the sleepers had apparently been aroused, for only one orderly officer remained, curled up on a palliasse, a red handkerchief over his face to keep out the light.

The dark panels of the walls were disfigured with notices, orders, and duty-lists nailed up with tacks.

'Good-bye!' said Radomski in Polish. 'Give my love to the Little Man! Tell him to call me at seven! I'll have breakfast with you, unless you've been shot for dereliction of duty! . . . Which is your Mess?'

'*C* Mess. With the *élite!*' said Anthony, and passed through the further doors into the workshop, laboratory, offices of the Emperor.

A vast apartment — the Hall of the Knights. As big as a church, with a high vaulted roof, lighted by innumerable hanging chandeliers. Four great bays, in which uncurtained windows with stone mullions looked down through the night upon the river, were opposed by four recesses — the size of chantry chapels — in which grim portraits of grim Electors of Brandenburg surveyed the tables whereat the Imperial office staff were feverishly at work. At the far end a dais, presided over by an enormous battle scene, in which Frederick the Great — more than life-size — rode placidly over a mass of dead bodies and exploded cannon against a background of smoke and flame. In the middle of the hall were islanded three long oaken tables with bulbous legs, two of them littered with papers, and the nearer spread with maps weighted down with at least twenty lighted candlesticks.

The plump white-breeched seat of someone leaning far over the table, and propped by his elbows among the maps, presented itself to Anthony's inspection. Other men in every variety of uniform and dress were clustered nearby or gathered in silent knots in the window-bays.

Anthony halted by the nearest chapel: the ministrants — young civilians — were writing for dear life with squeaking quill-pens; the one copying a dispatch onto gilt-edged vellum from a much-corrected draft, the other making a summary of the documents piled at his elbow on a dated and numbered work-sheet.

'What's *he* want now, Méneval?' he asked in a low voice of the dispatch-writer.

'God knows!' said Majesty's private secretary in a whisper, looking up over his shoulder to see who spoke, and returning to hostile study of a spidery correction. 'To kill us, I suppose! . . . I'll resign to-morrow!'

Anthony remained at anchor by the table awaiting summons from Plump-Seat forty feet away.

They were good breeches — well-cut! But the Little Man, to give him his due, always wore good clothes — plain clothes, gentlemanly clothes! Didn't get himself up like a harlequin, like Murat, for instance, or Ney. Still if you had a civil list of twenty-five million francs — to say nothing of the loot! And what loot! — you could buy good breeches! What sort of breeches did he wear when all he'd got in the world was a sub-lieutenant's twenty francs a week? What sort of breeches had he worn years ago when they had played chess together at the house in the mountains?

Plump-Seat, without altering his position, and as if he had an eye focused in the rearward part of his anatomy, suddenly said —

'Purvis!'

Anthony stepped smartly forward; clicked to attention.

'Sire?'

Colonel Bacler d'Albe — rotund and smiling — straightened himself up at the side of Plump-Seat. He held a pair of compasses in his hand, and gave his former assistant a friendly wink.

Plump-Seat, between the *chevaux-de-frise* of candles, remained recumbent on his tableful of maps, a pair of dividers clasped in one plump hand. The maps were studded with pins with tops of coloured wax. Said Plump-Seat —

'Who, Purvis, was Mistaire Silas Deane?'

'I never heard of him, Sire.'

That was all. Absolutely all.

Plump-Seat returned to the study of his maps. He debated — face-downward — with d'Albe; threw a stray remark to Marshal Berthier, Prince of Neuchâtel, a rather grotesque copy of his master, who strode up and down in the intervals biting his finger-nails, picking at his nose; streamed out dictation — still face-downward — to a wretched secretary with warty hands and a large note-book. He addressed no further word to the young officer of the Statistical Staff standing within kicking distance of his breeches.

Two hours went by. At the end of them Plump-Seat resumed an upright position and walked quietly away, his white hands lightly clasped under his green coat-tails.

The great folding doors to one side of the immense picture of Frederick II swung wide open; there was a momentary glimpse of the State bed-chamber and a carved and canopied four-poster as big as a mansion against which, like an out-house, nestled the little green curtained campaign bed of Imperial Majesty.

Plump-Seat passed through. The doors swung to behind him.

It was five o'clock of a winter morning.

Anthony went back to bed. Cursing.

Who anyhow was Silas Deane? It sounded like one of the prize conundrums in the *Journal des Débats?*

At half-past six a red-eyed orderly officer brought him a new summons to the ruler of Europe.

The duty-room was empty except for officer of the guard, page at the door, and Marshal Berthier's unshaven grandee who was playing solitaire with a pack of cards that looked as though it had been borrowed from the kitchen.

In the Hall of the Knights the great windows in the bays were still black with night, and the drab office staff drudged on in the brightly lighted chantry shrines of Brandenburg Elector and Prussian King. There was no one at the long central tables under the chandeliers except d'Albe, who, with a pile of his little topographical note-books beside him, was correcting one of the maps.

The Emperor stood at a buhl table on the dais, before the immense battle-scene, talking to two thin saturnine individuals in dark civilian dress. He walked round and round the tables as he spoke, twisting in corkscrew fashion both cuffs of his green uniform coat. On a side-table beneath the picture was opened a travelling book-case. Against this drooped Marshal Berthier, cocked hat under arm, apparently reading over the entries he had made in a small green leather-bound note-book.

Anthony halted twenty paces or so away, close — for moral support — to the preoccupied d'Albe, although he was far less alarmed than if he had been sent for by his late headmaster.

'Who, Purvis,' he said to his immortal soul, 'was Mistaire Thomas Brown? Citoyen Jean Durand? Herr Wilhelm Schmidt? Ali Mustafa Effendi? Signor Antonio Rossi? Señor Miguel Perez? Mynheer Arnold van Dam? Monsieur Nicholas Petrovitch?'

He realized that a plump white finger was beckoning to him. As he walked quickly toward the dais, the saturnine twins withdrew out of earshot.

He reached the table with its neat array of docketed papers, its silver standish and green russia-leather writing slope; halted beside it. The short square figure had ceased its peregrinations, and stood attitudinized in thought — chin sunk on chest, arms folded — gazing down the great nave of his shrine, a meditative high priest of war.

'Who, Purvis,' demanded Anthony of his immortal soul, 'is Missus Mary Brown? Citoyenne Jeane Durand? Frau Anna Schmidt? Fatima —'

Said his master, without shifting his regard —

'How many people are there who know you by sight in England, Purgis?'

Anthony was accustomed to the Little Man's impish habit of purposefully mis-naming people. It never, however, failed to irritate him. He answered curtly —

'Four, Sire! No, five! Perhaps six! Not more!'

'Who are they? Where do they live? Are they English or American?'

'Mr. Deane is not among them!' said Anthony to his soul. But aloud, 'A Birmingham manufacturer — name: Harradence — and his wife and step-daughter. I have not seen them or heard from them directly for over five years. I don't want to. I believe that they live in Wales . . . A French *émigré*. Name Courville. I don't know where he is . . . An English officer. Name Hurrell. But I don't suppose he would recognize me: he hasn't seen me since I was a child. You will recall him perhaps, Sire! You had his trousers taken off!'

The deep-set grey eyes were turned swiftly upon him: Anthony could have sworn that in their lustrous depths was laughter. A lock of dark hair had strayed over the Little Man's forehead: his pale olive face had black shadows about chin and upper lip — was, in fact, scrubby. He hadn't shaved! Emperors should always be properly shaved. They had no excuse. He recollected Harradence commenting acidly on Latin casualness with the razor.

'I remember!'

'There is also the American inventor, Fulton. But *The Times* says he is leaving for the United States this month.'

'Fulton!' said the Little Man. He started his travels round the table again, one hand behind his back, the other stabbing at the air with a mother-of-pearl-handled pen-knife. 'He was the man who invented plunging-boats and bombs-submarine! With a passionate hatred of the English! So he said — but he ended up by trying to get them to buy his devices!'

'According to our information, Sire, the English Ministry paid him fifteen thousand pounds!' said Anthony bitterly. He had added Fulton's name to the roster of Unforgivables.

The Little Man came to a stop beside his chair — a mahogany elbow-chair with an elaborately carved back. He stayed beside it shaving off slivers from the top rail with his little knife as if he were sharpening a pencil.

'There is no one else who would know you in England, then, Parvis?' said he.

'No one, so far as I know!' Paused. Suddenly added, impelled by he knew not what force — irritation, bravado, curiosity: 'Who *was* Silas Deane, Sire?'

Majesty sliced off an inch-long shaving from the reeding of the chair-back, before he replied acidly —

'So I have to teach you your business! But it's the same everywhere. I have to teach everybody his business — soldier, priest, dressmaker! Silas Deane, Purdie, was like yourself an American. He made the great and simple discovery that you can invade a country without landing armies and guns!'

He shot a glance over his shoulder at Marshal Berthier as though to indicate to him that he was included in the class for instruction . . . The Marshal closed his note-book and assumed an air of great attention.

'You must realize, young man,' continued the Imperial lecturer, not ceasing to sharpen his knife on the unfortunate chair, 'that a battlefront is not only the area wherein two armies face one another, but also the whole of a hostile territory. The English realized this during the war in America. They attacked morale behind the lines by speeding up the deterioration of your currency. They flooded the country with forged notes! It was a well-thought-out plan. But *your* people went a stage further! They carried actual warfare into Britain under Deane's direction!'

He turned to the mahogany chest which, opened and up-ended on the side-table under the great picture, made a bookcase holding on its three deep shelves such reference books as he might require on his journeys. Selected a dumpy volume bound in shabby tree-calf: sought in it, as he spoke, for the right place —

'The man Deane organized on behalf of the American nation, what might have been a most useful and important campaign of incendiarism in England. He was responsible for fires at the Royal Dockyards at Portsmouth, and at Plymouth, and on the quays at Bristol! Quite a lot of destruction! The docks at Chatham and Woolwich were also marked down for his attentions. Why he gave up after one of his subordinates was caught and hanged I do not understand. You Americans are easily disheartened!' He read out from the volume — ' "The scheme, involving as it did the destruction of naval dockyards and arsenals and military storehouses, aimed a blow at the efficiency of Britain's navy, which would

— if successful — have prostrated her whole maritime forces, and exposed
her shores to easy invasion." I hope,' added the Emperor with sardonic
courtesy, 'that I have now been able to satisfy your curiosity.'

As he put the book down something on a sheet of foolscap lying on
his writing slope caught his attention. He seated himself in the misused
chair and read the memorandum very closely.

Anthony remained standing at the side of the table, looking down
on a map so folded that only the table of conventional signs and an inset
plan of some city were visible. He recognized it at once as one of the half-
century-old maps of Saxony by Pétri, which were all the *Dépôt Générale
de la Guerre* in Paris had been able to provide.

He had not studied a map for a considerable time. But again he found
all the olden glamour in the table of signs — in the horn that marked the
post-station, the skeleton of a windmill, the starfish mark for the walled
town, the hieroglyphic outline of church and castle. The town, too,
wherever it was, was fortified and set amid gardened suburbs in a hollow
in some unknown mountains beside a winding river; was approached by
a narrow pass through the hills.

As he waited while the Little Man meditated, he found himself in fancy
riding up that mountain gorge to the city with its steep red roofs and
towers and spires set amid orchards; hearing the bells ring out and seeing the thin smoke arise from its hundred chimneys . . . His mind went
back to Camelot — the magic town of long ago, up whose tilted streets
he had used to ride as a child with his fairy companions, returning from
foray and high adventure. The heroes of his dreams had never whittled
away at their chairs of state with pen-knives in the knightly hall; nor been
surrounded by a clerical staff like tea merchants; nor appeared with jowls
blackening with unshaven beards!

'You will leave for London to-day, as soon as it is light,' said Majesty,
scribbling something in the margin of the foolscap sheet, pushing it to
one side, and drawing another paper toward him.

God! Did the Little Man propose to make an incendiary of him? He
was mistaken if he did!

'I mean to carry on where Deane left off!' said Majesty, idly stabbing
the pen-knife into the exquisite inlay of the table. 'My agent has instructions to pursue the campaign against the dockyards to the bitter end. He
has also instructions to effect a simultaneous rising in all the prisoner-of-
war camps. There are seventy thousand men interned in the big camps,
which are very poorly guarded, mostly by militia. This agent — his name
is Malone — has hitherto dealt only with the Ministry of Justice. He has
had big sums from Monsieur Fouché. Very big sums! I now want to see

results. I am not a charitable organization. Monsieur Fouché's large heart always permits him to give away big sums of other people's money — and to accept large sums from curious sources!'

He paused to let the implication sink in; gathered Marshal Berthier's attention again by a swift glance. Went on —

'As I invariably send out officers to make personal report to me on the military situation on any part of my battle front, so I now send you to make me personal report on the proceedings of my army in England. You will learn every detail of the plan for the attack upon the docks, and you will yourself visit the subordinate commanders responsible to Malone for undertaking the war in the camps. You will hear all they have to say, and judge the situation yourself. It is part of the scheme that the escaped prisoners, armed by various means, should undertake guerrilla war throughout the country, avoiding the larger centres of population at first.' He consulted the paper which he had taken up. 'These sub-agents are three. Their names are La Ferre, Denisham, and De Mussy. Remember them! They have landed as Americans and have their headquarters near Liverpool, Hull, and somewhere between Portsmouth and Plymouth. Malone will enable you to get in touch with them. You will return to me as soon as you have satisfied yourself that all is in order!'

'Where is Malone to be found, Sire?'

Anthony watched the plump small hands turn over the sheet of paper. Plump small hands and plump breeches — by God, he earned every penny of his twenty-five millions a year and colossal pickings! There was no detail small enough in war to escape his individual attention, nothing that he overlooked. Saw too that everybody about him earned their money: whether it was Berthier with his million and a half a year *and* the pickings, or d'Albe with his little pension of ten thousand plus salary! All provided — not by France, but from looted Europe.

Why did he continue to serve the little devil? . . . He had no material need. It must be because the enormous driving energy that was generated in that small frame awakened his response. Just as a glass would ring to a certain note, or a distant hill answer with echo to a shout; so his mind, or his soul, or just his body, replied obediently to the imperative summons of Napoleon.

The Little Man found the particulars. Read them curtly —

'Malone. The Strand. London. The pass-word is *Silas,* and the counter-word *Deane* . . . You will say nothing about this, even to Monsieur d'Ideville, except that you have been detailed for duty by me. Draw your expenses and be off! . . . Now, Berthier!'

Anthony backed away for a suitable distance from the Presence, negotiating the three shallow steps of the dais with caution.

Arrived at the great doors he paused and looked back.

Under the high vaulted roof the dais was a blaze of light. He had the fancy that the great hall was a church profaned to the worship of war, and that the small figure — so bowed over the table that there was visible the sheen of his dark oiled hair — was the very God of War incarnate, presiding at his altar beneath the vast picture of carnage and destruction as though under the East Window of his sanctuary.

. . . What would not his grandmother give to know of the errand on which he was about to start; to know that a Purvis was at last to become an instrument for the wreaking of her bitter vengeance? He had written to her last year after the bloodiness of Austerlitz, and again after the hideous slaughter at Jena to assure her of his own safety. She had written back through Buck to the same effect on both occasions. It was good — was the burthen of her reply — that he should have had this schooling of the battlefield against the day when the armies of the Emperor would be turned westward against the one enemy that mattered. Did normal folk bear hatred for so long, he wondered. He already was forgetting his own wrongs! . . .

God spoke: his cold, clear voice was audible to Anthony at the door — to everyone in the congregation; as doubtless He intended.

'And now, Prince, we'll make a move! We've been here long enough! Give orders to strike camp immediately!'

As the doors swung to behind Anthony he saw heads lifting everywhere; caught a glimpse of an aghast Méneval.

The little devil! Has everybody up most of the night, and then shifts camp at a moment's notice — just to keep them alive and active, and from getting stale! . . . The roads of Europe would no longer lead to the castle of Lauchstein from Paris and Milan; from Berlin and Vienna; from Naples and the Hague; from Madrid and London. The capital of an Empire was being moved.

He came chuckling into the ante-room.

Radomski was sitting on the small table by the further door, trying on alternately the guard officer's shako with its white aigrette, and the heavy plumed silver helmet of a protesting subaltern of the cuirassiers; examining the effect in a very small pocket mirror. The headgear did not harmonize with his short furred scarlet jacket. He set down the helmet with a grunt.

'Now what, my Tony, about that breakfast with the aristocracy of Imperial Mess C?' said Radomski.

'There won't be any breakfast for Imperial Mess *C*, Victor,' said Anthony in Polish, grinning as he donned his cocked hat. 'There won't be any breakfast for anybody! The Grand Imperial Stupendous Circus of Napolione Buonaparte and Company is on the move! The big tent is down, and the next performance will be — God knows where! . . . Good-bye! Mangez-bien!'

CHAPTER II

SILAS SEEKS DEANE

CAPTAIN ANTHONY PURVIS, an officer of the Statistical Office of the Private Cabinet of the Emperor Napoleon, rode peacefully on a coachtop across a wintry England.

The sky was a thin and sparkling blue as though the December sun shone upon a vault of ice: the smooth roads grey as steel: the fields a remorseless white, chequered by the black of hedges. It was Sunday, and the air all day seemed full of the melancholy music of church bells. The coach passed, so to speak, from peal to peal across a snowy undulating landscape, whose ridges were fretted with church towers and hamlets and little woods.

Dressed in the most English style imaginable — fawn top-coat with a precipitous stand-up collar of velvet, grey beaver hat worn to one side, and Hessian boots — Anthony sat on the box-seat next to the coachman. This professional gentleman was immensely fat, with a red face, crowned with a low round hat, housed in a vast green overcoat with three capes and pearl buttons the size of small saucers, muffled up to the chin by a neckerchief of vivid yellow, and wrapped about the lower limbs with a startlingly red rug.

The coachman was not stimulating company, although, owing to the condition of the frozen roads, his team of four could rarely exceed a walking pace. His idea of conversation was to put a question, apparently to the near-side ear of the near-side wheeler — a flea-bitten grey — and then, when he had had an answer, to repeat it and the original question aloud meditatively to himself half a dozen times at two minute intervals.

'Lose your arm fightin' Boney, sir, if you'll excuse me arskin'?' said the coachman.

'No,' said Anthony. 'In an accident at sea.'

Pause.

'Sez-I, "Lose your arm fightin' Boney?" Sez-ee, "No. In a n'accident at sea." ' . . . Pause . . . 'Sez-I, "Lose your arm . . ." ' And so *da capo*.

Arrived at a bare small hill, only steep because of the glassy road, Anthony got down from the box and walked ahead, while the guard at the bits of the leading pair urged and cursed and threatened the steaming skidding horses. The coach lurched and skirmished horribly between the hedge-topped banks of the narrow highway.

On the round sweep of the horizon five church towers were visible from the cross-roads at the hill-crest. On the triangle of grass in the middle a disintegrating beacon of tar-barrels and brushwood had been built on two upturned and dilapidated farm-wagons. It was nearly ten foot high and patches of snow had frozen against the pyramid.

A weather-stained notice was nailed to a board on the sign-post at one corner of the grass patch. It was headed in fat black type 'INVASION!' and Anthony paused to read whilst he awaited the arrival of the battling coach. It was addressed to the Inhabitants of the Hundreds of . . .

There followed a score of place-names, telling in their etymology of the ancient invasions of Roman, Anglo-Saxon, Dane, and Norman. 'In the event of the enemy effecting a landing,' it directed all farmers to burn their standing corn and drive their cattle further inland: it gave assembly points and routes for the evacuation columns of women, children, and aged, instructing them that the high roads must be left clear for the movement of troops: it called on all the able-bodied to spring to arms, with a certain amount of woolly rhetoric about freemen preferring death to slavery, and ended — also in fat black type — 'GOD SAVE THE KING'. It was dated some three years back.

Standing on that hill-top, hand thrust deep into pocket, he contemplated the subject of invasion from the viewpoint of the invaded for the first time, although he had ridden with the Imperial armies through a score of violated countries. Well, the English would get a taste, one day, of what they had inflicted upon America! . . . 'God save the King!' What a King! George the Third, the cod-faced imbecile of Windsor — as Harradence would have said!

The coach breasted the rise, was brought to a halt while the nervous horses steamed and calmed. A friendly hand helped him to regain the box.

In a small town smitten with the silences and emptiness of an English Sunday, Anthony bought the coachman a glass of 'hot with', as the horses were being changed. A trim secure little town, with a trim secure little inn, both looking as if they had always been trim and secure and would so continue whatever might happen.

He could not, somehow, picture to himself refugees streaming in endless procession through the wide street past all those neat little houses with scrubbed door-steps and shining windows, whose architecture told three centuries of English history. Nor visualize that trim security insulted by the passage of the Imperial troops in disorderly march, blue-coated, spatterdashed, and unshorn.

Unshorn!

He remembered the Emperor as he had last seen him. Berthier's *aide-de-camp*. D'Albe. D'Ideville — except on Wednesdays, Fridays, and Sundays. It was true what Harradence had said about the Latin being casual in his use of the razor. He glanced at the coachman. The man's weather-beaten countenance was as smooth as a rosy apple: every morning, it was obvious, he faithfully scraped his way through a foamy cloud of lather. Through the medium of the razor he suddenly felt himself akin to this man — name unknown — in the land of his enemies which was also the land of his fathers.

'Furrin' to h'England, sir, I see, if you'll h'excuse me!' said this kinsman, gathering short the reins, and flicking the fleabitten grey's successor for luck.

'What makes you say that?' asked Anthony, horrified that any variation of himself from ordinary English standards should have been so soon detected.

'We-e-ell!' said the other, scratching his head in an unsatisfactory manner owing to his hand being encased in a woollen glove. 'We-e-ell, as you might say, sir, there was you a-readin' that there notice on the top of Gallows Hill h'as if you'd never seen one afore! Then, just now, you looked twicet at the change the gal brought, and turned it h'over as though you didn't know what it were! You'll h'excuse me speakin' so plain!'

'I am an American,' explained Anthony, registering the determination not to examine his change in future no matter what the circumstances might be.

'American!' remarked Kinsman in high astonishment, shifting his regard from the near-side ear of the near-side wheeler to his companion. 'Now who'ld-a thought it? Blister my kidneys, but you talk English! May I be spavined if you don't speak as good English as any man!'

Anthony explained humbly that most Americans spoke English: permitted himself a trial run of the explanation of his presence in England. Been living in Berlin. Retreated before the French invasion. Escaped to Riga. Landed at Ipswich this morning from the Russian barque *Nikolai Chichikov* — 'Gawd! What a name!' interjected Kinsman. — Cargo: hides and tallow — 'Gawd! How nifty!' — Was going to settle up some family affairs before returning home to Virginia, which was a district in America where they grew tobacco.

This kept Kinsman supplied with mental cud until they pulled up at the Red Lion in Colchester, a dark timbered inn with a long courtyard, facing a broad and sleeping street whose gutters were littered with traces of Saturday's market in the shape of battered vegetables and an astonishing quantity of oyster shells.

'Lunnon,' said Kinsman throwing the reins neatly to the ostler and preparing to descend, 'is precisely fifty-one *h'and* a quarter miles. If you was a wise gem'man — you'll h'excuse me speakin' so plain — you'ld stop 'ere the night and take the morning mail. Fifty-one and a quarter miles of frost and dark and bleedin' fog — that's what it'll be, sir! That's what it'll be!'

The sky was already reddening toward sundown, and the shadows had become ominously long. Advice and hostelry both appeared to be good. Anthony expressed his determination to follow the one and sample the other; requested the pleasure of Kinsman's company at the bar. Whereat the coachman, acknowledging the invitation with professional celerity, seized Anthony's hand in a terrific grip and turned himself into a sort of human crane to lower his one-armed passenger bodily to the ground.

Two clumsy lads, arrayed in scarlet uniforms with green facings and plumed shakoes, swaggered by as he set foot upon the cobbles.

Kinsman noted his interest; pulled off his blue woollen gloves: spat somewhat contemptuously —

'Wolunteers!' said he: considered it necessary to explain still further to a foreigner. 'Wolunteers! . . . Been on Sunday drill! Spend all their money on uniform to please the gals, and h'ant got no guns, sir! One musket to three men — pitchforks for the rest! . . . What they want green and red uniforms and 'igh 'ats for to fight the Frenchies beats me! Them barstards'll never dare cross the water! They don't like water on the Continong! As you know.'

But on the great oaken doors at the entrance to the inn yard was another ominous notice, headed in fat black type — 'INVASION'.

'Englishmen!' it began — 'Your counties and shires are now assembling for the purpose of Local Defence. . . .'

'P'sha!' said Kinsman. 'Invasion — my breeches! Last year, *p'raps*, afore Trafalgar. And h'only *p'raps*, even then! . . .'

At an attentive waiter's suggestion he had for dinner a dozen oysters, a porterhouse steak, apple-pie, and a flat cream cheese packed in wheaten straw, accompanied by a pint of claret. It was served in a long narrow coffee-room — with a most disconcerting step down in the middle of it — warmed by a clear coal fire, and hung with sporting prints showing gentlemen in red coats performing all sorts of equestrian feats.

There was the same atmosphere of comfortable good nature about the place, that he had remarked among the customs searchers at Ipswich, about driver and guard of the coach, and at the inn on the road where Kinsman and himself had sampled a glass of 'hot with'. There was the same sense of permanency and orderliness about the place: it had always served good dinners and neat wines — it proposed to continue so doing.

When he had finished, following the waiter's direction, he crossed the draughty courtyard to drink a glass of port for company's sake in the landlord's parlour, a square snug bar with bright red curtains and a roaring fire, about which were seated four stoutish gentlemen arrayed in cord breeches and top boots.

The central shrine of the room was an enormous sash window facing the red curtains, flung up to its fullest extent, and revealing shelves loaded with every imaginable variety of bottle, decanter, puncheon, and glass keg.

An exceptionally pretty plump girl, with golden curls on her forehead, leaned over the ledge, engaged in deep conversation with a white-hatted sportsman in a green shooting coat and drab gaiters that came up to his thighs.

The four largish gentlemen about the fire looked up as he came in with a whistling draught, and the two in the centre politely shifted apart to make room for him before the blaze. He ordered a rummer of port, and drew up a wooden elbow chair into the gap.

His neighbour on the left turned a rosily placid face toward him.

'Good evening, sir,' he said. 'You have had a cold welcome to England, I am afraid. But not so cold as the farewell you got from Russia, I imagine!'

So already his history had been spread.

'Chinnery was telling us of your adventures,' continued Rosy-Face. 'You will be glad to get to safety and civilization and good port again! . . . Mary, you have brought the '74 for the gentleman and not that unmentionable muck you try on unwary strangers, I hope?'

Mary *had* brought the '74.

'I am glad to be on dry land once more,' confessed Anthony. 'The Baltic and the North Sea are not attractive at this time of year. Especially in a small ship!'

'Never was on the sea,' said Rosy-Face on the right. 'And by God's grace never will be!'

The conversation became general. Anthony found himself battered by a hail of questions.

What was the price of livestock in Prooshia? What sort of harvest had they had? Had there been much looting by the French? There was a report that Bonaparte had seized three million pounds' worth of British goods in Leipzig and all the bank balances in Hamburg — was it true? Had he ever seen Bonaparte? The Prooshians were kittle cattle: the other day they had been fighting us, and now they came in on our side when it was too late: was it true that they were utterly broke? Like the Rooshians who had been preparing war on us in 1801, fighting the French last year, and now said to be planning an alliance *with* them. Had the gentleman heard anything about that?

'We shall be alone, again, in Europe then,' said Rosy-Face Number One.

'The bastards!' said a more saturnine Rosy-Face at the outer edge who had not yet spoken. 'These bloody furriners — you never know what they'll do. We're better without them! What with French refugees, and Dutch refugees, and Belgian refugees, we've enough of them as it is!'

'We do not consider an American a foreigner,' apologized Rosy-Face Number Two explanatorily.

They appeared to be men of substance, not unintelligent, local squires and magistrates, staying overnight for the Quarter Sessions to be holden on the following day.

After that conversation turned on local matters. The cost of living — increase of vagrancy — increase of pauperism — increase of crimes of violence — increase of bastardy — lamentable behaviour of the Prince of Wales, of Frederick, of William, of Ernest, of Augustus, of Adolphus, all the younger male members of the Royal family. A conversation lubricated, mellowed by the consumption of much port. There was no mention at all of possible invasion, no hint of any sense of insecurity in all their placid speech: no shadow of doubts for the future upon their placid brows.

They were good fellows, he meditated, as flat candlestick in hand, he trod the shining oaken stairs to bed. He found himself irritated, nevertheless, by the calm assumption which they wore that they, being English, were superior to the common woes of Europe; that even the Emperor himself was not their equal in the eyes of God, being but a 'bloody foreigner'. God was unquestionably English, and wore cord breeches and a rosy clean-shaven face and a blue brass-buttoned coat and a neatly folded white neck-cloth.

He wondered as he got into bed what their reactions would be after Silas had met Deane, and Mr. Malone of the Strand — wherever that might be — London, had begun his sinister work. He recalled the phrase that the Little Man had read out from the shabby volume in his travelling library in the Hall of the Knights: 'prostrate her maritime forces and expose her coasts to easy invasion'.

The room was placidly substantial, like the rest of the inn: the candle burned with a consciously even flame: a black-jacketed Bible lay on the cotton cover of the night-table: a small fire blazed with grave respectability under a mantelpiece ornamented with a pair of toby jugs: the sheets glowed from recent application of the warming-pan.

He wondered what would happen when the Little Man's hard-bitten battalions should be let loose on Colchester as they had been on half a hundred continental cities. He wondered what would happen to the clumsy rosy boys in red uniforms with green-and-white facings when they met the 'Immortals' or the 'Glorious' Fifty-Seventh on a stricken field. He wondered what would happen to pretty plump Mary afterward . . . Or Garland!

Not for the first time he examined the question of his personal honour as it was involved in this errand; and then quenched argument with the reminder that he was a soldier acting under orders. At any rate his grandmother would have had no doubts about it. A pity for her sake that he had been unable to tell her!

He could see her now, a be-shawled figure in the depths of a large chair, staring out into space through the open French windows of her sitting-room, which was shadowed to the darkness of a mausoleum by a giant cedar. Her trembling fingers fumbling among folds of lace and wool in search of secreted comfits, she listened all day to the news of the world read by relays of readers. Never, however, could she glean a word of Hurrell: and no substitute could she find for Starkey who had unaccountably ceased writing after the renewal of war in 1803.

So helpless she was, and yet so terrifying that even yet he had not dared tell her about Jasmine, though he had been his own master for over three years.

Jasmine! Whose child, most peculiarly, had never been born!

Jasmine! Whose misliked uncle, most peculiarly, had appeared at their Paris home within a week of their elopement and marriage, and had been given an unaccountably warm welcome!

Jasmine! Whose pecuniary requirements were occasionally so great that once the Paris agent of wooden-faced Mr. Mason, of Marseilles, had refused to satisfy them without particular authorization from Anthony himself.

Still revolving these complexities he fell asleep. . . .

He drove post to London the next morning, at Rosy-Face Number One's suggestion. 'You'll never get there in one day by coach in this weather, my dear sir,' he had said. 'The extra expense will be less than what you would spend lying out the night. An economy, in fact!'

So he clattered away in a high chaise with his leather trunk strapped to the roof, behind four horses and a couple of red-nosed thick-gloved postilions in striped jackets and leather breeches — postilions who required a 'hot with' at every halt.

Clattered and jingled along winding roads across a chequer-board country snug under its blanket of snow, through snug villages with thatched roofs, and small towns whose red brick made them look snug and warm under the wintry sky. A yellow curricle behind a flashing pair of greys. A large bland house decorating a bland park. A pretty girl on horseback escorted by a young man in scarlet with a yellow beaver hat and supercilious nose. An ancient church, low-towered, guarding the long sleep of the uncounted generations of worshippers who lay about it under their grey gravestones. A pair of leather-faced naval officers — one square, one tall and thin — cocked-hatted, with golden epaulettes on their blue coats, drinking and laughing at the door of an inn while the post-chaise waited that should doubtless bear them to Harwich, and to the great black-and-white-striped ships that lay in the broad haven of the Stour. A pack of foxhounds at exercise streaming down a lane, with upright sterns, about a wizened small horseman in pink coat and black velvet cap.

An imperturbable England, he decided. Thought of the war-riven Europe whence he had come: of the vast armies moving across its face with their trail of destruction and disorder: of battlefields and cannon-aded dwellings: of The Man riding behind the storm and directing its fury. Unshaven!

An imperturbable England! He suddenly found that that very quality aroused his hostility. Too imperturbable! Too smug! Too placid! . . . After Silas had met Deane — !

The fools! Did they not realize the terrific host that should be turned against them, once the eastern phase of the war was over? And they were to oppose to it Sunday-drilled bumpkins sharing one musket among three!

He halted the carriage at a wayside public-house of inviting appearance: ordered a pint of ale, and, as he drank, listened to the conversation of three or four yokels who made up the company.

Polly Higgins was going to have a babby (he gathered) a babby she didn't ought. But — and everybody was very impressive about that 'But' — Polly had come back from France where she had been kitchenmaid at Clouds — or some such name — to Old Boney himself . . . For some little while Anthony did not realize who Old Boney was . . . And her mother said that Old Boney himself was the father. Well, stranger things than that had happened! Parson had said that there was a piece about it in the paper — in the *Essex Chronicle* . . . Had there now!

Anthony speculated on the subject. The Little Man's amatory net was very wide. Berthier, the Marshal himself, had on occasion to withdraw his attention from the duties of Chief of Staff in order to act as purveyor of loveworthy stock to the Imperial bed. That he knew for a fact. Talleyrand, Prince Murat, the Duc de Caulaincourt — all on occasion had dealt with the Imperial requirements. Radomski once had told him that the Little Man always paid an honorarium of two hundred louis to a casual light-o'-love. 'And I know,' had said Radomski, 'because I've had the same girls — for twenty francs!'

Well, it was possible!

The company babbled on. Wouldn't Polly Higgins's babby be a prince if his dad was an Imperor? . . . Prince Higgins . . . Roars of laughter . . . No. George and York and Clarence and Kent and Cumberland had, all of them, had bastards — and they weren't princes! Ah! But these bloody furriners! . . . And freeborn Englishman would have to keep a bloody furriner's babby out of the rates! Squire 'ld better issue a maintenance order against Old Boney!

'I reckon, bo-iy, that Polly Higgins wor a-playing mothers and fathers afore iver her went to France!' said someone. . . .

It was as the smoke from the hundred thousand chimney-pots of London obscured the reddening western sky, and hedgerows became gardens and gardens became streets, that Anthony was taken by the fancy that behind his carriage there posted those ghosts out of the past — the invisible companions of the journey of long ago. Father and Uncle Richard riding in silence behind the last Anthony Purvis on the way to the fateful meeting of Silas with Deane!

He inserted his hand under top-coat, under coat, under waistcoat, and sought till he felt beneath the linen of his shirt the hard outline of his grandmother's locket as it lay warm against his body.

CHAPTER III

SILAS MEETS DEANE

'YES, Mr. Purvis,' said Mr. Starkey.

'No, Mr. Purvis.'

'Quite, Mr. Purvis.'

Mr. Starkey, the author of so many angular letters to Madam Purvis, sat in a room no wider than a passage, with his back to a long window looking out upon the subdued shimmer of the River Thames, and a cloud-filled sky. He was quite other than Anthony had imagined as a boy. It was impossible to picture him listening in person at keyholes, or furtively dogging the footsteps of the Subject. Far from it. He looked like a wise lawyer, an attentive surgeon.

He had a queer triangular head on which unruly grey hair was plastered, and a lop-sided leathery face with a lop-sided nose, and bright and pale blue eyes. As he sat listening to Anthony, at a table covered with papers, he pulled and scratched with the nails of one large well-kept hand at some callosity at the base of the forefinger on the palm of the other. The walls on either side of him — he could have touched both at once if he had stretched out his arms — were lined with shelves, all neatly divided into small compartments and full of tubes of papers of varying size, dustiness, and discoloration, tied up with tape of different colours. It was rather as if he sat between two sections of a Brobdingnagian honeycomb.

A door in one of these walls gave on to a much larger room — from which Mr. Starkey's den had presumably been sliced off — wherein two secretive clerks were at work: and a door opposite the head of the establishment opened on a very long passage in which was a very long bench seating a large number of shabby little boys continually being hushed to silence by a wooden-faced man at an excessively inky table.

'I will now recapitulate with regard to our Subject,' said Mr. Starkey when Anthony had come to an end.

He drew forward a sheet of foolscap as he spoke, and produced a silver pencil with which he made notes.

'You desire me to find the present address of a lady living somewhere in Eastern England. A widow with one son, of the name of Parrish. She was a Miss Octavia Purvis, your grandmother's youngest child. She married an English officer, without her mother's consent, in Philadelphia in 1778. You believe her husband eventually became a general . . . That is all you know — absolutely all?'

'Absolutely all,' agreed Anthony.

Mr. Starkey, stabbing that hard spot at the base of a finger with his pencil, then repeated his instructions . . . The inquiries were to be made with the greatest speed and Mr. Purvis's name was not on any account to be mentioned. That was correct?

It was.

Mr. Starkey, satisfied, rang the silver hand-bell at his elbow, once. The summons was answered by one of the discreet clerks, who took the foolscap sheet and low-spoken instructions.

Mr. Starkey then rang the bell again — twice this time.

The wooden-faced man appeared: was handed a slip of paper: retired: could be heard shouting 'First Boy!' — a shout that was shortly followed by a clatter of hob-nailed boots and the crash of the hall door.

Anthony rose as though to go. In reality he had but little interest in unknown aunt and cousin, of whom his grandmother never spoke, even although they would be his rightful heirs should Jasmine continue to refuse to give him a child. This employment for Mr. Starkey, however, furnished the opportunity for broaching a matter of far greater and more immediate urgency. He said as casually as possible —

"There is one other small thing! A great friend of my family is staying here in London. A Mr. Charles Malone. Somewhere in the Strand. I had no idea that the Strand was as populous a thoroughfare as it seems to be, or I would have found out the number of the house before I left home. It would be hopeless for me to try and find him by myself. Could he be traced?'

'Charles Malone,' repeated Mr. Starkey thoughtfully. He ceased attacking the palm of his left hand to make a note of the name. 'Any peculiarities of personal appearance?'

'I have never seen him,' said Anthony, taking up his hat, and flushing. He explained lamely — 'I have been asked most particularly to meet him! I have messages for him.'

'Charles Malone!' repeated Mr. Starkey, raising his blue eyes to Anthony. 'I will do my best.'

Behind him on the glassy river, a string of long black barges swam slowly down with the ebb-tide. A few flashing gulls swirled up and down.

He rang the little hand-bell — twice — again: folded a scrawled note into a little cocked hat which he gave to Wooden-Face. The same shout of 'First Boy!' followed: the same clatter of young feet: the same slamming of the door.

'With regard to the first Subject,' said Mr. Starkey rising from his chair, 'I need hardly point out that the investigation may take a little time. The scent — so to speak — is old and cold. Where shall I be able to find you?'

Osborne's Hotel in the Adelphi had been recommended by Rosy-Face Number One at Colchester: and to Osborne's Hotel he had accordingly gone on his arrival last evening. He said so.

Gathering up his gloves, he added —

'Has anything been heard of Colonel Hurrell lately, sir?'

Mr. Starkey examined his client for a moment. Meditated. Hesitated. Protested, as he ushered him to the door:

'Now, my dear sir! Do consider! . . . I know that you have not seen your grandmother for some years, but she alone can speak to you of that business. I am not authorized to impart the affairs of any one of my clients to any other! Whatever their relationship! You *will* understand, Mr. Purvis? It would be very wrong, indeed!'

Mr. Purvis understood. Was impressed by the discretion of Mr. Starkey, who watched his elegance retreating down the boy-haunted passage with a peculiar expression in his pale blue eyes: returned to his room, scratching at his hand: produced a file of *The Times* for the previous month, and settled down to a profound study of its austere columns. . . .

Anthony spent the remainder of the day, after his visit to Mr. Starkey's chambers, in exploring London. He went to St. Paul's Cathedral and Westminster Abbey: inspected without interest the unimpressive and banal exteriors of the royal residences of Buckingham Palace and Carlton House: admired the snug red brick of St. James's: walked down Bond Street shortly after two o'clock — the time of high change for the world of fashion, according to his social mentor, William, the head waiter at Osborne's: shopped in unimposing shops that most surprisingly held imposing stocks. Found everywhere the same placidity, solidity, stolidity that he had remarked on the journey from Ipswich. London lacked the magnificence of Paris, but the splendours it possessed seemed to him to have some enduring quality that the other city lacked. Vienna — Berlin, that shoddy provincial town — The Hague — Brussels — the smaller German capitals with which he was acquainted, having been violated by their enemy, had none of the self-assured serenity of London and the Londoners whom he saw promenading in the region of Piccadilly.

There was — he felt — a galling arrogance and self-satisfaction about those lounging bucks in faultless coats and lacquered boots and glossy beavers; about the very few men to be seen in uniforms of red or blue; about those calm good-looking women in furred pelisses and Grecian helmets of almond green, or tasselled Polish caps neatly trimmed with sable.

What would happen to this unscarred city and these unscarred people — after Silas had met with Deane?

He dined — solidly — at his hotel, and afterward went to the theatre to see fifteen-year-old Master Betty, 'Young Roscius', perform *Hamlet* to the overwhelming applause of an adoring audience.

He went back to bed in a huge four-poster of black oak in a room papered in deep red. All very solid: all very dark: all very much like the setting for a Royal Lying-in-State.

He was breakfasting the next morning off cold pigeon pie and strong tea — a beverage with which he was little acquainted — in a coffee-room beset by mirrors and large sideboards, when the waiter brought him a note in Mr. Starkey's sloping script. It said —

'14 Buckingham St. Wednesday

'Dear Sir,

'With reference to Mr. Malone, this gentleman is no longer resident in the Strand, but I have been able to ascertain his address and have advised him of your intention to visit him. He would be glad to see you this morning as he leaves Town for an indefinite period this afternoon. As a stranger here you would find it most extremely difficult to find your way to his house; I have accordingly taken the liberty of sending a guide with a coach. The other Subject shall *in all circumstances* receive my most faithful attention.

'I am, dear Sir,
'Your obedient Servant,
'Ephvain Starkey.'

At the door of the hotel he found, accordingly, a hackney coach with — since it was a bitterly cold day — its floor deep in clean straw. Its exterior, so far as the box-seat was concerned, was crowded by an exceedingly fat driver, and a square man wearing an overcoat (which looked as if it had been cut from a green blanket) and a low-crowned once-black hat, the nap of which had worn so thin that it was now lead-coloured. The square man was engaged in talk with one of the shabby loiterers that always appeared to hang round the hotel door waiting to perform small errands for odd pence.

'I suppose you are the guide Mr. Starkey mentions in his letter?' said Anthony, being helped into that admirable fawn top-coat by an attentive waiter, and tucking the emptiness of the left sleeve into a pocket.

'Aye-aye, sir!' said the square man, touching the brim of his greasy hat in a rather grudging fashion.

'Is it far from here?'

'It h'ain't precisely far, and it h'ain't precisely near,' said the square man. 'It depends on 'ow you travel! We'll be there soon enough, sir, never you fear!'

They rumbled down Whitehall and Parliament Street; past the Abbey; into a perfect warren of side-streets; eventually into a clean quiet street of grave tall houses with hooded and fanlighted doors, and elaborately wrought lamp-brackets and torch-extinguishers to the iron railings fencing their areas from the pavement.

At one of the largest of these houses the coach halted, and the man in the greasy hat descended and opened the door.

He preceded Anthony up the wide shallow steps, and gave two re-sounding blows with the lion-headed knocker.

The hall door swung open at once, almost before the echo had died away, as if it had been awaiting that moment. A tall porter in scarlet livery with powdered hair stood bowing in the entrance of a wide vesti-bule floored with black and white marble.

'Mr. Purvis to see Mr. Malone,' said the greasy-hatted man in a loud voice. 'Mr. *Charles* Malone!'

'You are expected, sir,' said the porter, stepping to one side so that Anthony might enter the precincts.

A fire crackled in a marble-surrounded fireplace. A large clock ticked solemnly in a corner. There was a porter's chair near the door, leather-covered, hooded and studded with brass-headed nails. A wide staircase on the left wound upward to further silences and dimnesses. It was not the setting in which he had anticipated Silas meeting with Deane.

'Mr. Malone has been waiting for me for some days,' said Anthony. 'I have to see him on the most urgent business.'

Having admitted him to the house, the porter now appeared to wash his hands of him: passed him on to an equally large footman in a livery only a trifle less gold-laced. This latter bestowed him in a small panelled room facing the street, stirred the fire, assured himself of the name, and went away. Incendiarism and such-like could be made to pay — reflected Anthony — if they could maintain an establishment such as this. He had vaguely expected to encounter the secret agent, cloaked, masked, past a wicket with a password, in some attic up four flights of stairs.

In a moment yet a third menial made his appearance — a cat-footed man in black with an expressionless pale face. He assisted Mr. Purvis out of his heavy top-coat, secured that empty sleeve to olive-green coat by its gold pin as if he dealt with the toilette of one-armed men every morning.

Would Mr. Purvis be so good as to step this way? Mr. Purvis would.

They climbed the easy staircase, turkey-carpeted and hung with pic-tures of the Dutch school: penetrated a dark corridor: and, after a discreet knock, entered an immense cream-painted room ending in an immense bow window looking on the green grass and the bare black trees of St. James's Park.

At a table in this window, back to the light, sat a man in a blue coat and white neck-cloth busily writing. A large man with a short stroke of dark whisker, a straight mouth, and weather-beaten countenance. A typical Englishman, whom Anthony could imagine debating the increase in taxation or the price of consols with the Rosy-Faces, but not enacting the role of London agent to the Little Man of Lauchstein. Could Starkey have made a mistake?

'Mr. Malone?' he asked, almost before he had set off on the journey toward the window across a plain of turkey-carpet surveyed by large bland portraits and three or four chill bland busts on black marble columns. 'Mr. Charles Malone? Formerly of the Strand?'

The door behind him closed softly. The man at the table looked up. He did not rise.

'Charles Malone, formerly of the Strand!' he said in quiet even tones. 'What can I do for Mr. Purvis, of' — a long silence — 'America?'

'Silas!' said Anthony.

'Deane!' responded Mr. Malone.

He indicated a chair at the side of the table opposite him with the feather of his quill. He did not rise. He did not offer his hand. Anthony questioned, indeed, whether he could have brought himself to take it if the other had done so.

Mr. Malone laid down his pen, folded large hands — encased in tight-fitting lavender gloves — on the dark red leather surface of his writing-table, assumed an air of polite attention. His hazel eyes under bushy eyebrows closely inspected the young man before him — dark hair with a stray lock on the high forehead, long good-looking face with rather high-bridged nose, faint tan, cleft chin, grey eyes, green well-cut coat with the empty sleeve: his eyes returned again thoughtfully to that empty sleeve, when they had finished their survey.

'Silas!' said Mr. Malone almost as if to himself. 'Si-las! I may say, Mr. Silas, that you are not quite as I anticipated. You are certain that you are — Silas?'

'I will return the — compliment,' replied Anthony. 'You are not quite as I expected, either, Mr. Deane!'

Mr. Malone bowed.

'*Silas* and *Deane* should in the ordinary way have been sufficient password,' he remarked. 'In the circumstances, perhaps, you can evolve some other test of our mutual *bona fides?*'

Said Anthony, after a moment's thought —

'For a certain phase of your operations, Mr. Malone, you have three assistants. You shall provide me with the names of two of them. I will give you the third.'

'Denisham. La Ferre.'

'De Mussy.'

Mr. Malone made a note on a pad of paper before him.

'That verification having been performed,' he remarked, 'we can now get down to business . . . I presume that you have come from Paris?'

'I have come from East Prussia,' said Anthony, resenting what appeared to be the opening of an interrogatory. 'I have come from the Castle of Lauchstein.'

'East Prussia! Lauchstein!'

A flicker of interest appeared on Mr. Malone's rather expressionless face. He made another note.

'You will forgive me,' said Anthony curtly, and not in the least as though he required forgiveness, 'if I say that I have *not* travelled many hundreds of miles to answer questions, but to ask them?'

Mr. Malone bowed.

'I have been instructed by his Imperial Majesty —'

Mr. Malone bowed again at the mention of the august name of the Little Man. He seemed to restrain himself only with difficulty from a confirmed habit of note-taking.

' — to obtain a complete report of your activities. To interview your agents. To give his Majesty's orders. I am an officer of the Imperial Headquarters Staff.'

Mr. Malone this time was unable to prevent himself from writing something, or (perhaps) just idly drawing pattern or head upon his paper.

'Hitherto the only dealings I have had have been with Monsieur Fouché, of the Ministry of Justice!'

'The Police Minister was merely the channel through which the Imperial General Staff of his Majesty made contact with you. He is also paymaster.' — As he spoke Anthony allowed himself to survey the large bland room, the bland portraits, the bland busts, in a rather offensive manner. — 'For operational purposes henceforward you will receive your orders through the General Staff. His Majesty considers you as being in command of what he has termed in my hearing his "army in England".'

Mr. Malone had taken in the swift and insolent survey of his apartment and also its implication. He smiled for the first time, showing excellent large teeth.

'You are surprised at the lux — comfort with which I am able to surround myself? But when my old — friend, General Rapp, gets an annual *dotation* of over one hundred thousand francs, Savary a great deal more, and the marshals are all given dukedoms, you can hardly be surprised that the Emperor's G.O.C. *in* England should be well paid! He runs far greater risks than that gilded staff, Mr. Purvis! Or should I say General Purvis, or Colonel Purvis, or Major Purvis?'

'General Rapp and the others you mention have *earned* their money, sir! . . . I am Captain Purvis!'

Mr. Malone again permitted himself to smile. His eyes once more rested upon the empty sleeve pinned to the breast of Anthony's coat.

'And now, sir,' said Anthony in what he hoped was a brisk and business-like manner, 'I should be glad to hear the details of what you propose to do. When. How. Where.'

'Meaning?'

'Your complete plan of operations. Dockyards — prisons — guerrilla campaign!'

Mr. Malone opened one of the lower drawers of his writing-table. Stooped over, rustling among papers. As he did so, remarked in a casual tone —

'It is reported here that the Tsar has made tentative offers of peace to the Emperor. Was there any talk about it at Lauchstein?'

He turned over the documents that he had produced.

Anthony made no reply, and Malone did not repeat the question.

'Before I start,' said he, 'perhaps you will tell me exactly how much you know. It may save prolonged explanation.'

'Exactly nothing! The mere existence of the twin campaign. Your name, and the names of your adjutants. The passwords!'

'Then,' said Mr. Malone rising to his feet for the first time — and a big man he was — 'Then you are of little use to me, sir!'

He flicked up his right hand into sight. There was in it a long pistol which he directly pointed at Anthony across urbane table and neat heaps of correctly folded papers. The suggestion of violence was a solecism in that sedate setting of good breeding. With his other hand Mr. Malone rang very gently a little gilded bell, the handle made of a figure of Nelson, cocked hat and telescope and all.

As Anthony half-rose in that second of blinding revelation, a door in the panelled wall behind him swung open, and a tall man in scarlet uniform, with a lean intelligent face — who looked as if there was permanently a bad smell under his nose — materialized, loomed over him.

'It would be as well, Captain Joynes, to ascertain whether our mutual acquaintance is armed,' said Mr. Malone.

'Yes, Sir John,' said Joynes.

Big strong hands had swept over Anthony's person before ever he realized the indignity to which he was being subjected.

'Nothing except pocket-book, handkerchief, and a few keys, sir!'

'Thank you, Captain Joynes,' said Sir John. 'In that case I think I can deal with Captain Purvis unaided. You might, however, remain within call. There is, I believe, a guard at the garden entrance as well as in front?'

There was, and Joynes dematerialized as quickly as he had appeared. So Starkey knew more than he should, and had sold him! Starkey had betrayed his client! Silently Anthony cursed Starkey as he sat down again. There was nothing else he could do at the present — except that, or curse Fate and himself. He was utterly at the mercy of the enemy.

Sir John, too, had sat down again. Laid the pistol on the top of a pile of documents near his hand like a paper-weight, wrote for a few minutes with the utmost composure. Rang the bell. Joynes reappeared.

'Get an orderly to take this at once to his Royal Highness,' he said, sealing the letter with black wax melted in the flame of a taper burning in a silver holder.

'At — ?' inquired Captain Joynes, with one eyebrow raised.

'At — I should imagine!' responded Sir John.

Anthony could have sworn that the ghost of a smile was exchanged between the two men.

'You know, Captain Purvis, I really can't understand why you never had something done about that arm of yours,' remarked Sir John when Joynes once more had departed. He leaned far back in his chair, hands behind head, and spoke as though, business having been transacted, it was now but a social occasion.

'In what way?' said Anthony, a trifle taken aback by Sir John's manner as well as by his choice of topic.

'I imagine from the appearance of your sleeves that you have still a certain amount of forearm left — if you will forgive my curiosity?'

'Very little. My forearm was amputated pretty close to the elbow.'

'Exactly my case,' said Sir John rather proudly. 'But look at me!'

He unclasped those lavender-gloved hands from behind his head, brought them round and down so that they rested, fingers similarly spread apart, on his desk.

'Which hand is the artificial one?' asked Anthony, wondering if he could ever bring himself to the wearing of a false hand if it also involved the sporting of lavender kid gloves.

This inquiry was masterly so far as Sir John was concerned, for he opened out immediately into a long discourse on the capabilities and potentialities of what he called 'mechanical hands'.

He put the neat kid glove which sprouted from a neat blue sleeve through all its paces. He opened fingers and he closed a fist: with a little assistance from the other hand he picked up a penny: he pressed a knob hidden somewhere, and invited Anthony to try and wrest the coin from his grasp: he even demonstrated the ease with which the tight blue coat could be doffed, and thus stood for a moment or so in buff waistcoat and fine linen shirt-sleeves, astounding the decorum of his room. Donning the defeated garment was, perhaps, not quite so impressive a performance. Still —

'Remarkable!' said Anthony. 'May I ask where you obtained it?'

'My — own — invention, sir!' declared Sir John, sitting down again. 'I designed it *in toto*. I have very little spare time, but what I have I occupy in planning improvements. Finest mechanical hand in Europe! A little man in the Gray's Inn Road manufactured it from my drawings and instructions. There is no reason why —' He paused as though he had suddenly recollected the circumstances, ejaculated in reproof to himself, 'Come, come, this won't do!' and fell silent for a while.

Anthony returned to his thoughts and his private anger. The war would last for ever: so would his captivity!

'You know, Captain Purvis, this is a pretty kettle of fish in which you have landed yourself,' remarked Sir John at long last.

Anthony thought so, too. But he said nothing.

'Mr. Starkey's profession may be unpleasant, but he is not unpatriotic. By chance, or by reason of his trained memory, he recollected that Charles Malone was one of the many *aliases* of an unprincipled scoundrel who was arrested three weeks ago — about the time you left Lauchstein, I presume — and that one of his numerous dens had been in the Strand. Mr. Starkey is not unknown to us at the Horse Guards. Mr. Starkey approached me, being convinced that his duty to his country was more important than his duty to a client, even the grandson of a client of long standing. Mr. Starkey did what every true man should do!'

Anthony made no comment. He visualized Starkey sitting in his slice of a room, picking at the palm of a hand, revolving his position, ringing his bell twice; and then the ultimate clatter of a boy's boots along the passage and the crash of the door as the messenger went forth.

Said Sir John —

'Since the information can no longer be of any use to you, I have no objection to saying that Mr. Malone had little hesitation in answering every question we put to him. Very little hesitation! He was most obleeging! *Most* obleeging! That is how it comes about that I was acquainted with your mysterious passwords of *Silas* and *Deane*. Why, by the way, *Silas*? And why *Deane*? Mr. Malone was unable to tell me.'

'I fear, Sir John,' said Anthony, staring beyond him at the frosty blue sky, the still black boughs of the park, 'that I do not see my way to be as "obleeging" as your friend, Mr. Malone.'

'I am sorry,' said Sir John, taking a neat pinch of snuff — with his good hand. 'I assure you that it was purely personal curiosity. Perhaps, how-

ever, we might have a brief talk about Gen — the Emperor's staff. Its
constitution and system of work. A little talk which might make a great
deal of difference to you!'

'I don't quite understand!'

'I will be quite blunt and frank,' said Sir John. 'It might make all the
difference whether we hang you or not!'

He was very placid — but then *his* hanging was not in question.

'Hang?' echoed Anthony, blanching. '*Hang!*'

'We do not waste lead on spies in this country,' said the other, narrowly observing him.

'I am not a spy,' said Anthony indignantly. He struck the table with
his clenched fist. 'I — ' Paused . . . Was silent for a long time . . .
Spoke at last, as though asking himself an uncomfortable question out
loud, reflectively, very slowly, rather uncertainly. '*Am* I a spy? . . .
Am I?'

It was this honest consideration of the charge of being a spy that caused
Sir John to say nothing in reply, but await further comment with a look
of not unsympathetic interest on his weather-beaten face.

Said Anthony, still engaged in assessing his position —

'I am an officer of his Imperial Majesty's personal staff. My commission
is in the Regiment of *Chasseurs*. My instructions from the Emperor himself were to obtain a full report on their operations from his agents in
this country, and to convey to them his orders. With espionage I have
nothing to do!'

'Your position, sir,' said the other not ungently, 'is excessively compro-
mised by the fact that as a French serving officer you are found in this
country out of uniform, engaged to meet one of the most dangerous spies
with whom we have ever had to deal!'

To hang!

With pinioned hands and blindfolded eyes. A dangling scarecrow
upon a gallows for the edification of a phlegmatic English crowd! The
first Purvis had gone to America to escape a hangman's noose: the last
would have returned thence so that he might receive that delicate attention! The English had wiped out the generation before him: with him
they would now complete the destruction of the House of Purvis. The
scaffold was to be the end of the little boy who had dreamed such gallant
dreams, bent over Camelot in the cedar-scented library at High Pale long
ago: whose imaginings had always been bright with steel and glamorous
with victory: the scaffold, the rope, and goggling crowds! He recalled
those eight quiet men whom he had had to interview at Boulogne two
or three years ago. The eight men who had paid for their temerity in

landing on the Iron Coast, before a firing-party among the sand dunes. They had refused to talk with him the night before, but had been sedately preoccupied with two parties of sedate whist . . . There had been a young man of his own age who was dummy . . .

All this passed through his mind in the fraction of a second of time. He said, rising to indicate his readiness to take his departure whereso-ever required —

'This conversation, sir, appears to me to serve no useful purpose. I deprecate the vulgarity of the rope, but I am not well acquainted with the etiquette of such affairs. But I don't propose to talk "obleegingly", whatever the consequences!'

'No!' commented the Englishman. 'Perhaps a night or two in sur-roundings less — urbane may persuade you to change your mind!'

'Association with Mr. Malone, Sir John, has apparently dulled your perceptions!'

'It is possible!' admitted Sir John, courteously. 'But please don't think of going yet, Captain Purvis. Please to sit down. We must wait for a little. You see, the Commander-in-Chief has taken a great personal in-terest in this particular phase of General Bonaparte's operations. Very great interest! He wishes to see the emissary from General' — 'The Em-peror!' corrected Anthony, and Sir John bowed in acknowledgment of the emendation though he did not accept it — 'Bonaparte, for himself! . . . Incidentally we do not recognize General Bonaparte's empire in this country!'

'It is none the less a fact! A rather large fact!'

'None the less!' agreed the other.

'The Duke of York —' began Anthony.

Captain Joynes reappeared at Sir John's elbow, looking as if the un-pleasant odour under his aristocratic nose had greatly increased in strength. He said something in a very low tone. As he spoke, Sir John's tanned face became dark red, lost its Olympian calm, and a white scar that seamed his forehead and the beginnings of his receding hair grew bright scarlet.

'By God!' said he, throwing himself back in his chair, and looking up at the man at his elbow. 'This is damned monstrous! . . . To *my* house! . . . Treating *my* house as if it were a brothel! . . . What will my wife say? . . . It is an insult to Lady Damant! An insult to me! An insult to this gentleman! A gross insult!'

'This *gentleman* —' began Joynes, underscoring the word in a not inoffensive manner, as though doubtful of its application.

'Even in America,' said Anthony, a snob despite the proximity of the gallows, or — which was more likely! — because of it, 'we have pedigrees, and genealogies, and coat-armour! . . . And good manners!'

'Quite!' said Sir John. He sat up again, and struck the table so resounding and metallic a blow that it was obvious that it was done with his artificial hand. 'It is monstrous! I won't have it! I shall tell his Royal Highness so! Lady Damant will never forgive me!'

'She can hardly blame you, sir,' protested Joynes.

'She can!' said Sir John a little grimly. 'And she will! This is a warning to us, Joynes, against trying to work in pleasant surroundings instead of dutifully appearing at the War House!'

'I heard — I *did* hear that her ladyship was to meet Lady Nelson this morning immediately on her arrival in Town! In that case she is probably already out and will not be back before dinner!'

'You did, did you? You appear to know more of what goes on in my establishment than I do, Joynes. Dare I ask who your informant was?'

Captain Joynes now looked as though the smell under his nose was of *eau-de-Cologne,* attar of roses, or dried lavender —

'Miss Damant informed me, sir!'

'Oh, Libby told you, did she? Then it's correct! But it's my best hand to a sovereign that Lady Damant will know all about it before ever she steps from the coach!'

Sir John Damant appeared very seriously disconcerted. He rose and began pacing up and down the big room, leaving the pistol paper-weight on the table. Anthony regarded the weapon meditatively. Joynes, however, remained nearby.

'I must and will stop H.R.H. bringing the little bitch here,' said Sir John. 'He takes her to the Horse Guards, and I suppose he looks on this house as a sort of branch establishment. He's mistaken. Apart from everything else I'm damned if I'll be a party to making this officer a raree-show for a bloody strumpet! I'm eternally damned if I will! It is abominable treatment of an unfortunate gentleman!'

'As I seem to be somewhat concerned in whatever is troubling you, sir, may I ask what it is?'

Apparently there was to be some sort of interlude before the last act of the drama; before rope and gallows and hangman — an interlude of a bizarre nature!

Sir John halted half-way down the room, beside one of the bland busts on a black column.

'Joynes,' he said in a slightly embarrassed manner, 'perhaps you might explain to Captain Purvis! It would be a little indecorous for me, as a general officer on the staff of the Commander-in-Chief, to do so! . . . Explain exactly as if I were not here! . . . Imagine I'm not!'

Joynes appeared to relish the instruction. He regarded Anthony as though he were a trifle less odoriferous. He said in his rather affected tones —

'The C.-in-C., sir, has a little "keep" — a strumpet of the lower orders — to whom he is madly attached. As pretty as paint. As hard as they're made. She probably nails her chemise on!'

'Good!' commented Sir John to the periwigged bust — but obviously about other matters.

'As bad and as lovely as Sin itself. As we are alone I can tell you that she has him on a string. As we are alone I can tell you that nothing happens at the Horse Guards with which she is not acquainted. As we are *quite* alone I can tell you plainly that if you want promotion, or a commission or anything else in the army, you can get it — through her. In fact there's nothing you can't attain to if you don't mind helping to pay for H.R.H.'s pleasuring.'

'True!' said Sir John to the bust.

'This — er — female's tastes are simple,' said Joynes propping himself against the table close to Anthony, and speaking in a far friendlier manner; almost as if getting the plain truth about the lady out of his system were a great mental and moral relief. 'Next to money her interest is in bed. I am told, incidentally, that she is a very efficient bed companion! After that her main preoccupation in life is with crime. Reading every word of the newspaper reports of rapes and murders and forgeries and robberies! Sitting in a privileged seat through the trials of atrocious criminals! Visiting them in prison. Seeing them hanged. Seeing them lashed. She once watched — I know for a fact — a soldier getting four hundred stripes at the Tower. I feel certain that merely for the piquancy of the situation she would very much like to sleep with a condemned man on the night before his execution!'

'True!' said Sir John again to the bust.

'Is it suggested that she proposes to do me this favour?' inquired Anthony.

'My dear fellah — ' protested Joynes, by now feeling at peace with mankind, being (so to speak) thoroughly purged.

'By God!' said Sir John, obviously about somebody else, to the bust. 'She is quite capable of it!'

'What Mrs. Clark — Mary Ann: Polly to Highness — wants, is to have a look at a spy — excuse me! — when he is still fresh and gasping after being gaffed and landed. She will then be able to follow any subsequent developments with the greater interest.'

'By Christ, and she won't! By God, she won't! Not in my house! I will not have the place turned into a side-show!'

'As we are alone,' said Joynes, not answering the general, 'I must say that all that remains for us to do is to hang out a streamer across the front of the house — "Colossal Attraction! Boney's Large-as-Life One-Armed Spy! Admission One Penny!" And have a barker outside calling out in a hoarse voice — "Roll up, Ladies h'and Gents! Roll h'up! Roll h'up!" As if you were the Fat Lady, or the Bearded Lady, or General Thumbkin, or the Wild Man from Pongo, or the World's Largest Rat!'

This recital affected the general as though oil had been poured on the fire of his anger. He stalked back to the great bow window, stood with his back to them, staring out at the Park. A most remarkable tide of oaths rolled from his lips. Presently he turned round —

'I have no particular desire to put Captain Purvis in the way of a firing-party or the gallows. I find myself with a good deal of sympathy for a *gentleman* in his position. I have a fellow-feeling for a one-armed man. But I would also give a very great deal to disappoint York's whore of her entertainment. A very, *very* great deal, Joynes!'

'Yes, sir.'

'I will *not* provide a raree-show for Mary Ann Clark! . . . I will not! I will not!'

Captain Joynes's lean face was turned on Anthony; his intelligent eyes explored the younger man's face. The air of disillusionment was entirely gone from the Englishman — was replaced by an expression of concentration.

'If that is so, Sir John,' he said, 'and if Captain Purvis and I were again alone for a short time, I think I can guarantee you the required result!'

It appeared to Anthony that he might possibly escape the noose — that these respectable and patriotic Englishmen found it a matter of greater moment to avoid the contamination of a harlot's skirts than dutifully to send him to the gallows. He wondered for a passing moment about Lady Damant's temperament and characteristics.

'No dramatic escapes, Joynes,' protested the general doubtfully fingering his well shaven chin. 'I really couldn't stomach that! It wouldn't do! Wouldn't do at all!'

'Good God, sir, no! My duty —' asserted Joynes. 'If we might be alone — in the same way that we were before — I think things could be arranged. Perhaps I might use your desk?'

Sir John nodded. He took four long even strides back to his friend, the bust. He had admirable tight-fitting grey pantaloons — admirable legs.

Joynes spread his scarlet coat-tails, sat down in the elbow-chair of golden mahogany, leaned elbows judicially on the writing-table. There was something about his dark, intelligent, ugly face that reminded Anthony of an engraving of Charles the Second. Something quizzical and impish in the expression.

'Now that we have exchanged the passwords, Captain Purvis,' said Joynes, 'and you have satisfied yourself that I am Mr. Charles Malone, of the Strand, let us get to business! I suppose that as a French prisoner you are anxious for me to forward your escape from this country? That is so?'

'It is,' said Anthony taking the cue, although having no idea at what Joynes was driving.

'You were told of my existence and profession by one of your fellow-prisoners in the brig *Hearty?* . . . *Hearty!* . . . *Hearty!*'

Anthony memorized the ship's name.

'By which you were captured with a number of other officers and men while travelling from the mainland to Corsica in the sloop *Hirondelle* on October the 26th. That is what you tell me?'

'It is, Mr. Malone. The sloop *Hirondelle*. On October 26. I managed to escape on landing in England!'

'Ah!' said Joynes with a smile of appreciation. 'You were not the only one! All the prisoners got away. As no roster was kept nobody knows exactly how many prisoners there were, or the names of any of them!'

'I thought, when on shipboard, that it was a little remarkable that we were never mustered. In that case there was no nominal roll to hand over to the military, I suppose!'

'Exactly! Your escape has meant a lot of trouble for us. It has caused the Commander-in-Chief to go very thoroughly into the matter of the detailing of escorts for prisoners. I suppose that after you had bribed or intoxicated — you wouldn't need a great deal of money to do it! — the militia escort and their subaltern, you just broke out of the barn at Hawkhurst — Hawkhurst in Kent — and separated. In your case, I understand you to say that you made your way to London alone, buying civilian clothes *en route*. Is that so?'

'Yes. You have repeated pretty exactly what I have told you!'

'Not one has been recaptured so far, although of course you made your bolt over a week ago,' said Captain Joynes shaking his head. 'Not one! And you are the first to come to me!'

'The others know, perhaps, that you were not conducting your organization on purely philanthropical lines. They are probably incapable of paying your fees. In my case, however — '

From the tail of his coat he produced a fat russia-leather pocketbook: opened it: withdrew from it a packet of crisp Bank of England notes. One-hundred-pound notes.

'Let us come down to dots, Mr. Malone! The sooner I am out of this damned country the better! How much do you want to arrange my escape?'

Joynes rose. His face wore a seraphic smile. He was enjoying the game.

'I am not Malone, Captain Purvis!' he announced. 'I am Captain Archibald Joynes, an officer of the 50th Foot, *aide-de-camp* to Lieutenant-General Sir John Damant, K.C.B.' He sketched the motion of picking up and pointing the general's pistol which still lay, a deadly paper-weight, upon a few folded documents. 'I arrest you as being an escaped prisoner, on your own confession.'

Anthony, too, sketched rather amateurishly surprise and horror. His eyes, however, rested on the pistol which Joynes had replaced upon the pile of papers. The A.D.C. observed the interest: with a polite gesture implying the mere removal of temptation, he picked the weapon up and, with it in his hand, marched in military fashion up to Sir John and his bust.

'Sir!' His heels clicked together to attention. 'I have to report that the gentleman I interviewed on your instructions is one of the party of French prisoners who escaped from their escort at Hawkhurst. On his own showing. He is Captain Anthony Purvis, an American gentleman holding a commission in the *Chasseurs*. He will say nothing. I take it, sir, that I am to give orders for his return to the Transport Office as a recaptured prisoner of war!'

General Damant returned to his seat: he heaved a sigh of relief. Anthony felt that his altered status was of little importance or interest to Sir John except in so far as it might keep a harlot out of the house.

'You are an intelligent young man, Joynes,' said the general taking up a pen, and starting to write rapidly. 'You have saved my honour in regard to this gentleman. And if you go round quickly enough to the bitch's quarters you will also save my house the contamination of Clark's abhorrent presence. Tell the Duke yourself that our catch only turns out to be one of the Hawkhurst prisoners who will say nothing, and is being sent off for the Transport Office to deal with. They'll take no further interest . . . Good boy, very good boy! You'll be worthy of Libby — almost — one of these days! I am very grateful! So, I imagine is Captain Purvis! . . . Tell Henry to send round for an escort!'

Joynes bestowed a friendly wink on Anthony as he departed.

'You will give me your parole for a short time?' said the general. 'It will make things easier until they send for you.'

Anthony remembered that Joynes had placed the pistol in his coat-tails. He made, however, no demur.

The general gave a short cough. He continued —

'I do not imagine that for your own sake you will want to reveal what has just taken place!'

'I certainly will not,' said Anthony gravely. 'I am most grateful to you, sir! I have — like most people, I fancy — a constitutional dislike for being hanged. The prospect was by no means improved by the thought of being displayed as an About-to-be-Hanged Spy to the vulgar mistress of a duke — even if he is royal!'

'And in *my* house!' said Sir John. 'He would no more think of bringing that little devil here in the ordinary way than he would of dancing a minuet stark naked in St. Margaret's Churchyard. Because I do much of my Horse Guards work here, he thinks to treat my house as he does that establishment! What my wife would have said — what the world would have said, if it ever were known that the Duke of York and his impertinent little punk had visited my house, had entered its doors, I cannot bring myself to think. I break into a cold sweat at the thought of it!'

'For a royal duke,' remarked Anthony very primly, 'I consider that his Royal Highness appears to lack the essentials of good breeding! . . . If I may say so!'

Just what an Englishman might have said — he felt.

'Between these four walls,' said Sir John, 'there isn't a single son of the poor old King that I should call a gentleman. Not really! . . . Do you get much of this sort of thing happening with you?'

'I would hardly call life at Imperial Headquarters conventual,' said Anthony. 'But any interference by women with the routine or conduct of the army is simply unthinkable!'

They discussed army morale, and, afterwards, certain non-controversial aspects of the Austerlitz campaign very amicably, until someone knocked at the door.

'Well, Captain Purvis,' said the general rising and offering a kid-gloved hand across the table, 'I am glad that things have turned out as they have. Unfeignedly glad, damme! I may say that I should have hardly acted as I have done were I not convinced that you are a gentleman, that you acted as a soldier, under orders which you would not dream of disobeying, and that, in fact — though perhaps not theoretically — you are

not a spy! . . . As an American I suppose you would not think of joining us? No! Well, I expected nothing else. I am afraid you are in for
a bad time until the end of the war. Still it's better to be alive than dead.
Never forget that!'

A pleasant fresh-faced subaltern in shako and red jacket and blue
trousers stalked up the room, clicked to attention before desk.

'Ensign Weatherly, the Thirtieth! Beg to report with escort, sir!'

The general again shook hands — it was with his good hand — with
Anthony.

'Good luck,' he said. 'The name is, Andrews, 49 Gray's Inn Road.
Arms and hands, I mean. It would be worth your while! Don't forget,
49 Gray's Inn Road! . . . Good-bye!'

'The er-patient, sir?' inquired the subaltern, regarding Anthony with
boyish interest.

'You will treat Captain Purvis with every consideration, sir,' said the
general. 'He's a young officer for whom I have every respect — although
an enemy!' . . .

The Times of the morrow baldly reported —

> An officer of the French Chasseurs, one of the prisoners of war who
> escaped from an escort of the 3rd Battalion of the Cinque Ports
> Volunteer Regiment, at Hawkhurst in Kent ten days ago, was re-
> captured yesterday morning in civilian clothes, in Westminster. He
> made no resistance upon being arrested, and has refused to give any
> information with regard to his companions. He is said to have been
> of American nationality. The officers of the party are stated to have
> given their parole upon landing. In view of this breach of faith the
> man has been sent for a term to the prison hulk Crown in Porchester
> River, as is usual in such cases. No fewer than 104 French Officers
> have broken their parole this year and attempted to escape. Only 47
> have been retaken.

BOOK SIX

CAPTIVITY

Great Britain — Germany — France 1812–1814

★

CHAPTER I

A GENTLEMAN IN TEARS

'In three days' time I shall have been a prisoner for six years,' said Anthony flatly. 'For more than five of them here.'

The small private office of the superintendent of the Norman Cross prison was foggy with smoke from a miserable fire in a rusty grate; a variety of draughts whistled through crevice and crack in the ill-made wooden walls; and Captain Blewitt sneezed and swore, and wheezed and swore, and coughed and swore. He was an evil-tempered little man in a nautical coat of blue with brass buttons: he had a white fringe of hair to a shiny bald head, and perpetually mopped a very red nose with a very red handkerchief.

'There are perfectly innocent English non-combatants who have been held prisoners in France by your precious — Atishoo! — Emperor for *nine* years!' riposted Captain Blewitt without sympathy. 'Several thousands of them!'

And there, for the time being, the interview had ended, without Anthony knowing for what purpose he had been summoned at ten o'clock of that blustering winter morning. For at that minute one of the dusty-looking clerks from the outer office had tapped on the door, and tiptoeing over to the deal table set between fire and window, had said something to the superintendent in an undertone. Captain Blewitt had seized his very nautical cocked hat, and departed forthwith, sneezing and cursing, without a word of explanation or apology.

Anthony sat and waited. Time meant nothing to him. He had been robbed of six years: so what did six minutes or six hours matter? The round clock on the wall, above the mantelshelf's array of spikes stacked with dusty letters, showed the half-hour; jangled the hour; passed on to the half-hour again. The dusty-looking confidential clerk, who had been working at a ledger at another bare deal table by the door, cast a glance at the lean one-armed man in shabby green uniform sitting, wrapped in reverie, on a rush-seated chair opposite his superior's empty place: decided that he was harmless: ambled out with knock-kneed gait, to join in the crescendo of conversation in the outer room.

From where he sat, Anthony had a vista through the dirty window of heavy palisades, low wooden barracks, more palisades, more ugly buildings, and, rising amid them, the steep roof and semaphore of the octagonal block-house whence swivel-guns commanded the two broad roads that intersected the prison. Home!

Almost unconsciously he surveyed his six sordid years . . . Those first months spent in the *Crown* hulk, a floating charnel-house on the Porchester River, wherein seven hundred men ate their hearts out in degradation and misery . . . The yellow canvas suit, 'T.O.' marked on the back, with which his civilian clothes had been replaced . . . The miasma of the lower deck — where he was quartered — lighted and ventilated by barred scuttles which were closed at nightfall . . . The body of Giraud, the privateer who was drowned while trying to escape, stretched on the mud at the river brink, beset by carrion crows — and so left in sight of the prisoners for two days as an example to them . . . Bullock's head — decayed cod — bad bread — rations that were uneatable or short-weight, or both . . . Dirt past belief — vice beyond shame — disease surpassing cure . . . The earth-coloured half-naked herd, clad in yellow rags, that swarmed like vermin about the narrow decks, scurvy-ridden, their bodies wet with ever-spreading sores . . . Rotting blankets, rotting hammocks, rotting clothes, rotting boots: men rotting, too, in mind, body, and soul in a rotting ship . . . The day when the drunken brute who was their keeper-in-chief gave orders for the destruction of the prisoners' chief treasures — the tools and materials for their hobbies or for the pitiful manufacture of trifles for sale in the outer world.

God damn for ever the callous devils who penned live men up in dead ships! Merely to recollect the *Crown* was to stain one's thoughts.

The hands of the clock over the fireplace indicated against its smug English face that it was a quarter to twelve. The wind had changed direction, and the fire burned up brightly, and from the neighbouring cook-house came — as ever — the smell of the interminable stew. Captain Blewitt's table was littered with papers and forms placed under small ingots of lead. His ink-stained quill-pens were set in the holes round his pewter inkpot just as they had used to be in the inkpot in the schoolroom at La Cadière — like the head-dress of an Inca.

For over five years he had been here now. Five years behind wall and palisades, watched by sentries, and threatened by the swivel-guns of the block-house. For five years he had come to this grimy little office to collect his mail and his remittances after they had been inspected by authority . . . Pressland, whom Blewitt had succeeded, had incidentally been in the habit of levying a tribute of two and a half per cent upon all prisoners' moneys: had made no bones about it. The new man was more honest.

Five years!

By the time he had been sent here from the *Crown* letters had begun to arrive: from Jasmine — not many: from his grandmother — strange epistles in which, by implication, she blamed him for having permitted himself to become a prisoner; from Miss Buckley — full of underlinings and poetry, 'To a Warrior in Captivity', 'The Gyves', and 'The Prisoner's Companion'; from Radomski, and a few other friends of La Cadière or army days; from Mr. Mason, of Marseilles, about Jasmine's monetary needs; from Messrs. Lafitte, of Paris, about those self-same needs; from Solly, regularly once a month — letters written, to prove his proficiency in his new profession, in every sort of handwriting (including Anthony's) but his own.

He had gone to Pressland immediately after his arrival, and applied to be given parole. Pressland had said —

'My young friend, you *won't* get parole, however hard you try!'

'Why?'

'Because you were granted it once, and promptly broke your word of honour. That's why! And that's flat!'

'I utterly deny that I broke parole.

'The Transport Superintendent at Dover says you did!'

'Confront him with me, and see if he recognizes me.'

'Not my business!' said Captain Pressland. 'Write to the Transport Office! But I can tell you outright that you won't do any good! And now, blast you! Get out of my sight! I have got enough to do without arguing with you!'

But he had been right.

Damn Pressland! Damn the Transport Office!

Even Pressland, however, had proved not unsympathetic when the letter arrived that should have shattered him, and did not — not at least in the manner in which it might have been anticipated.

He had been sent for to the office, and Pressland had handed him the missive, saying a little awkwardly —

'No one has seen this letter except me. No one will ever know anything about it from me. I don't like reading other people's letters, but it's my job. Sit down here and read it. There's no good me saying I'm sorry, devilish sorry; but I am, all the same!'

With that he had bustled off, leaving Anthony in that self-same chair by himself, turning over a letter addressed to him in Miss Buckley's well-known hand. Instead of breaking the seal Pressland had cut neatly round it. The letter was not long, but before ever he read a word he had remarked on its peculiar appearance, owing to the fact that Buck, obviously under some great mental strain, had dipped her pen at random into the inkwells in his grandmother's writing-desk — one of which held violet ink, and the other red.

It ran —

'Versailles, February 3rd, 1808

'Dear Grandson,

'Count John Radomski paid a call on me this afternoon, in the course of which I learned that his brother, Count Victor, was killed in a duel shortly after daybreak to-day by an Irish adventurer named Pagan, uncle to the young woman whom I now understand you to have married. I will not comment on your matrimonial arrangements, beyond remarking that the cause of the duel was Count Victor's discovery of your wife's undoubted adultery with her uncle. He had apparently suspected this incestuous liaison for some years. On receiving irrefragable proof, he conceived it his duty in your absence, and as your friend, to call Pagan out. In the encounter he was shot dead. His behaviour was most honourable and I conceive that you will deal with the man Pagan on your return.

'Count John acted as his brother's second. He called on me almost immediately after the duel, as he believed that the guilty couple would at once elope with all the portables from your Paris establishment. He was obliging enough to place himself at my service, but when he and a representative of Messrs. Lafitte reached your house the pair had already gone; and with them, among other things, the remaining diamonds of the Muscovy necklace. In view of the circumstances Messrs. Lafitte have agreed to cancel your wife's authorization to draw on them, but would wish for your immediate confirmation of their action.

'The count informs me that your wife has been notorious even in Paris by reason of the multiplicity of her amours. Her name appears to have been coupled with a long muster-roll of men ranging from the King of Naples to one of her own lackeys. I should be glad if you will take steps to disembarrass our family of this *succube*. It is most inconvenient that you should be a prisoner of war at this juncture.

'I am glad to say that my health is greatly improved, the weather being unusually mild for the time of year.

'I have, of course, expressed the family's appreciation and regrets to Count Radomski.

'Your affectionate grandmother,
'Htte. Purvis'

The signature alone was in Madam Purvis's handwriting, faint and thin and shaky as though it were the tracing of a section of cobweb.

He had found it impossible in any way to conform in word or thought to the traditional behaviour of a betrayed husband. The furious anger that he felt against Jasmine and her paramour was only aroused because they had caused Victor's death. All his regrets were for the loss of his friend — and not the loss of his wife. He recalled Radomski at the Institut Putzger rinsing his mouth of a night to wash it clear of the foulness of the German language; championing Solly when he himself had been afraid; humble in hopeless adoration before Garland during his visit to La Cadière. And then he had gone to his death gallantly, chivalrously, performing what he considered to be his duty, because of the worthlessness of a woman!

Anthony knew that he himself would not have drawn sword or called for pistols on account of Jasmine. The Jasmine for whom he would have fought and died had had no existence except in his imagination: for the enchantment of his love had not been a spell potent enough to transform to reality his dreams. He admitted to himself now that he had realized this long since — even before she had deliberately refused to let her child be born alive.

He had reached that stage in his meditations when Pressland had returned to the office, treading very quietly as though in the presence of death. The superintendent had rummaged in a small cupboard, produced an unopened bottle of brandy and two glasses, and silently offered alcoholic consolation . . . They had emptied the bottle.

Even now he was amused to recall how Pressland's attitude toward him was changed from that day on. It had puzzled him, indeed, until he realized that his social status had been raised in the man's eyes because his wife had been mistress of a king.

He had sent word to Lafitte's that she should be traced and watched for a few months, and that a small allowance should be paid to her. After that it was as if she had never been. Like Garland, and Harrady, and Elizabeth Vane, and Fulton. It was because of Radomski that he took to the bottle.

Damn Jasmine! Damn Pagan! . . . Damn Garland, and Harrady, and
Elizabeth Vane! But for them — !

The clock struck twelve. The dusty-looking clerk slipped back into the
room: looked round suspiciously as if questioning himself whether
Anthony had made off with a half-dozen or so of the letter spikes on
the mantelpiece: found everything in order: removed the poker from the
fireplace as though afraid that the prisoner might waste English coals,
and took it with him to join the *conversazione* proceeding in the outer
office.

' 'E's a time, 'e is! 'E reelly is! 'E allus is!' he said as he passed out of
the door.

Damn Blewitt!

Five years! The very morning after his arrival a soldier had been
flogged before paraded troops and prisoners for some breach of discipline.
The man had been stripped to the waist and trussed to a timber triangle.
There had been two executioners to relieve one another in case of fatigue,
and a surgeon, and a drummer to beat correct time for the operation.
Tap — lash! Tap — lash! Tap — lash! So the duet had gone on — ten
times; hundred times; two hundred times; three — four — five hundred
times! And then the surgeon had stepped forward and the other five
hundred lashes of the senseless wretch's sentence had been postponed
until his back should be sufficiently recovered to be mutilated once again.
How the Duke of York's fancy lady, Mary Ann Clark, would have
revelled in it all — blood, screams, and solemn ceremonial tap-tapping of
drum! But she would never again enjoy the privileges of Concubine-in-
Chief to the Commander-in-Chief of the British Army (or disturb the
equanimity of Sir John Damant!) for she had temporarily cost her Royal
lover his job, and had passed into less exalted keeping amid much scandal.

Damn Mary Ann Clark! Damn Damant!

If it hadn't been for them he would probably have been dead long ago!
And would not any swift death have been better than this slow decay
of all his faculties?

Would the war never end?

Would it last for all eternity, while he wrote endless plays that would
never be acted, books that would never be read, epics that would never
be completed; brooded whole days together; paced in undesiring companionship with other 'broke-parole' officers the muddy — or dusty —
monotony of the palisaded south-eastern compound; visited the market
at the great entrance gate where the prisoners bartered or sold straw plait
and hideously obscene toys? Would it last for an eternity in which no

longer, even, would there be the faintest thrill upon the arrival of the mail from Stilton: when the few letters he got would mean still less than they meant now: when the hold of the newspapers on him would be entirely gone?

When Fielding's Bank first forwarded him the remittances for which he asked, he had subscribed to — and read — *The Times, The Statesman, Bell's Weekly Messenger, The Whig,* and *The Star.* Now although they still came, he rarely read them. He was sick of reading of war, of the making and unmaking of peace between France and every country other than Britain. Russia, Austria, Prussia had alternately fought the Little Man, and kissed and been friends — for a little. But not Britain! And while Britain remained in the ring, he remained her prisoner.

How was his position affected by the entry of the United States into the war? Worsened undoubtedly. The reports of M'Tavish, the Scottish overseer of the High Pale estate for more than a generation, had made increasingly gloomy reading during the last years: the British blockade would mean that the market for the tobacco crop would have vanished. Utterly.

Damn Britain!

She had murdered his father; slaughtered his uncle; mangled himself; and now would ruin him!

The tide of history was sweeping him and his family and his fortune away!

Even if the Little Man had found the Russian campaign less simple than he fancied, a devastated countryside before and behind his armies, and Moscow in flames — how Fulton would preen himself on that prophetic panorama painted for the delectation of Paris twelve years ago! — yet he was unconquerable. Of course he was unconquerable!

And even if the British expedition to Spain were to suffer the usual fate of British expeditionary forces on the Continent, and the attempt to stab at the soft under-belly of Imperial France were to end in dire disaster, yet her fleets remained afloat. In her way, too, Britain was unconquerable!

He would be ground into nothingness between the two Unconquerables!

He got up from the chair. As he did so was first aware that the knee-buttons of his breeches were undone, of carpet slippers, of hole in heel of stocking, of dust and stains and hairs upon green uniform. He examined himself critically. His hands were not particularly clean and the nails were grey. He had not shaved that morning: but then last night, one of the turnkeys — Richards, a venal creature — had smuggled to him a bottle of brandy which he had drunk in the dark. After that he had dreamed of the hulks . . . To-day, being Wednesday, was canteen day when beer was available! He wanted beer! Where the hell was Blewitt? Damn Blewitt!

On the wall, near the window, behind the superintendent's chair was a small square of looking-glass. He walked round and surveyed himself — shabby man reflected in a shabby mirror: surveyed a grey drawn face with sunken, bloodshot eyes, and colourless lips: realized, too, how stooped he had become: squared his shoulders.

Here was the adventurer of Camelot — the staff officer of an emperor — the romanticist — the companion of Garland — the husband of Jasmine — the Lord of High Pale!

He damned himself.

As he returned to his chair he caught sight of his name: written on a printed form which lay uppermost of a heap of papers on the ink-stained table. Without trying to excuse himself, he leaned over and read —

'Whereas the Commissioners for conducting His Majesty's Transport Service and for the Care and Custody of Prisoners of War have been pleased to grant . . . *Captain Anthony Purvis* . . . leave to reside in . . . *Morfa, Carmarthenshire* . . . upon condition that he gives his parole of honour not to withdraw one mile from the boundaries prescribed there without leave for that purpose from the said Commissioners, that he will behave himself decently and with due regard to the laws of the kingdom, and also that he will not directly or indirectly hold any correspondence with France or America during his continuance in England, but by such letter or letters as shall be shown to the Agent of the said Commissioners under whose care he is or may be, in order to their being read and approved, he does hereby declare that having given his parole he will keep it inviolably. . . .

'Norman Cross Prison,

'December 15, 1812.'

There was an illegible initial in ink in one corner, and his own signature alone was lacking.

He set the paper back under the weight, and went to his chair trembling. When he had seated himself he found that the tears were streaming down his face; he wiped them away with a grimy handkerchief, catching his breath as he did so, like a child that recovers from a fit of sobbing. . . .

On that same December day Mr. Harradence discussed high art with the Earl of Morfa in the Long Gallery at Morfa Abbey. It had been snowing in the Welsh mountains all night, and through the tall windows a fiercely white light was reflected from snow-covered terrace and park upon the squares and oblongs of the paintings hanging upon the neutral-tinted walls; particularly upon the unloveliness of an early Italian Master's conception of our First Ancestors in converse with a human-headed Serpent.

'Must I say that I like it, Charles?' complained Harradence, regarding the nudity of the newest acquisition with disfavour, and thrusting his hands deep into his pantaloon pockets.

'If you stand a foot or so more to your left, to get the light —'

'I shall still see it a foot further away,' grumbled Harradence. 'If you'd said a mile! . . . And it isn't even accurate. Why the fellow's given Adam a navel!'

'And why the devil shouldn't he!'

'Charles! Charles!' said Harradence, turning his grey head away from the picture and regarding his friend with an assumption of concern. 'How could Adam have had a navel? *Do* think for a minute! Adam didn't need a navel because he wasn't born of woman, and do you imagine that the Almighty provided him with a sham pit to his stomach just to ornament a blank space?'

'But, Henry —' began Morfa.

'Of course,' admitted Harradence with a large air, 'Browne suggests that Adam may have been in a "momental navel with his Maker", but he doesn't mean in a physical sense. A knowledge of midwifery —'

A very splendid servant, with powdered hair, and liveried in scarlet and yellow, swam deferentially toward them; presented my lord with a letter upon a large engraved salver.

He opened the missive with a word of apology; read it almost at a glance —

'It's all settled, Henry,' he said with an air of triumph. 'It's from Custis at the Transport Office. "The Commissioners have considered your lordship's representations . . . Instructions are being sent . . . Norman Cross . . . Captain Purvis will be granted parole in Morfa as soon as escort can be arranged."'

'Thank God!' said Harradence, and took the letter extended to him. He walked with it to a window, donned his oblong-paned spectacles; read it; and then stood, hands clasped behind plum-coloured back, staring out unseeing at the sparkle of the snow and the short noonday shadows of the Indian cedars.

'It's nearly twelve years since I last saw poor Rowley,' he said at length. 'Six of them he has spent as a prisoner. He was a boy then, and now he is a man of thirty! I wonder if I should know him? He must be altered by those years — by war — prison — bitterness.'

He had a sudden and almost overwhelming sense of physical nearness to the past.

But if for him the roads had reached out from France to the Welsh hills, and the years had reached out across nearly two decades; so, for the other, had the roads reached out from Virginia, and the years across a whole generation. It was no longer in the bland cold picture-gallery of Morfa Abbey that the two men stood, but in the apple-green library at High Pale — the lofty shadowy room in the house on the Toulon road; the small study at La Cadière with its dark cliff of books — the red-curtained cabin of the *Chesapeake*.

'All these years,' said Harradence turning, 'I've wanted to win back the lad I lost. You've given me the opportunity, Charles! I should not have had it but for you. Once again I have got to thank you.'

Morfa made no reply for a minute. He held up one long white hand in the other, and examined the great red stone in the signet ring on his little finger.

'As a matter of fact,' he said at length, 'I must tell you that in this business I have been serving myself! *I* have been looking for Anthony Purvis ever since I came in for — this!' — by a jerk of the head he indicated the picture-gallery, the great house of which it was part, the vast estate which lay about it, the peerage, the social and political influence — '*I* have been trying to find him ever since he vanished from Lauchstein — and it would have been easier if we hadn't thought that he had got swallowed up in Russia — to make my peace with him; with his father; with myself! . . . I don't know, Henry, how much you heard of what happened that night on the road to Toulon — of the charges made against me! One of them was true!'

Leaning against a glass-topped display table full of cameos and medals, twisting his ring, he told Harradence the story of what had happened in Virginia long ago. The unadorned truth.

Although a whole generation had passed by, there was about him still much of the look and lofty air of the young soldier who had debated strategy and tactics with the creator of Camelot, standing with one foot on the curb under the portrait of old Colonel Beriah, that night while the retreating English columns withdrew past High Pale.

The diamonds had been sold (he said) for an immense sum, many times the amount of the IOU he had made out and hidden. With the money he had bought his promotion — two steps — three steps. Always he had meant to repay: that was true, upon his honour!

'Do you know, Henry, that my first feeling when I heard about my uncle and poor George was one of relief! Because I could at last free myself from some part of the horrible burden I'd been carrying for years. I swear it! And the first thing I did was — '

He seized Harradence's arm and marched him up the shining length of the great gallery to the far end where, under the coldness of a tall east window, stood a marble-topped cabinet of satinwood. This he unlocked with a key from his fob pocket, and, stooping, fumbled with the spring of some inner secret receptacle; produced at last to view a small gilded casket, fantastically rococo; opened and placed it on the cabinet top.

Within a sepulchre of black velvet the icy fires of six great diamonds were resurrected, with the light of moonrise on a frozen waterfall.

'They must be of enormous value!'

'To get them back,' said Morfa, tilting the casket a little toward the window, 'I had to pay exactly twice what I was given for them! If they had asked me ten times as much I should have paid it. Without demur!'

Harradence was silent for a while, studying his friend's face with its arched eyebrows, high forehead, and high-bridged nose. Morfa had never, within his recollection, allowed himself to show much of what he felt or thought.

'So there are two of us — three,' he said finally, 'who want to make restitution to the House of Purvis!'

'Three?'

'Garland! . . . Your task is easier than ours. You can make your reparation remaining still unknown, but *we* must make *ours* in person! There is no other way, and it is going to be very difficult. All my letters — and I wrote many — were returned to me unopened!'

'It would be cowardly in me to avoid the personal issue,' said Morfa. 'And I shall not, when the time is ripe. If there is anything of the older Anthony in him — and from what you say, I believe there is — he will understand and forgive. In the end. I have never been haunted by the ghost of his father — it would be a whimsical, forgiving ghost, I'll swear! — but by myself!'

'Ghosts!' Harradence's eyes shifted from the jewels to the intense whiteness of the sky. 'I always loved Anthony for himself — as though he were my own. Because he *was* my own: I brought him back from the companionship of ghosts . . . And then, at last, betrayed him to them again!'

'What else could you have done but what you did?'

'Nothing — *then* . . . Any boy might have leaped at the adventure that offered, not realizing its dreadful possibilities. Or that the only excuse for destruction is a profound belief that you are serving some holy purpose. He was the ignorant instrument of his grandmother's insane desire for retribution . . . She *is* insane, you know! . . . But I'—and he drummed on his great chest with his fist as he spoke—'ought to have known long before where all the *Nautilus* business was tending. I wilfully blinded myself. I ramped on. I roared on all the old windy demagogy. I was in the position of a man who watches a gun being loaded and handed to a child, and refuses to believe that he can possibly fire it when he has it in his grasp! . . . Neither was I honest in hiding the change of heart which made me refuse to build the thing for Fulton! So dishonest, in fact, that I didn't even admit it to myself!'

Said Morfa, closing the lid of the sepulchre of the diamonds —

'I am afraid that it's not going to be easy for the three of us who want to make atonement, although I am sure of the ultimate issue!'

'We'll drive over and dine with you on Thursday, if you will give us a good dinner,' said Harradence, picking up his crop and hat from a chair. 'There'll be a moon. You and I can then go into full-dress committee with Elizabeth and Garland! . . . Of one thing I am certain, and that is we must keep well out of Rowley's way until new influences have got to work . . . If I know anything of the Almonds—'

CHAPTER II

INTRODUCTION TO A PRISON

ANTHONY traversed the breadth of a wet and windy England, of a snowy and frozen Wales. He made the journey in the comparative luxury of a post-chaise, to the infinite pleasure of his escort, a very young ensign of the West Essex Militia; who had mapped out their route for the official approval of Captain Blewitt with much care, and commented upon the countryside through which they passed as if he personally had invented it.

His last English journey had been in ragged orange uniform of canvas, from Portsmouth to Norman Cross—one hundred and fifty miles—in company with a herd of footsore prisoners, sleeping in barns and stables and churches on the way—a scarecrow procession to arouse the pity or the mockery of those who saw them pass. Now they slept in the best beds at the best inns, and sampled the neatest wines and the finest dinners producible—at Anthony's expense.

Mr. Thompson, the subaltern, enjoyed himself enormously: he was in hourly expectation of receiving a regular commission and being posted to the 44th Foot; and this foretaste of military duty seemed highly satisfactory. On the first night out, at the Angel at Market Harborough, he tucked Anthony — overcome by a new sense of freedom and a bottle and a half of old port — most solicitously up in bed. He was a large, amiable lad, straight from school; and, as he had only a beginner's head for wine, on the following night the position was reversed, and it was Anthony who put the escort to bed.

According to regulations they slept in the same room, and in the small hours of the morning Anthony was awakened by a spasmodic shaking.

Mr. Thompson stood at the bedside, holding a lighted candle unsteadily in his hand. Although garbed in his night-shirt, he had donned his plumed shako, presumably to convey the idea that he had resumed duty.

' 'Scuse me, shir,' said Mr. Thompson, enunciating the words with great deliberation. ' 'Scuse me, shir, but you — you — you — shtill on parole, o' courshe?'

'Of course!' Anthony assured him sleepily.

Mr. Thompson was apparently satisfied; but ten minutes later awoke from a brief nap, and appeared once more, requiring further confirmation.

On the third occasion, Anthony removed the shako, and hid it on top of the wardrobe; so that Mr. Thompson, being unable to find this insignia of office on re-awakening, finally composed himself to sleep. . . .

Anthony had told himself that he would never be able to speak to an Englishman again, except on the most indifferent matters and in the most frigid manner. But the boy was so like a large puppy — so certain of the friendship of all the world — that it was impossible to travel with him other than on terms of amity.

There was, too, one circumstance which occasioned Anthony particular amusement. Journeying, as they did, cross-country for a considerable distance, the spectacle of the captive's alien uniform of dark green with golden shoulder-knot and cocked hat, aroused interest and speculation at their halting-places. Mr. Thompson gathered much kudos from confidential explanation in coffee-room and bar-parlour that the officer he was escorting was a prisoner of great importance — no less an individual than one of the personal military staff of old Boney himself. After such explanation Mr. Thompson visibly swelled, and would look round as though suspecting that there were persons present who might contemplate a rescue. . . .

They joined the great coach road from London to western Wales at Brecon: came into a town that was a pandemonium of clanging bells, the crashing reiteration of guns, a purposeless movement of excited crowds.

When they stopped to change horses at an inn in the main street, Ensign Thompson had leaped from the carriage and was firing questions at an ostler almost before the wheels had ceased to turn.

Anthony was preparing to follow him when the other's large pink face appeared in the doorway.

'I say, sir! I think perhaps — if you don't mind! — you'd better stay in the carriage! You'll excuse me saying so, but you'd really better!'

The shadow of the palisades again! Ensign Thompson become turnkey! Anthony was conscious of a sudden anger at the reminder: his expression must have showed it, for the subaltern said hurriedly —

'For your own sake! . . . I'll bring you whatever you like, myself! . . . Please! You know these Welsh are very excitable! There's no telling what they mayn't get up to! . . . And — ' he hesitated before adding — 'if you *could* remove your hat! It's very foreign-looking . . . Thank you *very* much, sir!'

Ensign Thompson was away for some little while. When he came back, he brought a large rummer full of steaming punch in his own hands, and remained leaning by the door until they started again — as much like an affectionate country governess as a sentry.

'A bit beyond themselves to-day,' he said awkwardly as they rolled on once more. 'Just a bit!'

He offered no further explanation.

'Why?' asked Anthony at length.

'Well,' said Thompson with an air of apology. 'News came from London an hour ago that Bo — the Emperor's Grand Army has been annihilated in Russia! He's skedaddled back to Paris by himself. Of the six hundred thousand men he started with they say he's lost over half a million! . . . It's all in the papers, they say! *I* don't know, of course!'

They drove on in silence.

Was it so?

It was. Although not for weeks was it to be known how dreadfully and utterly had the Grand Army vanished into nothingness before the indomitable spirit and cruel snow of Russia, even as the Grand Armada of an earlier overlord had vanished before the indomitable spirit and furious seas of Britain.

They came out of a bleak, winding pass into a wide and snowy valley, through which a half-frozen river curved — a valley chequered with dark woodlands, hamlets set among bare orchards, grey castle rising on rocky spur. It was late afternoon, and the whiteness of the mountains was gold at the summits and shadowed luminous purple and blue.

So at last, across a pointed-arched bridge of stone, to ancient Morfa, with its tangle of streets and walled gardens rambling betwixt sinuous river and wooded bluff.

A little while before Thompson had said, with a sigh of regret —

'There you are! Only a mile to go!'

For beside the milestone opposite a wayside tavern was set a post bearing the painted notice —

'Limite des Prisonniers de Guerre'

It seemed, however, to Anthony considerably more than a mile before they came to the bridge and could set about finding their way to the Transport Office Agent's house; past one or two churches regarded reverentially by prim little houses; along narrow streets that went curving uphill and along narrow streets that went curving down; through two small and crowded squares — one of them presided over by a colonnaded market-house, and the other by a smug-looking inn built against the remains of a castle; and then all the way back again. Finally they plunged into another narrow street that descended sharply to the river — a shadowy row of sedate houses, with plane trees growing out of a pavement that accommodated itself to the slope only by a transformation into stairways at frequent intervals. . . .

In a little dim parlour in one of these houses, quite walled with faded water-colours and sketches of every imaginable sort of ship in every imaginable sort of frame, Ensign Thompson obtained a receipt for his prisoner from a dim little man with fluffy white hair, and bade Anthony 'good-bye'.

'I hope we shall meet again,' said the ensign, shaking him vigorously by the hand. 'It's been a most enjoyable trip . . . Captain Purvis has been a model prisoner, sir!' he assured the dim little man, anxious to give credit where credit was due; whereat the dim little man bowed and Anthony bowed. 'Perhaps the next time will be in America! I'm told the Regiment — the 44th, you know! — is going there! That's the best of a war: one sees the world! It would be a coincidence, wouldn't it? Good luck, sir!'

Anthony had almost forgotten that America was now at war with Britain. The reminder made his farewell less cordial than it might otherwise have been.

The Agent of the Transport Office, Staff-Surgeon Henry Strang, R.N. (retired), had the bedside manner of a deferential physician. In his dim little consulting-room he spoke to, and of, the prisoners in his charge as though they were patients needing gentle exercise and early hours.

'You are aware of the regulations, Captain Purvis?' said he, pushing a folded paper across the table to his client, as if it were a prescription.

'Here is your pass! I am afraid that I shall really have to ask you to be indoors by five of the clock nowadays and eight in summer. If you should require an occasional extension, you have only to apply to me; you won't find me unreasonable. Nor will you find the limit to your excursions out of town very irksome. It is surprising how far a mile can be! Very surprising! . . . I ask my gentlemen to muster twice a week. At eleven o'clock — a convenient hour, don't you think?'

It was a convenient hour — Anthony agreed.

'On Wednesdays in Castle Place. Convenient for the Mess, for shopping, and for the circulating library. On Sundays by the lych-gate of St. Teilo's — convenient for those who are of the Anglican persuasion! . . . Are you, by any chance, of this — er — inclination?'

Anthony was; and in the darkening afternoon Mr. Strang rambled on, getting dimmer and dimmer; until all that was practically visible of him, against a background of picture-frames and glass, was his crown of white fluff.

There were eighty patients in the town. The juniors messed in a large and airy loft in a builder's yard at the back of Market Street. The twelve senior officers had a room at the Four Swans Hotel in Castle Place — and very comfortable and snug they were, on the whole. He had consulted Colonel Millet, the doyen, and it had been agreed that Captain Purvis, although not of field rank, should be invited to join the Senior Mess, in view of his position on the Imperial staff. It would be a little more expensive, but he understood that that would not matter to Captain Purvis.

It did not.

Captain Purvis knew that he was also entitled to a parole allowance of eighteen pence a day, free medical attention, and a funeral costing not more than two guineas at governmental expense — gloves and hatbands to be bought by the mourners?

He did know.

Well, all that remained was to show Captain Purvis to his new quarters. Which accordingly Mr. Strang proceeded to do; wrapped for the expedition — although the journey was only one of a hundred yards or so down the slant of the street — in a huge many-caped coat, and topped by a beaver hat round the brim of which foamed a fringe of white hair.

Arrived on the doorstep of a grave Caroline house, which stood at the exact spot where the street finally decided to drop precipitously to the river, Mr. Strang said in a low voice —

'You understand, my dear sir, that this is no ordinary lodging!'

The house looked large and well-kept; bright brass knocker, shining paint, and glittering windows were obvious even in the dark.

Anthony understood.

'It is most difficult to find quarters for foreigners — and prisoners at that! — in Morfa. The Welsh are notoriously conservative. Fortunately Mr. Almond came to my rescue. A personal friend! He has a number of spare rooms. It's not a question of money at all with him, you know! He is extremely well-off — a very handsome estate, I should imagine!'

The door swung open. A small aged manservant appeared and gave them a respectful 'good evening!' and received Anthony into his care as though he, too, were connected with the medical profession; while Mr. Strang fluttered off as if he had an important maternity case awaiting his attention.

Anthony followed the servant through a spacious, dim hall, up a spacious dim staircase, to a door on the first floor.

The old man opened the door, and deferentially stood aside for him to enter.

An elderly couple — so small as almost to seem miniatures of the real thing — were at tea, sitting one on either side of the fire in a large white-panelled room. A snug warm room, bright with candle-light, full of old-fashioned furniture and rose-bowls and cabinets crowded with porcelain and silver, hung with many portraits, and smelling of lavender and China tea.

'Prison!' said Anthony to himself.

'Gaolers!' said Anthony to himself.

Both gaolers rose simultaneously to their feet: they had china-blue eyes, the pinkest possible cheeks and the whitest possible hair. Anthony felt that if Mr. Almond were to don his wife's white cap and black silk dress, and Mrs. Almond the black tail-coat and tights and the mighty neck-cloth of her husband, nobody would be any the wiser.

Mr. Almond hurried toward him with outstretched hand.

'My dear sir! So here you are! . . . Letty-my-dear, this is Captain Purvis! My wife, Captain Purvis! Now, have you had any dinner? We did not know when you would arrive, or, of course, we should have waited . . . You dined in Llandilo! . . . Well, I hope you will do justice to supper! . . . Jenkins, tell cook to advance supper! Say seven o'clock — could that be managed, Letty-my-dear? Can you wait till then, or will you have something at once. A little cold chicken? Some cold roast?'

'Prison!' said Anthony to himself.

Mrs. Almond considered the tall young man in the shabby green uniform with the empty sleeve. He looked tired, haggard, and worn — she thought.

'Captain Purvis won't decide anything for himself, Tom!' she said.

'He's too tired after his long journey. He will do as he's told . . . Jenkins, set a chair for the captain before the fire! Then bring up the cellaret! Captain Purvis is going to have a little brandy and water while we drink our tea. Then he will have a light supper. And then he will go to bed. "Sleep is better than medicine!" as Mr.——'

There she stopped abruptly, and sat down in her wing arm-chair before the great silver tea-tray.

So Anthony drank a little hot punch while they drank their scented orange pekoe: and listened to small talk — of a sort that he had not heard for how many years! — and had a light supper and more small talk: and was then sent to bed in a large room with a low ceiling and two windows that looked on the plane trees of the narrow street and two that looked on a precipitous slip of garden at the side of the house. His trunks had been unpacked: and his night-shirt put to air before a clear fire. . . .

'Prison!' said Anthony out loud to himself, sitting up in bed, and regarding the firelit room, the easy chairs, the sofa, the big writing-table, the bookcase with unexplored shelves, the swinging pier-glass, the blue and white of the willow pattern toilet set, and the shadowy portrait of a young man in tie-wig and regimentals over the mantelpiece.

'Prison!' said he very loudly, at that particular moment when a gentle tap sounded on the panels of the door.

The miniature gaoler peeped round the corner apologetically — inserted himself into the room apologetically — tiptoed apologetically to the bedside with the jerky tittup of a wagtail.

'Mrs. Almond,' said Gaoler-Wagtail, 'insisted upon my coming to see whether you had everything you required! Is your bed comfortable? Are there enough bed-clothes? I can assure you that it has been well aired. There has been a warming-pan in it every night for a week . . . I hope you will like your room. It used to be Young Tom's — our boy's, you know!'

From swift affectionate glance across the shadows of the room, Anthony deduced that the portrait over the fireplace was of Young Tom.

CHAPTER III

THE HOUSE OF ARMISTICE

As in course of time Anthony was absorbed into the ineffable calm of the household in Dark Wharf Gate, so he found that Young Tom was ever-present at all proceedings of the day — from the reading and discussion at the protracted breakfast of a three-day-old *Times,* divided in half so that both gentlemen could simultaneously enjoy it; up to the pleasant hour or so over the fire after dinner with tea and double acrostics until it was time for supper.

The names of places and people were all assessed according to their likeness to the names of places and people Young Tom had known; dishes were those that he had liked or disliked; his little traditional quips were quoted with much savouring of the jest; not a room but had some special association with him.

And so to the end of the peaceful day when Mrs. Almond would read the household prayers in a very special voice which she used on no other occasion, to a gathering of buxom elderly maids and withered elderly men-servants — all rustling rather creakily to their knees by the dining-room chairs; and would pause for an appreciable space when she came to return thanks for 'those we have loved, Thy servants, who, having put off mortality, await us with Thy hosts upon Jordan's further shore.'

Anthony asked the old butler about the picture in his room.

'Yes-yes, sir. It iss the young gentleman. And a fery fine young gentleman he wass!'

'It was painted a very long time ago,' said Anthony, looking on curled and powdered hair tied in a queue with black ribbon.

'The young gentleman died a fery, fery long time ago! A *fery* long time ago.'

There was another portrait, a magnificent painting by Romney, which had pride of place in the drawing-room; it was a three-quarter length and showed the lad in a wine-coloured suit and seated in the selfsame green damask chair that was drawn up underneath. In the dining-room, too, there was a family group by Gainsborough over the fireplace — Mrs. Almond in yellow satin with tiny pointed shoes and high powdered hair, having a chubby curly-headed boy standing in his smock upon her knee; and Mr. Almond in dove-grey satin with ruffles at his wrists.

This last was in its way remarkable, for it was the only portrait of Mr. Almond in anything but military attire. Otherwise the panelled walls of the dining-room were a perfect picture-gallery of Old Tom in the various uniforms he had worn during thirty years as a volunteer.

There was Old Tom over the immense bay of the sideboard, in scarlet coat with golden collar, and jack-boots and very plump breeches, and remarkable helmet having a sort of cock's comb of black fur to it, leaning against the fat hindquarters of a bay horse. That was when he was a major of the Loyal and Associated Volunteer Corps of Westminster.

There was Old Tom in much the same sort of uniform, with the addition of a flame-coloured plume to his hat, but minus golden epaulettes, waving on invisible troops to the attack, against the wooded background of Primrose Hill. There was Old Tom in a shako with a white plume, and Old Tom in a cocked hat with a blue plume, and Old Tom even in the three-cornered hat bound with gold of very long ago. Then, too, at one end of the room — between the windows — there was an aquatint of His Majesty reviewing the Volunteer Corps in Hyde Park on June 4, 1799; while at the opposite end was a large engraving, showing a vast and urbane confusion of men, horses, dogs, and plumes, entitled 'The Prince of Wales's Loyal Volunteers preparing for the Grand Review by His Majesty, October 28th, 1803.'

When they sat over their decanter of port after dinner — which was at four o'clock — the old gentleman would more frequently than not discuss such military matters as had come within his purview in the old days — the standardizing of the length of the military hair queue at six inches; the provision of velvet edging to the stiff black leather stock; the great field-day at Coxheath in '78; the failure of adjutants to earn their six shillings a day; forgotten triumphs at forgotten ranges; forgotten words of command and forgotten orders of drill; gracious praise dropped by Gracious Majesty in his hurried, flurried way; sins of omission or commission by subaltern officers now grandfathers or awaiting the Last Fall-In on the Parade Ground of Heaven.

Then the journey upstairs to the bright drawing-room with a halt on the way to tap and set the barometer at the foot of the stairs — an operation performed so frequently throughout the day that nobody ever really knew whether the glass was going up or down: Mrs. Almond would be awaiting them by a crackling fire, with knitting and tea-tray, her toes on a woolwork footstool, and shielded from the blaze by a woolwork fire-screen (depicting a large gentleman in a periwig against a blue house with a red roof, and executed by herself in the year '60) which always came sliding down its rod at the wrong moment.

The patterned damask curtains of Chinese blue would be drawn to shut out nightfall; and the three little gilded pagodas in the window-places, inhabited by a pair of bullfinches, and two pair of canaries, shrouded with identical covers made from an old Paisley shawl and embroidered with their hereditary names — William and Mary, George and Charlotte, Frederick and Caroline . . . There was some legend that they would not sleep peacefully at night if the covers were changed.

Anthony knew that now was the crowning moment of the day — the period looked forward to with gentle excitement throughout all the small busy-ness that filled life so fully and so satisfactorily. It was the Hour of the Acrostic.

Ah, happy hour, when at last Mr. Almond had settled himself in his chair; ascertained that the necessary works of reference were disposed on the little table beside him — Bible (on top of course), Johnson's *Dictionary*, Lemprière's *Classical Dictionary*, and a very ancient copy of Echard's *Geographical Index;* unfolded the latest *Enigma* broadsheet or the fortnightly manuscript compilation of the Morfa Sphinx Club — of which fourteen copies were made by the young gentlemen employed in the office of Mr. Davies, the attorney; put on his spectacles; coughed to attract his wife's attention; inquired eagerly, 'Well, and shall we see how sharp our wits are to-night, Letty-my-dear?'

So he would read the clues out loud very slowly and clearly, and Letty-my-dear, eyes focused on knitting, would attack the conundrum with a little frown of concentration and lips moving as they spelt out words to herself.

Ah, happy, happy hour! When away they could go hobby-horsically across the vast lexicographical spaces, delving into the classics, prying into the little-charted corners of the earth, fluttering over the two volumes of *Elegant Extracts* for all sorts of mysterious quotations.

Even on the second night Anthony — seated between them before the fire, provided with footstool and little table on which steamed his tea in a gold and red cup — was drawn into the tortuous game.

'Perhaps to-night,' said Mr. Almond breaking away from the conventional opening, 'Captain Purvis will be able to throw light on our problem. His mind will be more agile than ours. I must say I thought about it whilst undressing last night, and again when I was shaving this morning.'

He unfurled the sheet, and read out loud —

' "The recondite folds of a domestic work to secure which you are instructed to revolve the wards, resulting in a classical draught." There's a snorter! There's a horror! And we haven't got the first letter because we haven't got the left-hand pillar! As for the right!'

He shook his head.

But Anthony had no ideas at all. He had only a vague notion, in fact, of what he was expected to do.

And Mrs. Almond, after reciting to herself an immense laundry list of domestic articles that could be folded, also gave it up temporarily and plaintively inquired the clue to the whole pillar.

'Never say die!' said Mr. Almond (this was a standing remark) and proceeded: 'A word of eleven letters, of which we have only got the second — U, and the sixth — S. The clues are — "Part of a puss for example takes precedence of part of part of the church, and that it can we are assured. The result being very satisfactory to a good housewife." '

Solving these and kindred problems — such as whether or no there existed a place called Machrihanish in Argyllshire, and such a word as funambulist — kept them pleasantly occupied until supper-time.

Quiet old ladies paid afternoon calls in antiquated sedan-chairs: quiet old gentlemen, who still powdered their hair, came to dinner: quiet old servants moved about the quiet old house on quiet old feet.

Little by little Anthony was submerged beneath the tide of peace that lapped about the house in Dark Wharf Gate, where the only realities were the dreams and memories that filled its crooked walls. He did not resist. He welcomed the influence that blotted out the degradation and monotony of six years — and other things. He gave himself to it.

Of Staff-Surgeon Strang's other patients he saw no more than he could help. He attended the twice-a-week muster, and three times a week he took his noonday meal with the senior officers in their *café-au-lait* painted mess-room looking on to the courtyard of the Four Swans Hotel.

That last had been Mrs. Almond's doing.

'Anthony,' she had said — and 'Anthony' he had been after the first week — 'you must meet people of your own age. One can't have you getting old from infection, you know. It's bad for you living all your life with us old people. Now I really think that you should make a point of meeting these French officers more often. You must have a great deal in common to talk about . . . You speak the language, my dear, of course? . . . And don't hesitate to bring any of them home to dinner. I'm told they are a most gentlemanly lot! They are very well spoken of in the town. And the days you dine with them, take a good walk afterwards in company. You need more exercise. Stretching your legs — you gentlemen call it, I believe.'

Therefore, because he would have done anything she said, he dined thrice a week at midday in the Mess, which was ornamented by an engraving of Napoleon in cocked hat and grey overcoat over the mantelpiece, a likeness of Lord Cawdor in the uniform of the Cardigan Militia, a colour print of the Derby of 1800, a grandfather clock that did not go, and a notice that the hotel was a posting establishment which made wedding-coaches 'A speciality' and was in a position to supply a 'Hearse of the Latest Parisian design.'

Three only of the officers who constituted the Mess were French: the rest were representative of the vassal states of the Empire — Germans from Westphalia and the Rhineland, Italians from Lombardy, a Dutchman, a Dane, a Pole; in a medley of uniforms that were mostly shabby. In their company — in their superficial politeness, excitability, swiftly-aroused wrath, and general air of shoddiness — and in the pitiable shifts of their poverty, Anthony was recalled to the days of hulk and palisade. He hated the reminder.

Colonel Millet, the Mess president, an elderly bitter man, with recollections of earlier and more gentlemanly wars, seemed to realize and resent this, although he himself spoke of the assortment of races that surrounded him as 'This menagerie!'. He also obviously resented Anthony's affluence, and was at occasional pains to make himself unpleasant.

Anthony had succeeded with some difficulty in getting a new uniform made by a goblin-like tailor in a little shop in a steep dark street.

On the first day that he wore it at Mess, the colonel surveyed him sharply from his place at the head of the table — an ill-laid table with coarse linen cloth and earthenware, and clumsy glass — and asked in his thin bitter voice, without any preamble —

'And what uniform are you supposed to be wearing?'

As the new uniform differed in no particular from the old, Anthony did not at first realize that the question was addressed to him. When he did —

'That of His Majesty's staff of orderly officers, sir.'

'It is curious,' reflected Colonel Millet out loud, down the length of the table, 'that young officers take so little trouble to acquaint themselves with regulations!'

'In what respect?' asked Anthony.

'The uniform of His Majesty's orderly officers is blue and silver.'

'It was not six years ago, when I was taken prisoner.'

Colonel Millet added water to the half tumbler of cheap claret which he allowed himself with his meal.

'I have been a prisoner for nine and a half years precisely,' he said, 'but I do not permit myself to think that things have stood still in that time. If I were to buy a new uniform I should make certain that it was of correct cut and colour!'

'In the hulks, sir,' said Anthony, 'we wore yellow canvas. And at Norman Cross prison it was difficult to arouse much interest in the Imperial sartorial fiats!'

The word 'hulks', said loudly, brought utter silence for a moment to the entire table. It was as though the words 'death' and 'grave' had been pronounced at a wedding feast. And then a gush of criss-cross conversation surged over the stillness, as though everybody would bury the ill-omened word under a spate of talk.

Colonel Millet's morning exercise was to saunter slowly from his lodging by St. Teilo's Gate through the centre of the town, and down the slope of the long high street, to the candle-extinguisher-topped towers of the Bridge Gate, and back again. On this route he very frequently met Anthony escorting the old lady on her daily shopping expeditions, or accompanying the old gentleman to morning gossip over a glass of Madeira and biscuit with some other old gentlemen. Millet would salute sourly, if he could not avoid the encounter, and hurry past, or ostentatiously turn his back to examine the goods displayed in the bow window of tobacconist or hosier.

Later one day after such an incident, when Anthony had been in Morfa for some six weeks, he came upon the older man, warming himself in solitary state before the rather miserable fire of small coal and *pellau* which was all that the Four Swans felt itself called upon to provide. In the sunshine of the February afternoon the room — and the man — looked inconceivably shabby. The stuffing leaked from the shiny horse-hair-seated chairs: the sideboard under its fly-blown mirror was crowded with dirty dishes that had been overlooked from the midday meal: the table was still covered with a soiled dinner-cloth: the grey wallpaper was discoloured with damp. The darns, and the fraying, and the shininess of Colonel Millet's dark blue uniform were pitifully apparent.

The London coach that morning had brought Anthony a parcel of continental newspapers from Turner's of Cloak Lane. He had brought them for use of the Mess as usual, dumped them on the small billiard table at the far end of the room, and now, with a bow, was about to go.

Said Colonel Millet —

'Back to your English friends, Captain Purvis?'

'Yes, sir,' answered Anthony.

'I suppose,' said Millet, studying his own rusty shoes and frayed strapped trousers, 'we shall be hearing any day that you have applied for naturalization?'

'I fail to understand, sir.'

'Well, sir, it is very obvious where your social preferences lie!'

Anthony restrained his anger with difficulty.

'It is pleasant, sir, to be able to speak my native language. Nor have I been made so welcome here by my brother officers.'

'No?' said Millet, with a lilt of the voice and a tilt of the eyebrows implying that he found this a matter for no surprise. He added, after allowing the import of his monosyllable to sink in: 'We shall probably have you end by marrying a girl with teeth like a fence, and joining the British army!'

'That is your considered opinion, I presume, sir,' remarked Anthony, furious.

At this moment there was an irruption of half a dozen members of the Mess, returned from an excursion to the Black Ox, a thatched tavern conveniently situated at the extreme parole limits, and as remarkable for the strength of its home-brewed as for the amiable weaknesses of the daughters of the house.

Millet probably thought that he had gone far enough, for he said pacifically —

'The idle speculation of an idle man!'

Anthony made no rejoinder. What was the use? He took up his hat and made for the door. As he did so, Millet added as a sort of afterthought —

'Still it is almost as interesting a subject for speculation as the fact that you — of all people — should have been billeted with the Almonds — of all people!'

'I am, of course, quite unable to control the course of your speculations. But I should be obliged if you would tell me what you find remarkable about my billet!'

'You are an American!' said Millet dryly.

'Do you imply that it is surprising for an American to be billeted with a civilized household?'

'I made a statement of fact. You can hardly choose to consider yourself insulted in being reminded of your nationality —'

The colonel ended the sentence with a Gallic shrug of the shoulders.

Anthony resumed his path to the door, which was near the fireplace. As he put hand to door-knob, the other man said in a low voice: 'You don't know then! You can't, or you would be as surprised as I have been! . . . The Almonds' only son was hanged by the Americans in the War of Independence. Like Major André. He was caught in civilian clothes while carrying a message behind their lines. You wouldn't have expected them to welcome an American officer beneath their roof!'

'I see!' said Anthony.

He shut the door quietly after him. As he did, he registered an oath that he would not again set foot within the precincts of the Mess. And was ashamed of the oath: but was confirmed in the decision despite his shame. For he knew that he had no kinship with these people except a common captivity: abominated their garrulous talk of easy *amourettes* and such nothingnesses, their quarrelsome games of chance; saw in the sadistic bitterness of Colonel Millet the reflection of a mental state such as his own might become after ten years of restraint.

It did not occur to him for one instant to question the truth of Millet's assertion . . . So a tree and a rope had been the fate of Young Tom — Young Tom, the chubby infant in the great family portrait, the lad in the green damask chair, the youngster in regimentals whose portrait was the first thing that met his waking gaze! Young Tom, beside whose marble memorial tablet on a grey stone wall he sat of a Sunday in the dimness of St. Teilo's Church! 'Thomas Maitland Almond, Esquire, Ensign in the 55th Foot, Who fell asleep in Christ, on August the Eighth, 1779.' *Fell asleep in Christ* at the end of a hangman's noose! . . . Young Tom, whose name was on someone's lips each day in the quiet house in Dark Wharf Gate, and in certain hope of reunion with whom the Almonds passed every minute of their placid lives!

All the afternoon and evening, through the sedate ritual of dinner and tea-drinking and acrostic-solving, he was a little silent.

Old Tom put on his glasses: crossed his stretched-out feet: ascertained that the usual works of reference were in place: opened the silk-stitched foolscap MSS. which represented the Sphinx Club's fortnightly compendium: found the double acrostic which had sadly baffled them on the night before —

'I hope you are feeling really luminiferous this evening, Anthony! Because of all the snorters that we have had, this problem' — they were always problems, and never puzzles — 'is the most snorting! . . . I seem to recognize Lady Rhys-Hughes's hand in it, Letty-my-dear. The woman is a walking compendium of Hungarian hamlets and small Peruvian market-towns. And an absolute anthology of the minor poets.'

'She is, Tom,' said Mrs. Almond, rinsing the pretty red and gold cups in a little hot water before pouring out the tea. 'But,' with much triumph, 'I can tell you what the right-hand pillar is!'

' "Faction, ——'s restless child",' read out Old Tom, producing a pencil. 'Well, Letty-my-dear, I always said you'd got the brains! I certainly thought we should have to do all the cross-words first. We've only got an S, an I, an E, and a T. What is the answer, my dear?'

'Disappointment! " — Disappointment's restless child." That's what Faction is. And it comes from lines written by someone I've never heard of, about an attempted murder of His Majesty!'

'Now how,' asked Old Tom, regarding his wife from over the top of his glasses, 'now how in the name of all that is merciful, Mrs. Almond, did you arrive at that?'

'Never you mind, Tom,' said Mrs. Almond.

'Mrs. Almond,' said Old Tom tapping his knee very fiercely with his silver pencil, 'you've been cheating! You've been cribbing! You've been peeping, and you've been peering! If not worse!'

'It was on a strictly commercial basis,' said Mrs. Almond, assuming what was intended undoubtedly to be a business-like air. 'I met Miss Porcher this morning in the High Street. I exchanged "Adhibit" in the logogriph problem for "Disappointment". A reasonable transaction, Tom!'

'I'm prepared to wager all I possess that you had to treat Miss Porcher to a dish of chocolate and cream buns at Evan Jones's, as make-weight!' remarked Old Tom thoughtfully.

Mrs. Almond said nothing, but just looked a little more dignified, and proceeded to pour out tea.

Tom Almond resumed study of the acrostic —

'Well, now we've got a final T in the tenth word across. "You would enjoy this craft taken with two-thirds of an irriguous condition." '

'Now Anthony,' said Mrs. Almond pouring out cream and putting in sugar, 'you have been of no assistance at all this evening! What is a word for "irriguous" ending in T? And what is "irriguous"?'

But Anthony was wondering what Young Tom's feelings would be were he to know that an American occupied his room, tenanted his bed, and treated his home as home.

And knew the answer. It was told in those two faces on either side of the hearth, beautiful only as can be the faces of serene old age in sight of immortality. It was told in the nightly thanksgiving — that so soon followed — for him who waited so short a distance off, so short a time away; told in the nightly prayer for divine compassion upon our enemies and that their hearts might be turned . . . 'O blessed Lord, who in Thy bitter pains didst intercede with the Father for Thine enemies who crucified Thee — '; told in the quick upward smile that thanked him as he bent to help Young Tom's mother to her feet.

That night before undressing, he stood for a long time in front of the portrait above his fireplace — so brave in its youth and scarlet coat and gold-laced three-cornered hat worn a little to one side, so paradoxical in the smile in the blue eyes and the gravity of the lips.

He had the feeling that, though his mind seemed full of superficial thoughts, in reality it was the medium through which the dead were communing together on matters of great moment — Ensign Almond, of the 55th Foot Regiment of his Britannic Majesty's forces, and Anthony and Richard Purvis, of High Pale, Virginia, in the United States of America. The younger Anthony was as aware of their talk as if they spoke with one another in an adjoining room, the door of which was sufficiently ajar for him to hear the murmur of their voices without hearing what was said.

He undressed before the fire. Standing naked for an instant on the patchwork rug, viewing the maimed ugliness of his shattered arm, he

suddenly realized the burden and the pattern of the speech of the dead
. . . This house was the House of Armistice.

He wondered what his grandmother would have thought about it —
she who had imagined as grisly phantoms what were but quiet and
friendly ghosts: whose dictated letters even now caused Staff-Surgeon
Strang to raise a dim eyebrow and ejaculate an inaudible remonstrance
to the composer when he apologetically ran a censor's eye over the in-
coming mail.

It was because he knew the bond between this household in a Welsh
valley and the faintly remembered mansion in another continent, that
he began to think of High Pale as he had never done before — not the
High Pale that had been filled with the anger and the plotting of his
grandmother, but the High Pale of the apple-green library, and of . . .
Camelot.

Perhaps from the subconscious idea of perpetuating the link between
the two houses he found himself one afternoon mapping out and meditating on just such another city as his father had called into existence. From
that it was but a short stage to the purchase — in which Old Tom and his
wife took fascinated interest — of materials and tools. Cartridge paper
and pasteboard, glue and water-colours, brushes, knives, rules, protractors,
compasses, drawing-board, and a dozen other necessities. And scissors,
of course —

'No, Anthony, you cannot have my scissors! Cutting paper ruins the
edge! . . . Anthony dear, have you — just have you by *any* chance —
seen my embroidery scissors? I put them down on the work-table last
night. I know I did. I remember thinking as I did so, "Now is it safe
to leave them there for a minute or two?" And then I forgot all about
them. Of course I am not accusing anybody. But if the cap fits — !'

The growth of the enchanted town — and it grew apace although its
creator had but one hand — was watched with rapt attention by the
Almonds. At their suggestion, after its foundations (so to speak) had
been laid, the city lived in the drawing-room upon a Pembroke table
which was brought up to the circle of the fireside at night so that they
might keep in touch with all developments.

The acrostics suffered.

'"A not unusual journey for the feeblest",' would repeat Mrs. Almond
after Old Tom, with every appearance of concentration. 'Now I wonder . . . Anthony, who is going to live in that little house you are
making? I'm sure the roof is going to be too steep even for an attic!'

'That's just a fairy house where they never use the attics. Except to hang up the conical hats of the witches they've shot. From the central beam!'

'Ah!' with a satisfied nod of the head.

— Had someone watched with similar interest the rise of Camelot; questioned about the inhabitants of inch-and-a-half-high houses, and the names of winding alleys; and listened eagerly to all its dream history?

Twenty years ago, was it, that he had kneeled before Camelot, and ridden through its barbican on a grey charger, those only friends — what were their names? — on his right and left? All gallant in cloth-of-gold and silver and in blue . . . His mind went back to the impalpable tapestry of dreams that wove itself about the city, and to the child that was taken into its fabric even as Graelent or Ogier in olden legend had been drawn from mortal view into the other-world realm of their ladies.

There had been three fairy princesses who had dwelt under the crowded peaked roofs of the great castle of Camelot . . . There were none in this new city! . . .

And so, even as the other Anthony before him, he would lose himself in an enchantment of his own creating: and within the remote life of the house in Dark Wharf Gate lead a life that was yet more remote from reality. Remote from a world where threadbare prisoners ate out their desperate hearts in exile; where all Europe was a battlefield; where twenty years of war had but made grimmer the determination of a hungry Britain to endure to the end; where, as aconite and snowdrop sprang up on the lawns of spring, so rose new armies on the Continent to replace those whom the Tyrant had abandoned on the frozen steppes of Holy Russia.

His books, his writing, his enchanted city, the newspapers, the society of the Almonds, a little stately visiting in their company, and a morning walk that made the circuit of the area of his freedom: with these his time was fully occupied.

That morning walk was no mere promenade: the distance seemed greater than he would have thought it possible, keeping within parole limits.

Staff-Surgeon Strang explained the mystery one evening when he came in to make up a four at whist; very tightly buttoned up in his blue coat, his froth of white hair looking as if he had had a wig made of thistle-down.

'The Five of Hearts, did you ask for, partner?' said he, being dummy. 'Oh! *Magnificent!* . . . No, Captain Purvis, of course I know nothing officially, but I believe that the milestone at the Black Ox is one mile seven furlongs and six chains distant from the confines of the town by surveyor's measurement! Which is very odd! . . . The small trump, partner? Certainly! . . . And the notice at the old bridge at Bont-y-diafol is at least a mile and a half! You see there is some very good fishing in the pool by the bridge . . . Well played, partner! . . . A strict mile on the road past the Abbey is just before you get to Lord Morfa's south lodge, leaving the house well outside . . . The Queen? Certainly! . . . One day when I took my airing that way I found that overnight milestone and notice had removed themselves by the length of the park as far as the corner by the dairy farm!'

'That was done by Lord Morfa's men a month or so ago, on his lordship's special instructions,' said Old Tom reckoning up the tricks. 'I hear, by the way, that he and my Lady will be returning to Morfa shortly.'

'I know nothing about it,' said Mr. Strang. 'And it is nothing to do with me. All my instructions say, is that the parole limits of a prisoner of war shall be the first milestone beyond the confines of a town. I am not responsible if the milestones weigh anchor and set sail for ports several furlongs off. If you ask me — Who is responsible for the milestones? I shall say that I don't know where they are made, where they come from, or who says where they shall be. And I *don't* know!'

Neither did Old Tom or Mrs. Almond. Certainly Anthony did not.

Mr. Strang dealt the cards, carefully avoiding the glasses of mulled claret, and the plates of sandwiches which trespassed upon the red baize top of the card-table before the fire.

'The other milestones were moved by the townspeople themselves long before I came. There was much good feeling and sympathy shown to the prisoners in those days. I think you'll find the same thing in many of the parole towns. Now — ' He shook his head, presumably over a change of feeling; misdealt; apologized; covered his confusion in an appreciative draught of the claret.

'Nobody has bothered to shift them back,' said Old Tom. 'Probably — isn't that a misdeal, Mr. Strang? — probably they'll remain where they are long after your time and mine!' . . .

At Morfa Abbey and another home in the hills some twenty miles away there was much consultation whether or no the time was yet ripe.

'Yes!' said Garland.

'Yes!' said Morfa.

But Harradence was not so sure.

CHAPTER IV

'TURNIPS AND HARLOTS . . .'

SPRING was on the road. From his writing-table he looked out, over the steep slope of the garden and the wet roofs of the Sloop Inn beyond, to a silver-shining lake where the swollen river lapped the foot of hills wooded with bare black trees.

In the sunlight of the early morning the shadow of the house rested across one corner of the bright lawn. And the shadow with its delicate outline of gable and chimney was of no luminous black, but of white: for coincident with it, and vanishing with it as the sun rose higher, lay the thick hoar frost of the night. About the base of the apple trees at the far end grew golden and bright green aconites — small flowers as shining and prim as if they had been heraldic ornaments on the shield of the earth.

Spring! His seventh spring as a prisoner!

A furious desire burned in him to pass that silver water to its woodland coast, and cross the rim of the horizon of hills, walking into some enchanted land rich in the smell of running water, of wet shining trees, of dead leaves and of the brown earth.

But on church door, on pillar of colonnaded market-house, on the great gate of the Four Swans yard, on blank walls about the town everywhere was placarded that ominous reminder of the parole promise —

> . . . And if they shall exceed such limits or go into any field or cross-road they may be taken up and sent to prison, and a reward of Ten Shillings will be paid by the Agent for apprehending them.

The urge within him for freedom became almost uncontrollable; and, since his only barrier was honour, he began to hold himself yet more secluded behind the walls of the house in Dark Wharf Gate. Once, indeed, he even found himself theorizing — but only theorizing — on the question of withdrawing his parole so that he might be kept clear of temptation in Dartmoor, or Perth, or Norman Cross where he might honourably do all he could to escape.

He said something to this effect one morning to Staff-Surgeon Strang in his little dim parlour when he went to collect mail.

'Don't think of it!' said the little man in a horrified tone, putting on a pair of very misty spectacles to examine the pile of prisoners' correspondence that lay before him. 'The chances of a break-out are practically nil from any of the modern camps. Of getting away afterwards about the same. I'm talking as a friend and not the Agent of the Transport Office. Hang on! It can't be for long now!'

'Why?'

'*He's* come to the end of his tether. He's breaking! The war will be over inside a twelvemonth.'

'*He* won't break!' said Anthony with firm conviction.

'Perhaps I shouldn't have said "*He*",' said Mr. Strang rather apologetically, opening a cover in which there was an enclosure, and doffing his glasses in order to polish them before investigating. 'The weakest part of a chain is its weakest link. *He's* got a lot of weak links. All the vassal states, in fact. Holland — Westphalia — the Rhineland — Italy. Just waiting to turn on him. As the Russian threat grows and the menace of the British thrust from the south becomes nearer, so are cracks beginning to show even in France itself. I'm not saying this because I wish it to be so; I'm not saying this because I'm English and you're the enemy; but because I know — and everybody with sound judgment must know — that it is so.

'Wait and see — don't do anything rash! That's my advice to you. It is only a question of months.'

He pushed over a letter which had arrived by devious routes from one-eyed Mr. Mason of Marseilles, retaining however the enclosure, a draft on Coutts for four thousand francs, which he turned so that Anthony could see the amount.

'In accordance with regulations, as you know well, I must deal with this. I am afraid that the exchange rate is going still further against you, so that the sooner I get it cashed the better.'

Anthony nodded indifferently.

'And when I've done that and read the roll-call at this morning's muster, I shall have made my last official appearance as Prisoners' Agent in this town! And glad I shall be of it.'

'That's bad news, sir,' said Anthony shocked, for he had come to like the little man. 'Why?'

Mr. Strang rose to his feet. He flicked an imaginary speck of dust off one of the many dim pictures of ships with which the dim crowded parlour was decorated.

'When I accepted the office,' he said rather diffidently, 'I did so only because I thought I might do something to make things easier for the prisoners — always keeping within the letter of the law, of course! . A sort of fellow-feeling, you know! . . . I was a prisoner of war, myself, many, many years ago! During the war in America — the last war!

Your people kept me for a time with a herd of Loyalists and other suspects down the shaft of a copper mine!'

'Good God!'

'At Simsbury, in Connecticut! It was very dreadful: I have nightmares about it even now, after all these years. I doubt whether our prison hulks are anything like as bad! . . . Well, at first I got on pretty well here. In fact until the last few months there has always been quite good feeling between the prisoners and the townspeople. But now things have changed. It is the same in many other parole towns, I am told.'

'In what way have they changed?' asked Anthony.

'Quite suddenly there's been a sort of flare-up of mutual dislike. Our people seeing long-desired victory in the offing — the victory for which we have waited twenty years; your people very naturally resenting it! I'm being frank, you see! Then there's been all this talk of a general rising of prisoners. There are quite a lot of old ladies — and others — who don't sleep easily in their beds of nights because of it!'

'It's the first time I have heard of it since I have been a prisoner,' said Anthony truthfully, his mind going back to Silas and Deane and the organizers of mutiny whom he was to have interviewed.

'I don't suppose *you* know anything,' said Mr. Strang sitting down again and turning the draft over and over between his fingers. 'But there are others in town who do. And as there's no smoke without fire I don't mind saying that the Transport Office are very interested in a pedlar who visited Morfa in the autumn — and every other parole town and prison camp in the south and west — and afterwards vanished into thin air. Real name — Louis Vanhille! Believed to have sailed for Jamaica.'

He shot a sudden glance over the top of his glasses at Anthony, but it was obvious that the name conveyed nothing.

'And as the war wears on, and the cost of everything goes up and up, and taxes get heavier, and liberties get fewer, and atrocity stories get more and more livid, so you find hatred of the enemy growing! — I'm not being personal, my dear fellow. — There's a fine flourishing hate for Boney and the French even here in Wales. It grows every day. It vents itself in all sorts of ways. In the last month for instance pot-house loungers and the like have arrested seven prisoners for being without doors after curfew. And two for exceeding the bounds. A year ago nobody would have bothered. Then, too, all the local bastards are being sworn on them! Seven in the last three months, and I'll swear that five are put-up jobs!'

'And the other two?'

'In one case the girl has gone on the parish. So the authorities have thrown young Fortuna into the town gaol until he pays up. And he can't!'

'How much do they want?'

'Twenty-five pounds. Most of it will vanish on a jollification for the parish officers — "saddling the spit" they call it. Parish bastards don't live long — in Wales, or anywhere else for that matter!'

'Fortuna any good, or just the ordinary ne'er-do-well? . . . In that case I'll pay . . . And what's the other case?'

'A bad one. An ugly one, if all that they say is true. Commandant de Lisle is involved, and the girl is the daughter of the master of the charity school — a pretty little creature, nothing more than a child! There'll be trouble, for the father is a dangerous man — a violent and furious man!'

Anthony knew de Lisle slightly. A lean dark fellow with much shabby elegance of manner, who scraped together a pittance by teaching French and Italian at a seminary for young ladies in one of the prim old houses backing on the river near St. Teilo's Gate. He was for ever boasting of his conquests.

Staff-Surgeon Strang shook his silver thistledown over the situation.

'Since Christmas there has been a perfect epidemic of parole-breaking everywhere. Three from here, as you know. In the last twelvemonth one out of every nine parole-prisoners in the country has broken his pledge. Hundreds of parole-breakers, and two out of every three get clear away! It's a bad business, and now the Transport Office are going to tighten things up. New regulations! New restrictions! Transfer of prisoners to different areas! It's the wrong way to go about it to my mind, so I have thrown my hand in. The new man can deal with the situation. I am well out of it . . . Come in to-morrow morning and drink a glass or two of Madeira to celebrate my freedom. Bring Old Tom!' . . .

It was the very next night that Colonel Millet cut his throat with a razor, apparently standing in front of the small square of glass that had served him for shaving mirror. For four years past he had had no letter from home. The coroner's jury found a verdict of 'Suicide', and in accordance with the law his body, wrapped in a coarse shroud, was buried without ceremony by torchlight at the cross-roads on the Carmarthen turnpike, and a stake driven through it. None of his companions in exile could follow the farm-cart that took him to the grave, because the curfew had already sounded when the grim procession set out from the alehouse stable where he had lain.

A few days later a couple of young naval officers in the Junior Mess procured civilian outfits through two sisters who ran Morfa's most select milliner's and bonnet shop: broke parole, and disappeared with their lady-loves.

When Anthony passed by on his constitutional the morning after the news had become known, there was not one single pane of glass left in the bow window wherein the Misses Thomas had been wont to display their dainty things for admiration. Nor any of the usual contents except a notice that worn-out umbrellas could be made up into gipsy bonnets. The shattered shop door swung open on its hinges, and a ravaged garment of some sort lay on the topmost of the three steps up.

He remembered the girls, two pretty young creatures with golden skin and dark hair which had golden lights.

He was turning away when an old woman materialized directly before him, as though she were indeed the witch that she looked. An old woman with a small white flannel shawl folded over her shoulders and the high beaver hat of the country-folk pulled down over her hooked nose. She addressed him furiously in Welsh, striking with her stick on the flags of the pavement as she spoke.

'— — —,' said the old woman.

'I beg your pardon?' said Anthony.

'— — —,' continued the old woman.

Anthony made to go on, but the shrill voice had already attracted attention although it was a quiet enough side-street. Two or three children had arrived from nowhere in particular, and a cadaverous-looking man in a rusty black suit and puddingy white neck-cloth and round hat was also conjured up out of space.

Rusty-Black put out a detaining hand.

'You do not unterstand, prother?' he said. 'I will tell you what she says. *Derdyshefoni,* but she iss eloquent! . . . She says that that and worse shall be the fate off all harlots! That it iss to you and your like that all thiss harlotry and whoring iss due.'

'I have had nothing to do with *any* harlots,' said Anthony in a fury. 'Let me pass! . . . And I should dislike having anything to do with Welsh harlots more than any others!'

At that moment the bells of St. Teilo began to chime out over the town, a thin sweet jangle of song. It seemed to change the tenor of the old woman's thoughts, for she turned in the direction of the unseen belfry and spoke with such astonishing vehemence, stabbing at the pavement with her stick the while, that Anthony paused almost against his will seeking explanation.

Whatever it was she said was punctuated by a constant repetition of one phrase — 'Erfin, cawl erfin!' And every time she repeated it, the growing crowd of children took up an infernal chorus —

'Erfin, cawl erfin!'

Rusty-Black obliged once more.

'She says that once upon a time the pells sang of peace and plenty. Put now these many years, thanks to you and your like, and to the Man of Plood, your emperor, all their message to the poor has peen — Erfin, cawl erfin! . . .'

'Erfin, cawl erfin!' cried the chorus of children.

'And that means chust "Turnips, and turnip proth!" Yess-yess inteet, fair play to her, things iss fery bad for the poor! Fery bad! Turnips and harlotry! Turnips and harlotry! That's what you've brought us to, Misster Ploody Prisoner!'

'Christ!' said Anthony, and pushed his way past, pursued by shouts from the children.

As he continued his walk out of the town a tinkling song of childhood recurred to his mind; and he beat out new words to it, and found himself walking in time to the beat of the tune —

> 'Turnips and harlots
> Say the bells of St. Charlotte's . . .'

Arrived at the door of the Black Ox Inn, opposite the 'Limite' notice, he turned and looked back at the town, nearly two miles away. In the distance, and under the rain-washed blue of the sky, the wet shining roofs and white and grey walls lying between the silver curve of the river and the steep wooded bluff that hid Morfa Abbey, seemed those of some other city than the Welsh market town that was his prison.

On the way he had passed a little copse of twisted trees sunken in a shallow hollow beside the road. Their boughs were thick with lichen like a goblin leafage, and from every bough depended clusters of berries of mist-drops as clear as glass. At the edge of the hollow there had been a clump of pussy willow with the buds shining on bare twigs like moonstones.

He did not want to go back to that town where they drove posts through the stomachs of dead men and broke the windows of peccant ladies: he wanted to go down to the hollow and plunge through the thicket into the fairyland that lay beyond. He wanted to tear off the mockery of the uniform he must wear, and fare unidentifiable out into a world in which adventure should be compounded of both reality and fantasy: to find hours of excitement in the spectacle of running water, in the silences of a wood, in the journeyings of little winds under a rising moon.

He speculated about a sullen groom with the face of a bruiser, who was holding a knot of horses at the door, as he entered the dark flagged parlour of the inn.

There were tankards and hats and riding-crops on the scrubbed table, and before the open hearth were three gentlemen. Two of them faced the third, who stood straddle-legged with his hands behind his back, surveying the room with a lofty air of indifference. It was Count Pagan, superb in a violet-coloured coat with pale green lining — as shown by his parted coat-tails.

At first sight of him Anthony made a movement of retreat: changed his mind: advanced to the table, and, without sign of recognition, tapped a summons to the girl somewhere behind the sash-window of the bar.

The years seemed to have made no difference to the count. He stood there tall and slim, apparently dowered with the eternal and fantastic beauty of a faun. In the obscurity at any rate no grey showed in his black wavy hair. He said nothing, gave no sign that he had ever seen Anthony before, unless by the contraction of his eyebrows — those queer eyebrows that slanted upward at their outer edges.

One of his companions, however, swung about — a large young man in a red coat, with a jewelled brooch in the folds of his neckerchief, clutter of seals at his fob, and a diamond ring upon his finger. A young man with a twisted nose in a dark damp face, and hot dark eyes.

'God-dam-me!' said Damp-Face. 'Another of these bloody foreigners! The place is lousy with them! . . . Hi! Mounseer Frog, you can't stay here! This is a private room! *Ici privé,* you know!'

'Nonsense!' replied Anthony unpleasantly, and sat down in the window-seat.

'The Frog talks English!' said Damp-Face in high astonishment.

'And calls you a liar!' commented Count Pagan without emotion.

> ' "Turnips and harlots
> Say the bells of St. Charlotte's!" '

said Anthony to himself, paying no ostensible attention to the group by the fire. He continued making such poor rhymes while Damp-Face debated the situation with his soul.

> ' "Lechers and panders
> Say the bells of St. Andrew's!
>
> ' "Sharpers and — " '

Damp-Face had come down the room. He stood over Anthony — a large menace.

'Did you mean to imply that I am a liar?' he asked.

'Yes!' said Anthony, ignoring him, and looking across the room to an anxious face that had appeared at the window of the bar. 'Glennys, a tankard of "old"!'

The next instant he received a blow with the open hand on his cheek, so heavy that it sent him reeling against the window-frame. His hat fell to the floor and two pots of daffodils crashed from the ledge on to the seat.

He sprang to his feet, and stood confronting the other, almost breast to breast — green coat against scarlet coat. The girl behind the bar screamed.

But that unequal battle was never joined, for Count Pagan, without stirring from his place by the fire, suddenly addressed Damp-Face in a voice that was as chill and as languid as it had ever been.

'That was hardly gentlemanly, my dear George! Hardly gentlemanly! Now was it, my lord? I appeal to you!'

My lord, a little elderly man with the grey sad face of a sheep, registered disapproval of George, who withdrew a pace or so from Anthony with the sulky expression of a reprimanded schoolboy.

'There were several things you failed to take into account, George, if I may say so. That this gentleman has the misfortune to be one-armed. That you did not speak the truth. That he is not a Frenchman. That he is a prisoner of war and cannot therefore avenge an insult in the usual manner. And finally, that he happens to be an acquaintance of mine — of very long standing . . . I am of opinion that George should apologize, my lord. Do you concur?'

My lord, who looked as if he would always concur with the last speaker, obliged on this occasion.

George, thus brow-beaten, mumbled something, and retired to the sash-window to embark upon conversation with the daughter of the house.

'Well, well, Anthony! This *is* a surprise meeting!' remarked Pagan, still without making any movement or gesture. 'And how are we, after all these years? Enjoying life away from the war? I never fancied you as a soldier, you know!'

Anthony put his hat back on the window-seat in a deliberate manner; sauntered to the fireplace — to the manifest ill-ease of my lord — before replying. With his one hand he put his tankard of ale among the pewter dishes and bright brass candlesticks upon the mantelshelf.

'The meeting, so far as I am concerned, is entirely unwelcome,' he said at length. 'I had hoped never to see or hear of you again' — he paused, glancing at my lord's face which wore an expression of as acute intrigue as any grey sad sheep could be expected to muster up — 'until the moment I was free to meet you for a final settlement!'

'Tut-tut!' remarked Count Pagan easily, and turning a little to regard him. 'Really you ought to be ready to bury the hatchet after all these years! You seem to hoard up your — er — dislikes like your grandmother! A family trait, I suppose!'

'You have — er — pwivate things to talk of, my de-ah fellah,' bleated my lord, shifting uneasily from one neat boot to the other. 'I'll go and stwetch my legs for a bit, I think. Stwetch my legs for a bit. And take George with me — if I can get him away fwom the gal. Away fwom the gal.'

And he shambled in knock-kneed style — such beautiful breeches and perfect boots on miserable limbs — to the door, gathering up the sullen George with him.

'Shut your window, Beautiful!' said Count Pagan to the anticipatory Glennys, barely raising his voice, 'And go about your business! If anything interesting happens you shall know in good time!'

'Should I address you as Uncle?' questioned Anthony, propped against the chimney-breast, and examining dispassionately the slim straight figure of the man beside him — the man who had occupied his wife's bed. 'Or does one's wife's lover have a courtesy rank and status? Is he, so to speak, something in the nature of a brother-in-law? I should like to be accurate.'

Count Pagan did not alter his posture: still stared down the room indifferently, hands behind back, rising on his toes and then dropping on his heels in an easy rhythmical fashion.

'Still harping on that incident?' he remarked in a tone of gentle regret. 'It was really very remiss of Jasmine and myself. But habit makes one careless, you know; and we could hardly imagine that your lamented young friend would bribe the servants and burst in upon our slumber.' He shook his head. 'I deprecate, on the other hand, your rather selfish attitude in regard to Jasmine. If I could share her with you, I fail to see why you could not share her with me. Turn and turn about — I don't mean three in a bed, of course! . . . I don't think I should have let her marry you if it hadn't been that I was astonishingly short of money at the time, and quite incapable of supporting her!'

'I've got to thank you, then, for your generosity in letting me share your niece's embraces!'

'Step-daughter — of a sort!' corrected Pagan. 'I may as well let you into the secret of our relationship! She is the attractive pledge of a previous affection left on my hands by a little mistress who died of cholera in Smyrna. Adultery, but no incest! Not,' he reflected, 'that that would have hindered either Jasmine or myself! Still, it might have been awkward to have had a son who was also one's great-nephew, or grandson, or something such . . . I am sorry, by the way, that the affair ended so disastrously for your friend.'

'I reciprocate your sentiments,' said Anthony.

'You would hardly believe it possible that he should have tried to make me fight then and there! In my night-shirt! With swords: in a bedroom: without seconds! . . . He lacked *savoir-faire* and tact, did that young man: still, he was very young — '

' "*De mortuis* — " in fact!' suggested Anthony.

' "*De mortuis* — " ' agreed Count Pagan not unhandsomely. 'But I felt then — and I still feel — that if the young man had been at all reasonable I could have explained things to everybody's satisfaction. I mean, of course, everybody with common sense and some understanding of life . . . Now the business of consoling Jasmine — '

'Consoling?'

'Apart from your long absences, you *must* realize that Jasmine found marriage with you a trifle — what shall I say? — spiritual, perhaps! I provided the materialism. She was used to it. She found herself placed upon a pedestal when she wanted to be thrown upon a bed. I provided the latter ritual. You see, she began what I might call the fuller life rather early. At thirteen, to be exact. The oriental blood in her, I presume . . . She also had the notion, rightly or wrongly, that while professing the completest devotion to her, you had from the first the figure of some other lady ever present in your mind! I provided the consolation! Or shall we say some of it!'

'Ah!' said Anthony.

Had it been even then, so soon, that he had regretted Garland who had betrayed him in another way?

'And — a very small thing! — she found that a man with one arm and a stump cannot enfold with such ardour as a man with a full equipment of limbs. It was a disappointment to the girl!'

'Too, too bad!' said Anthony, more humiliated than he would have cared to admit to anyone.

'Yes,' concurred Count Pagan, still tittupping up and down. 'I should have explained all these things to you if it had been possible. Each one of them so thoroughly understandable when explained reasonably. But the young man had the Slav temperament very highly developed, and you were beyond reach . . . Hence the tragedy! And afterwards nothing except communications from your agent—not a very sympathetic person!'

Anthony drank off a long draught of ale, and set the tankard down on the mantelshelf with an air of finality. He did not propose to stay any longer; but before departure his curiosity made him ask—

'I wonder what your purpose was in seeking me out? . . . It can't have been for the pleasure of giving me a five-year-old explanation. Nor, in view of past events, could you have had any financial transaction on behalf of Jasmine in view!'

Said Count Pagan, turning to him as though with the belated idea of refreshing his memory as to his appearance before he departed—

'Seek you out! . . . I can assure you, Anthony, quite solemnly, that you are the last person I had any desire to meet, or the expectation of meeting! . . . Perhaps I ought to tell you—in case you were meditating a cheap revenge—that the British Government and I have kissed and made friends!'

'Charming!'

'My family and I decided to forgive one another. From that—for my people have a good deal of political influence—it was only a short step to the Government and myself also forgiving one another. To mark the era of forgiveness I resumed my family name of Dunscore, and the Horse Guards gave me a colonelcy in the Staff Corps! . . . I have already been very useful!'

'I am sure you have,' agreed Anthony. 'And how do you explain Jasmine in the circles in which you now move?'

'Orphaned niece of a dead wife! Very simple! A pleasing parallel to those Harradence connections of yours at La Cadière! . . . The woman, I remember as a good-looking creature! I wonder, incidentally, if the parallel goes any further?'

With a thoughtful air Anthony took down the tankard and looked inside. There was, perhaps, a wineglass of dark brown liquid awash at the bottom of the pewter. It was quite enough! In the most detached manner, with a quick flick of the wrist, he jerked the contents into the face that was bent toward him over a violet-coloured shoulder. Sighed out loud in so doing as though from supreme pleasure.

The beer, travelling as a solid rather than a fluid, struck—audibly struck!—Pagan-Dunscore between the eyes; splashed onto the upsweep of dark locks; spattered celestial perfection of raiment.

Anthony never knew why he laughed. Whether at the amazement in the other's expression as he realized what was about to happen; at the absurd temporary confusion of blindness that followed; or from sardonic amusement that he should thus avenge insult to people who had done him so great a harm.

In the ensuing moments the other recalled — by great effort at control — that he dare not risk his newly-recovered reputation by a brawl with a prisoner of war; least of all, in view of what he planned, with Anthony Purvis.

When he restored his wet handkerchief to his pocket, he had wiped not merely beer from off his face, but all trace of expression. He said not a word.

Anthony collected his hat; donned it. The bells of St. Teilo's started once more, and their distant music sounded clearly through the half-open casement, as he swung round again on the motionless count for a final word. Through his mind continued the jingle —

> 'Beware of the Pagans,
> Say the bells of St. Fagan's!
>
> 'Beware of the bitch,
> Say the bells of Shoreditch!'

He remarked —

'I can't fight you now, as you know, but I should like you to realize that when I am a free man I shall most certainly kill you. Not on Jasmine's account, of course. But on Victor Radomski's! . . . Good-bye!'

'Saundersfoot has just remembered something he'd forgotten, so the old fathead has gone baa-baaing away!' said Damp-Face to Pagan-Dunscore when the latter emerged a little later from the inn.

The elder man mounted his horse thoughtfully. It was not until the two of them had turned into a steep lane leading from the direction of the town, that he spoke — the sullen groom riding behind well out of earshot. Then he said —

'Do you know who that was?'

'Who who was?'

'The fellow at the inn to whom you were quite unnecessarily offensive. . . . You will have to do something about that manner of yours, George, or you will land yourself in serious trouble one of these days. You nearly created an awkward situation for both of us to-day! In fact you may have done so.'

'How was I to know that he was a friend of yours?' grumbled George, alternately spurring and reining in his unfortunate horse until the creature danced in anger.

'He is your cousin!'

George ceased making his beast gyrate. Consternation was printed on his somewhat sinister face.

'The fellow Jasmine divorced in Paris? . . . Uncle Anthony's bastard?'

'The fellow Jasmine divorced in Paris! Your Uncle Anthony's alleged son!'

'Bloody bastard! Bloody, bloody bastard!'

'That is what we hope to prove.'

'Mother always said that Uncle Anthony could never have had a child — was no use to the girls, you know!'

'You don't need to recapitulate everything we have discussed, George. We come here to get evidence out of Morfa about the original Anthony's death, and, lo and behold! we find the younger Anthony flourishing as a prisoner of war almost under his roof! There's something more than a coincidence about it. I don't like it at all!'

'Pity I didn't scrag him before you called me off! . . . What Jasmine ever saw in him — ' said George viciously, making his horse wince again.

'It is also very unfortunate that we should have run into him like this. Yet if we had stayed in the town, instead of with Saundersfoot, he would have been bound to have met me in the streets! He would certainly have suspected something if he had seen me about every day. The sooner Morfa reappears the better!'

'Pity I didn't scrag him!' said George.

Dunscore got off his horse, and, with the reins over his arm, stood in a gateway at a bend in the lane, admiring the valley below, spread all green and silver in the sunshine.

'Pretty, pretty place!' he said. 'Foul people! . . . George, I will have you understand that I am conducting this campaign! That there will only be violence when I say that there shall be! Prisoners of war on parole are peculiarly fragile creatures. They disappear, and people merely think that they have escaped back to France. They are shot or clubbed by patriotic Englishmen in the course of resisting arrest. They hide in queer places from pursuit, like drains, and get suffocated. Doing away with a parole prisoner is almost too easy. If we find that it is the only course, then we will do the job — but neatly, and as I plan it.'

'Pity — ' began George, surveying the scene without interest.

'You are a sullen, bad-tempered cub,' said Dunscore entirely without heat, without troubling to turn, but putting his elbows on the gate and admiring a whitewashed farm of many gables set against a copse on the further slope. 'What Jasmine sees in you I can't think — except she likes, perhaps, to have the kudos of having brought you to heel. Not a day has gone by since we left Hexgrave but that your ugly temper has caused us trouble of some sort. I suppose you inherit it from your grandmother!'

'Mother used to say —'

'I don't care a curse what your mother used to say. What I say is, you curb that temper of yours and do exactly what I tell you, and not one thing more. It's only because I took the trouble to find you out in your filthy Lincolnshire fens, and because of my knowledge and my staff work that you are being put in a position to claim the High Pale estate as your mother's son. I stand to take a third for my trouble — all written, signed and sealed! — and I am not going to lose it! Jasmine still respects her uncle — fortunately. She will do as I tell her — even if it comes to a question of marrying you or not, as you well know. I have also got a lot of rather peculiar paper of yours! Your problem is an easy one . . . Well?'

'You are making a lot of fuss about very little,' said George, slashing his boot with his crop.

'Very little? You bloody fool! Anthony is the sort of conscientious devil who would give up everything if he were persuaded that he had no right to it — if he believed that he had no moral or legal claim, and that his Aunt Octavia's son had. Do you think you have encouraged him in such an attitude by your gratuitous insolence, you damned hobble-dehoy?' Here, Dunscore turned on his companion a face of such frosty anger that the other instinctively backed away. 'If — if — it becomes necessary to remove him as an obstacle to an easy settlement of the question of the High Pale inheritance, do you think you have improved affairs by being seen by people — Saundersfoot, the girl in the bar — in a violent quarrel with him? Get on your horse, you poor imbecile, and see if you can ride back without getting any more blood on your spurs!'

CHAPTER V

THE BATTLE OF MORFA

FOR a few days after the encounter Anthony speculated at some length on the probable reasons for Pagan-Dunscore's appearance, and then, seeing no more of him, let the subject slip from his mind.

In the town things went from bad to worse. The new Prisoners' Agent did nothing to ease the situation: he was the local maltster, a hairy-faced and hairy-handed little man, whose sympathies lay where his business interests were — in the town. From his dusty little office at the maltings by the wharf there poured forth ukase and fiat after ukase and fiat, depriving prisoners of long-established small privileges, imposing new restrictions, warning and threatening.

The schoolmaster's little daughter died in giving birth to a still-born child: the town said she had been murdered.

The junior officers celebrated an entirely erroneous rumour of a new and startling victory in Saxony by Marshal Davout, within the privacy of their mess-room: the town said that they had drunk toasts to the perdition of Britain, the destruction of Wellington, and the damnation of the Royal Family.

There had been an epidemic of forgery, chiefly at the expense of the Carmarthenshire Bank: the town said that the aliens were responsible, and cited in support of the theory the undoubted fact that in the previous year no fewer than four French prisoners of war had been hanged in the West Country for forging bank-notes while in confinement; to say nothing of seven more charged with committing the same offence whilst imprisoned in Edinburgh Castle.

Anthony and old Mrs. Almond walked in the garden after breakfast, down the gravelled path that divided the oblong of the lawn, to the tiny orchard whose black bareness was now lighted by the thrusting buds of early spring.

'There never were such apples, that's what Tom — Young Tom — used to say,' said Mrs. Almond, pausing for a moment's inspection before they turned. 'Almost the very last letter I ever had from him said he'ld give all the luxuries in the world for just one apple from Jericho. That's the name he gave to the orchard and the high wall of the Sloop . . . Do you have apples in America, Anthony?'

Yes. They had apples in America.

'But I don't suppose they can be like ours. I'm sure, my dear, they must be very good — but just not *quite* the same. If you had ever tasted one of ours, I'm sure you would agree. I dare say, too, yours are very big apples. You see you are a very big country, so you have all your things in proportion. And we are only a little country, so we have to make up for lack of size by extra goodness.'

Anthony thought it possible.

'Tom — Young Tom — always loved apples better than anything else. I remember when he was very little — not two, because he could only just walk — that he got out into the garden by himself, and found a windfall, and ate it up, core and stalk and all. Every bit! And what a mess he made of himself!'

They had started to walk back to the house, up the steep slope of the path. She stopped and looked back now, her old face wrinkled with a smile as if she saw again that child of long ago marauding beneath the laden boughs of the apple trees.

'Every tree is different,' said Mrs. Almond, 'but Tom — Young Tom — used to say that he could tell from which tree an apple came by the touch and smell of it, even if he were blindfolded. And I believe he could!'

Anthony's mind went back to Harradence.

'I knew a man once who believed, too, that apples were the best and only fruit in the world. He even had theories about the number of pips that apples should have!'

Mrs. Almond's quick sideways glance at him was unobserved.

'He never ate an apple — *never* — without saying, "An apple a day keeps the apothecary away!" And he invariably counted the pips! If there were fewer than eight he would shake his head very gravely as though doubting if the dose had been full strength! A really perfect apple must have ten pips, said he!'

'A very sensible man, my dear! Was he an American?'

'An Englishman, ma'am. His name was Harradence. It's odd, but I now remember him speaking of Morfa. It must have been Morfa, because he spoke of the fishers using coracles, and showed me how they were made!'

As he mentioned the trivialities, it came to him with a sudden shock that he had forgiven Harradence — that he thought of him now as he remembered him in the old days, mentor, companion, protector, friend: that at some time during the years in which he had deliberately kept the big man out of his thoughts, the anger and the hurt had died away.

Mrs. Almond was spared the need of reply by the sudden appearance of Staff-Surgeon Strang in the French window of the study, and his emergence into the garden.

The little man carried his hat in his hand, and his fluffy white hair was blown about by the spring winds. He was buttoned very tightly into a short blue top-coat which was very close-fitting to the waist, and thereafter stuck out all around rather like a ballet skirt.

'Thank heavens, I am in time,' exclaimed Mr. Strang projecting himself into the garden. 'Good morning, Mrs. Almond! Good morning, ma'am! Good morning, Captain Purvis! I was afraid that you might have left before I got here. I told Sukey to stand at the window and make sure you didn't pass before I was ready.'

'I shall have to go in a couple of minutes,' said Anthony, looking at his watch. 'I've never yet been half a minute late for muster.'

'I knew I couldn't persuade you not to go,' said Mr. Strang, capturing truant locks and triumphantly imprisoning them under his white beaver hat, 'so the only thing to do was to go with you!'

'Go with me?' echoed Anthony in some astonishment.

'I sent down to Griffiths-the-Maltings as soon as I heard, and tried to persuade him to postpone the muster till to-morrow. But the man is as pig-headed as you make them. He won't budge an inch. So the only thing to do is for me to come too! I flatter myself that I have a certain amount of influence with the prisoners and with the townsfolk! I think we had better be going!'

'Dear! Dear!' exclaimed Mrs. Almond looking anxiously from one face to the other. 'What can be the matter? Must you go, Anthony? Do keep him out of trouble, Mr. Strang! This dreadful war!'

'If I don't go now I shall be late, and that would never do,' said Anthony. He took her mittened hand in his, and kissed it affectionately.

They fared forth together up the steep slant of Dark Wharf Gate, Mr. Strang discussing the early events of the day rather like a little dim doctor narrating obscure symptoms in a recalcitrant patient. Anthony gathered that the day — and a mart day at that — had begun extremely evilly. Children from the charity school had amused themselves by stoning, from a discreet distance, prisoners making their way to the Junior Mess in the builders' yard off Market Street. One of the brats had been caught by a young Frenchman and soundly and deservedly cuffed. In return the Frenchman had been mobbed by market-women and narrowly escaped a nasty mauling.

Then Doisy and Van Dam van Polanen, the Dutchman, were insulted by a couple of drunken cattle-drovers — 'On mart day they're usually lushed overnight!' The prisoners, a couple of stalwart young men, had remonstrated, and finally had retaliated. In the scuffle one of the assailants had had his head broken, and the other lost a few teeth. Their companions were vowing vengeance — 'And they're a rough, dangerous lot, if you like, Captain Purvis!'

Its accustomed peace, however, was still brooding over Castle Place, which was a very miniature square, having a dozen little shops in it as well as the inn and a doctor's house of red brick with brass plate on its green front door.

Pigeons strutted on the cobbles round the obelisk in the centre commemorating the Protestant martyrs who had been burned there in the days of Bloody Mary. Old Hughes the saddler was pottering about outside his shop with an armful of head-stalls and whip-lashes. The beadle in his gold-laced three-cornered hat and full-skirted coat — stippled with the stains of forty years of careless beer-drinking — leaned, picking his teeth negligently, against the nail-studded door of the town gaol — to which the gatehouse, last vestige of the ancient castle, had been degraded. Two or three of the charity schoolboys idled on the opposite pavement: they were dressed in hideous saffron-coloured livery, their tousled hair cut with a monkish tonsure for easier identification. Sunshine, in which diamond-paned and bow-fronted shop-window sparkled: clear, windy blue sky: a black kitten playing with a morsel of paper in the open doorway of the baker's: peace. The bizarre touch to the scene was in the variegated uniforms of the prisoners who were gathered in groups under the windows of the Four Swans coffee-room, and in the archway to the inn yard.

. . . On that very March day the patricide Emperor of Russia and the craven King of Prussia, alternately enemies and allies of Napoleon, wept in one another's arms in Breslau, and swore undying friendship, undying hostility to the Man in Grey . . .

'There doesn't seem much wrong here,' said Anthony.

'You never know with these Welsh!' replied Strang, walking across the square with Anthony. 'When the French landed in Cardigan Bay in '97 and promptly surrendered, it took us all we knew to prevent the local ladies from — well — er — emasculating them!'

He took his stand under the portico of the hotel where he promptly became the centre of a voluble knot of prisoners.

As the bells of St. Teilo chimed the hour, the men fell in, in two ragged lines before the hotel, and facing the memorial. Among them they wore every conceivable uniform of the Napoleonic armies — lancer, dragoon, hussar, cuirassier, gunner, infantryman; scarlet, blue, green, white; fringed with moth-eaten fur; edged with tarnished gold lace; helmets, shakos, schapskas, hats of all sorts; every kind of breeches; every kind of boot; a shabby medley of colour that was as variegated as a faded patchwork quilt.

Mr. Griffiths did not appear: he had the local discourtesy of unpunctuality very strongly developed.

Whilst he delayed Castle Place began to fill with spectators of the parade; more small charity schoolboys, climbing on the railings that surrounded the memorial; market-women in steeple-hats with their baskets; indeterminate hobbledehoys, and a steady drift of shaggy-looking men in riding-boots or gaiters, and coats almost to their heels, carrying the stout ash-plant sticks favoured by small farmer and cattle dealer.

'It's a poor muster!' said Anthony to his left-hand neighbour in the front rank, a little withered Gascon captain with a long grey moustache. 'Half of us can't be here. Where are the rest?'

'*Sacristi!* You may well ask! Those of our people who were mad enough to turn up at our Mess to-day have probably had to barricade themselves in. I could see a crowd outside the yard gates from the top of Market Street, on my way here!'

When Mr. Griffiths eventually arrived at the mouth of the narrow lane that led to the top of Dark Wharf Gate, there were knots of people everywhere about the square, eyeing the prisoners, discussing matters in high-pitched Welsh, edging all the time a little nearer to the double line of men drawn up outside the Four Swans.

Anthony did not like the look of them at all. Neither apparently did Mr. Strang, for, as Mr. Griffiths approached the parade, muster roll in hand, he came from out the hotel portico and minced across the cobbles to the Agent. It was impossible to hear what he said, but the other man shook his head — crowned by an astonishingly high black hat — at every period.

'The regulations must be observed, as you well know, Misster Strang,' he declared finally and loudly, unfurling the nominal roll, and advancing to within a few paces of the foremost rank. The beery-faced beadle, gilt-headed staff in hand, took up position behind him; assumed a portentous attitude.

Mr. Strang shrugged his shoulders: swept together his errant hair, and donned his hat anew: walked back to the entrance to the inn yard where he remained.

'Alagnon!' said Mr. Griffiths in a loud voice, reading the first name on the mustering list.

'Alagnon!' echoed beadle.

There was no answer to the double summons.

'Aversa!'

'Aversa!' bellowed the beadle, striking his staff on the cobbles in a most threatening manner.

Still no reply from the ranks before him.

'Bailly!'

'Bailly!!'

Nor apparently was the holder of that name present. But the crowd behind the Agent was beginning to thicken with new arrivals, to press inconveniently against the little man, to catcall.

'Barbazon!'

'*Ici!*'

The old Gascon next to Anthony stepped a pace out of the line, and,

according to formula, proceeded to fall in on the far side of the entrance
to the Four Swans yard. He passed between the ranks of his fellows and
the uneasy mob, very erect, head up, eyes front.

'Cock-a-doodle-doo!' said someone in the crowd.

There was an immediate outburst of farmyard noises and some horse-
laughter.

'Now, really, my good people, come, come!' said Mr. Griffiths, turning
on those nearest him remonstratively. 'Make room! Push back ⸱a bit
there!'

His voice failed to convey either command or appeal; was unheeded,
even when he repeated himself in Welsh.

'Jenkins, keep order! Keep order, my man!'

But the beadle had disappeared, three-cornered hat, gilt staff and all.

Mr. Griffiths gabbled on through the list. Not one man in two answered to his name. The others were presumably barricaded behind the
high doors of the builders' yard off Market Street.

'De Lisle!'

'Ici!'

Commandant de Lisle stepped out of the depleted ranks, and started
to walk toward the new assembly point.

At the calling of his name, at his appearance, a most appalling din arose
— not shouting; not jeering; but a deep and continuous groaning.

De Lisle was pale, but carried himself, cocked hat, shabby blue uniform
coat, as though he were going on parade before the Emperor. He walked
within arm's-length of the crowd without one look at the clenched fists
and angry faces, past the Agent; turned to step into place. At that
moment an enormous turnip struck him on the back of the head, and he
fell forward to the ground and his hat was shot into the mire of the
gateway, to the accompaniment of yells of triumph and ugly laughter.

Almost in the same instant de⸱Lisle was on his feet again. He turned
on the crowd, the blood streaming unheeded from his nose. He was
insane with fury, and it was obvious that if he had had a weapon of any
sort he would have made a single-handed attack upon them. He shouted
incredible blasphemies in French; stopped, picked up the turnip, and
hurled it back. The missile was thrown without definite aim, but found
a billet, for there was a shriek of pained surprise, and within a minute
the mob with multitudinous war cries were surging forward to battle,
swallowing up in their wave the futile Mr. Griffiths.

Anthony fancied that the whole business had been prearranged. He
noticed as soon as the roll-call was started that respectable onlookers and
women and small children were being hustled from the front ranks. The

rowdy element, perhaps a hundred strong, were mainly small, dark men and half-grown lads — cattle drovers, quarrymen, workers from the wharf, market hangers-on, and the general riff-raff of the town — with a sprinkling of yellow-liveried boys from the charity school. He thought that he had never seen at one time so many ugly faces and queer figures. The windows of every house were black with heads. Shopkeepers hurriedly put up their shutters.

He found himself and three other men cut off from the rest and isolated under the coffee-room windows. While it was obvious from the shouts and movement that there was actual fighting about the courtyard gate, the section of the mob that confronted him and his fellows was uncertain what to do; it included a large proportion of the yellow-coat boys, and confined its activities to screeching and fierce gesticulations, keeping well out of reach.

Someone on the outskirts of the crowd, failing human targets, began a long-range and extremely accurate bombardment with stones of the hotel windows. Glass showered down from the upper stories, and even above the din he could hear the noise of shutters being hurriedly closed, and the crash of the great bar dropping into position behind the hall door.

From out of the seething throng Staff-Surgeon Strang then appeared with startling suddenness as though he had been projected by a catapult. A different Staff-Surgeon Strang. Not the dim small doctor, but a furious warrior — white beaver hat rakishly to one side, arms akimbo, and his heavy Malacca cane with ivory knob pendent by its tasselled loop from a little finger. His eyes seemed to Anthony to have become startlingly blue, and his jaw to have become geometrically square.

'Keelhaul my bloody soul!' said Staff-Surgeon Strang in a new and roaring voice. 'Keelhaul my bleeding kidneys! What do you lousy bastards think you're at? Get back, I say! Get back, you damned mutineers!'

Standing before the handful of prisoners in his ballet-skirt-style blue coat and strapped white trousers, like a most peculiarly garbed guardian angel, he made fierce jabs with his cane at the demonstrators nearest him. They gave back before his fury: and as they gave back, so he advanced upon them.

What was happening in the meantime in the battle round the gates, it was impossible to tell. There was a terrific uproar, and from the heavy crashes it sounded as though the prisoners had sought refuge in the courtyard, and the mob were endeavouring to batter an entrance.

Just then Mr. Strang spotted a figure that he apparently knew, lurking in the milling throng before him. He hailed it in an enormous voice, shaking his cane as he did so —

'Hey! Mr. Jones — Mr. Bloody Jones! Call off your stinking brats! Call 'em off! Come here, and call 'em off!'

But Mr. Jones, who was master of the charity school — as well as workhouse porter, barber, and professional layer-out of the dead — showed no inclination to obey instructions. Rather he sought to hide himself in the crowd.

'Hey! Jones! Are you coming!' bellowed Strang. '*Are you coming!*'

Anthony watched with the detached interest he might have given to a crowd scene in a play. He could not bring himself to believe that he was physically involved in the turmoil any more than he was physically involved in the adventures which he had used to recount to himself as a boy. Then a stone struck his hat and knocked it off.

Out of the tail of his eye Strang appeared to have seen this, for he suddenly swept his own white hat from his head, and flung it into the mob before him with a wide gesture and a whole galaxy of loud oaths.

'I'm coming after it — and after *you!*' he cried.

With that he flung himself head-first into the crowd as though he were diving into breakers. A tremendous commotion marked his progress.

More stones came dropping down. Morier, one of the men beside Anthony, was felled. As though his fall were a signal, there was a sudden fierce surge forward of the human flood into which Strang had vanished. Anthony was being clutched by a dozen hands — clutched, not struck, until his fierce resistance angered his attackers.

He was hit about the head: was on the ground: was up again, he did not know how. And then down. Two men were fighting over him. He saw a shifting confusion of legs and boots. Somebody kicked him viciously and deliberately in the ribs as he lay, and then fell atop of him. Then there appeared to be a whole pile of humanity upon him. The stump of his left arm was kneeled on, or struck somehow. The pain was excruciating.

When the situation cleared itself into something that was identifiable as a situation, he found himself sitting on the pavement with his back against the inn wall. Morier was still on the ground, leaning upon one elbow and trying to staunch a wound in the scalp from which the blood poured. The other two were tightly held by a pack of boys. They were surrounded by a dense and excited crowd, who were obviously debating the next stage in the proceedings.

Anthony got to his feet with difficulty: would have stooped to help up Morier, but his solitary arm was roughly seized, and held twisted behind his back by an unseen assailant. Somebody else picked up his cocked hat, and crammed it fiercely upon his head broadside on.

The Little Man in Grey always wore his hat turned up in front: and presumably it was considered that a speaking likeness of the Emperor had been called into being.

'Nap! Boney!' said someone. And an excited jabber followed, to the accompaniment of much laughter and approval.

One man in particular appeared to direct the discussion, to make decisions, to issue instructions. He had his back turned at first; but when he swung round, Anthony recognized in him the cadaverous creature in rusty black whom he had encountered outside the looted bonnet shop a few days earlier. The recognition was mutual.

'"Erfin, cawl erfin!" You remember, inteet?' said the man. 'And now, Misster Prisoner *bach,* you shall pe Emperor for half an hour, and we'll give you a nice little ride round town. Chust like Boney — on a grey donkey!'

Over the heads of the crowd Anthony could see that some horsemen had entered the square.

He tore his arm free: flung his hat from his head: hurled himself on the man before him: went down with him to the flags: and was instantaneously submerged by the pack that went to their leader's rescue, although not before he had felt Rusty-Black's front teeth breaking under his fist.

Somebody had him by the nape of the neck: tore him from Rusty-Black and was most murderously endeavouring to smash his face against the stones.

Over all the snarling and the yelling he became suddenly aware of a very loud shout — an alteration in the character of the uproar, and then an entire dissolving of the scene. He was free of the pack; free of the unseen creature who was doing his best to kill him; Rusty-Black evaporated from beneath him.

He rolled over, very dazed. Blood was streaming from his forehead, and from the pain in his side he knew that a rib must have been damaged.

The crowd had broken; was running; was parting in waves before the riders, two of whom, swinging their horses on their haunches, were striking right and left with their whips. The third rode straight on through the passage thus cleared. Was a woman. Dismounted. Knelt beside him. Was Garland!

'Rowley!' she said. And the tears rolled down her cheeks.

'I made Paul walk on your picture!' said Anthony, and tried to smile.

CHAPTER VI

CONVERSATION PIECE — IN A BEDROOM

THE Earl of Morfa's carriage waited outside the house in Dark Wharf Gate. Postilions and outrider stood at their horses' heads. The lamps were already lighted, and in the gathering dusk the equipage seemed to fill the street, and yet to have something of fantasy about it, as though it were the fairy coach of the White Cat or of Cinderella.

My lord was within-doors: had paid his respects to Mr. and Mrs. Almond: now climbed the stairs alone to a room that he had known well many years before — the room of Young Tom, his boyhood's friend.

The door on the landing was ajar, so that as he approached he overheard the rustle of a newspaper and Garland reading aloud —

' ". . . Fulton, now completing the plans of a steam frigate, to be called the *Demologos*, of thirty guns. New York journals state — " '

Morfa pushed open the door, and stepped round an old nursery screen covered with scraps cut from valentines and coloured prints.

The room was softly lit by many candles, and snug with glazed chintz and ancient furniture and firelight. Facing him, a young man in flowered silk wrapper, with bandaged head, sat in a large arm-chair by the fire, under the portrait of Ensign Tom Almond: he was regarding absentmindedly the gay confusion of roof and tower and spire of the toy city established on the table before him.

Just such another young man had gazed unseeing at just such another fairy town a generation and more ago!

For a moment Morfa almost fancied that time had stood still since he had left the library at High Pale to investigate disturbances; and that now at length he had returned to report 'All Well!' and everything else was but a dream.

And when the second Anthony raised his head, Morfa saw in his face and expression every trait, every whimsicality that had been the first's. For so short a time had he seen the original Anthony, and yet the lineaments of the Virginian were more deeply etched in his memory than those of the companions of many years. Now in this stranger he saw once more the chronicler of imaginary voyages as when he had lifted his eyes from contemplation of Camelot, and prepared to talk of his fairy town and those travellers of whom he had written at such length, and of de Gribeauval and the generalship of Washington and Greene. The past was no longer a shadow — a memory, but something woven into the texture of the present.

Nothing of this was permitted to show in his expression; and Anthony, looking up, only perceived courtesy in the handsome face of the man who awaited realization of his presence.

Morfa was suddenly aware that Garland was watching him very curiously. She was no part of that fireside scene, for she had been sitting, a little withdrawn, on an ottoman at the foot of the chintz-curtained four-poster bed, skimming through *The Times* for the invalid by the light of a candle on the Pembroke table beside her. Now she rose, and beckoned Morfa forward.

'Charles,' she said, 'here's Rowley! In other words, the Earl of Morfa — Captain Anthony Purvis!'

My lord bowed.

Anthony bowed: indicated by an uneasy movement an attempt to rise that damaged ribs would not allow. Just such a gesture as another Anthony had made thirty years and more ago!

So this was Garland's husband! He had not realized that Morfa was so much older: old enough to be her father, although not old enough yet for his calm patrician face to show the tarnishment of age. Nothing, obviously, recalled to his mind the nightmare scene in the house on the road to Toulon, and my lord, realizing this, heaved an inward sigh of relief.

They talked easily enough of the events of the day before yesterday, as though the three of them were old and tried friends.

'The mob bolted,' explained Morfa, 'not so much because Howell and I attacked them as because they thought we were an advance party of cavalry from the barracks . . . I'll get that fellow Griffiths broken! He should never have been appointed to the job.'

Anthony said slowly —

'I can't help thinking — and I have thought a good deal about it — that there was a most deliberate attempt on somebody's part to make away with me!'

He looked up, as if fearing laughter, at Morfa leaning on the mantel-piece by the high nursery fire-guard; at Garland, in grey silk, sitting on the ottoman at the bed-foot, and framed as though a picture by the fluted slender columns of the bed.

'Have you been making incautious love to the local maidens, Rowley?' asked she. 'I can't imagine you as a "dragon among the chamber-maids," as Harrady would say.'

Recalled Hortense, and almost — but not quite — smiled to herself.

'I have had no — romances. Absolutely none! I have had little contact with the locals. And no disagreements with my fellow-prisoners, except one — and he's dead! Colonel Millet — who cut his throat the other day. You buried him at the cross-roads, with a stake through him!'

'Ah!' sighed Garland.

Morfa was not distracted from the subject under discussion.

'What makes you think it?' he asked.

'When I went down the first time,' said Anthony, 'someone — I don't know who — kicked me on the head. Kicked me not merely with enough violence to restrain my struggles, but with a violent violence. If you know what I mean. I moved my head only just in time, otherwise I am certain that my skull would have been smashed. I can see the boot now — a heavy riding-boot, better polished than the rest, with a peculiarly cut spur strap and plated or silver spurs, and a small patch on one side!'

'Somebody avenging a hard knock,' said Morfa. 'They are a revengeful lot!'

'They were on me before I was able to strike a blow at all,' said Anthony. 'Like a pack of jackals! The second time I went down with a fellow in rusty black. As he rolled away from under me the same boot got me in the ribs. I saw it!'

'Can you do anything about it, Charles?' asked Garland.

He shook his head.

'Nothing, unless Captain Purvis can recognize the boot again, and then he would have to swear to the occupant of the boot. Personally I believe that the whole riot was engineered — it certainly doesn't seem to me to have been spontaneous — but for what reason I cannot even attempt to guess!'

The thought of Pagan-Dunscore passed through Anthony's mind, as it had done before; and was dismissed as fantastic, as before.

'I do not think that there will be any more trouble,' continued Morfa. 'We have seven men behind bars on charges of riotous assemblage. They will *not* be tried before a local jury, so that we may get convictions.'

The presence of Garland's husband imposed no restraint upon the flood of reminiscence that had started on the previous afternoon — when she had first been brought upstairs in state by an excited Old Tom and by Mrs. Tom — and had continued at intervals during this second visit.

Anthony spoke of his grandmother without restraint —

'I always said that she was an old witch!' commented Garland, and glanced at her husband; but his face remained impassive.

Anthony nodded in token of agreement.

'I hear from her about once a fortnight. Letters she dictates to Buck. The most remarkable letters! . . . Especially as Buck sometimes breaks into parentheses of her own and poetry in the middle . . . The old lady has never forgiven me for allowing myself to be taken prisoner. It was a sin against the Purvis tradition!'

'Where were you captured?' asked Morfa.

Some instinct had refused to allow Garland to ask that question, since Anthony had vouchsafed no information. She was directly watching him as he answered briefly —

'In London.'

Morfa nodded as though satisfied, and went on to other subjects. Old Tom and Mrs. Tom arrived with acrostics and knitting, followed by Jenkins with all the materials for the making of punch. The evening passed very pleasantly until a sub-committee of the ladies decided that it was bedtime for an invalid.

'I shall come to-morrow,' said Garland, 'and spend all day. You don't mind, do you, dearest Mrs. Almond? I always say that where I lunch I dine, especially when it's with you.'

'As soon as you are well enough,' said Morfa, 'you must come to the Abbey whenever Mrs. Tom can spare you. There are books your father —'

He stopped: and Garland hurriedly said —

'You remember you told me, Rowley, about the book your father was writing? The history of all the imaginary travellers! Gulliver and Cyrano and so on!'

He did not remember. In fact he could not even recollect ever having, himself, been told about it.

He watched them as they stood by the screen bidding him farewell: Garland slim, proud, and dark: her husband tall, distinguished, with tanned face and high forehead that was very white above the brow. She had chosen a mate more wisely than himself. He recalled a querulous and lovely Jasmine lying on her couch in the house in Paris, bewailing the approach of maternity; recalled the defiance and pallor of her face when she announced to him that the child he desired would not be born; recalled, too, her ill-suppressed pleasure and excitement on the last day he ever saw her, as she stood in a long travelling pelisse of French grey by the door of the carriage which was to take her from Boulogne back to the capital.

Something of what he thought may have been obvious to Morfa, because as Garland and he were driving back to the Abbey he said —

'I think his marriage must have been very unhappy. Has he ever mentioned it?'

'He just said, "I married that girl! I suppose Harrady told you about her? It turned out badly — very badly!" That was all. Why do you ask?'

'I thought he looked rather enviously at us. It may have been just fancy. I don't know . . . Was he in love with you in those old days?'

'Are you getting jealous at last, Charles? After eight years!' said Garland.

She patted his hand with gloved fingers, and in the light cast into the interior of the carriage from the lamps in front he could see that she was smiling.

He smiled, too.

'I should not be jealous even if you were in love with him now, dearest. Only regretful — lest I might have spoiled things for you. I like him. He is a nice lad. And, by God! Garland, he resembles his father! I could have sworn that it was the other Anthony sitting there facing me over his magical city. I felt — felt — '

Garland helped him out —

'I was in love with him all those years ago, Charles! I'll confess it. He didn't know, of course. And I think he had just begun to be in love with me, when — when everything happened! I was only seventeen.'

'Your mother had married when she was no older! . . .' His mind veered to another subject. 'But it is curious that he should say that he was arrested in London! Did he say nothing to you about it?'

'Nothing at all. But why is it curious?'

'You don't expect officers of the Emperor's own staff to be gallivanting about London — unless — '

'Unless?' prompted Garland, a sudden chill at her heart.

'Well, it was just about that time, the winter of '06, that the traitor Malone was laid by the heels. And it was then, too, that the secret service people unearthed a big plot for mutinies in the prison camps combined with incendiarism at the docks!'

'Charles!' exclaimed Garland; and there was so much distress in her voice that Morfa checked himself in what he had been about to say.

'It is only assumption on my part,' he assured her. 'As a soldier of the Emperor he would have to do as he was told, however distasteful the duty may have been. Just like poor Tom Almond — or Major André!'

'It *is* true!' said Garland, and there were tears in her voice. 'That's why he never said anything to me about it . . . First the *Nautilus,* and then this!'

'In the first case, as you yourself have often told me, it was the spirit of adventure that involved him. In this other business — supposing him to have been concerned in it — his duty! A duty that demanded more courage than ever was needed to face the enemy in the field!'

The carriage came to a halt before the huge Doric portico of the Abbey.

They mounted the wide shallow steps. The great doors were flung open to the night, and light gushed out onto the colonnade. Immense porter — lackeys with powdered hair — solemn major-domo in black. Garland turned away for a moment.

The ground sloped sharply down in front of the house and its background of parkland and wood. Under a high moon the wide valley was spread beneath her gaze, threaded by the silver of the river. A few lights twinkled: the white walls of a farmhouse shone like frozen snow: the hollow unearthly cry of an owl sounded from amongst the trees.

Garland shivered.

'She *was* a witch, Charles,' she said. 'She *is* a witch!' . . .

Staff-Surgeon Strang had made his professional call the next day — his thistledown sadly tonsured by the barber and ornamented by strips of black sticking-plaster — and sent Anthony back to bed. Mrs. Tom had paid two visits — one of inquiry after health; and the other to bring the first bunch of early wall-flowers from the garden, and to announce in triumph that the chiff-chaff had been heard. Old Tom also had made two appearances; firstly to bring Anthony his half of *The Times*, and secondly to announce triumphantly that the solution of the right-hand pillar in last night's 'snorter' had been 'Galenical'. There was no question about it even although 'Number Five across' defied all attempts at solution.

Garland sat sewing by an open window, where he could watch her from his pillows. So he lay there very quietly regarding the curve of her cheek, the dark wave of her hair, the charm of the intent face bent over her work; with admiration; with affection; even with a certain sense of proprietorship.

If —

He broke a long silence.

'I suppose it was your — Morfa who got me out of Norman Cross and brought here?'

Garland looked up from the sewing. She broke a thread with her teeth. She smiled at him.

'He did, Rowley.'

'Why?'

She chose her words with great care.

'I asked him to. Harrady asked him to. Mother asked him to. And he needed no pressing!'

'And he arranged for me to come to this house?'

Garland said that that was so.

'To this house, because of . . . him?'

He raised his hand as he spoke, and pointed to the picture of Young Tom in scarlet regimentals over the mantelpiece. She looked toward the portrait, and was still looking at it as she answered —

'Because of *him*, Rowley!'

They were both silent after that for a long while. He lay staring at the gay patchwork quilt upon the bed, which was hummocked by his body, and looked (he thought) like the hedgerowed chequer of an English countryside viewed from a hill-top.

'Garland!' he said at length, apologetically.

'Rowley!'

She looked up at him again from her work, with a very special smile. He said —

'I think when they die this house will be transported with them to Paradise! . . . Why shouldn't a house go to Heaven? . . . And I think they'll still be old — because they have loved being old. And they'll still be excited because they've seen a new flower in the fields beside the Jordan, or heard a new bird singing in the woods of Eden, or solved so difficult an anagram in a celestial acrostic. But they'll have *him* to sit with over the fire at night and play three-handed whist. And *he*, of course, will always be young. I wish that I could be with them in that Paradise.'

'She *was* a witch!' said Garland.

His mind went back to the old woman in the dim room in the tower at La Cadière — to cobweb carpet and nibbled comfits — to the amulet of blood-stained paper and curl of fair hair — to that other room that seemed to have been excavated out of fog somewhere in the recesses of High Pale — to those invisible companions of his travels.

'You broke her first spell, you know, Garland!'

She nodded, threading a needle. He paused for a little, and then went on —

'*And* her second!'

At that she looked up directly at him. It was the first reference he had ever made to that night in March twelve years ago. She said nothing.

'You know when I set out in the *Nautilus* it was in the spirit of high adventure. I didn't visualize what might have been the results. I didn't visualize dreadful death for hundreds of men whom I had no business to help to kill — the maiming of others whom I had no business to help to maim. I saw only excitement and romantic endeavour. I realized the truth when for the first time I saw a great battlefield. When I rode over the field of Austerlitz after the Battle of the Three Emperors. On that day the enemy alone lost twenty-seven thousand dead! . . . I was glad then that we had failed!'

She knew then that she was forgiven, and that Harradence was forgiven.

'Oh, Rowley, if only you had known before, known what *we* went through!'

If only he had known then! All the might-have-beens came quickly to his mind, and were dismissed as disloyalties. He continued his self-analysis —

'And I was glad, too, that I was away from the murderous, violent side of war. Do you know, Garland, that I have never yet drawn my sword or fired a shot in anger?'

She had set down her sewing on her lap, and sat watching him, listening to him.

He said abruptly —

'And it was your idea that I should come here — to this house, as Young Tom's guest? You needn't tell me, because I know it! . . . And know why!'

She nodded; found that her eyes were full of tears, and that she could not speak.

'*Your* magic again, Garland! All your magic! Yours are very potent enchantments!'

'Many years have been lost all the same, Rowley!'

'Many years!' He agreed so slowly that she knew him to be thinking of other things that had, perhaps, been lost: went on — 'And while I have been here in this house of . . . of forgiveness, I have not merely forgotten the degradation of the hulks and the horrible monotony of Norman Cross. I have realized other things! . . . I used to enjoy the chessboard side of war — even that small part of it that falls to the lot of a junior officer of headquarters staff. The fascination of problems whose factors are men and guns and baggage, and roads and rivers and mountains, morale in your own and the enemy country, agents behind the lines, and invasions without armies or transport. *Now* I know that adventures with maps and reports can have even deadlier results than the adventures of mere violence. I have been the servant of a very great man — so great that he is a natural force rather than a man. I think that his glory and his genius blinded me to the fact that I had no personal purpose in the business at all!'

'You may have had no purpose,' said Garland, 'but your grandmother had! You were sealed to the purpose with that horrible amulet. You were taught history for the purpose. Your whole education was to the purpose — although even Harrady only realized it afterwards — that you should be fitted to carry on the war of Purvis against England on any front that offered. For that purpose she encouraged your interest in the *Nautilus*. And would you ever have thought of joining the French army by yourself?'

That was true! . . .

After dinner she came back to his room a little before the Almonds arrived, and sat again in the window-place looking down into the street. Through the dusk a trickle of worshippers passed on their way to evening prayer, at the Tabernacle round the corner beyond the Sloop Inn. Old women in tall beaver hats and white flannel shawls, their Bibles held against their breasts, and rushlight candles in their free hands wherewith to illumine the meeting-house when it grew dark. They were like grey ghosts. The grey ghosts of witches! Was the witch of La Cadière bereft of all her spells in her stricken age? — she wondered.

Then she heard Anthony say diffidently —

'I should like to see Harrady again — and your mother. He wrote to me many times. I returned his letters. Do you think that he — that I — that — '

Would Harrady not? — She assured him, already turning over in her mind ways and means for that first meeting.

And then a dammed-up stream of questions poured out, which she answered as she moved about the room drawing the curtains, putting the fire to rights.

They lived about twenty miles away. In one of Charles's houses. You see Mother had known Charles long ago. (It was not for her to impinge on Charles's problem: she did not think that he would find it so insoluble!) The two men had met, and had become fast friends. So there you were!

'When did your mother and Harrady get married? Why didn't they do it years before?'

But what he would have liked to ask was about her own marriage.

She did not even hesitate then.

'They aren't, though nobody knows it but Charles and me! You see, my father is still alive for all we know!'

'But — ' said Anthony.

'He was what we called a Loyalist during the War of Independence, and your people called a Tory. So he lost all his property. It was in Massachusetts. He came to England, married Mother, and then when things became more settled took her back with him to see what he could retrieve. I don't know what happened, but he went wrong when I was very little, and abandoned Mother. Then Uncle Harrady came out to

America and took us both under his wing. Can you wonder that Mother adores him?'

Anthony could well believe it: added —

'But —'

'Quite!' said Garland. 'Mother would have been perfectly happy to have lived with him openly, she loved him so much. She even pointed out that some of the Royal dukes had quite respectable mistresses. But that wouldn't do for Harrady! He drew up a declaration that my father, having failed to perform his part of the contract made between himself and my mother, had permitted his rights in her to go by default. In view of this the said Elizabeth Vane, considering herself free to — And so on for pages and pages. Mother signed, and Harrady signed, and Charles and Monsieur Courville signed as witnesses. Then there were all sorts of deeds and papers and affidavits to make sure that Mother would get his money without anything coming out. He *did* enjoy himself! You cannot imagine the state of confusion in which we lived for more than a month! And then finally we all went to some little church in Nottinghamshire — I don't know why; but we had the keys — and there he married himself to Mother with a wedding service which he had compiled partly out of his head and partly out of the Book of Common Prayer. It was all very solemn and reverent. There was nobody there except ourselves, naturally He was terribly pleased with himself, and, of course, Mother didn't mind! I don't know what Monsieur Courville made of it all.'

'Didn't he preach a sermon afterwards?' asked Anthony.

'He did. Indeed he did!' said Garland.

And with that they both fell a-laughing till Anthony's broken ribs were an agony, and the Almonds arrived and joined in their laughter without knowing the cause. . . .

She stood by his bedside saying good night — Old Tom and Mrs. Tom tactfully discussing acrostic problems over the tea urn before the fire.

She might be the Countess of Morfa, but yet also she was the Garland of old days. His eyes sought her face that held beauty and told of wit, and found in every loveliness a remembered loveliness.

She put her hand on that solitary hand lying on the sheet.

'In a little, when you are better, we will have a meeting of old friends. I think we even won't have Charles. Under my roof.'

'The past all conjured up and made the present!' he said very slowly. 'Your victorious magic, Garland, my dear!'

'It was not so victorious — *once!*' she said. . . .

And when she had gone, and the Almonds had gone, and he had been tucked up and left to the silence and the firelight he found that he wanted to weep.

CHAPTER VII

CONVERSATION PIECE — IN A DRESSING-ROOM

'Do you realize,' asked Jasmine, 'that you have abandoned me here for a month? In a house full of horse-faced women, horsehair furniture, horsey conversation, and the reek of the stable. They don't talk in this place: they neigh at one another!' She walked to the window and looked out into the sunshine. 'I suppose they gave you this dressing-room as being the best in the house because it has the finest view of the stable-yard dung heap!'

Dunscore, still in dusty travelling attire, paused in his task of selecting a change for the outer man. He had sent his servant away, and the narrow room was littered with the contents of his half-emptied valises and trunks. The wardrobe doors swung open wide: a pile of shirts was on the chest of drawers, and the floor was strewn with boots.

'You've no business in here!' he said. 'The proprieties exist even in savage Wales, and even for an alleged uncle and niece!'

'Your neighbour in the corridor,' remarked Jasmine, 'is nominally a female, but she is deaf from a fall out hunting, as well as lame and blind in an eye from being kicked by horses at various times!'

'In that case —' said Dunscore, eyeing her.

Even as himself she had changed nothing outwardly with the years — was as slim and as silvern and as golden as she had ever been. She was in a biscuit-coloured morning dress with a deep blue jacket — short-waisted and long-sleeved — and a high bonnet of grey silk, crested like a dragoon's helmet.

'No,' she said backing from a threatened embrace. 'I don't want to be fondled. I am all ready for the main excitement of the day — walking down to the Long Meadow, and watching the horses at exercise, and whinnying comments to one another. Too, too thrilling! . . . No, I mean "No"! . . . I am more than a little jaded from saying "No!" to George who is the most incurable optimist, and to Lord Saundersfoot who bleats round me like an amorous ram whenever he thinks his sisters' backs are turned and that George isn't about!'

Dunscore began to undo his muslin neck-cloth before a pier-glass set at right angles to the lofty window.

'Saundersfoot living up to his ideals as host — offering his guest every pleasure he can!' he commented. 'I shouldn't have stayed away so long if I could have helped it, but the government are still concerned about this business of prison mutinies. I have been to Launceston and all over the West Country to investigate . . . Heard anything of — our friends?'

'Lord Morfa got back the night before you left —'

Dunscore cursed in a motley assortment of languages.

' — and rode into the town in the nick of time to save Anthony from being murdered in some sort of riot the townspeople got up!'

'Ah, *that* little fracas!'

'What do you know about it? How do you know about it? You had gone when it happened!' she asked, and came up the narrow room, to watch him suspiciously as he stood admiring himself before the mirror.

'George wrote to me.'

'George *wrote* to you?' she echoed in the uttermost surprise. 'But George can barely hold a pen!'

His smile was such that illumination came to her.

'You and George planned the whole thing! You intended to put Anthony out of the way!'

Dunscore removed the cravat. He did not look round at her stormy face.

'It is true,' he admitted, 'that our proceedings would be greatly simplified were he to be . . . removed!'

'He will *not* be removed!' said Jasmine incisively.

'And why?'

'Because I say so.'

'And why so?'

She sat down on a grim unyielding sofa against the wall behind him, her hands lightly folded on her lap; and met his eyes unflinching when he turned to her.

'I've cost Anthony a great deal of happiness and many ideals. I've cost him the life of his best friend. I'm helping to cost him his inheritance. I won't go any further! And nobody else shall! *Nobody shall!* Just note the words, Julian! I mean them! . . . Go about the business as you like, but without — fatalities!'

He took off his coat, folded it very deliberately, put it over a chair back and turned again, in shirt-sleeves and almond-green waistcoat, to study himself in the glass: but could see nothing except youth — that seemingly eternal youth which he possessed.

She remarked the action with the slightest of smiles.

'You see, while you were away it came to me in a blinding flash that I was utterly weary of you — that you had just become a habit — that was

all. That I could get the . . . love I required from other men — in fact
from almost anybody — without all the imperative demands that you
make on me. I realized frankly at last that I am not so much interested
in the lover as in the love.'

'Surely you find this self-revelation a little humiliating?' he inquired,
watching her in his mirror.

'Not in the least,' she replied. 'I believe that if you had left me to my
fairy lover years and years ago, I might indeed have passed with him
into all the splendour of his dreams. But *you* didn't. And *I* didn't . . .
Incidentally I needn't tell you that I am more than weary of George.
I held him fast while you wound your coils around him. Now you have
got him all signed and sealed I propose to withdraw from the affair —
and from him! Oh, I know that it has been implied that I should be
part of the spoils of war — together with as much of High Pale as you
can spare him! But I don't care.'

'So you mean to cut adrift!' he said, and spoke quietly though she
saw his eyebrows tilt and meet across his nose. 'At the very moment
when we are in sight of success! . . . I found a very polite letter from
Morfa waiting for me. I am arranging to see him to-morrow. With his
evidence our case will be complete!'

'I am no longer interested!'

'On what do you intend then to live? *I* shan't support you, and Anthony's allowance won't — as he told me — do more than keep you
off the streets. If you want to keep off them!'

'Is it thanks to you that I — *we* — have lived in considerable comfort
during the past six years? How is it that you managed to get your claws
into George? How is it that we have been able to find house-room here
for all this time? How — '

'For Christ's sake — ' he began.

'I will wait until you have seen Lord Morfa — just to keep you in
countenance with George. I'm dissolving partnership — not betraying
it! Then I propose to return forthwith to London! Unaccompanied!'

She rose as she spoke, and walked down the room with infinite grace
toward the door: and he swung round and watched her progress, with
malignant attention. On the threshold she turned —

'It is a curious thing, Julian, that even when I loved you most I
abominated you. Not just hated, you know, or loathed — but abominated! The sort of feeling the damned must have when they worship
Satan with all that peculiar ritual you took such delight in recounting to
me when I was — when I wasn't what you've made me. When I was
very young!'

'Thank you, my pet!'

'I thought it might interest you!'

'It does.'

'I have told you this immediately you arrived so that you might have plenty of time to arrange your plans. This will be our last private talk together. The very last! My room has been changed — to the other wing. Next the eldest Saundersfoot female. I have been sleeping so badly!'

The face that watched her was dark with anger. He started as if to come down the room in a swift rush —

'Stop where you are, Julian! Otherwise I shall open the door and scream. George is lurking about somewhere if I know anything about it . . . I am no longer afraid of you! . . . Shall I tell you why?'

He said nothing, but stood quite motionless, still staring at her.

'When I go back to London, I am going back to a kind friend — a *Royal* friend! A friend I met in London before we came here, while you were away busy with your plots and counter-plots, and your spying and counter-spying, and other little treacheries and treasons! A *Personage!* Who made very handsome proposals to me through a most discreet intermediary sent here for the express purpose a few days ago. What merchants call "a firm offer", I believe. An offer that I have seen fit to accept. I shall be a very dangerous person to offend, Julian!'

He realized that.

'A member of the government, in fact!' he said: remained where he was.

Her hand was already on the door when he added —

'Is this sudden solicitude for Anthony connected with this new development, may I ask?'

She considered whether she should be frank about it. Decided that she would —

'No. It coincides. That is all . . . We women drove into Morfa the other day — thirty miles there and back over the foulest roads — to see a horse, of course!'

'But it was specifically agreed — ' he snarled.

'I know! But I was so wrapped in cloak and hidden by carriage bonnet and veil that no one could have recognized me. And in any case no one *did* see me, or recognize me — not even Anthony!'

'You saw him?'

'I saw him. Through the window of a milliners' shop where Amelia and Caroline were buying clothes that looked as if they had been cut from horse-blankets. He was in uniform with a bandage round his head . . . Who did it to him? It was filthy, brutal — and unnecessary. Who did it?'

'How on earth can I tell?'

She regarded him with contempt.

'Both you and George are capable of murder! — '

'Thank you again, my pet!'

'But you do not like crimes that upset the *toilette!* Rough-and-tumble is not your pattern! And George, who positively revels in bestial violence, could not be detached from me all that day. He was — ' She stopped. Understanding came to her. 'He was establishing his alibi, just in case! Wise George! . . . No, he didn't think of it. It was you! Wise Julian! And that, too, was why you went away! . . . I wonder whom it was you hired? You probably didn't have to go any further afield than George's man, who looks more like an assassin than a groom!'

'We were discussing your interesting encounter with your husband!'

'So we were! Well, he was with a prettyish dark girl! Talking and laughing. They stopped before the shop for a minute or so. She had quite a good dress — for an Englishwoman: and her bonnet wasn't too bad! I knew her at once. It was that cousin from La Cadière! I presume they've made it up and she's come to console him, because that big-nosed uncle of hers was just behind, with another man — very handsome; in the fifties. Some relation, I suppose, because both of them were beaming on the pair with a "Bless-you-my-children" expression!'

He turned over the situation in his mind.

'It is just as well that I should see Morfa to-morrow, if Anthony's friends are going to spring up round him like dragon's teeth. It is a most unfortunate coincidence that he should have been sent to Morfa of all places! . . . And what were your reactions to this romantic scene?'

'A trifle of jealousy at first, I suppose!' answered Jasmine, regarding the rings on a long pale hand. There was an immense solitaire diamond that he had never seen before. She glanced up, to note his interest.

'A souvenir of George, which I shall always value!'

'So I should imagine,' he remarked dryly. 'I wonder how he raised the money!'

'The very question that I asked myself! . . . You continually interrupt me. If you aren't interested — ' He apologized, and she went on: 'My first reaction was a trifle of jealousy, as I said. After that a pang of conscience! Or was it just giving rein to an elementary sense of justice? Anyhow I swore that he should have his romance, whatever else we robbed him of! . . . I know romance when I see it, although I doubt whether they themselves have realized it yet!'

'I do not imagine,' said Dunscore removing his waistcoat, 'that the girl's people will appreciate a romance with a married man!'

'That will be my contribution! When I reach London I propose to see that he's informed of what the American Ministry in Paris told you — that our marriage is only valid — at the best — in France and nowhere else! It will be no obstacle! . . . He would, of course, never dream of divorcing me, divorce is a far greater sin than adultery to people like the Purvises and their *milieu!*'

Dunscore had pulled off his boots on a folding mahogany boot-jack. He now proceeded to peel off his fawn breeches. He was the only man she had ever encountered — or heard of — who quite deliberately could strip himself to his under-clothes in the presence of a woman. There was something feminine in his realization of the fact that he adorned — and was not shamed by — his underwear! And that it was a fact, she admitted to herself, as she saw him straighten himself, and stand up attired only in shirt and white drawers.

'You are a fool!' he remarked without heat, and almost as if he had lost interest in her. 'That situation wouldn't have arisen but for your incredible elopement. *I* should have seen that the knot was tied more firmly than that.'

She gauged that he had recognized the finality of her decision, and was already dismissing her from his mind as no longer a factor in his life.

He started to pull his shirt over his head.

She opened the dressing-room door sufficiently wide to ascertain that no one was in the corridor.

'We shall meet at luncheon, dear uncle,' she said, 'when we will bray avuncularities to one another across the table over our horse-flesh and horse-radish!'

Was gone.

Standing naked in the angle between pier-glass and window, he wondered which of those large-size Royal dukes it was that had made the interesting and acceptable proposals to her. She had very carefully said 'Personage', not 'Duke'. Was it by any chance the Regent? No! His taste had notoriously declined toward the not-so-young and the over-ripe. . . .

CHAPTER VIII

THE RECIPE FOR HONOUR

'HE's cracking at last!' said Morfa out loud to himself.

And as he spoke he let go the cord of the roller map which he had been examining, so that it wound itself up on the wall like a spring blind, with a click as though to emphasize his words.

Subject Europe was reacting in such manner as might have been expected after the vast extent of the disaster in Russia had become known. The satellite states meditated treachery to a hated alliance: the enslaved states nerved themselves to revolt. Before Russia's advance, before resurgent Germany, the invading forces had fallen back from Berlin and Dantzig; had abandoned Dresden. British supplies and money were pouring into Russia in ever-increasing volume. To-day news had come that He—there was only one man in all the world who could just be 'He'—had left Paris, bound hot-foot for a shuddering front. Somewhere, somehow, he had raised a huge new army—farm labourers torn from the plough, sailors of an immobilized navy, conscripts levied from unhappy allies, anybody, everybody; whilst malcontents had begun to plaster the walls of his cities with 'No Conscription!' posters. After years of torment the end was in sight!

Morfa had been studying the defensive line along the river Elbe and its tributaries with professional interest, with human interest. Could he? — Would he? . . . What was about to happen on the second front?

He was crossing to the other map alcove, on the further side of the great Flemish fireplace when a deferential voice breathed —

'My lord!'

His butler, reverentially garbed in black, was at his elbow: indicated by respectful inclination of head two gentlemen who were advancing toward him, under the escort of a liveried servant, across the shining floor of the Long Gallery.

'Sir George Parrish and Colonel Dunscore, my lord!'

The visitors introduced by Saundersfoot! He cared neither for Saundersfoot, nor for stray callers! He permitted himself, however, to shorten their journey between high cold windows and picture-covered wall by a pace or two; waited for them, with the correctest of expressions, under the picture of Adam and Eve of which Harradence had so much disapproved.

Sir George was a large young man with a dark and dampish face, in a bottle-green coat and Hessian boots.

Colonel Dunscore was astonishingly good-looking: wore a violet-coloured coat and the most admirable grey leather breeches: appeared to do all the talking. After the self-presentation ceremonies had been completed, it was he who, despising the Englishman's customary conversational opening of weather or the news, broached the subject of Italian Old Masters with particular reference to the picture beside them, and talked easily and with a certain amount of knowledge on the subject.

Decanters of very excellent port and superb sherry were produced.

Colonel Dunscore debated the wine with connoisseurship and appreciation. Morfa found himself thawing to the man. Before the process went
too far, and they became too deeply and amicably involved in the question of vintages and soleras, it might, however, be as well, he thought, to
delve into the purpose of the call —

'Your letter to me, sir, said that I might possibly be of service to you
and Sir George. In what way can I assist?'

Colonel Dunscore at once proceeded to broach the business with many
expressions of thanks, with many regrets.

'May I ask your lordship,' he concluded, 'to cast your mind back some
thirty years? Thirty-two, to be precise! For a moment!'

Thirty-two years ago! Although his face showed no flicker of expression, yet behind it for a moment or so he battled with absolute panic.

Thirty-two years ago!

High Pale, and a room tapestried with books, and a man in a flowered
banian drooping over a long table, and a toy city — gay-rooted as a basket
of flowers — and a necklace of diamonds like burning ice! . . . A necklace of diamonds! . . . A necklace of . . .

But apparently Dunscore was not interested in the question of the
diamonds. He went on —

'It is a matter, my lord, which only calls for an effort of memory.
Memory of a rather dramatic incident! But for my friend, Sir George,
a matter of supreme importance!'

What was the fellow leading up to?

Morfa rose from the small round table at which they were seated in
the recess to one side of the vast hooded fireplace; and stood looking down
on Julian with an expression of polite inquiry, one hand resting on the
high ledge from which the carved chimney-breast sloped.

'You served in America, I believe, my lord, with Tarleton's Legion?'
He nodded. 'Were eventually attached to Cornwallis's headquarters
staff?' Nodded. 'Were at a house called High Pale, in Virginia, on the
night when the owner was shot by a drunken Hessian? A bad aim!
The bullet was meant for the fellow's trollop.' Nodded. 'You remember
that, of course. Do you chance to remember the date, my lord?'

'It was my birthday,' said Morfa. 'I am not good at remembering dates,
but I have a land-mark for that incident naturally.'

'You actually saw Mr. Purvis die, I believe?'

Now why did the fellow want to know that? Why?

Dunscore rose, too, and faced him. He pressed his case.

'You see, my lord, my friend Parrish has every reason to believe that
there was a most abominable conspiracy to rob him of a great estate —

that Mr. Purvis died almost at once, and did not linger for many hours afterwards, as the world was led to believe. Your evidence as to Mr. Purvis's immediate death can blow that conspiracy sky-high — the evidence of an entirely disinterested witness, who was present by chance.'

'There were a number of other people in the house at the time.'

'Tainted evidence!' said Dunscore. 'Suspect evidence! Slaves! Niggers!'

How could the High Pale estate belong rightfully to any one other than the son of Anthony Purvis — that second Anthony to whom he proposed to make confession at last when next he saw him? That very Anthony who had been in and out his house almost every day during the last four weeks. No one had ever breathed a word in his presence implying that there was any mystery attaching to the birth of the second Anthony. If Garland, if Harradence had ever heard anything, they would have told him.

It seemed to him that the conspiracy — the 'abominable conspiracy' — might possibly be against the son of the man whom he had wronged.

'It sounds a very strange story,' he commented in a non-committal tone.

Dunscore recognized the tone: set out to rectify affairs. He told with much dramatic skill the story of the strange bridal at High Pale more than a generation ago, as he had been able to reconstruct it from what Earle had told him in his cups — from the confused denials of Rasselas's widow. Told it as an act of treachery by a mother to ensure the disinheritance of an unforgiven daughter and her descendants.

Morfa, recollecting that letter which had been the dying man's last concern, wondered whether the drama had not symbolized loyalty to a son, rather than loyalty to a daughter.

'May I ask the name of the lady who figured in this ceremony?' he inquired.

'The dead man's cousin,' answered Dunscore. 'Miss Fell. Lavinia Fell.'

Morfa remembered well the superscription of the grey square of blood-smeared paper that had lain on the library table near the pile of diamonds, as clearly as every other detail of that night of memories — the creaking of the wheel-chair in which the dead chronicler of imaginary voyages travelled slowly from the room; the contemptuous regard of Colonel Beriah, magnificent in green, from out of his Florentine frame; that first I O U on a sheet of manuscript which he had burned because of the luckless number of the page, 1313 . . . So the girl to whom Anthony Purvis's last thoughts had gone out, was wedded to his empty shell, was mother of Garland's playmate! He knew death when he saw it: knew the ghastly wound that a big-calibred pistol would effect at close range: knew quite well that there could have been no living bridegroom. But what had been the dead man's wish was clear to him: it was not for him to betray once again that friend of one night. On no account would he do so.

He shook his head.

'An extraordinary story!' he commented.

'Most families have a skeleton in the cupboard,' said Dunscore. 'This family of Sir George's appear to have it in the marriage-bed!'

The remark incensed Morfa as an insult to a dead friend — to a dead friend's bride.

'I am sorry that I am quite unable to help you, Sir George,' he said acidly, addressing himself to the younger man who had sat in silence, twirling his half-empty wineglass between his fingers. He offered no explanation.

Parrish's dark face reddened. He looked down his twisted nose and said nothing, although Morfa noted that beads of sweat started on his forehead, and that the wineglass revolved the faster in his hand.

Morfa looked the length of the gallery, across the shining pools of reflected light in the glass tops of the display-tables, to the tall eastern window and the satinwood cabinet beneath it. The two men would be interested to know what souvenir of that night of thirty-two years ago was hidden within! . . . His lost honour could not be returned to him by the mere return of those few jewels!

Dunscore protested.

'But surely, my lord, you can recollect? My information is that you were present actually at the moment he died . . . Very great issues are at stake!'

Morfa made no denial. He simply remarked —

'You realize that nothing in any case can be done at present while Great Britain and the United States are at war?'

'The war,' responded Dunscore, 'can't last for ever. It is doubtful even if it lasts the year out.'

'I think you are optimistic!'

The demon fury that beset his grandmother — and was by her restrained — was unbridled in George Parrish. He raised his hot dark eyes from the table in an insolent study of Morfa; turned his regard then toward Dunscore, who was standing at his side; questioned him —

'Is this fellow going to tell us what he knows, or not? Let's have straight answers to straight questions!'

'Control yourself, George,' answered Dunscore. 'You are an incredibly insolent cub!' He turned apologetically to Morfa. 'I trust you'll forgive Sir George. His natural uncouthness has been accentuated by repeated setbacks and disappointments! When he gets older he will realize that a gentleman remembers his manners, however great the stress or the stake! If, ignoring this bucolic ebullition of youthful temper, you would be so very good, my lord — '

'I am ready to overlook Sir George's ill-temper,' said Lord Morfa with the far-away expression of one no longer interested in his company. 'He asks, however, for a straight answer to a straight question. I will give it to him — I do not propose in any circumstances to allow myself to be mixed up in this business. Please don't imagine that I doubt your sincerity; but there may be other aspects of the case and other motives, with which you are unacquainted. I cannot be compelled to give evidence, and I am afraid that I do not see my way to volunteering it.'

Dunscore noticed the expression: remarked the tone. His eyebrows began to slant, to draw together across the nose. From deferential faun he was in process of becoming malignant satyr. Nevertheless he made a final polite effort —

'I trust, my lord, that you will not allow yourself to be prejudiced by the boorishness of this wretched youth! . . . Be silent, George! . . . I pray you not to permit yourself to be dissuaded from an act of common justice by reason of his stupidity. An immense fortune — a really immense fortune by any standard — is at stake! The extraordinary plot was devised and carried out by Lady Parrish's mother — whom I can quite safely describe as a she-devil, if there ever was one! — in order that the daughter might be robbed of her rights! That is beyond doubt. She never forgave her for marrying an Englishman!'

She-devil!

There came back now to Morfa every detail of the horrible incident in the house on the road to Toulon. With a certain sardonic amusement he reflected that, by remaining silent, he was making of himself an ally for the old woman who had put upon him so great a humiliation.

'Quite frankly, Colonel Dunscore,' he said, 'while I am sorry to appear disobliging, I shall abide by my decision. I have no intention whatever of embroiling myself in this affair.'

'Surely, my lord, when a few words from you can right a great wrong — ! . . . You will admit it is unreasonable — '

'Unreasonable?' echoed my lord in his iciest manner.

'I withdraw the word,' said Dunscore quickly. 'But you will permit me with all deference to point out that your standpoint might easily be misconstrued. People *might* say that for fear of being involved — and God knows how you could be! — in a possibly unsavoury affair, you are prepared to withhold vital evidence. I ask you, my lord, to consider in what light your conduct *might* appear to the ordinary individual. I beg most earnestly that you will reconsider your attitude.'

The girl to whom that urgent letter had been sent over a generation ago, could rely on him! He answered coldly —

'Really, Colonel Dunscore, I do not feel inclined to debate the matter with you!'

He turned as he spoke, and his left hand flickered toward the embroidery bell-pull that hung on the wall of the recess, as if about to summon servants to attend his visitors to the door. It was a gesture that was suppressed almost as soon as it was begun: the damage, however, was done.

This time it was Dunscore who took offence. He recognized defeat — complete defeat: was infuriated by it; required revenge for it. He — who had carried through all his adventures an almost satanic pride — saw in Morfa's gesture a contemptuous readiness to inflict humiliating dismissal upon an inferior: was infuriated by that also; required revenge for it, also.

He said, his fingers fidgeting with the buttons of the praiseworthy violet coat —

'Your lordship's attitude has, *of course,* no connection with the presence in your lordship's town of the late Mr. Purvis's bastard son!'

Morfa realized that he had to some extent brought the insolence upon his own head. He ignored accordingly the insult to himself: did not — could not — overlook the insult to that other whose father he had seen die. He said —

'I should be obliged, sir, apart from all else, if you would recollect that you are speaking of a friend!'

'So that's the yolk in the egg!' exclaimed Sir George.

The young man rose: his big shoulders twitched as if against the restraint of his coat: his fists closed. He did not directly regard Lord Morfa, although he was turned toward him; but kept his head slightly bent, looking up from under his black brows like some evil-tempered beast. The short curls along his forehead were damp with sweat. Dunscore did not reprove him.

There was a nightmare quality about the interview, of which Morfa had had enough. His hands closed on the bell-pull. He rang.

'Lord Saundersfoot shall know how his friends are treated by you, my lord!' said Dunscore, with malign expression.

'He shall certainly be informed of those friends' peculiar conduct in my house!'

'Conduct not so peculiar as your own, my lord. Conduct from which one can only infer — '

'Your inferences, Colonel Dunscore, are of no concern to me!'

'They may become so!'

'Possibly — ' began Morfa, when George Parrish interrupted —

'I am sick,' said he violently, 'of this bloody bandying of words! I say that this bastard is deliberately suppressing the truth because he's hand-in-glove with his Yankee confederate! He hasn't got a leg to stand on, and he knows it! You can take that or leave it!'

He beat a large fist against a large palm. It was the action of an angry orang-outang.

'I prefer to leave it,' said Morfa, entirely unstirred. 'In my position I can fortunately ignore the outbursts of stupid young men such as your friend, Colonel Dunscore! I should, however, be glad if you would remove him! I find him displeasing!'

He took up his stand before the imposing fireplace, in which great logs had crumbled into a red-hot bed edged with feathery ash: appeared to await their departure.

Said Dunscore, confronting him —

'My young friend does not mince his words, my lord! I am afraid that he is too honest for polite society. Now I will say much the same thing in slightly different words . . . I will say that, while your conduct has become comprehensible, it has not become honourable!'

'Ah!' said Morfa meditatively. His head was turned away, and through the nearest long window he watched the boughs of a great cedar battling with the wind.

'Now *I*,' continued Dunscore, 'am not a juvenile hothead! As Saundersfoot told you in his letter, I believe, he first met me seventeen years ago, when I was an officer in the Sardinian service. He is acquainted with my brother, Lord Dunscore. He is aware of the fact that I have just been appointed to the Staff Corps as British liaison officer with the force raised in this country from French refugees. In view of these facts I do not presume that you will ignore *me!*'

' "Not honourable" was the expression I thought to hear you use?' remarked Morfa gently, still watching the tree.

'It was!' said Dunscore. 'If you don't understand the word, I'll repeat it in almost any language you like — except Welsh!'

Sir George was wisely enough helping himself — surreptitiously — to more wine.

The butler's impassive face presented itself.

'Are any of the gentlemen within-doors this morning, Evans?' asked my lord.

'They have all accompanied her ladyship to the horse fair, my lord . . . No, my lord, I am wrong — Colonel Tudor-Lloyd is in the billiard-room.'

'Present my compliments to the colonel. Ask him if he will be good enough to favour me with his presence for a few moments. On a matter of some urgency!'

A minute or two later a small gentleman in a snuff-coloured coat — sandy hair brushed up into a tremendous mountain peak on top of his head, lobster-red face, china-blue eyes — came trotting into the picture-gallery; trotted down it; pulled up with a jerk (as if he had suddenly been reined in) before the group by the fire.

'Evans told me you wanted me, Morfa,' he said in a toneless voice, looking from the earl to the two strangers.

'Colonel Tudor-Lloyd — Sir George Parrish — Colonel Dunscore, of the Staff Corps.'

Everybody bowed.

'To begin with, Colonel Dunscore, perhaps you will repeat to Colonel Tudor-Lloyd the insult you thought fit to inflict on me in my own house,' said Morfa. 'It will regularize proceedings for it to be said before one of my own circle.'

Dunscore was quite ready to oblige. He bent a little toward the new-comer, who was at his side facing Morfa, and said —

'I have just informed Lord Morfa that I do not consider him to have acted honourably in a certain matter.'

Colonel Tudor-Lloyd did not appear to realize that he was being addressed until Dunscore had almost finished speaking: then he looked at the younger man with entire lack of comprehension.

'I beg your pardon! I did not understand you were addressing me! Would you mind repeating what you said?'

Dunscore sensed rather than saw the smile on Morfa's face. He repeated what he had already re-said, in a voice that was pitched considerably higher than before. And with increased venom.

But Colonel Tudor-Lloyd, who had been watching the movement of his lips very closely, shook his head.

'Don't follow you,' he said in his flat voice. 'You people mumble your words so nowadays!' Sought in his coat-tails: produced an engraved silver ear-trumpet of most elaborate design and cornucopia-like convolutions, which he placed to his ear: inclined his head a trifle in Dunscore's

direction so that the mouth of the trumpet was brought a little nearer to
him. 'Would you mind repeating what you said,' asked Colonel Tudor-
Lloyd, 'and speaking close to the instrument, until I get accustomed to
your voice?'

Dunscore cast a furious glance at the politely attentive Morfa: surveyed
the guileless face and the queer instrument bent toward him: gritted his
teeth.

He stooped: roared into the hollow of the trumpet —

'I said, sir, that Lord Morfa was a dishonourable cur! I repeat it!'

Whatever Colonel Tudor-Lloyd had expected, it was nothing of that
sort. For he lowered the instrument, and looked from Julian to Morfa
for a moment in a blank astonishment that was succeeded by horror.

'In your own house?' he appealed for confirmation to Morfa.

'In my own house!' said Morfa, nodding to make things still clearer.

'Most ungentlemanly! Good Gad! Devastatingly ungentlemanly!'
Morfa nodded.

Colonel Tudor-Lloyd continued the conversation as if he and Morfa
were alone together: waved the horn in Dunscore's direction —

'Is the fellow a gentleman?'

'Supposed to be,' replied Morfa, and nodded in confirmation.

'Don't care for his manners — or his looks!' said the colonel. 'You will
ask satisfaction, of course?'

Morfa shook his head.

'Good Gad, my lord!' said the colonel, directing his ear-trumpet in
Morfa's direction, as though hoping to hear words that contradicted gesture.

'I shan't,' said Morfa to the ear-trumpet, 'because I am entirely indifferent as to Colonel Dunscore's opinion of me. But I have something else
to say to him which I should like you to hear!'

Colonel and hearing-apparatus were barely a yard away, in an attitude
of acute attention. Dunscore waited — with a sneer; Parrish, obviously
with some new outbreak bubbling to his lips.

'On reflection,' said Morfa, 'I find that Colonel Dunscore has most
grossly insulted a friend of mine, an American gentleman long dead, to
whom I owe more than I can say. He has most grossly insulted that
gentleman's wife, a lady of whom I can and will believe nothing that
is not good. In insulting the dead he has also most grossly insulted their
son, who is unable at the present to defend their memory. For these reasons, and these alone, I shall be happy to meet Colonel Julian when and
where and how he likes! Very happy, indeed!'

The colonel's face brightened.

'You would like me to act for you?'

Nod.

A new briskness filled the old warrior. He pivoted himself and his ear-trumpet from one to the other of the strangers as though he were a brass swivel-gun in action, with a fire of questions as to names and addresses and times — the replies being invariably misheard, the corrections misunderstood, and the conversation seasoned with 'What-says?' and adjurations not to mumble.

With a malicious smile Morfa watched him escort Dunscore and his violent friend to the door at the far end of the gallery, where they were taken into convoy by attendant lackeys.

Then the colonel came trotting briskly back, holding the trumpet to his ear with the mouth of it projecting forward, as though he were some odd relation of the unicorn.

'I shall call at the Four Swans at two o'clock this afternoon to make arrangements formally. To-morrow morning early will be the best for our little *rencontre,* I think . . . What-say? . . . Get everything done decently and in order before breakfast! You won't say anything to my lady or the other woman, of course! Only makes them nervous! . . . What-say?'

Morfa drank a cup of coffee, standing before the mirror on top of his high dressing-chest, while his man-servant put the last touches to the black cravat that was wound about a high black military stock. The unshuttered windows of his dressing-room showed a daybreak that was still darkly grey.

By the light of the candles on either side of the looking-glass he could see Barney's long disapproving face over his shoulder. Although more than ten years had gone by since Barney had last assisted at this early morning ceremony, yet he had obviously not forgotten what black cravat and stock and coat meant at a dawn toilet.

Barney knew without being told. Evans probably had guessed. But apart from those two discreet servants, there was no one in all that great house, with the exception of Colonel Tudor-Lloyd, who knew what was to happen so soon on the oblong of turf under the walls of the ruined chapel half a mile away.

'Charming — charming!' had commented the deaf warrior when he had walked with Morfa on a visit of inspection, down the grassy ride between beeches and chestnuts, and out onto a secret lawn girdled by trees except on the side whence it surveyed the peaceful valley. 'Charming! What-say? Perfect for the purpose!'

There was a tap at the grey-painted door, and a brief whispering when Barney answered it.

'Staff-Surgeon Strang is here, my lord,' he said on his return. 'He is taking coffee with Colonel Tudor-Lloyd in the Stone Parlour!'

Morfa looked at the gilt French clock on the mantelpiece, flanked by miniatures of Garland and his mother. It was not yet five. He was really getting too old for these hours and this sort of assignation, he reflected. He finished his coffee; picked up his gloves; cast a glance round the room. It was in the perfect order that he liked — that Barney liked. Although the operation of dressing was only that moment finished, yet all the appurtenances of the toilette were returned already to their place, every mahogany door and drawer of wardrobe and chest was tightly shut, every discarded garment had vanished; only before the bright fire his flat brass bath steamed and shone on the rose-coloured bath-blankets spread on the Turkey carpet.

So very ordinary, and pleasant, and sensible a room to quit! And so extraordinary, and ugly, and foolish an errand for which to leave it!

With rust-coloured beaver and gloves held behind his back, he stood for a minute or more in one of the windows, saying his prayers erect, as was his custom, looking on the beauty of the awakening world — the faint flush in the sombre sky above the dark stillness of the wall of trees across his lawns.

Was it so ugly and foolish an errand after all?

The stupid words addressed to himself mattered not at all. It was the honour of a friend of long ago — the honour of a lady whom that friend had loved — which he must avenge. Here on a Welsh lawn could he expiate the folly, the crime and the dishonour of which he had been guilty a generation ago. It was with a smile that he turned away from his window and went from the room.

He halted on his way downstairs, outside the high grey-and-gold door of his wife's bedroom. He would have liked for an instant to enter and look down on the sleeping Garland, flushed in slumber, dark hair spread upon the pillows; and bless her, and from the mere sight of her be fortified in return by a blessing unconsciously bestowed . . . He even put his hand on the gilded handle of the door; withdrew it; passed on with the shadow of a sigh.

As he walked down the great staircase with silent footfall, he asked himself whether she had had last night any unformulated suspicion of portending evil. Even Harradence amid all his volubility had remarked the shadow that lay over her wonted brightness. When they had said 'good night' outside her bedroom door she had clung to him for a moment longer than was usual, and her kiss had been more than ever that of a very cherishing mother — perhaps a daughter; for deep affection and devotion she had given him, but passionate love she had neither promised nor pretended. He had been content.

He walked down the grassy drive to the ruined chapel of Our Lady, between Colonel Tudor-Lloyd — enveloped in a long many-caped coat, chatting briskly with his ear-trumpet glued to his ear — and Staff-Surgeon Strang, wrapped in an old blue boat-cloak with a cat-skin collar, and breathing very strongly indeed of the lozenges of liquorice and horehound with which he was protecting himself against the raw air of early morning. A pair of queer acolytes for the ritual of death, he reflected . . . Made certain that he had his spectacles.

Suddenly he knew quite well that someone else was walking with him. Knew, and was glad. . . .

The valley below was hidden by a billowing sea of white and silver mist: the rim of the further hills was gilded by the rising sun, sharp-edged against the pallor and the clarity of the dawn sky. Not a whisper of wind stirred in the bluebell-haunted depths of the woods that clasped chapel and lawn. Pigeons flurried and murmured in the ivy of the ruin and the tall pine trees that guarded the broken western door. . . .

The handkerchief dropped from Tudor-Lloyd's outstretched hand. It opened as it fell, so that it seemed to flutter quite slowly to the grass. Because he had watched its fall, his pistol spoke the fraction of a second after the other.

His hand was still straight out before him, the smoke still drifting lazily upward, when Dunscore toppled forward with a bullet in the brain — did not crumple, but fell flat, like a pillar that has been overset — and remained unstirring.

With heavy wing-beatings the frightened pigeons took flight.

George Parrish was running across the sparkling dewy grass toward the fallen man, when Morfa himself fell. . . .

Someone was on his knees beside him, supporting his head. Even in this ultimate agony he recognized the smell of liquorice and horehound: smiled. Someone else kneeled beside him. Even with fading vision he saw the silver convolutions of the ear-trumpet close to his lips: smiled. He tried to speak: could not.

And then he became aware that Another bore his head and was bent over him, whispering to him, listening to him. A friend. A friend he had known long ago. A friend whose whimsical loving smile told him of so many things — the very least of which was the unimportance of this moment of agony.

CHAPTER IX

THE RECIPE FOR DISHONOUR

'THEY are sending us away to-morrow,' said Anthony, leaning against the mantelpiece, and watching Garland's back.

She stood at a tall window surveying the green splendour of a valley dappled with slowly-moving cloud-shadows and barred with the black shade of woods drowsy under the sun of a July afternoon.

She had chosen that small square corner room for her own because its windows looked down the valley as well as across to the opposing hills. It was lofty and cream-panelled, furnished with severity, and there were no pictures on the walls except a seventeenth century sea-battle scene — murky with the smoke of cannon, and crimson with the flames of burning ships — above the fireplace. 'A man's room!' Morfa had always said, but he had liked to sit there pretending to read though in reality watching her at work — writing, sketching, embroidering.

There was an appreciable moment before she replied, and she did not turn round as she asked —

'Why, Rowley? Where?'

'Abergavenny, to start with. Afterwards I don't know. Probably Stapleton Prison at Bristol . . . Griffiths read out a Transport Office order at the muster to-day. Apparently people are being shifted everywhere — retribution for "indiscipline", "infraction of regulations", and an "epidemic of parole-breaking". . . . So to-morrow we set march under guard, bed down at night on straw — I hope it's clean: it wasn't last time! — and get sixpence a day on which to keep ourselves!'

He spoke as lightly as he could, but deep in his heart anger was mingled with despair.

'Oh, Rowley, this is terrible!' said Garland, and turned, at last being certain of herself. 'Can't I do anything — or Uncle Harrady — to stop it? . . . If only Charles — '

'Morfa could have done nothing, either! There would have been no time — even for him. One day's notice, they've given us. That's all!'

When would he ever see Garland again? It was the thought of parting that weighed more heavily upon him than the misery ahead. Quite deliberately he set himself to imprint upon his mind her picture as she stood there in the window-place, black-gowned for the dead Morfa. Grave face a little golden from the sun, with long-lashed eyes, short nose, straight brows, and chin that seemed always to be tilted at so proud an angle: the waves and curls of the dark hair that grew to a widow's peak upon her brow: the jet ear-rings: the long curve of her throat and the whiteness of the slim shoulders that rose from the high-waisted dress of soot-black silk.

The love for her, which he had realized at the very moment when he found himself looking up at her tears from the cobbles outside the Four Swans; which he had pretended to himself to be merely the old affection renewed; which he had admitted and honourably repressed — that love became a torment.

Garland ceased twisting a handkerchief. She said —

'Oh, Rowley dear, I prayed and hoped that we had you here until it was peace. Until — '

She came toward him, stood opposite him by the fireplace whose emptiness was masked by a Chinese screen of golden lacquer.

'Until — ?' he prompted her.

She hesitated for a second before replying.

'Until — until all the bitterness had gone from you!'

'Bitterness?' he echoed in some astonishment.

'Have you ever seen yourself, Anthony dearest? There used to be a sort of surprised look about you — but now it's a lost look! You used to look as if you were remembering fairy tales, and now you look as if you remembered nothing but horrible things!'

'In those days,' said Anthony, 'I had day-dreams. Now I have nightmares. In those days I hadn't seen the unspeakable degradation of men to beasts. I hadn't eaten greedily a stew of rotten bullock's head with my bare hands. Or watched men fight a mortal duel with pointed stakes. Or seen a corpse left on the foreshore mud to the crows, as an example of the fate of an escaper to his comrades. I hadn't — '

He catalogued the facts unemotionally enough. It was, perhaps, that very lack of emotion to the recital which assured her of the depth of his feeling, which made her say almost in anguish —

'Don't, Rowley! Don't! I can't bear it!'

The quick look of surprise that he turned upon her was yet more evidence to her of his own lack of realization. She found that she was near again to tears.

He said —

'But I've had *you*. And Harrady. And your mother. And Morfa. And the Almonds!'

'For a time,' she answered, 'you have succeeded in isolating us in your mind, together with all the fantasies with which you live, from the external world. We are as apart from the realities of life as all those fairy tales you used to tell yourself! But for how long can you keep us apart from those realities?'

'What realities, Garland?' he asked, looking down at the glittering varnish of his riding-boots, the thin straps of his silver spurs.

'The reality that you are American and we are English: that our countries are at war: that the suspicions, anger, and vengeances of a whole generation lie between us . . . Dear God, what hatred, what unhappiness!'

She turned a little so that she no longer looked at him, but at the battle scene over the white mantel — at a foam-flecked sea in which men clung to submerging spars, and the sides of lofty ships were stabbed with flame.

'Garland — ' he began afresh: stopped as abruptly . . . Morfa had been barely three months dead!

Said Garland, examining the tangle of cordage trailing over the side of a dismasted warship: and it was as though she knew what he would have said —

'We were always very honest with each other in the old days, weren't we, Rowley?'

He responded thoughtfully, with memories of Hortense and Jasmine —

'You were more honest than I!'

'There were no comparisons present in my mind . . . Let's be honest now! Very honest! . . . What did you think when Harrady told you about Charles — Charles's story of High Pale, I mean?'

He answered by an action before ever he said a word. His solitary hand went up to his high black stock: his fingers fumbled for an instant between it and his throat, retrieved, and produced to view a thin gold chain — a locket. A locket that she knew. A locket that she herself had worn many years ago.

He broke one of the thread-thin links of gold with a sharp jerk: held the trinket reflectively in his open palm for perhaps a minute: opened it clumsily, and extracted a square of paper which he unfolded. Garland saw the word 'I O U' and the signature 'Charles Hurrell' before he started to tear it into shreds. It was tough paper, and difficult for a one-armed man to deal with; but in the end he reduced it to a pile of tiny fragments which he pushed along the mantelpiece top toward her with locket and broken chain.

Then he answered her in words —

'I knew, of course, his story must be true. It would be impossible for anyone who had known him to think otherwise . . . Morfa and my father were friends. In half an hour can you not make a friend for life and beyond life? Shall not one friend borrow from another? If you had ever seen the picture of my father at High Pale you would have known that he understood, that he would always understand. My mother used to say that when she met him after she died she would have to tell him how much she loved him, even before she humbled herself before Almighty God!' She shot one swift sideways glance at him — at his downbent head with a dark lock astray upon his temples. 'You know, Garland, that I'm sure my father was waiting on the Other Side to present him to Mother! That they are walking together in the shimmering colonnades of Paradise . . . Shall I ever forget that Morfa died in avenging their honour? . . . I wish that it had been I!'

She had intended bringing him from admission of belief in Charles's story to acknowledgment of the erroneousness of his grandmother's conjectures, and thence to avowal that all her virulent hate was sprung mainly from similar misconception and misjudgment. But now she knew that, so far as Rowley was concerned, Charles had joined the first Anthony in some fairy-tinted fantasy utterly dissociate from the world of the living, and that his evidence could no more affect earthly things — like hate and vengeance — than the whisperings of ghosts.

And her knowledge was confirmed when Anthony went on —

'My poor grandmother' — Garland was as shaken by his sympathy for the dark woman of the tower as if he had expressed his love for one of a witches' coven — 'was wrong — dreadfully wrong! But can you be surprised at her bitterness? Robbed of both her sons! And now me — a prisoner of war for over six years!'

Was 'bitterness' an adequate word to use, she asked herself, for the spirit that had hounded Charles for years, that had launched the *Nautilus* against the English ships in La Cadière Bay, that had educated a small boy to be the instrument of its vengeance?

'Oh, God!' whispered Garland to herself.

She stared with tears in her eyes at the sultry splendour of the ancient sea-fight. Anthony still examined his boots. And thus they stood and talked, not looking at each other, against the mantelpiece, with the great picture and the golden lacquer screen between them.

After a silence she went on —

'I'm going to continue being very honest, Rowley!'

'Yes, Garland?'

'And since you are going now, and no one can tell when we shall meet again, I am going to say things that I would have preferred to say much, much later — if, indeed, then they had to be said at all!'

It came to him then that there was something which it was imperative that he should say first — something which he had tried to say a minute or so before. He said —

'Garland, I love you very much!'

Did not look up.

'*I* loved *you* so much, long ago, Rowley, that I did my duty the more readily — when I helped to warn the ships — because I knew you would be the less lost to me if you were killed than if you succeeded. That is how much I loved you, Rowley my dear! . . . But you were lost to me all the same!'

'What a fool I was!'

'And then, by and by, I married Charles. He was kind — always, always kind. He was old enough to be my father, but I was tired of young men who were just brave and brainless. England seemed full of them. And I had left my girlhood behind me, that night at La Cadière. I can't describe our relationship. I loved him — but in a different way. He was a comrade and a friend. And then . . . you came back to us again!'

'Yes, Garland?' he prompted her in a very low voice.

She turned now again, and regarded his stooped head.

A buzzard swung high above the valley in the gold-dusted sky of the early afternoon. Harradence — puffing at a long clay pipe filled with some unsatisfying combination of raspberry and hazel leaves, for tobacco was short since the blockade of the American coast — passed the long windows unperceived.

'And then I found that I was still in love with you . . . I think Charles guessed. I think he was sorry . . . that . . . he — And you were married too!'

He did not look up when she paused, but began to fumble for the tail-pocket of his dark green coat. Whenever she saw him do any small thing that would be so much easier performed with the assistance of a second hand, she often found herself biting her lip, restraining herself from going to his help. He produced at last a letter; handed it to her, still without raising his eyes.

'This has some bearing on what you are saying, Garland! It isn't an interruption!'

The letter was in writing which she did not know — flowing, ornamented, Italian. It was dated from London a few days before; it was signed 'Jasmine'.

It was not long. Narrated the utter capitulation of a Royal duke on a most satisfactory financial basis. Congratulated themselves on the removal of Julian Dunscore. Informed him of the disconsolate retreat of the man whom he now knew to have been his cousin to the wilds of Lincolnshire. 'I never believed the story Julian brought back from America; and now the only person left who could prove its truth is your grandmother! Remembering correspondence George Parrish had with her, he is not likely to make much headway.'

What story? — she asked herself; even as Anthony had done. But there was no hint of it in the letter. Uncle Harrady had known nothing at all; and Colonel Tudor-Lloyd, waving his ear-trumpet, had been only able to say, in an embarrassed fashion and extraordinarily loud voice, that Anthony's mother and father had been insulted — grossly insulted . . . It was not until she came to the last paragraph that she saw why Rowley had given her the missive.

'It is but a few weeks since I saw you, although you did not know it. In Morfa. With the girl who was my rival years ago at La Cadière. She was called Garland, but I have forgotten her surname. I watched you, and saw how it was with you. I told myself that I had been very right when I warned myself in the earliest days of our marriage that I had two rivals — one the Me-that-had-never-been, which lived in your imagination alone; the other the rival whose continued existence in your heart you did not even guess yourself . . . Anthony, if it had not been for Julian, I believe that I might have become the Me-that-never-was! Think of me sometimes like that. Remember too that I am now giving you your freedom. We married in such innocence — after all, I had never been married before! — and with such speed that the ceremony is valid nowhere in the world — except perhaps in France. Julian found that out last year . . . Perhaps *she* will thank me for this!'

It was not until she had read and folded the letter and was holding it out to him that he spoke.

'Dearest, dearest Garland, when I saw you kneeling by me as I lay on the cobbles outside that wretched inn, I knew that nothing mattered beyond the fact that we had found one another once more . . . Again and again during those first days I was on the verge of telling you how much I loved you. Not to excite your compassion, not in any way to dishonour Morfa; but because it seemed so natural and simple a thing to be in love with you.'

Garland said —

'So you are free, then! It *would* have made no difference to me if you had still been tied to her, Rowley. I am like Mother: when I give, I give everything . . . *Now*, too, it makes no difference!'

He looked up swiftly and hopefully; stirred as though he would have taken one step nearer; did not. Could not read what was written in the eyes that looked beyond him to the smoky purple of the distant hill-tops, and to the chiaroscuro of the cloud-mountain that piled itself slowly above them.

'You see, Rowley, *now* I cannot, will not risk our love!'

'But, Garland —' he objected.

'Supposing that in course of time I became no longer isolated from your hates, that my own deep love for my country involved me in your hatred of it! Supposing that your anger awoke in me an answering passion against an enemy!'

'But, Garland, you would always be a thing apart!'

'How could I be? . . . Think what happened but so few years back! . . . Do you remember, too, when we were children in the *Aventurière* how you sang the "Marseillaise" and I dug a fork into you? Do you remember on the terrace at La Cadière when they first talked of Mr. Fulton and his *Nautilus*? . . . I should always live, Rowley my darling, in a panic of fear lest there might one day be mingled with all my love for you some horror of you. And our children — how could I bear it for them? . . .'

Even as he murmured passionate protest he sensed the rigidity of her decision.

'The house in Dark Wharf Gate, myself and Harrady — you have deliberately excluded us from our setting. Perhaps you are right in the case of Old Tom and his wife — already their eyes are turned toward the glory of another world. But *I* cannot be set apart from the world in which I live, apart from my faiths!'

She could — she could: he reiterated.

'Supposing something happened such as might have happened on that March daybreak twelve years ago . . . And we were married and I had a baby! Where would my hopes be for our child, or for ourselves?'

He thanked God in his heart that she knew nothing of Silas and Deane.

'I would not go back to the army,' he assured her.

She shifted her gaze to him as he stood utterly dejected, his left shoulder against the high mantelpiece, idly turning Jasmine's letter over and over in his right hand. There was every love in all the wide world for him in her eyes.

'It isn't that,' she said. 'It's what has been implanted in you of which I am afraid. Planted within you in childhood without you realizing it. A tradition of hate which has been nourished ever since by your own misfortunes. Do you remember the history lessons your grandmother gave you? Sometimes you recited them to me afterwards. I have never

forgotten! . . . Who was the governor of New York who used to parade
the Battery dressed in women's clothes, Rowley? . . . Who signed the
death warrants for innocent men in his cups, Rowley? . . . How many
American soldiers were killed by the panicked firing of red-coats when
Braddock's force was ambushed on the way to Fort Duquesne by the
French? That was the sort of history the old witch taught you! Dreadful
history, but, alas, dear God! true history! History that *you* must forgive
and allow *us* to forget! . . . One day you might look at me and suddenly
discover in me the representative of the race that killed your father and
your uncle, and devastated your property, and clapped you into coffin
ship and prison camp! . . . You might, Rowley! You might, indeed!'

He reached out, and took her hand in his. She let it lie there, warm
within his clasp so that it might comfort him for her irrevocable words.

'And, Rowley, I might come to look at you as representing a nation
that, having equal grievances against England and France, chose of the
two to make war on us when we were fighting almost alone not merely
for our own liberty but for the liberty of all enslaved Europe. When the
seaboard of the continent was arrayed against us . . . I know so well
that now we are fighting for freedom, just as in the Revolution we fought
against it . . . And then I might come also to think of you as one whose
hands were stained with English blood because of your service with
Napoleon! . . . And so there would be incurable heart-ache for both of
us! Such unhappiness by very reason of our love!'

He battled with her for long, as though he might wear her resistance
down. But she was inflexible. Battled with her until she was in tears.
Battled with her until, within the light clasp of his arm, she sobbed with
her face hidden against him, the dark curls of her lovely hair against his
lips. But she remained inflexible.

Presently she straightened up; withdrew herself a pace.

'It isn't any good, Rowley dearest! I know that I am right. Can't we
still be friends all the same? Mayn't I go on helping you where and how
I can? . . . I shall never stop loving you, Rowley! Never! Never! . . .
I'm going to be yours only, now and always!'

'Mine!' he said a little bitterly.

And then for a short moment he thought that he had won, for she
came to him again, under the fierce seascape on the wall, and kissed him.
A kiss that was more than the mere meeting of lips; that was passionately
symbolical of a love that surpassed passion. . . .

He found himself walking down the avenue under the great chestnut
trees. Reciting to himself arguments that he might have used. Ques-

tioning the justice of her assertions. Interrogating himself . . . Why had
he become the servant of the Little Man? From no love of his political
theories. From no impellent belief in the hegemony of France in a
European confederation. No. From an immediate anger, which soon
was dead, but from which had risen all the shadows that now surrounded
him — the shadows of hulk and prison camp, *and* of lost love. Why —
he asked himself — had he gone on when his anger was dead, before
there had been fresh cause to seek retribution? And admitted the intel-
lectual fascination of the problems of war, regardless of what the solution
of those problems meant in death and destruction and sorrow; the over-
mastering magic of the small man in the grey coat and cockaded hat
who had made all Europe a graveyard that he might rule over it.

He pounded down the avenue, unaware that he had left his hat behind
him, regardless of the salute and curious look from the green plush
magnificence of the servant at the gate-lodge.

Suddenly he slackened his pace, so that he came very slowly down
the steep road to the town between the slanting woods of Morfa and
slanting orchards of apple and of plum. He was making up his mind to
return. There were other arguments to use, other promises to be given.
Garland must be made to understand. Garland *could* be made to understand.

He was just about to halt and return when he reached a sharp bend
in the road, where it sloped steeply downward between high banks of
reddish earth and was over-arched by lofty trees.

A soldier stood negligently in the middle of the road, red-coated with
black spatterdashes and cockscomb-crested helmet. He was standing with
crossed legs, propped — as if it were a staff — by his musket, which had
the bayonet fixed. Hard by four or five other men were sitting with their
feet in the ditch, eating and drinking, firearms and spades stacked against
the bank.

'Hey! Sergeant!' said the soldier loudly, without altering his posture, as
Anthony appeared at the bend. ' 'Ere's anuvver on 'em!'

One of the men rose from the roadside; came toward Anthony, his
empty bayonet sheath flapping against the short tail of his jacket.

'Wot you doin' 'ere, mister?' said the sergeant, who was a little bandy-
legged man with a wizened sallow face.

'What the hell is it to do with you?' asked Anthony peremptorily,
halting.

'Beg pawdon, sir!' said the sergeant coming to attention. 'British
n'orfisser? Didn' unnerstan'! We on'y jest got 'ere, sir.'

'British be damned!' said Anthony, about to turn back.

'It's a bloody Yank prisoner, sarge!' said the soldier.

'Jesus Christ! So it is! Hey, you! Stop!'

Anthony paused irresolute —

'What the devil? Why shouldn't I be here? I am not out of bounds!'

The sergeant stood squarely across the road.

'Ho, you aren't, aren't yer? I mought tell yer, mister, that y'are per-cisely three paces out-er bahnds! By statootary measurement! . . . And Gawd knows where yer've come from!'

Anthony's astonishment at this announcement was so obvious and real that the sergeant guffawed, and not unsympathetically.

The man pointed to the bank by which his fellows rested; Anthony now saw that a milestone was propped among the spades.

'It's come 'ome!' said the sergeant. 'Four furlongs, five chains, an' seventeen yards nearer town, where it did oughter be. All on 'em 'as been put right to-day! . . . You go back, sir! Str'ight! Like a good boy! 'N we'll say no more abaht it!'

'What —' began Anthony.

But what did it matter? Of what importance beside the pressing need to get back to the Abbey, with all the new weapons in his armoury.

'Can I go back to the Abbey?' he asked. 'It's a matter of — it's most important! I will promise to return!'

'Dunno nuffink abaht no h'Abbey,' said the sergeant. 'We're noo to these parts 'ere. 'N don' mind h'if we don' see 'em again! You can't go back, and that's flat!'

'One of your men could come with me to the door. It's the Countess of Morfa's. I should not be long. Let me go, as a good fellow!'

'These 'ere Yanks want bleedin' nursemaids, sarge,' said the soldier, 'It's like their bleedin' sauce, sarge! Whaffor should we go trapesin' the bleedin' country arter them, sarge!'

'Go back 'ome,' said the sergeant, 'h'or it'll be the wuss for yer! Come h'on!'

'Be reasonable,' said Anthony. 'The place wasn't out of bounds an hour ago.'

'Well, it *is* naow! Come *h'on!*'

For one moment Anthony meditated immediate disobedience: but it would have been the sheerest folly.

He set off downhill without another word.

' 'E's in a n'urry!' meditated the sergeant, watching the retreating figure with some surprise. 'Now I wonder — ! Smithy, foller 'im! . . . Take yer musket, you bloody fool! . . . 'N see there's no 'anky-panky!'

One of the resting men straightened himself to his large feet, seized his gun, and shambled rapidly after Anthony, who went quickly on, unaware of escort.

'Don't like the look o' the feller!' further meditated the sergeant. 'Wilson, Hughes — go arter Smithy!'

Half a mile further on a lane branched off between hedgerows, along the foot of the hills, eventually joining the highway out of Morfa to the west. From that road there was another approach to the Abbey.

Without a minute's hesitation Anthony turned into the lane, and began to run. All his preoccupation with Garland was against a background of fury with these fools who obstructed his return to her. The regulation forbidding a prisoner to leave the main road was entirely out of mind; it is questionable, indeed, in any case, whether he would have regarded it.

Smith, rounding the bend, saw the road stretch empty before him. He whistled shrilly, waved wildly to the men following him, shouted ' 'E's mizzled!' and broke into a rattling gallop.

Anthony heard the cry; disregarded it; went on with one quick glance over his shoulder.

The soldier had reached the entry to the lane, a bare hundred yards behind him: shouted a summons to halt: was down on one knee, raising his musket to his shoulder. There was a loud explosion, and simultaneously something sang past Anthony's ear like an enraged hornet, and smacked on to the upward slant of the byway with a puff of dust twenty feet ahead of him.

The fact that he was under fire meant little to him: it was just part of the insane confusion of everything. The only thing that counted was the fact that he must see Garland, now, at once, before he was torn irrevocably away to the jungle of a prison camp. He increased his speed, as he heard from the shouts behind that other men had joined in the hunt . . . Another shot cracked out; but the aim was wild, and he did not even remark the passage of the bullet.

At the end of a quarter of a mile the lane degenerated into a mere cart track, grassy, between high hedges, with ancient and deep ruts full of brown rain-water. It divided a screen of tall poplars to pass into a level meadow at the very foot of the precipitous wooded hills. At the far end of the field were horse lines stretched from the wheels of limbers; at one corner a knot of very muddy tents, before which shirt-sleeved soldiers were busied with saddlery and about a camp fire.

The sound of the shots and the cries had obviously attracted attention, for an officer was coming toward the entrance to the lane through the long golden greenery of the grass, buckling his sword-belt as he came. A couple of troopers with unslung carbines followed him.

He could not go forward . . . Equally he could not go back . . . Had he been seen?

Anthony flung through the hedge to his left and into a thicket of bramble bushes that fringed the nearer side of the wall of poplars . . . The thicket became a jungle, through which he passed as silently as he might; in which he lost all sense of direction; from which he could hear all round him the uproar of an intensifying chase.

Presently he came to a deep cleft, through which flowed a fast-running stream in a boulder-strewn bed, almost completely arched over by woodland tangle. He lowered himself into the rift, and followed the course of the brook under overhanging banks. Once he fell on the mossy wet stones and not only drenched himself, but cut his forehead and gave so severe a blow to the stump of his amputated arm that he remained sitting in the water for nearly ten minutes in a sick agony.

Much later he reached the mouth of the gully: peered cautiously out.

The stream ran betwixt stunted willows across a field cropped short by grazing sheep and horses. Beyond the further hedgerow, a road. A coach swirled by. He could see the shimmer of its yellow and black panels, and the glint along the guard's horn as he raised it to warn the expectant town that the Royal mails were in transit from Western Wales to His Majesty's good city of Gloucester. A little to his right lay the Black Ox Inn — where he and Julian Dunscore had met — with its whitewashed outbuildings, smoke idling up from the squat chimneys on its thatched roofs. Just beyond the tavern the by-road, that led to the western entrance to the Abbey, joined the highway. . . .

From the shelter of a hedge he looked onto a great bay in the road, with a semicircular sweep of high grey wall broken by gates of wrought iron and by a squat stucco lodge faintly resembling some mausoleum of Homeric Greece.

The gates were shut. A scarlet soldier with fixed bayonet leaned against them: others were talking to the gorgeous lodge-keeper. From distant halloing it was clear that the vigour of the hunt had not abated.

The hopelessness of the position was borne in on him as he lay crouched beneath the bright green of a hedge speckled with the light green of slowly ripening hazel nuts.

They had realized his interest in the Abbey. And since now the gates were guarded, and the ten-foot wall that surrounded the miles of park — as was the way with lordly estates — was unscalable by a one-armed man, he was in an utterly hopeless position.

Fury with those who had — he thought — so wantonly excluded him from the paradise that might have awaited him; anger with his hunters; these mounted within him — burned more and more furiously. And with them, too, rose the consciousness that he had broken his parole undertaking not to leave a main road — that he had disobeyed a lawful summons to halt — had fled from authority — had absented himself from the special muster of prisoners ordered for that afternoon — was now a fugitive against whom any man might turn his hand or his weapons . . . What a pity for the demon-ridden Parrish that he did not know it! . . . Only three days before Griffiths, the Prisoners' Agent, had read out a solemn warning from the Transport Office at morning parade —

> 'The Commissioners desire that all prisoners of whatever rank be informed that, in consequence of many breaches of parole and recent defiance of authority, any future infraction of the regulations laid down for their conduct will be punished forthwith by the immediate transfer of the offender or offenders to a prison ship.'

The hulks!

Garland!

He was sick with love for her; with fear of them.

Every horror of the *Crown* came back to him — the naked *raffalés* seething in the darkness of the lower deck like the blanched insects that are revealed beneath an upturned stone; the miasma as of a charnel-house that rose through hatchways from depths in which the bestialities of unnatural sin provoked as little comment as they would in hell itself.

Garland!

And other things, small things! A prisoner — stripped to the filthy skin — squatted by a barred gun-port, scratching, scratching, scratching like a demented monkey, and devouring a raw dead rat . . . The moment when he discovered that he himself was vermin-infested . . . A drunken surgeon puking over the hammock of a dying man in the sick bay . . . The filthy scum that loitered round the ship so that she, like her consorts, seemed to float in excrement. Ship? — Craft that prostituted the word! . . . . The wife of the doctor of the *Crown* whose house was said to be completely equipped with bedding intended for the hospital ship, whose household was petticoated and under-garmented in cotton and flannel taken from the prison stores. He could see the woman now — loose lipped with an amorous roving eye, a questing bitch!

If he went forward, it would mean infallibly the hulks! If he went back to the town to surrender, it would also mean the hulks! . . . The hulks!

He suddenly swore to himself that he would not go back to be coffined in those floating sepulchres! He could not — would not face them a second time.

And at that moment *Dewi Mawr,* the big bell of St. Teilo's, began to toll. Its solemn clangour — each new outburst of brazen resonance overtaking and drowning the dying vibrations of the last — sang to him of no glory of resurrection, but only of finality . . . Requiem for love . . . Requiem for honour . . . Diamond-shaped heraldic hatchments hanging on sombre walls, crowned by skulls — undertakers' mutes in funereal cloaks — shuffling feet of coffin-bearers — gaping excavation hideous with raw earth glistening at its side. . . .

It was late in the afternoon when he came back to the high road again, a mile or so further from the town, and, with every precaution, looked out from a gate upon a highway barred with the long black shadows of maple and lime and chestnut.

A few yards away alongside the grass verge of the road a battered post-chaise — that had once been painted purple and green — was halted. The postboy, in an equally battered beaver hat and a sleeved waistcoat of blue and white stripes, was busied at the straps of luggage fixed behind, with turned back.

The man suddenly looked over his shoulder and had seen him before Anthony could step back into the shadows. The fellow straightened himself then: glanced up and down the road: tilted his hat, and set to scratching his head. Then he whistled sharply between his teeth, and beckoned.

Anthony had no plan, but to escape somehow, anyhow. He had plenty of money. He stepped out into the road, and walked briskly toward the carriage.

He knew the man at once — the one-eyed ostler from the Four Swans, an Englishman, an obliging enough fellow, who had often done errands for him, and been well-paid for them.

'You know, sir,' said the postboy shaking his head over venial naughtiness, 'that they are looking for you h'all over the town! They are arter you right enough! It'll be the 'ulks, sir, if you're cotched! It'll be the 'ulks right enough!'

'Who's in there?' asked Anthony in a low voice, jerking his head toward the carriage.

The postboy's long leathery face split in a wide grin that showed a few yellow fangs.

'H'empty in a manner of speaking! And not h'empty in a manner of speaking. A bit o' both, sir!'

'I've plenty of money, Varley,' said Anthony. 'Plenty! . . . Where are you going?'

'I'm goin' a mile or so the other side of Carmarthen,' said Varley reflectively, still scratching the top of his head and surveying the American. 'You allus treated me like a gentleman should! Is it worth a couple of jimmy-o-goblins to you?'

Anthony had already extracted red silk netted purse — already extracted two golden sovereigns — was at the door of the post-chaise.

'You'll have to ride with *him!*' said Varley, and flung the door wide open.

A long stiff bundle, enfolded in a brown blanket, was propped up in the nearer corner of the mildewy box that was upholstered in shabby wine-coloured cloth. Varley leaned within; pulled down an edge of the wrapping.

The glazed eyes of a dead man glared out of a chalk-white face. The jaw was dropped, and the coarse grey hair tousled; it was as though death had come on him as he saw a ghost.

'Good God!' said Anthony.

'Reg'ler picter, ain't he?' said Varley rather possessively. 'He 'ad a fancy piece down in Morfa — a sojer's wife she is — in Abbey Walk. He died on 'er. Appleplexy, the doctor says. Anyhow she don't want no funeral from 'er 'ouse. Bad enough h'as it is. 'E 'ad plenty in 'is pockets to pay to send him back, post, to his 'ome. And so 'ere 'e is, and 'here h'I h'am! There is a cloak in there and a 'at. I should 'elp yerself — they'll 'ide the furrin-ness of you! Put a quid in 'is purse, so there'll be no ill-feelin'!'

Anthony mounted the step, and pushed inside past his fellow traveller, and seated himself as far away as possible. Varley slammed the door after him; and then, as one recollecting matters that had been overlooked, thrust his head in over the rim of the window.

' 'E's quite fresh, sir!' he informed the new passenger considerately. ' 'E only died last night!' Paused; broached another topic tentatively: 'I suppose you'll get to Lunnon somehow, by 'ook or by crook!'

Anthony had not even arrived at the stage in his plans of having a settled destination.

'The address is, Number Fower, Pratt Street, Camden Town,' said Varley confidentially.

' 'What is?' asked Anthony.

'That's where they 'elp you. To get acrost to France. There's Madam Glion, in Pulteney Street, too. But I don't recommend 'er, sir! Dearer and more posh, as you might say, but a bit of the amatchoor! Worth another quid, sir?'

It was.

It had not occurred to him before that war and the consequences of war should have called a brand new profession into being — that of escape agent. How reasonable and natural that the practitioners, since they could not advertise their calling in the public Press, should employ touts in the parole towns!

Varley accepted another sovereign with a touch of the forelock, and in a few moments they were rattling away in a cloud of dust. . . .

What communings he held with the dead man Anthony never knew, for as they drove the fifteen miles along the valley toward the sunset the post-chaise seemed full of ghostly travellers . . . A smoky mist was rising from the river against the empurpled hills, and the conflagration of sunset shone before them and in the dead man's eyes . . . He could not bring himself to risk touching the dead in pulling up the blanket that should have veiled its face.

Was it the Thing in the corner, or Julian Dunscore, or those two returned companions of his earlier travels that eventually said to him in most conversational manner:

'But you are a bastard, of course, you know! Your mother never — '

He suddenly opened the door and flung himself from the carriage as it went at a swift trot round some sharp bend between dark jutting woods and the River Towy. He stood — hatted and cloaked by the dead — looking after the carriage, and then was gone even before it came to a halt out of sight. . . .

The details and the route of the Odyssey that followed were never clear to him. He must have had plenty of money, because he could not recall at any time being embarrassed through lack of funds. He made his way over the hills to the coast by night journeys; crossed the Bristol Channel by fishing-boat to North Devon: found himself on a Sunday in a town that he later learned to be Ilfracombe.

There, in a tavern by the small hill-girt harbour, someone recognized the enemy uniform beneath the cloak. They loved neither Americans nor Frenchmen in Ilfracombe, for sixteen years before the American adventurer Tate had landed his Black Legion on a piratical expedition hard-by. A growing crowd chased him pitilessly through the streets. A brick or a bottle struck him on the shoulder. . . .

He went through the half-open door into the dusk of a small church. The light of a cloudy morning filtered through the stained window above the Holy Table. A great voice spoke and was made sonorous from the vaulting of the roof. Even as he stood uncertain of his refuge, panting from the hunt, hand upon the serge curtain that shielded the door, the words echoed down the nave —

'Ye that do truly and earnestly repent you of your sins, and are in love and charity — '

He then saw that there were many worshippers within the church, for, with the rustle and the hushing of a wood in a small wind, they rose; streamed up the aisle between high pews towards the dim chancel — the sanctuary — the altar.

' — draw near with faith — '

Already he had taken his place unperceived in that slowly-moving procession up the nave; was kneeling with the rest upon the flagstones in a semicircle . . . Above the murmur of the General Confession he heard a babble of voices outside; the creak of the west door as someone peered in, and was apparently satisfied, for voices and heavy feet passed on.

There was a large signet ring upon the hand which the kneeling priest had rested upon the bare altar as he recited the confession . . . There were words incised upon the iron-grey stone upon which he himself kneeled: he could make out the lines —

> 'What wee gave, wee have;
> What wee spent, wee hadd;'

He did not like to shift back far enough to see how the epitaph continued; was still puzzling over it when the Paten of the Eucharist was presented to his downbent gaze, and rejected as later he was to refuse the Cup. He was in no love and charity with his neighbours; there was no comfort to be had of the Holy Sacrament. . . .

That night — or was it, perhaps, some other? — the woman of an inn, her grey hair tightly screwed in curl papers, a horse-pistol in her hand, discovered him searching for clothing in a press in an empty room.

They had some difficulty at first in understanding one another; but in the end she proved quite ready to sell him a broad-cloth tail-coat, green corduroy breeches, and a pair of generous-sized boots with yellow tops — presumably the property of her husband now deceased. She had also given him food, general directions for the road to Exeter, and pressed upon him a gig and bay mare belonging to a customer who was sleeping off deep potations: even helped him to harness and put the creature into the shafts.

Years afterwards he could recall her standing outside the stable, in the drizzle and the darkness, holding a lantern above her head, the better to watch his departure. She was shaking with suppressed laughter: he wondered ever since to what sinister jest he was made a party.

He abandoned the vehicle in the dawn on the outskirts of a market town beside a broad estuary over which the sea-gulls whirled . . . Walked for all a day beside a fierce tattered girl with an angry baby bound to her by her shawl — a girl whose man had been hanged a month ago for some trivial offence which he could not wholly divine . . . Rode for a day within a vast hooded carrier's wagon, drawn by eight horses, and lumbering along the narrow roads like some clumsy galleon of the land. The straw-covered space that was not occupied by crates and sacks he shared with a weeping miserable creature escaping from the consequences of some minor misdeed, and now more afraid of the wrath of the Almighty than the vengeance of man. The fellow spent his time in abject prayer: he reminded Anthony of Solly in the degradation of his abasement . . . Was on the roof of the Exeter-London mail, the pageantry of summertime England speeding by to the music of horses' hoofs, the jingle of harness, the rattle of wheels.

It was on that last stage of his journey to London that he realized that he was running away *from* things and not *to* them — that his escape had no true objective. It was, in a sense, symbolical of a flight from a world in which there was no Garland, but an armada of prison hulks — nothing more . . . He supposed he would go back to the Little Man . . . Or would he not?

As he descended to the cobbles of the inn yard, where the coach came to a final halt, a man stepped forward from the little crowd that attended its arrival, and tapped him on the shoulder.

'I rather think, sir,' he said in a hoarse voice, 'that you and I ought to have a few words together! I'm Mr. Lavender, from Bow Street Police Office.'

And as he spoke he let his coat open so that there was displayed the brilliant red waistcoat which was the hall-mark of the Bow Street runner.

Tap that meant Hulks. Words that meant Hulks. Waistcoat that meant Hulks.

So to the prison ship again! To the *Blenheim* anchored off Chatham marshes. To an orlop deck where no grown man could stand erect; where four hundred and sixty prisoners lived in a space one hundred and twenty-five feet long and forty feet wide, and drew their light and air from twenty-eight portholes seventeen inches square, that were shut fast at night. To vermin, and rags, and hunger, and sin, and typhus — and overwhelming hate.

CHAPTER X

REQUIEM FOR AN EMPIRE

THE Conqueror of the West sat steaming in his bath in a rococo palace in Dresden.

Great square malachite bath, set in midst of a lofty room of black and green marble with white panels sculptured in deep relief with a tale of the loves of mermen and sea-witches. As dense a cloud of warm vapour as any sea mist. Piles of green towels upon a sea-green slab supported against a wall by silver Tritons. Marble bench upheld by writhing dolphins.

A tray, furnished with silver inkstand and paper, was set before him across the bath so that he could write if he wished. But all he did was listlessly to scrawl circles and squares and elaborate initial letters, as, with the sweat pouring down his face and over his chest, he simmered there where formerly had simmered the fat mistresses of Saxon Electors, their immense turrets of powdered hair protected by oiled silk bags.

Latterly there had been occasional spasms of horrible inward pain, and periods of utter weariness; times when the prospect of defeat seemed not so bitter as it would once have done, because defeat meant rest.

And whilst on that early October afternoon in 1813 the Little Man loitered in his bath, lingered over decisions that would once have been immediate, the pulse of the vast headquarters that he had created — and alone could operate — beat deadly slow. Whilst he loitered in his bath, whilst he lingered over decisions, the sands of his hour-glass trickled swiftly away.

The one implacable enemy that had given him but a few months' respite in all his career not merely still ruled the seas, but her armies at last looked down from the high mountains of Spain upon the broad plains of France. More and more millions of money was England providing from her accumulated wealth, more and more munitions of war — cannon, powder, boots, a million muskets — for those who would use them to bring liberation to Europe. The despoiled and the dispossessed and the vengeful were gathering on his flanks and before him and in his rear. The blue-eyed Russian, who for a space had been his loving friend: the big-lipped Austrian, his unloving father-in-law; the market-gardener's son who had stolen his sweetheart and now ruled Sweden; the Prussian who had been his unhappy jackal — were pressing on to crush him past recovery . . . The shadow of the conqueror was about to lift from a ravaged and terror-filled world.

He sat in his deep hot bath, drawing a pattern in which the letters 'N' and 'I' were repeated across all the sheet in front of him. Napoleon — Imperator . . . Napoleon — Imperator! The sweat dripped from his hand, as he wrote, on to the paper so that the ink of the letters ran, merging into a pale grey-black blot.

'Marchand!' he said suddenly, curtly, without turning his head.

The man in black, who had stood by the door at the far end of the room behind him, for one hour — for two hours, silent and motionless except to summon fresh supplies of hot water, stepped forward, throwing a great bath-wrap over his arm.

'Send for Monsieur d'Ideville and Colonel d'Albe!'

'They are already waiting, sire.'

He sat up, drawing nearer to him the broad tray which was covered with green oilskin. His shoulders and upper arms, glistening white, showed above the rim of the bath. His thin black hair was streaked across his beaded forehead.

Marchand ushered in d'Ideville — with black portfolio; Bacler d'Albe — with roll of maps, and, with a secretive smile of welcome, the man who accompanied them. A one-armed man wearing a shabby green uniform and golden shoulder-knot such as the Emperor's orderly officers had worn — how many years ago, was it?

'We are too near the mountains here, d'Albe!' said the Emperor abruptly, ignoring the presence of that third man, of whose arrival an hour ago he had been advised; whose attendance he had personally commanded. 'Why are we here?'

'It was your own decision to make the headquarters at Dresden, sire!' replied d'Albe acidly. He looked round for a place to spread his precious map, in a prim, old-maidish way.

'Put it on the floor!'

Incisiveness had come back to the Little Man's voice: he pointed with an abrupt gesture of a plump white arm.

With distaste d'Albe spread the great map on the black and sea-green diamond pattern of the sopping marble floor, close to the bath. He weighted down the edges with cut glass flagons full of brilliantly-coloured scent.

The Emperor hung over the rim of the bath, pointing, demonstrating with a hand from which sweat and bath-water dripped on to roads and hills and great cities.

'Dresden was a mistake,' he admitted. 'I allowed myself to be over-persuaded by Berthier.' — A grim smile of amusement twitched the corners of d'Albe's mouth. — 'The result was that when I beat the Army

of Bohemia I had no room and no time in which to turn their retreat
into a rout. They found refuge almost at once in the intractable mountains . . . Now they want me to fall back on the marshlands of Leipzig
— Point me out Leipzig, d'Albe! — but I won't be over-persuaded again!
Berlin — that's where our new headquarters shall be!'

The fog of indecision and lethargy that sometimes clouded him was
swept away. He quoted the saying of Danton, ' "*Ce qu'il nous faut pour
vaincre, c'est de l'audace, encore de l'audace, toujours de l'audace!*" '
Emerged from the bath to be enveloped by the waiting Marchand in a
large green towel: stood steaming amid the uniforms of blue and green:
went down on his knees to trace the trend of the northering roads from the
Saxon capital.

'Anything new about Bernadotte, d'Ideville?' he asked. 'Send for Berthier! . . . Send to the *salle-de-service* — I want an officer to report on the
castle of Düben . . . D'Albe, this map was perpetrated by a *coglione!*'

'It's the best I can get,' said d'Albe in an aggrieved voice. 'The Saxon
war department is preposterous, and those they have just sent me from
Paris are Pétri's maps, drawn over fifty years ago!'

The Little Man rose to his feet. He stood on the map as though it
were a bath-mat, holding the folds of the wrap toga-wise about him.

'There was precisely the same difficulty, sire, seven years ago,' said Anthony Purvis from the background.

'Nobody on my staff ever has a map that is accurate!' said the Little
Man, shifting his wet feet so that he straddled the whole sheet as a colos-
sus might bestride a kingdom. 'Nobody ever speaks a language other than
his own! Nobody ever has a watch that goes! I am a nursemaid to my
staff! . . . Where's your watch, d'Ideville?' D'Ideville made an apolo-
getic gesture. 'Yours?' D'Albe shook his head. 'Yours?'

He turned toward Anthony, and then for the first time permitted himself to realize the presence of one long absent, to note the outmoded uniform. His bright grey eyes became yet brighter. Amid all the cares of
empire and wars and love there still had been tabulated in the wonderful
brain the essential facts about that one-armed man who bowed in his
presence, very low — just as there had been indelibly recorded for use a
million other facts about an infinitude of other matters.

'Comrade!' he said — and his voice was very musical — 'I welcome
you back! You were too long gone!'

'Long gone, indeed, sire!' said Anthony, and kissed the well-shaped
hand that was offered him from the folds of towelling.

The Little Man let the toga fall to his waist so that it became a skirt.
He dipped two fingers into a jar of lavender water which Marchand

offered him, and thoughtfully rubbed the scent into his plump white chest. For all that he was an Emperor he had become corpulent.

Anthony realized that other men were silently entering the room, were standing at discreet distance: the splendour of their uniforms seemed to him almost as out of place in the mist of that place of ablution as nudity in a hall of State.

'When we found out what had become of you,' said Napoleon, taking another dip into the scent flagon, 'we tried to effect an exchange. But the British would not play! We tried several times!'

He looked to d'Ideville for confirmation, and the tall man bowed.

'At least twice every year, sire,' he agreed. 'And Your Majesty offered good measure! You took the bidding up to two colonels and a major in exchange!'

'You see, comrade, you were not forgotten!' said the Little Man, and he stretched out wet scented fingers and tweaked Anthony's ear in his peculiar gesture of affection. 'I did not forget my playmate of the house on the road to Toulon! . . . Where do you come from, Parvis? . . . Marchand, bring me some clothes!'

'I come from the English hulks,' said Anthony grimly. 'Where they herd eight hundred — perhaps twelve hundred — prisoners of war into the space that they ordinarily use for four hundred convicts!'

'They are monsters, these shopkeepers!' said the Little Man, absorbing this fact, and obviously meditating in what connection use could be made of it . . . He stalked up and down the long bathroom in his sea-green skirt, with bent head. 'Send for Méneval! . . . Ah, I want you, Berthier! . . . Well, and what else?'

'The English papers have themselves stated that fraudulent contractors are making over a million pounds sterling a year. By giving prisoners short rations and incomplete issues of clothing and bedding!'

Méneval, that prince of secretaries, entered — note-book and pencil in hand — against an escaping billow of steam.

'Méneval, take a note of that! . . . What else?'

'They sent us a boatload of new prisoners, who had just come from overseas. Thirty of them, not even "walking sick" but delirious with fever, lying in rags at the bottom of the boat. Our captain would not have them for fear of infection. They remained in the boat while he carried on a long argument with the hospital ship about their reception. Before they were allowed on board they were bathed in icy water. Many of them were hauled up dying!'

'Have you got that, Méneval? . . . Take him away and get all you can from him. Lies and truth are equally good! Circulate the report, Ber-

thier, to all commands so that the men shall know what will happen to
them if they fall into British hands! Good propaganda! Worth a divi-
sion! . . . How did you escape, my little Pargis?'

'Bribed the drinking-water contractor, sire, after I'd been aboard ten
weeks — ten weeks in Hell! — and went ashore with a load of casks for
re-filling. It cost me £150 — nearly four thousand francs. It was cheap!'

He looked back as he followed Méneval to the door.

The Little Man had sat down upon the marble bench, hands upon the
tinted flying-fish that formed the arm-rests. The steam from the bath
hung in a cloud under the lofty ceiling. The map had been set again at
his feet. With his naked torso, and folded robe, and with the grave classical severity of his face, the Emperor seemed to be a deified Caesar presiding over the destinies of mankind. The brilliance of the staff gathered
in half-circle before him was commonplace against his divinity.

He heard the Little Man say in reply to somebody, employing words
that he had used to the Austrian envoy a few short weeks before—

' . . . One such as I cares little for the lives of a million men!'

The irony of this remark from the critic of British brutality escaped
him . . . He was forgotten.

He was passing through the door when he heard the voice rise —

'Purgis! . . .' — He halted — 'Captain Purgis! . . . Colonel Purgis! . . .
Berthier! We move to Düben Heath! To-morrow. No, to-day!'

He was not forgotten. The Little Man was a great master . . . And
so he had come back to him at last. . . .

And so back to his post: to be taken up by the furious whirlwind of
war; to be borne almost at once to that overwhelming defeat at Leipzig
where he stood beside the Little Man watching the disorder of the Imperial army streaming in rout from a field of carnage. A raw October
morning. Eighty thousand dead. Retreat over a single bridge across the
river Elster. The Little Man stood in grey overcoat, hands behind back,
whistling maddeningly between his teeth the refrain of the ancient air —
'Malbrouk s'en va-t-en guerre!' Anthony recalled Fulton in the Nautilus,
in just so infuriating a way, whistling, humming the negro song, 'Keep
me from sinkin' down!'

'All is not lost!' said the Little Man, and pulled his hat forward over his
nose.

And therefore the whirlwind of war did not die down: bore him to
daemonic campaign of defence in the valley of the Marne: swept him as
Imperial emissary far to the south where Soult, Duke of Dalmatia, fell
back before the advancing forces of England. And then in one last tur-

bulence at Orthes, swirled him away amid panicked fugitives in the head-long flight of autumnal leaves: at sunset had done with him, and left him fallen amid the dead and wounded somewhere between the torrent of the Gave de Pau and the River Adour. . . .

He was convalescing from a great wound in the side, under the acacias at La Cadière — whither his grandmother had recently returned — when he received his first letters from England. Some of them had been writ-ten as soon as he was traced to the hulks, and had been more than a year upon their journeyings about Britain and war-torn Europe.

There were letters from Garland. Kind and loving letters, in which there was no reference to what had passed between them under the great picture of a sea-battle; in which there was no criticism of what he had done — only prayers and hopes for him, and the small news that might interest him: Harrady had been to London, had bought an interest in Finlayson's of Birmingham; Mrs. Tom had had rheumatism, had recov-ered; the roan mare had thrown her yesterday.

Ah! Garland! Garland! Wise, beautiful Garland! He closed his eyes — feeling the tears hot against the lids — so that he might see her again. Saw the frost-white façade of Morfa Abbey aloofly regarding all the valley; the many windows of the immense house reflecting the early sunshine, and the great Doric columns of its portico silhouetted against their own shadows. And, thus reconstructing the mansion, was able to visualize her standing behind one of those shimmering windows look-ing down to the valley and the silver glint of the river . . . Not yet eight o'clock — hatted and habited for her morning gallop in the park — dark brown beaver hat, short russet jacket and long russet skirt, gay Chinese scarf knotted about the frilled ruff at her throat!

It was a long time before he could return to his correspondence.

Letters from Harradence himself — long letters, each most painstak-ingly copied out three times so that one at least should be certain to reach him.

Letters from Old Tom and Mrs. Almond.

A letter from Fielding's Bank reporting that the former Mrs. Anthony Purvis had returned to them the allowance that they had been instructed to pay quarterly to her account. On the occasion of her marriage with the Earl of Saundersfoot. And what should they do about it?

So Jasmine had decided in favour of respectability instead of a Royal duke — or was Saundersfoot just in addition?

Jasmine — Dunscore.

Dunscore — Parrish.

His grandmother was close by him, sitting in her wheel-chair beside the worn balustrade of the terrace, looking out across the tangle of the garden toward the still blue sea and the islands where the English ships had lain on the night when he had first lost Garland. She was enveloped in a black shawl, fastened with the brooch depicting a sarcophagus that was his earliest memory. Her parchment-coloured bitter face, now etched with a hundred lines, was as immobile as ever. For all that she was more than eighty years old she needed no glasses. Her long yellow fingers, twitching and trembling, crumbled to dust some morsel of cracker or biscuit on her lap.

Little had he said to her of his sojourn in Morfa. She had asked for no detail beyond what he volunteered; had listened without comment; had understood what was sheer confusion to him — for, until he had heard Colonel Tudor-Lloyd's vague report of the scene in the Long Gallery, he had been utterly unaware of doubts about his birth. Now, with news of Jasmine before him, he was reminded of what she had written to him last year; just that Dunscore had brought back some other mysterious tale from America on which George Parrish had based a claim to High Pale, and that his grandmother alone could prove its truth. A fantasy — not even a legend! A foul insult to his mother's memory! One does not dissect a fantasy, but yet —

He said diffidently: 'My cousin, ma'am, appears to be under the impression that I am illegitimate. It's monstrous, of course — '

'Is he, Richard?' she replied, unstirring, and without interest.

It was no new thing for her to call him Richard. She had done it when he was a child. He did not even remark it.

'Some cock-and-bull story, I suppose, ma'am?'

'Some cock-and-bull story!' said Madam Purvis. 'I can assure you that your mother was most scrupulously married. I was present!'

After that he lay silent, with the letters in his grasp, watching the windows of the house, staring down the colonnade of acacias, seeing everywhere Garland — the child, the girl, the woman. It was true what she had said last year, that he deliberately excluded her, as he did, too, Harradence and the Almonds, from her setting — the England that was his enemy; the England of hulks and prison camp; the England that had shot away his arm, had put a bullet in his side; the England that had killed his father, and his uncle. Dissociated her, but . . .

His grandmother said, while still she stared out to sea, and into the past —

'There was a letter from M'Tavish which came before you were capable of dealing with any correspondence!' M'Tavish was the Scots overseer

of the High Pale estate. 'You had better see it, though there is nothing
you or anyone can do . . . except smash the British!'

It was a letter showing how disastrous indeed for the planter grandees
had been blockade and war. The export market for tobacco had vanished,
said M'Tavish. Last year a miserable five thousand hogsheads had been
sent oversea from all Virginia: this year the exports would probably be
halved again.

'When I was a girl,' said Madam Purvis, 'we reckoned on a net profit
from every slave on the plantations of sixty-five dollars a year. M'Tavish
shows that there is now a loss of over fifteen dollars on each negro . . .
You must get well quickly, Richard, so that you can go back to America
and beat the British before they make peace! *Beat them!* Then bring
the Emperor back from exile in Elba to beat them again!'

But before Anthony was on his legs the futile fratricidal war had
reached its end: the British had burned Washington and the Americans
had smashed invasion at New Orleans. A war which resulted in nothing
but a century of embitterment, souvenirs looted from the Capitol on a
few British mantelpieces, and razor-strops made from the hide of a Red
Indian chief in a few Congressmen's dressing-rooms.

He was still incredibly gaunt when he stood on the steps of the Tuileries
on a wet and foggy March evening, to welcome back the Emperor Napoleon to a palace from which only that morning had the weary cynic of
a Bourbon king departed . . . He saw the Little Man step from his mud-
stained carriage, grey-coated and cocked-hatted, as if he had returned
from some resounding victory instead of from the prison-paradise of
Elba; saw him borne within the great doors shoulder-high by shouting
generals . . . Were these men there just because they were loyal, or just
because they thought to follow the fortune of a rising star? Was he come
to serve an Emperor who was not his, from personal loyalty and devotion, or for the purposes of his own private war? He did not know.

But as the fateful One Hundred Days of 1815 wore on amid a fury
of preparation, of planning, of the marching of giant armies, of statecraft,
of diplomacy, he became doubtful of the outcome — and knew that others
were so, too; and knew that loyalties could be built on sand . . . In
agonized shame at his uncertainties, Berthier, Prince of Neuchâtel, Marshal of the Empire, flung himself from his window and was broken to
death. Berthier, the copyist of the Little Man, the magnifico with the bitten finger-nails! Just exactly what Junot, Duke of Abrantès, Marshal of
the Empire, had done two years before! Just exactly what Solly, the Jew,
had done — or tried to do — sixteen years before!

Waterloo! A muddy, bloody confusion! And thereafter hideous confusion of flight to Paris, of flight to Rochefort.

Now at the end of all this confusion, he watched through his spy-glass from the shore a boat slowly pulling toward a great ship lying in the roadstead with open gun-ports; a ship from whose poop stirred the flag of Britain. He knew that a figure in grey coat and cocked hat was sitting in the stern, although he could not distinguish it. . . .

Ever since they had reached Rochefort in their flight and found the port blockaded by the British, they had debated ways and means of escape. They had talked — Heavens, how they had talked! Of mad schemes — wild schemes — brave schemes.

'If your friend Fulton was here with his *Nautilus,* or his steam-engine boat — !' said the Little Man, who seemed the least concerned of all. And he smiled.

'He died six months ago, sire,' said Anthony.

They became silent.

The Little Man fell a-whistling, almost beneath his breath, '*Malbrouk s'en va-t-en-guerre!*'

Requiem for a lost empire! Anthony thought. The tolling of *Dewi Mawr* — requiem for lost love! 'Keep me from sinkin' down' — requiem for a lost submarine! Thought of Solly, and his requiems. Of Putzger, the half-Englishman, who had made an end of Solly's music. Of the sailor of long ago, with the pale belly, who had frightened him in the *Aventurière.* Of Starkey tearing at some callosity on his hand whilst he prepared betrayal. Of the crowd of bestial faces surging about the thin line of prisoners outside the Four Swans at Morfa. Of the man in the red waistcoat whose touch had meant — Hulks . . . Of the hulks. Of Norman Cross.

A bird flew through the open window into the room.

'A good omen, sire!' said Gourgaud, the principal orderly officer, a swaggering figure of theatrical mood and gesture; and caught it in his hands.

'There are enough unhappy things in the world,' said the Little Man. 'Let it go!' As it flew away, added — 'Watch the augury! Which way does it fly?'

'It is flying to the right, sire. It is flying toward the British men-of-war!' . . .

And now the Little Man was following the direction of the bird. He was on his way to surrender himself up to the one enemy.

Anthony suddenly found himself without an object in life.

BOOK SEVEN

THE GUARDED ISLE

St. Helena — 1818

★

CHAPTER I

RAREE-SHOW AT WORLD'S END

ALL the highways of the desolate sea led to the desolate island.

The lofty peaks and rocky walls rose from the grey-green swell of the Atlantic without welcome for the traveller who had journeyed for many weeks across a thousand, two thousand, three thousand unfathomable miles. They had survived, it would seem, from some lost continent for one purpose, and for one man.

For that one man came ships from Europe, with timber for his house, with books for his library, with shirts and saucepans and rat poison for his household, with letters — opened and scrutinized by His Majesty's Secretary of State for the Colonies — for his attention. Ships from the Congo and the Cape with fruit and wine and provisions for his table. Ships with red-jacketed soldiers for his guard. Ships with dispatches — reams and reams of them! — about him.

For that one man — a retired French military gentleman, who must never be given a higher title than 'General', although he had been the maker of kingdoms and the overlord of kings — this remote and precipitous island at world's end, guarded by the vast seas and eternal wind, was sentinelled as never had island been before.

For that one man, by day and by night a patrol of warships circled the precipices from whose summits sixty miles of tossing water could be surveyed. Because of him, those vessels, which by prescriptive right or valid excuse could come to anchor in the only harbour, lay under the guns of a quayside battery, under the guns of a sentinel frigate, under the guns of a fort: the hill-tops bristled with signal-stations; the ravines, the hill-sides clothed with cabbage palm, the high plateaux, echoed to the challenge of sentries. For that one man a garrison of three thousand men kept watch and ward upon an island of forty-seven square miles.

For that one man, too, the sightseers flocked ashore. Sightseers from ships India-bound, freighted with pink-faced young subalterns and dashing young ladies; from ships out of Bombay and Calcutta with liverish colonels, and yellow civilians, and sallow ladies wearing Paris fashions of the year before last — their trunks full of Kashmir shawls, Tibetan silks, and Madras muslins. There could be no more stupendous exhibit in the world menagerie than a sullen emperor pacing his rocky prison.

Merely to have seen St. Helena was to secure distinction; to have made the toilsome pilgrimage from Jamestown to the windy upland where was the dwelling of the former master of Europe, was to have earned fame: to have glimpsed, even if only through a spy-glass, a short figure in cocked hat and green hunting coat, was to become an author. To souvenirs in silk and ivory and silver of Hindoostan in those brass-nailed chests were added precious relics of Europe's prisoner — dark grey fragments of lava from the beetling hills, skeleton leaves of a willow, or a pressed flower or two from some combe on the way to Longwood.

Relentless censorship and unremitting sentry-go were no impenetrable barrier to the secret messages and the secret messengers that came and went for the one man. Messages written on silk and sewn into waistcoats, folded small and hidden in snuff-boxes, placed under the false bottoms of innocent-seeming trunks, left under boulders by the roadside to await collection by an illicit intelligence service. All sorts of people involved in that service: narrow-eyed naval surgeon playing traitor to his oath, mulatto servant, gouty banker who (they said) was a by-blow of the Prince Regent, ship captains earning by their dishonour fees of six hundred pounds, court botanist to the imperial majesty of the captive's unloving father-in-law in far-away Vienna, as well as a herd of lesser characters — slaves, sailors, Chinese labourers.

The messages came from all the corners of the earth, whispering of mysterious plots, of mysterious expeditions that were preparing, of mysterious ships that were being built, of . . .

'So everything has been arranged, then?' said Madam Purvis reflectively, as she rested against the pillows in her sleek mahogany cabin.

'For the first stage of operations — yes,' said Anthony.

He sat at a small writing desk under a square port-hole, surveying stiffly a mass of papers, his chin propped by a high black stock, the gold-embroidered stand-up collar of his dark green uniform rising almost to his ears. Upon his left breast, above the bend of the empty sleeve, glittered the immense silver star of some knightly order.

His grandmother's eyes were turned to him for an instant: she admitted that he looked to be distinguished. Then her gaze went back, as ever, to the shore of St. Helena.

The green reflections of the bay — sheltered from the tireless trade winds — and the sombre landscape beyond, swung gently up and down and to and fro, framed by the open port. Above the bastions of the landing-place a line of stunted thorn-trees: beyond them, the prim grey tower of a small church and the long whitewashed bulk of a largish building that might have been a barracks or a school but was dignified by the name of the Castle. Beyond them again, amid dark verdure, James-town was strewn along the narrow valley between high ashen hills toward the forbidding bulk of yet another peak. Upon the bare walls of the great furrow were etched sharply precipitous winding paths. As the ship swung at her anchorage there came into view the few white cottages lining the shore path under a headland to the adjoining bay. As she heaved a lit-tle with the swell, so dipped into sight the gun embrasures of the fort crowning the summit of Ladder Hill which sentried the town upon the other side.

Those guns had spoken yesterday. Madam Purvis had not heard the voice of British guns for more than a generation — not since she had listened to the distant slamming crash with which retreating artillery disturbed the misty twilight at High Pale. Yesterday the emptiness of the Atlantic had echoed to the salute with which the hill-top battery had replied to the cannon of the ship reported to shore authority as His Prus-sian Majesty's 36-gun frigate *Königin Luise*. Madam Purvis had been by herself at the time: she had permitted herself to laugh dryly: and since then something that might have been the beginning — or the end — of a smile never quite left her face.

'You will send a message to the *Conqueror* at once, then, explaining why we are temporarily leaving anchorage and putting out beyond ter-ritorial waters? You will sleep ashore to-night?'

'Yes, ma'am,' said Anthony.

He turned and spoke in German to a bald-headed man in a blue coat with golden epaulettes, who stood against the cabin door; a man with drooping eyelids and high shoulders that gave him the appearance of a deferential vulture.

'You are satisfied that this melodrama can be staged effectively? *Quite* satisfied?'

'No one would know that he's been in pickle for a month, even if we were to carry out the performance in harbour,' said Captain von Velhagen. 'I am perfectly satisfied with all the arrangements.'

Anthony turned over the documents before him — a strange variety, in all sorts of handwriting on all sorts of paper with all sorts of signatures; the work of one man.

'Solly is a genius,' he said to himself, completing the inspection. 'You might sign this memorandum to me, Captain von Velhagen! It will be the only genuine signature in the batch . . . You know what it is!'

The captain approached the table — he had a most peculiar walk, straightening his knees after each individual step with a violent jerk. He took up the paper: read it quickly. It ran:

> 'Memorandum to Lieutenant-Colonel Count von Schauenstein, Privy Councillor and Commissioner of his Majesty the King of Prussia in St. Helena, from Captain Wilhelm von Velhagen, commanding his Majesty's frigate, *Königin Luise:*
>
> 'In accordance with your request, search of the ship and inspection of the belongings of the crew were made yesterday. In the result I regret to report that a large number of letters for General Bonaparte, of a compromising nature, were found in the possession of Franz Hermann, a quartermaster, contrary to the orders read to the ship's company at the beginning of the voyage and on quitting the last port of call. I enclose these documents for your Excellency's attention and disposal. The offender will be dealt with in accordance with the decision of a court-martial held this morning.'

With a grim smile von Velhagen accepted the pen that Anthony offered him, and wrote a small jerky signature.

He went back to his post by the door; stood with his hand on the latch —

'I will go now and arrange about the message to the British ship and for a boat for yourself . . . You will not be alone, of course?'

'I shall take secretary and servant. That's in accordance with the voluntary restriction which we are supposed to have announced to the British cabinet, and of which the Governor has been informed.'

The captain produced another grim smile — which reminded Anthony of Knotty at the Institut Putzger — and remarked, as he opened the door —

'I am not a flatterer, as you know, but I myself could never tell that you are not a German, not Count von Schauenstein — if he exists otherwise than in your person, — not the Royal Commissioner to St. Helena.'

Anthony bowed his acknowledgment of the compliment.

'It's just my good luck to have been born,' he said, 'with a natural ear for the rhythm of language. Just as Klasing has an eye for the flow of line and curve. I can forge a pattern of speech in the same way that he can forge a letter and signature.' Added lightly — 'My secretary and I, in fact, are a pair of dangerous men!'

'I well believe you,' said von Velhagen, and departed with a jerky small bow to Madam Purvis.

Anthony swept his papers together: rose to his feet.

For a moment his regard lingered on the distant mountain which hummocked the end of the valley. It was mist-capped. Somewhere beyond it, up in the clouds, was the prison of the Little Man who once had ruled the greater part of Europe — had vied with Alexander and Caesar and Charlemagne. The Little Man who once had been an emperor and was now only a retired general: who once had palaces by the score wherein to dwell, and now was tenant of a gaol.

He came back to the immediate present; returned his gaze to his grandmother and to a cabin luminous with the reflections of the sea. At the far end, over a cushioned settee, the dark panelling was masked by a chart of the Atlantic, upon which the ship's course had been daily pricked. Before her, as she sat up amid her pillows, Barnes's new map of St. Helena — showing soundings and anchorages — was spread upon an adjustable writing slope. She wore usual lace cap with black ribbons, usual black shawl fastened with usual sarcophagus brooch; a startling contrast to the whiteness of the bed-linen and the honeycomb quilt. It seemed to him that she had not altered in appearance at all ever since first he could remember.

At the foot of the berth was coiled a smoke-grey kitten with applegreen eyes. Madam Purvis permitted its presence: she may even have liked it: but she never spoke to the little creature or took cognizance of it.

'So at last we open our campaign!' she said, as much to herself as to him. '*At last!* . . . There are no suspicions so far as you can judge?'

He thought over events since their arrival just before dark on the previous day: shook his head.

'None at all, I am prepared to swear . . . And Sir Hudson is a suspicious man — whether by nature or by force of circumstances, I don't know. As I told you last night, ma'am, he even produced his official despatches from Whitehall — so artistically prepared by Klasing — and asked if my instructions tallied! He wouldn't have done that if he had had any suspicions!'

She admitted this by a nod of her head. Her trembling hands were engaged in shredding to pieces a sheet of paper. The tiny scraps littered the quilt and dripped on to the maroon carpet that covered the floor.

'Then he was impressed too by the moderation of the views we fathered

upon the Prussian government . . . I had been instructed to stay here
only if in my opinion Prussia was justified in incurring the expense of
having a commissioner resident. Very sensible! — said he . . . The fact
that Russia and Austria and the Bourbon king of France were represented
on the headquarters staff of the Emperor's prison was no reason of itself
why Prussia should send an envoy here to add to the circus. Very, very
sensible! . . . And then our voluntary decision to hold the ship *incom-
municado* — that no one should go ashore except myself and my personal
staff. Very, very, *very* sensible! When to-day's proceedings have been
duly noted, I fancy that we shall have the Governor eating out of our
hands!'

With a shaky sweep of a long hand Madam Purvis swept a pile of
the shreds of paper to the carpet, as though she were presenting Sir Hudson Lowe with a diet of finely minced forgeries.

'I have lived a good many years for this,' she said. 'I do not grudge
them, now that I can take part, *myself!*'

'With all deference to you, ma'am, it is just as well that Cardinal Fesch
was able to persuade Madame Letitia that she should not come too!'

'Madame Bonaparte merely has a live son to set free,' said Madam Purvis coldly. '*I* have two dead sons to avenge!'

'There are very few of us on board who can be called really disinterested,' commented Anthony thoughtfully. 'Except Klasing!'

'Why Klasing?'

'He is a Jew.'

'What has that to do with it?'

'Gratitude! The gratitude of Jewry to the man who recognized their
rights of equal citizenship in his empire. The gratitude of the liberated
ghetto!'

'Captain von Velhagen, then?'

'He'll never see his native land again unless the Emperor returns.'

Madam Purvis made no comment. It did not appear necessary to Anthony for him to tell her that von Velhagen had been one of the many
Prussians who had played traitor to their country after the Little Man
had overwhelmed it in disaster at Jena eleven years ago.

'Yourself?' she asked, and looked up at him from the chart which
showed all the hilly confusion of the island.

'I haven't analysed my motives, ma'am,' he said, hand upon door.
'Perhaps allegiance. Perhaps also the fellow-feeling of one who has been
a prisoner of the British! I will send word to you, ma'am, how matters
proceed in the course of the next day or so. Good-bye!'

He bowed, and was gone.

Why was he so like her elder son — she asked herself. The son who could not have been his father. She saw that other Anthony in his thin dark face, in his grey eyes, in the black lock that strayed upon his forehead, and in the rather haggard expression of weary inquiry that he habitually wore. But in all the work of organization that had preceded and made possible this expedition financed by herself and by the mother of Napoleon, she had seen the quick realistic mind of Richard coupled with a fixity of purpose which Richard had never had — a fixity of purpose transmitted from herself, she was sure.

After he had left the ship, however, she sent for von Velhagen again. When the yellow face and great beaked nose of the captain appeared in her cabin she said, in passable German, watching him intently —

'There is one small matter, Captain von Velhagen, about which I wish to make certain.'

'Please?'

The question was a simple one . . . Did Captain von Velhagen understand that by far the greater part of the funds of the expedition had been provided by Madam Purvis? . . . Captain von Velhagen did so . . . And his officers? . . . They did so, too! . . . Was it understood, then, that being paymaster-in-chief Madam Purvis was also — ? . . . There was no need to finish the sentence for Madam Purvis's position was understood and thoroughly appreciated. . . .

Outside the guard-house under the ruggedness of the mountain, a red-coated sentry stood to attention, facing the landing-stairs. He wore a top-heavy shako and white trousers, and his face was wet and scarlet in the heat of the early afternoon. A little way beyond, looking to the bay over moat and rampart and line of stunted trees, the unimposing huddle of white buildings, so grandiloquently called the Castle, drowsed under a drooping Union Jack.

A small negro boy carrying a large flying-fish in one hand and a rod in the other provided the only token of public interest in Anthony's arrival. A moment or so later, however, a young officer — also shakoed and red-coated — arrived hurriedly from the guard-house: saluted.

'*Bitte, Herr Graf, seine Excellenz —* ' began he in schoolboy German.

'You can speak English to me,' said Anthony, permitting himself the slightest of foreign intonations.

The other sighed with relief: introduced himself as a Captain William Forsyth, temporarily attached to the Governor's staff.

'His Excellency has had to leave for Plantation House earlier than he expected, sir. He ordered me to tell you, sir, that the horses in the Castle stables are at your disposal if you should care to ride out this afternoon. His Excellency also told me to remind you, sir, of your dinner engagement this evening with him . . . I am to act as your guide, sir, if you wish.'

'That will be very obliging,' said Anthony with a stiff bow.

'There *are* some pleasant rides here,' said the Englishman, leading the way along the short quayside, and accenting the sentence as though he had to reassure himself on the subject. He was a beautifully complexioned lad with a permanently discontented expression and a dusting of golden down upon his cheekbone that was a romantic curl rather than a side-whisker.

'Interesting, if not beautiful, I am sure,' remarked Anthony, wondering whether Captain Forsyth would prove to be one of the class of Englishmen who look upon all aliens as 'bloody foreigners' or of the type that being unpopular with its fellow-countrymen for one reason or another seeks its companionships among strangers and casual acquaintances.

'If you like ferns,' said Captain Forsyth with an air of general disparagement, 'you'll find them here, sir! They grow fifteen feet high under the cabbage trees on Diana's Peak! . . . This way, sir — under the arch!'

They turned left-handed from the walk above the seaward battery into the most miniature of town squares, surrounded by the toy official buildings of the colony — in front of the most unimposing of which four toy cannon menaced nobody in particular. A toy church, looking as if it had just emerged from a child's box of bricks, was at the far end. The place was entirely deserted. Anthony felt that the outfit was arranged afresh and dusted with a feather brush by housemaids each morning so that the inhabitants might play with it if they were good: felt, too, that a wooden soldier or a brightly coloured Mr. Noah was needed to complete the scene.

'The roads are frightful! I should like to do nothing except walk on London pavements for the next ten years,' continued Forsyth as they crossed the little square. 'There's nothing to shoot except pea-fowl, and then you are lucky if you get off with a four-mile walk between each shot!'

He became plaintively garrulous as they made their way to the far side, whence, beyond a garden of dark and dusty trees, variegated by a single palm, opened Jamestown's only thoroughfare, basking in the sun. It was also deserted.

'The pleasantest trip, sir,' meditated the youth, 'would be to go up past the Devil's Punch Bowl — you'll see Longwood from there! — round Diana's Peak into Sandy Bay — where old William Doveton lives — and then back over the ridge to Plantation House . . . The horses aren't bad. Cape Arabs!'

He came to a halt before the first house on the left in the main street, a modest building of two stories, shaded by the foliage of the garden which adjoined it. Like most of the other buildings in the street its entrance was considerably above the level of the pavement and approached by a flight of stone steps with an iron handrail. At the foot of the steps a small door — from sound and smell obviously opening on a bar.

'Here you are, sir! I understand that you are staying at Porteous's, until you can make other arrangements . . . Thirty shillings a day, sir, and fifteen shillings for servants! Daylight robbery! Albacore steak and yams! Ugh! . . . But there isn't another hotel in the place except Solomon's boarding-house — and that's worse! . . . Shall I come back in an hour with the horses? or would you prefer to make it later? I'll send an orderly over so that your man can go direct with your dressing-case to Plantation House!' . . .

Captain Forsyth was yet more garrulous and yet more plaintive when they rode out of Jamestown a little later in the afternoon. Up a street of houses and shops and warehouses that was vaguely reminiscent of a small Welsh town. A negro servant, her head bound in a yellow handkerchief, sunned herself in a doorway; a pig-tailed Chinese labourer, under an enormous straw hat, regarded speculatively a well-worn elbow-chair in the window of a furniture store.

'Even this is an excitement for me, sir!' said Forsyth surveying superciliously two pretty coffee-coloured creatures who were coquetting with a soldier — with much swaying of slim hips and flashing of white teeth. 'I've been leading a Robinson Crusoe sort of life until yesterday. Orderly officer at Longwood for the past month!' And he whistled rather shrilly in unspoken criticism of the duties which he had had to perform.

The lad took on a new interest and importance.

'You did not care then for the post?' asked Anthony, unbending a little in the quest for information.

'It was frightful, sir! How Poppleton of the Fifty-third stuck it for over eighteen months I can't think!'

'Why?'

'The General, sir, hasn't put his nose outside the place for a month!'

'That should make an orderly officer's position very simple!' remarked Anthony in his stiffest English, remembering the tribulations of the *salle de service* rather grimly.

'No, sir! You'll forgive me, sir, it does not. Not in this case.'

Forsyth spoke of other and indifferent things as they emerged from the town and slanted upward from the verdure of the valley bottom, and Anthony did not press him.

They left behind them the variegated greenery of fields, and gardens, and groves of oranges and pomegranates and lemons gathered about snug white dwellings with slated roofs.

Their unfenced road wound round the tormented ridges of dark mountains. The barren hummock of the central peak of the island was now hidden from view by intervening hills, boulder-strewn, cleft with deep ravines — rocky chaos dating from that day immeasurable aeons before when a continent had been overwhelmed and sank, leaving St. Helena a flaming crater, solitary in wreckage-strewn seas.

The ferocity of the landscape seemed a rightful setting to the climax of the Napoleonic tragedy. To such confusion of splintered hills might have withdrawn the older gods after Ragnarok, that day of fatal battle, to brood in the twilight of their divinity.

The Englishman reverted eventually to his grievances.

'Talking about Longwood, sir, the position is that the orderly officer has to report the presence of the General *to his own knowledge* night and morning! He's supposed to satisfy himself that the General is there, without being obtrusive. It's damned well not possible, sir! No, sir!'

Anthony looked a question.

'The orderly officer's got a room of sorts, of course; but it's beyond the kitchen premises, and opens onto the garbage heaps! . . . There'd be literally hell to pay if he showed up in the General's part of the house! . . . I've spent hours at a stretch trying to get a glimpse of him! I was on my legs for ten solid hours playing bo-peep the day before yesterday! Christ Almighty, sir, ten hours!'

The plaintive Forsyth needed no encouragement now to embark upon his tale of woe; to recount how the Chinese coolies at work in the garden had cackled with laughter at his antics and how even the sentries were grinning.

'Montholon — he's the worst of the lot! — tells me the General has gone across to Bertrand's house — that's in the grounds, you know, sir! When I got there they said he had left, and gone to the garden. So back I trundle, sir. Find Gourgaud airing himself on the grass before the house, looking more like a stage Frenchman than ever. Ask where the General is. Never left the house, says Gourgaud! "His Majesty" — you can't stop 'em calling him that, you know, sir! — "is in the library reading about ten books at once!" I creep up to the library and peep in over the window-sill. Not a soul there! I go round the house, bent almost double so that they shan't see me from within. When I get to the billiard-room somebody shuts the shutters, and I can hear them, sir, laughing like hell inside! . . . Hours after I peer into the dining-room. All I can see is the top of the sort of cocked hat he wears. Do Frenchmen wear their hats at dinner, sir?'

Anthony ostensibly meditated this problem of etiquette as they navigated a twist in the steep road up an iron-grey hillside that was bare but for a few scattered pines, bent by the wind. At the summit was a shapeless sort of building, from whose roof sprouted the black arms of a semaphore against the sky that had suddenly become grey. It recalled the octagon guard-house at Norman Cross . . . As they rode they had now once more a view of the whole length of the valley, of an illumined sea, of the *Conqueror* lurching a little under bare poles at her anchorage, and of the pyramid of sail under which some other vessel moved slowly in the distance.

'I didn't have a smell of the General for my first ten days of duty,' said Forsyth in his irritating tone of complaint. 'I got desperate, sir, I assure you. Then one afternoon somebody said he was having a bath — he sits in them for hours, you know, sir! So I went round the house, and looked in over the sill. And there he was, right up to his neck in a sort of lead-covered sarcophagus! Of course he saw me! He leaped out of the bath like a squirrel, and ran to the window and made faces at me through the glass! He did really, sir, I assure you! . . . I've never seen a naked emperor before! Not a very impressive sight, sir! Indeed not very impressive!'

Would the fellow never have done? Anthony asked himself, wearied at length of the whine, and shaken a little by details that appertained rather to farce than to great tragedy.

But there was more to come —

'The final blow so far as I was concerned, sir, was when they found that all sorts of surreptitious letters were leaving Longwood in the laundry bundles. I was told that it was the orderly officer's duty to search the dirty linen. So I paraded and respectfully declined to do the job without a written order. Then they shifted me! Fancy if Countess Bertrand heard that I'd been rummaging among her soiled petticoats and chemises! She's Irish and Creole: she'ld have had hysterics for a week! Albine de Montholon wouldn't have minded so much, sir! But then — well, they say she's —. But, of course, I don't know!'

A path turned off to the right — up a rocky barrenness stippled with stunted cactus and spiky aloes — to the wooden telegraph house on the bare crest. As they approached, the semaphore above the building suddenly came to life: its arms began to gesticulate dramatically and jerkily in urgent message to some distant colleague. Its inhuman animation emphasized the bizarreness of the chaotic landscape.

A red-coated man appeared in the doorway, which was barely a couple of hundred yards off. He had a telescope in one hand, and beckoned with the other.

'It's Tom Barlow — something of a pest!' said Forsyth, eyeing the signalling figure with distaste. 'But if you'll forgive me, sir, I had better go and see what he wants. I will catch you up in a few moments!'

He was, however, absent for a little longer than he had promised, and when he reined in his sweating pony at Anthony's side, his expression was that of one who had had his appetite for excitement whetted. He was bubbling over with questions.

'Did you know there was going to be an execution on board your ship to-day, sir?' he asked.

'It had passed out of my mind,' remarked Anthony with an air of complete indifference whether or no there had been execution or a holocaust.

Captain Forsyth cast a glance at his companion, as though assessing him afresh.

'Well, sir, they've got a fellow hanging all right by the neck from a yard-arm. Barlow says he could see the whole thing. I had a look through his telescope. I could see the chap's face. He looked pretty dead!'

And so he should be — thought Anthony — considering that he had been kept in spirits of wine for over a month specially for the occasion. It had been his grandmother's idea to make such use of the dead.

'A quick death!' he commented courteously aloud.

'Barlow says he could hardly walk . . . had practically to be carried! . . . What had he been up to, sir?'

'Attempting to smuggle letters to the — General!'

'By God, sir, that's a pretty sharp punishment!' said Forsyth in some surprise, and rode on in silence for a considerable way. Added at last — 'If we hanged everybody here who was engaged in the business, half the population would be swinging, I give you my word. As it is, anybody who plots Bonaparte's escape here is liable to the death penalty — even the foreign commissioners themselves, you know, sir?'

'*So!*' remarked Anthony sententiously. 'But we Prussians insist on discipline. The orders were definite, and the penalty for infraction stated! The offence was committed and the punishment exacted. What else would you have, Captain Forsyth?'

The glance that the other gave him was full of the shocked realization of one who discovers that he has been fondling a tiger and not a cat.

Upon the left of the road a huge and wide ravine full of dense shadows.

Small damp winds stirred in the chill air. High and vaporous clouds blanketed the sky. Anthony imagined that such might be a landscape among the lunar craters.

On top of the far side of the gulf, a trifle over a mile away, a cluster of low buildings showed against a background of dwarfish pine-trees. They had no clarity of outline, but were filmed over with a thin mist.

'Longwood, sir!' said the repressed Forsyth, and pointed with his whip.

'Yes?' said Anthony, displaying no interest.

He felt deep within himself — though not confessing it — that the fallen majesty of a dethroned emperor should have been granted the drama of confinement behind the towering walls of some fabulous castle amid these mountains at world's end.

CHAPTER II

GARDEN PARTY AT PONTIUS PILATE'S

THEY walked together on a most magical greensward in the enchanted garden of Plantation House, talking very amicably — the man responsible for the safe-keeping of Europe's prisoner, and the man who came to rob him of his captive.

The narrow lawn was colonnaded on either hand, as though it were a temple, by tall date-palms: ended in a high curved wall that was masked by a snowdrift of white bougainvillaea, before which three fountains splashed and sparkled. The lustrous velvet of the grass was barred by the slim afternoon shadows of the palms; and, through the archway of the trees, the dense hedge that enclosed the pleasaunce was illumined by flowers as bright as ice and as flame. The sky was deepening to sapphire: in the still air the eternal anger of the sea against the iron coast was transmuted to a murmur.

This was the innermost green sanctuary of a strange and wonderful garden at world's end. A garden where apple and bread-fruit, pear and orange, plum and guava, gooseberry and tea-shrub grew side by side. The Garden of Eden — of Cyrus — of the Hesperides. Standing for a moment by the stone basin of the middle fountain, as they turned in their walk, Anthony watched a spray of small drops being torn from the jet of water by a whispering breeze and scattered — momentarily like beads of crystal — on the grass. It recalled to him phrases from the leaf of his father's manuscript which had served as an I O U. Something about 'the islands of the Happy Other-World' in the Western Sea —

'Emain and Aircthech, whereon drop dragon-stones and crystals'. He had never been able to find out what were dragon-stones.

The small sandy man with a worried expression, who stood beside him with folded arms — a favourite attitude — appeared to read part of his thoughts; remarked in fluent German —

'Fifteen years ago Bonaparte had a report on St. Helena from one of his "lookers-round". It described the island as an "earthly paradise where health blooms in every cheek!" Now he says it is the ante-room of death. That liver diseases are endemic. That the climate is abominable. That we have deliberately brought him here in order to kill him off as quickly as possible!'

'Did you not?' said Anthony; but he said it to himself. It was the Prussian Commissioner — with silver star on the left breast of his green coat, and the ribbon of the Order of Merit about his neck — who remarked —

'It was a pity that von Blücher's flying column did not catch him. We should all have been spared much trouble if he had been shot out of hand!'

'If I were to agree with you even below my breath, and alone as we seem to be,' said Lowe, 'that whisper would be caught up by the breeze and become a shout which Longwood would hear! Which all the island would hear! Which all the world would hear! . . . I have already been accused of proposing that *he* should be poisoned! They say he is ill, but hint that every doctor I suggest is a potential assassin! . . . I sent him the other day a present of some special coffee. Really superfine Brazilian! I am told that there was much debate whether or no it might be safely used! It was felt that I might have mixed arsenic or strychnine or rat-bane with the berries! . . . I am Borgia! Nero! . . . No, they even call me Pontius Pilate, and speak of this as Napoleon's Calvary!'

His melancholy hazel eyes from under sandy eyebrows scanned the high walls of flower-starred verdure as though suspicious that they might hide eyes and ears.

A rather dyspeptic Pontius Pilate, with a long fanatical and not un-humorous face, wrinkled at the corners of the eyes like a sailor. A lean spare Pontius Pilate in the late forties, in scarlet coat with golden shoulder-knot and infinitude of great golden buttons, the broad crimson ribbon of the Order of the Bath about his neck, and against his high black stock the jewel of some other knightly decoration.

'If there is a Calvary,' said Pontius Pilate after a pause, 'he has made it himself — for himself . . . And for me!'

They resumed their pacing of the long green lawn with silent footfall. They carried their cocked hats under their arms.

'He has fallen very far,' said Lowe. 'He has toppled like Lucifer. Kings were his servants. Kingdoms his playthings. Eighty-three million people were his slaves. Would you not think that in adversity the supreme dignity of such a man would shine undiminished? Even perhaps be brighter because of the darkness surrounding it? But just as his empire has shrunk to a bungalow on a remote island, so has he shrunk, too, from a great man to a little!'

'Between ourselves I think that he might have been allowed to retain the title of Emperor!'

'Does to be addressed as "Majesty", "Holiness" or "Excellency" mean anything at all to a man who is really imbued with majesty, or holiness or excellence? Personally I would call him "Your Godship" if it made him any happier. But I have no choice. The convention of the Allied Powers speaks of him simply as "Napoleon Bonaparte".'

Anthony was unconvinced. Lowe noticed the fact. He said with earnestness —

'The tragedy of Napoleon ends in anti-climax. He should have died at Waterloo. There is no grandeur or dignity about this episode. All the galvanic current that flowed from him to animate armies and empire is streaming forth through cracks in the dam of his character. Is occupied in fantastic details of a fantastic propaganda that he thinks may affect public opinion in his favour. Propaganda that will blacken the character of his gaolers; that will depict his circumstances as infinitely harsher than they are in reality!'

He brooded for a minute with a lost and rather friendless expression: went on —

'I am only a little man, you know! I never really thought that I should ever rise above a colonelcy, or pictured myself as governor of an island — however small! He — the Emperor-that-was — has lowered himself to my level — no, lower! He has become the Apostle of the Parish Pump. The instigating spirit in a campaign of petty conspiracy and espionage and complaint and irritation — a campaign that may seem well suited to the pettiness of my islet, but ill-suited to his former greatness. It is Lucifer reduced to cocking snooks! . . . But I suppose he'll ruin me in the end! I never thought to get into the history books, but I shall — as a simile for the horrific turnkey, just as Herod is synonym for a slayer of little children, or Henry the Eighth for the murderous husband! . . . I am but a servant obeying orders . . . The Emperor has reverted to the Corsican — the Corsican with a vendetta!'

Anthony felt a faint stirring of sympathy for the man caught up in great events.

He asked —

'What did you mean exactly when you used the word "propaganda", Sir Hudson?'

'I could give you a hundred instances,' the other replied, coming to a halt. 'Did you never hear about the affair of his silver plate?'

Anthony shook his head. The opportunity was a suitable one to emphasize once again to Lowe the remoteness of his interlocutor from the remoteness of St. Helena.

'Your Excellency must remember that for the past five years I have been employed on missions in America where they are now doing their best to forget Europe and Europe's problems!'

Lowe nodded. One long well-kept hand kneaded slowly a sleeve — a trick that reminded Anthony of the Emperor.

'Little things here are watched and noted and spied on and reported throughout Europe. My mail bags from Europe are full of dispatches and instructions about trifles. My daily correspondence is one about wallpaper, carpets, bread, servants. Minutiae which have lost their reality and become immense obsessions. It's difficult for me to recall that somewhere in the world people may really not be concerned about the daily life of Bonaparte . . . Oh! His silver! He brought a great deal with him, you must know. Fine stuff — salvage of the Imperial grandeur. Soon after I came he had much of it broken up and sold in the town. His staff said that the reason was that they were going short of provisions, and that there was no money to buy any! That is not true! First of all, they have everything that it is humanly possible for me to get them. The waste and extravagance of that household is utterly fantastic. I could show you the accounts. Secondly, *he* has plenty of money, although he thinks I don't know. At least twenty thousand pounds here in cash, as well as five million francs or more in Paris and Amsterdam, and very large sums in America! So I starve them, you see! . . . Then two days ago he had his bedstead chopped up for firewood, although as much as they required was to be had for the asking. They use ten bags of coal a day and three hundredweight of wood — which isn't a bad ration even if they keep all their twenty-three fires going at once! I am trying to freeze them to death! . . . He has an old green hunting coat turned by the local tailor. Actually he has refused to wear English cloth, but the story is, of course, that I won't provide the material, so that otherwise he must go in rags and tatters! . . . I am Pilate! Pontius Pilate!'

Lieutenant-General Sir Hudson Lowe halted, and stood looking with a forlorn air down the garden, still pulling at his sleeve.

At the far end of the lawn, against the flower-hung wall, there now appeared three slim figures in silk dresses as delicately tinted as flowers themselves. Flounced dresses of apricot and the silver-green of almond. High bonnets with ostrich plumes.

'It's Susan!' said Lowe, and his face lost its look of tragic reverie.

He took his companion by the arm and led him toward his wife.

She was accompanied by her daughter and another young girl. They were three charming creatures. Their bright beauty reminded Anthony again of Garland, as it had done when first he met them. In the older woman something of an older Garland: in her slender daughter and niece — no longer children, but not yet women — something of the Garland of La Cadière.

Lady Lowe smiled and bowed. The girls dropped curtsies, dipping until their dresses swept the grass and their lace-fringed pantaloons were hidden from view.

'I am glad that you are here, *Herr Graf*,' said Lady Lowe. 'There are very few people, beside his staff, that Hudson can talk freely to . . . But I suppose it was the *one* subject?'

'I did not raise the topic, ma'am,' protested Anthony.

'I can believe that,' she replied, watching her husband's weary face. 'When next he starts, change the subject! Talk about Virgil or Horace, or about Cervantes or Calderon, or Molière or Tasso, or Kotzebue or Goethe. He's a strange man for a soldier, you know. He likes books. He likes foreign languages. And there's no one here that is interested in such things excepting yourself.'

From some hidden place there came the preliminary scratching and wailing of violins being tuned. Liveried servants were whisking muslin covers from off trestled tables, spread in the side-aisles of the green temple between the columns of the palm-trees and the flower-spangled tapestry of the shrubs: were setting chairs in the shade.

A tall officer with a disillusioned face approached deferentially. He held a paper in his hand, and Sir Hudson turned abruptly to speak to him, his face already puckering with the foreboding of new anxieties.

'You are not in the least my conception of a German, Count von Schauenstein,' said Lady Lowe. 'I wish you could stay. I know I should not say it — but to no other commissioner could I truthfully express that hope! When first I heard you say that you could see no reason for your continued presence here I was glad. Now I shall be sorry when the *Königin Luise* comes back from Africa to take you away. I feel that in so short a time you have become Hudson's only friend in this Bedlam! He needs one — a man of his own calibre!'

Anthony felt that he flushed. If Lowe was called a Pilate, might he not well be compared to a Judas? He had stolen a friendship only that he might betray it?

He said frankly —

'What can the Commissioners of the Powers do here? We have no authority in the island or over the prisoner. Bonaparte refuses to see any of us or even to hold communication with us. We have no occupation except to intrigue and quarrel, to spy on one another and the Governor, and to write reports about anything and everything. I should be failing in my duty to my master if I did not use the discretion he gave me in the matter, and return to Europe.'

'Quarrels!' said Lady Lowe with lifted eyebrows. 'There are more on this speck of an island than in a thousand square miles anywhere else. And the French are the worst. Bertrand — Montholon — Gourgaud; they quarrel with *everyone* and keep in practice by quarrelling among themselves. Madame Bertrand told me that the General is always inciting them against one another!'

'Mamma — !' — 'Aunt — !' began Charlotte and Caroline simultaneously.

'I — ' said Lady Lowe.

'Mamma!' pleaded Charlotte, taking her mother's hand. 'Mamma, we *must* tell you! Mustn't we, Caroline?'

'He called her a cow!' said Caroline, the younger, dancing up and down, her long black ringlets swinging within the vast brim of her apricot-coloured bonnet.

'Who called Charlotte a cow?' asked Lady Lowe in an accent of extreme horror.

Charlotte explained.

'We went to Solomon's this morning with Miss Mason. She wanted some ribbons. While we were there Count Montholon came in to buy some things his wife had seen. But they had all been sent up to Countess Bertrand on approval. You cannot conceive, Mamma, the fury into which Monsieur Montholon worked himself! Everybody listening, and Mr. Saul Solomon just smiling apologetically and washing his hands together, and Mr. Lewis Solomon dancing up and down and washing *his* hands. Monsieur Montholon said that things ought to be submitted to *his* wife before Count Bertrand's wife. He said that the Solomons insulted him by such treatment. That Bertrand was a schemer and his wife was a cow! . . . And then Baron Gourgaud, who was with him, chimed in, and said that Madame Bertrand had a frightful mind. Whenever he visited them she always sent away a pretty maid she had . . . And then Miss Mason said "T'ch! T'ch!" and hustled us away to the other end of the shop!'

Lady Lowe sighed.

A bright uniform and two pretty frocks approached across the grass on which the shadows of the palm trees slanted under the westering of the sun.

Lady Lowe sighed again.

'Will you content yourself with my two hoydens until I can find you more suitable entertainment?' she begged him as she made her way toward the new arrivals.

Charlotte took his arm possessively. He found himself promenading between the two pretties, and kept well clear of the increasing throng around Lady Lowe.

'Mamma hopes that one of the "yamstocks" will catch you, and then you might stay, perhaps,' said Charlotte. 'Yamstock' was the name given by the temporary inhabitants of the island to the permanent British residents. 'The young ladies are most extraordinarily pretty. Look at Betsy, and Rosebud, and The Nymph, for instance! . . . But Laura — you should have seen Laura! . . . It's hard luck on me and Caroline!'

'Neither of you have any need to be envious,' said Anthony, glancing at each bright and pretty face in turn. 'If only you were a couple of years older, Miss Charlotte — '

Charlotte gave his arm a tender squeeze.

'If I can't have you, I shall have Count Balmain, the Russian Commissioner. He is *too* good-looking! . . . Monsieur de Montchenu at any rate doesn't think I am too young! He tried to kiss me the other evening!'

'Charlotte!' exclaimed Caroline, horrified at the unmaidenliness of the confession.

'Well, he did! And he got his face so close to me that I could see all the powder in his wrinkles!'

'They've got the ice-machine working just in time,' said Caroline, indicating by gentle pressure against Anthony's side her desire for early exploration of the buffet.

'What did you do?' asked Anthony inclining his steps toward one of the long tables with statuesque servants presiding over arrays of decanters and crystal and all the gallantry of confectionery and dessert.

'I said,' said Charlotte in her primmest manner, ' "Now, Mr. Munching" — that's what the troops call him, because he's so greedy! — "None of that, or I'll pull your pig-tail!" And I should! Fancy still wearing a pig-tail and hair powder in 1818!'

'Ah! But fancy becoming a *marquise* of the *ancien régime!*'

'His intentions were dishonourable!' said Charlotte. 'But I respect him for still having dishonourable intentions at his age! . . . He said to me, "But Mees Charlotte, *belle, charmante* Mees Charlotte, I have already keessed four t'ousand Angleesh ladees! *You* would not deny me so gr-r-reat a plaisir, *hein?*" He does not know that *I* know that he wrote a six-page love-letter to Mamma! Mamma doesn't know that I know!'

'Ices!' said Caroline, who had a single-track mind. 'General Bonaparte broke the thermometer of his ice-making machine the day it arrived! Betsy Balcombe told me! . . . I wonder what sort Foster has made! I *do* hope that there are ginger ones!'

Charlotte mimicked the high falsetto voice, the gesticulations, the shoulder-shruggings, of Monsieur le Marquis de Montchenu, Commissioner of His Most Christian Majesty of France at the prison island of St. Helena —

' "Zat Bonaparte, 'e is not a chentleman! . . . I know! I was 'is col-o-nel w'en 'e was a little boy officer before ze Revolution!" Wretched old man! . . . I'm going to eat two ices! Don't tell Mamma!'

They had reached the table farthest away from the bougainvillaea-tapestried sanctuary of the garden where Lady Lowe was receiving her guests. An elderly coffee-coloured mulatto with a pleasant face, liveried in dark blue, appeared to divine the requirements of the ladies without instruction.

'You've been careful, Jackson?' said Charlotte rather anxiously examining the yellow-tinged ice-cream in a cut-glass plate.

'Yes, Miss!' said Jackson rubbing his nose very vigorously with a large white handkerchief.

'Poor Jackson suffers from nose-drips,' explained Charlotte in a high clear voice of commiseration. 'I *have* known accidents! I like to be sure!'

'Very natural!' said Anthony, hearing and seeing once again a very young Garland commenting upon a similar failing on the part of Paul.

Garland! . . . He suddenly found that he wanted to kiss both these young creatures with the childish kisses of La Cadière, in a sort of sacrament of memory.

'Would you marry me, Count, if I were two years older?' asked Charlotte, looking up beguilingly from the rapidly vanishing ice.

'Yes! If you gave me the chance,' said Anthony, in a tone of great seriousness.

'That's practically a proposal,' said Charlotte with much delight. 'Your intentions are quite honourable — quite, quite honourable? . . . There's the admiral, Caroline! He doesn't look in the least upset!'

A sturdy figure in cocked hat and blue coat, a great bunch of seals at his fob, was ambling across the grass towards refreshments.

Caroline ceased attack upon her ice and watched with trepidation the approach of the naval commander at St. Helena. The great man had been disreputable enough to bring out a little mistress with him from

England instead of discreetly outfitting himself with that commodity from among the amoral ladies of various shades of chocolate and yellow who were available upon the island. In consequence the Reverend Mr. Boys had felt impelled to administer public rebuke to him in a sermon preached last Sunday. It was the sort of thing the Reverend Mr. Boys *would* do!

'What shall I say to him, if he speaks to me?' asked Caroline. 'I shall faint if he talks to us! I shall, Charlotte! I shall, indeed!'

But Rear-Admiral Plampin did not cause further consternation to virgin bosoms, and in a moment or so Lady Lowe appeared, to whisk Anthony off upon a dutiful round, and to distribute extreme youth amongst a group of young subalterns in the Honourable East India Company's service.

Funny old Mr. Doveton wanted to know when Count von Schauenstein was coming again to have breakfast and drink home-made orange shrub on the cedar-shaded lawn at Mount Pleasant . . . Miss Mason wanted him to come and sip Madeira and see her new ponies one morning soon at Orange Grove Cottage . . . Major Lascelles wanted to know when he was going to dine with the 66th . . . Major Blakeney had a notion for a picnic under Diana's Peak which was ardently supported by sundry very pretty young ladies in clothes that were very pretty, even if they had not cost very much and had come from Mr. Solomon's store rather than Corbin's in the Rue de Richelieu or Mrs. Bell in St. James's Street: or even had been designed at home from the fashion plates in old numbers of the *Repository* or *La Belle Assemblée!* . . . Dr. Henry wanted him to see the shell of an eight-hundred-pound turtle with which he had just been presented . . . Baroness Sturmer, young French wife of the Austrian Commissioner, wanted — he wondered very much of what desire her dark eyes spoke. Someone — who was it? — had whispered to him that through her the Emperor knew all that passed at Plantation House and the councils of the Commissioners . . . Assistant Commissary-General Ibbetson wanted to know if he were coming to the performance at the Jamestown Theatre to-morrow night — Colonel Dodgin was going to play Falstaff — everybody (including Excellencies) was coming — it was going to be a first-class show! Yes. Count von Schauenstein hoped to be present. . . .

He stood withdrawn a little from the crowd, in the luminous shadow of a high hedge of evergreen starred with blue passion-flowers. At his side the buffet table presided over by the grey-haired mulatto Jackson, with its array of gold-topped bottles in ice-pails and jugs frosted by beverages of straw gold and purple red. A pair of young officers were at the farther end drinking hock and seltzer water: no one else.

With a glass of claret-cup in his hand, he watched the scene framed between the shafts of the palm trees in front of him — a scene staged in a garden at world's end, on the last peak of lost Atlantis, one thousand miles distant from the nearest continent. In the clear golden light of the late afternoon, in that setting of greensward and magical flowers, there was a fairy quality about the pageant of gay silks and muslins and nodding plumes and lacy parasols and brave uniforms. Distant enough from him it was for the sound of speech to be but a susurration punctuated by the tinkle of laughter.

He was aware of a spasm of regret. In a few days' time, the *Königin Luise* would return: there would be no garden parties in Pontius Pilate's garden, then, after he had done what he came to do. They would break Lowe — he supposed — and Charlotte would have to find a husband in whatever second-rate watering-place a half-pay and disgraced officer could find refuge. There would be courts-martial and courts of inquiry — perhaps even shootings and hangings. And then the island that was both at the end of the world and yet the centre of the world would sink back to its obscurity. The regiments would march down to Jamestown and sail away; the warships would sail away; the stream of British gold would dry up.

One of the officers suddenly said in a rather loud haw-haw voice —

'They haven't seen him for eleven days! . . . Gorrequer says that they're going to give the orderly officer orders to break in and make sure he's there if he doesn't show up soon!'

The other — it was the plaintive Forsyth — said —

'Why the hell can't he behave like a reasonable human being?'

You could not get away from *him* on the island even if you never saw him. Lowe himself had not seen him for two years — the Commissioners never. *He* sat remote, withdrawn, brooding within a prison which existed but for him. *He*, like a God, was omnipresent although unseen. *He* was the reason, the riches, the mystery, the one topic of the island.

Said one of the two men —

'They say he's as fat as a pig through taking no exercise!'

Forsyth drank off his tumbler and had it refilled.

'Well, he's invented a wooden rocking-horse, which he rides for exercise every day! I know it for a fact because Darling made it and he showed it to me in his workshop! "Gee-hup, you ugly devil! H'up,

Dobbin!" Can't you imagine old Boney spurring along across his bath-room floor? He's got a wash-ball seat, anyway!'

There was a cackle of laughter from the other.

A gust of anger seized upon him.

Damn these chattering jailers, who made mock of the fallen Master of the World — the blood and spirit brothers of the warders and turn-keys of Norman Cross and the hulks.

The hidden band swung into some stately and old-fashioned dance ... For no reason that he could imagine, he thought of Solly — the Solly who made music — not forgeries — and his fantastically entitled tunes ... This ought to be the Pavane of the Turnkeys! He was still savouring the phrase when someone addressed him in a very quiet whisper, appar-ently from the hedge immediately behind him —

'Do not turn round!'

By an effort he remained as he was, staring at the pretty pageantry of the lawn. Out of the corner of his eye he could see, however, that the officers were still unsuspectingly talking and drinking.

'To-morrow night, after the theatre! . . . The sign will be "Silas" and the countersign "Deane". That is all! Just nod if you understand!'

So at last he was to see the Emperor. Secretly — so that authority should find no starting-point for suspicion in the Little Man's sudden reversal of his decision to see none of the representatives of the Powers that held him captive. News of the progress of his plans — now complete — had all been given by surreptitious letters, at surreptitious meetings with Gourgaud in the back-premises of Solomon's shop, or in the garden pavilion of The Briars half-way to Jamestown . . . 'Silas' and 'Deane' after all the years that lay between Lauchstein and St. Helena! None other than the Emperor could have devised such passwords. What an astonishing memory he had got!

He nodded in token of comprehension: looked round after the lapse of a minute or so. But there was no one to be seen nearby — only the mulatto, Jackson, with a large white handkerchief up to his unfortunate nose. He was near enough to have heard — or was he not? Or had he spoken through the cotton folds?

'. . . He's got holes cut in all the shutters so that he can stick his tele-scope through and see everything without being seen!'

'They've done the same thing for him at the Bertrands' house. He went there yesterday and watched the Deadwood races.'

'He'd better enter his Dobbin for the next meeting. General Bona-parte's Dobbin! Ridden by the owner!'

Further laughter: after which Captain Forsyth changed his tipple to planter's punch.

Had he let the anger burning within him show in his expression? He found that Jackson's eyes were on him — seemed to be conveying some warning. He set down his glass and prepared to move away.

At that moment Rear-Admiral Plampin, who had been obviously undergoing a certain amount of ostracism, drifted up in search of liquid consolation. He was a pink-faced choleric man with black eyebrows and white hair, and a shiny pink nose which twitched like a rabbit's when he talked, and white trousers very much puffed and pleated at the waist.

'A'rternoon!' said the admiral. 'Bloody weather, isn't it? Bloody island, too! Hear you've decided to go! Don't blame you! Wish it was me!'

Anthony mumbled some reply.

'S'pose your ship'll be back any day now. Ought to be!' The admiral left it to be inferred that if the *Königin Luise* had been a British ship she would have long since returned from her voyage to the West Coast: but from 'bloody' foreigners anything might be expected. 'She's a queer-looking craft! American-built, you said?'

Anthony repeated the mixture of truth and falsehood about the vessel which had been adjudged suitable as a reply to all enquirers. She had been constructed in Adam and Noah Browne's ship-yard on the East River, New York, for the Prussian Government. In addition to her ordinary armament (said he, with a great show of frankness) she carried four columbiads — guns capable of firing a hundred-pound projectile under water — Mr. Fulton's last invention before he died. He did not add that in her hold she bore — as a mother carrying a child in her womb — the submarine boat *Mute*, on whose construction Fulton had actually been engaged at the time of his death. A craft compared with which the *Nautilus* of seventeen years ago was a mere toy. Such a craft as alone could guarantee secret approach to — or departure from — the guarded shores of St. Helena. He wondered if the *Mute* had been assembled by now. . . .

'Fulton!' said Admiral Plampin, mopping his brow with a red handkerchief. 'Remember him well! Met the man often! Helped prepare his submarine bombs for the attack on Boulogne Harbor in '04. The clockwork in each of the damned things cost fourteen pounds!'

'I recollect!' said Anthony.

And he recollected, better than ever Admiral Plampin would know, the infernal uproar and confusion of that British raid on the invasion base, in a night illumined by gun-fire and reverberating with heavy explosions.

'I towed one of the bloody bombs in myself — just for the fun of the

thing! Paddled in with it at the end of a tow-line in the dark, with
my face blacked and dressed in a black jersey and trousers. Hooked the
beggar to the cable of a brig that was riding at anchor and made off. It
exploded prematurely. All we got for our bloody trouble was one bloody
pinnace and her crew. *"Veel geschreeuws, en luttel wol!"* as the Dutch
say! . . . Queer fellah! Mad! Borrowed money from me, too! Thought
he wouldn't return it, but by God he did!'

So a younger Plampin, like himself, had been involved in Mr. Fulton's
activities! Like himself, for the fun of it! Plampin would have personal
as well as official interest in the history of his empty sleeve; in the cargo
of the *Königin Luise* which might already be swimming in these deep
seas over sunken Atlantis! . . . Had Fulton whistled and hummed that
damned negro tune 'Keep me from sinkin' down' on the night he had
turned his inventive genius against his former employers? He would
have liked to ask the admiral.

He said rather coldly —

'One must admit his cleverness, but I did not care for his character —
so far as I was acquainted with it!'

'What d'ye mean?' asked the admiral, draining his glass.

'He was what you call a turn-coat!' said Anthony, airing his old grievance against Fulton.

The admiral was obviously about to make some outspoken comment
on a parallel with Prussian foreign policy: thought better of it: but with
legs apart and hands under coat-tails, came out in somewhat bellicose
fashion in defence of the American.

'That's where you're wrong, *Herr Graf!* That's where you're wrong!
The little fat fellah we've got here under lock and key — Boney, I mean!
— is the reason why he came over to us. He used to talk about it to me.
Never came across such a man for talk! Blah-blah-blah! — all day long!
. . . He was one of these radical republican democrats who are always
spouting about liberty and the freedom of the seas and so on! Believed
in it, too! Became quite oratorical at times. After Boney got into power
he soon saw that it was all up with liberty, equality, and fraternity and
the rest on the Continent. So he upped anchor and set sail for England!
And I believe he was telling the truth!'

Had then Fulton been just such another as Harradence? Had he
really believed in what he had said in those extraordinary epistles to
the Directory, which an eager pupil had helped him to write so many
years ago? Had his beliefs been so important to him that — like Harrady — he had been ready to sacrifice the world's conception of honour to
them?

An elderly naval lieutenant approached . . . He had a face like a slice
of under-done roast beef that had been left too long on the plate . . .
He addressed a few respectful words in a low voice to the admiral.

'Your ship's just been sighted, Count!' said Plampin. 'She should make
the bay before breakfast.' He asked of his subordinate a question about
the wind. 'Yes. Soon after dawn. That avoids all awkwardness, y'know!
I couldn't break the bloody regulations and let her anchor between sunset and sunrise, even for you, my dear fellah! Not even for you! Why,
the shore batteries fired on my predecessor when he arrived here, because
the damned ass forgot some regulation or other. They knew quite well
whose the ship was!'

The *Königin Luise* and her crew had been kept out of mischief during
the long weeks of waiting by a voyage to the Guinea Coast, ostensibly for
the purpose of collecting tropical plants for the royal gardens at Potsdam.
Out of mischief by collecting plants: and *in* mischief by assembling the
Mute. At some time during the darkness to-night, then, the plunging-
boat would be sent forth from the parent ship, and by to-morrow would
be lying invisible at her secret anchorage in a small rocky cove near Old
Woman Valley. In a few nights' time again she would slip out to sea to
rendezvous with the frigate — with a passenger bound for the New
World.

Presently he escaped from Plampin and joined the Lowes in the bay
of verdure by the bougainvillaea-covered wall, which was reserved for
Excellencies and their intimates by an entirely invisible barrier. Lady
Lowe was narrating some exciting news to a tall woman with a face like
a horse's, surrounded by an immense straw bonnet.

'So I've sent a carriage,' said Lady Lowe. 'You see, my dear — .'

Sir Hudson, with a far-away expression, his arms still folded, was
listening to a heated argument between two civilians — a long lean man
with a white beaver hat on the back of his head, and a short fat man with
a white beaver hat tipped over his nose. He invited Anthony to join them
by a glance.

'I say,' said the fat short man, 'that if he had shot the fellow he would
have had to be tried for manslaughter. There's no getting away from it!'

'How could you punish him?' asked the other, 'if he were found
"guilty", considering that he is already undergoing a sentence of imprisonment for life? It is absurd to try a man for an offence if you can't
punish him!'

He! — Him! — There was but one staple subject of conversation.
He! — Him!

Anthony raised an eyebrow in enquiry.

Lowe explained.

'Our mutual acquaintance, the General, shot a bullock this afternoon. The problem is what would happen supposing he had missed the bullock and shot a sentry!'

'What did he want to shoot a bullock for?'

'Somebody had left the gate open, and the creature had strayed into the outer garden . . . They never shut gates after them. Just as they are always breaking down fences and hedges when they go out on horseback, and usually ride across a lawn when they visit their acquaintances!'

'Shooting the creature seems a little drastic!' said Anthony.

'He's always doing it,' said Long-and-Lean. 'He keeps a gun by his study window, and shoots anything in sight. He's already killed a stray goat or two belonging to Legg, blown off the heads of some of his own chickens, and wounded a bullock of Robinson's! To say nothing of "bag" rabbits!'

It had been — he recollected — a constant habit of the Little Man in the old days to have a loaded gun somewhere to hand so that he might shoot at any creature that came within range of his windows, if he felt so disposed. The ranks of the Empress Joséphine's pet peacocks at Malmaison had been sadly depleted owing to the Imperial marksmanship.

' . . . at Toulon!' concluded Lady Lowe to the horse-faced woman. 'He was much senior to Hudson. He was, of course, old enough to be her father! . . . There was no heir to the title: the estate wasn't entailed: she inherited everything! *Everything!* . . . And here she comes!'

Without turning to see, Anthony knew quite well whom Lady Lowe was advancing to meet. Knew, too, that this meeting at world's end was no fortuitous coincidence. . . .

'Count von Schauenstein? . . . There were some people of that name with whom I was very friendly in London a few years ago. Relations, I suppose? . . . There was Theresa — a most amiable girl! And Count Frederick. And Count Henry. The last had something of your expression! Definitely! . . . Ah, cousins! That will explain it!'

The wonderful Garland stood before him — Garland whose coming spelled disaster, perhaps even the gallows. Garland in a gown of blue-green silk girdled with gold at the high waist, with a Tudor ruff of fine gauze about her graceful neck, and a milk-white bonnet trimmed with milky lace and milky plumes — a bonnet that came quite obviously from Minette of Paris or somewhere such, and must equally obviously, too, become sole topic of feminine conversation throughout the island.

She offered friendly hand and gave friendly smile to the one-armed man in dark-green uniform who bowed so low before her: bowed very low, and afterwards stood with bent head, because he could not bring himself to see what tale there should be in her eyes.

CHAPTER III

THE HOUSE OF FOUR MILLION GHOSTS

'FOUR million dead!' said Sir Hudson very slowly, resting his folded arms upon the ebony dining-table. Repeated still more slowly: 'Four — million — dead, Lady Morfa!'

His melancholy eyes under their sandy eyebrows did not look at her; stared at the symmetrical folds of the thin gauze curtains before the windows as though penetrating them and surveying the velvet blackness of the night.

The four of them were silent for a little while. An errant sigh of a breeze stirred faintly the flames of the great silver candelabra, and the shadows of the piled fruit dishes and the glittering decanters quivered in the sheen of the table-top like shadows in the sheen of a pool of ink. The foliage rustled in the dark gardens that lapped the house: from the foot of the valley came the subdued uproar of a thousand miles of sea.

'Pity is wasted on him,' continued Lowe at length. 'Regret for his vanished splendours is a false sentiment. When next your kind heart aches because of our prisoner, Lady Morfa, harden it! Remind yourself that four million men died because of that one man! Died in the wars of aggression and brigandage that he unleashed. Wars to make him an emperor, his brothers kings, and his generals princes! Wars to make all Europe a confederation of puppet states subordinate to one super-race — the French: and to one super-man — himself!'

All through the monologue which Garland's expressed sympathy for the fallen Emperor had produced, Anthony had been conscious that her very lovely eyes had been fixed upon him, as though she were assessing the effect of what Lowe said — were hoping for some sign of deviation from the purpose that she had divined.

'Four million! How do you arrive at that figure, Sir Hudson?' he asked.

'Lafayette estimated the losses on the French side in Bonaparte's wars at two millions. It is impossible to reckon that the forces opposed to him would lose fewer!'

'Four million!' echoed Garland in a low voice: and then again, 'Four million!'

She was willing him to look up at her; but he would not raise his eyes from the wine-glass that he twisted round and round between finger and thumb of his solitary hand.

Lady Lowe — in geranium-coloured velvet — sketched a movement designed, in vain, to attract Garland's attention: it was time that they left the two gentlemen to themselves and the port, before Hudson was utterly carried away by his obsession.

'If you should ever feel yourself inclined to grow sentimental about Bonaparte,' said Sir Hudson — still staring into the folds of the faintly stirring curtains, as though in those two long panels, set in the cream-coloured walls, he saw the ghosts of the events of which he spoke — 'you should remind yourself, too, of the fate of Benasco . . . Benasco was burned to the ground; its entire population massacred. Just to teach Italy a lesson — the meaning of the word Fear!'

'Benasco!' repeated Garland in a low voice, as though to imprint that tragic name upon her memory: Anthony knew that her purpose was to incise it in his.

'Remember, too, that two thousand five hundred prisoners were slaughtered in cold blood at Jaffa by his orders!'

'Two thousand five hundred!' said Garland in just above a whisper.

'Remind yourself that the municipality and magistracy of Pavia were shot for resisting his requisitions!'

Would Garland never cease regarding him?

'That the Duke of Enghien — whom he knew to be innocent of offence — was seized on neutral territory and murdered. Merely to intimidate the Legitimist party . . . The publisher Palm — executed for daring to print criticism of him! . . . Three thousand people flung into concentration camps without trial because they thought differently from himself. Because they disagreed with a government by espionage, secret police, and propaganda organized from the Bureau of Public Opinion!'

Lady Lowe was making small protesting noises, heeded neither by her guests nor by her husband who sat forward in his great carved elbow chair of Indian ebony, and continued to detail his indictment of the man who had wrought for himself an empire stretching from Denmark to Sicily by violence and bad faith, enriched it by pillage, cemented it with blood and tears.

Lowe did not change his attitude: did not alter his tone from that of one dispassionately reciting a list of criminal charges already known by heart: did not once shift his gaze. Anthony felt of him that so might the clerk to the Eternal Magistrate in the Court of Heaven recite the offences to which the accused must answer.

The motives of that epic war, in which endurance had beaten violence, had been no concern of Colonel Purvis. He had accepted war, just as one accepts the weather: had taken it for granted that the leader, whom he had chosen to serve, must be right — always right. He wanted now to protest — to raise his voice in a sudden shout of 'Lies! Lies!'

Garland was still watching him: Garland who had defeated him: at whom he dared not look. In her eyes, he knew, there was no triumph, but only assessment and appeal.

'When next you feel inclined to pity his fate,' said Lowe, 'remember that he kept prisoner the Pope and the King of Spain!' And so continued with the charge sheet.

How greatly he loved Garland, he knew: so greatly that his anger was only with God or Fate. How greatly she loved him, he knew too: although she had come there to betray him — for a second time — to his death, if all else failed.

'. . . to disembarrass himself of his wounded by having them poisoned with opium . . . Twenty-five thousand men were killed at the battle of Borodino. He viewed the carnage and he wrote — "The finest battlefield that I have yet seen!" "Yet!" — as though he anticipated bigger and better battles, richer slaughter over which to smack his lips! . . . It is true. I saw the letter! . . . He —'

But had Garland defeated him — yet?

'He escaped from Elba . . . And so tens of thousands of men died — millions of money were poured out! . . . He — will — not — escape — from — St. Helena!'

There was so great a change in Lowe's voice that Anthony instinctively looked up. The man's face was transfigured by something fanatical: his body was stiffened: he gave out challenge: he told the night and the powers of darkness that the Destroying Spirit who was his captive should not again be let loose upon an agonized world. He was the Guardian of Decency and Order, of Peace and Justice. He stood Sentinel for Civilization. He was no longer just a lean small man with an upstanding crest of sandy hair.

They were very silent.

Lady Lowe remarked, 'My poor brother, Sir William de Lancey, the Quartermaster-General, you know — was killed at Waterloo.'

She had initiated a fresh effect at withdrawal, when Garland said —

'Dr. Henry told me that he sleeps very badly!'

'He always has,' said Anthony.

'Instead of sending himself to sleep by counting sheep through a gate, he should count the dead — his dead — his four million dead!' said Lowe.

The two women were rising. Lowe and Anthony came to their feet.

Lady Lowe said apologetically —

'They say that Hudson is a glum and silent man . . . So he is usually. But when he lets himself go — !'

She ended the sentence expressively with arched eyebrows.

'Four million!' repeated Garland once again, in a tone implying that the dreadful total furnished the argument which, above all others, crushed any incipient sympathy which she might have entertained for the Prisoner at Longwood.

She brought the scene back to a less tense level.

'I will promise not to help him escape, or even to ask for an audience of him like other tourists, if Lady Lowe and you really mean to give me house-room until my ship comes! . . .' Anthony listened, wondering what explanation she had provided for her appearance on that mid-Atlantic speck. Whatever it might be, it was obviously satisfactory . . . 'But I suppose that I could survey Longwood from afar? I should like to do that!'

'Let me see! I can drive you over — ' began Lady Lowe, obviously sorting out her engagement list to accommodate this unexpected and important guest.

'Any time! Any time!' said Garland. 'I wouldn't upset any of your plans, dear Lady Lowe, for worlds. All I want is exercise — after a month at sea. If I might borrow a horse to-morrow morning before breakfast — ! I always say that there is no exercise like riding!'

Of course! Every beast in the stables was at her disposal. Now Nada would really be better than Sultan — Nada was so sure-footed. That unfenced road round the Devil's Punch Bowl! . . . Lady Lowe didn't ride, and Sir Hudson unfortunately would have to be at the Castle soon after dawn, but Major Gorrequer would prove quite a pleasant escort! A very amiable fellow! Or there was young . . .

Lady Morfa needed no escort. She often rode unaccompanied on her early morning rides at home. Even without a groom!

Anthony knew without looking up that she was regarding him — waiting for him to speak: knew what he was expected to say . . . How well he recalled those morning rides at La Cadière. To Cap Pinède, through an endless crypt of forest with fawn carpeting of pine-needles; the metallic glitter of the sea at the distant end of an unvarying vista of dark tree-shafts.

He said diffidently —

'If Lady Morfa would condescend to a one-armed cavalier — !'

Lady Morfa protested politely.

'I ride each morning,' said Count von Schauenstein. 'It's a long time

since I had a companion . . . There's nothing I should like better than
to act as your escort to-morrow!'

He looked up as he spoke; met her frank gaze at last, and regarded
her in silence for an appreciable space of time. There was such truth in
her brow, such pride in the carriage of her head, such loveliness in her
every feature, as he had always known. He remembered everything —
the smooth texture of her skin, and the warmth beneath the pallor of
it — the angle of her chin — the inquiring lift of her eyebrows so that she
ever had the air of being a little puzzled by life — the curve of cheek
and throat — the sheen of her dark piled tresses, and the position of every
curl and ringlet about her temples — the slender beauty of white shoulders rising from the low-cut dress of smoke-grey silk shot with flame.

'You will be breaking no engagement for me?'

'None.' Realized the fullness of her meaning: added — 'Even if I had
an appointment with Bonaparte himself it should be postponed!'

Everybody smiled at the comical notion of the General granting an
interview to one of the Commissioners.

He was holding the door for the ladies — a little clumsily, perhaps,
since it was hinged on the wrong side for a man without a left hand —
when the house stirred about them. It did not shake: it did not tremble:
it just stirred with the faint shudder of someone experiencing a sudden
chill. The movement was only made visible in the restlessness of the
Chinese dragon tapestries in grey and primrose and floss silver on the
wall, although there was no breath of wind: was to be felt in the merest
suggestion of unsteadiness of the feet.

At the first tremor Lowe had whipped out a watch from his fob; held
it close to his eyes in the palm of his hand.

'Ten seconds!' he announced. 'Only a ten-seconds shock!'

He spoke (Anthony told himself) as though he were a Minor Prophet
who was a trifle discontented with the tardiness and the scrimpiness of
a manifestation required and expected from the Most High.

Garland dismounted. With the reins over her arm she stood beside
Anthony on the coarse turf of the high upland.

At some little distance to their right the low buildings that housed the
fallen Emperor were huddled behind a fringe of shrubby garden, flanked
at either end by three tall cypresses. The long spikes of the hedge of aloes
that fenced the garden front looked like a palisade of spears. High above
the wet slate and shingle roofs loomed the misty outline of Diana's Peak.

The sun was a silver blur in the veil of low vaporous cloud that hid the
sky. In the mournful light, almost without shadows, the wide parkland

of blue-green gumwood trees — bare-stemmed, their meagre caps of foliage all bowed to the north — took on the desolation of a landscape in the spirit world. The place was a remoteness within a remoteness. It was here that the physical world seemed, in geographical fact, to end.

Even a distant high bugle call had thin unreality, as though it were the echo of a bugle call out of history, and not sounded for the attention of living ears.

The grass tussocks at their feet were alive with field-mice, and swarms of small birds with crimson beaks twittered and fussed about the dark foliage of the trees.

Garland shivered.

'There are too many ghosts!' she said.

Anthony knew what she meant. That here in this strange twilight that was the shadow only of day, upon this hill-top more than a thousand miles from anywhere, the ghosts of four million dead pressed about the house beyond low stone boundary wall and the hedge of aloes.

Until then their talk had all been of old times and an exchange of news — Elizabeth — Monsieur de Courville, who had died last year — Miss Buckley: 'She's here with my grandmother!' said Anthony, jerking his head in the direction of Jamestown Bay; and Garland wondered if Buck knew that she was liable to be hanged — Harradence. . . .

'Harrady adopted a baby three years ago!' Garland announced.

'Whatever for?' he asked in astonishment. 'What did your mother say?'

'It was a negro baby — a month-old girl!'

Anthony's jaw dropped. He repeated the word 'negro' with varying shades of expression in his voice.

'In the name of heaven, why?'

'There is never any good in trying to guess why Harrady does things . . . He found it in Liverpool. Its parents were runaway slaves from South Carolina who had smuggled on board a ship at Charleston. The mother died . . . He invited half the county to the baptism!'

'Did they come?'

'Did they not! . . . I am one of the godmothers. The other is the blind woman who sits by St. Teilo's lych-gate. He says that it was an old custom to choose a beggar as a godparent, before the world became plutocratic and snobbish! . . . The child was christened "Liberty"!'

'What did your mother say? And what did the haughty Countess of Morfa say to a black step-sister,' said Anthony, and he rolled in his saddle with laughter.

'Mother did what you are doing — laughed until I thought that she would die! The haughty Countess of Morfa was too busy trying to find a white wet-nurse for a black baby to worry about the problems of relationship!'

After that they had ridden for a while in meditative silence along the narrow ridge that led — between deep ravines — to Longwood.

Then he had told of his voyage with an indomitable grandmother to New York — the visit to the house near East Hampton which she had not seen for fifty years; the house where (although he did not know it) he might have been born — the almost incredible journey to High Pale.

'The journey south from Philadelphia recalled nothing to me. Only the trivialities that impress themselves upon the mind of a child! . . . A grey-bearded negro in a pink-striped apron summoning buyers to a tobacco sale by blowing a horn. The horn was quite three feet long! Just the sort of thing a small boy would notice! . . . Then once we passed a man bringing his tobacco to market, horse and steer harnessed to huge casks and dragging them along the road just as if they were drawing garden-rollers . . . I had seen that before! . . . A strip of cabbage-coloured carpet hanging out of the upper windows of a store on Chestnut Street! I'll swear it was the same carpet I saw more than twenty years ago!'

'And High Pale?'

'It was just as I remembered. A little smaller, perhaps. We reached it at nightfall. There was at first sight something rather ghost-like and insubstantial about it. It was just a white glimmer across wide lawns . . . But when we got inside there was a warm scent of cedar-wood and dried roses which I used to tell myself about in my dreams. And the polished floors shone and shadows masked the stairs — as I used to dream.'

He thought again about High Pale, where they had awaited the secret completion of the *Mute*.

'I remembered very little about the house — except, vaguely, a big portrait of my father and my uncle. And a huge old doll's house which stood in the passage outside the nursery — covered with red paper printed to resemble brickwork: why, I don't know: I never played with it in my life! . . . And, of course, Camelot?'

'Camelot!' said Garland. 'Do you know that the Almonds have put *your* Camelot in a glass case under the picture of Young Tom in the drawing-room!'

He smiled.

'When I saw my father's Camelot on the long table in the library, where it had always been, I knew that I had forgotten nothing about it. I could recall the names I had given every house and street . . . Mine was but a very poor shadow of his city. His was fourth-dimensional. I am convinced that he could withdraw into it when he wished! . . . He was more successful in his dreams than I!'

'He had less contact with the outer world!'

Now they stood together looking at Napoleon's prison-house, whilst their sweating horses cropped the scanty herbage.

He stole a sidelong glance at her thoughtful profile. He wondered whether the Emperor were watching them through his telescope from behind closed shutters. It would be difficult for Majesty to realize that that slim figure — in riding-habit of dark green, with gold-buttoned hussar jacket, and high-crowned hat — had brought all their schemes to naught. Or had she not? Was there any way in which . . .

'Shall you go back there now?' she asked, without turning.

He knew then that the crisis had come. He did not answer, but himself posed a question —

'How did you know?'

'Not by chance!' she answered still watching the grey-blue wood smoke rise in slow spirals from the chimneys of Longwood. 'Harrady and I heard that you stayed with *him*' — and she nodded in the direction of the house — 'until the last: that in the days of his humiliation and ruin you remained with him. So reasoning and imagination told us what next you would attempt to do! . . . We were proud — so proud, Rowley! — of your loyalty! I am so proud of it now!' Her voice trembled: she added, 'I would to God that it were loyalty to some other cause!'

He did not say anything, but continued to watch her so that he might imprint her likeness indelibly upon the tablets of his memory. This might be the last time that they could ever talk together as Garland and Rowley!

'We had you watched — Harrady and I — after that! . . . We had you spied on!' At the disgraceful word she looked suddenly at him: but there was no change in his friendly melancholy face. 'We knew when you went to Rome to see Madame Bonaparte — when you went to Parma to see the Empress Marie Louise. We knew when you went to America; found out about the *Mute*, but too late to stop you sailing. If only we had, what frightful risks would have been avoided!'

'Risks!'

'The peril to the world of *him* being let loose on it again! . . . The frightful risk you yourself incur! . . . The horrible, unthinkable risk that I again might have to — ' She could not put into words the possibility that she might have to betray him. 'You know the penalty for what you are doing?'

'The penalty Young Tom Almond paid! I've run the same risk before. Twelve years ago I practically had the rope round my neck, and the hangman waiting for me! It's nothing new!'

They had started walking slowly alongside the rough stone wall that marked the Longwood boundary, halting at every other step while their led horses snatched at the more succulent tufts of grass.

'So I came,' said Garland, 'to stop you doing this dreadful thing. To persuade you — if I could! But to stop you . . . anyhow! . . . You *must* not do it, Rowley!'

'I must,' he answered.

'You heard what Sir Hudson said last night?'

'That's only one side of the story!'

'Do you think that, if *he* were to escape, he would be content to settle down like a retired general? Do you think that he would be content to remain a country gentleman in an American wilderness? Do you think that he would give up all idea of reconquering his empire?'

He could not be sure of the answer to that question; and, since he would not reply to her otherwise than truthfully, he remained silent.

'You must accept the inevitable, Rowley my darling, and sail away! At once! I shall stay on guard until you have gone!'

They were facing one another now, standing under one of the goblin trees. The colourless landscape was blurred with fine mist. The roofs of Longwood and the cypresses about it were a dark blot against a monotonous grey.

'You must go!' she repeated. 'To-morrow! For the peace of the world! For your own safety. For — my sake!'

In her eyes, appeal. In his — unshaken love.

'I suppose that really I have no choice,' he answered. 'I am checkmated!'

He asked himself — 'But *am* I?'

'Two thousand soldiers and four warships on guard, Rowley! You know quite well that on the merest breath of suspicion they would double their watch! What chance would you have then, even if that suspicion were not directed against you or your ship? What chance if that suspicion *were* turned toward you?'

'Little!' he said.

'None!'

He asked himself — 'But *would* I have no chance?'

'In any case you have but little time now!'

'Very, very little! It is unlikely that Lowe will have failed to notify London of my arrival. The least time in which he could get an answer is three months. The reply will be a surprise for him, I'm afraid.' He let himself smile rather wryly. 'But things have taken longer than I expected. In a week the three months are up! After that every day means great and increasing peril! So —'

'Are you very angry with me, Rowley?' she asked, still holding his grey eyes with hers. 'You aren't! Even now, you aren't!'

'I would never be angry with you,' he answered truthfully. 'Not even if —'

'Not that! Don't say it, Rowley! I couldn't bear it — even saying it! ... I can't bear it, anyhow! First, *that!*' — and her eyes sought the empty sleeve pinned to his coat below the star of the order of the Red Eagle — 'And now *this!*'

'I'm only angry with Fate,' Anthony went on. 'With Fate because we've been given different loyalties!'

'Then it is only from loyalty that you are doing this, Rowley! ... I knew it! Was quite certain! I knew it wasn't from a traditional hate. Or revenge for those years you lost! I *knew* you were not made to hate, but only to be loyal!'

'After the *débâcle* I watched them fall away — the men he had raised from nothing to be as great as kings. I went to Parma to interest — if I could — the Empress in our plan. I found Napoleon's wife nursing a bastard fathered by her one-eyed chamberlain. I —' He broke off: continued after a moment, in answer to Garland's other statements. 'As for hatred — my grandmother is filled with enough for both of us, enough for the whole State of Virginia! She has some hidden reservoir from which the flames are fed! It is rather terrible. I always feel that she might suddenly be utterly consumed by her hate. And yet she has lived to be eighty-five!'

'The Witch in the Tower!'

He saw again that squat round tower at the end of the acacia terrace — the cobweb carpet and the queer table in the middle of the lair — the brass-bound writing-case — the miniature of Uncle Richard lying on a folded handkerchief — the morsels of comfits that had been nibbled and rejected and left strewn about the polished top of console or commode.

He went on —

'I know that those lost years of mine were just the misfortune of war. But my memories of the *Crown* and the *Blenheim* are a nightmare. They are too horrible for words. They surpass the imagination. When I escaped from the *Blenheim* I was angry and bitter and filled with desire for revenge. Now all I have is fellow-feeling for a prisoner, and loyalty to a master. I swear it!'

'A prisoner who must never go free!' she said; and regretted it as soon as she had spoken. Had a new determination stamped itself upon his face? She could not be sure. 'Rowley! A prisoner who must never go free — even — if — my — heart — breaks! You do understand, Rowley, don't you?'

He understood quite well.

'Give me till to-morrow to decide! This time to-morrow. We might ride together again?'

'But — '

'I will give you my most solemn word that the Emperor shan't vanish in the meantime. I will give my oath that we will not do what we have come to do for forty-eight hours, if you like!'

'The position can't alter in that time, dearest Rowley! I can't change my mind! I love you so very dearly, but I can't!' He saw the tears welling in her eyes as she spoke, and the quivering of her lips. 'You can't do anything! You know you can't!'

She took his hand in hers in the urgency of appeal.

'Rowley, I implore you!'

'I have others to consider. Others to consult! Give me until to-morrow!'

The mist had grown more dense. Longwood had been swallowed up. Reality had diminished to themselves, the munching horses behind them, the naked grey stem of the tree beside them, the rough grey wall in front, the wet grey-green tussocks at their feet. All else, except for the phantasmal trees, was blotted out. A patrol marched with almost noiseless tread out of invisibility, passed across the limited stage of their vision — shakoed, with fixed bayonets, their red tunics dulled with a thin film of mist; marched on into invisibility. In Anthony's mind their appearance laid a sudden new stress upon the prison and The Prisoner.

When they had passed out of hearing, Garland said —

'Till to-morrow, then! We will ride again together . . . And think, oh! my dearest! of what you are trying to do. Think of what the world has suffered because of him! Think of the four million dead! Think of what might happen were he free! Rowley, you are defeated now! You know you are! One day you will realize that your defeat is a victory for humanity! . . . I wish and pray that that "one day" will be to-morrow!'

Her heart went out to him as he stood before her in all the consciousness of defeat —

'Rowley, will you marry me?'

It was so little what he had expected her to say that he could only repeat her words, dumbfounded —

'Will I marry you?'

'Will you marry me?'

The look as of one that is lost, deepened upon his face, lightened even though it was by the tenderness of his smile.

With clumsy fingers he pulled off the glove she wore so that it was her bare hand that he raised to his lips.

When he looked up —

'You'll marry me out of pity for my defeat, dearest Garland!'

'From love.'

He corrected himself —

'From pity and love!'

'Love.'

'My dearest, do you remember what you told me five years ago? Is not this — this business what you feared might happen? . . . And might it not happen again?'

'I will risk it!'

'— And if there were children?'

She knew then that she, too, was defeated.

When she was in the saddle again, looking down on his bare head as he adjusted her stirrup leather, she sought assurance —

'You'll still love me, Rowley, won't you, whatever happens?'

He did not answer in words. Only he bent his head a little lower till his lips touched her bent knee. He remained thus a long, long time.

Presently he said —

'And you, too, will go on loving me?'

Neither did she answer in words. Only she placed her hand upon the mist-dampened disorder of his hair, and let it stay in blessing.

The mist had lifted not at all, when, on their way back, they reached the white guard-house at the entrance to the Longwood grounds. The place might have been the lodge of a city merchant's neat suburban residence but for the sentry standing by the door, a rigid image of a man, his musket held at the peculiarly wooden position of 'support'. In the gateway a small boy — a very small boy — in nankeen trousers and absurd frilled collar, battled with an equally small white kid which he held by a leash attached to its broad red leather collar. By the screen of mist the whole world was reduced to that small setting.

The kid — at full length of its lead — leaped into the air on all four feet. The small boy, still grimly hanging on to the creature, fell flat on his face. The kid, content with the effect, fell to nibbling the rough grass at the foot of the wall as though its master's fall was of minor importance. Wooden Image snorted appreciation of the entertainment.

'This,' said Anthony reining in, 'is the son of Count Bertrand, Grand

Marshal of the Imperial Palace of Longwood!' And he inclined his head
in the general direction of the invisible huddle of bungalows.

The small boy had recovered his feet, still clinging to the leash. He
ducked his tousled head politely to Anthony with a grin of recognition.

'Henri!' said Anthony in French, 'This is the Countess of Morfa! Lady
Morfa — Count Henri Bertrand, one of the prisoners of St. Helena!'

Count Henri ducked again: completed the circle of introductions —
'This is my goat, Polissonne! I am now going to beat her!'

And beat her he did.

At Hutt's Gate, where all the misty roads to everywhere were knotted
about a tangle of misty ravines darkened by the shadow of Diana's Peak,
they were taken back into the everyday life of the island . . . Miss Mason
returning from her morning's shopping in Jamestown. A tough elderly
spinster in a dark red habit, riding — side-saddle — a large red ox, a
market basket on her arm, her aquiline nose shaded against an invisible
sun by an enormous straw hat . . . A gang of pig-tailed coolies rolling
empty watercasks uphill . . . General Baron Gourgaud in a new white hat
cantering — with very long stirrups — to town, to the manifest discom-
posure of his escort . . . A pair of young negro slaves, shoeless, in striped
cotton trousers, carrying baskets of fruit upon their heads. . . .

Anthony stood at his window looking onto a bright green grass plat
set about with a high hedge of magnolias in full bloom. The little lawn
was spattered with rose petals from the sweet-briar growing on the rustic
trellis-work of the porch, and the garden was full of the song of birds
and the rustle of a waterfall.

A few days after his arrival he had rented the place, a three-roomed
pavilion in the grounds of a house called The Briars, a little over a mile
from Jamestown. Napoleon had occupied it during the first weeks of
his captivity on the island. It was isolated, and yet accessible; lying amid
a garden of pomegranates and orange and mango trees, at the foot of the
mountains that closed the valley. It was convenient for visitors who came
at dead of night; it was convenient for residents who did not desire attention called to their movements.

The sitting-room was furnished without any graces, in a horsehair-and-
misty-mahogany sort of way. Its only decoration — if decoration it could
be called — was an engraving over the fireplace of the Prince-Regent of
England, very bland and plump, his Royal hair dishevelled in an elegant
and wind-blown manner . . . Mr. Balcombe, the landlord, who was son
of a Brighton publican, liked to foster the St. Helena rumour that he
was a by-product of Royal Highness.

At a table in the middle of the room, Klasing was busied with papers, lists, a large-scale map. Anthony found it quite impossible to associate in any way Solomon Klasing, his secretary, with Solly Klasing, his school-mate, even apart from the fact that the once-red hair was now a quite unbelievable black. The man made so efficient a secretary that Anthony often wondered whether he ever really had had the makings of anything more than a repetitive musician within him. If Klasing were interested any longer in music, he did not show it. His only known interests, indeed, apart from his work, were to watch himself enacting the stage Jew, to study the philosophy of Spinoza, and to collect violent-coloured handkerchiefs. He maintained — and insisted on maintaining — toward Anthony the attitude of a secretary, of a privileged and confidential sec-retary, nothing more and nothing less.

'I have told Lady Morfa,' said Anthony, speaking with stiff lips, 'that I will call for her at half-past seven to-morrow morning, to ride to Sandy Bay. The road is very narrow and steepish, and runs into a jungle of tall fern as you cross the ridge. Stuff that is fifteen feet high if it's an inch. Even higher!'

'Yeth. I underthtand,' said Klasing, scratching his bony red nose with the end of a quill pen, and studying the map. He had no need to lisp, but did so at odd intervals because he felt that it was in character.

'There's cover for an army to lie in ambush along the road,' said Anthony, continuing to stare into the garden.

'Yeth!' agreed Klasing, still scratching his nose and studying the map.

'The whole hillside is torn with great ravines and bottomless fissures.'

'Yeth!'

'When her horse goes back riderless, and they can't find her, they will naturally think —'

But he could not go on: could not continue coolly outlining the thing that he proposed to do . . . So Garland must have felt all those years ago when she and Harradence had found that their loyalties and their love for him were at variance! He swung round on Klasing to find the Jew looking up at him with a most charming and understanding smile.

'You leave me to fill in the detail,' Klasing suggested. 'An abduction wath mere child'th play to uth at the Polithe Minithtry! I can lay my handth on a dozen Chinethe — men of the Red Leopard *tong*. Ying, their headman, ith a firtht-clath fellow. A gentleman, although he'th a heathen Chinee! We'll take her to Burroughs's farm, and then move her to the Bertrands', as you wish, as soon as it'th dark. I'll see Madame Bertrand. They can't continue the hunt after sunthet, and it'll be quite safe then. Quite safe!'

Anthony turned back to the window. For a moment he had the fancy that he saw Garland coming toward him across the grass, dressed in the biscuit-coloured habit and primrose beaver hat that she had worn when she went riding with him at La Cadière in the days before the *Nautilus* had finished building. Thought to hear her high clear voice calling him. Felt all the awareness of her presence that sight and sound could give — and some other unknown sense . . . He cursed, and out loud, the intervening years whose fruition was to be this act of violence . . . Judas!

He pictured her being torn from her horse by a dozen clutching yellow hands; being borne — vainly struggling — in sinister procession through the bizarre depths of the fern forest . . . Judas!

'Klasing — ' he began: and found that his voice was not steady.

The secretary appeared to be wholly occupied in altering the trim of his pen with a little sharp knife: essayed a stroke or two: pared yet another minute shaving off the quill: tried again. But he answered the unspoken —

'No harm shall come to her! She shall be treated with every respect! I am guarantor. I swear it — by Abraham's beard! . . . That's a thuitable oath for an Israelite, isn't it?'

. . . The acacias on the terrace at La Cadière were whispering to the night; the restless sea below the tangle of steep garden was whispering to the night. As though it were only yesterday he could remember that session of Harradence's Parliament which debated the possibilities and future of Robert Fulton's submarine boat; could see the faces round the table and catch the very timbre of the voices; could hear the indignant Garland's low-voiced protests. It was the night which more than any other had shaped the fashion of his life! The night when his imagination had first been stimulated by the wonder and the possibilities of the *Nautilus;* the night when he had met Jasmine!

From *Nautilus* to *Mute!* The circle of events was complete. That which had been begun at La Cadière was to be finished at St. Helena! . . .

He had in his pocket-book a two-line note she had written to him in Morfa five years ago. It was creased and blurred and the folds had split. He had kissed it. He had carried it with him everywhere. He took it out, and stood looking at it now, and at a small engraving of Garland — torn from an old number of the *Belle Assemblée* — which was enfolded in it . . . He was Judas!

CHAPTER IV

'IF' AND 'WHEN'

HE did not see who touched him as he emerged from the theatre into the night. The short lane was filled with people making their way, with bobbing lanterns, to the main street where the carriages waited — was filled with the babble and bustle of their departure through the darkness. One minute he had been hearing old Doveton narrate, for a third time, how he had seen David Garrick play Macbeth in a bob wig and scarlet breeches: hearkening to Baroness Sturmer's complaint that seven shillings and sixpence a pound for fresh butter was monstrous: striving to distinguish Garland's voice amid the clamour. And then —

'Silas!'

It was a low whisper in his ear; and whoever spoke urged him gently to one side so that the stream of theatre-goers passed him by.

He said, 'Deane!'

How many years ago was it since last that sign and countersign had been used in the Emperor's service?

And then he found himself on the slant of the hill-side, enfolded by night, the life and movement of the small town now reduced to a distant murmur of voices and a few pin-points of light — and now silenced and extinguished.

A strenuous two hours later he came up through a trap-door, masked by a large billiard-table, in the middle of the raftered hut that was the Longwood servants' hall. Of the route that had brought him there he had no notion: at some point, he fancied, they had climbed out of the Devil's Punch Bowl, crossed the road, and plunged down the precipitous ravine that passed behind Longwood and opened out into Fisher's Valley.

There, for the first and only time, had they evidence of constant guard, for they heard the challenge of a sentry on the ridge above them, and the sound of feet. They froze in their tracks. But a crisp voice answered the order to halt — the voice of the orderly officer going his rounds. They moved on, his guide preceding him by a few yards, as he had done throughout the journey, without the exchange of a word. After that a dry torrent-bed up which they climbed — a fissure masked by some ferociously spiked shrub — a short low tunnel — and then emergence through this aperture to light and the sound of voices and a panorama of white silk-stockinged legs.

A grave tall servant in well-remembered livery of green and gold assisted him to extricate himself from beneath the table.

A large shaded lamp hanging from a beam illumined the green baize surface and the intent faces about it. All the rest of the room was in shadow, except in one corner where two small candles burned, one on either side of the diminutive mirror set in the open lid of a mahogany ship's washstand.

He was washed: he was brushed: he was groomed.

The rough plank walls were decorated with a motley collection of unframed prints, mostly invisible in the gloom: but above the washstand was a tattered engraving representing the opening of Waterloo Bridge in London . . . Waterloo!

'If you will come this way, sir,' said the grave tall servant, 'I will announce your arrival to the Grand Marshal. He will inform his Majesty.'

He was shepherded out of that place of sedate faces and low voices into a wide uncarpeted corridor; into a dark small vestibule — from which mounted a staircase that was little more than a ladder; into a dining-room filled by a large table of golden oak, lighted by a single candle, painted light blue, and full of doors.

. . . Into a yellow and green room, lighted by a small chandelier with glass lustres hanging from it.

On a settee between the two heavily-curtained windows, facing a blazing log fire, sat the Emperor. He was reading aloud in a declamatory voice from a book upon his knee, and did not raise his eyes from the page when Anthony entered.

'For who liv'd king, but I could dig his grave?
And who durst smile when Warwick bent his brow?'

The room, which was of very moderate size, was papered in pale yellow with an ugly pattern of green flowers. A misty mirror over the black marble mantelpiece. Ebony chairs of Empire pattern, upholstered in dark green with yellow binding — all a little shabby. Heavy curtains of dark green serge. A peculiarly hideous carpet of a startling geometrical design. A chess-table, with the pieces still in position, in the nearer corner. In one of the recesses that flanked the farther door, a large clock, brassily gilt, with a bright blue face, under a glass shade. At the Emperor's feet a few open books flung carelessly upon the floor.

'Lo, now my glory smear'd in dust and blood!
My parks, my walks; my manors that I had,
Even now forsake me . . .'

On the wall above the bent head with the thinning dark hair, a portrait of the faithless wife, high-bosomed and voluptuous-lipped, having in her arms the ringleted King of Rome.

> '. . . and of all my lands
> Is nothing left me but my body's length!'

In this setting, as tarnished as the parlour of a London or a New York lodging-house, the Imperial Court were grouped respectfully about their master. Three men, in full-dress uniform, their breasts glittering with decorations, the fringes of their epaulettes and their high erect coat collars heavy with gold . . . Gourgaud, romantical Master of the Horse, with runaway chin and runaway forehead, fidgeting wearily from one foot to the other, seeking surreptitious support from the chess-table behind him. Montholon, Court Chamberlain, black-side-whiskered, with bowed attentive head, at the farther side of the settee. Bertrand, Grand Marshal, in the centre of the room facing the Principal Lodger: Bertrand, the always-loyal, with a square, lined, honest face, holding himself formally erect. The star of the Legion of Honour was upon his breast, and three medals were suspended from a button-hole; but the seams of his coat shone, and the light directly above him showed a large patch upon the elbow . . . Anthony was not ashamed of the tears that filled his eyes.

> 'Why, what is pomp, rule, reign, but earth
> and dust!'

The Tuileries — Fontainebleau — Montebello — Schönbrunn — Charlottenburg — Sans Souci — all the fantastic splendour of fairy-tale palaces reduced to the compass of a lodging-house parlour! Gala theatrical performances, at which satellite Kings and princes applauded only where Imperial Majesty applauded, replaced by the entertainment that he himself provided from a French translation of Shakespeare's tragedy of King Henry the Sixth!

The Principal Lodger, having now come to the end of the scene, laid down the book upon his knee. He raised his eyes. He extended a white well-shaped hand — a hand as cold to the touch as stone.

'You find us studying Shakespeare instead of the battlefield, my little Purgis!' he said as though they had only parted on the yesterday. 'Does he lose much in translation?'

Anthony bowed low over the fingers that he kissed — lower than he had ever bowed to that small seated man in the plenitude of his power.

'A quarter of a century ago almost precisely you saw the beginning!

Now you see the end,' said Napoleon. 'The accommodation is very little better than in that house on the way to Toulon!'

'Not the end — another beginning, sire!' replied Anthony.

He realized that the other had as little belief in the venture of *Königin Luise* and *Mute* as he had had in any of the schemes of escape promoted by mere scatter-brained adventurers.

The Principal Lodger was a little heavier in face and figure, a little more sallow, than when he saw him last. His chin and cheeks were dark with the unshaven stubble of a day's growth. There were shadows under his bright grey eyes. He wore the coat of an infantry general — green with white facings — and white breeches and stockings. Oval buckles of gold glittered on his lacquered shoes.

'Another beginning?'

It seemed to Anthony that the voice was somewhat altered, too; had become a thought more harsh, and to its remembered tone was now added a suspicion of the Corsican speech of childhood.

'In America, sire!' suggested Gourgaud. 'A new kingdom to be carved!'

The Principal Lodger shook his head; paid his meed of regret to the notion —

'After the Carlovingian empire, the Aztec!' Meditated for a flash on the fabulous glories of other vanished dynasties: shook his head again. 'I was a *coglione!* I should never have sold Louisiana! Nine hundred thousand square miles practically given away! What an empire to have been carved west of the Mississippi!'

There was a dark patch of damp on the yellow and green wall-paper in the corner by the chess-table. The candles in the chandelier had guttered, and the yellow and green carpet was speckled with grease marks beneath them. The gilt metal ornamentation on the woodwork of the yellow and green settee was broken. In fact all the yellow-greenery had the mildewed, second-hand appearance of the yellow-greenery to be found in a lodging-house sitting-room.

Fifteen years ago the small man sitting in this shabby jungle had disposed of nearly a million square miles of land with less thought than the owner of a large estate would give to the sale of an outlying farm!

Gourgaud sighed rather gustily. Bertrand shot a disapproving look at him. Montholon shot a disapproving look at him. Gourgaud in a rather guilty manner transmuted sigh of weariness into sigh of regret —

'And then, sire, we should not have been on this execrable rock!'

'Gourgaud is young,' said the Emperor. 'Gourgaud needs a woman! Your wife had better let him have that little mulatto maid of hers, Bertrand! Or what about Albine's maid, Esther, my dear Montholon? . . . Perhaps he could have both?'

'The Baron would have to arrange that with your Majesty's principal valet,' said Montholon acidly. 'I am not the guardian of Esther's uncertain morals, but I suspect that she would be found in Marchand's bed at this moment.'

'Marchand is a good judge! I have paid a great deal of money for women far worse-looking than Esther!'

Gourgaud threw out his chest in a histrionic manner: his face was very stormy —

'Your Majesty did not share their embraces with lackeys!'

'Who knows?' replied the Principal Lodger, supremely indifferent.

'Baron Gourgaud had better buy himself a female slave, sire,' said Bertrand severely, 'instead of upsetting his colleagues' domestic staffs! It may be a little expensive, but I, for one, will subscribe . . . My wife's maids vanish like frightened rabbits at the sight of him!'

'Gorgo, Gorgotto, my son! What is this I hear about you?' said the Principal Lodger impishly. 'Can it be that the advances of my Master of the Horse are rejected by the Grand Marshal's kitchen wenches?'

It could not be true, Anthony told himself. It was not possible that the man who had been master of the destinies of kings and kingdoms, should now be preoccupied by the bedtime adventures of the lodging-house staff. It was a joke — a charade — amateur theatricals by the inmates of the Longwood Boarding Establishment, in seedyish uniforms and decorations hired for the occasion. They would put off their gay clothes in a little, and make for a dingy dining-room and scramble for a tripe-and-onions supper.

Gourgaud stammered in wrath. His eyes filled with tears of self-pity.

The Principal Lodger passed on to another topic, apparently revived in his mind by mention of the Montholons' maid, Esther.

'Who washes your wife's baby linen, Montholon?' he suddenly inquired.

Montholon did not know.

'It won't be Mrs. Quilton!' meditated the enquirer.

Montholon agreed. It certainly would not be Mrs. Quilton.

'Then it must be either Joséphine or Esther!'

This seemed logical to the Chamberlain. He said as much.

'Then,' said the Principal Lodger, 'please give instructions to whichever of those two women is concerned, that your diapers are not to be set out to dry on the grass under my library windows!'

It was Montholon's turn to flush. He apologized most humbly. Gourgaud assumed the expression of one whose baby linen would always be kept well out of range of the Imperial eyesight.

'It gives the house,' said the Principal Lodger severely, 'the air of being inhabited by the *petite bourgeoisie!*'

How could anyone ever say that this man had been responsible for four million dead? The room was insufferably hot. The fire roared up the chimney. The wind was rising, and one of the outside shutters, loose on a fastening, rattled continuously . . . It could not be a charade! No amateur actors would stand so woodenly, so respectfully, so wearily around one seated man. For how long had he stood there? Half an hour — an hour? For how long had those others stood there? The brassy clock under the glass shade registered the hour as midnight.

The Principal Lodger, from criticism of his fellow guests, turned his attention to the proprietorship and management of the establishment. With each sentence that he uttered, his fury mounted. It was not the fury of an emperor, felt Anthony, but the fury of an aggrieved lodger. It was a fury about little things: things which, he was persuaded, were barely more important than the missing laundry, the imperfectly polished boots, the cold mutton, the lack of hot water, the insolence of a servant, which might arouse the ire of boarders at some 'select' establishment. It was a fury which became an antiphon, for to each sentence there was a response from the other lodgers — a murmur of profound agreement, like the mumble of the congregation replying to the priest.

The censorship of letters — the wall-paper — the ever-present orderly officer — the quality of the meat — the fact that he was provided with the London *Times*, that 'infamous newspaper subventioned by the Bourbons at six thousand francs a month!' — the various restrictions upon his freedom of movement: and then recurrence to the major theme, British treachery, and the assassin-like qualities of the *sbirro*, Lowe.

'He has the face of a mangy dog,' declared Majesty. 'It wants treating with mercury and sulphur! . . . Sulphur!'

The irritation which the fretful monologue began to produce in Anthony's mind was suddenly swept away by an intense pity. Even as he himself had begun to break, at Norman Cross; even as Millet (buried with a stake through his intestines) *had* broken; even as a dozen other men he could remember had broken before the prospect of indefinite imprisonment; so was Majesty breaking. Europe had decided that he was her Eternal Enemy; for him would peace never be declared; for him freedom could only be obtained by guile or force — or death. Anthony found, too, that mingled with the pity was regret that there was so little dignity amid so great disaster . . . Garland was wrong — the peace of the world would never be disturbed again by this man. . . .

He said in abrupt interruption —

'In less than a week, sire, you should be free from Lowe for ever!'

There was silence for an instant. Napoleon sat meditatively on the sofa twisting his right coat-sleeve until it was as tormented as a corkscrew. It was clearer than ever that up to the present he had refused to take the *Königin Luise* seriously.

He knew that Bertrand was watching him, had read all his thoughts, was bidding him remember that utter loyalty must place a sordid present in its rightful relation to a splendid past.

Then, the next instant the lodger had again become the commander: had begun a hail of questions with regard to the expedition — its organization, its schedule. It was such hail of questions as the Emperor of the French had fired at his staff in the past when he cross-examined them, muster-rolls in hand, map spread upon his table.

No, it was no charade. It was the genuine thing. It was a real general, surrounded by real generals, probing relentlessly into every least particular of a forthcoming operation.

He was satisfied at last. 'And afterwards?'

'My house at High Pale in Virginia is at your Majesty's disposal. A house in New Orleans is also ready should you prefer to stay in Louisiana while you settle your plans!'

'Plans!'

The Emperor rose to his feet —

'Plans!' he repeated with rising inflexion. 'To be able to plan again!'

He walked slowly, with bent head and with hands behind his back, up and down the room. There was a green-painted door at each end, and he would unfold his hands and tap a panel with the nail of his right forefinger before turning, as though to assure himself of the continuing reality of things.

He halted on his journeyings, under the chandelier. He addressed himself to Anthony although he did not raise his eyes from the grease spots on the ugly carpet —

'Little Purvis! Did you not find, too, that what you missed most in captivity was — Planning? . . . Dreaming — Bah! Anyone can dream. The drunkard and the opium-eater and the laudanum-drinker! But to plan the bending of reality to the shape of your dreams — that is another matter! Let me plan plans: I do not care if others have the execution of them! Let me plan battles for generals to fight, laws for lawyers to codify, bridges and roads for my engineers to construct, empires for a nation to win!'

His hair was very thin on top. Perhaps it was the reflections from the lustres that made his skin seem more sallow than of old.

'Plans! To make real plans again, instead of to dream them!'

To and fro. 'Plans! . . . Plans! . . . Plans!'

Stopped, and frostily regarded Gourgaud who did his best to convey the impression that he had not been propping himself wearily against the wall. There was a dark mark that was not part of the green pattern on the yellow background of the wall-paper, level with his head.

'The next tenants will complain of the condition of the decorations, my Gorgo,' said the Tenant of Longwood. 'The British Government will undoubtedly make me pay for new wall-paper. Use less hair-oil, please! Or don't rub your head on the wall! Or both!'

The sombre Bertrand was expressionless. Montholon permitted his apple cheeks to wrinkle in the beginnings of a smile. Once again tears started in Gourgaud's eyes: Anthony decided that he must be an infuriating companion in captivity.

The Tenant continued his march, repeating to himself the single word 'Plans!' at a gradually increasing interval, slowly, and — finally — triumphantly. Flung himself down at last on to the settee; sat forward with his hands upon his plump knees, staring into the blazing fire.

None of the other men — not even Gourgaud — had shifted their position by more than a few inches since Anthony had arrived. How long ago was it? An hour — an hour and a half — more? The hands of the brassy clock had not altered. The airless heat of the room was intense: the wind was rising, and the loose shutter increased the tempo of its rattle.

'For nearly three years I have said "If — !" ' said the Emperor. 'Now I can say "When!" '

'If — !' had become 'When — !'

The yellow and green walls of the lodging-house of Longwood had vanished, as in some Grand Transformation Scene: the riven mountains of St. Helena had been obliterated: the leagues of wild sea overpassed. The miserable audience-chamber of a dethroned emperor was of a sudden filled with all the glory of earthly opportunity.

'When — !' had replaced 'If — !'

'When I escape, I will — .' Not 'If I escape, I will — .'

'You, too, know something about English hospitality, Purvis! Life in the hulks! *I* remember! . . . What were your first reactions when you escaped?'

The Emperor leaned back as he spoke, crossing his white-stockinged legs at the ankle, the heel of a varnished shoe resting on the back of a large book which lay, with ruffled leaves, face downward on the floor.

Anthony, brought up to the observance of a most rigid etiquette towards books, was always shaken by the cavalier treatment meted out to them by Napoleon; leaves covered with scribbling, turned down, torn out; the volumes themselves wrenched apart, hurled upon the floor, or out of the window — things emptied, gutted, finished.

He meditated for a few moments before replying —

'I suppose, sire, that my principal feeling was one of intense appreciation of my freedom . . . But I know, too, that I also wanted very greatly to get my own back! To exact some kind of payment for the indignities that I had undergone! I was extraordinarily glad; I was extraordinarily angry!'

'Angry?' said the man who was giving up the tenancy of Longwood. 'Angry? . . . You were just angry?'

He kicked the book beneath his feet so that it was propelled, with scrabbling leaves, for a short distance across the carpet. Anthony felt certain that if Harradence had been there he would have gone immediately to the rescue of the hapless volume, smoothed its leaves, consoled it as though it were a child . . . Had Harrady read yet Peacock's new book, *Melincourt?* Had Harrady read yet *Guy Mannering* or *The Antiquary* by the author of *Waverley?* He would have liked a bookish talk with Harrady again.

'Angry!'

How much longer must they continue standing about the short pale fattish man upon the settee, whose eyes were fixed brooding upon the fire? Was it — brooding? Or was it — planning? . . . The blue and gold monstrosity of a clock had unquestionably stopped, or did not go at all — like all lodging-house clocks!

'I have had one enemy all my life,' said the man on the settee. 'I have beaten her again and again — but she has still endured, relentless, resurgent, vindictive! England! The others were to be cozened, cajoled, frightened, or conquered; would assume the mask of friendship. But never England! She fought alone: she withstood me alone: she hated me. My God, how she has hated me! How she hates me still! . . . How *I* hate her!'

No matter how passionate the anger, the chill marble of that Roman face had never altered in the past. It did not alter now. The voice vibrated: white plump fingers pulled at white plump knees; but the contours and lines of the countenance remained as unmoved as those of a mask.

'I was advised badly!' he said. 'I was served worse! . . . There was only one obstacle to my Empire of the West. Britain! Only one obstacle to the New Order in Europe. Britain! I should have dealt with her first. Russia could have waited — should have waited! . . . And now — !'

What plans already were formulating themselves in his mind? Not dreams — but plans that a free man, a free Napoleon could carry out!

He said harshly, and looked from one to the other of those weary attendant men, as though a school-master seeking answer from his class —

'What has changed the whole business of generalship?'

Gave no time for reply; himself answered —

'Steam! . . . Fulton! . . . The maiden voyage of the American steam frigate *Demologos* three years ago! A heavily-armed ship that could travel against the tide and against the wind! Twelve years before that I had written to Champagny of the Marine Ministry ordering a commission to report on the *pyroscaphe* that Fulton was experimenting with on the Seine! I said "the project may change the face of the world!" Was that report ever made? No! I was evilly served . . . The Americans have laid up the *Demologos*. Why? She did all that was asked of her. She was a deadly thing! The equivalent of a fleet at the cost of a single frigate! The British Admiralty start to construct a steam sloop. They don't complete her! Why? . . . Because it is peace-time! Peace! The fools! Have they not learned yet that peace is but the preparation time for war? Must peace always be the time for disarmament, and great projects need the incentive of war for their fulfilment? Britain is no longer an island protected by the unpredictable wind and seas. I should have a fleet of these things —'

Were these plans, after all, or just dreams? Had the reality of 'When' become mingled with the unreality of 'If'? . . . With what cynical appreciation must Fulton be listening now, recalling the drudgery of writing letters to which authority made no reply.

When — If: Plans — Dreams!

How long had he been standing there?

The little man on the settee continued to corkscrew his sleeve: continued to tell his thoughts aloud —

'. . . Once I landed I would push on to London. I would publish proclamations broadcast. To *coglionare il popolo!* I would declare that I came only as a friend to free the masses from the rule of an oligarchy! To restore the rights of the people! To establish a new order of better things! I would abolish the monarchy and the House of Lords. I would share their property among the people. I would make such promises as would bring over to my side all the *canaglie* in London and elsewhere, and all the idle and disaffected. I would promise everything! There are traitors to be found amongst all nations! . . . Afterwards I would annex England to France; or, if I were not strong enough for that, I would establish a government that would do as it was told.'

The old policy of interlocking treason with violence! The policy that had conquered almost all Western Europe! He experienced a sense of chill. 'If' becoming 'When' meant dreams becoming plans, meant freedom becoming conquest . . . And then saw a pale small middle-aged man with his waistcoat strained across his middle and his hair thinning on top —a pale small man from whom was diffused a rather overpowering scent of lavender perfume, sitting on a rather shabby settee in a rather shoddy room. It was absurd to think of this little fattish fellow as though he were the Angel of Death himself. It was somebody quite other who had shot the prisoners at Jaffa, had filled the concentration camps, had executed Enghien and Palm, was responsible for four million graves! He took grip of the realities, and almost smiled . . . Even Garland must agree that here was just a middle-aged gentleman whose sole desire was to find more suitable lodgings.

CHAPTER V

VIOLENCE IN THE FOREST OF FERNS

KLASING was waiting up for him when Anthony arrived back at the pavilion, weary and dishevelled. He was very busy with pen and ivory ruler at the table, in his shirt-sleeves, his watch hanging up before him on a stand made to represent the triangular gallows at Tyburn. Face, watch, and the large sheet of paper over which he was bent were illumined by a single candle. All the rest of the room was in darkness.

'Well?' said Anthony, the door not yet closed behind him, sopping cloak still about his shoulders.

'Everything will go off very thweetly!' answered Klasing, looking round into the shadows, from contemplation of his neatly ruled columns. 'All the arrangementh are made. I opine that it'll be the quicketht, politetht, neatetht abduction that ever wath! We've found a beautiful thpot for it! Be-yoo-ti-ful!'

'My God!' snarled Anthony, 'there's no occasion for humour!'

'None!' agreed Klasing, and his voice lost its lisp. 'I am merely telling you incontestable facts. I really think our scheme is fool-proof. I spent practically the whole of yesterday on it. Look here!' — He pulled out the map of the island from under a mass of papers, as Anthony flung off his cloak and stalked across to the table. Stabbed at a point with the quill pen from behind his ear. — 'The bridle track from Plantation House runs down into a deep combe here before it breasts the topmost ridge of the hills. It burrows its way through the fern. Literally! You can't see the sky overhead. In the middle of the valley there is a very small clearing where the path forks. The left-hand branch tunnels downwards through a ravine to Burroughs's farm at the edge of the forest of fern . . . See, the house is marked! . . . The other track emerges from the fern after about half a mile on to the top of the ridge. Most extraordinary place — just like Dante's Inferno. You have been there?'

Anthony nodded. He had ridden that little-frequented path only once before, but he remembered well the chaos of the torn hill-top, split with ravines and cracked with great fissures; with pinnacles of rock and queerly coloured cliffs — streaked with violet and emerald and orange — rising from thickets of yellow gorse. He had fancied that such might be a lunar landscape.

'The men will be waiting, hidden round the clearing in the fern. All you will have to do is to stop on some excuse when you get there. To adjust your girth, or something such, I suppose . . . I've also made all arrangements with Burroughs. He's got a good room where she will be quite safe — and comfortable — until we can move her. One of the men will bucket her horse about until it's in a muck and then loose it with broken reins among the ravines. Half the garrison and most of the island will be out searching for her in all the gullies before the day is over. "Mystery of the Missing Countess". Might be a romance by Mrs. Radcliffe!'

'Judas! Judas!' said Anthony to himself, still regarding the curve in the hachures on the map, that represented the scene of betrayal.

'You've got your story planned, I imagine, sir?'

'Yes!'

'I've arranged with Countess Bertrand — '

'So the Count told me. For Christ's sake spare me the detail! I don't want to know it . . . I suppose it's necessary for me to take part personally in this filthy business?'

'Absolutely necessary, sir, I am sure! Take just one point. Without you Lady Morfa would not ride alone across strange country! There is your answer, sir.'

His secretary, after one quick glance up at him, pushed the map to one side and bent his eyes to the operations *schema*.

'You have no alternative, sir!' he said. 'Absolutely none! It's this — or failure, and possibly the hangman!'

Anthony knew it to be true. It was no consolation. He stood in silence whilst Klasing's large copper watch loudly ticked time away, suspended from the noose on the little ebony gallows.

In that silence he told himself that Garland must some day come to realize that he had been right, that she had been wrong: that his loyalty to the Emperor entailed no hurt to her loyalties . . . But then it would be too late! . . . Some day she would know what he already knew — that Europe's Prisoner was no longer an enemy to be feared, had become old before his time, was a fretful middle-aged gentleman (Yet, *was* he a gentleman?) who only wanted a more comfortable chair in a more comfortable corner in a more comfortable lodging, where he might abide peacefully day-dreaming life away . . . Judas! . . . Some day she would come to understand that the detention of the Emperor as prisoner at St. Helena was not continued in order to ensure the peace of the world — because he no longer menaced its security — but merely in order to exact retribution for the past. It was punishment in keeping with the spirit of British Justice, the most vengeful and the harshest in the Western world. Justice which enforced the penalty of death for forging a penny duty stamp upon a scent bottle; inflicted three hundred lashes upon a soldier for a day's absence without leave; and provided prisoners awaiting trial with neither bedding nor fuel, and for ration only a daily penny loaf . . . Judas!

Garland would realize all this some day. *Some* day! Too late a day!

Klasing, bent over the table, grumbled —

'I've had to make out an entirely new operations schedule owing to this business. It has taken hours . . . It's based on our heaving up anchor at a quarter past four on Tuesday next. Clockwork! Synchronization! Co-ordination! . . . The time still stands?'

'It does.'

Anthony examined automatically the double sheet of foolscap with which Klasing was concerned.

It was a masterpiece of a time-table. There were columns for everybody and everything: for 'N' — for the *Mute* — for the *Königin Luise* — for Anthony — for Klasing — for the Red Leopard *tong* (whose multifarious activities included a diversionary raid upon the huts of their rivals of the Society of a Thousand Bridges) and for all sorts of people ranging upwards from mulatto guides to the venal Mr. Balcombe, Anthony's landlord, and the lieutenant in charge of the post at Mason's Stock House in Fisher's Valley, an even more venal gentleman. Reading down the columns the commander could see detailed the complete story of each factor in the scheme; reading across the columns he could see what every unit should be doing at any given time. There was an additional column on this schedule now as compared with its predecessors. It was headed 'Lady M.' It showed how 'Lady M.' was to be transported across country by stages at night and finally to her eventual prison in Count Bertrand's house on the Longwood estate, where she was to be kept hidden until all danger was over . . . No harm could come to Garland (he told himself) in charge of Fanny Bertrand!

He looked again at the watch upon its little gallows — an old-fashioned watch without a minute hand, so that it was difficult to tell the time in such obscurity. He walked to the window, and drew back the curtains. The garden was greying with daybreak. It was just five o'clock . . . In little over two hours he was to meet Garland! Had Judas felt like this before he betrayed his Master? Had Judas loved his Master even while betraying him?

'Everything stands!' he asseverated harshly. 'The Emperor must be got down Old Woman Valley to the *Mute* on Monday night. We shall sail at a quarter after four on the following afternoon. Thank God, the winds here are as constant as your clockwork, Klasing! I told Lowe last night that the dispatches which the *Königin Luise* had brought back meant that we must leave at once . . . He asked if I could take some personal letters for him!'

Klasing sniggered. He wiped his narrow-lensed spectacles with a yellow handkerchief decorated with red foxes; put them on; regarded his employer. Realized with concern how grey and weary was his face, how muddied and torn the dark uniform he wore.

'You'ld better get a little sleep, sir! You've had a strenuous night, and you have an unpleasant day in front of you. You've got an hour or so to spare!'

Anthony shook his head.

'I could not sleep now. I'll get bathed and shaved and changed. Otto shall make some coffee. I want daylight and fresh air. I feel as if I had been skulking in a rabbit burrow!' . . .

And so once again they rode together — as they had ridden yesterday; as they had ridden in the park at Morfa; as they had ridden in the pine forests above La Cadière years and years ago.

They had had little to say to one another as they passed down the gravelled carriage-sweep across which the green-shuttered windows of the great white house regarded — with a supercilious Englishness — wide lawns, and rolling hills studded with plantations of Scottish fir. Even overwhelmed, as he was, by consciousness of what was so soon to happen, Anthony realized a quick pang of anger at the comparison between the smug perfection of the Governor's residence and the shoddy makeshift of the Emperor's lodging.

They rode through a plantation of evergreen oaks and turned into a country lane whose hedges were swamped with large starry flowers of deep blue. A prim small bare church — of the New England type — looked down on them from the top of a low rounded hill.

There was between them, not the silence of old friends but the desultory conversation of new acquaintances. He found himself planning small banal remarks with which to fill any pause in their talk. When he spoke it was with stiff lips that fought against being made to shape words. His forehead was damp with sweat.

Down into a dingle with a small white cottage lost in the verdure. Now the road began to mount again . . . How much farther was it to the appointed place?

He stole a glance at Garland. She was looking straight before her thoughtfully, as though his last trivial remark deserved careful attention before answer. Then she became aware of his surveillance, and suddenly turned her face toward him, and smiled.

'We are just being absurd, Rowley,' she said. 'Let's either say what we've got to say now, or else be silent until we reach the sea. I always say that it is easier to talk important things within hearing of the sea. Its tremendousness restores one's sense of proportion!'

He did not know afterward what reply he made, because at that moment they had rounded a bend, and the track sloped down into a fold in hills over which billowed a sea of immense fern, islanded with the plumed tops of palm trees, and moving restlessly in some light eddy of the wind . . . How far was it, now?

The road became a corridor passing through the cool green depths, gothic-arched overhead by the giant fronds, lighted only through the golden translucency of the roof, and scented with the heavy scent of fern and damp earth.

. . . A mile? Half a mile? . . .

Once he thought to hear above the whispering of the giant cryptogams some other — and harsher — noise, but the close pattern of the great stems, rising from the bright brown tangle of dead stuff at their base, revealed nothing.

The track was barely wide enough for them to ride abreast, and sunken below the level of the hummocked rootstocks of the plants. With arm and riding-crop at full stretch Garland yet found that she could not touch the vaulted roof. It was some older world into which she and Anthony had travelled — a world that had been aeons out of memory before ever that continent had sunk to the ocean floor, of which St. Helena was the last fragment. She, too, heard some rending, snapping noise within the labyrinth; such noise, she fancied, as might have been made by giant slate-grey reptiles — huge as elephants — browsing in the fern forests of a million years ago.

Fifty yards ahead the end of the tunnel showed its pointed archway outlined against a gold-green shimmer that was like the reflection of sunlight in a woodland pool.

She looked at her escort.

The haggardness of his long dark face was emphasized most cruelly by the unearthly light: sweat streamed from his brow so that the high-lights on cheek and chin and bridge of nose shone as though upon a mask that had been rubbed in oil. His lips worked as if he spoke to himself.

She reined in.

'Rowley! Are you ill? . . . What is the matter? . . . Rowley!'

Her voice was imperative — anxious.

His horse automatically stopped when its companion halted. He would have pressed it on, as he answered her —

'No . . . Why? . . . What — ?'

But she had already leaned a little forward and taken his rein in her left hand; was repeating her question as a statement of fact —

'Rowley! Stop! . . . You *are* ill!'

He stammered in reply something about the heat.

. . . Fifty yards? Thirty-five yards? . . .

She disdained his answer —

'Dismount, Rowley dearest! You must dismount! I'll hold your horse! Sit down till you feel better!'

Dear God! It *would* happen in this way — that all her thought and love for him should be made manifest even when the moment of betrayal had come! Involuntarily he groaned aloud, and immediately her grip on his bridle was tightened.

'Get down, Rowley! I insist! You *shall,* even if I have to pull you off your horse!'

Thirty-five yards away — he knew — a ring of men were attending on their emergence from the catacomb of verdure: slant eyes in yellow faces peering between the great tufts of lofty fronds, or watching from lairs burrowed in the tumbled débris about the roots! He could not wait here and be ministered to by her tenderness in very sight of the trap he him-self had set for her.

He clambered — rather than dismounted — from his horse; so awk-wardly that his cocked hat fell off. He made no effort to recover it, but moved on with the reins looped over his arm.

'Better in the open!' he stammered. 'I'll be better in the open! It isn't anything! It's nothing at all! It's all right, Garland!'

They were in the clearing — a circular space of spongy black earth barely forty feet across. The wall of immense fern fronds leaned inward over it so that only a small round patch of turquoise sky was visible, as though at the bottom of a funnel.

... It was *now!* And *here!*...

His nerveless hand loosed his horse. He was standing by Garland's side, looking up into her dark, lovely, and pitiful eyes in desperate appeal ... He touched her olive-coloured habit. Cried in a broken voice —

'Garland!' and then an almost indistinguishable word which she did not grasp — 'Judas!'

She thought for the instant that he was going to die. She dropped the reins upon the grey mare's neck: was about to leap from the saddle, when suddenly she knew all the meaning of his piteous look. Knew quite clearly the thing that he had planned. Knew it all before ever his henchmen had begun to stream out from their hiding places in the fern.

In that flashing second she had gathered up her reins again — had begun to lift her horse round, in order to fly by the way she had come. And in that second, too, he had flung himself at her, and caught her with his one arm round the waist, and held grimly on against her struggles and the rearing of the startled mare.

'Rowley!' she cried ... The yellow men were almost on her, now! ... And it was no cry of anger or of hate, but — of apology. For with it — in last effort at escape — she brought down the riding-crop that she held in her free hand upon his upturned face. And saw the blood start from the stroke along his left temple.

Two men were at the horse's head. Another had seized the reins from her hand. She was in midst of a crowd of pig-tailed Chinese in faded tunics of blue and yellow. Someone said —

'It's no good, my Lady!'

... She was standing on the ground, still in that crowd of yellow faces. Rowley stood a pace in front of her, his face so tortured that it was almost unrecognizable, the blood trickling down his cheek and chin and on to the dark green breast of his coat. Beside him a big square man in cotton trousers and shirt, and black handkerchief tied so as to hide all his face below the eyes.

Said the big man in a high disguised squeaky voice — like a Punch-and-Judy show —

'No harm'll come to you, my Lady! You'll be as conformable as at Plantation! There's no use in makin' a fuss! Take my word for it! There's a snug little 'ammock slung on a pole to carry of you. And a clean silk handker' to a-bind up yer eyes! . . . Is the word "Go!", my Lordship?'

'Yes!' said Anthony, looking up at Garland for an instant, and quickly looking back to the ground again.

. . . How many years ago was it since she had stood at a window looking out into a darkness pin-pricked only by the lights of two anchored ships, tormented beyond endurance, as are the damned, because she must betray the lad she loved? The wheel had swung full-turn.

She made no appeal, no reproach.

All that she said was —

'Poor Rowley! . . . Poor, poor Rowley!'

In such tone as spoke only of sympathy for the bitter anguish of his soul.

CHAPTER VI

ACCORDING TO THE BOOK OF NUMBERS

FOR five days the island had forgotten the existence of the Emperor. Ever since Captain Forsyth, riding back from breakfast at Mount Pleasant, had encountered Count von Schauenstein, sitting dazed and bleeding by the roadside; and a riderless horse had returned to the Plantation House stables, sweating, with broken reins and side-saddle twisted under its belly.

The Prussian Commissioner had been thrown and stunned almost immediately after Lady Morfa's horse and his own had taken fright and bolted for some inexplicable reason. He knew no more . . . Nearly a thousand men of the garrison had fine-combed the countryside for the missing countess . . . Sailors from the *Conqueror* had clambered into the great ravines, had swung on ropes over the hideous depths of narrow volcanic fissures, had descended the iron-grey precipices overhanging the swirling sea . . . The Prussian Commissioner had offered £200 for my Lady's rescue . . . A slave had discovered a coroneted handkerchief in one of the gullies running into Old Woman Valley . . . The Prussian Commissioner had given the man £50 . . . The Governor and Admiral Plampin had disagreed upon the best method of search . . . The Prussian Commissioner had offered £500 for my Lady's rescue . . . A negro had heard a woman crying somewhere in the fern forest last night . . . The Prussian Commissioner himself had assisted in the systematic quartering of the tangle by five hundred troops . . . A soldier on picket at Deadwood had seen a grey filmy figure glide past him wringing its hands . . . Yesterday the Reverend Mr. Boys, who was always at his best on topical

matters — such as the fornication of Admiral Plampin, or Mr. Charles De
Fountain's treatment of his slaves, had preached a flesh-is-as-grass sermon,
mentioning Lady Morfa by name to a crowded congregation in St. James's
Church . . . She could no longer be alive. The Prussian Commissioner
was leaving to-morrow for Europe, but he had deposited £500 in Sir
Hudson's keeping, to be paid for the recovery of her body — living or
dead.

To-morrow the nightmare of lies was at last to end. To-night the
Emperor was to be smuggled down Old Woman Valley to the *Mute,* and
at a quarter after four o'clock of the following afternoon the *Königin
Luise* would nose out into the Atlantic, the smoke of her farewell salute
puffed like cotton-wool from her gun-ports.

And so a little after dawn Anthony — with bandaged head — rode out
again to the uplands where the Emperor was held prisoner . . . where
Garland was held prisoner.

The sky was mother-of-pearl. The gumwoods — so much less like real
trees than a child's drawing of them — striped the coarse drenched turf
with their long shadows. From the Longwood chimneys grey-blue smoke
trailed in mare's-tail streamers across the heavens before the north-east
wind.

At the door of the white guard-house, by the entrance gate in the fierce
high hedge of spiked aloes, stood the same wooden image of a scarlet
sentry that he had seen on the morning when he had ridden there with
Garland.

Count Henri Bertrand — very small, very tousled as to head, very
muddy as to yellow nankeen suit — made his appearance round a bend
in the rutted road to Deadwood Camp. He was engaged as usual in
skirmish with the white kid, Polissonne, which was under his nominal
control at the end of a red-leather leash. He passed the time of day with
Anthony courteously if abstractedly, but greeted the sentry as an old
friend and ally in very fair English. During the exchange of salutes, kid,
boy, and leash became much involved with the soldier's legs.

Anthony rode on. Longwood itself, guarded by its six slim cypresses,
was in sight. The green outside shutters of the house were thrown back,
and a Chinese servant was washing down the steps of the porch. The
wide lawns were frosted and sparkling with dew . . . The place was
undoubtedly the residence of a retired general officer, established for old
association's sake near a barracks gate! A house which had proved inconvenient and undesirable — which the tenant desired to sub-let! An
unpretentious house in which one might *villégiaturer* for a few weeks

— if one was not too particular: not the sort of house to be haunted by four million ghosts, or even by one!

At the foot of the gentle rise to the house was the Bertrands' home, embowered in dark trees. He wondered whether Garland's rooms were lighted by one of the three small dormer windows that he could see: whether she were looking out by any chance . . . could recognize him: whether she had forgiven him.

'Poor Rowley!' she had said. 'Poor, poor Rowley!'

He had turned his horse and was riding back along the aloes hedge when the shot rang out.

He came out into the road and in sight of the guard-house within two or three minutes.

The wooden-faced sentry was sitting on the door-sill, his musket propped against the wall: against his scarlet coat he nursed Count Henri who was sobbing as though his small heart were about to break. A wooden-faced sergeant stood in the doorway, hatless, saying 'There! There! There!' in a barrack-square voice of consolation. A wooden-face peered over his shoulder. A wooden-face peered round a corner of the lodge. Yet another wooden-face — attired as to the body in trousers and singlet — emerged from the gateway, carrying in his arms, as though it were a child, the white kid. A torrent of blood poured from the little creature's mouth. The man in the singlet set it down upon the ground.

Count Henri tore himself from the sentry's clasp, and flung himself down beside his pet.

'Poli! — Ma p'tite Poli! . . . Poli!' he cried in a choking voice and encircled the kid's bloody head in his small arms.

'Poli!'

The white kid raised its little head.

It answered its master. It bleated excuse for all its offences. It died.

'Bastard! Bloody, bloody bastard!' said the sergeant.

As Anthony dismounted, he saw that there were tears in that wooden-face's eyes.

'Take the child inside, and give 'im some rum, Joe!' said the sergeant. 'There, there, there, 'Enery, you'll feel better in a minit . . . I tell yer wot we'll do! We'll give 'er a bang-up, slap-up milingtery funeral!' . . . He answered the question in the raised eyebrows of the lean dark man who confronted him across dead kid and weeping child. 'The little crittur got away from 'im, sir. W'ile 'e was a-lookin' for it in the scrub, it come roun' in front of the guard-'us and skipped inter the gawden. That bastard Boney, sir, sees it from 'is winder, and 'e ups with 'is gun and pots it, clean as a whistle! Bloody swine, sir! 'E knew 'oo's it was h'as well as wot we does! 'E seen it h'every day of 'is life, sir! H'if 'e could see ter plug it as 'e did, 'e could see the collar and lead on it! . . . 'E killed the Regimental's little dawg last week, sir, that 'e did! 'E's always a-doing of it! . . . Brown, take up yer gun and get back to yer post! . . . Come h'on, 'Enery—'

Anthony mounted his horse.

So the Emperor had shot a child's pet goat!

He cast one look at Longwood. The wet shingles shone with the reflections of the gold-washed blue of the early morning sky. The wind had died down, and the streams of smoke from the chimneys rose in straight columns. A young man was hurriedly crossing the grass, buttoning himself into a scarlet coat as he came—presumably the orderly officer on his way to investigate.

'For why did 'e want ter do it, sir?' asked the sergeant in valedictory explosion. 'The bloody bastard!'

With gentle firmness he detached the child from his dead pet and carried him screaming and struggling into the guard-house.

Anthony shook his head: he gathered up his reins.

The Emperor had shot the playmate of his most loyal friend's child! Just for target practice!

Henri Bertrand's wails came muffled from within the guard-house. The sentry stood woodenly at attention above the little white body that lay in a mess of blood by the door-sill . . . 'Joe shall make yer a luv'ly corfin, if yer a good b'y!'

Anthony rode away: did not look back.

He found himself furiously angry at this wanton slaughter of a small boy's pet. A killing without excuse. A brutal act of heartlessness. . . .

He rode down into a shadowed ravine, among whose splintered rocks and barrenness chill night winds seemed still to linger.

Rode very slowly because it was there that he became suddenly aware of the vast importance of the small dead thing in the road outside the Longwood gate. Of its vast importance to himself—to the man who had shot it—to St. Helena—to the world!

The shot which had wakened the hollow echoes of the dawn-bright uplands a few minutes ago was one of the most momentous shots in history, because it would cause history not to be made!

Was it an absurd thing—he asked himself—that the spilt blood of a baby goat should convince him of what even Garland had not been able to persuade him? Was it absurd that that act of trivial ruthlessness should stamp with the seal of truth the tales of great ruthlessness in the past, foreshadow great ruthlessness to come? Was it absurd that because of it he should know now beyond all possibility of doubt that everything which had been alleged against the Emperor was true — quite true?

He saw again those weary men standing respectfully about the shabby green settee. Montholon had told him afterwards that thus they had stood for five hours in the Presence since Imperial Majesty had omitted to give them permission to sit.

He remembered all sorts of other things — little things — very little things that bore evidence to the truth . . . More than ten years ago. At Lauchstein. There had been a chair, a very lovely chair. And the Little Man had whittled with a knife at its loveliness as he paced to and fro under the great battle-picture above the dais . . . Only a few nights ago. There had been a book in a lovely binding of red leather, lying with crumpled leaves face downward upon the floor. The Principal Lodger's heel had rested negligently on it.

A dead kid and three weary men! A mutilated chair and a disfigured book! . . . Four million corpses and a devastated Europe!

How came it that he had ever forgotten those damning words pronounced in his hearing — 'One such as I cares little for the lives of a million men'? . . . Everything was true!

The veil of illusions was rent. Behind the overwhelming splendours, the allurement of gigantic battles, the glamour of titanic enterprises, was revealed in stark reality the man whom he and others had served with blind loyalty. As in Jasmine he had beheld the lady of a dream, half-goddess and half-saint, passionless, remote from desire; so in this man — filled with the malign spirit of destruction — had he seen a high-priest to Glory, an Almost-God. Two mirages!

The semaphore of the telegraph station was gesticulating like a wind-blown scare-crow as he began to ride down into the green valley.

Klasing, with his gold-rimmed spectacles pushed high up on his forehead, was standing on the small lawn before the pavilion, throwing crumbs to the red-beaked sparrows when he returned. He was in his shirt-sleeves: he had not yet donned his shabby black satin cravat, and the bedraggled frill of his shirt bosom was speckled with ink. His rusty pantaloons terminated in a pair of ancient scarlet slippers. With his immense bony red nose he looked rather like a sort of Israelitish sparrow himself.

'Pleathing picture of a good-natured criminal!' he remarked, dusting his hands together; hurled a large slice of bread at the nearest bird, and turned to follow Anthony into the cottage.

Anthony walked to the deal table in the middle of the room, and

looked down on the elaborate schedule of operations that were to have
dovetailed together into an emperor's escape from captivity. The shot
that killed a white kid had made it a meaningless jumble of times and
places and names!

His secretary surveyed him for an instant with his head on one side —

'You don't need to break the news gently to me!' he commented, as
if he had read the other's mind. 'I'm only a thecretary — a creeping
thing! . . . It'th all canthelled?'

He made a gesture as of tearing up the escape scheme.

Anthony nodded.

'Because of Lady Morfa?'

There was a new peremptory note in Klasing's speech, which Anthony
did not resent. He remembered telling his grandmother that he thought
Klasing to be the only altruist in the expedition.

'No. Upon my honour! A reason that Lady Morfa could not possibly
know of, or even guess!'

Klasing said — and he no longer lisped —

'All the months of preparation, all the vast fortune, all the hopes poured
out — spilled — wasted!'

But Anthony knew, without the man saying so, that he had believed
him, had loyally accepted his decision.

He brought out his watch from the fob pocket of his grey breeches.

'It is half-past eight. You will have your work cut out to cancel all
our arrangements and tie up the loose ends in time. You had better
go to the Bertrands first and tell them whatever lies you can concoct for
their benefit.'

Klasing nodded. He was obviously already turning over schemes in
his mind.

'You will insist on seeing Lady Morfa personally. Nothing can happen
to the Bertrands because of her. She won't help any investigation — of
that I am sure! She will have to remain in their charge for another ten
days to make things safe for us. You will give her a letter from me!'

'Quite!' said Klasing: paused: added tentatively, 'I wonder what made
you change your mind?'

'A white goat!' replied Anthony uninformatively, and walked to the
window.

Klasing made no comment except in so far as he reiterated slowly the
phrase repeated so often in the Book of Numbers — 'One kid of the
goats for a sin offering! . . . One kid of the goats for a sin offering!' as
though he were testing its applicability to the present circumstance. He
folded the *schema* thoughtfully: refolded it until it became a long thin

spill, to be lighted from his tinder-box — to be reduced to blackened
ashes — to be ground into dust upon the floor.

'"A white goat!"' he echoed, and nodded his goblin head as if the
answer were entirely satisfactory.

'You will send word to the *Mute*,' Anthony went on, 'that she will sail
as planned in time to rendezvous with us two hours after sunset to-
morrow. At the point arranged, three miles nor'-nor'-west of Egg Island,
where the two lights above Ladies' Chair are in line . . . Passenger or
no!'

'"Passenger or no!"' repeated Klasing, making rapid notes. 'No passenger, I opine!'

'I shall have to make my round of official farewells. It will take all day.
You will have to see that everything else is settled satisfactorily.'

Klasing nodded again.

'Your white goat,' he remarked, 'appears to have butted you into quick
decision!'

'Yes!'

'I wonder,' said Klasing, a little sadly, to unresponsive back and bent
head, 'what satisfactory explanation you can offer *them!*'

'As I shall be honest with them,' replied Anthony, 'I can be honest with
you . . . I have gone over to the other side!'

Klasing made no comment. He said, with abrupt irrelevance —

'You don't know the signalling code here, do you? . . . I do! Interesting messages this morning! I amused myself reading them!'

Anthony recalled the fluttering arms of the semaphore at Alarm House.
He looked round.

'Well?'

'The schooner *La Estrella* arrived this morning from Ascension. She
reports speaking the British frigate *Speedy* 15° south, 7° 41' west.'

Anthony calculated.

'Roughly a hundred and forty miles off?'

'Thereabouts, I fancy. The *Speedy* was less than six weeks out from
Plymouth! A phenomenal voyage! She was delayed when the *Estrella*
spoke her, repairing damage done to her mainmast and foremast in a
gale on the previous night. She instructed *Estrella* to report that she had
on board General Sir John Damant —'

'Damant!'

'— bound for the Cape with his staff, and Sir Grover Portland of the
Foreign Office! *Estrella* says she should arrive in four or five days' time!
Six weeks! . . . Foreign Office! —'

'Sir John Damant!'

Across the years Anthony remembered the John Bull figure of the one-handed man in the lavender-coloured kid gloves: the man who had not been Malone: the man who had considered it less serious that a spy should escape the gallows than that a royal concubine should pollute by her presence his elegant but respectable home.

'The *Speedy* is a better excuse than a white goat,' said Klasing, sitting down and preparing to write, 'if I may venture to say so. We will advance the time of her arrival by a few days in our story, and then nobody can question our failure to produce the Emperor!'

Anthony answered —

'I'm still going to be honest! It won't affect you. You are just doing as you are told. No one can blame you. Nothing can happen to *you!*'

Klasing suddenly became in attitude and bearing a caricature of the stage Jew: he rubbed his hands together and he spoke in a whining voice and stumbled over all his sibilants.

'You mayn't believe it, thir,' he said, 'but it'th you I'm worrying about. Odd — very odd, I know! Not expected in a poor Ithraelite and therefore almotht improper! True nevertheleth! There are thome of our friendth in the *Königin Luithe* who will be very annoyed. Very! Madam Purvis, Captain von Velhagen, and Colonel Theimer, for inthtance! If you thtay here you will infallibly be hanged: if you go on board you will infallibly be murdered — unleth you make a very thmall adjuthtment of the truth! *I* should lie. Anything elthe ith undiluted madneth! . . . I shall agree to anything you thay! They'll get nothing out of me!'

Anthony stared out of the window.

Above the loveliness of that pool of grass before the cottage — rimmed with a flowering hedge of snowy white, and sunk in the golden verdure of trees — towered the black precipitous mountain wall against the glittering clarity of the morning sky. From near at hand came the whispering, tinkling, splashing music of a torrent.

He was touched by the loyalty of the queer-looking creature —

'You're a good fellow, Solly, but — '

And then was silent while he and his immortal soul debated the situation . . . Nothing on earth, he decided, would induce him to play the hypocrite any longer than he need. If he were to stay in the island he would want to shout out loudly to all St. Helena that he was on the side of the turnkeys and not the prisoner. All those weeks he had been living a lie: he was not going to continue to live one for a moment longer than he need. He could not endure to have to profess a loyalty he no longer felt during the long journey home. He felt that he would lose his soul were he to remain on board the *Königin Luise* pretending to be what he no longer was. It would not be possible. His conscience told him that he must betray the cause he had served: but his conscience told him, too, that he must abide openly by that betrayal, with full knowledge of its consequences . . . It would be, moreover, an insult to Garland were he to rate his new loyalty more cheaply than his life, when he had kept faith with his old loyalty at the cost of love.

' —but it's not possible! When once we have sailed, and the *Mute* has been met and sunk, I shall tell the plain truth! There'll be no way for them to retrieve the situation then, even by the most desperate adventure.'

'Do you think,' said Klasing dryly, 'that you are a good enough actor to disguise the truth even for the few hours between sailing-time and rendezvous?'

Privately Anthony was by no means sure, but he replied acidly, 'I believe so. At any rate I have lived a lie for over two months! Very successfully!'

It was obvious that Klasing did not concur. He blew his nose on a cornflower-blue handkerchief in a manner that absolutely trumpeted denial. Shook his head.

'You have walked the part, and spoken the part of Prussian Commissioner, if I may say so. That is all, sir! You are not cut out for the hypocrite! My heart has been in my mouth all the while! I do not think for an instant that you could disguise your real beliefs, for example, before your grandmother!'

Klasing had reason! He did not believe that he could maintain any secret before the cold black eyes in that yellowed mask of a face. Once she had looked at him, she would know.

From under his papers Klasing produced a pile of coloured handkerchiefs, bought the previous morning at Solomon's store in Jamestown. He regarded proudly the pick of the collection — an affair in yellow and reds depicting Napoleon Bonaparte as the Devil bestriding St. Helena and shrinking from the effulgence of a noonday sun which loyally bore the well-known features of the Prince Regent and — to make things quite clear — was surmounted with a representation of the Prince of Wales's armorial feathers.

'A fine piece!' said Klasing in the tone of a connoisseur. 'A most unusual piece. I shall have to keep it quiet on shipboard! . . . I suppose that's how you look on *him* now!'

Anthony came back to the table; seated himself.

'Is one always a traitor when one changes one's earthly loyalty?' he demanded, as much of himself as of Klasing. 'Is not there some transcending faith, to deny which is the only treason?'

He wrote a few lines in pencil on a sheet of paper —

'Dearest Garland: The whole scheme is abandoned. You have nothing more to fear from me. Since that is so I know you will not implicate anyone that matters. The worst that can happen to the Bertrands is that they will be sent back to Europe. I am sorry that I did what I thought was the only thing to do. You will be free in a few days. God bless you. Always. Always. — Rowley.'

There was no more to be said. There must be no 'good-byes'. Nothing to suggest to her the price he might have to pay. He would not see her before he sailed for fear of her guessing how final that parting might be.

He folded the letter; sealed it; addressed it; handed it to Klasing without a word.

The man took the missive in his hand. He regarded it for a minute and then scrutinized Anthony in silence. The golden-green light, reflected from the foliage without upon his narrow spectacles, made the lenses look like peeled grapes. He said —

'There were two goats, you remember, according to the Mosaic Law. One for a sin offering to the Most High. And one for an atonement. One presumably has already been sacrificed. You, I opine, are to be the other — the scapegoat!'

He shook his head as he put on his coat.

CHAPTER VII

THE SPELL OF THE WITCH

' . . . KNEW that it might mean murder,' said Anthony finally. 'The murder of Liberty!'

He sat back on the low green-cushioned locker facing his grandmother in her big state-room; behind him the great chart of the Atlantic upon which the course of the *Königin Luise* was daily pricked in red. He was outwardly calm, but he knew that the hand which rested upon his knee was trembling a little: remarked to himself that Mr. Mason of Marseilles would have found consolation in the thought that a one-armed man must necessarily tremble less than one not so handicapped.

The movement of green-carpeted floor, of wine-dark panelling — lightened by the whiteness of the charts — was just perceptible. The softly glowing bracket-lamps, above the bedside table and above the small mahogany dressing-chest at the foot of the berth, oscillated slightly: the classic masks engraved upon their frosted globes would appear to shake their heads at him in gentle disapproval.

'So accordingly you betrayed us all!' remarked Madam Purvis in cold assessment of facts. 'Your associates. Your Emperor. Yourself . . . Me!'

'The alternative was to betray humanity!'

The old woman was sitting erect against snowy pillows. On the adjustable table in front of her were a two-handled cup of chicken broth, a plate of Bath Oliver biscuits, a little pile of elderly English newspapers that had arrived on the previous day by an outward-bound East Indiaman. Her ivory face — under frilled cap with black satin ribbons — was silhouetted against the map of St. Helena on the wall. It seemed to Anthony that the hachure strokes marking the jumbled hills were repeated in the innumerable lines engraved upon the still features.

'You have betrayed everything for which I have worked,' she said, and her voice was unemphatic, although with a black-mittened hand she broke one of the biscuits into fragments — crumbled it into powder. 'You have robbed me of my vengeance, after I have waited more than a generation for it! You have gone over to the enemy — an enemy that did his best to enslave your country!'

'I have good cause to dislike the British,' he answered, looking at the floor. 'I mildewed — rotted — for months in the hulks. I ate out my heart at Norman Cross for years. For more than five years! But the God who made America free did not intend that Britain and Europe should be made slaves!' — 'T'cha!' interjected his grandmother. — 'However much I might want to exact payment for what I underwent I could never run that risk! A sane man doesn't burn down an ancient church because a slate has been blown from the roof and in falling has just missed his head!'

She watched him for a little while, across the stretch of green carpet, with an unblinking stare — her sight was very good despite her great age . . . Richard would never have used metaphors! But then Richard would never have done this!

'Why did you lie to me when first you returned on board?' she asked at last. She pushed the plate of ruined biscuits aside, and fell to smoothing out the folds of one of the newspapers with narrow yellow hands.

'I did not mean you to know until return to St. Helena was impossible — an adventure too desperate even for the most desperate!'

Another thought occurred to her.

'It is a peculiar coincidence that with the arrival of Garland you undergo this change of heart!'

He flushed. But, again regarding him, she knew that it was from indignation, and not from shame: recognized reproof in his voice —

'I trust you have not thought of it as otherwise than a coincidence? . . . You should know me well enough by now to be sure that my personal relations with Garland — or anyone else — would not affect a matter of my conscience!'

Even amid her anger she admitted the truth of this to herself. Recognized in him, again, her own strength of will and singleness of purpose — dower of a New England ancestry. In the much-loved Richard she had never seen any such mirroring, only the easy-going nature of her husband, of the typical Virginian.

'I apologize, Anthony!' — He acknowledged the withdrawal with a stiff small bow: remained silent, waiting — 'None of this altruism, however, was obvious when you went ashore!'

'The possible consequences had not then dawned on me!'

'What, may I ask, caused the revelation?'

'Many things. Each of them small, but each a link in an unanswerable chain of reasoning.' He paused for an instant, and his grandmother, looking at him from under lowered eyelids, remarked the humorous twist to his mouth. 'It was the matter of a small white goat which finally, I believe, brought all my subconscious doubts to the light of day.'

'A goat! How very interesting!' commented Madam Purvis to the grey kitten which had risen drowsily to its feet and was arching its back and kneading the quilt, small pink mouth a-yawn.

'You know, ma'am,' said Anthony leaning a little forward, 'I came into this business for no reason of personal or family vengeance. Perhaps I wanted an objective in life, it is true, but in the main I joined out of loyalty to the Emperor. Because I knew what imprisonment at the hands of the British meant! But it was his personal freedom I wanted to give him — not freedom to begin a fresh European holocaust!'

A travelling-clock in a red leather case stood on the small square table against the head of the berth. It struck the quarter-hour past eight. The sunset gun on the island had been fired at sixteen minutes past six. At any moment now the *Mute* should be signalled. Nevertheless he had the feeling that he and his grandmother, and that lighted room with its mahogany panelling and its charts and green carpet and the smoke-grey kitten — once more curled up on the white honeycomb quilt — were no longer part of the ship, but cradled in infinite isolation in the midst of the heaving wilderness of the Atlantic.

Madam Purvis continued her watch.

Anthony had not changed out of the uniform in which he had said

farewell, on the quayside at Jamestown, to a galaxy of feathered and
flowered bonnets, of gold-embroidered coats and stupendous cocked hats.
He was as dapper, indeed, as when he had climbed the high sides of the
ship from the launch, to the salute of tossed oars, whose wet blades —
erect like a parade of spears — had glistened in the sun. He bore his chin
thrust out over a palisade of black stock hedged by the high embroidered
collar of his coat. He was very pale, and one lock of his dark and wavy
hair was astray upon his forehead. There was on his face an expression
which she could not define . . . It was in fact a look of resolution, mingled with some apprehension and with a good deal of sardonic amusement . . . She did not attempt to define it because at that moment she
saw in him an earlier Anthony. Saw in shape of face, expression, pallor,
that eldest-born of whom she rarely thought. Saw suddenly the dead face
on the pillows of the Black Bed at High Pale, smiling whimsically at her
whilst they made ready to receive the bride. Before she could stop herself,
she had said out loud in a low voice, even at that juncture, for reassurance
as she had so often done before —

'Richard! Richard!'

For the first time in his life he answered her, denying that reassurance;
corrected her in a yet lower voice —

'Anthony! Anthony!'

Again there was silence. The old woman turned over the newspaper
that she held. Laid it on the invalid table. Pressed down the folds with
thumb and with nail of forefinger.

He had been able to lie sufficiently for the time being to von Velhagen,
to General d'Aubrac, to the Alsatian, Colonel Theimer, when they had
attempted to question him upon his arrival on board. But he had not
relished having to lie to his grandmother, even for a few hours. It was
because of this that he had deliberately remained on deck for a long time
while the ship moved slowly out of the bay . . . The band of the 66th —
with peculiar and painful appositeness — had sped them on their way
to the tune of the traditional military farewell, 'The Girl I Left Behind
Me!'. . . The gulls swirled screaming up and down the wind. Beyond
the shelter of the land the long billows chased one another, snowy-fringed,
over a slowly-heaving sapphire sea. The light was golden, the shadows
in the valley purple, and the island peaks ashen. Somewhere amid those
hills he was leaving Garland! . . .

'What decided you to admit the truth to me?' asked Madam Purvis at
length.

'I never had any intention of keeping it secret from you — even if it
were possible,' he answered. 'These others — what do they matter? Von

Velhagen with a name which no one can redeem for him but the Emperor. Theimer lusting for the flesh-pots of Paris, where he can only return with the Emperor. General d'Aubrac, a regicide forgiven by the Bourbons, now under death sentence himself because he betrayed during the Hundred Days those who had pardoned him. All of them serving nobody except themselves. But to you I must tell the truth — because of your ghosts —'

'Ghosts?'

Barely spoken: more nearly a sigh.

It seemed a long time before he went on —

'The ghosts that hunted me across America when I was a little boy. And across the Atlantic. That set me aboard the *Nautilus* and brought me to the hulks. That cost me Garland. They are *your* ghosts. They are things which you yourself have created. *My* ghosts have demanded none of this — no retribution, no blood vengeance! . . . I tell you this — *my* ghosts answering yours! In what I have done to-day my ghosts answer yours!'

Across all the years again she recalled the other Anthony. In the dusk-haunted library at High Pale. She had said then that the recollection of the outrages of the Revolutionary war would endure to the fourth and fifth generations, and he had answered that he prayed to God they would not . . . Was Anthony speaking through Anthony? Was one generation fulfilling the prayers of another?

As if he heard the question she never put, he answered it aloud with emphasis —

'I know, ma'am! I *do* know! . . . I am nearer death to-night than you are. Nearer the dead!'

And at that moment, even as he spoke, from overhead a scurry of feet and muffled shouting told that the tiny secretive sparkle of a lantern, low upon the dark waters, had answered the lights of the great ship; had announced the presence of the *Mute*. The passengerless *Mute!* It was true — she told herself — that now he was very close to death, indeed.

'The *Mute!* . . . When she comes they will all know that you have played traitor!'

'They will, ma'am! . . . I shall not lie again when the inevitable questions come.'

He was sitting, chin in hand, elbow resting upon his knee. One of his green coat-tails had been brought forward and lay on his thigh. A small double-barrelled pistol was in the pocket: he could feel its weight upon his leg. A singularly inadequate weapon of defence against an entire ship's company! He smiled.

'You smile!. . . Even my influence could not save you — supposing I exercised it!'

He knew it to be true.

'I am aware, ma'am.'

'I doubt whether your life is worth five minutes' purchase!'

'Forty-five minutes!' he corrected, with the air of one being meticulously careful about pending financial operations. 'Thirty minutes for the *Mute* to come alongside, and fifteen minutes for them to sort matters out!. . . After that! — I am under no illusions!. . . I'll quote you some lines from your favourite author, Young:

> 'While man is growing life is in decrease;
> And cradles rock us nearer to the tomb.
> Our birth is nothing but our death begun.'

She was very very old. She did not face death with equanimity: although the preoccupation of most of her life had been with it, and her enduring anger because of its finality . . . Suddenly she knew herself to be intensely proud that her grandson could await the certainty of almost immediate death serenely, with a tag from *Night Thoughts,* with a half-smile as though he would apologize for causing any unpleasantness — as though it were a matter of but small importance.

She pressed back against the high pillows, and once more set to folding and re-folding the newspaper. She did not raise her eyes again to look at the silent figure under the chart that showed the course of the *Königin Luise* on her mission of vengeance. She did not need physical sight to see that pale long face with the little twisted smile and the dark lock upon the forehead.

Which Anthony was he who waited there? Was he, perhaps, the same Anthony that had died more than a generation ago in his apple-green library at High Pale, fallen forward among his papers, before his fantastic toy city? He was not Richard's son, although he must be. He could not be Anthony's son, although he was. He was the child of two fathers — in him implicit the venturesomeness of Richard and the imaginative idealism of Anthony. In him were both her sons . . . If she were to raise her eyes she knew that she would see them standing at his side. If she were to listen she knew that she would hear them speaking, the one proud that their son faced death so unafraid, the other proud that their son faced death for the reason that he did.

She suddenly said in a loud, firm voice —

'Anthony! Richard!'

And looked up.

And knew that in that instant — that very instant — two other figures had merged into the man who had raised his eyes quickly to hers as though startled by some change in the quality of her voice. They had been hers. He was hers. Nothing else was of any account. She was no longer concerned by the purpose for which she had bred him — the dead had repudiated that purpose: himself was a purpose of far greater importance.

She said in a minute or two, looking back at that ancient copy of *The Morning Herald* —

'You may go now! To your cabin. You will return here when the *Mute* comes alongside. Immediately! You understand?'

To him it seemed purposeless that she should be witness of his inevitable condemnation. He would have protested. But she already appeared to have dismissed him from her thoughts, because as she spoke she set her hand to the red silk bell-rope that hung down the panelling at her bed-head. He rose to go wondering who it was she summoned. . . .

He had returned again: seemed to have been waiting for an eternity in the silence of the big cabin, sitting with his knees crossed, chin sunk thoughtfully on the folds of his white neck-cloth. Waiting for the irruption of von Velhagen, hunched and vulturine — the great animal, Theimer, with his huge hands and blue-black chin — d'Aubrac with his white and wavy hair and coal-black eyebrows.

Overhead the noise had been continuous.

Now, suddenly and easily, that bright and luxurious room — swung over the profundity of the Atlantic a thousand miles from any continent — tilted steeply. The papers on the little writing-desk under one of the curtained windows cascaded to the floor, and the chair in which he was sitting by it started to slip toward his grandmother's berth . . . The room recovered its balance: bent a little outward over the sea: recovered its balance again, and remained comparatively stable.

They were changing course. The *Mute* had been met and left to sink. He pictured the small dark hull sliding down into the pitchy night of the undersea. Would she remain suspended in perpetual equilibrium somewhere in those immense depths, or sink into the ooze of the ocean floor? Would she go silently, or would there be a violent hiccough of escaping air as she slipped finally below the surface?

Any instant now they would come seeking him!

He no longer carried the pistol in his tail-pocket. Resistance would have been foolishness. Undignified foolishness. In all the great ship there were only two men of whom he was sure. Solly Klasing with his toothpick limbs, and Lieutenant Guillaume, the gaunt commander of the *Mute,* who had sailed years and years ago in that other ill-fated expedition in the *Nautilus.*

His grandmother had not spoken since he returned. She had not lifted her eyes, to all appearances at least, from the open pages of a book — *Night Thoughts,* he was prepared to swear. She was aware, nevertheless, that he had changed out of uniform into a plain coat of night-dark blue. He preferred to meet fate as a private gentleman, and not in comic opera attire! Quite right!

Approaching voices! Excited voices! Many of them. A crisp knock upon the panels of the door.

Madam Purvis did not look up. She turned over a leaf of her book; glanced at the first lines as though to make certain that she had not skipped a page; indifferently rang the small hand-bell by which she signalled permission to come in.

'Enter the First Executioner!' said Anthony genially.

He rose to his feet. It seemed to be more gentlemanly to stand, for that momentous presentation to death.

But it was Garland who stepped within.

Garland who said very quietly —

'Good evening, Madam Purvis! . . . Good evening, Rowley!'

The three men, that he had known would come, entered after her. Von Velhagen closed the door and remained standing by it, listening and watching, his yellow bald head between high shoulders bowing rhythmically the while like the head of the nodding porcelain mandarin on the Almonds' mantelpiece. D'Aubrac stood by him, close to the end of the settee, watching, too, from eyes as peculiarly round as those of a monkey.

Garland advanced a few steps into the cabin; took off her dark hooded cloak, handed it to Colonel Theimer — an uncouth squire at her heels — as if he were there for no other purpose; adjusted a stray black tress with the utmost nonchalance.

Madam Purvis answered in her collected tones —

'Good evening, Garland!'

None of the men understood any English: their eyes ranged from old woman to young: saw nothing in the expression of either to suggest that the encounter was unexpected or held anything of the unusual.

'I am sorry to be late,' said Garland still composedly patting curls into place. 'But I stayed on deck to see the end of the *Mute.* There has been considerable consternation lest we should go up as she went down!'

'Why are you here, Garland?' asked Anthony: added the assurance — '*They* can't understand at all!'

She did not answer him in words, but flashed at him a look — a smile.
Madam Purvis repeated the question —

'Why have you come?'

'It seemed a pity that the passenger accommodation in the *Mute* should
not be used. I was very definitely a guest whose presence the Bertrands
might find it difficult to explain to authority. So no one raised any objection when I suggested that I might occupy the Imperial state-cabin . . .
It was not luxurious. I measured it with a ha'penny. It was exactly two
feet six inches by three feet. And one couldn't stand upright! I have
had eighteen hours of it. I do not know that I particularly care for submarine travel . . . I am afraid that Countess Bertrand's pretty dress —'

She glanced a little sadly at the frock she wore — high-waisted, violet,
with a dark purple bodice and sleeves. It was badly creased.

Theimer seemed to be mesmerized by her. He was a bull-like stupid
creature, as capable of enormous generosities as of vast bestialities. He
looked from her to the cloak over his arm, furtively stroking the folds
with his free hand as though to assure himself that it was no fairy garment
of invisibility or some such enchantment.

It was von Velhagen who demanded —

'Who is this lady? Why is she here? What does she say?'

General d'Aubrac's pale intelligent face and black round eyes were
turned to Anthony. He asked —

'Where is the Emperor? Has this lady's appearance any bearing upon
the matter?'

'None!'

The two men bowed.

'Why have you come, Garland?'

It seemed to him that she must be dead: that her wraith had come
from some other world to strengthen him to face the swift travel of
death to her side . . . Or else he dreamed! And this cabin had no reality.
And it was years and years ago. And he would wake up and find that it
was time for the early morning ride in the pine woods above the sea. And
the *Nautilus* had not yet been built — he would not sail in her; so then
there would be no hideous memories of Jasmine, of hulks, of prison camp,
of folly of war, of yellow men streaming out from the forest of fern.

Garland did not answer him for a moment; by one swift glance at
Madam Purvis asked him a question: to which he replied —

'I have told *her!*'

Then she said —

'Did you think that I should leave you to face this alone, so long as
there were means within the world to bring me to you? If you had done

what you have for my sake, I should still have come. But because you did it from your own conviction of the right, how much more gladly have I come! There can never be anything between us now. Not even death . . . I shall be beyond death, Rowley darling! I am above death. To me and you it will be no barrier!' She paused: went on — 'Do they — ? Will they — ?'

'I think so, dearest!'

She turned her very lovely head and surveyed for a little while the three silent men. Von Velhagen, blue-uniformed, hunched and suspicious by the door; Theimer, who smiled at her uncertainly, in some strange way tamed by her cloak; d'Aubrac, with his white-wavy hair and watchful eyes. Turned back from them, and met the dark gaze of the old woman sitting so erect against the pillows — the witch of the tower! A gaze in which there was some message that she could not read.

Said General d'Aubrac, examining his beautifully-kept finger-nails, speaking in a well-bred voice of chilled politeness —

'We understood that the Emperor — instead, this lady — ! Perhaps she will explain in French. My colleagues and I — we do not understand English.'

She stepped across the floor to Anthony with rustling skirts. She took his hand in hers. She was at his side. She would be at his side. For ever, and for ever, and for ever. In life. In death. Beyond death.

Von Velhagen said in his rasping French —

'I insist on knowing what has happened to the Emperor!'

'When General d'Aubrac has finished stammering and Captain von Velhagen concluded his insistence,' remarked Madam Purvis, mittened hands now folded placidly upon the beetle-black cover of *Night Thoughts*, 'I should be glad to remind you that my state-room is not a committee-room . . . As you express an interest in the matter, I have no objection, however, to informing you that the lady, whose presence arouses your curiosity, is my grandson's betrothed. Her friends in St. Helena — *our* friends — considered that she would be safer out of the island. I concur with that decision. I concur with the action taken. She is an English-woman, and the part she has played in this business might have very serious consequences for her!'

She surveyed with sublime indifference those alien people at the far end of the cabin, by green settee and chart of the Atlantic, barring the door which faced the bed-foot, as though on guard.

They were her own folk, the two who stood at her side, who had defeated her, and over whom, in their victory, she must cast the mantle of her protection. They were so near that, if she had stretched out her hand, she could almost have touched the grave slim girl who was watching her in intent and wondering speculation. She remembered hearing what the grave slim girl had called her long ago — the Witch in the Tower! She would soon show them what witchcrafts and spells and sorceries she possessed!

D'Aubrac minced a few steps across the green carpet . . . . He wore a dark blue coat that had something of the naval uniform about it, and white pantaloons pleated at the waist. He was like a good-looking monkey. He was by far the most dangerous — because the most intelligent. He insisted —

'Where is the Emperor? It is fantastic that we —'

Anthony moved as though he were about to speak: the pressure of Garland's hand restrained him — Garland, who was saying to herself, praying to herself, 'She has a spell! She has a spell!'

Madam Purvis turned a snake-like gaze slowly upon the general.

'This lady, General d'Aubrac, knows nothing at all — but that he has not come! How can I answer you in that case! Has not Lieutenant Guillaume reported yet? Why has he not reported to me?'

Von Velhagen said harshly —

'He knows nothing . . . He has hurt himself in disposing of the *Mute*. There seems something very curious —'

. . . What spell had she got? What spell?

The chill regard continued on its path. To von Velhagen. To the door he guarded.

. . . Yet was that regard so chill? — Garland asked herself. Did not the flicker of some emotion for a moment disturb the rigidity of a face that she had thought as changeless in expression as that of a priestess of Thebes?

And then, as though the old woman had evoked her enchantment just by that concentrated gaze, there came a sudden untidy thump upon the panels of the door.

Von Velhagen stepped away as the door flew open. The loose-jointed shabby figure of Lieutenant Guillaume appeared, crossed the threshold, came into the room. Behind him in the opening, and visible only to the old woman in the bed, stood Klasing: she could not see his expression, but knew that he nodded reassuringly to her before he was shut without.

Guillaume wore a thin cotton shirt which was extraordinarily stained with oil and sweat and blood — as dirty as his cadaverous face — and was hatless. He looked round the cabin: ignored everybody except Anthony, whom he saluted with a smile, touching a bedraggled forelock with a bandaged and bloody hand.

'Beg to report that the *Mute*'s sunk, sir,' said Guillaume. 'The bitch gave us just the same sort of trouble we had with the *Nautilus*. The lanyard of the bomb fouled something. Nearly blew up the ship! Nearly took my hand off!'

He shook his bleeding hand, so that blood drops spattered upon the green carpet.

He appeared then to recollect something — to chide himself for forgetfulness.

'There is a letter! It was brought when they brought the lady down to the cove. What with the trouble we've had one way and another it had gone out of my mind!'

He sought in his trousers pocket: produced a crumpled cover: tried to read the superscription: failed: made to give it to Anthony, who shook his head.

'Give it to General d'Aubrac,' said Madam Purvis. 'I dislike letter-reading by lamp-light.'

. . . What spell had the witch?

The general took the letter from the outstretched hand with a little bow in Madam Purvis's direction. Examined the inscription on the cover with his head on one side: examined it yet more closely. An intrigued monkey! His face suddenly lightened.

'It is the Emperor's handwriting,' he announced. 'In all loyalty, and with all due respect, the worst writing in the world!'

With a little penknife he deliberately cut round what remained of the seal; withdrew the content of the cover; and held out for inspection a sheet covered with incredible scrawl.

'The Emperor's fist!' agreed Theimer nodding.

'But — ' began Anthony. Was aware of the quick bleak regard of his grandmother, of a renewed pressure of the hand.

'The Emperor!' said von Velhagen, and relaxed his air of vigilance.

D'Aubrac stepped aside to hold the letter under the light of the lamp above the mahogany chest.

'It is dated from Longwood, last night. It is addressed to you, madame,' he said, speaking in a reverent tone. And then he read slowly, and stumbling more than once over the shapelessness of words —

'Brave and loyal friends,

'At this late hour I have realized that it is impossible for me to contemplate escape. I must not shirk my martyrdom. On the rock of St. Helena I expiate the imaginary offences of France. I have been made the ritual scapegoat of Leviticus. Upon my head have been placed "all the transgressions of my people in all their sins", and bearing them I have been sent away into the wilderness. Should I escape, then full retribution would be exacted from unhappy France, and the day of the evacuation by the Allied armies indefinitely postponed.

'Never shall it be said that their Emperor added to the torment of his people merely in order to escape the hard fate laid upon himself. . . .'

'Ah! The brave! The brave!' said Theimer, the tears running down his large red face. With the back of his free hand he unashamedly wiped them away.

'When the Allied armies evacuate the beloved fatherland then the call will come, and I shall answer it. . . .'

'He has reason,' commented d'Aubrac, interrupting his own reading. 'He is, perhaps, right!'

'The expenses of the expedition will be borne out of my funds in Europe, and this letter shall further be for an authority to Madame Henriette Purvis to divide the sum of one hundred thousand francs between MM. d'Aubrac, von Velhagen and Theimer as a token of my appreciation of their loyalty. To Madame Purvis and to Colonel Purvis, her grandson, I can offer nothing but my thanks and undying gratitude . . . One day — '

'One hundred thousand francs! . . . Ah! The brave!' said Theimer. He smoothed the cloak upon his arm as though in imagination he were already caressing the sleek cool flesh of Creole lights-o'-love in New Orleans.

So the Emperor himself had relieved him of the need for confessional! Anthony, utterly at sea over this new development, realized only that fact, and that the face bent in scrutiny of the missive, although frowning in the effort at decipherment, had cleared of all suspicion.

Clever, clever Henriette! Clever, clever Klasing! Loyal Guillaume! — thought the old woman. The estate in New York would have to go. It did not matter. The house at East Hampton would have to go. It did not matter. Nothing mattered but the result . . . *He* shall never know that this letter is Klasing's supreme masterpiece! Never know that *I* have given him his life! Any more than he shall know that *I* gave him his name and his father! He shall owe me everything, and never know!

She turned her head a little so that she might see Anthony: saw Garland — found her eyes fixed on her, and in their depths a realization that some miracle past comprehension had been performed . . . Neither should

Garland ever know! . . . The dead were not dead. In him they lived. In him *she* would live. And so would they continue alive in those yet to be. . . .

The room upon the Atlantic tilted a little upward: tilted a little sideways. Very little. And the silent people within swayed a little with it. Everything became for just a moment instable, reflections in water ruffled by the wind, images in a dream ruffled by reality.

Anthony knew that there were other passengers aboard that ship — within that room. Knew past any manner of doubt that Tom Almond, who had died for England, spoke with Uncle Richard, who had died for America; that Charles Hurrell, who had died for his mother's honour, spoke with the father he had robbed. Was aware, without knowing why, that all was well — very well. Was aware that Garland was on her knees beside the berth, her face hidden in the bed-clothes; that his grandmother, with inscrutable expression, was slowly smoothing the dark tresses with a hand stiff because unaccustomed to caress.